MOUNTAIN *Christmas* BRIDES

*Nine Historical Novellas Celebrate Faith
and Love in the Rocky Mountains*

MOUNTAIN
Christmas
BRIDES

Susan Page Davis, Carrie Turansky
Mildred Colvin, Mary Davis, Lena Nelson Dooley,
Darlene Franklin, Debby Lee,
Tamela Hancock Murray, Gina Welborn

BARBOUR BOOKS
An Imprint of Barbour Publishing, Inc.

A Trusting Heart © 2008 by Carrie Turansky
Home for the Holidays © 2012 by Mildred Colvin
One Evergreen Night © 2012 by Debby Lee
All Ye Faithful © 2012 by Gina Welborn
A Carpenter Christmas © 2012 by Mary Davis
Fires of Love © 2010 by Tamela Hancock Murray
The Best Medicine © 2010 by Lena Nelson Dooley
Almost Home © 2010 by Susan Page Davis
Dressed in Scarlet © 2010 by Darlene Franklin

Print ISBN 978-1-63409-890-8

eBook Editions:
Adobe Digital Edition (.epub) 978-1-63409-976-9
Kindle and MobiPocket Edition (.prc) 978-1-63409-977-6

All scripture quotations are taken from the King James Version of the Bible.

This book is a work of fiction. Names, characters, places, and incidents are either products of the author's imagination or used fictitiously. Any similarity to actual people, organizations, and/or events is purely coincidental.

Published by Barbour Books, an imprint of Barbour Publishing, Inc., P.O. Box 719, Uhrichsville, Ohio 44683, www.barbourbooks.com

Our mission is to publish and distribute inspirational products offering exceptional value and biblical encouragement to the masses.

ecpa Member of the
Evangelical Christian
Publishers Association

Printed in the United States of America.

Contents

A Trusting Heart

by Carrie Turansky

Dedication

To my twin daughters, Megan and Elizabeth,
who are a treasure and blessing.

Trust in the LORD with all thine heart;
and lean not unto thine own understanding.
In all thy ways acknowledge him,
and he shall direct thy paths.

PROVERBS 3:5–6

Chapter 1

An intelligent widower of twenty-eight years from a fine family wishes to correspond with an honorable maiden or widow eighteen to twenty-five years with a loving disposition who is interested in matrimony and would like a good husband and a life of plenty in Wyoming.

October, 1880

The shrieking blast of the train whistle shook the platform of the Chicago Central Train Station. Annika Bergstrom clutched her twin sister, Sophia, and swallowed her tears. She must be strong for Sophia's sake.

"I don't know how I shall ever get along without you." Tears ran down her sister's cheeks. She reached up and brushed them away with her gloved hand.

Sophia's new husband, Lars, stepped forward and tenderly placed his arm around his wife's shoulder. "We'll pray for you, Annika, every day."

"Thank you, Lars." Annika studied the man who had won her sister's heart. He would take care of Sophia. They were a good match and had a wonderful future ahead, serving the Lord at a small, rural church in northern Illinois.

Would her future husband treat her with such love and tenderness? Annika forced a smile. "I promise to pray for you both as well. I'm sure God will keep us safe in His loving care." She truly believed that, but she said it aloud to reassure herself as well as her sister and Lars.

"And you must write to us often," Sophia said. "I'll be waiting for your letters."

Annika's hands trembled, and she grabbed her sister once more. "I will. I promise. And you must do the same. I want to hear all about your new church as soon as you're settled."

Annika stepped back and gazed at her sister, memorizing the curve of her cheek and the look of devotion in her blue eyes. If she didn't love Sophia so much, she could never leave her like this. Since the day they were born, and even those nine months before, they had never been parted. How would she survive without Sophia?

The huge, black locomotive hissed. Puffs of steam and smoke filled the air. All around her travelers said their last good-byes, gathered up their belongings, and moved to board the train.

The conductor, dressed in a black uniform and cap, walked toward them. "All aboard," he called.

A shot of panic raced through Annika. Was it too late to change her mind? But if she did, how would she support herself? For the last five years, since their parents' deaths, she and Sophia had worked as maids at the Hillman School for Girls. Even when they combined their meager salaries, they barely made enough to scrape by. She could never afford to live on her own now that Sophia was leaving Chicago.

No. Her decision was made. She had accepted Charles Simms's proposal of marriage, and she was a woman of her word. She would travel to Wyoming as his mail-order bride and make a new life for herself. But more importantly, she would free Sophia to make a new life with Lars.

"It's time, Annika." Lars nodded to the conductor as he approached.

"Are you headed to Omaha, miss?" the gray-haired conductor asked.

Annika gripped the handle of her bag. "Yes, sir, and then on to Laramie, Wyoming."

"My goodness, all the way to Wyoming?" He chuckled and turned to Lars. "Don't worry. I'll keep an eye on her this first leg of the trip." He took Annika's bag and walked toward the train.

Sophia kissed her cheek. "Good-bye, dear heart. I love you."

Annika was afraid her reply would come out as a sob, so she kissed her sister, then followed the conductor to the train.

He checked her ticket and directed her to the second-class coach.

She lifted her skirts and mounted the steps. Making her way down the aisle, she looked for an open seat by the window so she could catch one last glimpse of her sister and Lars. How long would it be until she saw them again? Six months? A year? Five years? Would her sister be holding a baby in her arms the next time they met? Would Annika? She gulped and pushed that thought away. The possibility of having a baby with a man she had never met was too much to consider at the moment.

The train creaked and groaned as the engine built up steam. The car lurched forward and rolled away.

She waved to Sophia, then pressed her face against the cool, dirty glass, watching her sister grow smaller and disappear from sight as the train rounded a curve. She let her tears fall, but only a few. This was the right decision. Her parents' loving and selfless example had taught her to put Sophia's needs above her own.

Sophia had initially refused Lars's proposal because she didn't want to leave Annika alone in Chicago. It was only after Annika found a suitable groom through Mrs. Mayberry's Matrimonial Society for Christians of Moral Character that Sophia had finally agreed to move ahead with her wedding plans.

Annika took a handkerchief from her bag and wiped her nose and cheeks. Perhaps if she read the letters again it would calm her heart and strengthen her for the journey.

She pulled the small packet from her bag. A pale blue ribbon tied the five envelopes together, one from Mrs. Amelia Mayberry and four from Charles Simms. She scanned Charles's first letter dated June 18, although she had read it so many times during the last four months she had almost memorized it.

A man's penmanship told a great deal about him, and Charles's writing was neat and precise. Even though he had been raised in the West, he was obviously an intelligent, educated man with a caring heart.

His description of the family's large cattle ranch intrigued her. She'd lived on a small farm in Sweden until her family immigrated to America when she was twelve. Living in the country again after spending the last ten years in Chicago sounded wonderful. The Simms's ranch was only six miles from Laramie, a small town on the Pacific Railway Line about halfway between Omaha and San Francisco. Life would be different in Wyoming, but she was strong, she knew how to work hard, and she was willing to learn how to be a rancher's wife.

She looked down at the letters again, and her gaze rested on the last paragraph where Charles mentioned his prayers for a loving wife for himself and a kind and caring mother for his seven-year-old daughter, Mariah. Annika had prayed for a thoughtful and understanding husband. His willingness to allow them a month to get acquainted before the wedding convinced her she had made the right choice. And Mrs. Mayberry had assured her she only referred responsible Christian men who provided good references for their character and position.

So many nights she had prayed for God's direction. Finally, everything had fallen into place. This had to be His answer. Her parents' marriage had been arranged by their families, and it had been a loving union. Surely she could build a new life with Charles Simms. She might not love him at first the way Sophia loved Lars, but in time love would grow. She clasped her hands and stared out the window.

Dear Lord, let it be true.

❄

The aroma of fresh-brewed coffee, ham, and eggs greeted Daniel Simms at the back door. He stomped the mud off his boots and hustled into the kitchen. Warmth radiated from the cast-iron stove, drawing him closer. He rubbed his hands together and held them out toward the heat. "Breakfast almost ready?"

Song Li, their Chinese cook, looked up and scowled at Daniel. "You come in too soon. Breakfast not ready."

Daniel held back a grin. Song Li might work for them, but he owned the kitchen. "I'll just get a cup of coffee while you finish up."

Song Li muttered in his native tongue, then returned to flipping ham slices with a vengeance, while his long, black braid swung across his back.

"Uncle Daniel, look what I made." Mariah hurried over, carrying a tin plate of puffy, golden biscuits.

"Mmm, those sure look good." He smiled at her and ran his hand over the top of her head, smoothing down her wild hair. "Why don't you run up and get a brush, and we'll see if we can tame these curls."

Her face puckered into a frown. "My hair don't need brushin'." She placed the biscuits next to her plate and pushed her hair back with floury hands. " 'Sides, Song Li needs my help."

"You done now," Song Li said. "Obey Uncle Daniel. Go get brush."

She huffed. "Why does everyone fuss about my hair?" She stomped off toward the stairs.

Daniel shook his head. That girl was too smart for her own good and cute enough to get away with it. She needed a firm hand, or she was going to turn out as ornery as a wild mustang.

Charles Simms Sr. strode into the kitchen.

"Morning, Pa. Why are you dressed up?"

"I'm going into town after breakfast."

"How come?" It wasn't Sunday, and his father hadn't mentioned a meeting of the cattlemen's association.

His father frowned, ignoring the question, and glanced around the room. "Where's Chase?"

Daniel shrugged. The last time he'd seen his older brother he'd been sound asleep, snoring like a grizzly bear. But he didn't want to set his father off with a report like that, especially when he already seemed bothered about something.

His father huffed. "That boy will be the death of me yet. Where's Mariah?"

"She went up to get a hairbrush."

"Well, at least someone's getting ready for the day." His father turned toward the stairs. "Chase, get yourself down here!"

Daniel stifled a groan. His father shouldn't treat Chase like a kid, but the way he'd been acting lately, staying out late and carousing around with a wild bunch of cowboys, he almost deserved it.

"Grampa, I can't find my hairbrush," Mariah called.

His father growled and pounded up the stairs.

Daniel hustled after him, ready to protect his niece from the older man's temper. Charles Simms loved his granddaughter, but he had a short fuse, and the fact that Chase did little to care for his daughter infuriated him.

"I'll help her, Pa," Daniel said as he reached the top of the stairs.

His father ignored him and banged on Chase's door. "Time to get up!"

A low groan issued from the bedroom. "Go away."

Daniel shook his head, knowing exactly what was coming.

His father shoved the door open with a bang and marched into the room. "Charles Joseph Simms, get out of that bed!" He yanked back the covers and snatched the pillow off his son's head.

Daniel watched from the doorway, praying for a quick end to the confrontation.

Chase blinked and lifted his head. "Pa, what are you doing?"

"You need to get up and get dressed. We're going to town."

"What?" Chase squinted toward the window, then moaned and flopped back on the pillow. "I can't go anywhere. My head's killing me."

"You'd feel a whole lot better this morning if you hadn't been drinking so much last night."

"Don't lecture me, Pa. I'm a grown man."

"You're still living under my roof, so you'll do as I say. Now get out of bed."

Mariah grabbed Daniel's leg and looked up at him with a trembling chin.

Daniel patted her shoulder. "It'll be all right." Whenever his father and Chase raised their voices, she sought refuge with him. He didn't blame her; all their hollering made him wish he could head to the barn, but he wouldn't desert Mariah.

His father picked up a wrinkled shirt and a dusty pair of pants off the floor and tossed them toward Chase. "Put those on and be downstairs in five minutes."

Chase groaned. "Ah, Pa, what's the hurry?"

"We're meeting the eleven o'clock train." His father straightened. "Your future wife is on board, and you need to be there to meet her."

Chase's mouth gaped open. "My what?"

"You heard me. Your bride arrives at eleven. We need to leave right away."

"What? Are you crazy?" Chase grabbed his shirt and stuffed his arms in the sleeves.

"No, but I'm tired of watching you waste your life."

"My life is just fine."

"No it's not. You need to get married again and settle down, so I found you a wife."

"You *are* crazy!" Chase jumped into his pants, grabbed his hat, boots, and jacket, and charged out of the bedroom door.

"Papa, wait. Where are you going?" Mariah reached for Chase as he flew past, but he didn't even slow down.

Daniel blew out a disgusted breath and shook his head. His father had really done it this time. He hustled down the stairs after them with Mariah close behind.

Chase dropped his boots on the kitchen floor and shoved his feet into them. "You can't run my life, Pa." Glaring at his father, he jammed his hat on his head. "I'm not going to town, and I'm not marrying some woman I never met!" He stormed out the door and slammed it behind him.

His father jerked open the door. "Come back in here, young man!"

Chase marched straight for the barn.

His father spun around, his face flushed and his gray moustache twitching. "Go after him, Daniel. Talk some sense into him."

"Me?" Daniel huffed. "What am I supposed to say?"

His father pulled a photo from his jacket and held it out. "Show him her picture. Tell him she's a decent woman who'd make a good wife and mother, and he ought to think about someone besides himself for a change." He glanced down at Mariah, and his angry expression softened a bit.

Daniel examined the photo. A fair-haired young woman with large, pale eyes and a shy smile looked back at him. "Who is she?"

"Her name's Annika Bergstrom. She's from Sweden by way of Chicago. She speaks English and writes a fine hand, and she has good references from her minister and head of the school where she worked."

Daniel rubbed his chin. "She looks mighty young."

"She's twenty-two and never been married. She can sew, tend a garden, clean, and cook."

Song Li gasped, banged a lid on the frying pan, and began ranting in Chinese.

His father spun around. "What's the matter with you?" he boomed.

Song Li waved a wooden spoon and shouted back in Chinese, then switched to English. "Song Li cook! Song Li clean! Song Li take care of family!"

Mariah burst into tears and clutched Daniel's leg.

Daniel laid his hand on Mariah's shoulder and closed his eyes.

Lord, help us!

Chapter 2

The conductor tapped Annika on the shoulder. "We'll arrive in Laramie in a few minutes, miss."

"Oh, thank you." She rose from her seat and hurried down the aisle to the curtained area referred to as "The Necessary." She combed her hair and secured it with a ribbon. Frowning, she tried to brush the dust and cinders from her skirt. The stench from the toilet combined with the swirling cloud of dust set her coughing.

She sagged against the wall of the swaying coach and closed her eyes. Four days of smoke, baking sun, cold nights, unpredictable meals, and little sleep had taken a toll on her. Her head pounded from the noise and smells. Her back and neck ached from the cramped conditions, and her stomach twisted from nervousness and lack of food.

"Next stop, Laramie," the conductor called. "Larrrrramie, Wyyyyyoming!"

Annika gasped and hurried back to her seat. Looking out the window, she scanned the rolling hills dotted with scraggly pine trees. Then they passed a few scattered homes, a small church, a blacksmith, a livery, a general store, a hotel, and a saloon. The train screeched and slowed.

She reached up and wrestled her bag from the overhead rack. Gripping the handle, she stared out at the dozen or so people waiting on the platform. Off to the side, two men and a young girl stood together. The older man looked about sixty and had a bushy silver moustache. The girl with brown curly hair and an impish smile wore a faded blue dress and scuffed brown leather boots. The younger man was tall with broad shoulders and long sturdy legs. His wide-brimmed, wheat-colored hat shaded his tanned face, dark hair, and eyes. He was clean-shaven and handsome in a rugged sort of way.

Her heartbeat picked up. That had to be Charles.

Oh, why did she have to meet him looking so travel-worn? Well, it couldn't be helped. Her mother had always said a pleasant smile and warm greeting made anyone look becoming. She hoped it was true because that was all she could offer today.

The conductor took her bag and set it on the platform, then offered his hand to help her down the stairs.

Mr. Simms walked toward her, followed by his son and granddaughter. He swooped his hat off, revealing a thick head of silver hair. "Miss Bergstrom?"

She smiled and nodded. "Yes, I'm Annika Bergstrom, and you must be Mr. Simms."

"That's right. And this—"

The girl rushed forward and tried to tug the bag from her hand. "I can carry your bag for you. I'm real strong."

"Hold on, sweetie." The other man reached to help the girl. "You better let me get it." He nodded to Annika, but his expression seemed cool.

Her stomach clenched. Was he not pleased with her? Did she look that bad?

"This is my granddaughter, Mariah." Mr. Simms patted the girl on the shoulder.

Then his expression faltered. "And this is my son. . .Daniel."

The name jolted her to a stop, and she blinked. This wasn't Charles? She glanced around the platform, searching for her future groom.

Daniel frowned and looked away. "Do you have any other bags?"

"Yes." She pointed to the baggage car, where a man unloaded her dark brown leather trunk. "That's mine as well."

"I'll load them in the wagon." Daniel strode off down the platform, Mariah at his heels, lugging the smaller bag.

Mr. Simms's moustache twitched, and he turned his hat in his hands. "I suppose you're wondering about Charles."

"Yes. . .I thought he'd be here to meet me."

Mr. Simms nodded and glanced down the platform. "We had some trouble at the ranch this morning, and Chase, that's what he goes by since we're both named Charles, needed to take care of it. But you'll meet him later at the ranch."

"Oh, I see." Although she really didn't understand why Chase would send his family to meet her, rather than coming himself.

Mr. Simms escorted her to their wagon. Daniel joined them and helped the station-master lift the heavy trunk into the back. Mr. Simms invited her to sit up front with him, but Mariah begged her to sit in back. Annika settled in with Mariah on a pile of folded blankets behind the bench seat. Daniel sat next to his father.

As they rolled out of town, Mariah chatted away, telling Annika about all the things she wanted to show her at the ranch, including her doll and her horse, Buttercup. "Let's lay down and look at the clouds." She tugged on Annika's arm.

Annika joined her on the soft quilts and gazed up at the puffy clouds drifting by.

"My Uncle Daniel taught me to find things in the clouds. See that one?" She pointed to a cloud on the left. "It looks like our cat, Precious. My momma named her that. She's mostly black, but she has a white tummy and paws." She was quiet for a moment. "That one over there looks like a milk bucket."

Annika nodded and yawned, trying to take in everything Mariah said, but soon her eyes drifted closed, and she floated off to sleep, dreaming of a dark-eyed cowboy with a wheat-colored hat.

❈

Daniel glanced over his shoulder as the wagon rounded the curve and rolled toward the house. Both Mariah and Annika had fallen asleep only a few minutes into the hour-long ride back to the ranch. They lay side-by-side now, nestled in the blankets.

He studied the young woman and frowned slightly, concern tightening his stomach. She looked much younger than twenty-two and didn't appear to weigh more than an armful of firewood. How would she handle the hardships of ranch life? He'd hate to see her get sick and waste away like Mariah's momma, Eliza. Her death had hit them all hard, especially Chase. His brother hadn't been the same since.

Daniel sighed and shook his head. He, Pa, and Mariah adjusted over time, but

Chase continued to run wild since losing his wife. And the fact Mariah looked more like her mother every day didn't help.

Was that why Chase spent so little time at home? When he was there, he rarely gave his daughter the affection and attention she longed for. It wasn't right. He'd tried talking to Chase about it, but that hadn't helped. Maybe this young woman would give Chase a reason to stay home and spend time with his daughter again, but that seemed like an awful burden to place on her, especially with the way Chase had been acting lately.

Would he treat her kindly or break her heart? That was what really worried him. He didn't like the idea of his father springing a bride on Chase. It wasn't fair to either of them. But he could understand why he'd done it. Somehow, he'd have to get Chase to give the girl a chance.

"Whoa now." Pa reined in the horses, and the wagon rolled to a stop.

Daniel scanned the barnyard and corral looking for Chase, but he didn't see him or his bay gelding, Sundancer.

"Time to rise and shine," Pa boomed to the girls.

Annika sat up quickly and looked around; then she gently brushed the hair from the sleeping girl's face. His father helped Annika climb down.

"I'll take Mariah in." Daniel lifted his niece into his arms and glanced at Annika. Uncertainty creased her pale brows as she looked at the ranch house.

He turned and took in the view as a newcomer might. The large, two-story log house looked sturdy with a fine rock chimney and wide front porch. A small stream wove through the rich grasslands beyond the barnyard, and granite hills rose in the distance. His family had lived on the property for almost twelve years, since the Pacific Railroad came through and brought them here. He and Chase had been fourteen and sixteen at the time. Their mother had died two years later. It wasn't an easy life, especially for women.

He climbed the porch steps and called Song Li. The cook pushed open the door but scowled when he saw Annika. As soon as Daniel and Mariah passed through, Song Li let the door bang closed.

Pa yanked it open. "Come in, Miss Bergstrom."

"Please, call me Annika."

He nodded and set her bag on the floor. "Daniel, you and Song Li get Miss Bergstrom's trunk. I'll take Mariah upstairs."

Daniel nodded and passed him the sleeping girl, then headed out the door. Song Li trailed behind him, muttering in Chinese.

Daniel and Song Li hauled the heavy trunk upstairs. When Daniel reached the top, he stopped and glanced back at Annika. "I suppose you can stay with Mariah for now."

Her cheeks bloomed pink. "Yes, thank you. That will be fine."

They set her trunk down, and she stepped in the room, taking a wide path around him. The poor girl looked scared as a fawn separated from her mother.

He took off his hat and wiped his damp forehead. "Why don't you get yourself settled and then come downstairs? I'm sure Song Li will have supper ready soon."

Song Li glowered at Daniel then hurried out the door.

Annika watched the cook with an anxious expression.

"Don't mind him. He's just worried you're going to send him packing."

Her eyes widened. "Why would he think that?"

"Song Li has been our cook for the last three years since Eliza passed away."

"Eliza?"

"Chase's wife."

Her face flushed. "Oh yes, of course."

"He doesn't like change or anyone telling him how to do his job. But he'll settle down and accept you by-and-by."

She sank down on the edge of the bed where Mariah slept. "Thank you." Her voice came out in a hoarse whisper, and tears collected in her blue eyes.

Daniel nodded and backed toward the door, uncertain what he'd do if her tears overflowed. "Take your time. There's no hurry," he said and ducked out the door.

Chapter 3

Sunbeams slanted through the window the next morning, waking Annika. The other side of the bed was empty, and the angle of the sun told her it was already mid-morning. She flipped back the covers and hopped out of bed. The cool wood floor sent shivers racing up her legs. She washed and dressed quickly, hoping Chase and his family wouldn't think she was a lazy woman intent on sleeping the day away.

Buttoning her dress up the back without her sister's help was a challenge, but she managed it with a bit of wiggling and tugging. With a final glance in the mirror, she smoothed back her hair, ready to face the day and hopefully meet her future husband.

Her stomach fluttered. Would he be as handsome as his brother? What a silly thought. A man's character was more important than his outward appearance. Chase had shown who he was through his letters. That was enough for her. But if he did resemble his brother, she certainly wouldn't mind.

Energy hummed through her as she opened her trunk, took out her apron, and slipped it on over her dress. Today she would begin her new life on the ranch and make a place for herself in the family.

As she descended the stairs to the kitchen, the aroma of coffee and bacon rose to greet her. Her mouth watered.

The only person in the kitchen was the Chinese cook, Song Li. He stood at the counter kneading dough.

"Good morning." She greeted him with a smile.

He glanced her way and continued kneading. "You late for breakfast."

"Oh, I'm sorry." Her face flamed. "I don't usually oversleep. I'm used to rising early. I suppose it was the long trip and the wonderful feather bed."

His somber expression didn't change.

A plate covered with a pie tin sat on the back of the stove. Had they saved her some breakfast? Should she ask about cooking her own?

Straightening her shoulders, she faced Song Li. She was going to be mistress of this house when she married Chase. He ought to show her more respect or at least common courtesy.

But memories of the rude way she had been treated by some of the wealthy students at the Hillman School came flooding back. Looking down on him or treating him unkindly simply because he worked for her would not be wise. Kindness and teamwork would more likely win him over. "Something smells wonderful. What are you making?"

"I cook meat for dinner."

"You certainly are an accomplished cook. The chicken you prepared yesterday was very tender, and the dumplings were delicious, the best I've ever had."

Song Li gave her a curt nod.

She heard voices and the sound of footsteps on the back porch. "You look busy. Shall

I cook myself some breakfast?"

Song Li gasped, and his dark eyes flashed. "You no cook in my kitchen! Song Li cook! Song Li clean! Song Li take care of family!"

Mr. Simms, Daniel, and Mariah walked in during Song Li's outburst.

"I understand. I simply asked if I could make myself some breakfast."

"Your food on stove!" Song Li slammed the bread dough down and wrestled with it as if it was alive.

Daniel hustled over and snatched the plate off the back of the stove. "Morning, Annika." He set it on the table and lifted the lid, revealing a stack of pancakes, scrambled eggs, and several slices of bacon. "Would you like some coffee?"

"Yes, please." Her voice trembled slightly.

"Song Li, I want to speak to you outside." Mr. Simms motioned the cook to follow him.

Song Li slapped the dough down and stalked out of the room. The front door slammed.

Bowing her head, she prayed and asked God to give her peace in the midst of this unexpected storm. After a whispered, "Amen," she lifted her head.

"How'd you sleep?" Daniel asked as he passed her a cup of coffee and took a seat across from her. His gentle tone and smile soothed her.

"Fine, thank you. The bed was very comfortable."

"You didn't mind sharing with me?" Mariah asked, climbing into a chair next to her uncle.

"Not at all. I'm used to sharing with my twin sister, Sophia, so it was a comfort to have you there." She smiled at Mariah, pleased to see the girl's eyes sparkle.

But then, Mariah's warm expression melted away. "I don't have any sisters or brothers, and my momma is in heaven."

Annika's heart clenched. She looked at Daniel.

He didn't seem bothered by the turn in the conversation. His warm gaze rested on Mariah. "Your momma is probably looking down right now proud as can be to see the way you're growing up." He laid his hand on Mariah's shoulder and winked at her.

Her smile resurfaced, and she turned to Annika. "You gonna eat all those pancakes yourself?"

Annika held back a grin. "I believe there are too many for me. Would you like some?"

"I sure would. I been cleaning stalls with Uncle Daniel, and I'm real hungry." She hopped up and got a plate and fork from the stack of clean dishes on the counter.

Annika slid two large pancakes onto Mariah's plate, and the girl sat down again to eat.

Song Li marched back in the kitchen, followed by Mr. Simms. The cook bowed to Annika, his expression grim. "I sorry for bad words. You most welcome in this house." He almost choked on his apology, and Annika suspected he only spoke under threat of losing his job.

"Thank you, Song Li." Annika turned to Mr. Simms. "Has Chase returned yet?"

Mr. Simms exchanged an uneasy glance with Daniel. "Not yet. I think I'll ride out with a few men and see if we can find him."

Annika's stomach tensed. "Do you think something's happened to him?"

Mr. Simms rubbed his chin. "Well now, I wouldn't worry. He's probably fine, just taking his time to settle some things before he comes back."

What did that mean? She glanced at Daniel, hoping he might explain.

But he got up from the table and turned away. "I'll go with you, Pa."

"No, you stay here, show Annika around, and keep an eye on Mariah."

The muscles in Daniel's jaw tightened, but he didn't argue with his father.

Mariah stuffed the last piece of pancake in her mouth. "I don't need no one to watch me. I'm big 'nuff to take care of myself." Then she jumped up from the chair and grabbed her uncle's arm. "Could you take me and Annika for a ride? Please, Uncle Daniel, please."

Annika froze, her gaze riveted on Daniel. She'd welcome a tour of the ranch, but getting on a horse was the last thing she intended to do.

❄

Daniel grabbed his hat and strode out the door. Some days he'd like to tell his father exactly what he thought of his harebrained ideas. He didn't mind staying behind or keeping an eye on Mariah, but he disliked keeping the truth about the situation with Chase from Annika.

The struggle between his controlling father and freedom-loving brother was a long-standing battle. He usually tried to stay out of it or work behind the scenes to help them forge a temporary truce. But bringing Annika here added more fuel to the flames, and he wasn't sure he could stop the smoldering argument from turning into a raging wildfire this time.

He could see why Chase was upset, but running off and leaving them to deal with his unexpected bride wasn't right either. And shoot, it wasn't Annika's fault. What was going to happen to her?

He glanced over his shoulder. Mariah and Annika walked side-by-side a few paces behind him.

"That's the smokehouse where we put all the ham and bacon after we butcher the hogs," Mariah said. "And that's the chicken coop. I feed them every morning and collect the eggs. Over there is the springhouse. That's where we keep all the milk and butter."

Annika smiled. "My family used to have a dairy farm back in Sweden. I helped my parents make butter and cheese."

"Song Li lets me help make butter, but we never made cheese before."

"Well, maybe I can teach you how."

Mariah grinned and took Annika's hand. "That sounds good."

Daniel slowed so they could catch up. It was nice to see Mariah happy for a change. Having Annika around would be good for her, and it would be good for Chase, too, if he'd get himself back here and take some time to get to know her. She had a real pleasing way about her, and those blue eyes of hers looked like the sky on a summer day. Chase would have to hunt a long time to find another bride as fine as Annika.

Well, there was nothing he could do about his brother right now. He might as well help Annika find her way around the ranch. "Over there's the bunkhouse." Daniel pointed past the corral to a long, low building off to the left. "We have about a dozen hired hands. They have their own cook and eat their meals out there, so you won't see too much of them. They're all hard workers, but they can be a little rough around the edges."

Annika's golden brows dipped, and she bit her lower lip.

"They shouldn't give you any trouble. If they do, just let me know. I'll take care of it." Her expression eased, and she nodded. "Thank you."

"That's the old barn next to the bunkhouse," he added. "We store hay there and use the stalls during calving season. And this is our new barn." He lifted the latch on the big double door and pulled it open. "We mainly use this for the horses."

Annika hesitated in the doorway then she hurried in, staying close to Daniel. The sweet smell of hay mixed with the pungent aroma of horseflesh floated out to meet them.

"That's Buttercup." Mariah dragged a stool over to the second stall. She stood on top and reached up to rub her horse's nose. "Isn't she pretty? Come pet her."

Annika shook her head, her face pale.

"It's all right. She's real gentle. She won't hurt you." Mariah's voice was soft and coaxing, but Annika stayed by Daniel's side.

He tipped his hat up and studied her. "Have you ever ridden a horse?"

"Yes, I used to ride when I was younger. But a horse bucked me off. I broke my arm and ankle and had to stay in bed for weeks. A few months after that, we left Sweden and came to Chicago. I've never ridden since."

Daniel rubbed his chin. "That could be a real problem."

She looked up at him, her blue eyes wide. "What do you mean?"

"That's how we get around out here."

"But you have a wagon and carriage." She pointed to the carriage parked at the other end of the barn.

"They're made for the road. If you're going anywhere else on the ranch, you have to ride. . .or I suppose you could walk, but it would take a mighty long time to cover sixteen hundred acres."

Annika's eyes widened again. "Sixteen hundred?"

"That's right." Daniel nodded. "We raise more than three hundred head of cattle, plus all our own grain for feed. Riding is a necessity out here."

Annika bit her lip and stared at the horses, looking like that was the worst news she'd heard since she'd arrived.

Annika sat on the porch steps with Mariah seated in front of her, brushing out the girl's hair. It was so tangled she could only do one small section at a time.

"Owww!" Mariah reached up and clamped her hand over the brush.

"Just a little more and we'll be done," Annika said gently.

Mariah sighed and let go. "All right, but my head feels like it's gonna come off."

"I'm sure you'll be fine. And once we get these tangles out, we can braid it. That'll keep it nice and neat."

"Can we just stop for a minute?"

"All right." Annika leaned back and scanned the rocky peaks and grassy, rolling hills beyond the barn. There was no sign of Mr. Simms and the other men who were still out searching for Chase.

Late-afternoon sunshine slanted across the Ponderosa pines, giving them a golden glow. Even in late October, this was a beautiful spot, so different than the busy streets of Chicago or quiet country lanes in Sweden. Even the sky looked different here, so broad and clear and somehow closer, as though she could reach right up and touch it.

"You think they're gonna find my papa?" Mariah asked, gazing toward the hills.

Annika tensed. "Of course they will." She began brushing Mariah's hair again.

"My grampa says my papa misses my momma, and that's why he's always running off."

Annika's hand stilled. "What do you mean, running off?"

"Sometimes he leaves and doesn't come back for a while."

Annika frowned. "How long is he gone?"

"Two or three days, sometimes longer. I get real worried, but he always comes back."

Chase had told her he was a widower, but he'd said nothing about feeling so distraught over his wife's death that he left home for days at a time. In his letters he sounded strong and steady and eager to marry again. Perhaps Mariah misunderstood her grandfather, or she was talking about something she had heard months or years ago.

Mariah made a small circle in the dirt with the toe of her shoe. "I miss my momma, too, but I don't go runnin' off cause of it."

Annika stilled, a silent prayer for wisdom forming in her heart. "When people lose someone they love, it affects them in different ways."

"What do you mean?"

"When I lost my parents, I cried for days. I wondered if I'd ever be happy again." The memory of that dark time passed over her like a cloud hiding the sun. Five years was long enough to lessen the pain, but not to wipe it out completely.

Mariah looked up at her, sympathy filling her eyes. "You lost both your momma and your papa?"

Annika nodded.

"What happened to them?"

"They died in a carriage accident when I was seventeen. It changed everything for Sophia and me. We had to leave our home, find jobs, and learn to live on our own in a very big city. It was hard, but we made it through by clinging to each other and to the Lord."

Mariah leaned back against her. "I'm sorry about your momma and papa."

Annika swallowed past the tightness in her throat and wrapped her arms around Mariah. "Thank you, Mariah. I'm sorry you lost your momma. I'm sure she loved you very much."

Mariah sat quietly while Annika finished the last section of her hair. Finally, she released a soft sigh. "My momma used to brush my hair just like this."

Tears burned Annika's eyes, and she bent and kissed the top of Mariah's head. "Well, I'm happy I can do it for you."

Hoofbeats sounded in the distance. Annika looked up. Three men rode across the pasture toward the house.

"Here they come!" Mariah jumped up.

Mr. Simms rode in the lead on a big black horse. Annika's heartbeat sped up as she searched the other men's faces. The one on the left was stocky, gray-haired, and had a grizzled beard. The other was middle-aged with dark brown skin and eyes and a drooping moustache. Neither of them looked anything like Daniel or Mr. Simms.

Mariah ran to her grandfather. "Did you find my papa?"

Mr. Simms dismounted and passed his reins to the older man. "Sorry, not yet."

Mariah trudged back to the porch, her shoulders drooping.

Daniel jogged over from the barn. "Any sign of Chase?"

His father shook his head, looking more irritated than worried. "We rode out past Marshall's Creek and talked to the men working out there, but they haven't seen him." He stomped up the steps and strode past her into the house. Mariah followed him inside.

A chill traveled through Annika, and she pulled her sweater more tightly around her. Where was Chase? When would he come back? He'd seemed eager to meet her in the letters they exchanged. Why had he taken off on the day she was due to arrive? She turned to Daniel. "I don't understand."

He was quiet for several seconds, the muscles in his jaw jumping. "Me neither."

"What happens now? Will your father keep looking for him?"

He took off his hat and ran his hand through his dark hair. "We'll find Chase. You can be sure of that."

Chapter 4

Daniel carried a load of firewood into the sitting room and stacked it on the hearth. That should keep the fire blazing for a couple more hours and give them time to enjoy the evening together.

He glanced around at the cozy scene. Annika and Mariah sat side-by-side on the settee holding a book between them. A lantern on the end table nearby gave off enough light for Mariah to practice her reading. His father sat in the large chair on the right of the fireplace with his newspaper and pipe.

His niece scrunched her face as she focused on the book. "The man. . .can see the cat in the. . .tree."

Annika smiled and nodded. "Very good. Try the next line."

"The cat will not. . .come down. What. . .will the man do?" Mariah huffed and lowered the book. "He's gonna have to climb up there and carry that old cat down, that's what."

His father chuckled and lowered his newspaper. "Sounds like you ought to be writing those stories rather than reading them."

"Well, I could make a better story than this." She closed the book and set it beside her on the settee. Her eyes lit up. "Maybe Uncle Daniel could read now."

"Well, I don't want to interrupt your lesson."

Annika looked up and sent him a shy smile. "I think we'd all enjoy hearing the next chapter of *The Adventures of Tom Sawyer*."

Daniel nodded and took the book from the mantel, pleased that Annika as well as Mariah was enjoying the story. He hoped it would ease the worry lines around her eyes and distract her from her concern for Chase. Seven days with no word was wearing on all of them, but she had to be feeling it more deeply.

He settled into his chair and opened the book, determined to do his best to fill the next hour with a lively story and hopefully lift everyone's spirits.

❄

On Thursday afternoon, nine days after Annika had arrived at the Simms's ranch, Annika and Mariah carried two empty laundry baskets outside to the clothesline. Annika set her basket down, scanned the rolling pastureland, and searched for any sign of Chase, but there was none. Where could he have gone? What if he never came back? What would happen to her then?

Her parents had taught her that worry was a sin, so she did her best to catch her anxious thoughts and turn them into a prayer. Pulling in a deep breath, she reminded herself that God knew where Chase was and when he was coming home. Her duty was to trust God and make the best of her situation.

The scent of fresh air and sunshine drifted from the clean cotton sheets dancing in the brisk breeze. Annika tested one of the sheets for dryness. She nodded and plucked a wooden clothespin off the line, then dropped it in her apron pocket. "Pick up that corner, Mariah."

The girl lifted one side to keep it off the ground while Annika unpinned the other. "Uncle Daniel said it might snow soon. I sure hope so."

Annika looked up and searched the blue sky. The few wispy clouds overhead didn't look as though they carried snow, but she'd come to trust Daniel. His years of working on the ranch had taught him common sense and life skills one couldn't learn at school. It amazed her to see the way he could tame a wild horse, mend a broken fence, nurse a sick calf, and even coax a tired and cranky seven-year-old into finishing her supper.

Yes, Daniel was a fine man—smart, patient, and caring.

Too bad his father didn't seem to appreciate him. Why did he overlook Daniel's efforts and continually talk about Chase? Was he trying to convince her she'd made a wise choice by accepting his older son's proposal, or was this always his habit?

Some days she wished she could give Mr. Simms a good shake and make him notice all that his younger son did around the ranch. Even though she'd only been there a little over a week, she could see how much his father's uncaring attitude hurt Daniel.

Lord, help them all see how much they need each other.

She put those thoughts aside and glanced at Mariah. "So, it sounds as though you like the snow."

Mariah nodded and grinned. "Last year, Uncle Daniel and I had a snowball fight, and Grampa took us for a sleigh ride."

She couldn't help noticing Mariah hadn't mentioned her father very often the last few days. She sent off another prayer for Chase as she placed the folded sheet in the basket. "When the snow comes, maybe I can teach you how to make a special treat."

"What kind?"

Annika took the next sheet off the line. "It's a delicious candy called Sugar-on-Snow. You make it by pouring hot maple syrup over some clean snow."

Mariah's eyes widened. "You pour syrup outside on the snow?"

Annika chuckled. "We usually bring the bowl of snow indoors."

"I never made that before."

"I'm sure you'd like it. Do you think your Uncle Daniel—"

The sheets on the line parted, and a man in a dark gray hat poked his head through. "Hello, ladies!"

Mariah spun around. "Papa!" She dropped her end of the sheet in the dirt and jumped into his arms.

He laughed and twirled her around, then tossed her up in the air.

She screamed with delight and dropped back into his arms. "Where've you been? Grampa's been looking all over for you."

"Oh, don't worry. I'm home now."

Annika stared at her future groom. Dust covered his face and clothes, but it couldn't hide the shadows under his bloodshot, gray-green eyes or the scraggly, reddish-brown whiskers on his chin and upper lip.

"Oh, Papa, I missed you." Mariah gave him a big kiss on the cheek.

He set her down and looked Annika over with a lazy smile. "Well now, you must be that gal from Chicago. What's your name, darlin?"

She blinked and swallowed. How could he forget her name after the letters they'd exchanged?

Mariah took his hand and tugged him closer. "That's Annika, Papa. She came all the way out here on a train to marry you."

"Mariah!" Daniel charged around the end of the clothesline, worry etched on his face. "Are you all right?" He caught sight of Chase and skidded to a halt.

"Hey there, brother." Chase staggered over and slapped Daniel on the shoulder. "How ya doing, Danny boy?"

Daniel glared at Chase. "Where've you been?"

"In town and around, takin' care of a little business."

"It's been nine days, Chase."

"Don't worry. I'm fine. . .fine and dandy." He turned and sauntered back toward Annika. "You sure are a quiet little bird, aren't you?" He laughed and slapped his leg like that was the funniest joke he'd ever heard.

She tried to form a reply, but her mouth suddenly felt as dry as desert sand.

"Well, you might not talk much, but you sure are pretty." He wiggled his brows. "I really know how to pick 'em, don't I, Daniel?" He reached for her. "Come here, sweetheart. Show me what—"

Annika froze.

"That's enough!" Daniel grabbed his brother's arm.

"Hey, what ya doin? I wanna talk to my bride."

"You aren't talking to anybody until you sober up." Daniel hauled his brother off toward the barn.

Mariah looked up at Annika. "What's wrong? Where's he takin' my papa?"

Annika shivered. "It's. . .all right. He and your uncle just need to talk."

❄

"You're a skunk! You know that? A dirty, rotten skunk!" Daniel punched his fist into his palm to keep from busting his brother's jaw.

Chase leaned back against a stall door and chewed on a piece of straw. "Why are you so riled?"

Daniel whirled around and faced his brother. "You take off for nine days and never tell us where you're going.

We have to search over half the territory, not knowing if you're dead or alive. Finally, you show up drunk at three in the afternoon. You upset your daughter and insult your future bride; then you act like there's nothing wrong!"

"Ah you're just mad 'cause you had to do my chores while I was gone."

Daniel clenched his fists. "Oh, I'm mad all right, but it's not the extra work or the worry. It's the way you're hurting Mariah and Annika."

Chase scoffed. "I don't even know that gal. I've got no power to hurt her."

"That *gal's* name is Annika. Did you catch it this time? Annika! And you've got more power over her happiness than you know."

"What kind of name is that? German? I thought Pa said she was from Chicago. Well, she better speak English, or I'm not wasting my time with her."

Daniel glared at his brother, wishing he could kick him all the way to Cheyenne. "You have got to be the most small-brained, stubborn fool I ever met!"

Fire flashed in his brother's eyes. He spit out the straw and pushed off from the wall. "I'm not listenin' to any more of your insults."

Daniel hustled after him and grabbed his arm. "Hold on."

Chase growled and pulled away. "It ain't gonna work. I can't stay around here and marry that gal."

He'd better think fast, or his brother was going to climb on his horse and disappear over the hills again. "I thought you cared about Mariah."

Chase stalled in the doorway. "Of course I do."

"You'd never know it from the way you're acting."

Chase swung around and clenched his fists. "You better take that back."

Daniel stepped closer. "It's true, and you know it."

All the starch drained out of Chase, and his eyes glittered with shame. "I love Mariah, but every time I look at her, I see Eliza. I can't take much more of that."

"That's not her fault. She needs you to stick around and do what's right instead of running off every time you and Pa have a fight."

Fire smoldered in Chase's eyes. "I can't abide living in the same house with that man. He's always riding me about taking over the ranch. But there's only one way to do things—his way! Well I'm tired of it!"

"I know he's hard to deal with, but he just wants you to stop running wild and face up to your responsibilities. He doesn't mean to anger you."

Chase huffed and crossed his arms. "You should'a heard him yellin' at me in town yesterday."

"What? He talked to you yesterday?" Why hadn't Pa told them he'd found Chase in Laramie?

"That's right. He told me I'd never inherit one acre of this ranch unless I came home and got ready to marry that little gal."

Daniel sighed and ran his hand down his face. Poor Annika. What had she gotten herself into? Would Chase marry her just to lock in his inheritance? What kind of marriage would that be?

"Listen, Annika's a sweet girl with a good heart." Maybe if he kept repeating her name, it would sink in and his brother would remember. "She's been working real hard to learn how we do things around here. And she's real good with Mariah. She's been teaching her how to read and knit. I think she'd make a fine wife."

Chase scowled. "Not sure I can marry some gal Pa picked out for me."

"Don't hold that against her."

He shook his head. "You think she's strong enough for ranch life? She don't look like she's got enough meat on her bones to make it through winter."

The worry in his brother's eyes hit Daniel hard. He'd wondered the same thing. If Chase married Annika and lost her as he had Eliza. . . His stomach twisted. He straightened and shook off those fearful thoughts. "She seems strong and healthy, but none of us has a guarantee on tomorrow. We've all got to put ourselves in God's hands and trust Him to carry us through whatever's ahead."

"Don't know why I should trust God. He hasn't done me any favors lately."

Daniel studied the lines sin and sorrow had cut in his brother's face, and he felt as though they sliced into his own soul. He loved his brother. Seeing him struggle was hard, maybe harder than going through it himself. But he'd never make the same mistake Chase had by trying to overcome his problems without God's help.

"You're wrong, Chase. God's done more for you than you realize."

"Like what?" He clamped his jaw and narrowed his eyes.

"He's kept you alive and given you a chance to have a home and a family. I'd say those are pretty big favors for a man who's been running away from God and breaking most every commandment in the Good Book."

His brother's face hardened. "Don't preach at me, Daniel. I don't want to hear it."

"Maybe not, but someone's got to tell you the truth. You need to surrender to God and drop that load of grief and bitterness you're carrying, or it's going to destroy you and hurt all the people who love you."

Chase snorted. "Not many people on that list."

Daniel clamped his hand on Chase's shoulder. "I'm on it, right up there with Mariah."

Chase dropped his head and shuddered. "I don't deserve it, Dan, not after everything I've done."

"Chase!" His father strode across the yard toward them, his stern glare slicing a path ahead of him.

Chase turned and nodded to his father. "Pa."

"So, you finally decided to come home."

Daniel winced. Why couldn't his father treat Chase with a little dignity or at least understanding?

"You didn't give me much choice, did you?" Chase and his father locked gazes for several seconds.

"Let me make your *choices* clear. You've got one month to court Annika and convince me you're serious about this, or I'll send you packing myself." His father spun away and marched off toward the house.

Daniel studied his brother's mottled face. If glares could shoot bullets, his father would be a dead man.

Annika pushed aside the curtain of the upstairs bedroom window and bit her lip. Her gaze bounced from Daniel and Chase, standing together by the barn doorway, to Mr.

Simms, striding back toward the house. Even from a distance, she could read the tension between the men in their rigid postures and drawn faces.

What had Mr. Simms said to them? Had Chase really been off drinking all this time? Was that what Daniel meant when he hustled him off to the barn and said he needed to sober up? She didn't have much experience with men who had been drinking, but Chase's voice had certainly been loud, and his actions bordered on obnoxious.

How could he be drunk in the middle of the day? That didn't sound like the man who had written to her. This must just be a lapse in his behavior, a way he dealt with his grief over losing his wife.

Grief could make people act in unusual ways. She'd been through that herself when her parents died. But being a woman, she'd had the freedom to cry and pour out her troubles to her sister and friends. It must be harder for a man like Chase, especially when his father was such a stern, strong man. Maybe Chase never had been given the freedom to grieve for his wife so he could move on and put his sorrow behind him.

Annika clasped her hands. She was no expert at helping people sort out the deeper issues of the heart, but she could pray that God would help her be a good wife to Chase so he might not need to run off or turn to a bottle for comfort or companionship. Surely the warmth of family and the love of a new wife would be enough to keep him on the right path. But could she learn to love and trust a man like Chase? The bedroom door squeaked opened, and Mariah walked in. "Song Li is all done in the kitchen. How about we bake a cake for Papa?"

Annika let the curtain fall back into place and forced a smile. "That sounds like a nice way to welcome him home."

Perhaps it might also make up for the way she'd acted when he surprised her out by the clothesline. She certainly hadn't made a very good impression, gawking at him without a word of welcome. The next time she saw Chase, she'd greet him with a warm smile and a freshly baked apple cake.

Chapter 5

After supper the men settled in the sitting room by the fire with their coffee. Annika carried in a warm, cinnamon-scented apple cake. She'd dusted the top with sugar and placed it on a pretty white plate with a scalloped edge, hoping Chase would be pleased with her efforts.

"Something sure smells good." Daniel smiled at her and then winked at Mariah as she brought in the bowl of whipped cream.

"Me and Annika made apple cake, 'specially for Papa."

Daniel chuckled. "You gonna let your grampa and me have some?"

Mariah's grin spread wider. "Of course you get some, too."

Annika placed the tray on the low table by the settee. Mr. Simms sat in the large upholstered chair to the left of the fireplace. Daniel shared the wooden bench on the right with Song Li. Mariah's small rocker was pulled up close to the settee, where Chase sat on one side, leaving the only empty seat next to him.

She exchanged a brief glance with Chase, and a shiver traveled up her back. He'd changed clothes, washed his face, and slicked back his curly auburn hair, but rough whiskers still covered the lower half of his face. His gray-green eyes held no warmth or invitation. In fact, he had avoided looking at her altogether during supper.

Annika swallowed and focused on cutting the cake. "Who would like some dessert?" The forced lightness in her voice didn't fool anyone.

"Cut me a big slice." Chase sniffed and wiped his nose on his sleeve.

"You want whipped cream, Papa?"

"Sure do."

Mariah added a dollop and passed him the plate. "I helped chop all the apples and mix up the batter."

He nodded to Mariah. "That's nice." Then he glanced at Annika, and his forehead wrinkled for a second. "Thank you, Annie."

Daniel grimaced and looked as though he would correct his brother for calling her by the wrong name, but Annika gave her head a slight shake. Daniel sighed and sat back.

"You're welcome, Chase. Would you like more coffee?"

Chase took a big bite, grunted, and shook his head.

Annika passed plates to the others, and they ate in silence. Annika's spirits wilted like a flower picked and left out on the porch steps in the sun. Even though the fire crackled, spreading its warmth in the room, the temperature seemed to have dropped several degrees. Without Daniel's usual stories and laughter, the atmosphere seemed gloomy and tiresome.

Daniel finally broke the silence. "You girls sure did a fine job with this cake."

Annika looked up, meeting his gaze. Empathy filled his dark eyes, and she forced a smile. "Thank you, Daniel."

Mr. Simms cleared his throat and glared at Chase.

Chase shoveled in the last bite, then glanced at his father and sat up straighter. "Yes, it's real good." But he sounded a bit like a puppet, mouthing words his father wanted to hear. He grabbed his cup and gulped down the last of his coffee. "Well, I think I'll go out and check on the horses."

Daniel blinked and frowned at his brother.

"But, Papa, I was gonna show you how I've been learning to read." Mariah hopped up and took her primer from the basket by the hearth.

"Not now. Maybe later." Chase walked out of the room. A few seconds later, the back door banged shut.

A heavy silence hung over the room. Annika stared down at her half-eaten slice of cake and wished she could dissolve into the floor. Chase obviously didn't enjoy her company.

Song Li got up and bowed slightly to Annika, his expression grim. "You make good cake. I go write to family." He bowed again and fled the room.

Mariah put her primer back in the basket. "I don't feel much like reading."

"That's all right, sweetie," Daniel said. "Why don't you go on up and get ready for bed. I'll come tuck you in after a bit."

Mariah nodded and trudged off toward the stairs.

Annika's heart sank as she watched her go. Poor girl. Couldn't Chase see how Mariah longed to spend time with him?

"That was mighty fine dessert. Thank you, Annika." Mr. Simms got up. "Oh, I almost forgot, I picked up these letters for you when I was in town." He pulled two envelopes from his jacket pocket and held them out to her.

Annika gasped and reached for them with a trembling hand. "Thank you." One glance at the handwriting confirmed they were from Sophia. She clutched them to her chest as though they were gold.

Worry lines fanned out around his old blue eyes. "Hope they bring good news."

"Any news from my sister will be a blessing." She started to open the first envelope then looked up. "I have several letters I'd like to mail to her. Will we be going into town soon?"

Mr. Simms frowned and rubbed his chin. "I think we could go in for church on Sunday if the weather's not too bad."

Daniel glanced toward the window. "I think we're in for some snow soon, Pa."

Mr. Simms nodded. "Long as it's not too deep, we could take the sleigh."

Daniel turned to Annika. "The post office is closed on Sunday. But we could give your letters to someone to mail on Monday."

"Thank you." Annika bit her lip, her face warming. "I was wondering if. . . Well, I don't have any money for postage—"

"I'll take care of it," Daniel said. "And anything else you need, just let me know." Kindness shone from his eyes.

"Thank you, Daniel."

How could two brothers be so different?

❄

Early the next morning, Annika peeked out the kitchen window. Snowflakes fell at a steady pace, covering every rock and dusty patch of dried grass with a powdery white blanket.

Daniel trudged through the snow and tied a thick rope from the barn and outhouse to the back porch so no one would lose their way in the blowing snow. Then he and Mariah went to check on the chickens.

Song Li muttered under his breath while he flipped hotcakes then scooped a heap of scrambled eggs into a bowl.

Annika looked up as Chase entered the kitchen. "Good morning, Chase." She handed him a hot cup of coffee.

"Morning," he grumbled and sat down at the breakfast table.

She tried to engage him in conversation while he ate, but he gave her one-word answers and focused on shoveling in his food.

Finally, he pushed away his plate and rose from the table. "I've got to go outside."

Annika's heart sank. Gripping her coffee cup, she watched him stomp off and slam the back door. Why did he spend almost all his time out in the bunkhouse or barn?

❄

Friday morning, the temperature rose a bit, and the sky finally cleared. Mr. Simms pushed his breakfast plate aside. "Looks like it would be a good day to go into town. Let's head out as soon as we finish our chores."

Annika's heart leaped. Finally she could mail her letters to Sophia and see if any more had arrived.

Mariah hopped up from her chair and ran to put on her coat. "I'll hurry up and feed the chickens!"

Annika laughed and helped her with her buttons. "Don't forget your mittens. Hold on to the rope and stay out of the drifts so you don't get too wet."

"All right." Mariah pulled her mittens from her pockets and dashed out the door.

Daniel smiled as he watched her go then turned to Annika. "We may not get into town again before Christmas. Is there anything you need from the store?"

Song Li faced them. "I already make list."

Daniel and Annika exchanged a glance. "We'll get whatever you need, Song Li, but Annika might like to make something special for Christmas."

Song Li scowled, but he didn't argue. "I check list." He marched off to the pantry with a scrap of paper in one hand and a stubby pencil in the other.

Annika leaned toward Daniel. "Thank you."

"You're welcome."

"There are a few recipes I'd like to make, and maybe we could get some fabric and yarn. Mariah and I want to make some Christmas gifts."

Daniel nodded, looking pleased. "It's nice what you've been doing with Mariah.

She seems real happy."

Working with Song Li, they cleared the table, washed the dishes, and banked the fire in the stove. Then they dressed in their warmest clothes and climbed into the sleigh.

Annika sat in the back seat with Chase, although Mariah sat between them. Song Li placed hot bricks wrapped in cloth at their feet, and Daniel tucked heavy blankets around them before he climbed up front with his father and Song Li. Mariah chatted away, exclaiming over everything she saw as the sleigh flew along the snow-covered road.

Chase barely spoke the entire trip, but Annika was determined to enjoy the beautiful day, no matter how somber and distracted he seemed.

By the time they reached Laramie, the bricks had cooled, and Annika's teeth began to chatter. Her nose felt frozen, and the tips of her fingers were stiff from the cold.

As they pulled into town, they passed the hotel, café, post office, and bank. The one- and two-story brick and stone buildings were smaller than those in Chicago, but most looked relatively new and well kept. Several horses were tied to hitching posts, waiting for their owners to finish their business in town. But only three other sleighs passed as they glided down Second Street.

"Whoa, now." Mr. Simms guided the horses to a stop in front of Iverson's General Store. Mr. Simms jumped down and saw to the horses while Daniel helped Annika and Mariah.

Chase climbed out of the sleigh and tugged up the collar of his coat. He cast a longing glance across the street toward the Silver Nugget Saloon.

Annika's stomach tightened. "Shall we go into the store?" She smiled up at him and took his arm. He nodded, then walked up the steps and opened the door for her.

A small brass bell jingled overhead as they stepped inside. The delightful scents of nutmeg and fresh-cut wood greeted her. Her eyes widened as she looked around. Shelves filled with every kind of food and household item she could imagine covered the walls. Glass jars holding lemon drops and peppermint sticks stood next to the cash register. Baskets of apples, walnuts, potatoes, and onions sat on the floor in front of the sales counter. Bolts of cloth and baskets of thread and notions covered the far wall.

Mr. Simms introduced Annika to Ed and Jane Iverson and their daughter, Mary. Then he joined three other men seated near the potbellied stove, who were discussing the price of livestock and the effects a hard winter might have on their herds.

Daniel spoke to Mr. Iverson about a rifle he hoped to order.

Song Li read his list to Mrs. Iverson. The shopkeeper quickly packed the items into a wooden crate.

"Come on, Mariah, let's see if we can find the fabric and ribbon we need for your dress." She took the girl's hand, led her to the back of the store, and looked at the material on display. As Mary measured and cut three yards of white fabric for them, Annika glanced over her shoulder.

Chase stood by the front window gazing outside, hands in his pockets, shoulders sagging. Suddenly, he straightened and stepped closer to the window. Two seconds later, he hurried over and spoke to Daniel in a low voice, and then without a word to anyone else, he slipped out the door.

Annika clutched the folds of her skirt. Where was he going?

Mariah tugged on her hand. "How much red ribbon do we need?"

Annika swallowed and turned to Mary. "Two yards should be plenty. Thank you."

"Are you making something for Christmas?" the young woman asked as she unrolled the ribbon.

Mariah's eyes danced. "We're making a special dress for me for St. Lucia Day, but don't tell my papa. We're gonna surprise him."

Mary smiled. "Your secret's safe with me. I've heard about that holiday from some other folks." She measured and clipped the ribbon. "I remember they made some special buns and needed saffron. I think we still have some if you'd like it."

"Thank you." Annika followed her to the front of the store. While Mary checked through the spice jars, Annika glanced out the front window, searching for Chase.

She didn't have to look far. Across the street between the saloon and the café, a pretty young woman with long dark hair and a tattered brown cloak stood with Chase. The woman was obviously upset about something. Chase placed his hand on her arm and leaned toward her, his posture tense.

Annika's stomach dropped like a bucket tossed in a well. Who was she? What was Chase saying to her?

Chase shook his head, then turned away and strode back toward the store, his mouth set in a jagged line. The woman called to him, but he didn't look back. Her face crumpled, and she turned and fled down the street, disappearing into the small opening between the saloon and the café.

Annika gulped and glanced around the store. Had anyone else seen Chase and the woman? What should she do—ask him about her or pretend she hadn't seen them?

Before she could decide, Mary held up a spice jar. "Here it is! How much do you need?"

Annika blinked. "Oh, just two teaspoons or so."

Mary nodded and spooned a small amount into a little paper envelope.

Daniel turned and looked at her. A frown creased his forehead. He crossed to meet her. "Are you all right?" he asked in a low voice. "You look almost as white as that material." He nodded to the folded fabric on the counter.

"I'm fine." But her voice trembled.

Chapter 6

Daniel grabbed the pitchfork, scooped up a pile of dirty straw, and tossed it in the wheelbarrow. Mucking out stalls wasn't his favorite way to spend the afternoon, but it sure beat being cooped up inside all day. Too much time sitting by the fire with Annika and Mariah had left him feeling fractious and out of sorts.

Strange, he usually enjoyed the slower pace of winter with more time to read, relax, and repair things that had broken since last winter. But everything seemed different now that Annika had arrived.

It wouldn't be so bad if she and Chase were growing closer and making plans for their wedding, but his brother continued to treat her like a distant cousin, never taking her hand and rarely sitting next to her in the evening. More than six weeks had passed since their father had given Chase the ultimatum, but he still hadn't pressed Chase to follow through on the marriage plans or even confronted him about his standoffish attitude. Even when they'd all taken the day off to celebrate Thanksgiving, Chase had not seemed to enjoy their celebration or his time with Annika.

So what was his problem? How could he not want to marry Annika?

Daniel shook his head and heaved more straw on the pile. The whole situation was about to drive him crazy!

The barn door squeaked open, and Annika stepped in. She looked around and smiled when she saw him. "Afternoon, Daniel."

His chest tightened, and a strange sensation flooded through him. He shook it off. "Afternoon."

"Have you seen Chase?"

"He and a couple men rode out to check the cattle up north past Grier's Peak."

"Oh." Her smile faded and little lines creased the area between her golden brows. "When do you think he'll be back?"

Daniel leaned on the pitchfork. "Maybe not till suppertime."

Pressing her lips together, she turned away and paced across the barn. Then she spun around and marched back, determination in her steps. "Teach me to ride."

"Right now?"

"Yes!" Her bright blue eyes sparkled with life. For the first time, he noticed the pale freckles dusting her nose and cheeks. They looked almost like cinnamon sprinkled on apple pie, sweet and tempting.

He swallowed and looked away. "Well, I wouldn't mind teaching you, but it's awful cold out for riding lessons."

She laid her hand on his arm. "I don't care about the cold. Please, Daniel, I need to learn."

The warmth of her hand melted through him. He stepped back and leaned the pitchfork against the wall. "What's your hurry?"

"That seems like the only way I'm ever going to catch up with your brother." Her voice cracked, and she quickly looked away.

Daniel's heart clenched. He was going to have to talk to Chase. Couldn't he see how much Annika wanted to please him? She'd even get on a horse, though she was terrified of them, just to win his approval.

He straightened. "All right. I'll teach you, but you've got to go change first. Those skirts will just get in the way."

Annika's cheeks flushed a pretty pink. "What shall I wear?"

Talking to her about changing clothes seemed awfully personal, but there was no way he could teach her to ride in that outfit. "Eliza had a split skirt. Check the trunk in Chase's room. It might be a bit big, but you'll probably find a belt in there, too."

Her smile resurfaced, and her eyes glowed. "Thank you, Daniel." She stood on tiptoe and kissed his cheek. Then she turned and dashed out the door.

Heat burned Daniel's face as he stared after her. The sensation of her soft lips brushing across his cheek lingered, making his heart gallop.

Why'd she have to go and kiss him like that?

❄

Less than ten minutes later, Annika brushed her hand down the brown wool split skirt and tried to smooth out the wrinkles. Daniel was right, the skirt was several inches too big around the waist, but she cinched it in with a leather belt.

Wrapping her blue knit scarf more tightly around her neck, she tucked the ends into the front of the jacket. Then she followed the frozen path to the barn.

Her stomach quivered as she pushed open the side door. The thought of getting on a horse again after so many years made her want to turn around and run back into the house, but she had to do this and prove to herself and Chase that she could be a rancher's wife.

Daniel stood in the center of the barn by a huge bay mare, tightening the cinch strap of the saddle. He looked her over with an appreciative smile and nodded. "That's better."

Heat flooded Annika's face. "I hope Chase won't mind my wearing Eliza's clothes."

Daniel frowned slightly then shook his head. "I think he'll be pleased to see you ride."

"I hope so." She sent him a shy smile.

"Come on over and meet Lady Jane." He patted the horse's neck. "She's a good horse, steady and gentle."

"She looks. . .big."

"She's actually one of our smaller horses."

Annika moved closer, but several feet still separated her from Lady Jane. She looked at the animal's big brown eyes, and fuzzy memories of her childhood in Sweden returned. She'd loved riding before the accident, but weeks in bed recovering and her mother's anxious response had squelched her desire. She bit her lip, still hesitant to touch the horse.

"It's all right. Give me your hand." He gently guided her as she stroked the horse's neck. She pulled in a slow, deep breath and relaxed.

Daniel was so kind and caring, always going out of his way to make her feel a part of the family. How many times had he sat with her, listening to her talk about how much she missed her sister? And every morning he carried in extra firewood to lighten her workload. He always seemed to be watching out for her, making her feel safe and protected. Even her two older brothers had never treated her with that much care and attention. Why didn't Chase treat her like that?

She cast a sidelong glance at Daniel. He had deep brown eyes, a fine straight nose, and a firm square jaw. He wasn't bold and flashy like Chase. Instead, he had a quiet strength that inspired her trust and confidence.

He looked down at her, and his hand stilled. His gaze grew more intense and hovered over her face, seeming to take in each detail.

Her stomach fluttered, and her heartbeat sped up. For one second she imagined he was going to lean down and kiss her.

She stepped back. What was she thinking? She'd always had an active imagination, but this was pure foolishness. Daniel didn't think of her like that. She needed to put a harness on her thoughts and keep them in line, or she was going to be very sorry.

She patted Lady Jane's side, willing her heart and breathing to slow down. "She seems very gentle. I'm sure I can ride her."

He cleared his throat. "All right." Then he helped her mount.

For the next hour, she held on tight and tried to follow Daniel's directions. He worked with her in the barn and then took her out to the corral. She focused on staying on the horse and tried not to let her thoughts drift back to those moments in the barn with Daniel. She was promised to Chase. She must not let her affections shift to Daniel. That would only lead to heartache and discomfort between all of them. Her fingers grew cold and stiff inside her gloves, but she didn't complain.

Finally Daniel called her over. "You look mighty chilled."

"I'm all right." But a big shiver raced through her, negating her words.

"We can work on it again tomorrow."

Annika gave in and nodded.

He led her back into the barn and helped her dismount. His warm hand lingered on her waist for just a moment. "You did fine. With a little more practice, you'll be ready to ride wherever you want."

"Thank you, Daniel." She didn't look at him. She didn't dare. Instead, she turned and hurried toward the side door, scolding herself all the way.

Just as she reached for the door, it flew open and smacked her in the face. Her head jerked back, and a thousand white stars exploded around her like the fireworks on Independence Day, and then they rained down and burned into darkness.

❄

At the sound of Annika's muffled cry, Daniel whirled around. She crumpled to the ground like a puppet whose strings had been cut.

Chase stood in the open doorway with his mouth agape. "What. . .what happened?"

Daniel ran to Annika, his heart pounding like a runaway train. He grabbed her limp hand and searched her pale face. A red bump on her forehead was already rising. He looked at his brother. "You big lout. Look what you did!"

Chase stared at her, his eyes wide. "Is she still breathin'?"

Daniel scowled at him. "Yes, but she's out cold."

"It's not my fault. I didn't even see her." Chase squinted at Annika, and his face grew red. "Hey, why's she wearing Eliza's clothes?"

Daniel scooped her up and clutched her to his chest, struggling to keep his anger under control. "You really are an idiot, you know that?"

"What? Why are you mad at me? I didn't knock her out on purpose."

Fire flashed through Daniel. "Don't say another word." He elbowed his brother out of the way and stepped through the door.

"Well, she shouldn't be poking around in my trunk and taking Eliza's things without askin'," Chase called after him.

Daniel clenched his jaw and carried Annika into the house. As he passed through the kitchen, Song Li looked up from chopping carrots. His mouth dropped open.

"Get me some snow and a towel. Bring them upstairs."

The cook hustled off.

Mariah met him coming up the stairs and gasped. "What happened?" The look of fear in his niece's eyes tore at him.

"She'll be fine. She just hit her head." He prayed it was true as he laid her on her bed.

Mariah followed him into the room but hung back.

He gently brushed Annika's soft blond hair back from her forehead. The goose egg was growing bigger by the moment. "Go tell Song Li to hurry up with that snow."

Mariah turned and ran from the room.

He rubbed Annika's hand and called her name, but she didn't respond. A cold knot twisted in his stomach. What if that smack on the head was harder than he thought? What if she didn't regain consciousness? "Come on, sweetheart. Wake up." He rubbed her hand again and whispered another prayer.

Her eyelids fluttered, and she slowly opened her eyes. "Daniel," she whispered. "What happened?"

Relief washed over him. "You ran into the door and got knocked out."

She slowly lifted her hand to her forehead.

"Whoa, be careful. You've got quite a bump there."

Song Li bustled in carrying a bowl of snow. He scooped some into a cloth and handed it to Daniel.

"This will help keep the swelling down." Daniel placed the cold cloth on her forehead.

"Thank you," she whispered then closed her eyes, still looking pale.

Chase leaned his head in the door. "How's she doing?"

"She's awake," Daniel said, "but she's going to have quite a knot on her forehead."

Chase turned his hat around in his hand. "I'm sorry, Annika. I didn't know you were on the other side of that door."

Daniel huffed. *Well, at least he got her name right this time.* He motioned for his brother to come closer.

As Chase approached, Daniel nodded toward Annika, hoping he'd get the message he needed to take over her care.

Chase gave him a pained look but pulled up a chair and sat next to the bed.

Bile burned in Daniel's throat as he strode out of the room. His brother had better change his attitude and start treating Annika right, or he was going to take him out to the barn and teach him a lesson he'd never forget.

Then he remembered how he'd almost kissed Annika, and a load of guilt dropped onto his shoulders. He had no right to be upset with his brother. He'd just about crossed the line and kissed the woman promised to Chase.

❄

A slight headache returned each day the following week to remind Annika of her run-in with the barn door. And if the headache was not enough, each time she looked in the mirror, the purple shadows under her eyes and lump on her forehead brought it all back.

Her hopes to look pretty for Chase were dashed, and she ducked her head whenever he came in the room. He had been a little more attentive after the accident, but soon he returned to spending most of his time outdoors or with the ranch hands, only coming in for meals and when it was time for bed.

Annika had almost grown accustomed to Chase ignoring her, but when Daniel started treating her in a similar fashion, she thought her heart would break. He'd given her one more riding lesson, but he'd kept his distance and avoided conversation. Whenever her thoughts drifted back to that time she thought he was going to kiss her, she scolded herself again and pushed those thoughts away.

She and Mariah retreated to their room for a good part of each day to work on their Christmas preparations in secret. But the truth was she didn't want to face either brother, and for totally different reasons.

"Tell me about St. Lucia Day." Mariah wrapped her doll in a small blanket Annika had made.

Annika smiled and looked up from hemming Mariah's new white dress. "Lucia was a young woman who lived in Rome about a hundred years after the time of Christ. She is remembered for her strong faith and the way she used to go out early in the morning to give food to the poor. She wore a wreath of candles on her head to light the way. In Sweden, people celebrate her feast day on December 13, and the oldest girl in the family portrays Lucia. She wears a white dress with a red sash and a wreath of candles on her head. And she brings special buns and coffee to her family early in the morning. It reminds us we can bring Christ's light and love into the darkest times."

"And I will be our Lucia!" Mariah announced, her face glowing.

"That's right. We'll make the buns this afternoon and get everything ready. Then tomorrow morning you will be Lucia."

Mariah jumped up and danced around the room with her doll.

Annika laughed, and memories came flooding back. She and Sophia had traded off being Lucia every other year. She would never forget the joy that filled her when her mother placed the wreath of candles on her head and handed her the tray filled with fragrant buns and steaming coffee.

Annika and Mariah spent most of that afternoon in the kitchen preparing the saffron-infused Lucia buns. Mariah stood on a stool and helped Annika knead the dough. After it rose, Mariah tucked raisins in the curls of each S-shaped bun. Their sweet fragrance filled the house as they baked.

While they waited for the buns to turn golden-brown, Mariah and Annika wove pine branches into a wreath for Mariah's head. Finding a way to secure the candles to the wreath stumped them for a few minutes. They finally decided to take Song Li into their confidence, and he found some wire to secure the four white candles to the wreath. Now everything was ready for their St. Lucia Day celebration.

❄

The next morning, before the first rooster crowed, Annika and Mariah climbed out of bed. With hushed laughter and whispered words, Annika placed the new white dress over Mariah's head and tied the red ribbon around her waist. Then they crept downstairs to the kitchen and stoked the fire to warm the buns and make coffee.

"Where did you put the wreath?" Mariah asked, her eyes reflecting the glow of the lantern on the table.

"In the pantry on the bottom shelf," Annika whispered.

Mariah tiptoed off to find it.

"Be careful," Annika called in a soft voice.

Mariah returned with the small evergreen wreath made from pine branches they had clipped and woven together the day before.

Annika placed it on Mariah's head. "There. You make a beautiful Lucia, but you have to promise to be calm and walk slowly."

"I will. I promise." She sneezed, and Annika passed her a handkerchief to wipe her nose.

Annika frowned slightly, hoping Mariah wasn't coming down with a cold. "Good girl." She kissed her cheek. "Remember, we want to surprise your father, but we don't want to burn the house down." She reached for the pan of warm buns on the back of the stove.

Footsteps sounded on the stairs.

Mariah gasped. "Uncle Daniel, go back to bed!"

Annika's hand stilled. My, Daniel certainly looked handsome, even with tousled hair and an unshaven face.

He stopped midway down the stairs and squinted at them through sleepy eyes. "What are you girls doing up so early?"

"It's St. Lucia Day!" Mariah announced.

He padded down the steps in his stocking feet and peeked over Annika's shoulder. "Mmm, those sure smell good."

"If you want some," Annika said with a teasing grin, "you'll have to go back to bed."

Daniel cocked his head. "Sounds like a fun idea, especially if you'll bring 'em to me."

Annika's cheeks flamed. She stepped away and took a plate from the shelf with a trembling hand. "I guess you can come upstairs with us if you're quiet."

Daniel grinned. "I'll be as quiet as a fox sneaking up on a hen."

Annika filled the coffee cups and set them on the tray with the buns. Daniel's gaze remained fixed on her, making her stomach flutter. "All right. We're ready."

"But what about the candles?" Mariah pointed to her wreath.

"We'll light those just before you go into your father's room."

Mariah nodded and rushed toward the stairs. Her wreath slipped, and she slowed.

"Let me take the tray for you." Daniel's fingers grazed Annika's.

Tingles raced through her.

"Annika, I—"

She looked up, and his tender gaze rested on her.

"Pssst!" Mariah leaned over the railing. "Come on! We've got to hurry before the sun comes up."

"We're coming." Annika's voice quivered, but not as much as her knees. Lifting her candle, she took a deep breath and followed Mariah upstairs.

Daniel walked just behind her, but she didn't look back.

What had he intended to say? Had she truly seen affection in his eyes, or was her imagination playing games again? He was probably just grateful she'd helped Mariah with this fun surprise.

Mariah stopped by Chase's door, beaming an angelic smile.

Annika carefully lit the candles in her wreath, and a warm glow spread around them, pushing back the darkness.

"Here you go." Daniel gave Mariah the tray and opened Chase's door.

"Good morning, Papa!" Mariah walked toward the rumpled bed. "It's St. Lucia Day, and I made a surprise for. . ." Mariah stopped and stared.

Annika's stomach dropped. The bed was empty. Chase was gone.

Chapter 7

It took Annika well over an hour to calm Mariah. Through her tears, she complained of a headache and stomachache. So Annika climbed back in bed with her, holding her close while they both cried for all Mariah's broken dreams. Finally, Mariah fell asleep. Annika tucked the quilt around her and slipped out of the room.

Down in the kitchen, Song Li slowly stirred a pot of oatmeal and muttered in Chinese.

"Did Daniel and Mr. Simms go looking for Chase?"

"No. They go out to work. They say he not come back till he ready."

Annika slumped in the chair. Ready for what? To run the ranch? To marry her? Would he ever be ready?

How could this happen? Hadn't she prayed and asked God to lead her from the beginning? She'd stepped out in faith, trusting God, Mrs. Mayberry, and Chase with her future. And look where that had gotten her—stuck out in the middle of Wyoming, waiting to become the bride of a man who didn't want her. Was she that unlovable?

Tears stung her eyes, and she wearily pushed her long blond hair back from her face. She'd been so distracted this morning she hadn't bothered to braid it and wrap it around her head as she usually did. She must be a sorry sight.

But it didn't matter. Chase was gone, and so was her hope of being a bride, a wife, and a mother. What would she do now?

Song Li touched her shoulder. "Sorry Chase no like you."

Annika pressed her lips together. He meant to comfort her, but his words tore at her heart. It was true. Chase didn't love her. He didn't even like her. And there didn't seem to be anything she could do to change his mind.

Song Li huffed. "He foolish man. Very foolish."

Annika looked up.

Compassion flowed from Song Li's dark eyes. "You make good wife."

She swallowed against the tightness in her throat. "I'm not so sure about that."

He patted her shoulder. "Song Li see. Song Li know."

A strange moaning cry and a wild thrashing sound came from upstairs.

Annika stared at Song Li, trying to make sense of the noise. Then she turned and ran up the stairs, following the frightening sound. "Mariah?" She dashed down the hall and into their room.

Song Li's steps pounded right behind her.

Mariah jerked and thrashed wildly on the bed, eyelids fluttering.

Annika gasped and ran to her. "What is it? What's wrong with her?"

Song Li shook his head. "I not know. Maybe falling sickness." He bunched up the blankets around Mariah so she wouldn't hurt herself.

Her thrashing finally slowed.

Song Li laid his hand over her forehead. "So hot!" He pulled off the heavy quilt and fluffed the sheet to let in some cool air.

Annika dampened a towel in the washbowl and gently wiped Mariah's forehead, but her face was still flushed and burning. "Mariah?"

She moaned softly but didn't open her eyes.

"She need doctor," Song Li said in a hushed voice.

"I'll stay with her while you ride out to find Daniel and Mr. Simms."

Song Li's eyes grew large. "I not know where they go! I no ride horse! You go!"

Annika shivered. Should she try to find the men or ride to town? The road to Laramie was snow-covered and most likely impossible for her to follow. But she had to get help for Mariah. "Keep her as cool as you can."

Song Li nodded and wiped the girl's forehead.

Annika grabbed her cape and ran down the stairs.

❄️

Daniel shifted in the saddle and gazed out across the snowy hills. A chilling wind blew through the valley. He pushed his hat down and tightened his scarf. That stopped the draft down his neck, but it did nothing to keep his mind from the troubles surrounding his family.

How could Chase take off again? There was no excuse for his brother's heartless attitude toward Mariah and Annika. He didn't deserve such a sweet bride or loving daughter.

Memories from the morning filled his mind—Annika dressed in her long white nightgown with that blue shawl wrapped around her shoulders and her long blond hair flowing down her back. Watching her prepare that tray and light the candles almost did him in. If Mariah hadn't interrupted him, he'd have told Annika exactly how he felt about her.

He had no idea if she had feelings for him. Well, there was that quick kiss on the cheek in the barn the day he'd agreed to teach her to ride, but that seemed more out of gratefulness than anything else. Could she grow to love him the way he loved her? If she did, what would his pa say? And what about Chase? Well, he was tired of waiting for his brother to follow through on the plan to marry Annika.

"Doesn't look like there are any more strays out this way," his father called. "Let's head back to the house and get something to eat."

Daniel nodded. With a gentle nudge of his knees, he urged his horse forward. As they reached the top of the next rise, he spotted someone riding their way.

His father tipped his hat back. "Who's that on Lady Jane?"

Squinting against the sunlight reflecting across the snow, Daniel pulled in a sharp breath. "It's Annika."

"What's she doing riding out this far from home?"

Daniel kicked his horse to a gallop and rode toward her. His father followed.

"Daniel!" Her blond hair blew in the wind as she raced to meet him. The crazy girl wore no hat or gloves. Her cheeks were wind-whipped red and her hands practically blue.

"What's wrong?" Daniel called, reining in his horse.

"It's Mariah. She needs a doctor."

"What happened?" His father demanded, pulling his horse to a stop beside her.

"She had some kind of convulsion or seizure. She's burning up with fever." Tears flooded Annika's eyes.

"I'll ride to Laramie for the doc. You two head home." His father spurred his horse and galloped toward town.

"I was so scared. I didn't know what to do. Song Li said he couldn't ride for the doctor. None of the men were in the bunkhouse, so I saddled Lady Jane, but I didn't know the way to town. I followed your horses' hoof prints and prayed I'd find you—" Her voice choked off in a sob.

Daniel swung down from his horse and reached for Annika. She slid off the horse and into his arms. He held her close while she cried and shivered. "You're freezing."

She sniffed and looked up at him, tears lacing her eyelashes. "I didn't want to take time to dress any warmer. Oh, Daniel, I'm so worried about her."

"She'll be all right," he said, pushing the words past his clogged throat. "You did fine coming out here by yourself." He took off his scarf and put it over her head, covering her ears and crossing it under her chin.

"Come on. You can ride with me." He tied her horse behind his then boosted her up in the saddle. He sat behind her and pulled her back against him. "Put your hands inside and tuck them under your arms."

With one arm wrapped around her, he held her close and rode toward home. Annika soon relaxed against him, and he breathed in the sweet scent of her hair. At last the ranch house and barn came into view.

Daniel rode up to the house and dismounted, then helped Annika down. He tied the horse to the railing and followed Annika inside. "Why don't you warm yourself by the fire? I'll check on Mariah."

Annika headed for the stairs. "I'll be fine."

They found Song Li in the bedroom hovering over Mariah.

Lines creased Song Li's brow. "You bring doctor?"

"Pa went for him." Daniel took off his hat and leaned over his niece. "Mariah?" But she didn't answer. His stomach clenched, and he shot Annika a glance. "How's she been, Song Li?"

"She not talk. Fever still high."

Annika touched Mariah's forehead and nodded. She drenched the cloth in water and gently wiped the girl's face and neck. "Song Li, can you dump that water and refill the pitcher?"

He grabbed the bowl and pitcher and fled the room.

Annika looked up at Daniel. "We need to pray."

He nodded and bowed his head, but his throat felt too tight to speak. Annika slipped her hand in his, and new strength flowed through him. He pulled in a deep breath. "Father, we ask You to have mercy on Mariah. Please bring her fever down and heal her of this sickness."

Annika squeezed his hand. "Father, please watch over Mariah. Bring her back to good health. And help us trust You now and always. In Jesus' name, amen."

Through the next hour, Daniel paced the room, prayed, and watched Annika tenderly care for Mariah. Every few minutes he glanced out the window toward the road, searching for his father and the doctor. Surely he should've been able to reach Laramie and bring him back by now.

Finally, he saw three riders approaching. "Here they come."

Annika crossed to the window and looked out. She gripped the windowsill. "Chase is with them."

They exchanged a glance, and Annika returned to Mariah's side.

Emotions stormed through Daniel. Mariah needed her father, but he hated to see Chase return. He quickly shook off that selfish thought. It was better this way. As soon as Mariah was better, he'd tell Chase how he felt about Annika.

Chase pounded up the stairs. "Mariah!" He ran through the doorway and tore over to the bed.

Pa and the doctor followed him in.

"Oh, Mariah, I'm so sorry I wasn't here." His voice tore from his throat.

"Step aside now, Chase. Let me take a look at her," the doctor said.

Chase moved back and turned to Annika. "Pa told me how you rode out to find him. Thank you." He crushed her to him in a tight hug.

She slowly lifted her arms and wrapped them around him.

He held her close and rocked her slightly back and forth. "I'm sorry, Annika. So sorry."

Daniel stared at his brother holding Annika. His chest constricted, and he felt like a boulder rolled over him, crushing out his breath.

He clamped his jaw, then turned and walked out of the room. There was no way he could stay here and watch Chase take Annika and make her his own.

❄

Annika spent the afternoon nursing Mariah, trying to keep her as cool and comfortable as possible. But Mariah's condition didn't change. Chase came in for a few minutes every hour, and Mr. Simms checked in often. It wasn't until suppertime she realized she hadn't seen Daniel for quite a while.

As the room grew darker, she lit the lamp on the table.

Song Li brought her a plate of stew and corn bread. "You not eat all day." He scowled at her. "Eat now, or you get sick."

Annika took the plate and thanked him. "Where's Daniel?"

Song Li turned away and straightened Mariah's covers.

"Song Li, I asked you a question."

The cook spun around. "He go hunting."

"Hunting? In this weather?"

Song Li shrugged and hurried out the door, a guilty look on his face.

What was going on? Why would Daniel leave when Mariah was so ill?

She set aside the plate and checked Mariah once more. She was still warm but resting peacefully.

Annika hurried downstairs and passed through the quiet kitchen. Maybe Chase or Mr. Simms could explain where Daniel had gone. She heard the two men talking as she approached the sitting room.

"I'm sorry, Pa. I know I should've said something sooner."

"How can you just up and decide to marry some gal you met in town when you've got a bride out here at the ranch waiting for you."

Annika froze. Surely she'd misunderstood them.

"It wasn't my idea to bring Annika here. That was all your doin'. If you'd let me pick my own bride, we wouldn't be in this mess."

Annika gasped then strode into the sitting room. "I can't believe this. Who wrote the letters?"

"That would be me." Mr. Simms's moustache twitched. "I'm sorry. I thought when he met you, everything would work out fine."

Chase stared at her, a pinched expression on his face.

She grasped the back of the settee. "So you never wanted to marry me?"

He hesitated then shook his head. "It's nothing against you. I've been courting a woman in Laramie since September."

Suddenly, Annika remembered the young woman who had spoken to Chase that day they'd gone into town.

"She's a real sweet gal. Her pa died last summer. He was a miner. She'd already lost her ma years ago, so she came into town looking for work."

His father groaned. "Don't tell me she works at the Silver Nugget!"

"No, she works at the café, but that's no life for her. We want to get married so she can live out here with me."

"Why didn't you tell me before?" Mr. Simms demanded.

Chase straightened. "Her name's Angelica Morales. She's Mexican."

Mr. Simms's face flushed. He turned away and braced his hand on the mantel.

"She's a good woman, Pa. I love her. It shouldn't matter where her parents came from."

Mr. Simms turned to Annika. "I never should've written those letters." He sighed and rubbed his forehead. "We'll buy you a ticket back to Chicago tomorrow. That way you'll be home by Christmas."

Annika stared at him. Home? She had no home in Chicago. She'd given up the room she and Sophia rented. Sophia and Lars lived in northern Illinois with another family until their parsonage could be built next spring. Her brothers lived in Sweden, and she had no money to pay her passage back to her homeland. Where would she go? What would she do?

Chapter 8

D aniel trudged through the snow to a small hunting cabin halfway up Grier's Peak. He and Chase used it each fall when they hunted elk, antelope, or white-tail deer, but he'd never come up this late in the year. He wouldn't be here tonight if there was anywhere else he could go to get away from Annika and Chase.

But leaving the ranch didn't blot out the image of Chase taking Annika in his arms. That tormenting memory sent a searing pain through him each time it returned.

"Why, Lord? Why did I fall in love with Annika when she was promised to my brother?" He struggled against the unfairness of it as he built a fire and tried to warm his hands.

It wasn't right. Chase would crush her spirit and heap a load of burdens on her shoulders unless he changed. Closing his eyes, Daniel clasped his hands while he wrestled with his conflicting feelings. He had to stop thinking of himself and how he hated to lose Annika. If he truly loved her, it was time he put her needs first.

He bowed his head. "Oh Lord, for Annika's sake, help Chase become a better man and a loving and faithful husband. Protect her and bring her all the love she deserves."

A sense of calm settled over his soul. He'd won the first battle, though he knew many more would come.

He could never stay at the ranch and watch Annika and Chase together. It would be too hard. He'd have to head west and make a new life far from Annika and the rest of his family.

❄

Song Li burst into the sitting room. "Come quick! Mariah wake up."

Annika hurried upstairs with the men right behind her. As soon as she entered the bedroom, she could see that Mariah's coloring looked better.

Chase rushed to the bedside, nearly knocking Annika out of the way. "Oh, darlin', are you feelin better?"

"Papa!"

"That's right, darlin. Your papa's here, and he's never leaving you again."

Mr. Simms and Song Li huddled around, while Annika stood back, no longer feeling a part of the family. But Mariah called for her.

Song Li brought a bowl of broth, and Annika tenderly fed it to her. They left Mariah in her care, and not long after, the girl settled back in bed and fell peacefully asleep.

Annika's eyes burned as she tucked the blanket around Mariah. Would Chase's new wife continue teaching her to read? Would she help her learn to knit or sew or bake cookies? Who would help her finish the Christmas gifts?

And what about Daniel? Mr. Simms and Chase had no idea where he was hunting or when he would return. As she thought of never seeing him again, she felt like a flower crushed in the road by a hundred wagon wheels.

Oh Lord, this is too much to bear. Please carry it for me.

With an aching heart, she lifted the lid of her trunk and began packing. They'd leave the ranch tomorrow morning by nine so she could catch the ten-thirty train headed east. Heaven only knew what would happen to her then.

❄

The jingle of sleigh bells filled the air as Annika and Mr. Simms sped down the road toward Laramie.

Mariah had begged to go along and see Annika off at the station, but Chase felt it would be too upsetting for her, especially since she was still recovering. So Mariah and Annika said a tearful good-bye at the ranch. Chase and Mr. Simms stood nearby looking grim. Song Li cried and fled the kitchen, clutching a dishtowel to his mouth.

She stared across the snow-covered landscape feeling as numb and frozen as the stream they'd just crossed. So much had happened in the last twenty-four hours that she could barely take it in.

How could she be leaving Wyoming? The thought of returning to the crowded, busy city weighed her down, but not as much as leaving without saying good-bye to Daniel. If only she could have seen him one more time.

Mr. Simms flicked the reins, and the horses picked up their pace. He glanced up at the overcast sky as they entered Laramie. "Looks like we're in for some more snow."

Annika lifted her face as the first few flakes drifted down in a lazy dance then flew past the sleigh. She pulled her coat more tightly around her, trying to keep out the cold wind.

Mr. Simms rounded the corner and approached the train station. "Whoa, now," he called to the horses, and the sleigh glided to a stop. They climbed down, and Mr. Simms made arrangements for her trunk. They walked inside, and he purchased her ticket.

In five days she'd be back in Chicago. What would she do then? Who would take her in? Where would she find a job? A shiver passed through her, and she gripped her bag.

Annika glanced toward the windows. "You don't need to stay. I can wait in the station until the train comes."

Mr. Simms's silver brows dipped. "I wouldn't feel right leaving you here alone."

"I'll be fine." The truth was she didn't think she could take one more extended good-bye.

"Looks like the storm is picking up. I suppose I should head back."

Annika nodded, her throat feeling tight and dry.

He removed his hat and looked at her with sorrowful eyes. "I'm truly sorry for the way things turned out. I just wanted to help Chase. I hope. . ." He stopped and cleared his throat. "You're a sweet girl, Annika. You deserve a good husband who'll love you and take care of you."

"It's all right," she said, forcing out her words. She thought of Mariah and how much she loved her. "A parent will do just about anything to help a child."

He nodded and sent her a sad smile. Then he placed his hat on his head and walked out the station door.

Annika sank down on the bench and blinked back her tears. Now she was all on her own.

Chapter 9

Daniel rode to the top of the hill and reined his horse to a stop. His heartbeat kicked up as the barn and ranch house came into view. Gripping the reins, he debated his decision a few more seconds. Should he ride on past and avoid the pain of seeing Annika with Chase, or should he stop and say his final good-bye to his family?

He shook his head and huffed out a disgusted breath. He couldn't put them through the same worry they'd experienced when Chase up and left without a word. How could he think of heading west without knowing Mariah was on the mend and Chase was finally treating Annika as he should?

He spurred his horse to a gallop and headed for the house. When he walked inside, he found the sitting room empty. He straightened his shoulders and entered the kitchen.

Song Li looked up from stirring a big pot on the stove. He nodded to Daniel, his expression somber.

Chase sat at the table drinking a cup of coffee, but Annika was nowhere in sight.

"Welcome back," Chase said. "How was the hunting?"

"Not good." Daniel shook his head. "How's Mariah?"

"Better. Her fever broke last night. Doc says she needs to stay in bed, but it's not easy keeping her there." Chase chuckled and took another sip of his coffee.

Daniel glanced toward the steps. "Is Annika upstairs with her?"

Chase's smile faded, and he exchanged a wary glance with Song Li.

"What?" Daniel's gut clenched. "She's not sick, is she?"

"No." Chase stood and put his coffee cup in the sink.

"Well, where is she?"

Chase turned and faced him. "She's on her way to Laramie to catch the ten-thirty train to Chicago."

"What! You're sending her back?"

"That's right." Chase snatched his hat off the table and jammed it on his head.

Daniel grabbed his arm. "But you're supposed to marry her!"

"I can't. I met a gal in Laramie, and I've been courting her since September." Chase stepped back, as though he expected Daniel to take a swing at him.

Daniel's jaw fell slack. "You're not marrying Annika?"

He shook his head. "I know you and Pa want me to, but I can't do it. I love Angelica. We're getting married as soon as Pa settles down and gets used to the idea."

Daniel stared at Chase for a second, and then his face split into a big grin. He gripped his brother's shoulders. "You just made me the happiest man in Wyoming!" He turned and dashed toward the back door.

"Hey, where are you going?" Chase called.

"To Laramie! I've got to beat that train!"

"But you'll never get there by ten thirty."

Daniel jumped on his horse. "Watch me!"

❄

Annika sat on the hard wooden bench and stared at the huge snowflakes swirling past the station window. Her thoughts drifted back to the ranch. Was Mariah still improving, or had her fever returned? Was Chase spending time with her, or had he left her alone in her room? Surely now that he'd revealed his reason for spending so much time in Laramie, he'd be more open with his family and give Mariah the attention she longed for.

Please, Lord, let it be so. She needs her father's love so much.

Her thoughts shifted to Daniel, and her heart grew heavier. Was he safe and warm? Had he returned from his hunting trip? Was he sorry she'd left? Would he miss her even a little? Tears clogged her throat, but she refused to let them fall. Instead she swallowed and clasped her hands tightly in her lap.

The truth was clear now. She loved Daniel. But she'd never know if he returned her affection. She'd be back in Chicago soon, and Daniel would return to his life on the ranch. Chase would bring his new wife home, and they'd all settle in together and forget about Annika. She'd be just an uncomfortable memory—that mail-order bride who'd arrived unexpectedly and been sent home when no one wanted her.

A terrible pain stabbed her heart, and she squeezed her eyes shut.

The stationmaster cleared his throat as he stepped out from his office. "The train should be here any minute. It's running a little late because of the snow."

Annika lifted her head and thanked him, but her voice came out in a choked whisper.

He nodded and sent her a concerned glance, then crossed the room to add coal to the stove. "This storm looks like a bad one. But don't worry. The train will plow right through. You'll be back in Chicago before you know it."

That was exactly what she was afraid of.

The station door burst open. "Annika!" Daniel strode in, snowflakes covering his hat and shoulders.

She gasped and rose on trembling legs. "Daniel. . .what are you doing here?"

He rushed across the room and took her in his arms. "Thank the Lord you're still here." His voice was rough with emotion.

Her tears finally overflowed. He'd come all this way in the storm just to say good-bye. But now that he was here, how could she ever make herself get on that train and leave him. She stepped back and looked up at him with a trembling smile. "Thank you for coming. I didn't want to leave without saying good-bye."

"Good-bye?" He stared at her. "No, please, don't go."

"I can't stay. Chase is marrying someone else."

Daniel clutched her shoulders. "Then stay and marry me."

Annika stilled. "What?"

He took hold of both her hands. "I love you, Annika Bergstrom. I have from the first day you stepped off the train, but I. . ." His voice choked off, and he looked at her through glistening eyes.

"Oh, Daniel." She flung her arms around his neck.

Laughing, he picked her up and spun her around. "I take it that means you'll stay and marry me?"

She nodded, still struggling to believe the love shining in his eyes. "Yes, Daniel! Yes!"

Chapter 10

Christmas Day arrived bright and clear with a fresh snowfall covering the ground. Inside the Simms's house, happy preparations gave way to a merry celebration. Mariah wore her St. Lucia dress and served buns and coffee to the family early that morning.

A happy glow filled Annika's heart as she lit the candles around the house and on the small pine tree they had decorated with dried fruit, straw figures, popcorn, and cookies.

After breakfast Mr. Simms read the Christmas story as they all sat by the fire. Then Annika and Mariah gave hand-knit scarves to each of the men. Chase delighted Mariah by giving her a beautifully illustrated book titled *Young Folks Christmas Book*. Song Li gave the family a Chinese tea set.

Daniel presented Annika with a lovely gold locket. Her heart nearly burst with joy as he fastened it around her neck.

In the early afternoon, Chase brought Angelica Morales to meet the family. Her dark laughing eyes and warm smile delighted everyone, even Mr. Simms. She presented each person with a little tin of homemade cookies.

Angelica gave Mariah a little doll she had fashioned for her. Mariah promptly named her Angel and carried her everywhere, even seating her at the table for Christmas dinner.

"This is the nicest Christmas we've had in a long time." Daniel winked at Annika then slipped his hand into hers under the table.

Her stomach fluttered, and she smiled at him. What a blessing to be chosen and loved by such a fine man.

"It certainly is," Mr. Simms added. "The best part is seeing everyone together around the table." He smiled at Chase and Angelica, then at Annika and Daniel. Finally, his warm gaze rested on Mariah. "Merry Christmas, everyone. Let's pray."

Annika bowed her head and held tightly to Daniel's hand.

"Dear Heavenly Father, we thank You for Your kindness and goodness to our family. Thank You for healing Mariah and for bringing such fine wives for my sons. You've blessed us, and we're grateful. Help us remember the best gift of all, Your Son, Jesus. Let us welcome Him into our hearts today and always. Amen."

Annika lifted her head and glanced around the table, basking in the knowledge she had a special place in the family now. She looked across at Angelica, and they exchanged a smile. Right then, Annika made up her mind to do all she could to help the young woman feel accepted and welcome.

Mr. Simms shook out his napkin. "Well, what are we waiting for? Song Li, bring on the feast!"

The cook carried in a big platter of glazed ham. Soon bowls of mashed potatoes, green beans, beets, spiced plums, and applesauce covered the table. Laughter and lively conversation filled the air as they enjoyed the special meal.

When it was time for dessert, Annika brought in a big bowl of rice pudding sprinkled with cinnamon. "This is a special Swedish tradition."

Chase frowned. "It looks like rice pudding."

Angelica's eyes flashed, and she nudged him with her elbow.

"Well, it is rice pudding, but there's a surprise in someone's bowl," Annika said as she passed them around the table.

Mariah's eyes grew large. "What is it?"

Annika's cheeks grew warm. "There's an almond hidden in the pudding, and Swedish tradition says whoever finds it will marry soon."

Mr. Simms chuckled. "Well, eat up, and let's see who gets the prize!"

They all dug into their bowls, while Chase and Daniel teased each other about finding the almond first.

"I'm too young to get married," Mariah said, "but I sure like this pudding."

Annika laughed then crunched down on the almond. "Oh my. . .I got it!"

Laughter and cheers rose around the table.

Daniel grinned and lifted his coffee cup. "Here's to my beautiful Christmas bride. Almond or no almond, we're getting married next Sunday." Then he leaned closer and kissed her tenderly. "Merry Christmas, sweetheart."

His kiss left her breathless. "Merry Christmas," she finally whispered. Then, with her heart overflowing, she lifted a prayer of thanks to God for His faithfulness.

All the time, even when she couldn't see it, God had been working on her behalf, bringing everything together to give her the desires of her heart—a loving husband and wonderful family.

What an amazing blessing—what a wonderful plan.

Carrie Turansky has loved reading since she first visited the library as a young child and checked out a tall stack of picture books. Her love for writing began when she penned her first novel at age twelve. She is now the award-winning author of 15 inspirational romance novels and novellas, including "The Governess of Highland Hall" and "Where Two Hearts Meet." Carrie and her husband Scott have been married for thirty-seven years and make their home in central New Jersey. They enjoy traveling together on ministry trips and visiting their five adult children and four grandchildren. Carrie also leads women's ministry at her church, and when she is not writing, she enjoys spending time working in her flower gardens and cooking healthy meals for friends and family. You may connect with Carrie through her website: http://carrieturansky.com/, and on Facebook, Pinterest, and Goodreads.

Home for the Holidays

by Mildred Colvin

Dedication

To Jim and Jon for letting me bounce ideas off them.

For we are his workmanship, created
in Christ Jesus unto good works,
which God hath before ordained that
we should walk in them.

EPHESIANS 2:10

Chapter 1

October, 1888

Anna Wilkin missed her trousers. Not that she wore them all the time, but they were a lot more comfortable than the new party dress she'd made for her best friend, Larkin's, birthday party. The lace around her neck scratched, and the bustle Larkin talked her into adding felt like a cage attached to her backside. She ran her finger around her neck for the tenth time.

"Stop that," Anna's older sister hissed in her ear. Kathleen could be so bossy. "You're scratching like a hound dog, and you're liable to tear that nice dress."

Anna ran her finger under her chin again just to annoy her sister. "I shouldn't have listened to you and Larkin in the first place. The only reason to wear something this fancy is if you're trying to snag a man, and I'm not."

She didn't wait for Kathleen's next comment but moved to stand by Larkin near the refreshment table. Looked like she needed rescuing from Abigail Leonard anyway. Although a friend of Anna's, Abigail didn't like Larkin for some reason.

"What are you two talking about?"

Abigail turned and looked right past Anna. Her eyes widened and a smile curved her lips.

Anna swung around. All she saw were four men standing in the doorway looking uncomfortable. Maybe she'd missed something. She looked back at Abigail. Oh, but of course. Abigail always took note of new men. But even Larkin seemed focused on them.

Why? Anna narrowed her eyes and studied the men. The tall, dark-haired one might be all right. Another one was maybe an inch shorter with lighter hair. He had a square jaw with a cleft in his chin. Another, some might consider the most handsome, stood between those two. He glanced their way with bright blue eyes but didn't seem to take notice of any of the girls. An unfriendly sort maybe. Anna didn't bother with the fourth man.

Larkin's father greeted the four newcomers, welcoming them as if he'd always known them.

Kathleen moved beside Anna. She leaned forward to look at Larkin. "Didn't I see you talking to those men last Sunday after church?"

When Larkin didn't respond, Anna turned to look at her friend.

Larkin's hazel eyes had a glazed look, the kind she got when she was deep in thought, something she often credited to her mama's Chinook blood.

Anna frowned. Larkin couldn't be interested in those men, could she? Of course, she was nineteen years old now—plenty old enough to marry. In another three months, Anna would be eighteen. Little more than a year younger, but she was in no hurry to grow up.

Anna sighed. If Larkin was smitten, she wouldn't give away her secret. In fact, a change of subject might be a good idea. She swiveled around to face the table. "Hey, what happened to all the cookies? They're almost gone."

From a group of girls gathered at the other end of the table, Abigail's younger sister Elizabeth stepped closer. She giggled and held up a half-eaten cookie. "Maybe I should offer some to our new guests."

Abigail frowned. "Hush, Lizzie, you're too young to even be thinking about such things."

Elizabeth's eyes opened wide. "What? Eating?"

"No. Men." Abigail lifted the tray off the table. "Someone may as well eat what's left of these. I'll take them around." She smirked at Larkin. "Maybe you should have let your cook make the refreshments."

Larkin didn't flinch at the jab, but the words had to have hurt her. Anna glared at Abigail. She might be her friend, but she could be so cruel sometimes, and she never had a good thing to say to or about Larkin. Everyone else loved Larkin.

"She didn't make them, Abigail." Anna stepped between her two friends. "I did. There's more in the kitchen. I'll go get them while you ladies drool over the new men."

Anna spoke over her shoulder as she left. "You can carry cookies to them if you must, but you'll never catch me falling all over myself just to get attention."

What made girls act so silly when it came to men? Maybe someday marriage to the right man would be all right, but not yet. Being free to be herself meant so much more. Working with Papa in the woods, helping him the way he'd expect a son to, that's what she liked. A husband would be a hindrance for sure. Maybe that's why she and Larkin had become so close. Larkin liked fishing, climbing trees, and swimming, same as she did. Larkin was sweet and kind, too. She and her family often delivered food to the needy, which was something to respect.

Anna admired Larkin's home as she crossed the room. Tonight, the formal parlor had become a festive faux ballroom to celebrate Larkin's birthday. The elegant room had been emptied of furniture, so there'd likely be dancing later. Anna snickered. If her parents gave her or Kathleen a birthday party, it'd probably be held in their barn. They mostly stayed at the logging camp, but they owned a big two-story house in town where they spent their weekends. They didn't have a room as large as this one, or as nice. Considering where Larkin lived, most people might expect her to be a snob, but she wasn't. And the fifteen months separating them didn't stop her from being Anna's friend.

A small orchestra in the music room played one of Anna's favorite songs. She could hear it in the kitchen as she worked. She arranged the tray of cookies while she hummed with the music then sang the chorus to the catchy new tune called "Clementine." "Thou art lost and gone forever. Dreadful sorry, Clementine."

Her feet itched to dance when the band switched to a lively polka. She headed back down the wide hall, carefully holding the tray of cookies. A quadrille had started. Oh my, Larkin and Kathleen were dancing with two of the newcomers. Abigail and her brother, Garrick, along with the reverend's son and daughter, Matthew and Natalie Bollen, made up the other set. She shook her head. Couldn't they have mixed it up so Abigail and Natalie didn't have to dance with their brothers?

She held the cookies high to navigate past the swinging dancers. She'd almost made it to the refreshment table when Garrick stepped back against her shoulder, knocking her off balance.

"Oh." She stumbled, and her tray tilted. Garrick grabbed for it and hit her instead, knocking her into a hard wall of warm flannel.

"Oomph!" A male voice huffed in her ear.

The aroma of bay rum aftershave surrounded her. His arms closed around her, and she landed in a very undignified heap on the floor, or more precisely, on his chest while he sprawled on the floor.

Again he *oomph*ed in her ear.

Anna scrambled away and turned to stare into the most beautiful light blue eyes she'd ever seen. The man shook his head as if to clear it and rolled to a sitting position, holding his stomach. Cool air rushing up past Anna's ankles brought her to her senses, and she jerked her dress back into place. She should have worn her trousers. The uncontrollable urge to burst out laughing took over, and she buried her face in her arms before she gave in. Everyone's stares and the poor fellow trying to get his breath filled her awareness, yet the music played on. Her shoulders shook from the laughter she held in. Didn't the musicians know she'd taken their job of entertaining? A very unladylike snort escaped her nose.

"Miss, are you all right?" a deep voice asked while a warm hand cupped her shoulder. "Are you hurt? I'm sorry. I got my feet tangled in your skirt when you hit me."

That remark, and the effort to keep from laughing, brought tears to her eyes. Her shoulders shook again.

"Anna, are you all right?" Larkin knelt beside her.

Garrick joined Larkin. "I'm sorry, Anna. I didn't see you."

One peek at the worried expressions on their faces broke Anna's control, and her laughter pealed forth. A moment later, Garrick laughed, too.

With a crooked smile, Larkin stood and waved at the others who'd pressed close. "All's well. Papa, would you have the orchestra play something new so we can begin another dance?"

When he nodded, she turned to Anna and the poor man struggling to get off the floor. "This seems the appropriate moment for introductions. Anna, this is Jeremiah Tucker from Seattle. Mr. Tucker, I'd like you to meet my dearest friend, Anna Wilkin."

On her feet again, Anna smiled at the tall, dark-haired man who watched her as if she might break. "I'm glad to meet you, Mr. Tucker. I'm sorry I bumped into you. Garrick hit me in one of the turns. Did my. . .did I hurt you?"

Her face burned. She'd almost mentioned her bustle. She still felt bruised where she'd landed on the thing. Why she'd agreed to wear it, she had no idea.

He chuckled. "No, I'm fine, except I believe you owe me a dance, Miss Wilkin."

Anna motioned to the scattered cookies. "I can't. The mess—"

"Go ahead." Larkin touched her shoulder as if to guide her away. "I'll—"

"We'll clean it up." The blond man with the cleft chin drew Larkin closer to him and out of Anna's way. "Go dance."

"Thanks, E.V." Mr. Tucker motioned to where the other dancers were lining up. "I became quite concerned when I thought you were crying."

"Crying? Me?" Resigned to dance with the poor man, Anna shook her head. "I assure you, I would not be crying over a silly spill such as that."

❄

Jeremiah Tucker kept a close eye on his dance partner. She was a petite young woman. He'd hate it if she were injured. Thankfully, she didn't seem to be. A pleasant smile brightened her pretty face while her quick, sure steps kept time to the polka. Something about her struck a chord in his memory. Rebekah would be about the same age if she'd lived. She'd always been as plucky as this girl, too.

They locked arms and twirled in a circle. He grinned at her. "Tell me, Miss Wilkin, what's a fun activity you enjoy even more than dancing?"

"Fishing." She giggled and moved away.

She was teasing, and he was intrigued. They came together, and he took her small, gloved hand to lead her through the steps. He could tease, too.

"So you sink worms and like it?"

"Of course, every chance I get. Mama thinks it's unladylike, but she cooks all the fish I catch." Her dark brown eyes sparkled with humor.

How refreshing to talk to a girl who didn't bat her eyelashes. "Go fishing with me Sunday afternoon. Maybe you can show me how."

A light flickered in the depths of her eyes before the dance carried her away from him. She'd caught on to his skepticism. The girl was fun, cute, and smart.

When she returned, she accepted his hand, twirled, curtsied, and stepped into place beside him, graceful and light on her feet. "I will, with my friend. Right after lunch. Meet us at the lake."

"I'll be there, Miss Wilkin." He hadn't expected her to accept. His grin remained as the set came to a close. He bowed, and she offered a little curtsy.

"Mr. Tucker, there you are." A beautiful young woman resembling Anna, her sister perhaps, hurried toward him. "The orchestra has agreed to play some popular songs for us to sing. Please say you'll join our group."

"I'd be delighted." Jeremiah turned toward Anna in time to see her long blue skirt flare out as she pivoted away. She stopped beside Garrick Leonard, one of the workers at the logging camp. They exchanged words then walked to the refreshment table where E.V. and Miss Whitworth were talking. About time his friend found a female who could woo a conversation out of him.

Movement at his side brought his attention back to Kathleen. "Your sister and Garrick Leonard seem to be good friends."

A frown touched her brow. "Yes, they are."

Jeremiah chuckled.

"Is something funny?"

"Sorry, your kid sister just doubled up her fist and punched Leonard."

Home for the Holidays

Kathleen shrugged. "Anna is a child. Garrick—Garrick is—" She turned away with her fingers pressed to her eyes. "Will you excuse me? Something's in my eye."

As she hurried away, Jeremiah wondered if he should follow, but Anna's laughter rang out, capturing his attention. Rebekah would have loved her, but his little sister was gone, taken in the same fire that killed his parents. He watched Anna, captivated in a way he'd never been before. A fishing companion? He chuckled again. He couldn't wait to watch her touch a worm. If she even showed up.

Chapter 2

Anna sat beside Abigail and tried to listen to Reverend Bollen's sermon. If Mama knew how Anna's insides skittered in anticipation for this afternoon's fishing excursion, she would withdraw the privilege of leaving the family pew to sit with the Leonards.

Would Reverend Bollen ever finish preaching? If nothing else, she'd have a fun outing with Larkin. Competing with Jeremiah would add to the fun. Her lips twitched upward. She really shouldn't think of him by his given name. Mama wouldn't like that any more than she would the squirming, but she couldn't call a fishing buddy Mr. Tucker, could she?

"Please stand for the benediction."

Anna rose with the others and bowed her head. As soon as the amen sounded, she darted into the aisle.

Garrick stopped her. "Where are you headed in such a hurry?"

The light of curiosity in Abigail's eyes cautioned Anna. If she told them about the fishing contest, Garrick would want to come. Then Abigail might tag along. She didn't want anyone but Larkin there, and Abigail could never get along with Larkin. "Home for dinner of course."

"You must be hungry." Garrick moved closer.

Her stomach growled on cue, and she grinned. "I am."

She turned toward the back. Already a line of folks had formed at the door to speak to the minister and his wife. Mama and Papa had just reached them. Kathleen stepped out the door—with Jeremiah.

A fist of dread slammed into Anna's midsection. Kathleen had taken over Jeremiah last night at the party, and she was doing the same today. It wasn't fair. Just because Kathleen had Mama's dark auburn hair and porcelain skin and everyone said she was beautiful didn't give her the right to take Anna's friends away.

She couldn't take Jeremiah if he didn't want to go.

Anna ignored the voice of reason in her mind. Men always liked Kathleen best.

She turned back to her friends. "I really do need to go. The preacher's family is coming for dinner today, and Mama will need my help."

Abigail fanned herself with her lacy white glove. "That means the Bollen sons will be there. If your mother needs extra help, let me know."

Anna laughed. "All right, but it isn't likely."

She hurried past several people waiting to talk to Reverend Bollen. She couldn't honestly say she knew what he'd preached about today, so she slipped past.

Jeremiah stood in the churchyard, grinning at Kathleen as if he'd been smitten just like every other fellow in Tumwater. Oh! If Anna wasn't such a lady, she'd stomp her foot—right on top of Jeremiah's toes. Obviously, Kathleen hadn't dragged him out of the church and held him hostage. She wasn't even touching him.

Anna ran to catch her parents. "Papa, I'm going to walk home today."

He nodded. "All right. Be careful."

"I will." She turned on her heel and set a brisk pace through an unusually sunny day. Too bad Kathleen had to put a damper on it. She'd probably talk Jeremiah into doing something else this afternoon and the fishing competition would be cancelled. As if she cared. She'd have won anyway. She'd turned on Division Road when footsteps pounded behind her.

"Hey Miss Wilkin, wait." Jeremiah skidded to a stop.

Anna looked past him, but didn't see Kathleen.

"So are we still going fishing?" His lopsided grin held her attention. "Or did you chicken out? Decide you don't want to touch a worm after all?"

"Ha! I'm not the chicken here. I've probably baited more hooks than you have." Anna glared at him, one fist landing on her hip.

He threw his head back and laughed. "Not likely, little one. I'm going to eat with my friends, but I'll see you after that—if you show up."

"I'll be there." Little one? She'd show him little when she caught more fish than he did. He was halfway to the church when she called after him. "My name's Anna."

She didn't wait for him to respond, but set her mind to getting away from the house. If she was lucky, she'd be able to slip out after dinner. Of all days for the Bollens to come, why did it have to be today?

❄

Anna rushed about, setting out the pies Mama baked the night before. She started the dishwater and had the pots scrubbed clean before Mama called her into the dining room. The fact no one seemed to notice the work she'd done should have bothered her, but today she didn't care. She only wanted to have dinner over with so she could be on her way to the river.

Reverend Bollen ate the last of his potatoes then leaned back in his chair "Mrs. Wilkin, you've outdone yourself today. Everything was delicious."

Mama's cheeks grew pink, and she smiled. "Thank you. My girls are a big help."

Anna began clearing the table. Maybe if she washed the dishes, Mama wouldn't say anything about her leaving in a few minutes.

Kathleen stood and motioned for Natalie. "Come upstairs, and I'll show you the pattern I was talking about."

In *Godey's Lady's Book*, no doubt. Anna carried the first load of dishes to the kitchen while the others left the table.

Mama hurried after her. "Anna, we don't need to clean up right now. We'll let it rest and visit. I've already told Mrs. Bollen we don't need help."

Anna set the stack of plates on the counter beside the sink. "I don't mind, Mama. You and Mrs. Bollen go visit. I've already done the pots. The rest will be easy if I do them now before they stick."

Mama took a couple of tea towels from the drawer. "If you're sure you don't mind. I'll cover the table in case anyone wants something later."

"Mama, I promised Larkin I'd be over this afternoon." Anna held her breath.

"Are you coming?" Papa stuck his head in the kitchen.

Mama ignored him. "Anna, you need to stay here while the reverend is visiting. How would that look if you up and run off?"

Papa gave Anna a wink. "Anna's done her duty. This is Sunday. The day of rest. The reverend will understand her need to get out of the house on such a pretty day. See that sunshine out the window? Days like this are few and far between. Makes me dream of a fishing pole on the riverbank."

"But—"

"But nothing." Papa touched Mama's shoulder. "Come. Your company's waiting."

"Thank you, Papa." Anna's held breath rushed out.

He gave her another wink and ushered Mama from the kitchen.

Anna washed dishes faster than ever then carried the water to the back door and threw it out. Would Jeremiah still be at the lake? She'd taken far too much time, but what else could she do? If she hadn't offered to clean up, Mama would never let her go. And if Papa hadn't intervened, it wouldn't have mattered how much cleaning she'd done.

In the garden shed, Anna changed from her dress slippers to the work boots she wore at the logging camp. She grabbed her fishing pole and held it so her body shielded it from the house. If Kathleen looked out an upstairs window and saw it, she'd be sure to tell Mama. Anna didn't relax until she turned the corner and the house was no longer in sight. Then she set long strides to Larkin's house and found her ready to go.

They walked to the edge of town, stopping not far from the lake. "Next to go is this skirt," Anna said. She stepped behind a tree to shed her skirt and petticoat, revealing the trousers hidden beneath. After rolling them together, she propped them in the fork of a tree.

Larkin smiled and shook her head. "If your mother saw you now, what would she do?"

Anna shrugged. "I imagine she'd faint dead away. But Mama doesn't understand how important fishing is. She doesn't love the forest, the trees, and the river the way I do. If not for Papa, I'd have to act just like Kathleen." She spotted Jeremiah by the lake and grinned. "Can you imagine anything more dreadful?"

Jeremiah found a likely spot on the riverbank and baited his hook. A quick flick of his wrist, and he sent the worm into the water. He leaned back against a tree, letting his muscles relax. So Miss Wilkin didn't show after all. She'd looked so cute boasting about being the best fisherman. He chuckled. Sure would've been fun to show her up. Like he used to do to Rebekah. Of course, no one could take Rebekah's place, but it might be fun to have a substitute sister.

By saving every penny he could from his job, he'd soon have enough to start building a new house on his land. He sighed. A home of his own without the bad memories.

A tug on his line alerted him to a bite. He grinned. The only thing missing was a certain female to listen to him gloat.

He reeled in his first fish and dropped it in a pail of water beside him. A quick glance down the trail toward town revealed nothing. She wasn't coming. He might as well give up. He sank another worm and leaned back to do some serious fishing.

Kersplash! Jeremiah jumped a foot off the ground. Water arched from the lake and soaked his feet and legs. His heart took off running without him. Something had hit the water right in front of him, and it wasn't a fish. He swung around at the sound of giggles—out-of-control giggles.

Miss Wilkin and the Whitworth girl stood behind him, clasping hands and laughing at him.

He deliberately placed his pole to the side and anchored it with a rock. Keeping his quarry in sight, he rose, speaking in a low tone. "Did you throw something at me?"

Anna's eyes grew to twice their normal size, and the other girl stepped back. A squeal such as he hadn't heard in a long time almost shattered his eardrums. Anna took off running with him right behind. He caught her waist and swung her around as a loose pebble threw him off balance. He fell, taking her with him. This time when she slammed against him there was no bustle to knock the breath from his lungs.

She hadn't stopped giggling. Her laughter was just as contagious as Rebekah's had been. He could never stay angry with his sister. Looked like his substitute sister would be the same in that respect. His laughter joined hers. He released her, letting her scurry away.

"You little scamp. What'd you throw at me?" He sat up and rested his arms on his bent knees.

She shook her head, still laughing. "Nothing. Not at you. I threw a big rock in the water."

"You could've hit me." He took a second look at her. "What is this? Does your father know you're wearing trousers?"

She stuck her pert nose up. "Maybe. Mama doesn't know I went fishing though, and she wouldn't understand if I came home with dirt and grass stains on my skirt." She grinned and tugged at her pant legs. "She'll never see these, so it's okay to get them dirty. Come on, I want to fish. Larkin has already started."

Jeremiah watched Anna and her friend bait their own hooks, and his eyebrows rose. Within minutes Anna pulled a fish as big as his from the river. He shook his head. Rebekah would have loved going fishing with Anna. Larkin was a nice enough girl, but Anna seemed to bubble with fun. "You know what?" he asked.

She turned her pretty dark brown eyes on him, and her lips curved the least bit. "Not unless you tell me."

He grinned. "I think I'll call you Little Bit. Yep, that'll be my special name for you. Miss Wilkin sure doesn't fit." He laughed for no special reason, but he'd done a lot of that this afternoon. "Little Bit fits you just fine."

A wide smile lit her face. "Okay, then I get to call you Tuck like I heard your friends doing."

He chuckled. "Sure, but you'd better be careful around your mother."

She rolled her eyes, and he laughed long and loud.

Chapter 3

Here, Papa." Anna handed the hatchet she'd been using to her father. A misty rain hung in the air, but she didn't mind. She'd rather work in the rain with Papa any day than be cooped up inside cooking. "I need to go. Mama will have a fit if I'm late again. She sure didn't like it when I was late on Tuesday."

He set the hatchet aside and grinned. "She runs a tight ship, does she?"

"Oh, you can't imagine." He was teasing, but Anna shuddered as if she took him seriously. "Between her and Kathleen."

"Maybe I work you too hard. This isn't a job for a girl."

Now this was no joking matter. "I like working with you, Papa. I love the woods and the fresh air."

"Next time I need some help, I'll see if I can get you another hour of freedom." He chuckled as she started away. "You got a skirt stashed around here somewhere?"

"Oh, I almost forgot." Anna turned and ran back to the stump where her skirt lay. She quickly pulled it on over her trousers. Mama would have more than a fit if she showed up looking like one of the lumberjacks. At least Papa let her be herself. On impulse, she gave him a hug. "Thanks, Papa."

She ran toward the logging camp, her father's love as warm and secure as his arms had been around her. At the large mess hall, she walked in the back door. Kathleen didn't bother to greet her—she just handed her a potholder. "Take one end of this pot and help me carry it to the serving table."

Anna hung her jacket and ignored her sister's glares. She carried her end of the large pot of pinto beans through the kitchen door to set it inside the dining area. What was the matter with Kathleen? Anna had permission to help Papa.

"You're late." Kathleen whispered the words.

"I am not." Anna took her place behind the serving table as the outside door opened.

Men poured into the crude building, forming a line where the tin plates and utensils sat. They grabbed what they needed, and the first man held his plate out toward Kathleen just in time to keep her from scorching Anna's ears. Anna grinned at Garrick for saving her, but he was looking at Kathleen, reaching for the slice of bread she held. Their fingers touched, and Kathleen blushed. Good, she should be embarrassed for almost yelling in front of the men. She could be a real prude.

That group of men had no sooner cleared out than another came in on their heels. Anna dipped a ladle of beans and plopped them on Jeremiah's plate. "Hey Tuck, how ya doin'?"

She almost giggled at Kathleen's lifted eyebrows.

He grinned. "Good. How about you, Little Bit? Been fishin' lately?"

This time Anna did giggle at the soft gasp from her sister. "Not for a few days."

"Then how about Sunday afternoon? I plan to be at the lake then if the weather holds.

Maybe I could give you some fishing tips." He took the corn bread she handed him.

She hesitated, but couldn't think of anything she'd like better. Why not go? Papa would let her even if Mama didn't like it. She flashed a quick grin at him. "All right, but you'd better plan to learn a few things from me."

Jeremiah's laughter brightened her day until movement to the side let her know Mama had returned. The scowl on Mama's face told of her disapproval more than her rebuke might have. Nothing unusual about that. When did Mama ever approve of her? It wasn't that Anna disliked ladies' activities. She enjoyed making her own clothes, and she loved to embroider. Cooking and cleaning were okay. But what she absolutely loved the most was being outdoors and running through the woods or sitting on the riverbank with a fishing pole. She felt useful when she helped Papa with his chores.

Anna turned to the next man in line. She'd find some way to go fishing Sunday. Tuck was fun. Even more fun than being with her best friend, but she wouldn't tell Larkin that or she might not go with her.

❄

Jeremiah ate his lunch and watched Anna bustle about helping her sister and mother. Little Bit. He chuckled under his breath. That name fit her perfectly. Little and as pretty as a china doll, she looked just as feminine.

He walked out of the warm mess hall and back toward work with the other buckers. Yep, Anna was a little thing, but he had a suspicion she was also a bit of trouble just waiting to happen. The question was what kind of trouble.

"Hey Tuck!"

Jeremiah turned toward the sound and realized he was walking beside the railroad track leading into the woods. His mind had been so locked on Anna, he hadn't seen Frederick or the Shay locomotive he drove to haul logs to the sawmills around Tumwater.

"I've been yelling at you. Anything wrong?" Concern covered Frederick's face.

"Naw, just getting back to work after a good meal." He couldn't tell his friend he'd been thinking about a little slip of a girl. He'd never understand. "You getting a load ready to take down?"

Frederick nodded. "I'm heading into the woods here in a minute. Want a ride? Beats walking in the cold."

"I would, except you're going the wrong direction for me." Jeremiah waved and started walking again. "I'll catch you Saturday. I'm staying in town with Willum so I can go to church."

"Okay, see you then." Frederick turned back to his locomotive, and Jeremiah went on.

Nope, Frederick wouldn't understand his fascination with Little Bit. She continually popped into his head. Had since they'd gone fishing. He needed to get her out of his mind and start looking for a suitable wife. Saturday he'd talk to Willum about building a house. The other men would pitch in to help, too, when they had time. The desire for home and family filled Jeremiah's heart. He had neither anymore. Only memories that impressed on him the longing to replace what he'd lost.

Although Anna stayed fresh on his mind, he shoved her image aside and replaced it with one after another of the girls he'd met since moving to the area. He thought of the birthday party he had attended in that big, fancy house. Larkin. She was attractive and seemed nice. Then there was Abigail Leonard, Garrick's sister. Anna sat with her at church Sunday. He shook his head, pushing both Abigail and Anna from his mind. What about her sister, Kathleen? While the other girls were pretty, Kathleen was beautiful. Yet he felt drawn toward Anna.

Jeremiah picked up his ax. He'd be helping cut a log into sixteen-foot lengths for boards this afternoon. If he didn't keep his mind on his job, he might cut something besides a tree. He didn't need Anna intruding in his mind so much. Yep, the little bit of trouble he sensed about her could be something more than a physical injury. She had the potential to cause pain in his heart. He needed someone who wouldn't tear his heart out if she left the way everyone else he'd loved had done.

Chapter 4

Anna pushed from the table and, like the Sunday before, began stacking plates.

Kathleen stood. "Mama, we can put the food away. You go relax with Papa."

Mama smiled. "You girls are spoiling me, but I'll take advantage of it this time. I don't think we'll want anything until later. Thank you."

"You're welcome, Mama." Anna tossed the words over her shoulder as she carried her load to the kitchen. Last week she'd done everything alone. Maybe with Kathleen's help the work would go quickly, and she could get to the lake before Tuck gave up on her. Anna had the dishwater prepared in the sink before Kathleen pushed through the door with a dish of food in each hand.

Kathleen put the pie in the safe and the bowl of potatoes on the counter. "We'll eat this tonight, so I'm leaving it here. Maybe make potato patties. What are you doing this afternoon?" Her question was tossed out too casually.

Anna looked up at her sister, who didn't even glance her way. "I thought I'd go see Larkin for a while."

That wasn't a lie. She did plan to go by Larkin's to see if she wanted to go fishing, too. Maybe Tuck would invite one of his friends the next time. Then Larkin would have her own fellow. Heat rose in her face at the direction her thoughts were taking. Tuck was not courting her. She needed to remember that.

Kathleen continued putting away food while Anna washed dishes. After a while, Kathleen picked up a dish towel. "I'll dry the dishes. You go see Larkin."

"Thank you." Anna didn't waste time untying her apron. She hung it on a hook by the back door, grabbed a coat hanging there, and slipped outside into a damp cloudy day. Why couldn't the sun be shining like last week? Anna shrugged. At least it wasn't pouring down rain. She spoke back into the kitchen. "If Papa or Mama ask, you can tell them where I am."

"Sure."

Anna ran across the backyard to the garden shed. She changed into her boots and grabbed her pole. If only she could stash her skirt here. No, she had to wear it in town. Someone would see for sure and tell Mama.

As she turned to leave, the door opened and Kathleen stepped in. "I didn't think you were going to Larkin's."

"I am, too." Anna flushed under her sister's steady gaze.

Kathleen shook her head, her smile knowing. "No, you're going fishing. You're running off to meet Jeremiah Tucker, aren't you? I heard you make plans with him the other day, so don't deny it."

"With Larkin. What's wrong with that? Papa doesn't mind if I go fishing with friends."

Kathleen's eyebrows lifted. "Mama does."

Anna wanted to stomp her foot, but Kathleen would love that show of frustration. "You're going to tell, aren't you?"

"No." Kathleen folded her arms. "I don't care. Go meet your beau if you want." She laughed. "How long do you think he'll stay interested if you keep acting like a hooligan? You're almost eighteen. Don't you think it's time you grew up and became a lady? I know Mama and Papa are getting tired of your tomboy ways."

"Not Papa." Anna's protest sounded weak even to her. Hadn't he said she shouldn't work in the woods?

"I wouldn't be so sure." Kathleen shrugged. "I heard them talking about a school back East. A finishing school. Mama says it's the only way now to turn you into a lady."

An angry flush rose in Anna's face. "Papa won't let her send me away."

Kathleen's laughter rang out in the shed. "Papa agreed with her. I'm sorry, Anna, but everyone's getting tired of your behavior. It's past time for you to grow up. I think it'll be good for you. Look at this as an opportunity, not a punishment. I wish I could go."

Kathleen left, and a tremble worked its way through Anna's body. She leaned against a table. Kathleen had to be wrong. Papa wouldn't do this to her. Emotions raced through her until her mind whirled without direction. She shoved her pole back into place with the others and pushed out of the building, slamming the door behind her.

She ran toward Larkin's through wisps of fog that hung in the air and added to her dismal emotions. She had to tell someone who would understand. At the Whitworth house, Larkin let her in. "Anna, what's wrong?"

"Mama and Papa are sending me away." Anna knew she didn't make sense, but Larkin led her upstairs to her room. There, with tears pouring down her cheeks, Anna told what she'd just learned.

"Oh Anna, how terrible." Larkin's tears of sympathy blended with Anna's.

Anna dried her eyes with the back of her hand and straightened her spine. "I'll show Papa and Mama I can be a lady. I'll act like Kathleen. They'd never send her away."

"There's nothing wrong with you the way you are," Larkin sympathized. "You aren't like Kathleen. They shouldn't expect you to be."

"But they do." Anna forced a smile for her friend. "It's all right. I can do it. I have to because I would simply wilt away without my forest."

Jeremiah set a rhythm Monday morning with another bucker on the two-man saw. The scent of cedar filled the air and sawdust flew over him while they sliced a six-foot-diameter log into shingle bolts. He hadn't seen Anna at breakfast. Where'd she been yesterday? He'd caught enough fish for Frederick to fry for him, Willum, and E.V. for supper, but they didn't make up for Little Bit's company he'd missed earlier. Something must have happened.

When the noon whistle blew, he strode toward camp and the mess hall, eager to talk to Anna. His eyes adjusted to the dim light inside as he moved through the serving line. "Hello, Mrs. Wilkin. Mmm, boiled potatoes and gravy. Looks good."

She smiled. "I imagine anything would look good after working all morning the way you boys do."

"That may be true." He grinned, but let his gaze roam down the table. Kathleen handed out bread and dished up heaping ladles of green beans near the far end. Where was Anna? He moved down the line.

Kathleen glanced up with a smile. "How are you today?"

"I'm fine." He held his plate under her ladle. "I haven't seen your sister lately."

"She's working in the kitchen today." Kathleen set the ladle in the pot.

"She wouldn't be avoiding me for some reason, would she?" Why had he asked that? He sure didn't need Anna's sister thinking he cared.

"Not that I know of." Kathleen slanted him a glance. "Why would she do such a thing unless you've done something you shouldn't? Like enticing her to go off alone with you for the last two Sunday afternoons."

Heat crept up his neck. Had Kathleen twisted a few hours of fishing into a romantic interlude?

Before he could defend Anna, Kathleen handed him a couple of slices of bread and smiled. "If you want to see Anna, why don't you come by our cabin tonight? You know where our family stays here at camp, don't you?"

He nodded.

She glanced down the line and back at him with a bright smile. "Please do come to the cabin tonight, Jeremiah," she said in a strong voice. "We'd love to have you visit."

Someone cleared his throat. Jeremiah turned to see Garrick waiting behind him with a frown on his face. "Oh, sorry." He gave Kathleen a nod. "I'll stop by later tonight."

Kathleen's invitation didn't sound sincere. Maybe she'd only asked to get him to move on so she could serve Garrick and the rest of the men. Jeremiah let her words play through his mind until late afternoon, but he couldn't find the answer. Whatever her reasoning, he appreciated the chance to see Little Bit.

❄

Long strides took Jeremiah through the cold November air to the log cabin set back several yards from the mess hall. Anna hadn't served supper either. She must be avoiding someone. If not him, who?

Kathleen opened the door at his knock. "Oh, Jeremiah."

"You said for me to come by tonight. To see Anna." He shifted his weight. Maybe he shouldn't be here. He looked past her. "Is she home?"

"No, she's out somewhere with Papa." Kathleen stepped back. "Please, come in. They should be back soon, and Mama's here."

Jeremiah accepted a cup of coffee and slice of cake from Mrs. Wilkin. "Thank you, ma'am."

She and Kathleen sat across from him sipping coffee. Mrs. Wilkin lowered her cup and gazed at him. "How do you like working in the woods, Mr. Tucker?"

He allowed a smile. "I imagine it could be worse."

"I'd guess logging isn't your calling?" Her smile answered his. "What would you rather do?"

That was an easy question. "Farming."

Mrs. Wilkin's eyebrows lifted. "Doesn't a farm require land, animals, and equipment?"

"Yes ma'am. I hope to have all that within a year's time." Truthfully, he had most everything except a house to live in. After the fire that took Rebekah and his folks, he sold the farm and all of Pa's animals except his best team. When the next-door neighbor offered to board them and store Pa's plow, wagon, and other tools, Jeremiah accepted.

"I see." Mrs. Wilkin stood. "I'll take your plate if you're finished. Would you like more coffee?"

"No ma'am. Thank you." Jeremiah stood until she left the room. He turned to Kathleen. "I should be going."

Kathleen walked him to the door. "I'm sorry you didn't get to see Anna. She's probably wandering around in the woods like always. She's angry right now because Mama and Papa are sending her to school next spring or early summer. By then she'll have had plenty of time to get over it and see this is best for her."

Jeremiah narrowed his eyes. "What do you mean, sending her to school?"

"Back East. Chicago, I think. Where Mama went. She should be glad to go. I would be, but Anna is such a tomboy, she's the one who needs polishing."

"Finishing school?" Jeremiah frowned. Little Bit didn't belong in finishing school any more than he did. She'd smother there. No wonder she'd been avoiding him.

"Yes." Kathleen smiled. "She has to grow up someday."

Jeremiah's mind whirled with images of the two sisters after he left. Beautiful, graceful Kathleen and fun-loving, cute Anna. So different. Why'd Kathleen invite him tonight? For Anna or for herself? Why wasn't Kathleen married? She'd make a wife any man would be proud of.

Chapter 5

A leaf, dried on the tree and only now letting go, drifted toward the ground in front of Anna. She bent, picked it up, and twirled it between her fingers. The days were slipping past and she still had no solution to her problem. How long had she walked? An hour? Two? She'd been so upset when she left the kitchen, she hadn't even changed into her trousers. A short laugh escaped her lips. Mama would be proud of her.

She lifted her gaze toward heaven and the top of the stately old pine beside her. *Lord, where is the answer? Must I go to school? Is that Your will for me?*

So many questions, but no answers. She couldn't leave her woods. She just couldn't. And what about Tuck? Their friendship was new but precious. A tear escaped, and she brushed at it. Why would Papa do this to her? Her insides churned when she thought about confronting him. Maybe Kathleen was wrong, and they wouldn't send her away. It was just talk at this point anyway, wasn't it? She should ask Papa tonight after supper and find out the truth. Or maybe even now. He'd gone to the shed to sharpen axes. She could help him before she had to help with the evening meal.

Again, her stomach rolled. She couldn't talk to Papa if she got sick just thinking about it. She shuffled her toe through old, soggy leaves and soft pine needles on the forest floor then turned toward camp. Maybe if she offered to help, he'd tell her Kathleen made up the story about school just to be mean, or maybe she'd mention it to Papa first, and he'd tell her she could decide if she wanted to go. That sounded more like Papa.

Anna set off with long strides toward camp. How hard could it be to tell Papa she didn't want to go away? He always understood.

At the tool shed, she stopped and took a deep breath before opening the door and slipping inside. Papa sat on a stool with an ax across his knee. He ran a long file along the edge of the blade then stopped and looked up at her. "Anna. Did you come to help?"

She nodded. "Yes. What can I do?"

He grinned. "Take your pick."

Anna straightened the tools on Papa's worktable. The steady rasp of his file on the blades scraped her nerves in a way it never had before. How could he sit there acting as if nothing was wrong? How could he send her away?

"Papa?" She turned to meet his questioning gaze. "Does it bother you for me to wear pants when we're in the woods?"

A soft smile lightened his expression. "I wouldn't let you if it did."

"Oh." She looked down. "Mama doesn't like it, and Kathleen's always the perfect lady."

He chuckled. "Your mama doesn't know, does she?"

She grinned. "She knows, but not how often I wear them. I don't think Kathleen knows either."

"Kathleen's a good girl." Papa smiled and turned back to his work. "Just like her mother. She'll make a fine wife someday."

Air huffed from Anna. "Like I said, always perfect."

Papa shook his head. "Not perfect, but she knows what's important." He looked up. "Don't worry, little one. You'll learn, and one day you'll be ready for marriage, too."

Anna wrinkled her nose and turned back to stack wedges, alternating them so they were even. She sighed. Papa wanted her to learn—to get ready for marriage. He'd confirmed what Kathleen said. Papa wanted her to go to finishing school. Maybe if she started acting like a lady all the time, they'd let her stay home. She could do that. Surely she could. Only she wouldn't give up wearing her trousers when she went into the woods alone. Or with Papa. Or Tuck.

Tears burned her eyes, and she blinked them away. "Papa, I'd better go. Mama will want me in the kitchen before long."

"Okay, that's fine. Thanks for your help." He didn't even look up.

Outside, Anna saw no one. Today, Kathleen helped Mama prepare the food. Tomorrow would be Anna's turn. She had at least an hour before she was needed to serve. Her heart weighed a ton. How could Papa be so unfeeling? To send her away was cruel. A cool November breeze brushed past as her feet carried her toward her beloved woods and the tall pines that gave her solace. Their scent was like balm to her soul. Tears blurred her eyes because of the unfairness of her situation. She loved her parents, yet they found her lacking. Under the cover of her trees, she ran while the forest passed in a blur of movement and tears. Finally, she collapsed at the foot of a fir tree in a soft bed of damp moss, her body shaking with sobs.

❄️

Jeremiah headed back to camp early. He'd cracked his ax handle, and the foreman told him to go see if Mr. Wilkin had another.

A flash of red to the side caught his eye. Anna's long, dark braid flew out and bounced against her red plaid jacket. Her dad's, no doubt. He chuckled. Only Anna would wear a man's jacket with boots and a skirt. His smile faded when she fell to the ground and curled into a tight ball with her face against her knees. Had she hurt herself?

Jeremiah's strides lengthened as he altered his course toward Anna. He leaned the ax on the opposite side of the tree and knelt in front of her. She sniffed and sobs shook her shoulders.

"Anna?" He murmured her name, not wanting to startle her. "Little Bit, what's wrong?"

Her head lifted. Tears trailed down her cheeks. He brushed a damp tendril from her cheek and tucked it behind her ear. "Tell me what it is."

She swiped her sleeve across her eyes. A hiccup brought a curve to his lips. No other girl could be so adorable in the midst of a crying spell.

"Is this about you going away to school?"

Her eyes widened.

"Kathleen told me."

"Oh." She turned away from him so he couldn't see her face. "She would. She wants me to go. So do Mama and Papa."

"But do you want to go?" He touched her chin and brought her back toward him. "You're the one who needs to decide, right?"

She shook her head and blinked as her eyes filled. Two big tears ran down her cheeks. He caught them with his thumbs and brushed them away.

"Oh Tuck." Her voice caught. "I don't want to. I have to. I just talked to Papa. He wants me to go."

If he could, he'd wipe the worry from her face. She should always smile and be happy. Her hurt brought heaviness to his heart. "I thought Kathleen said you'd leave in late spring or early summer. That's months away. Your parents could change their minds by then. I wouldn't worry about it now."

Anna's eyes brightened for a moment. Then, as a cloud covered her countenance, she shook her head, and another tear eased from her eye. "No, Mama will never change her mind. Papa said I should learn to be a good wife. He wants me to be like Kathleen. He wants me to go away."

Another tear fell and yet another. Jeremiah's heart broke. Without thought of the consequences, he reached for her, and she fell into his arms. He patted her back. "Hey Little Bit, don't cry. It's cold out here. You'll freeze your face."

Her only answer was a sniffle. A tremble moved through her body. His arms tightened, and he tucked her head more securely under his chin. He'd do the same if she were truly his sister. Only his heart had never acted up like this when he consoled his sister. Emotions, having nothing to do with brotherly love, surged through his awareness.

His muscles tensed, and she looked up. Tears glistened in her lashes. Her full lips pulled down into a pout. His heart pounded as if he'd run a mile. He stared into her wide, chocolate eyes until they blurred, and his nose touched hers.

He jerked back and fell to the ground as if he'd been hit. What just happened? He'd almost kissed the pout from her lips. He'd wanted to kiss Little Bit. His nose still tingled from the brief contact. What on earth had he been thinking?

Chapter 6

He was crazy. That's all there was to it. Taking advantage of Anna's innocence that way. He felt sorry for her. Nothing else. No reason to start kissing her.

He scrambled to his feet. "I'm sorry, Little Bit. I need to get this ax to your father. The handle broke."

She sat on the ground looking up at him with wide, luminous eyes. No doubt calling him a few choice names for his behavior.

He grabbed the ax. "Well, I better go. You take care now."

She never spoke, and he didn't look back. Better if he didn't. Seventeen years old. Same age Rebekah would have been. Little Bit. Little sister. He thumped his forehead with the heel of his hand.

Sure, he cared about Anna. She was fun to go fishing with. Her chatter would keep anyone entertained. But to court? To kiss? Not likely. Her father would have his job if he knew what had almost happened. Better if he took a second look at Kathleen. At least she was closer to his age.

Jeremiah strode through the forest's carpet of leaves and broken sticks, stretching the distance between Anna and him. What appeal drew him to Anna? He searched his heart and had to admit he cared. Far too much. Girls like her were the ones who could tear a man's heart out. She was family, pure and simple. Only more. Could be a lot more. Enough to get hurt again, because family didn't always stay.

He dodged a tree branch and took a deep breath of the pine-scented air then let it out in a rush. His plans didn't include waiting around for a little girl to grow up. Sure, he needed a wife, because come spring, he planned to be living on his own farm. He'd carry on the tradition of farming his grandfather and dad had left him. He needed a woman suited for marriage. Someone who didn't turn his emotions inside out and set his heart pounding like a drum. Maybe Kathleen would be the best choice. Her mother seemed to like him, and Kathleen did invite him to their cabin. Wouldn't hurt to think about it, pray about it, and maybe ask her father for permission to court her.

Camp came into view, and he quickened his stride. His heart had returned to normal. He shoved both sisters far from his mind. Willum had promised to build a house for him. He'd even joked about it, saying it would be one less man taking up space in his tiny cabin on weekends, so he'd be glad to do it.

❄

Clouds blanketed the sky, releasing a gentle rain when Anna tugged the horse to a stop in front of Tumwater's grocer and set the brake. She hopped from the wagon, her skirt flaring out before settling back down to cover her ankles.

"Anna, be careful." Kathleen climbed down, scarcely exposing the toe of her shoe. "You could fall and get hurt jumping like that. What if your foot got caught on something or you slipped in the mud?"

"It won't." Anna twirled toward the mercantile three doors up the street. "Oh Kathleen, there's Larkin. She's wearing the new dress she got for her birthday. You won't need me for a few minutes, will you? I'll be back in time to help load the wagon."

Kathleen sighed. "Go ahead. At least you drove."

"Thanks." Anna ran up the boardwalk steps, her boots clomping on the wood. Her green calico looked shabby next to Larkin's fancy blue dress, but Anna didn't care.

Larkin turned, a dimpled smile brightening her face. "Anna, I didn't see you."

"Kathleen's in the grocery. Mama didn't feel well and asked us to shop for her. I'll have to help, so I don't have a lot of time. I wonder if they have any new embroidery floss."

"I don't know, but I'd love to see, too." Larkin held the door open. "Are you feeling better? You've been in my thoughts and prayers all week."

Anna stepped into the mercantile. She'd like to forget this past week, except for one special part. Every time she thought about Tuck's nose brushing hers, her stomach jumped just before her heart took off like a horse in a race.

"I'm fine." She tossed the answer over her shoulder, her boots beating a hollow staccato against the wood floor. What would Larkin say if she knew? They had shared a lot of secrets in the past, but maybe not this one. It was too new. Too unsure. Tuck sure had acted funny after it happened.

Larkin caught up with her at the thread counter. "Have your parents said any more to you about finishing school?"

Anna fingered the embroidery floss. "Mama hasn't, but Papa says he wants me to learn to be a lady, so that's what I'm doing." She sighed. "Sure do hate to give up fishing."

Larkin's eyes widened. "You're giving up fishing? You can't. You love to fish."

Anna glanced around the store and grinned as she leaned closer to Larkin. "Maybe ladies can still fish."

"Of course they can." Larkin picked up a violet hank of floss and grimaced. "This is Mama's new favorite color for next year."

"It's pretty."

"Try wearing it all year."

"So is this green one. Kind of reminds me of the woods." Anna couldn't stop the catch in her voice.

The warmth of her friend's hand on her arm almost brought tears to Anna's eyes. Larkin patted her arm. "I'm so sorry. Why don't we plan a fishing party to prove to your mother you can fish and still be just as much a lady as your sister? Once she sees that, you can stay right here in Tumwater. My Chinook grandfather always said a fish fry makes everything better, and the *Farmer's Almanac* predicts this dry spell will continue through the next month at least."

At Larkin's mention of the almanac, Anna smiled, her tears banished. "You and your weather talk. And tempting me with fishing. When can we have the party? How many shall we invite?"

"As many as you want. Would next Sunday afternoon work?"

Tension seeped from Anna as excitement took its place. "Yes, we can bring food and cook the fish we catch."

"Now, how about this embroidery floss? Do you want any?" Larkin began picking out several hanks of brown and gold shades.

Anna took the green one she'd admired earlier. She'd make something she could take to school that would remind her of her woods. Maybe ivy on a pillowcase. "I'm getting this one, then I've got to get back to the grocery before Kathleen tells Mama I ran off."

Larkin gave her a quick hug. "I need to look at some other things, but I'll see you tomorrow at church."

"All right." Anna paid for the floss and hurried out the door, almost bumping into Abigail coming in. "Oh, I'm sorry."

"That's fine." Abigail looked into the store with a frown marring her face. "I see Larkin is here."

"Yes, we were just talking." Anna stepped onto the boardwalk.

Abigail followed, letting the mercantile door close. She fell into step with Anna. "I don't know why you hang around with her. Just because her father's the richest man in town doesn't lessen the fact she's a mixed breed."

"Most people around here are. I'm a mixture of Dutch and Scots."

Abigail patted Anna's shoulder as if she were a foolish child. "Sometimes you say the strangest things. What were you and Larkin talking about?"

Why don't you like Larkin? If it'd do any good, she'd ask. "We've decided to have a fishing party out at the lake. Everyone's invited. Why don't you and Elizabeth come? And Garrick. It's for the fellows and girls, both. We'll bring potluck and fry the fish. It'll be lots of fun."

Abigail nodded. "I'm sure it will. I haven't been fishing in ages."

"Then it's time you did." Anna's heart lifted at the thought of everyone gathered around the lake. Larkin always knew how to make her feel better. Now to convince Kathleen their idea was a good one.

"Anna, the order's ready. Are you?" Kathleen stood in front of the grocer, her hands on her hips.

"Yes, I said I'd be right back." Anna frowned. What was wrong with Kathleen?

Kathleen headed toward the wagon. "You could have stayed and helped instead of running off."

"I didn't. . ." Oh, what was the use? She could argue all day that Kathleen gave permission, and still her words would get turned around somehow. "Larkin wants us all to meet next Sunday afternoon for a fishing party at the lake."

"I don't like fishing." Kathleen wrinkled her nose and shifted toward Abigail. "Are you going?"

Abigail nodded. "Yes. I'm sure Elizabeth and Garrick will, too."

Kathleen's eyebrows lifted. "Well, I suppose I could." She looked back at Anna. "Mama should approve of your fishing with a large group rather than going off by yourself or alone with—"

"I know, Kathleen." Anna climbed to the high wagon seat. "You don't need to complain. I've decided I'll be a lady from now on."

"Ha." Kathleen laughed. "I can't wait to see this come to pass. If you can act like a lady at a fishing party, it'll be a miracle. Abigail, it was nice seeing you. We've got to get home. Most of what we bought is for the camp."

"I understand." Abigail walked on down the street.

Anna shook her head at her friend's behavior. She'd been going into the mercantile until she saw Larkin. What could she possibly have against Larkin? Anna picked up the reins and flicked them above the horse with a click of her tongue. There was no understanding some people. But one thing she knew. Mama would have nothing bad to say about this fishing trip. Not with Kathleen going. Now all she needed to do was spread the word. Would Tuck and his friends come? Her tummy did its familiar little jump, and she smiled. He'd better come. If she didn't have a chance to ask him at church tomorrow, she'd make sure to during the week. Maybe they could bump noses again.

Chapter 7

Jeremiah squinted at the overcast sky above the church. "Looks like a good day for fishing. At least it's not raining."

"Good thing." Frederick grinned. "I've got a craving for fried fish and good company."

E.V. nodded. "So the plan is to head to the lake this afternoon and fish for our lunch, right?"

"Right." Jeremiah's gaze shifted to the Wilkins' buggy pulling to a stop beside the church.

Anna climbed out and turned toward him. His rebellious heart raced without his permission. His eyes refused to look elsewhere. What was wrong with him? He'd kept his distance ever since he'd almost kissed her. She wouldn't have stopped him either. Would she have known to? She'd probably never been kissed, and he almost took advantage of her. She'd been crying. Upset, vulnerable. Disgust for his actions landed on his heart, bringing it under control.

"There's the Wilkin family." E.V. nodded toward the girls. "Didn't I see you talking to the little one, Tuck?"

Little one. Jeremiah almost laughed. Even his friends thought she was too young. "Yes, she gave me the invitation for this afternoon. Said to invite all of you, though I can't imagine why."

Frederick gave him a playful shove. "Watch it, buddy."

Jeremiah laughed. His gaze shifted to Kathleen. A chestnut ringlet brushed her smooth cheek. Her eyes, dark and wide, looked across the yard. He looked, too. Garrick and his sisters walked toward them from the opposite way. Jeremiah looked back at Kathleen. A soft smile brought out the loveliness of her face. She was a real beauty. A woman any man would be proud to claim for his wife.

Anna twirled and ran back to the wagon, taking his attention from her sister. He shook his head. Kathleen's beauty paled next to her rambunctious sister.

Kathleen walked past and smiled. Every man lifted his hat and acknowledged her presence. What better time to set his plan in motion? He stepped forward but felt a hand on his arm.

"Tuck?" Anna smiled at him. "Are you going to the lake this afternoon?"

His heart melted at the sparkle in her dark eyes, the endearing tendril of hair blowing across her face. He resisted the urge to catch it and tuck it behind her ear. Instead, he grinned. "Miss a chance to go fishing? Now, what do you think?"

"You'll be there." She laughed. "I will, too. I plan to catch more fish than you do, you know."

"Ha, as if that's possible." His heart pounded. "Hey, I need to catch someone. I'll see you later."

"Okay." A crease between her eyes told him she didn't want him to go.

He resisted the urge to stay with her and ran up the steps just before Kathleen disappeared through the door. "Miss Wilkin?"

"Yes?" Kathleen turned with her eyebrows lifted.

Jeremiah ignored the buzz of male voices behind him. He'd probably shocked his friends, but he had a goal to fulfill. More than anything, he wanted a family. Kathleen could give him that without danger of losing his heart. He'd already suffered more loss and pain in his life than he wanted. He could learn to care for Kathleen, but not too much.

He pulled his hat from his head. "Would you mind if I sat with you this morning?"

Kathleen hesitated only a moment before a smile crossed her face. "I would be honored by your company, Mr. Tucker."

She slipped her hand through his arm, and he felt no more than her gentle presence. Perfect. He nodded with his best smile. "Please, call me Jeremiah."

"Of course." She seemed pleased by his invitation. "I'll expect you to call me Kathleen from now on."

❄

Anna's foot hit the ground and her arms crossed. How could Jeremiah do such a thing? *I need to catch someone.* Who might that be? None other than Kathleen! To walk away in the middle of their conversation just so he could smile and offer his arm to her sister. Oh! Again, her foot stomped.

"Anna, is something wrong?" Larkin stopped beside her.

"I'm sorry, I didn't see you." Anna turned from the scene at the door to force a smile for her friend.

Abigail and Elizabeth joined them. "Hi, Anna. Are you sitting with us this morning?"

Garrick waved then walked toward the church with Jeremiah's friends.

Anna sighed. "I suppose I might as well."

"Are you all right?" Larkin persisted. "You seem so sad this morning. Aren't you excited about the fishing party?"

"Oh yes, of course. I'm fine. Maybe we'd better go in and find a place to sit. Church will be starting soon." At least Larkin didn't press for a more honest answer. What could she say? *Oh, I'm just jealous of my sister because she's so beautiful every man in the territory falls at her feet. Even Tuck, who almost kissed me, is at this very moment sitting beside her. Mama will be thrilled of course. Papa, too. Kathleen is so perfect, she'll be the perfect wife.*

The perfect wife for Jeremiah. A sob caught in her throat. She would not cry. No matter how angry or hurt she was, she would not let anyone know she cared.

She latched on to Larkin's arm when they reached the door. "I haven't done very well being a lady. I need to try harder."

Larkin patted Anna's hand. "Oh Anna, you're exactly the way God made you. You don't need to change a thing."

Spoken like a true friend. Anna smiled. "Thank you. When I need lifting up, I know who to come to. You're my best friend, Larkin."

Larkin nodded. "Always."

Anna didn't want to look when she walked past the pew where Jeremiah and Kathleen sat. She tried not to—and lost. One glance told her everything she needed to know. Jeremiah held his Bible in his lap, a satisfied smile on his face. So he thought he'd caught the best fish in the sea, did he? If he only knew Kathleen, he wouldn't think that. Anna loved her older sister, but there were times when they didn't get along. *Humph.* Like now.

Anna sat beside Abigail and tried to pay attention. She sang the right words to the songs. She closed her eyes during prayer, and she sat quietly while Reverend Bollen preached. She even caught a few words before her mind wandered again. Maybe she should try harder to be a lady. Mama said ladies should walk, not run. She could do that. What else did a lady do? She should know. She'd heard the rules all her life, but at the moment every one of them fled her mind. She sighed. How would she ever change if she couldn't even remember what to do?

"Let us stand." Reverend Bollen's voice and the rustling across the church brought Anna's mind to the present. She stood and bowed her head for the closing prayer.

❄

An hour later, Anna slung her fishing pole over her shoulder and turned to her sister. "Aren't you taking a pole?"

Kathleen stood just outside the open door of the shed with her umbrella. She rolled her eyes. "No, Anna. Just because we're going to a fishing party doesn't mean I have to act like you." She wrinkled her nose. "I'm going to visit, not fish."

Anna shrugged. "Suit yourself. I plan to fish. And don't tell me ladies don't fish, because the other girls will. You'll more than likely be the only one who doesn't."

Kathleen's laughter trilled behind her as she headed toward the street, picnic basket in one hand and umbrella in the other. "I seriously doubt it."

Anna let her bonnet hang down her back, and she didn't carry an umbrella. Larkin said it wouldn't rain, and she usually knew. Of course, Kathleen had to have both bonnet and umbrella. A little rain might muss her hair. Then who would sit with her at church?

No, she would not think about Jeremiah sitting with Kathleen. Why had he done such a thing, anyway? It didn't make sense. Anna clutched her smaller basket that held a bowl of potato salad and another of baked beans and willed her mind away from Jeremiah. The food should keep well now the weather had turned cooler. After all, November would soon be past.

"I told Jeremiah I'd catch a bigger fish than he does."

Kathleen looked toward Anna's fishing pole. "I don't know why you'd want to even try. It certainly isn't ladylike. How do you ever expect to catch a husband if you're continually trying to outdo men? Besides, impaling a worm and throwing it in the lake is so barbaric."

Anna laughed. "Papa says the worm doesn't feel a thing. God made them for bait."

"Oh really?" Kathleen's eyebrows lifted. "Mama told me God made worms to loosen the soil in our garden. That's still a lowly job, but at least he doesn't have to die doing it. And no one has to force him to."

"Maybe." Anna shrugged. "Could be God made worms to do both jobs. Besides, fishing's a lot more fun than gardening."

"Not for the worm." Kathleen met Anna's eyes with a twinkle in hers.

When she laughed, Anna joined in. Sometimes, Kathleen could be fun.

They turned onto the path leading to the lake and Anna quickened her stride. Larkin and Abigail would be there. Would Jeremiah? He promised before he sat with Kathleen at church. He'd be there. Why not? He probably made plans with Kathleen.

Voices rang out. And laughter. Anna ran ahead around the gentle curve where she saw her friends. There must be twenty people. She laughed and turned. "Come on, Kathleen. We're late. I think everyone's already here. The Bollens and the Leonards. There's Larkin and Tuck, and some of the other fellows and girls, too. This should be lots of fun."

"Anna, wait."

What for? Anna stopped until her sister caught up.

"Maybe this would be a good time for you to behave like a lady."

Anna stared at her sister. Was she trying to help or hinder? "I know, Kathleen. I intend to."

"Good." Kathleen smiled. "Mama said I should help you. She's counting on it."

Which meant Kathleen would tattle if she did anything unladylike. Anna turned away and walked as fast as she could toward the others. Larkin had a pole in her hand. Good. She intended to fish.

Someone had brought a wagon. Probably the Bollen brothers. They had the tailgate down with a tablecloth spread on it. Anna ran over and left her basket with the rest.

"Anna, come on." Larkin waved.

Anna trotted across the ground toward her friend. "Hey, I see you have a pole, too."

"Of course, that's what you do at a fishing party."

A group of young men sat on the bank, talking and casting out their lines. Tuck laughed at something Frederick, the engineer who carried logs on the Shay engine, said. They seemed to be awfully good friends. As close as she and Larkin.

Larkin nudged Anna. "Want to join them?" Her dark eyes sparkled.

A slow grin spread across Anna's face. "Sure."

"Anna." Kathleen's call stopped her in her tracks.

What now? Anna turned toward the wagon where Kathleen and some of the other girls stood.

"You need to come and help. Did you see this fish?" Kathleen pointed to the makeshift table and a bucket sitting on it.

Anna sighed. Fishing with the men wasn't the most ladylike thing she could do. If she didn't help, Kathleen would tell, and Mama might send her away before Christmas. She turned to Larkin. "I want to fish, but Kathleen's going to tell Mama if I don't act like a lady."

"I'll help." Larkin's gentle smile sympathized. "It'll be fun. You'll see."

"I know. I just wanted to fish." Anna flashed a quick grin. "Maybe later."

Anna took over the job of cooking the fish the men had cleaned. Tuck seemed to be having a good time with his friend. He pulled a fish in while Anna watched. She ached to run across the grass to sit beside him. They'd laughed and talked that first time when they scarcely knew each other. Now look at them. One almost-kiss and they scarcely spoke.

Larkin helped set out food while Anna arranged the pieces of fish in a cast-iron frying pan. She crouched beside the fire pit someone had fixed and set her pan across the hot rocks at the base of the fire. While the fish heated, she glanced toward the lake. Tuck's place was empty. Her pan sizzled and spit hot grease, making her jump. She grabbed the spatula to turn the fish.

She sensed his presence just as his hand covered hers. Tuck. She turned toward him.

"Hey Little Bit, be careful there. Why don't you back up and let me do this?"

She met his gaze. "I can do it. This is woman's work."

He chuckled. "Not outside on the ground over an open fire. Besides, you're too close. Your skirt might catch fire. You back up now just a little."

Anna slid her hand from under his and missed the contact. Her heart spoke with a mind of its own. She scooted back while he deftly scooped the fish and turned each piece. She loved him. No, she didn't. How could she? Papa wanted her to go to school. She didn't have time to fall in love. But she did love him, with all her heart. She'd never forget Tuck as long as she lived. She'd love him forever.

"There you go." He looked at her with a wide grin and stood, holding out his hand.

She slipped hers into the warmth of his and allowed him to help her stand. Her heart fluttered dangerously and broke in two when he looked away—toward Kathleen.

"Be careful." He glanced back at her, concern in his eyes. "Tuck your skirt out of the way if you're going to cook, okay? I don't want you hurt."

"I should have worn my trousers." She clamped her hand over her mouth. Tuck didn't want a tomboy. He wanted a woman like Kathleen. One who knew how to act like a lady instead of run around in men's clothing, fishing, and helping Papa in the woods all the time.

His laughter rang out, and he cuffed her jaw. "That's my Little Bit. You remind me of my sister, you know? I like that."

Anna stared after him. *His sister!* How could he make such a remark then turn and walk away? Her foot hit the ground and her arms crossed. He walked straight toward Kathleen and stopped with a smile on his face. Tears burned Anna's eyes and her shoulders slumped. Why wouldn't he prefer her sister's company? Kathleen was beautiful, and she always acted like a lady.

Chapter 8

A nna ran up the stairs to her bedroom in their house in town. Although the cabin in the woods should seem more like home since they spent more time there, it didn't. This house was where they spent every weekend and where she kept most of her belongings. Here, she didn't have to share a bedroom with Kathleen. Since Tuck had started paying so much attention to Kathleen, sometimes just looking at her sister was a chore.

It had been two weeks since the fishing party. Maybe today she could stop thinking about Tuck and Kathleen. Larkin always made shopping fun, and they'd be looking for Christmas gifts, which would be even more fun. Her soft green dress lay on the bed where she'd placed it before lunch. She dressed and started to smooth her errant hair back into place when a deep voice drifted up the stairs and through her open doorway. Tuck. Her heart thudded. Here? At their house? He must have only now arrived in town from the logging camp.

Anna knelt beside the floor vent in her room and bent low to hear.

"Certainly. We'll go into the parlor where it's private."

At Papa's words, Anna straightened. What would Tuck have to say to Papa in private? A problem at camp? She stood and peeked out her door. Assured no one else was upstairs, she crossed the hall to her parents' room, which was above the parlor. She slipped inside and closed the door without a sound then knelt beside the heating vent on Mama's side of the bed.

"I've secured the land I'll need for my farm, and Willum has started building a small house for me. If I need more room later, I can add on."

Tuck had land and a house of his own? Weight pressed against Anna's heart. But how could she have known? They'd spent so little time together, and when they did, their conversation had been fun, lighthearted. There was so much she didn't know about him, but she wanted to know everything. If only he wanted to court—oh my!

She clamped a hand across her mouth, her eyes opened wide. Could he be asking Papa's permission to court her? Then why had he been acting so friendly with Kathleen? Her stomach leaped and her heart pounded.

". . .to court your daughter."

Anna almost fell on the vent. What had she missed?

"Let me get this straight." Papa's voice rose through the vent. "You want to court Kathleen, not Anna?"

After a pause, Tuck repeated the one name. "Anna?"

Anna pressed against the vent. *Don't pick Kathleen, please don't.*

Silence filled the room before he spoke. "Isn't she a little young? I understood she'd be going away to school in a few months."

"Yes, that's true." Papa's deep sigh sounded, then a rustle below as if the men stood. "All right, you have my permission to court Kathleen if she agrees."

"Thank you, sir. I think she will."

Anna didn't wait for Tuck to leave. She ran to her room, grabbed her coat, hat, and mittens then rushed down the back stairway to the kitchen and out the door. For a moment, she stood in the backyard, lost. Where was she going? What should she do? He didn't love her.

A sob caught in her throat. She'd fallen in love with Tuck. How long ago? Since October and it was December now. Two months since she'd knocked him to the floor at Larkin's party. Time didn't matter. She loved him as she'd never loved before, and she could never tell him now.

Larkin. They were going shopping. She'd be waiting at her house, wondering what had happened. Anna held her skirt just high enough to run without hindrance. So what if ladies didn't run? She'd never be a lady now. Not ever. Her vision blurred before she realized she was crying. Of their own accord, her feet slowed to a walk, and she brushed the tears from her cheeks with her woolen mittens. More took their place, so by the time she reached Larkin's house, sobs shook her shoulders.

Larkin let her in. She tossed her own coat aside and led the way upstairs. In Larkin's room, Anna fell into her friend's arms and cried even harder. "How could Tuck do this to me?"

Larkin rubbed soft circles on her back. "Oh Anna, I'm so sorry. First school and now this. But maybe you won't go away, and maybe Kathleen will tell Mr. Tucker no."

Anna took a shuddering breath as she pulled back. "He chose my sister. That's what matters. I want to go to school now. Maybe I'll marry someone back East and stay there."

"But your family?"

"Papa might miss me, but Mama and Kathleen won't. I'll go, and I'll never come back."

Tears glistened in Larkin's eyes. "Oh Anna, where is your faith?" She picked up her Bible from the bedside table and flipped pages toward the back. "Here it is in Romans. It says, 'All things work together for good to them that love God.' Don't you believe that means you?"

Anna stared at the scripture verse while conflicting emotions ran through her soul. Anger, fear, jealousy, remorse, and love were a few she recognized. Finally, she nodded. "I know you're right. I've been acting like a spoiled brat. But if Kathleen and Tuck fall in love and get married, I'll have to stay away. I couldn't bear to watch them together." She lifted a moist gaze to her friend. "A person can't help who they love, can they? Not Tuck, but not me either."

With a soft smile, Larkin shook her head. "No, they can't. But this verse also tells me God has the perfect man picked out to be your husband. 'All things work together for good.' That means if Kathleen and Mr. Tucker marry, it's for your good as well as theirs. Isn't that right?"

A sigh escaped Anna's lips. "Yes, you're right, as usual. Maybe someday my heart will stop hurting so much and then I can accept this. Come on, let's go to town."

Anna walked beside Larkin, but her mind wouldn't shut out the sound of Tuck's voice asking to court Kathleen. Her heart still felt as if a log had fallen and crushed it. Would she ever get over Tuck? Any other man would have to be very special to take his place in her heart.

Garrick stepped out of the feed store as they neared it. "Hey, what are you two up to?"

Larkin stopped, so Anna did, too. "Just Christmas shopping."

"Really?" Garrick looked at Anna. "You look like you're going to a funeral. Where's the happy girl we're used to seeing?"

Anna shrugged. "I guess she grew up."

"What's wrong, Anna?"

"Nothing." She turned from his questioning gaze. Garrick was the big brother she'd never had. He'd protected her more than once, even took blame when the rock she threw at a bird broke a neighbor's window. She didn't want to burden him with this, too.

"Did Kathleen do something to you?"

Tears filled Anna's eyes just when she thought she'd used them all. She shook her head, then nodded. "If you must know, Jeremiah Tucker came to the house before I left and asked Papa's permission to court Kathleen."

Garrick's eyebrows shot up. "You heard him?"

Anna nodded. "Yes, and Papa said yes." Tears rolled down her cheeks, and she covered them with her mittens. "Kathleen doesn't love Tuck. I do, but he wants her. Oh, it doesn't matter anyway. Papa's sending me away. Kathleen's perfect, and she's staying here."

❄

Jeremiah stepped off the Wilkins' front porch. He should be walking on air, but he felt as if his feet were dragging through six-inch-deep mud. He had permission to court Kathleen if she agreed. She hadn't been home, but he'd talk to her tomorrow at church. That didn't concern him, but Anna did. How could he spend time with Kathleen without running into Anna? He couldn't. When had she become more to him than a substitute sister?

He turned and walked toward the lake, his mind and emotions roiling. He should be happy. He'd just been given the opportunity to win the hand of the prettiest girl in Tumwater. Or so everyone else seemed to think. Why had her father asked if he'd meant Anna? A man should want his oldest daughter to marry first.

Jeremiah shook his head and stood at the lake, taking little note of his surroundings. He might as well go to town and pick up a few things from the mercantile. Retracing his steps, he broke into a run. Maybe the exercise and the cold wind would clear his mind. A few minutes later, he slowed to a fast walk and concentrated on Kathleen. Beyond her outward appearance, she seemed attractive inside. Her manner was gentle. She worked hard at camp just as she had at their fishing party. She was—

Jeremiah slowed to a stop, his gaze locked on Anna. She stood across the street by the feed store with Garrick and her friend, Miss Whitworth. His heart ran faster than he had. What was wrong with him? A glimpse of Anna turned him into a smitten schoolboy.

Garrick held his arms out to Anna, and she fell against him for a tight embrace.

Jeremiah's stomach twisted. His heart constricted. Anna always sat with Garrick and his sisters in church. He'd seen them together talking before. A harsh, short laugh tore from his throat. He'd fallen in love with a girl who belonged to another. Good thing he'd asked for her older sister instead.

Disgusted with himself, Jeremiah turned away from the cozy scene and almost bumped into E.V., who was stepping off the boardwalk. "Oh, sorry, I didn't see you there."

E.V. grinned. "That's pretty obvious. What's got your dander up?"

"Nothing." He heard the growl in his voice even before E.V.'s eyebrows rose.

E.V. looked toward the feed store. "Ah, I see. I thought you were spending more time with Miss Wilkin than mere friendship. What was she doing hugging Leonard?"

"How should I know? It's none of my business." Jeremiah took off at a fast walk down the street. So what if they hugged? Pain squeezed his heart.

E.V. fell into step with him. "None of your business? If you have feelings for Miss Wilkin, why don't you let her know?"

"Because I plan to court her sister."

"What?"

"I just got permission from her father." Jeremiah couldn't resist a quick glance over his shoulder. He breathed better when he saw Anna heading one direction and Garrick the other. He forced a laugh. "Besides, Anna's only a kid. I'm looking for a wife. I just need to convince Kathleen she wants the job."

"Job? How romantic." E.V. stopped and turned as if to walk away.

Jeremiah looked at him. "Where are you going?"

"Somewhere away from this foolhardy path you're trodding." E.V. waved over his shoulder. "Good luck, my friend. You'll need all you can get."

Chapter 9

Jeremiah sat with Kathleen the third Sunday in a row. Even after two weeks of courting her, his gut instinct was to run. Fine. That's exactly what he wanted. A woman who wouldn't tear him up inside if anything happened to her. He glared across the church where Anna sat beside Garrick. Ever since he saw them hugging in public, they'd sat side by side.

"And 'the just shall live by faith.'" Pastor Bollen's voice brought Jeremiah's attention to the front where it belonged. He forced himself to listen. Better to focus there than across the aisle. A lot better than what he wanted to do. Especially since asking a friend to step out of church for a round of fisticuffs would shock more than a few in the congregation.

He'd lost Anna, and he might as well accept it. No, he'd never had her. Marriage with Anna would never work anyway. She was too young, and crazy as it sounded, he cared too much for her. He'd never been in love before Anna, but he'd get over her.

"Let's talk about faith now." Again the reverend's voice intruded. "The Bible says faith comes by hearing and hearing by the word of God."

Another glance revealed Garrick leaning toward Anna while she whispered something to him. Jeremiah looked away and squirmed, bringing a sharp look from Kathleen.

"Sorry," he whispered.

She smiled.

He couldn't ask for a sweeter girl than Kathleen. She'd make a perfect wife. Must run in her family. Anna was sweet, too. She was fun, smart, beautiful—and lost to him. He slanted a glance toward Kathleen. His choice was best. Anna had his heart in a twist now, and she wasn't even his. Kathleen would never do that to him. Maybe he should ask Kathleen to marry him right away. Why wait? Get it settled. Then he wouldn't be pestered with thoughts of Anna all the time. He gave a decisive nod and settled back with his arms crossed to listen to what was left of the sermon. Before he had time to make sense of the reverend's words, they were standing, and it was time to go.

He turned to Kathleen. "Would you go for a walk with me this afternoon? I'll pick you up around two if that's all right."

She nodded. "Yes, that would be nice."

"Fine. I hate to go off and leave you now, but I need to catch up with the other men. We're all eating together. Since we don't work in the same area, we try to get together at least once on the weekend."

"I understand. I don't mind at all." Kathleen smiled and touched his arm. "You go ahead. I have a way home with my parents."

"All right." Jeremiah returned her smile and headed outside where the others waited.

Anna breezed past him as if he were standing still. "Anna," he called out when he should have kept his mouth shut.

She froze for a second before turning with the fakest smile he'd ever seen. What was wrong with her?

"Hello, Mr. Tucker. What are you doing?"

He frowned. "What happened to Tuck?"

She waved a gloved hand in front of her face. "Oh, I think Kathleen wouldn't like me calling her beau that."

"Why would she care? She seems agreeable." A lot more than her little sister. A lot more boring, too.

Anna laughed. "Yes, she's agreeable most of the time. Well, nice talking to you. I need to get home."

She crossed the street before Jeremiah got his breath. He might have watched her until she was out of sight, but Frederick called to him. "Hey Tuck, we're heading out. You comin'?"

"Yes." Jeremiah turned on his heel and followed the men.

E.V. dropped back beside him. "Sure you know what you're doing, buddy?"

Jeremiah glanced toward Anna hurrying down the road. The muscle in his jaw ticked, but he nodded. "I'm positive."

"I hope so. Your girl is pretty, but her sister is, too, don't you think?"

"Yes." Jeremiah nodded. "Pretty young."

E.V. gave a sad shake of his head. "Is that what you think?"

Jeremiah drew his brows together and lengthened his stride. Maybe he didn't really think that, but it made a good excuse. He'd been hurt enough for one lifetime.

He followed the others in the diner where his stomach rebelled against the tasteless food they complimented. Their conversation turned from friendly banter to deeper issues as the food disappeared.

"The talk about statehood's been getting serious lately." Willum leaned back after cleaning his plate. "Won't be long until it's signed, sealed, and delivered."

What difference did it make? Jeremiah pushed his plate away. At the moment, he didn't care one way or the other what became of Washington. Territory or state, it was all the same to him. If he was going to talk Kathleen into accepting his proposal, he needed to go. No wonder he'd been unable to eat. He was nervous. Perfectly normal reaction. He just wished the unease stirring his insides would stop. Maybe when she agreed to marry him, it would.

He stood. "Sorry, but I promised Kathleen we'd go on a walk this afternoon. I'm due to pick her up pretty soon."

Frederick lifted his eyebrows. "Sounds like things are getting serious."

Jeremiah shrugged.

E.V. met his gaze, looked as if he might speak, but didn't.

A quick nod and Jeremiah headed toward the Wilkins' house.

After greeting Anna's—or rather Kathleen's parents, he walked beside her down the street. Anna hadn't been at the house. Or hadn't made herself known. After church, when he stopped her, he recognized the hurt in her eyes, as if he'd disappointed her. But he couldn't think about Anna now. Not when he intended to ask for Kathleen's hand. "I thought you might like to go out to the falls. It's always nice there. You're warm enough, aren't you?"

She gave him a sweet smile and clutched her coat lapels with both hands. "Yes, I'm fine, and I'd love to see the falls."

"Good." He lapsed into silence to match hers.

As the falls came into sight, he slowed and Kathleen did, too. He turned to face her, only then taking her hand in his. "Are you all right?"

She nodded, watching him with wary eyes. Wary? Why? Surely, she wasn't afraid of him. He attempted a smile. "I have a farm not far from town. My friend, Willum Tate, has been working on a small house out there. It isn't finished. He can only work between jobs that pay better, but progress is being made. Do you like the country?"

Her gaze skittered away for a moment before returning with her nod. "Yes, but not as well as Anna does. She'd live in the woods if she could."

"Yes, that's probably true." Why did she say that? Didn't he have enough trouble keeping Anna from his mind? He shook his head. "But I'm talking about you. You and me. I want to know if you'd consider marrying me."

Kathleen sucked in her breath as if he'd surprised her. Surely, she'd had some suspicion of his intentions. Of course, he was rushing things.

"I know we haven't had a lot of time together. We've known each other only a few months, but I'm serious about this. If you need to see the house first, I understand. I just thought maybe we could be engaged right now. There's no rush to marry." He gave a quick laugh. "I mean the house isn't even built yet. It will be soon, though. Definitely by spring."

When she only stared at him, he tried again. "Kathleen, will you marry me?"

She nodded, her eyes wide and solemn. The word whispered through her lips. "Yes."

That one word slammed into his midsection then wrapped around his heart as if he'd been chained. His voice sounded rough when he spoke. "That's good."

Her eyes puddled with unshed tears until one and then another rolled from her lower lashes to slide down her cheeks. She covered her face with her gloves. "I'm sorry, Jeremiah. I thought I could do this, but I can't. I just can't."

Sobs shook her shoulders. He pulled her into his arms and let her cry against his chest. He'd never asked a girl to marry him before, but surely this wasn't a normal reaction. He hated when women cried. He patted her back then pulled a handkerchief from his pocket and tucked it into her hands. "What's wrong? Did I do something?"

"I can't marry you. I love s–s–someone else. I love G–Garrick. He s–scarcely looks at me. If I try to talk to him, he stammers and leaves."

Garrick? Did Garrick feel the same for Kathleen? Images filtered through Jeremiah's head as he remembered Garrick standing nearby more than once when he'd been with Kathleen. Garrick scowling at him, and he hadn't known why. But what about Anna? Didn't Garrick want Anna? Why else would he have been holding her that way in front of the feed store? Poor Kathleen. He knew what it was like to love someone you couldn't have.

❄

Anna sat on the Leonard's front porch in the cold December air, her back propped against a corner post, her coat wrapped around her bent legs. If they were lucky, it would snow.

Garrick leaned against the opposite post. "Life isn't always fair, Anna. The both of us might as well face it."

She blinked the burning from her eyes. Abigail had been her excuse for this visit, but she'd been glad when Garrick told her the girls weren't home. He was the one she wanted to see. He understood. She knew why when he admitted he loved Kathleen.

Anna shrugged. "I guess, but if that's true, how does anyone ever find happiness?"

"Not by the abundance of the things you possess, but by every word that proceeds from the mouth of God." Garrick met Anna's gaze. "I guess that means you don't need everything or everyone you want. All you need is God."

Anna giggled. "You're wonderful, Garrick. I'd love for you to be my brother-in-law, but you need to study your Bible a little more. You got the verses mixed up."

"I did?" Garrick frowned. "So my meaning isn't right either?"

"No. I mean yes." Anna giggled again. "The meaning is right, especially if you consider both verses. The first was from the Gospel of Luke. It really says, 'A man's life consisteth not in the abundance of the things which he possesseth.' The other is in the New Testament, too. I don't remember where, but it's where Jesus was being tempted by the devil. 'Man shall not live by bread alone, but by every word that proceedeth out of the mouth of God.' You memorized verses when you were little. I know you did."

"Sure, how else would I have known those two?" Garrick lifted his chin as if offended.

"And thought they were one." Anna grinned at him then dropped her chin to her knees. "But you're right. It doesn't matter how much we love someone. The important thing is our love for God. I guess what we need to do is forget them."

"How?" Garrick looked as glum as she felt. "I've loved Kathleen since I was a kid. She's beautiful and kind. Sweet, gentle, and smart. She never looked my way, and I was afraid to tell her how I felt. Good thing I didn't. She'd have broken my heart. 'Course, she did anyway. At least, I've had most of my life to prepare for this."

Anna searched his face and saw sincerity. "I never knew you loved my sister."

"No one knew but me."

A long sigh escaped Anna's lips. "I'm in love with Jeremiah, and I haven't had any time to prepare. I wish I could go to school now. What are we supposed to do while they keep company right in front of us?"

Garrick's mouth curved. "I guess we could get married. We're good friends, we get along, and who else are we going to marry? How about it, Anna? Think that's a good idea?"

Anna's heart skipped a beat. She looked into Garrick's eyes and the little patient smile that begged for acceptance. What would it be like being married to Garrick? Pleasant for sure. He was right. They liked each other, even loved each other. As friends. But maybe they could learn to love as husband and wife. Not everyone married for love. Why not?

A smile tugged the corners of Anna's mouth upward. "You have a point. If you think you can put up with me—"

At the sound of a familiar voice, Anna stiffened and turned to look out toward the street beside Garrick's house. Jeremiah and Kathleen. They walked past as if lost in their own world. She couldn't hear more than an occasional rumble from Jeremiah then

Kathleen's soft tone answering. Neither looked toward the house. Kathleen clung to Jeremiah's arm as if she belonged there.

The sharp pain shooting through Anna's heart brought tears to her eyes. She brushed them away to see the stricken look on Garrick's face. "Garrick." She called his attention back to her. "If your offer still stands, and I can get out of going to school, I think I'd like to accept."

Chapter 10

Jeremiah woke far too early and stared into the darkness above his cot, wrestling with the same tormenting thoughts that had kept him awake the night before. Snores from the men sleeping around him vibrated the bunkhouse, but they hadn't awakened him. Visions of Kathleen's tears and Anna's pain-filled eyes danced through his head. What sort of mess had he gotten them all into? He should have stayed in Seattle. Maybe after Christmas he'd pack up and go back.

He huffed a laugh. Go back to what? There was nothing in Seattle for him anymore. That's why he'd jumped at the chance to go south when Willum suggested it. In one night and a raging fire, his entire family had been taken from him. The house was gone and most of their belongings. Only the stock, barn, and farm equipment had survived. And the land he'd sold for a new start.

Anna.

His heart yearned for the young woman with the heart-shaped face, the pert nose, and ready grin. How had he fallen in love with her? A girl in love with another man. The memory of her sitting on the Leonard's front porch with Garrick taunted him. He'd tried to ignore them, but he'd seen just the same, and his heart had twisted at the sight.

So Anna loved Garrick, and Kathleen confessed her love for Garrick, too. Unless he was mistaken, Garrick loved Kathleen. Poor Anna. Maybe sending her away to school was the best thing her father could do for her. Maybe then Garrick and Kathleen would tell each other their true feelings.

Jeremiah watched dark shapes of the night take form and color as dawn crept into the sky. He sat up and buried his face in his hands. *Lord, I've made a mess of things. You are sufficient to meet our every need. I pray for Your will to be done. Seems the only two who might find happiness here are Kathleen and Garrick. They're good people and need Your blessing. Jesus, help them find each other and happiness in serving You together. Amen.*

At breakfast, everyone seemed to be ignoring everyone else. When Jeremiah went through the line, he recognized Kathleen's red-rimmed eyes for what they were. She was grieving over Garrick. All Jeremiah had done was open an old wound for her.

Anna didn't meet Jeremiah's gaze. Garrick followed him into the mess hall, but sat across the room from him. The only time their eyes met, hostility glared from Garrick's. Jeremiah ate eggs, sausage, biscuits, and gravy, but scarcely noticed the taste. If he wasn't the villain here, he didn't know the meaning of the word. Someone needed a happy ending and since it wouldn't be him, he'd better see what he could do to help Kathleen and Garrick.

When Garrick got up to leave, Jeremiah stuffed the last bite of biscuit into his mouth and followed.

"Garrick." Jeremiah ran to catch the departing form of a man he still considered a friend. "Wait. I've got something to tell you. Something you'll want to hear."

Garrick looked over his shoulder but didn't slow his pace. "Not interested, Tucker.

Keep your news if it makes you happy." He stopped then and turned around. "Oh, speaking of news. I've got some, too. Yesterday, Anna Wilkin and I decided to get married as soon as we get her father's blessing."

Jeremiah stopped as if he'd taken a hit to his gut. Garrick laughed and strode away.

"Tucker, come on." One of the guys from his crew called, and Jeremiah turned toward the sound. Pain twisted his heart. Anna couldn't marry a man who loved her sister. Her life would be miserable. A rock settled into the cavity where his heart should be. He needed to talk to Garrick, but he probably wouldn't see him until evening.

Jeremiah joined the other men heading to the work site. While he manned one end of the bucksaw to cut slices from a log, Garrick's face stood before him. Garrick hadn't understood Jeremiah's news. He thought he was going to announce his engagement to Kathleen.

Had Garrick been serious about marrying Anna? No, he'd only been trying to get even. What a mess. Jeremiah's grip on the saw slipped, jerking him back to his job.

"Hey, watch it!" Henry, his partner on the saw, yelled. "This is the second time you've done that."

"Sorry. My hand slipped. I'll pay better attention." If he didn't, he could get himself or someone else hurt. He'd seen injuries happen when men were careless. He'd have to deal with Garrick later.

The sound of something crashing through the forest brought the men's work to a halt. Jeremiah turned to watch a horse and cart hurry past. In the back of the cart, calking boots below a blanket-covered form told the story. A man had been hurt. How bad was hard to tell. Who it was remained a mystery. Jeremiah sent a prayer for the man toward heaven as he went back to work until the lunch whistle blew.

On the short walk back to camp, Jeremiah listened to the buzz of speculation about the injury. He followed the others into the mess hall and met Anna's gaze. She stood behind the serving table, her eyes luminescent and red rimmed.

When he stood in front of her, he searched her face. She'd been crying. "Anna, what's wrong?"

"Oh Tuck, it's Garrick." Two big tears hovered on the edges of her eyelids before rolling down. "He's hurt. His leg—" She sucked in a breath.

Her tears tore at his heart. He ached for her, but he also ached for himself. She loved Garrick, not him. "Little Bit, don't cry. He'll be okay. How bad was it?"

"I don't know. Papa and Kathleen went with him to the hospital. Oh Tuck, they said he wasn't paying attention and a limb hit him. He fell, and his ax cut his leg. What if he dies?"

"We'll pray and he'll be fine. They'll take good care of him." Jeremiah longed to take Anna in his arms and wipe the tears from her eyes. He wanted to make her forget Garrick and love him instead. Each silent tear trailing down her face burned his heart, but he was powerless to stop them. She belonged to Garrick now. He let her fill his plate then moved to a far corner to eat.

Jeremiah ignored the conversation around him and dug into food that held no appeal.

Anna finished serving and moved into the kitchen. Her mother covered the bowls and pots on the table. Where was Kathleen? When he didn't see her, Anna's words came to the surface of his mind. Kathleen went with Garrick to the hospital. Kathleen? Why not Anna? Just this morning Garrick said he and Anna were getting married. Something didn't add up.

Still puzzling over his discovery, Jeremiah left his unfinished plate and walked into the woods to be alone. He wanted to pray for Garrick, but soon the cleansing power of repentance poured from his soul. He'd been out of God's will in pursuing Kathleen. While he admired her, he didn't love her. She might like him, but she didn't love him, and was smart enough to realize it. But that wasn't where he'd failed God. No, he was like Abraham, who'd moved ahead of God's will for his life when he took Hagar as his concubine. Jeremiah's reason was different, but the lack of trust was the same. His fear of losing another loved one seemed foolish under the ray of God's loving conviction. Why hadn't he trusted God to take care of Anna? To take care of his hurt. Now he'd lost her without her ever being his.

He fell to his knees. "Lord, I'm sorry for not trusting You. I ask Your forgiveness. Maybe someday I'd have lost Anna, but at least she'd have been mine for a while. Now I've lost her anyway. I'm sorry."

Jeremiah lifted his head and rose. The hurt was still there, but God forgave him, and he'd do his best to trust Him from now on, even if he never married.

❄

Garrick might die. Hot tears ran from Anna's eyes and dripped into the dishwater. She turned her face first one way and then the other to blot them on her shoulders. Her heart ached for Garrick. And for Kathleen. She'd never seen her sister so worked up over anyone as she was Garrick. Mama was shocked but adjusted well when Kathleen confessed her love for Garrick. She said it was better to find out now than later. Anna agreed.

Lord, please spare Garrick's life. Let him know how much Kathleen really cares. He loves her, and she loves him. If she doesn't know her own heart, help her see it now. And please, Lord, forgive Garrick and me for talking about marrying each other. I see now we were wrong. My love for him is of a good friend, not a wife. Please don't let him die. Touch him and give him healing. Amen.

Anna pushed her worries aside and worked hard throughout the afternoon. She knew that praying then continuing to worry showed a lack of faith, but she was afraid that even if he lived, Garrick might lose his leg. She dropped the broom.

"Anna, are you all right?" Mama looked up, her hands stilled on the bread dough she'd been kneading.

"What if they cut off Garrick's leg?" Anna fought more tears.

A crease formed between Mama's eyes. "I don't think that will happen. Garrick will be fine. Your worrying will do him no good."

"I know." Anna picked up the broom. "But Kathleen is in love with him. He loves her, too. He told me so yesterday. I've always thought of Garrick as a sort of brother. Now he could be, and this had to happen."

Mama smiled. "Yes, but don't worry, I believe Garrick will be fine. Kathleen isn't one to let a missing limb stand in the way of her love. I thought from the start Jeremiah was wrong for her. They'll come through this."

Anna turned back to sweeping. Maybe Kathleen and Garrick would be all right, but would she? She loved Jeremiah. He'd be hurt that Kathleen loved someone else. Why couldn't he love her? Mama was glad Kathleen loved Garrick. She wanted her daughters to be wives and mothers in their own homes. Anna wanted the same thing. But she wanted to be true to the way God made her, too.

She should have stood up for herself long ago. Now, just before Christmas, might be the best time to talk to Papa and tell him she didn't want to go away. Maybe tonight she'd get a chance.

She kept watch for Papa and Kathleen while she worked, but Papa's wagon wheels didn't crunch against the ground outside. It seemed they were taking an awfully long time. After supper, she and Mama closed the mess hall and went to their cabin.

"It isn't a good sign for them to be so late, is it, Mama?" Anna hugged her arms close to ward off a chill more from unease than from the cool December air.

"I wouldn't worry, Anna." Mama's smile looked tired. "Kathleen may have wanted to stay with Garrick as long as she could. You'll understand someday when you fall in love with a young man."

Her mother's words cut deep into Anna's heart. She'd already fallen in love, and she did understand, but there was no point in saying anything. Jeremiah didn't love her. She followed her mother into the cabin. "I'm tired. If you don't mind, I think I'll go to my room."

She climbed the ladder to the loft room she shared with Kathleen and lay across the bed. Her eyes drifted shut while exhaustion lulled her to sleep. A sound in the quiet darkness of night woke her, and she sat up.

With only moonlight filtering into the room, Kathleen sat on the edge of the double bed. "I'm sorry, I didn't mean to disturb you."

"Is Garrick—"

"He's going to be okay." Tears mingled with relief in Kathleen's voice. "He plans to be at the Whitworth's Christmas party."

Anna's breath rushed out. "I'm so glad."

"Papa let me stay until he woke." Kathleen turned to face Anna. "I thought I'd lost him. Did you know he was afraid of me?"

"No, why would he be?"

"I don't know, but he said I was too good for him. Too pretty. Too perfect." Kathleen caught Anna's hand. "He's loved me for years, and I thought he didn't care."

Anna laughed. "Poor Garrick. Did he propose?"

Kathleen's head bowed. "Not yet. I think he will though, when he's better."

Anna changed into her nightgown and crawled into bed beside her sister. She'd talk to Papa later. As soon as possible. She lay in the dark, no longer sleepy as Tuck filled her thoughts. Kathleen hadn't mentioned him. His heart would be broken when he found out

Kathleen didn't love him.

Long into the night she lay awake imagining how life as Jeremiah's bride might be until sleep and dreams took over, renewing her determination to win his love if it took the rest of her life.

❄

Thursday after Anna finished her work, she found Papa in the tool shed where he often spent his evenings. He turned with file in hand when she stepped in and closed the door. "Anna. What are you doing out here?"

She grinned. "Tagging along after you like always."

He chuckled. "That's my tagalong Tootsie."

Even as she laughed with him, a lump caught in her throat. He hadn't called her that in years. Now she felt seven years old, and like a child, she blurted out her complaints. "Papa, I don't want to go away."

His eyebrows shot up. "To school?"

"Yes." Tears threatened her eyes. "I love our life here. I want to stay home. God made me just the way I am, and I don't see why everyone wants me to change. Why do you want me to go away?"

"Anna." Papa's voice was calm in the midst of her storm. "You know I love when you help me. I'd like to keep you with me, but if you don't go to school, you'll miss a chance to better yourself. It's a good opportunity, don't you think?"

An invisible cord tightened around her insides as she looked into the pleading in his eyes. He really did want her to go. She blinked against the burning tears that threatened. "All right. If you really want me to, I will. I'll go for you, Papa, not me."

Papa's chuckle returned. He held his arms out, and Anna stepped into his warm embrace. His chest rumbled when he spoke. "It won't be for me, Anna. Your mama came up with this idea and convinced me it's for the best. If you're sure you don't want to go, I'll talk to Mama and set things straight. I'd rather you stay here. I'm happy with the girl you are. I'm pretty sure God is, too."

The tears Anna had tried so hard to keep under control rolled down her cheeks. She didn't have to go away, but what had she gained? Jeremiah didn't love her, and now she'd be here to watch him find someone to take Kathleen's place.

Chapter 11

Anna studied her reflection in the mirror. Where had the sparkle in her eyes gone? Her family was staying in town through Tuesday for Christmas, so she hadn't seen Jeremiah all weekend, and she missed him. Today she should be looking forward to the Whitworth's Christmas Eve soiree, but all she could think about was Jeremiah.

"Aren't you ready yet?" Kathleen stepped around the edge of the doorway. As usual, she looked beautiful.

Anna sighed. "Yes, I'm ready."

What difference did her appearance make? Jeremiah might not even be there. Just because he had an invitation didn't mean he would come. Anna listened to Kathleen chatter with Mama on the short buggy ride across town and shook her head. At least her sister had found love with Garrick.

At the gaily decorated Whitworth mansion, Anna followed Kathleen in and stepped aside to allow her parents room. The house buzzed with activity as townspeople spilled from the formal parlor through wide double doors into the entrance hall.

Anna looked for Larkin, but Kathleen grabbed her arm and pulled her toward the parlor. "There's Garrick."

"Let go, Kathleen. I'm coming." Anna jerked her arm free and hurried after her sister. They stopped beside Garrick's chair. His leg stretched out, resting on a footstool. "What's your rush? It isn't as if he's going to run away."

"Anna, what a horrible thing to say." Kathleen scowled.

Garrick laughed. "She's right. I won't be dancing tonight either." He looked up at Kathleen. "If I could, I'd fill your card."

Pink tinged Kathleen's cheeks, and Anna turned away. She didn't hear her sister's response because there by the front door stood Jeremiah. The waltz, played by the small orchestra in the music room, faded to background music for the dance steps of her heart. Hers and Jeremiah's, only his heart wouldn't be dancing with hers now that it was broken by Kathleen's rejection.

Her breath caught in her throat as his eyes held hers, and he stepped forward. A shadow moved between them, blocking him from her view.

"Anna, you're here." Larkin clasped her hand and stepped back. "You look so much older with your hair fixed that way."

Jeremiah stepped past Larkin. After giving Anna a quick glance, he shook hands with Garrick. "Glad to see you're able to be here. I want you to know I wish you the best."

Anna didn't hear more as she allowed Larkin to lead her away. Jeremiah lost Kathleen and was stepping graciously aside. She turned for one last look and saw the sadness in his eyes. Why couldn't he have loved her instead?

She smiled for Larkin's benefit. "Your family always has the best parties."

"Thank you. Mama and Papa both enjoy entertaining."

As Anna went with Larkin from one person to another, visiting for a few minutes before moving on, she kept her smile in place. She danced with one of the Bollen brothers and then forgot which one when she saw Jeremiah scowling at her. He looked so unhappy. Tears burned her eyes, but she refused to let them fall. Why did Jeremiah keep watching her? She slipped out of the parlor into the hall. If she could get away from him, maybe she could catch her breath. She stood against the wall, smiling at no one in particular. If only she could forget Jeremiah. She leaned her head against the flocked wallpaper and closed her eyes. Still Jeremiah took form in her memory. So near, yet so out of reach.

"Anna."

His deep voice sounded in her head, and she smiled.

"Little Bit, are you all right?" He sounded concerned.

She jerked, her eyes popping open. "Tuck."

He stood before her, a frown darkening his eyes. He touched her wrist. His fingers burned through her gloves as his hand surrounded hers. "Come with me, Anna. Away, where we can talk."

She tugged against his hold, but he didn't let go.

"Please?" His brows drew together. "It's important."

As if a magnet drew her to him, she nodded and stepped forward. How could she resist? Even if he wanted to talk about Kathleen, she would listen. She loved him.

❄

Jeremiah nodded toward a closed door. "Where does that go?"

"The library, but we can't go in there."

"Why not? We'll leave the door open." He guided Anna inside. A soft light glowed in the corner near a desk, but he didn't move away from the door. No need to risk Anna's reputation.

He kept her hand in his and looked into her questioning eyes. "I love you, Anna."

Only the slight widening of her eyes gave indication she heard.

He took a deep breath. "I didn't intend to fall in love. You're too young. Then there's school. I was afraid of you, so I courted your sister."

"Afraid?" Anna shook her head. "I don't understand."

"When you love someone and lose them, it hurts—more than you can imagine. That's what happened with my family. I didn't know if I could go through that again. What if I lost you? Then I realized my error when I saw you with Garrick. I'd already lost you. I tried to tell Garrick Kathleen loved him, but he wouldn't listen. Then he got hurt."

Anna rubbed her forehead. "Aren't you in love with Kathleen?"

He shook his head. "No, Anna. I fell in love with a little tomboy. My love is for all time, whether you are mine for one day or for the next sixty years."

He released her hand and stepped back. "I wanted you to know how I feel about you. I know you can't marry me now. I'm willing to wait, but there's no other girl who can ever take your place in my heart. When you finish school, if you haven't found someone else, I'd like the chance to court you. I understand if you don't love me."

Jeremiah swallowed the lump in his throat. He'd laid everything out before her and had nothing more to say. He walked out the open door.

"Tuck." Anna's sweet voice followed him.

He stopped but didn't look back.

"I'll be eighteen in two weeks. I'm not a child."

Jeremiah took a ragged breath. Still he didn't turn. "What about school?"

"I'm not leaving."

At her touch on his arm, he turned and searched her face.

"I've talked to Papa. He never really wanted me to go. It was Mama's idea."

Jeremiah grabbed her hand, and with his heart pounding the rhythm of his love, he knelt before her in front of anyone who wanted to see. "I love you, Anna. Can you find it in your heart to care even a little for me? Will you marry me?"

❋

On the fringes of her vision, Anna saw people standing in the hallway, making a semicircle around them, but she couldn't tear her gaze from the insecurity in Jeremiah's eyes. He truly loved her. Not Kathleen, but her. She laughed, and her feet bounced as she tugged at him to stand.

"Yes!" As quickly as he rose, she threw her arms around his neck. "Yes of course, I love you. I'll marry you, and don't you dare back down."

"Never." His voice choked on the one word. His cheek touched hers as applause filled the hall where they stood.

Anna released her hold and turned with Jeremiah to see Larkin standing in front of a group of their friends, her lips curved in a smile. Garrick sat behind them with Kathleen by his side. All smiled and clapped their approval then surrounded them, offering congratulations.

Jeremiah took Anna's hand. "This isn't official without your father's blessing."

"Then I suggest you ask now." Papa pushed through and shook Jeremiah's hand. "You know, I don't think this is right. A father shouldn't lose both his girls in the same night."

"Garrick and Kathleen?" Anna bounced inside.

Papa nodded. "Yes, and now you." He turned to Mama. "What do you think about this?"

Anna held her breath when Mama looked from her to Jeremiah. Finally, she shrugged. "Just one question. Are you sure you want this tomboy?"

Jeremiah threw back his head and laughed. He pulled Anna close and looked into her eyes. "Oh yes. I'm positive."

Mama smiled. "Then you have my blessing as well. When do you plan to marry?"

Jeremiah raised his eyebrows in a question. "Before spring planting?"

Anna looked toward her sister. "Maybe we could have a double wedding."

Kathleen stepped close and hugged Anna. "Garrick says he plans to walk before we marry, so we are thinking about March."

Anna laughed. "That's perfect. We'll be married in March and everyone's invited. We'll have the biggest wedding Tumwater has ever seen."

She turned to Jeremiah as he lowered his head to cover her lips in the first of what she hoped would be many kisses.

Mildred Colvin is the author of more than thirty romance novels in both contemporary and historical time settings, including the bestseller "Mama's Bible" which is the first in a series of Oregon Trail stories. She is a member of American Christian Fiction Writers as well as a wonderful critique group. Mildred often sets her stories in her home state of Missouri where she lives with her husband of almost fifty years. They have three adult children and three grandchildren. You can find Mildred online at http://www.infinitecharacters.com and on Facebook at Romantic Reflections by Mildred Colvin.

One Evergreen Night

by Debby Lee

Dedication

This is dedicated to my mom, who has helped me along the way; to my dad, who helped me with the technical stuff in the story; to my husband, Steve, and my five children for putting up with me; to my four classmates and friends, Jeff Pratt, Nick Sorensen, Steven Stover, and Del Ray "Buzzy" Hughes, for giving me this idea; to Mr. Hoglund, my high school English teacher, who was the first one who thought I could write a book; to my friends at Crossroads Church who prayed for me and helped me discover God's calling on my life; and last but not least, to my Savior, Jesus Christ, for not giving up on me.

Except the LORD build the house,
they labour in vain that build it.
PSALM 127:1

Chapter 1

Frederick Corrigan piled firewood into the furnace of the locomotive. The rattletrap he'd given the pet name Inferno swayed violently from side to side as it careened down the hill. Frederick braced his hands against the walls and struggled to remain in a standing position. At the speed the train was going, he would have no time to jump if it derailed.

Steam poured from the engine. Frederick's chest ached as he sucked the sweltering air into his lungs. The furnace door burned red hot and could potentially explode from the pressure at any moment, but getting the load of logs to the mill on time was crucial. His job depended on his ability to deliver the timber as quickly as possible.

When he reached the bottom of the steep slope, Frederick pulled hard on the brake lever in order to round Widow's Bend looming ahead. The brakes protested with a grinding shriek. The screech of the wheels pierced his eardrums with a painful force. Sparks flew from the wheels that gripped the flimsy rails. *Lord, let the tracks be stable*. The corner approached with frightening speed. He was going too fast. . .again.

As the landscape alongside the tracks flew past with a blur, Frederick held his breath. He stood frozen for what felt like eternity.

"Turn. . .turn," he whispered, prayed. He leaned opposite of the turn. His two hundred pounds wouldn't make a difference in a true emergency, but the action made him feel better. For a brief moment, he thought he felt the wheels lift from the tracks. He white-knuckled the sides of the car as if sheer force of will could push Inferno back onto the rails.

The rickety wheels somehow stayed on course. With the corner behind him Frederick relaxed his grip and breathed a little easier, especially since the path ahead was clear of animals. Such wasn't always the case. Derailing would surely curtail his chances of getting the promotion with Kenicky Logging, the company he worked for, and then where would he be?

The rolling hills of Tumwater came into view. Small farms where cattle grazed in green fields skirted the town. Farther down the line, he spotted several wooden structures clustered along Main Street. Few people were milling about the lively town he called home when he wasn't stuck up in the logging camp.

Clutching the throttle, Frederick checked the pressure gauges as a short wooden bridge approached. He gave a cursory glance behind him to check on the logs and make sure they were still on the flatcars. It was a wonder they were considering the way he drove, but he hadn't lost a load yet, and he didn't intend to.

The wheels rolled onto the bridge with a shaky bump and again Frederick held his breath. Pieces of twisted metal and broken railroad cars lay on both sides of the tracks in the creek below. Remnants of a recent crash that killed one of his coworkers, one of his friends. Frederick shuddered. *But for the grace of God. . .*

As Inferno rolled over the tracks, the wheels made an eerie *thumpity-thump*, drowning out the sound of rushing water in the creek. Slowly the locomotive passed over the bridge. Frederick relaxed when it was on solid ground on the other side.

He blew out a sigh of relief and mopped the sweat from his face with a red bandana. He was going to make it in one piece. The last guy who rode these rails wasn't as lucky, as evidenced by the wreckage behind him.

As the small businesses that dotted the landscape began to whip past his line of vision, Frederick applied the brake again. More sweat caused his hair to stick to his forehead. The noise made him want to cover his ears, but he had to keep his hands on the levers and his eyes on the gauges. Renier Lumber Company lay just ahead, and the team of men waited to take this load of logs and turn them into lumber.

Frederick pressed hard on the brake lever and steam poured from the locomotive. The heat caused his muscles to grow weak as he came to a stop at the loading dock of the mill. "Thank You, Lord," he whispered under his breath.

He climbed down the rough metal ladder. "Morning, E.V."

E.V. strode up and gave Frederick a slap on the back. "Looks like you had a good run there." He raked his fingers over what had to be at least three days' stubble on his chin. E.V. only shaved on Wednesdays and Sundays.

"Sure did." Frederick stood back and took a breather as E.V. pulled on a pair of worn leather work gloves and joined a team of men nearby.

Frederick couldn't help but feel pride in his accomplishment of getting the train safely to Tumwater. If all continued to go well, he just might get that promotion. If only the boss could overlook the recent loss of the previous engineer. The accident hadn't been Frederick's fault, but he felt somewhat responsible anyway. He should have been there that day.

"You all right?" E.V. asked with concern buzzing through his tone.

"Yeah, I'm fine. Let's get this thing unloaded so I can get back up to the landing and get another load." Frederick moved with precision, although his thoughts vacillated between a gnawing hunger to impress his boss; Albert, his coworker's widow with two fatherless children; and anxiety at his own father's home teetering toward the auction block.

❄

"Shoo, shoo!" Emma Pearson charged after a rat, knocking over a wash bucket as she chased the vermin out of the bunkhouse. Once the rat darted into the woods, she halted her chase and paused to catch her breath. She looked over her shoulder into the open bunkhouse door. "Oh no," she groaned at the mess she'd created.

Getting the sheets off the beds, washed, and dried was proving to be much more work than she had originally anticipated. Nonetheless, the job had to be done before the men came back in from the woods, or she would be in a heap of trouble that night.

Muttering under her breath, she traipsed back inside. She picked up the water bucket and winced as the dirty soapy water sloshed on a recent burn she received while taking dinner rolls from the cookstove.

Emma hated living in the rough and dirty logging camp. The work was so hard and the conditions were so. . .primitive.

Mr. and Mrs. Wilkin were kind enough to offer her a loft in their cabin. The tiny room offered little privacy, but it held her most prized possession, her mother's dark green ball gown. The garment had frayed around the collar and sleeves over the years, but to Emma it was a dress fit for a fairy tale.

"Lord, I know Your Word says to be content in all circumstances, but this?" With no place to go and nobody to turn to for help, she gritted her teeth against the pain in her burned fingers and resigned herself to finishing the sheets. First she had to get a bucket of fresh water to replace the one she'd spilled.

"Stupid rat." Emma stomped down to the creek, her thoughts drifting in the direction of town and all the excitement going on there. Many of her friends were attending fancy parties at the Whitworth mansion, plays at the local theater, and a real church on Sunday mornings. If only she wasn't stuck in this isolated and dirty place. Immersed in her dreams of all the activity in town, the pain she felt in her burned fingers subsided.

About the time she unpinned the last sheet from the makeshift clothesline, the sound of the men arriving in camp brought her back to the present. Emma's older brother, Jake, sidled up to her, gave her a pat on the head, and then began gathering the clothespins. "You look like you've had a hard day," he said with a lopsided grin.

"Every day is a hard day," she replied, grimacing as the grin fell from his face like a giant oak crashing to the ground.

"I'm doing my best, sis, to support us."

With dark hair and dark eyes mirroring hers, he was the only living relative she had left in the world. She was glad he was home safe, at least for the night. "I know," she answered, "and I'm sorry for complaining."

"I start training for driving the loads into town tomorrow." Jake eyed her as if to gauge her reaction. "Frederick Corrigan has been kind enough to put in a good word for me and is willing to show me the ropes."

Emma tried to smile but couldn't, not any more than she could count on her burned fingers how many times a day she prayed for her brother's safety. From what she heard of Frederick Corrigan's driving, they could use the prayers tomorrow, and the days after to boot!

"Don't be angry, Emma. Compared to the job I'm doing now, it's twice the pay—"

"And five times the danger!" How could she make him understand that, after losing their parents, she couldn't bear to lose him, too?

"Fred is a good man. He's a skilled driver and will teach me well." Jake rambled on about Frederick Corrigan's proficiency, but few words soaked through the dry and brittle exterior of her heart. The company's driver took daring chances on the rails—chances she didn't want her brother taking.

"Emma, I need you to come and help me take up the potatoes, please." The voice of the camp's cook, Mrs. Wilkin, floated to Emma, drawing her from her thoughts.

"Go on, sis, I need to wash up." Jake strode to the creek. "I'll see you at dinner."

Emma quickly picked up the basket full of clean sheets. "Be right there," she called toward the kitchen. She hadn't taken more than two steps before she bumped into someone and nearly dropped the laundry basket. Clothespins fell to the ground and rolled every which way. Exasperation bubbled within her.

"Of all the—" Emma bit her lip to stifle the exclamations swirling in her head.

When she looked up, Frederick Corrigan stood blocking her path.

Chapter 2

Afternoon, Miss Pearson." He tipped his hat and nodded.

Emma noted the twinkle in his sky blue eyes as he smiled down at her. What, pray tell, he had to smile about was beyond her. From what she heard, his father's house was in foreclosure and one of his lumberjack friends had just died in a horrible accident.

"Afternoon, Mr. Corrigan," Emma said, noting all too well the cold flatness in her voice. She had once thought him to be handsome and daring, but now that he had agreed to teach her brother—her only living kin—his reckless ways, she could only see him as a means to her brother's death.

"May I help you with that basket?" Mr. Corrigan reached for the load she carried, and she shied away from his touch.

"No, thank you, I can manage just fine on my own." Emma's curt words dripped with disdain.

"Since your brother will be riding with me, I would think we could at least be friends." He cracked a bright grin.

"I'm really very busy." Emma adjusted the basket on her hip and turned toward the bunkhouses. Since when would she like to be friends with the likes of this rough scoundrel?

"You don't approve of me, do you?" He stood in her path like a towering pine, with his hands on his hips. His eyes reminded Emma of the sky on a cloudless summer day, much as she hated to admit it.

"It isn't that I dislike you. I just don't care to see my brother taking the same reckless chances on the rails that you do."

He glared at her with stormy intensity. The eyes that were a lovely shade of blue only a moment ago now took on a thunderous darkening. "I'm the best engineer this company has, and I'll teach your brother well."

"I've no doubt you'll teach him to properly deliver the timber, but will you teach him to be safe? Speedy delivery didn't fare well for the last driver, now did it?" Emma didn't wish to be confrontational or tell Mr. Corrigan how to do his job, but the last thing she wanted was her brother becoming the next casualty in the logging camp.

He aimed an icy glare straight at her.

"Do you think I'd intentionally endanger another man's life?" Rage and hurt pride were evident on his tanned face. His nostrils flared and his jaw was set in hardened lines.

Emma sucked in her breath. Something in her gut coiled as the hair on the nape of her neck prickled. She had seen men angry like this before. If she lived to be a thousand years old, the sight would always trigger fear.

He sneered through clenched teeth. "I'll see to it your brother's kept safe." Without another word, he turned on his boot heel and stomped away, leaving a gasping Emma to cope with his blunt words.

❄

"Emma Pearson is sure angry with me." Frederick spoke with E.V. the next morning at the sawmill. He could almost feel his blood heating in his veins. "She doesn't want me showing her brother the ropes of train engineering."

"Can you blame her?"

E.V.'s words gave Frederick pause, and he thought about Emma's situation. Having lost both her parents, she probably lived in daily fear of losing her brother, too. And with an engineer's recent death, her fears had to be multiplied.

Frederick shook his head. "No, it's dangerous work, much as I hate to admit it. I just wish she'd understand I'm not the dare-devil she thinks I am."

Even though E.V. owned the sawmill and had his employees to do the grunt work, he pulled on a pair of leather gloves and began to help Frederick with the current load of logs. "Why don't you do something nice for her?"

"I don't want Miss Pearson thinking I'm sweet on her."

E.V.'s gaze shifted to the street where Larkin Whitworth exited the mercantile, holding boxes precariously balanced. "Doing something nice doesn't mean you have to start courting. See a need and then meet it." He dropped a log onto the pile then patted Frederick's back. "I'll catch up with you when you bring the next load in."

Frederick watched as E.V. ran across the street to the mercantile and helped Miss Whitworth with her packages. *See a need and then meet it.*

With that thought in mind, Frederick tromped back to Inferno and climbed aboard.

The afternoon went by with a blur, quite literally, as he sped back to the woods, refilled his string of flatcars with timber, and returned to Tumwater. This didn't allow for any time to check on Miss Pearson at camp, but it did allow for time to pray for compassion and insight as to what made Miss Pearson tick. She had to have some type of need.

Yet the only answer he heard from the Lord was *"Seek, and ye shall find."*

As Inferno's engine cooled from the day's frantic pace, Frederick pulled his red bandana from his trouser pocket and wiped his face. He climbed down, helped unload the logs, then headed down the street looking for a nice peace offering.

An hour later, with his nerves frayed at the edges, Frederick stomped down the wooden-planked boardwalk. Everything he "sought" had too high a price.

"I could use a little help here, Lord," he grumbled.

"Seek, and ye shall find."

Not sure where he was supposed to seek, Frederick stopped walking and looked around. Karl's Feed and Seed was the only business he hadn't visited. "All right, Lord, I'll keep seeking."

He hurried across the street. After entering Karl's, Frederick walked around, examining every shelf before roaming to the pens in the corner. Baby pigs rooted around and climbed over each other in an effort to get to the food plate. Two of the scrawnier ones looked up at him with big dark eyes.

"Just came in this morning," Karl called from the side counter where he scooped grain from a large bin into bags.

"Twelve, that's a good-sized litter."

"Thirteen, actually. I heard the runt in the litter had to be disposed of."

"That's too bad." Frederick studied the wiggling creatures.

Karl reached for some twine to tie off a full bag. "You heading back to camp tonight?"

"Yup—do you need me to do something?"

Karl walked to him, carrying a gunnysack. "Johnny isn't back from the last delivery, and I have all these customers. Could you take this watering can to Mrs. Wilkin? She ordered it awhile back for her chickens and it just arrived."

"Sure thing." Frederick took the sack, slung it over his shoulder, and headed out the door. Within minutes, he and Inferno were on the rails again. His father's house was still in foreclosure, Miss Pearson still hated him, and the guilt he felt every time he saw the bridge continued to grow. As the bridge approached, Frederick slowed the locomotive in an effort to be extra cautious.

"Lord, I pray You'll take Albert's family by the hand and walk with them through the valley of the shadow of death. Give them a comfort that only You can bring."

When God's peace washed over him, he glanced over the bridge. *What in creation?*

He leaned far out the locomotive's window to get a better view. A tiny pink piglet clung to the wreckage. Probably the runt piglet Karl had mentioned. The water was plenty cold for late September.

Frederick jerked Inferno to a stop. He climbed down and slowly made his way to the riverbank. With great care, he maneuvered across the wreckage and managed to grab the creature by the head and pull it from the icy water.

The piglet protested at this treatment with a series of ear-piercing squeals and wiggled with more force than what Frederick thought possible.

Climbing back up the ravine to the train, Frederick bundled the piglet inside his wool coat. He whistled a lullaby all the way back to where Inferno was parked on the tracks in hopes the tune would help calm the squirming animal. Once they were back inside the train, Frederick pulled the watering can out of the gunnysack.

"Not sure why I saved you. All you're good for is a few strips of bacon," he said, wrapping the squirming piglet in the gunny-sack. He placed it in the kindling bucket. "Can't have you falling out on the way home."

The piglet lay down, content.

Frederick grinned as he fired up the locomotive and headed off in the direction of camp. Large, fat raindrops descended from the gray sky. He needed to hightail it home. The rails were a temperamental part of logging equipment, as moody and unpredictable as a woman scorned. He shuddered, thinking of Widow's Bend. The curve of slippery metal lay only a few miles ahead.

Chapter 3

Weary of life in the primitive logging camp, a determined Emma would use any excuse she could to go into town. Now if only such an excuse would present itself.

She sat a few feet from the kitchen door and plucked another feather off the chicken. Cooking was a dirty job and not in her normal duties, but when Mrs. Wilkin ran behind schedule, she needed Emma's help. It was difficult, to say the least, keeping up with the appetites of the hordes of hardworking lumberjacks.

Ridding the deceased poultry of their feathers was a job she especially disliked, but a job she had to do for dinner. The dead birds stunk to high heaven, causing her to gag. She considered lighting a match to get rid of the smell, but the wet feathers stuck to her fingers with frustrating tenacity and would make lighting matches difficult at best.

Finished with the second bird, she grabbed the next one in line, submerged it in scalding water, and yanked at feathers till her forearms ached. She tried not to look at the pen containing nine more waiting their turn for a neck wringing and a dunk in the boiling pot.

Emma longed for her quiet time after dinner when the washed dishes were put away for the night. Then she could crawl into a hot tub of water. If only she had some dried rose petals to take away the stench of dead chicken. Resigned to her duty, she focused on the only thing she could make a difference in—praying for her brother's safety.

"Lord, please protect Jake from danger—and Mr. Corrigan, too," she added for good measure, hoping God would hear her prayers. A decent and worthy way to pass the time even though, in her opinion, prayers hadn't done much good for her mother, who had been left to support two children after their father had died. Warm clothing had been scarce in cold winter months, not that they had any finer clothing in the summer. She remembered frequent hunger, but Mama had always prayed before every meal, no matter how meager it might be.

"Oh Mama." With tears pooling in her eyes, Emma pulled in a ragged breath of air. "I wish you were here."

"Emma, could you come in here, please?" Mrs. Wilkin called out the kitchen door.

"Be right there." Emma dropped the half-plucked bird and strode toward the small but sufficient kitchen.

"Mr. Corrigan would like to speak to you." Mrs. Wilkin jerked her thumb at Frederick Corrigan, standing in the corner with his arms folded across his barrel chest. "I'll attend to the chickens." She walked outside carrying what looked like a shiny new watering can.

Mr. Corrigan pointed to a little wiener pig rooting through the rancid garbage pail in the corner. As small as the creature was, it had no difficulty in tipping over the bucket and spilling the contents onto the floor. Another mess for her to have to clean.

"Would you accept my peace offering?" Mr. Corrigan had a cheesy grin plastered on his face, as if he expected praise for the "offering." "I thought you could raise him for a while and then we'd butcher him when the time was right. Or you could sell him."

Emma stood speechless.

The piglet lifted its nose and looked her way. Brown smelly gunk covered its tiny snout. It eyed her with what had to be curiosity and sniffed.

"Um, thank you." Emma raised her eyebrows and hoped it was enough of a response. What else could she say? No one had given her a gift in years. While it wasn't rose petals, she supposed it was still sweet of him.

"Go say hello, Bacon," Mr. Corrigan chided. He gave the piglet a tap on his two-strips-of-bacon belly. Much to Emma's horror, the animal let out an ear-piercing squeal and limped straight toward her.

❄

The locomotive's wheels rolled along to the tune of a well-oiled machine. Frederick stood next to Jake Pearson, ready to take control of Inferno in case an emergency arose. He hoped things would continue to run with smooth efficiency. After a week of intense training, Jake had done quite well. He hadn't even been intimidated rounding Widow's Bend. Fear could be as dangerous as rain on the rails. But then, so could cockiness.

As the landscape passed during a straightaway, Frederick asked Jake how his sister and Bacon were getting on.

"She was busy with dishes last time I seen her and didn't say much about it." When Jake didn't say more, Frederick decided to let the matter go.

But he couldn't forget about it, about Miss Pearson. There was something about her that kept invading his thoughts. He wanted to know more about her. He wanted to convince her he'd keep her brother safe. He wanted to see her smile.

The locomotive rolled over the bridge leading into town. Just a few more miles to go and then another few dollars would be added to the precious hoard in the bank. Dollars meant for saving his father's house in town.

Much to Frederick's chagrin, Jake piled more wood into the furnace. An uneasy feeling did a slow roll in Frederick's gut. In almost no time, the train picked up speed.

"I know you're getting good at managing the engine," Frederick warned the greenhorn, "but its best not to get too cocky with the rails."

"I've got control over this thing!" Jake shouted above the racket of the locomotive. He seemed quite confident in his abilities.

Frederick wished he could say the same. Anxiety and a rising anger twisted around his heart.

"We're going fast enough!" he yelled back. He braced himself against the wall of the car as it rocked and swayed. He knew how to handle Inferno at that speed, but Jake didn't have enough experience yet.

Images of Miss Pearson flooded Frederick's thoughts. If her brother died on the rails, she'd never forgive him, and Frederick doubted he'd ever forgive himself either. And he wasn't about to have another accident like the one that killed his good friend. No. Not on his watch. Miss Pearson would survive if he died, but she'd never recover from the loss if anything happened to her brother.

He pushed himself off the wall and grabbed Jake's arm. "Jake, put the brakes on," he ordered. They were approaching the mill with unsettling speed. Sweat beaded on Frederick's forehead, and not just from the heat. "Do it, or this thing will jump the tracks when we get to the end of the line at the sawmill."

"I've got it. Back off, will ya?" Jake hollered at Frederick and gave him a rough shove to the side. "I need to learn how to do this so I can take care of my sister."

"You can't take care of her if you're dead," Frederick bellowed.

Jake pushed him again. "I'm going to make more money at this than you do and give her all the pretty things she deserves."

Frederick would have loved to debate the issue, but time was of the essence. He wrestled the controls from Jake and shoved him up against the wall of the locomotive. "Until you've proven yourself, this is *my* train. Now step aside or you'll be back logging trees." He released Jake and focused on the tracks in front of him.

The mill up ahead loomed closer still. If he didn't slow Inferno down, they'd crash into it. He didn't want to think of the number of possible deaths.

"Think of your sister, for pity's sake!" Frederick reproved.

For what seemed like an eternity in slow motion, Frederick pulled hard on the brake lever. Jake slumped against the wall and sneered at Frederick with a red face and fists clenched at his sides. Frederick didn't care. He wasn't about to have another casualty on the roster of Kenicky Logging.

❄

Bacon squealed with the force of a lumberjack yelling "timber" as Emma bathed the gunk from his body in the creek. Careful inspection of his back legs explained why he had been rejected by his owner. The left leg was stunted and twisted at an odd angle, making it difficult for him to move easily.

Emma ran her hands over the disfigured part of Bacon's body. If anyone understood the pain of being small in a big world without a mother, it was she. No wonder the poor thing squealed all the time. Tenderly, she wrapped a towel around him then held him close so he could get warm.

An hour later, while sitting outside the cookhouse shucking corn for the evening meal, Emma eyed her new wiener pig. Wariness and caution sat on one end of her heart's seesaw while pity and protectiveness balanced on the other. He was a cute little creature, even if he was from Frederick Corrigan.

A pig as a peace offering. A new hat or a bouquet of flowers or even material for a new dress would have bought her more pleasure, but the strangeness of the gift actually brought a curve to her lips.

Bacon let out a squeal, and Emma looked down in time to see a rat scurry past them. The piglet loped inside with as much speed as he could muster and hid behind the woodbox in the corner. Emma laughed so hard the shucked corn dropped to the ground. Whoever heard of a wiener pig being afraid of a rat?

When she regained her composure, she moved to comfort the poor thing.

"It's all right, Bacon. A rat's nothing to be afraid of. I'll protect you," she soothed as she squatted in front of the woodbox. She reached behind it and grabbed the squirming creature, pulling him out from his hiding spot. Not caring who might see them, she cradled him close. He let out a few grunts and rubbed his wet snout against her neck. It tickled, and she couldn't help but laugh and squirm.

"What's so funny?" Mrs. Wilkin asked as she strolled into the kitchen. "That little pig Frederick got you causing a stir?" She chuckled and set about peeling potatoes.

"I think he's starting to grow on me," Emma replied. A quick shudder went through her. What would Miss Abigail Fancy Pants say about her having a pet pig? She pulled Bacon closer and kissed the top of his soft head. The Bible said all creatures needed loving-kindness, especially the motherless ones. A determined Emma decided to give that to Bacon.

"Emma, could you please finish shucking the corn? It's getting late." Mrs. Wilkin's voice rose above the noise of a few men who were trickling in a little early, to Emma's surprise. "I'm going to stoke more wood on the fire."

While Mrs. Wilkin hustled into action, Emma set Bacon on the floor and resumed work.

She hadn't been shucking corn for more than a few minutes when one of the men came running up to her. The expression on his face spelled disaster, eerily reminiscent of when Jake told her their mother had died. Was her brother dead now, too? Why else would the men come in early?

Chapter 4

After the close call they had at Renier Lumber Company that morning, Frederick and Jake had gotten into a fistfight. Now Frederick's hands were bruised and burns covered his forearms from where he fell against the hot furnace. He sat in the bunkhouse and winced in pain while the doctor examined his wounds. Jake glared at him while waiting his turn to be seen for his apparently broken fingers.

Frederick cast his gaze at the floor. How could he make Jake understand that he cared for his sister a great deal and wished to see her at peace about their job?

Groaning with frustration as the doctor finished, Frederick stomped from the room. Perhaps a walk would do him some good. He wandered down the path that led to the creek. The water rippled over the moss-covered rocks with bubbly enthusiasm. Dipping his hands into the cool refreshing stream, Frederick splashed water over his arms and sighed at the relief. He lifted a drink to his mouth. The cold liquid felt good going down his parched throat. He never failed to appreciate how refreshing it was after a day of slaving over a blazing furnace.

When the ache in his fingers subsided to a dull throb, he stood and walked farther into the mass of towering trees. A few birds called to one another against the distant grating of the bucksaws. Before long the rest of the crew would come in for the night. It was moments like this that Frederick loved.

The buckers might need some extra help—that is, when his hands were healed properly. The pay was just as good as driving Inferno and would provide a way for him to get away from Jake Pearson and his sister. If he volunteered for the most dangerous job, he could make money that much faster.

Frederick ventured with care over fallen dead logs and through blackberry brambles, closer to the sounds of the bucksaw. No wonder the lumberjacks enjoyed their work. Here in the midst of God's handiwork, peace and tranquility permeated the air. He should fit right in, or so he thought.

A sharp, loud crack split the silence like a jagged bolt of lightning. Frederick jumped. A tree was falling. The swishing of tree limbs was followed by a long drawn-out "Tiiiimmmbbbeeerrr!"

With a rapid glance to his left and then to his right, Frederick had little time for making an assessment as to which direction was safest. Additional creaks and groans from the monumental tree reverberated throughout the forest.

"Lord God, protect me." A prayer uttered out of sheer desperation.

Looking up to the top of the hill, Frederick spotted the crew scrambling to the left. He quickly followed suit, leaping over sword ferns, clawing his way through blackberry brambles, and digging through the dirt on his hands and knees. God forbid one of those towering pines came down on him. It would squish him flatter than a pancake.

No more than a few seconds had elapsed when he heard a thundering boom followed by squawking of birds and the shattering of tree limbs. The tree had landed. Shouts filled the air as Mr. Wilkin, the crew boss, called to check on everyone's well-being.

A voice cut through the chaos. "Look out! That widow-maker's coming down, too!"

One Evergreen Night

The racket of creaking, crunching, and the splintering of wood grew louder and more menacing. Observing the mass of timber above him moving to the right, common sense told Frederick to run to the left. He sprinted as fast as his legs and the terrain would allow, stumbling and panting with every step. He didn't know much about falling timber, but he had enough sense to know that he had get out of the way.

Frederick could see that it was going to be a close race for his life.

Emma swept the bunkhouse for the tenth time and filled the woodbox for the old stove. The nights were getting so cold, and she pitied the men sleeping in these damp and freezing quarters. That included her brother. And it was only early October. How much colder would it get in January? Oh, if only they could leave.

An argument just outside the bunkhouse caught her attention. From what she heard, Frederick Corrigan had nearly been killed by a falling tree!

Emma clasped her hand over her mouth. What, pray tell, was he doing traipsing through the woods? He had to have known how unsafe that was. Mr. Wilkin was arguing with a man, and Emma decided to investigate.

"You need to be more careful when you're felling timber, especially widow-makers!" Mr. Wilkin's face was red. "Corrigan could have been killed."

"I'm fine." Mr. Corrigan rubbed the back of his neck.

She took a step back in surprise. He didn't look fine—he looked as if he were going to topple over any minute. Couldn't the other men see he was in no condition to stand outside arguing about whose fault it was?

"He should have never been out there anyway!"

"I hate to say it, but he's right, Corrigan. Stanley, just try to be more careful," a calmer Mr. Wilkin said.

Emma was quite surprised to see that the boss's son was the one arguing with Mr. Wilkin. Stanley Kenicky, not a day over twenty-one, lugged at least that many extra pounds around his thick middle.

"You can forget working in the woods, Corrigan." Stanley jabbed his finger in Frederick's direction. "I'll see to that."

Frederick stepped forward, but Mr. Wilkin held him back.

Emma drew back against the door and tried to keep from trembling.

"Don't worry about this, Miss Pearson," Stanley said. "You go back inside now."

The condescending tone of his voice made Emma shift from one foot to the other with mounting discomfort. He didn't seem like a pleasant person to work with. She felt sorry for the cutting crew. She turned and headed back into the bunkhouse. The sound of arguing filled her ears as she went.

Frederick lay propped up in bed and grumbled at the bandages the doctor placed on his hands all the way up to each elbow. No thanks to Stanley Kenicky, they were now scratched and bleeding besides burned and bruised. His head ached horribly, and he had lost his chance to work in the woods.

He needed to get back to work. Not only did he need the money, but Jake was placed in charge of training another new man how to drive Inferno. That was a recipe for disaster. Jake was nothing but a greenhorn himself and not in any position to be training anybody in how to get the timber to the mills.

And what about his father's house? Frederick should take some time to visit the aging man, but couldn't afford to take time off work. His body could heal just as well at the helm of Inferno as it could lying around.

Heaving himself up and off the bed, he wobbled as his head swam.

"Frederick Corrigan, shouldn't you be resting?" Miss Pearson set a tray on the table, hurried to him, and grabbed him around the waist. Even in his wounded condition, it felt good. Her touch was something he could definitely get used to.

❄

For the past three days after Frederick Corrigan's near brush with death, Emma had wrestled against pity knotting in her stomach for him. He had been nearly crushed by a widow-maker, but insisted on doing as much for himself as possible.

"Here, Mr. Corrigan, why don't you lie down? I've brought you some food." Emma advanced toward him, carrying a tray.

The aroma of the fresh meal wafted upwards and it smelled delicious. Corn and potato chowder—his favorite—along with some fresh-baked bread and a cup of coffee.

"Thank you, Miss Pearson." He grimaced as he looked at her. His stomach growled loud enough for her to hear.

She stifled a giggle. "Sounds like you're hungry." She handed him the napkin.

He took the cloth and tucked it around his neck. He reached for the bowl of steaming chowder and began to eat.

"Mind if I keep you company?" she asked.

"Not at all." A bit dribbled down his chin.

This time she couldn't help but giggle out loud. "It's not easy eating with thick bandages from fingertips to forearms. Allow me to help you, and please, Mr. Corrigan, call me Emma." She helped him hold the spoon in his hand so he wouldn't drop it. He spooned a few more bites into his mouth before he replied.

"Pleased to have your company, Emma. You can call me Frederick if you like." A genuine grin curved across his tanned features and caused Emma's heart to jerk and skip a beat.

"Thank you, Frederick." Heat rose to her face as if she were standing in front of a blazing hot stove. "I'm glad you weren't hurt too terribly bad, and I'm glad you're on the mend."

She sounded like a giddy schoolgirl. She ducked her head with embarrassment. Several quiet moments elapsed as Frederick polished off his bowl of chowder.

"That was delicious."

"It's my mother's recipe. She made it often when Jake and I were small." Emma shifted in her seat with nervous energy. She was sorry they had gotten off on the wrong foot and wished she hadn't said such horrible things to him.

"I'm sorry for the terrible things I said to you, Frederick. I know they wounded you deeply. Please forgive me."

Frederick gazed at her with uncertainty written in his expression. His eyes were so incredibly blue, and she gazed into them, into his very soul. Could he see the longing in her eyes? Momentarily startled, she wondered where that longing had come from.

"It's all forgiven, Miss Pear—um, Emma. Don't you worry your pretty little head about a thing." Frederick cleared his throat once and then again a second time. He reached for his coffee and took a long slow drink. "And would you please forgive me for the things I said to you?"

Emma's cheeks grew even warmer. She fanned her face with the hem of her apron and gasped to catch her breath. She desperately wanted to believe him.

Time and again she had seen her stepfather say he was sorry only to imbibe again and again. And in the dark of night he slunk home to take his rage out on her mother while Emma cowered under her blanket. She'd rather be boiled in hot laundry water than make the same mistakes as Mama. It was best if she just left and didn't get attached.

"All is forgiven, Frederick. I'll take those dishes to the kitchen now if you don't mind. I've work to do before the men come from the woods." She grabbed the tray and hurried from the room. Experience had taught her well the dangers of trusting daring men who said they were sorry for their heedlessness.

Chapter 5

Several days later, with his hands and forearms mostly healed, Frederick stood on board Inferno with Jake Pearson and Stanley Kenicky. He struggled to move within the crowded space. Jake was stoking the engine with his usual arrogance, while Stanley looked ready to jump off before the train had a chance to move.

The company was in the process of acquiring a new locomotive to replace the one that had gone over the bridge and crashed. At least one more engineer was needed to run it, and Stanley's father had decided that Stanley was ready for the job.

"Nothing to worry about, kid," Jake said. "Just keep the fires burning hot and know when to use the brakes." He gave the young man a slap on the back and then threw more wood into the furnace.

Stanley looked even paler than a moment ago.

Frederick groaned. It was going to be a long day. Jake had done well learning to use the brakes and the furnace. The problem was that he hadn't learned to use them at the appropriate times. Frederick hoped to get a moment alone with Jake and ask him about his sister. He wanted to spend more time with her and become a true friend.

The furnace grew hot as the locomotive picked up speed.

"I think I'll be spending the afternoon in town running some errands for Father," Stanley stammered as he cowered against the wall. Frederick wondered about the truthfulness of his statement but wasn't about to question it. Grateful for the opportunity to have Stanley gone, he hoped to speak with Jake alone.

The locomotive rolled along the tracks at a normal speed. "We're doing real well, boys. Let's not get carried away." Frederick didn't want Stanley reporting to his father that they were reckless engineers.

"If I've said it once, I've said it a hundred times," he reiterated, wishing he could toss Jake from the engine. "You need to watch the speed and not get rolling faster than what the brakes can handle."

The temperature rose within the small quarters of the engine car and sweat blurred Frederick's vision. Widow's Bend approached.

"We're going too fast!" Stanley screamed, white-knuckling the side of the locomotive.

"We can handle this just fine!" Jake shouted.

"Just hang on. Don't worry, she always leans a little," Frederick instructed. Wheels screeched as the engine rounded the most dangerous part of the bend and lifted.

"Lean this way!" Frederick yelled.

❄

Emma jumped up and down with excitement at the chance to go into town and do some shopping. Counting her meager savings, she prayed for money enough to purchase some lace or new buttons for her mother's green dress. Christmas was coming up, as well as a

124

number of parties to celebrate Washington being signed into the Union. She needed time to sew something pretty to the gown.

"Let's go, Emma," Mr. Kenicky hollered above the noise of the company's new locomotive. It was good to see that the company had replaced the one that had plunged off a bridge a few weeks ago. This one had a few seats for passengers, unlike the one that crashed and left one train engineer dead. If only she could do something to help the widow and her children. Knowing the deceased man had been Frederick's friend, Emma made a mental note to add the family to her list of folks to pray for.

Hustling to the train, Emma took care while boarding to not get her best dress dirty. Mrs. Wilkin had decided to join them, so squeezing into the small space wasn't an easy feat. Emma didn't wish to rub against something that would turn her pale blue dress a horrid shade of charcoal black.

Mr. Kenicky, who also happened to be a skilled engineer, piled wood into the furnace and soon the wheels turned round and round along the tracks. Emma squirmed like a child in church the entire way. It soon grew hot in the car, but not any hotter than standing in front of a mammoth caldron of boiling wash water.

Mr. Kenicky was a cautious driver, and Emma didn't flinch in the slightest as the train rounded Widow's Bend. If anything, she enjoyed the gentle breeze that wafted into the car and cooled her flushed face.

The town's buildings soon came into view. Emma craned her neck to soak up every image she could. Three new stores and a large barn had been built on the end of one very long street. She could hardly wait to browse through each one of them.

The engine's whistle blew, startling her. She covered her ears, and the brakes screeched as if in protest. Once the train had rolled to a stop, Emma all but leapt from the locomotive.

"I'll be back in time to ride home for dinner." She waved a hand over her shoulder and rushed toward the nearest mercantile.

Strolling up and down the aisles, Emma rubbed her fingers over one bolt of fabric after another. Soft cotton, crisp taffeta, and smooth cool silks all cried out to be sewn into something beautiful, but they were out of her means. Even so, she could hardly wait to get back to camp and make use of her needle and thread.

"Oh, how are you today, Miss Pearson?" Abigail Leonard waltzed down the fabric aisle as if she clung to the arm of a prince of England. "I hear you have a pig for a pet, and a beau." Abigail's cackling echoed off the walls of the store and sank deep into Emma's heart.

"I don't have a beau."

"Oh, no? I hear you're sweet on Frederick Corrigan, and he's sweet on you." Abigail jutted her chin in the air. To Emma, the haughty girl's ruddy cheeks belied a look of pea green jealousy.

"You're wrong. Now, please just let me be," Emma snapped as she turned on her heel and stomped away. The Wilkins were such a great family, Emma couldn't figure out how their youngest daughter, Anna, could be friends with Abigail.

As she walked away from the sneering girl, a bolt of fine imported material all but leaped out at Emma. A gasp escaped her lips, followed by a soft groan of disappointment.

She caressed the fabric that would never be hers, and then she jerked her fingers back as if she'd touched a rat. No sense in dreaming over something she couldn't afford. Her complaints to Jake about the drudgery of her job came back to her in a rush.

Emma wandered through the mercantile with twinges of guilt following close behind her. She shouldn't be putting so much pressure on Jake to make more money. No wonder he worked so hard. She decided to forego a dress for herself and make him a nice shirt instead. She could afford the material, and she'd pull some buttons off an old shirt to finish it.

Moving farther down the aisle, her eyes fell on a cream-colored spool of eyelet lace. It equaled in softness the finest dress she'd ever owned. She could use it to patch a few worn spots on her mother's dress and wear it to the Christmas Eve service. But she didn't have the money to buy both the lace and the shirt material.

No matter. Jake deserved a new shirt for taking such good care of her. Emma moved past the expensive dress material and the lace and proceeded to the counter.

She pulled several coins from her reticule. "I need a few yards of that new green plaid flannel, if you please."

"Yes, of course," the clerk replied, and went to retrieve her supplies. He returned a few minutes later and tallied up her purchase. Emma paid the man and was about to gather up her package when she heard an unfamiliar voice behind her.

"Why, you're Emma Pearson, aren't you? Jake's younger sister."

The hair on the back of Emma's neck bristled and her hands grew cold and clammy. She made a slow turn on her heel to gaze at a leering Stanley Kenicky.

"Good afternoon." Emma tried to keep her voice from quavering, and failed.

"Did you hear? Dad's gonna give me a job running the rails on the new train."

"Oh." It was all Emma could think of to say. She was getting an eerie feeling deep in her stomach from the way he looked at her.

"I've seen you cleaning for the crew, helping out Mrs. Wilkin, and hanging around Frederick Corrigan."

A small gasp flew from Emma's lips. *What's he doing watching my every move?* She had to get away from this man.

"If you'll excuse me." Emma clutched her package and fled from the store.

"I'll be seeing you around, you can be sure of that, Miss Pearson." Stanley's laughter echoed behind her, but she dared not turn and give him the pleasure of knowing how much he unnerved her.

Chapter 6

The early November morning had dawned crisp and clear while Inferno rolled along the tracks. Much to Frederick's relief, Jake began to show some signs of restraint and care when it came to running the rails.

"So how is Miss Emma today?" Frederick held his hands close to the furnace to warm them against the chilly air.

"She's doing fine. She's all excited about the territory becoming a state. Been sewing on one of our mother's dresses, trying to patch it, for the occasion." Jake's hand rested on the brake lever, ready for any emergency, or so Frederick hoped.

"Er, Jake." Frederick paused and cleared his throat. "I'd like to escort your sister to the Christmas Eve service, with your blessing of course." There. He'd said it. He rubbed his hands together and then held them to his face for warmth.

"That'd be fine with me. I know you're a good man, Fred, but it's up to Emma, and she's real cautious with gentlemen."

"I see." Frederick noted the expression on Jake's face. Not used to seeing the man so serious, he raised his eyebrows and almost questioned Jake further, but then thought it best not to pry.

Perhaps a man had broken her heart in the past. But plenty of women had been spurned and went on to love again. There had to be another, more deeply rooted reason for her feelings.

The lumber mill came into view and Jake put the brakes on. When they stopped, Jake climbed down ahead of Frederick.

"I've got some business in town. I'll wait for your next trip and catch a ride home with you then," Jake called over his shoulder as he walked toward town.

"Sounds good, enjoy your lunch." Frederick waved then helped the sawmill crew unload the logs from the flatcars. He was soon on his way back to the camp, with images of Emma dancing in his head like tree branches in a gentle breeze.

"Lord, why am I thinking about her so much?" Frederick shook his head. He probably shouldn't have given her a pig for a gift. Of course he cared for her, but he was loath to admit he was falling in love, because he wasn't. At least that's what he kept telling himself.

The sound of a loud pop and then a hiss brought Frederick back to the present. Another hose had burst, and now he'd have to stop and repair it. He slapped the side of the engine then applied the brakes. Time was money on the rails, and he growled at having to stop.

An hour went by as Frederick removed the bad hose with his pocket knife and installed the new one. It wasn't a perfect fit, but with some extra twine tied and twisted here and there, he made it work. Such was life in the logging business. Men made do with what they had and learned to think on their feet.

"Thank You, Lord," Frederick murmured. At least the hose had been to something else and not the brakes. "Now back to work."

Two miles passed by uneventfully and Frederick began to breathe peacefully again. He could go extra fast and try to make up for lost time, but after some thought he decided against it. His hand clutched at the brake lever when a doe and her fawn leapt across the tracks. He relaxed his grip as they cleared the rails with mere seconds to spare. The last thing he wanted was to stop yet again.

Frederick's eyes scanned the tracks ahead, wary of anything else that could slow his trip back to the mill.

About a mile ahead, he spied a downed tree trunk lying across the tracks. "Lord, no!" He groaned and kicked the furnace so hard his foot hurt.

❄

Emma sewed with frantic speed on Jake's shirt. She had gotten up a little earlier to have a few precious minutes to work on it before beginning her duties for the day. Thankfully, it was nearly done. All she had left was the buttons, and he'd have something nice to wear for Christmas. Bacon interrupted her thoughts as he trotted in from outside. She pulled him close to her chest and hugged him so hard he squealed.

"I'm sorry, little friend. I didn't mean to hurt you." She stroked the top of his head and Bacon looked up at her with dark eyes and grunted as if he actually understood. He had grown in the six weeks or so since Frederick had brought him to her. In another few months he might live up to his name and be on the breakfast table as opposed to cuddled in her arms. A part of her wanted to shove him away and not allow her heart to love him, but there was something about this motherless creature that nobody but her seemed to care about. Whether she willed it or not, he was winning her love.

After setting Bacon on the floor to root around, Emma finished two buttons on her brother's shirt. She would have to wait until the next day before it was finished. She tucked it in her sewing basket then swept the bunkhouse, carted fresh water up from the stream, and tended to the many other duties of her job.

The cold afternoon drifted by as she filled the woodboxes and dried the dishes for Mrs. Wilkin. She ironed Jake's Sunday clothes and lugged water from the creek for Mrs. Wilkin to cook supper with.

"Emma, where are you?" Jake's voice carried down to her as she was fetching another bucket of water from the stream.

"Down here, Jake." Emma lugged the bucket along as fast as the awkward load allowed. Much to her relief, Jake quickly came alongside her and took the pail from her hands. It warmed her heart to know how protective her older brother was of her. She was glad she had decided to make him something nice for the holidays.

"You've been working hard, sis. Abigail told me in town that she saw you and Stanley talking at the mercantile last week. Anything I should know about?" Jake asked like it was the simplest thing in the world to answer.

"Why, I'm sure I don't know what you mean." Emma's feelings vacillated. She wanted to be honest but feared the repercussions if she told him everything. She didn't want to tell her brother about Abigail's snooty comments or Stanley's creepy remarks.

"I heard Abigail flirting with Stanley." Jake's face turned into a thunderous cloud of angry emotion. "She told me you were doing the same, with Stanley and with Frederick. Try as I might, I can't make myself believe that."

"What? That's not true, Jake. You know I'm not like that!" Emma gasped and clutched handfuls of her skirt in her fists.

"I know it isn't true, but I don't take kindly to folks referring to my sister that way. I don't want Stanley getting any funny ideas. It's bad enough I had to protect Mama from a monster of a stepfather. I don't wish to do the same for you!"

"I'll take extra care to mind my manners," Emma said.

"And stay away from Stanley," Jake ordered. "I don't trust him."

"Yes, Jake," Emma conceded. God forbid, what if Stanley watched her when nobody was around? Would he attack her or something awful like that?

Indignation rose within her. No, she would not allow herself to suffer the way her mother had. She'd defend herself if any man attacked her, and she didn't care if it meant her brother's job or not. After what had happened to their mother, she was sure Jake would feel the same way.

❄

"Morning, E.V." Frederick climbed down from Inferno quite happy about his new raise from the boss. Soon he'd have his father's house out of foreclosure. If only he could buy Emma something girlie and nice to show her how much he cared for her.

"Morning," E.V. replied, pulling on his work gloves.

Frederick met E.V. at the end of the first flatbed. "Is that a bunch of ladies' bonnets in your office I saw the other day?"

"Yep." While his tone had E.V.'s normal good-natured optimism, the sadness that momentarily flickered in his brown eyes dampened Frederick's mood. "I need to return them to their rightful owner."

"Are they Larkin's?"

"I seem to have a knack for finding them around town."

"I take it your efforts with Miss Whitworth haven't produced any positive results?"

"Not yet." E.V. grabbed the end of a log and then paused. "Fred, if something's truly important to you, you don't give up, no matter what the obstacle is. Now let's get this timber unloaded. I've got paperwork to do."

Frederick grabbed the end of the log and lifted. The temptation to spend his raise on Emma clawed at his heart. Maybe he could find something little to let her know how he felt.

Once the train was unloaded, Frederick headed into town. The little money he had jingled in his pocket.

Inside the mercantile, he found a multitude of things any woman would fancy. Then his eyes fell on a spool of ivory-colored eyelet lace.

"Miss Pearson gazed at that same lace just the other day." The store clerk nodded toward Frederick.

"I bet this would go perfect with one of her dresses." One yard cost a fraction of what a new bonnet did. Frederick could hardly wait to give it to her.

He paid for his find. Once the lace was wrapped, he hurried back to the train.

Careful to not get the wrapping dirty, Frederick placed the package in the corner on the floor, out of the way of the furnace's soot and grime.

He stoked the furnace as full as he dared. He was in a hurry to see the look on Emma's face when he gave her the lace. In hardly any time, Inferno chugged up the hillside. Widow's Bend came and went. No trouble there, but then a mess of deer grazing on the tracks caught his eye. He pulled on the whistle, but the stubborn animals remained on the tracks and simply stared at him with their noses in the air.

"Come on, move it!" Frederick bellowed. Frustration mounting, he yanked on the whistle one last time.

Chapter 7

Emma was just finishing hanging the clean sheets on the line when a call went out for the company's doctor. Frederick Corrigan was hurt. Again.

Dropping the clothespins to the ground, she lifted her skirts and raced toward the wagon pulling into the camp. Thankfully some crew members had found him on the tracks and brought him back to camp. Jake could bring the train in later that night.

Emma stopped by the wagon. *Lord, please don't let him be seriously injured.* She was beginning to care for Frederick, and her heart couldn't take another loss.

"Is he badly hurt?" she asked.

One of the men waved a hand at her. "Nah, he'll be fine. He just went a few rounds with some bucks on the tracks."

"And lost." Stanley chuckled as the men carried Frederick to the bunkhouse.

Emma aimed her meanest scowl at Stanley but held her tongue. She could see that Frederick bled from the head and right shoulder. "I'll get some water heating and tear some bandages."

Poor Frederick babbled on about how crazy deer acted in rutting season, and something about lace for a lady's dress.

Lord, he must have taken quite a lick to the head.

Emma reached the kitchen and could see that Mrs. Wilkin was one step ahead of her. The pot of water sat on top of the cookstove. Emma piled wood under the fire to get it blazing. Next she raced back to the clothesline and snatched the most ragged sheet down. She tore several strips with lightning speed.

When she had a sufficient amount, she grabbed the bundle and hurried to the bunkhouse, gasping for breath. Frederick was semi-coherent when she stumbled inside.

"Afternoon, Miss Emma," he mumbled, his blond hair soaked red with blood.

"Hello, Frederick, I'm glad you seem well—um—as well as can be expected." Emma breathed a sigh of relief and hoped she didn't sound scatterbrained. Heat rushed to her face, and she ducked her head, lest he guess her feelings.

"I got you a more appropriate present than a pig, but it got dirty on the way home. I'm sorry." Frederick's tone lost some of its sparkle.

"Don't be sorry. I'm growing quite fond of Bacon."

"I'd be fond of him, too, on the breakfast table." Frederick grinned.

Emma bristled with mock indignation. "I can assure you, the darling little thing won't meet an untimely death and wind up alongside your pancakes one morning."

Frederick let out a chuckle that shook the bed he was lying on. The man had a sense of humor and for that Emma was grateful.

Mr. Kenicky rushed into the room at that moment followed by Jake.

"Thank the Lord you're all right, Corrigan." Mr. Kenicky folded his arms over his chest and studied Frederick through narrowed eyes. "You know, one of these days your luck is gonna run out."

The doctor maintained that Frederick's wounds were minor. He told him to keep everything clean and change the bandages often.

"Rest assured, Doctor, I'll do that." Emma patted Frederick on the arm and smiled at him. It would be her pleasure to care for this wonderful man. Jake eyed her with suspicion. If he guessed she was now sweet on Frederick, she didn't think he would understand, let alone be happy about the situation. She didn't want either man to think of her as childish, so she straightened herself and acted like a proper lady should.

❄

Later that evening Frederick lay back on the bed and tried not to let on how much pain he was in when Emma brought him his dinner. He pasted on a smile. But Stanley stoked the woodstove and stared daggers at him. Did Stanley admire Emma also? If they both wished to court her and Frederick won out, the boss would probably hear all about it. This was a situation he'd have to gauge carefully, or it could become as dangerous as rounding Widow's Bend without brakes.

"Are you all right?" Emma's sweet voice drew him to the present, and he gazed across the room at her. She stared at him with one eyebrow cocked and her head tilted to one side.

"Um, yes." Frederick cleared his throat. "I'd like to thank you for helping out the doctor."

"You're more than welcome." Emma set a basin of hot water on an end table along with a fistful of bandages. She then pulled a chair over to where he lay and tenderly pulled the dried bloody bandage from his head. He gritted his teeth against the pain. God forbid he yelped in the presence of a lady. She began to sponge the goose egg on his right temple with a wet cloth. The coolness was soothing against his skin. He sighed then laid his head back against the pillows and closed his eyes.

As good as the nursing felt, he still chided himself for the stupidity of his actions. How much work would he miss due to this injury? He was determined, not more than one day. Even with his new raise, he couldn't afford to miss work.

After a moment, he heard the chair scoot back as Emma rose to her feet. "I must be going now. Mrs. Wilkin needs me to help cook supper tonight."

He smiled. "I'm looking forward to seeing you more. Perhaps this Saturday we could go for a walk and have a picnic."

❄

Emma froze. Her heart skittered along like a pebble on smooth water's surface before sinking into the depths below. Elation that he cared and fear of getting too close wrestled in her heart like two squirrels over the last hickory nut of the season.

"Why, yes, Frederick, I'd love to go."

"Glad to hear you say yes."

"I'm looking forward to it already." Emma prepared to leave the room but couldn't help grinning with excitement.

"Great. We'll leave first thing Saturday morning." Frederick beamed, his blue eyes twinkling.

Saturday morning arrived with a wan mid-fall sun that tried desperately to warm the frigid air, but didn't quite succeed. Emma took Frederick's arm as they strolled down a path in one of Tumwater's most beautiful parks and watched the waterfalls.

Frederick spread the red-checked tablecloth on a picnic table while Emma pulled a plate of fried chicken from the basket. The aroma made her mouth water.

Throughout their meal, Frederick and Emma discussed everything from their favorite books to the places they'd like to visit.

"Emma, I'd like to take you down to Toledo for a short trip. I spoke with Mr. and Mrs. Wilkin, and they have friends down there they'd like to visit. They would like us to go along. They've offered to cover the cost of the train tickets." Frederick gazed at her with his dreamy blue eyes.

Emma blushed and turned away for a moment to gaze at the water. Again her heart seesawed with emotion, but the desire to get away from the logging camp won out.

"I'd love to, Frederick. When will we go?" She turned back to him and felt goose bumps on her arms, and not from the cold weather.

"We'll take the train next weekend. If I work extra hours this week, I can afford to take off a day, maybe two. You're going to love it."

❄

The November morning was perfect, with one exception. Emma hadn't finished sewing the lace Frederick had gotten her onto her mother's gown. She was resigned to her best Sunday dress of plain blue cotton as she and Frederick boarded the train, followed by Mr. and Mrs. Wilkin.

The whistle blew steam toward the sky with a loud racket. Emma started and clutched Frederick's arm tighter. He laid a tender hand over hers and smiled down at her.

"This is so exciting, Frederick. I don't know how I'll ever thank you." Emma felt heat rise in her cheeks and ducked her head in embarrassment. She was growing quite fond of the wild train engineer and wasn't sure how to handle that fact.

Her thoughts were interrupted when Frederick took her by the hand and held her steady as the locomotive lurched to life and pulled away from the station. A *clackity-clack* sound filled Emma's ears as the wheels rotated in rhythm.

Emma noticed Abigail standing on the station platform with an angry expression marring her features. Jealousy was evident in her furrowed brow and the clenched fists at her sides. Emma cringed, remembering Jake's words. Abigail seemed bent on causing trouble.

❄

Frederick and Emma rode along, chatting about Tumwater and life in the town. They entered into a lively discussion about Shakespeare. Jake had done a good job of keeping Emma educated after the deaths of their parents. Her dark eyes seemed to hold an odd mix of haunted pain and yearning for adventure.

The train slowed to a crawl and came to a stop with a jerk. The Wilkins and Frederick and Emma crowded to the doors to debark. From there the party boarded a stagecoach and rode to Toledo.

"We're about to round the bend and then the town should come into view." Frederick directed Emma toward a window and pointed past a clump of evergreen trees in the distance.

"The scenery is beautiful, Frederick. Thank you for bringing me here today." Emma looked up at him with longing in her eyes. How he wanted to lean down and kiss her rosy lips. As they rolled into town, Frederick noticed a number of buildings that had sprung up since he had been there last. My, how the place had grown. The stage finally rocked and then lurched to a stop. It felt good to stretch his legs as he stepped down from the cramped confines.

"Allow me." Frederick held his hand out to assist Emma down the stagecoach steps.

"Why don't we get some lunch at the Koontz Hotel?" Mr. Wilkin asked.

"That sounds lovely," Emma replied, her eyes sparkling in the sunshine as she kept her gloved hand in Frederick's strong one.

A stern-wheeler on the river whistled. Emma emitted an unladylike squeal and craned her neck for a better view. She held onto Frederick's waistcoat as if to steady herself.

"Mighty exciting, eh?" he asked, boldly wrapping his arm around her slender waist to keep her from falling as she turned this way and that, looking at everything. The gasp that escaped from her lips caused his heart to beat faster. She looked up at him with dark ebony eyes that brimmed with anticipation and. . .passion?

"Thank you kindly for your assistance." She blinked as if specks of dust had landed in her eyes.

"You're most welcome."

The town of Toledo had turned into a bustling place since he had last been there. Crewmen loaded and unloaded cargo from the boats lining the riverbanks. They made quite a racket. Frederick was pleased to see the steamboat the town had been named for. The *Toledo* blew its whistle again as several passengers scrambled to board before the boat sailed south again, down the Cowlitz River.

Sidewalks lined a few of the streets while others weren't much more than muddy paths. Ladies strolled along the walkways holding parasols.

Just up and over the hill was Frederick's childhood home, the one his family lived in before they moved to Tumwater to seek better medical care for his mother. The structure could be seen from downtown, and Frederick squirmed with anxiousness to see the old clapboard house once again. Memories came flooding back.

"Right this way, Emma." Frederick guided her along the plank sidewalk that lined the muddy street. Their shoes made a *clompity-clomp* sound as they bustled along. "After lunch, I'd like to show you my childhood home."

"Oh yes." Emma wrinkled her pert little nose and lifted her skirts to avoid getting mud on them from a recent rainstorm. He held out his hand and escorted her across the nasty patch of ground. She looked up at him with that same look in her eyes that made his heart skitter like the clanking of Inferno's wheels across a length of steel rails.

One question popped into Frederick's mind and haunted his thoughts. Would this fragile flower dare to love a rough and reckless man like himself?

❅

Emma glanced this way and that, studying the town. The polite nods of men in suspenders and women carrying baskets of goods made for a cozy atmosphere. Through her gloved hands, she could feel Frederick's muscled arms, making her feel safe. Mr. and Mrs. Wilkin were there, too, of course, following them around like proper chaperones.

"I beg your pardon?" Emma asked as the sound of Frederick's voice drew her from her thoughts.

"I asked if you'd like to have lunch here. It is highly recommended by Mr. and Mrs. Wilkin." Frederick motioned to the hotel they were standing in front of.

He was so handsome. Emma's breath caught in her throat and for a moment she was unable to speak.

The aroma of fresh beef roasting caused her mouth to water. The cold biscuits she had eaten that morning weren't sustaining her. "I think that would be delightful." She gave his arm a squeeze.

After they had eaten their lunch, they walked up the hill leading to Frederick's childhood home. It wasn't much to look at. A medium-sized house with a towering redbricked chimney and a lovely rose garden along one side and a vegetable garden on the other. Frederick chatted about the place as if it were Buckingham Palace. Emma's thoughts drifted as he rattled on about the boyhood pranks he'd pulled.

Emma finally understood Frederick's enthusiasm. It wasn't the clapboards and bricks that made this house so wonderful to Frederick. It was special and cherished because he spent a happy childhood there.

A barb of pain jabbed at Emma's heart. How comforting it must feel to have had been raised in such a home. She vowed if she ever had children of her own, they would not be privy to the horrors she had witnessed as a young girl.

On the way back down the hill, Mr. and Mrs. Wilkin interjected with some rather wonderful news. Their friends in town had offered to take them all out for dinner that night.

"This is such a delightful little town, Frederick. The people are generous in spirit and kind to one another."

"Yes, and Lord willing, it will stay that way."

Excitement flooded Emma's heart, and she fairly burst with gratitude for such wonderful friends as the Wilkins. They had provided this adventure for her, and she knew she would never forget it.

❅

The next afternoon, they boarded the train for the ride home. Emma had enjoyed the trip so much and was glad she had gone. She was thinking of the Lord and His promises while standing next to Frederick on the passenger car's loading platform. Was it really possible for

God to heal her deepest hurts and provide her with a husband someday?

The sun was still shining in an iridescent sky, colored with streaks of gold and purple. A cool breeze wafted across the platform as Emma listened to the birds calling to each other. Finally, the whistle blew, signaling their impending departure.

A near frenzy ensued as the locomotive lurched to life and ladies waved handkerchiefs and men hollered good-bye. Conductors busied themselves with ticket collecting and shouts of "All aboard!"

As Emma gazed up into Frederick's tanned face, her heart pounded harder in her chest. The intense gleam in his eyes mirrored a passion that burned in her veins. His strong calloused hands wound their way through her hair and caught on a few strands.

Frederick wasted no time in tilting her head back and placing his lips on hers. For a moment, time seemed to stand still. Emma drank in the warmth of his kiss as her knees went weak. Her heart opened a slight crack and feelings of love for Frederick poured in.

"Oh Emma," he whispered in her ear with a husky voice. "Please forgive me if I've been too forward." He pulled back and stared deep into her eyes as if to search for some flicker of emotion.

"Please forgive *me*, Frederick, if *I've* been too forward." Emma sighed after finding her voice. He simply pulled her closer and held her as the train departed and made its way north to Tumwater.

When the town of Tumwater came into view, Emma excused herself to the powder room to freshen up. She'd cringe and wither away if Abigail saw her in a disheveled state and made fun of her. Especially in front of Frederick.

Chapter 8

Emma held Frederick's hand as they disembarked Inferno later that evening. Her dress would need a good washing, but she didn't care. She'd had a wonderful time, and her feelings for Frederick were blooming like fresh apple blossoms under the warmth of a spring sun.

As they walked back to the camp, Emma was about to ask where her brother was when a frantic shout rose above the commotion coming from the bunkhouse.

"Dear Lord, Emma Pearson, there you are," a logger exclaimed as he bolted toward her.

Emma's blood flowed like cold stream water through her veins. Her heart threatened to stop beating but pounded in her chest regardless. Air came in ragged gasps. No, not the last blood relative she had left on this earth.

"Is it Jake?" Emma blurted.

"Yes, he's got a nasty gash on his head, and the doctor thinks his leg is busted."

The man's voice sounded as though he were speaking the words into an empty barrel.

"No!" Emma shrieked as she lifted her skirts and sprinted toward the bunkhouse.

When she burst through the door, she saw Jake lying on a bed with a bloody bandage wrapped around his head. The doctor pulled the bandage away for a moment, and Emma became light-headed at the sight of so much blood. His shirt was stained red and his eyes were closed. He looked dead. If Frederick's strong arms hadn't circled her waist and supported her, she'd have slid to the floor in a faint.

"Oh Jake, you promised you wouldn't leave me all alone in the world." Emma stumbled forward, laid her head on Jake's shoulder, and wept.

"Get this hysterical woman out of here!" the doctor barked. Frederick grasped her by the shoulders and escorted her from the room.

The night crawled on, as if it were passing by on hands and knees. Frederick brought Emma a warm blanket as the chilly night air set in. He held her hand as the minutes ticked past. Without saying a word, his presence radiated strength, and Emma found no shame in leaning into it.

Bacon's warm body lay at her feet, his occasional grunts and snorts telling her he was comfortable. Jake hadn't made a sound.

When the last of the crew members left Jake's side, Frederick reluctantly had to leave Emma alone. She understood the impropriety of his staying in the room all night with her. He left a lamp burning on the table for Emma's convenience. She sat back in her rocker and thanked God for his care and concern.

Orange rays of the sun finally crept over the horizon and soon morning followed. With sore aching muscles, Emma shifted in her chair. Jake had survived the night and for that she was grateful. But how had the accident happened?

A crew member walked in. "Morning, ma'am,"

"Good morning," Emma mumbled, running her hands over her brother's chest, reassuring herself that he still breathed. She looked up at the man. "Do you know how the accident happened?"

"Stanley and Jake were out on a day that we were supposed to have off," the man explained. "According to Stanley, Jake cut down a tree and didn't jump out of the way soon enough. He got caught in the branches."

The details didn't matter to Emma. She was just praying that Jake would wake up. A moan escaped from her brother's bruised lips and drew her attention to the present.

"Jake, it's me, Emma. Please wake up." She grasped his strong calloused hand in her own. Relief flooded through her when he slit his eyes open.

"Emma, what happened?" Jake's hoarse whisper caused her to flinch. He was alive, for now, and that's what mattered.

"There was an accident. You were hurt, but you're going to get better now. I'm here, and I'm going to take care of you." Emma choked back tears as she brushed her fingers through the few wisps of hair not wrapped in bandages. Jake smiled back at her and then, by the time the doctor was summoned, he drifted back to sleep.

The doctor did a thorough examination.

"I think he's going to be fine, but he's not out of the woods yet. He needs some time to recuperate and much rest."

"Thank you." Emma turned back toward her brother, her mouth dry as she wrung her hands with anxiety.

"I'm going to get some coffee and some breakfast. I'll check back in an hour or so. You should get some rest yourself, young lady." The doctor yawned.

Frederick came through the door a few minutes later, and he brought Emma a cup of coffee.

"You look worn out." He plopped down on a straight chair beside her.

"I am." She stifled a yawn and took a sip of the warm, invigorating coffee. The aroma alone was comforting, or was that Frederick's presence?

"You know, if there's anything I can do to help, all you have to do is ask." The sincere look in Frederick's eyes made Emma feel more secure, but the future still held many questions she didn't have answers for.

"Thank you," she replied. "Now if you'll excuse me, I'm heading off to my room to try and get some rest." She finished her coffee and stood to leave. She was exhausted and was unsure if her world would ever be the same.

✻

Every evening when Frederick was finished with his shift, he went to visit Emma. For three days she stayed by Jake's side caring for his every need. Much as he hated to admit it, a part of him longed to be cared for by her with the same concern she showered on her brother. And he desperately wanted to let her know how much she meant to him.

One night on his way to the bunkhouse, he heard voices coming from behind the boss's office. He slowed down and listened, straining to hear their words.

"Stanley's been untruthful and negligent in his work, and he's the one who's responsible for Jake's injury."

"Yeah, but what can we do about it? Who's going to believe us over the boss's son?"

Jake recognized the voices—they were two of the newer crew members. He didn't want to believe what they said. Was the boss aware of Stanley's guilt? If so, then why wasn't he doing something about it? These questions haunted Frederick, and he debated whether or not to broach the subject with Emma.

What he needed was some solid proof, but that might be hard to come by. Then he could approach the boss, and then the boss could break the news to Emma. But how would Emma react when she knew her brother had almost lost his life and his livelihood because of negligence on someone else's part? It would infuriate her. Frederick sure didn't want to see her get so upset that she did something rash and lost her job. And what would happen if she thought he went behind her back?

"Lord, give me wisdom in knowing how to handle this," Frederick prayed.

If he knew exactly how the accident had happened, he'd have a better idea about how to proceed. The crew boss, Mr. Wilkin, would have the best guess as to what happened out there that day. Without wasting more time, he decided to speak with the man and see if he could find out a thing or two. This teetered on gossip, but the boss needed to know the truth, considering what was at stake—the lives of the crew.

❄

On the fourth night after Jake's accident the full moon cast a romantic light over the quiet and still earth. The stars shimmered in the heavens and the crickets chirped in blissful-sounding harmony. Emma began to believe her brother would live—probably with a limp in his leg for the rest of his life—but at least he would live. Mrs. Wilkin's sister had come out from town to help for a week or so, and they seemed to be doing fine without Emma's help.

Frederick brought dinner to the bunkhouse for Emma and Jake and asked if she wanted to go for a walk afterward. She agreed. With a sparkle in his deep blue eyes, he took her by the hand and led her down to the creek.

Emma chuckled at Bacon, who trotted alongside her on their late-night stroll. Frederick talked of his day at work, but Emma, so enthralled at being by his side, her hand clutching his strong arm, hardly noticed what he said.

Frederick paused to run his strong hands through her long dark hair and laid a tender kiss on her eager lips. Emma responded by leaning into the kiss, as if to absorb some of his strength.

"Tomorrow's Saturday and we usually have the afternoon off. Let me take you into town and get you away from this for a while," Frederick said between kisses to her forehead. Emma sighed. She didn't want to leave her brother until he was at least able to get up and about.

"As long as I know Jake will be taken care of." Jake had been through so much, and if she left him and something terrible happened again, she'd never forgive herself.

"I'll ask Mrs. Wilkin to keep an eye on him," Frederick suggested.

Emma saw hope in his eyes, so she conceded.

The next afternoon she rode into town on Inferno with Frederick at her side. He didn't seem to go all that fast, and she wondered why everyone made such a fuss over what a reckless driver he was. Then it occurred to her he was probably being extra cautious with her along.

When they got into town, she held his arm as they strolled in front of the shops. He escorted her down the road that led to his father's house. Much larger than the one in Toledo, it gave off an aura of grand elegance, with a porch swing and tall white columns.

"It really is lovely," Emma said, leaning against his strong shoulder, wishing she could do more for him. For a short minute, she understood how her mother must have felt at times. She was learning to praise God even in the face of imminent hardship.

"I made some extra money selling a share of the land, and along with my savings we made a large payment to the bank. If Pa takes in boarders for about a year, he can pay off the house, and the bank will hand him the deed."

Emma couldn't help but notice how much straighter he stood, obviously proud of himself. "It's not as grand as the Whitworth mansion, but it's Pa's home."

"I heard there's a party at one of the hotels in town right after Thanksgiving to celebrate Elisha Ferry being sworn in as governor," Emma said, to change the subject.

"I'd like very much to escort you to it," Frederick said.

"I'd love to, if it's okay with Jake." Emma's hand rested in the crook of his arm, and he patted her hand with his. The gesture brought comfort to her.

On their way back into town, they stopped in at the post office. There was a letter for Jake and Emma from a man they had lost contact with for more than a year.

"It's from Uncle Irving!" Emma exclaimed, clapping her hands. She'd assumed the old man had died, and she was delighted to know he still lived. "I can't wait to tell Jake when we get back to camp. He's going to be thrilled."

"I take it Jake and this man were very close." Frederick smiled down at her.

"Oh, they were, and once Jake speaks with Uncle Irving, maybe he'll invite us to live with him in Chicago." Emma dreamed of getting away from the dirty camp. This would be a perfect opportunity.

Frederick's expression indicated he was less than pleased and she understood why. They had begun an earnest courtship, but was she falling in love with him? She didn't know for sure. She couldn't help but wonder what would happen now.

✼

Frederick stormed across the lumberyard the next day, full of gruffness.

"What's wrong?" E.V. asked, his eyebrows raised in question.

"After all this time of guarding my heart, I think I'm falling in love." Frederick scratched his chin with the back of his hand. Knowing E.V. understood, Frederick explained the new developments in Emma's life.

E.V. placed a hand on Frederick's shoulder and gave a reassuring squeeze. "If you really love her, you'll want what's best for her."

"I do," Frederick groaned. "That's why I know I'm going to lose her."

"Just keep praying about it."

"I will," Frederick replied before his friend walked back to the sawmill office.

When the load of lumber was stacked and ready for the saw, Frederick boarded Inferno and steamed back to the landing for another load of timber. The entire time, he talked to the Lord, asking for direction and guidance. Soon he felt God's peace and he began to relax.

That didn't last long however, as he pulled into the loggers's landing to find it in utter chaos. Had someone gotten hurt again or was something else terribly wrong? Was Stanley to blame this time as well?

Chapter 9

Emma bolted from the bunkhouse with anxiety and heartbreak making chase behind her. Their uncle from Chicago had offered Jake a well-paying job, and it didn't matter if he walked with a limp. He'd offered to provide Emma with employment, too.

But Jake wanted to leave her behind. If Jake thought he could run off to Chicago while she stayed behind in this God-forsaken mudhole, he was sadly mistaken! He knew her worst fear was being all alone in the world. After walking off her temper, she returned to the bunkhouse to present her case to him.

At last, after some heated discussion and much pleading on Emma's part, Jake agreed to take her with him as soon as his leg mended enough for him to travel. She blew her breath out in a tired sigh and tramped to the kitchen to help Mrs. Wilkin peel a mountain of potatoes for dinner that night. Now if only she could find a way to tell Frederick she was leaving.

Bacon grunted and lay down in his usual corner.

"Emma, is everything all right?" Frederick asked, mopping his forehead with his customary red bandana.

She hadn't seen him approach.

"Yes, everything is fine," she said. Later she'd ask God to forgive her for leaving this wonderful man who had done nothing but show her kindness.

"I have something I need to speak with you about." The serious expression clouding his features caused the hair on her skin to tingle. A niggling intuition told her it had something to do with her brother's accident. She knew Frederick wasn't entirely convinced they knew what had happened out in the woods that day.

"I spoke with Mr. Wilkin, the crew boss, the other day. He examined the logging equipment after Jake's accident. He believes it wasn't an accident. He thinks Stanley neglected to set the safety, and that's what caused that tree to roll over your brother."

Emma clenched her teeth to keep from screaming aloud. How could someone be so careless when working with such dangerous equipment? Wasn't it dangerous enough just to be a logger? "I see," she managed to mutter with her jaw set. "Just what do you intend to do with this information?"

"I'm going to the boss first thing tomorrow morning. He needs to send that kid packing before somebody else on this crew gets hurt or killed."

"Do you have any evidence?"

"I've got Mr. Wilkin's opinion. That's as good as any evidence you'll find." Frederick's face flushed deep red as the fire in his eyes burned with obvious indignation.

By Frederick's demeanor, Emma guessed he wanted to tear Stanley limb from limb, and for a brief moment she felt sorry for the young greenhorn. "Well, I do hope you're able to get through to Mr. Kenicky. Please let me know how it goes."

"I'll sure do that." Frederick stuffed his bandana in his back pocket. "Now if you'll excuse me, I'd like to speak with the rest of the crew and get their opinion on how Stanley's holding up out there."

Emma went back to peeling the potatoes. Even though she was numb from the news, she still managed to finish the job. She dumped a bucket of slops onto a plate for Bacon and gathered firewood for the bunkhouse. Frederick's words churned in her head like rushing river water around a sharp and rocky bend.

The boss had to understand what a danger his son posed in the woods. But how would he react once he understood that fact? Worse yet, what if he didn't believe the crew boss? He would more than likely keep his son on the crew. Would Stanley go after Jake again, and with a vengeance?

Remembering how Stanley treated her with such disrespect, Emma shuddered at the prospect. The sooner she and Jake got out of there, the better.

❄️

"But sir!" Frederick growled and clenched his fists at his sides. "Have you even heard a word we've been saying?" He wanted to toss his boss down the side of a steep slope at his obvious obtuseness, followed by Stanley, who stood off to the side with a smug expression plastered on his face.

"I said that's enough." Mr. Kenicky slammed his hands on his makeshift desk and rose to his full height from his chair. "Don't you two have things to do? Get out of here and get back to work."

"And wait until the next man gets killed?" Frederick glared at his boss, loathing coating his words.

"Now see here!" Stanley took a menacing step forward.

"Let's go, Fred." Mr. Wilkin grabbed him by the shirt and dragged him out of the office. It was a good thing, or he probably wouldn't have a job by sunset.

"Come, Fred, let's get back to work. We've got a large clearing of trees to cut down and get to the mill today. We need all the hands we've got." Mr. Wilkin turned Frederick around and aimed him toward Inferno.

"That fool needs to wake up and learn how to run a logging business!" Frederick struggled to control his frustration. The last thing he wanted was to bury another crewmate. "And that kid needs to find a job where his negligence won't get somebody hurt, if that's even possible."

"I'll keep an eye on the kid. With any luck he'll learn a few things, and we can avoid another tragedy."

"Thanks." Frederick paced the ground in front of the bunkhouse as the crew was getting ready to head out for the day. The men filed past him, and he couldn't help but wonder if they'd all come back in one piece at dinnertime.

"I'll talk to you tonight." Frederick waved at Mr. Wilkin and headed for Inferno. He had to cool his head, or he'd lose focus and risk his own hide. One thing was certain, he'd be praying for the crew and his friend. But would that be enough?

❄

Emma threw herself into her brother's arms two days later with gratitude seeping from her heart. He had announced to her that he felt they could leave for Chicago very soon. She couldn't wait to get away from the camp and all the drudgery that went with it.

"But it breaks my heart to leave Frederick." Emma bit her lip.

"Bear in mind, sister dear"—Jake interrupted her thoughts—"there are many men in the city who will be vying for your hand."

"Oh no, I'm going to get a job and learn how to care for myself."

"Well, I'm not going to allow you to live by yourself, not in the city," Jake said with enough force to knock over a tall pine tree.

"Of course not, but I can earn my own money, and not be such a burden to you. Maybe get a little something nice to wear—nothing too fancy of course."

"Always pretty things. I can see you haven't learned much during these long hard months," Jake teased.

"Let me go check and see how Mrs. Wilkin is coming along with dinner. I'll be back later to check on you and bring you a plate." Emma stood and hurried from the room before her brother could object.

Even if Frederick was filthy rich and able to provide luxuries, she was still afraid to give her whole life to a man. It was hard enough to give him a piece of her heart.

"Lord, I'm afraid," she prayed as she walked. Guilt wiggled in her middle. She really should tell him that she was leaving soon.

But she wanted to attend the party at the hotel after the governor was sworn in. Who wouldn't want to witness such a historic moment? A part of her didn't want to be put down anymore. She wanted to wear pretty things and silence Abigail's jeering tongue. Was it such a sin to defend oneself against such cruelty? More tangled thoughts wound through Emma's head as she trudged toward the kitchen. Just a few weeks left to cook for the rough men in camp.

She walked into a stifling hot kitchen filled with chaos and in the usual uproar. Mrs. Wilkin stirred some corn and potato chowder with a vengeance, a kettle of water threatened to boil over, and Bacon squealed in the corner, his plate empty. Mrs. Wilkin's sister must have gone back to her own house.

Stifling a groan, Emma pulled the pot of water off the cook-stove and dumped a bowl of slops onto Bacon's dish. His hearty grunts communicated gratitude. Rubbing his soft head, Emma thought of Frederick. Bacon had been a gift from Frederick after all.

Granted, he had kissed her and expressed admiration and a desire to court her. So how could she convince herself that he wouldn't care if she left? How could she put off telling him? She knew he'd be angry, and she cringed in terror at the thought of an angry man who might throw things in his rage.

Besides, ladies of better means were best suited for a man like Frederick, and he'd come to realize that, in time. He wouldn't miss her for very long.

Mr. Kenicky glared at Frederick as though he had brought the plagues of Egypt into the camp. Frederick shook his head to clear cobwebs from between his ears. Had he heard the boss correctly?

"Don't you have anything to say on your own behalf?" The man's eyes narrowed into two snakelike slits.

Yep. He had heard the man right. He was being accused of carelessness with the equipment—breaking it and not reporting it, so the next man who used it got hurt. The same equipment that had gone haywire and caused Jake's accident.

A part of him wanted to leap across the desk and shake the man silly, but he knew that wouldn't do any good. How on earth was he going to defend himself against such wild accusations?

"You wouldn't believe it anyway, so no, I guess there isn't anything I can say," Frederick growled. But there was something he could do. Leave Tumwater for good. Just as soon as the loose ends were tied up regarding his father's house. Where he'd go remained a mystery, but parts beyond the horizon looked better by the minute.

"That will be all for now, Corrigan. We'll talk more later." The boss went back to studying the paperwork before him, and Frederick stormed from the office.

He jumped into Inferno and stoked the stove to overflowing with wood. In only a matter of minutes, the engine burned hot and in even less time, Inferno raced down the tracks. He braced his arms so taut around Widow's Bend they actually hurt when he rounded the corner.

Frederick rolled into Tumwater with an aching jaw as well, from clenching his teeth so hard. By God's protective grace he made it without crashing. Instead of moving lumber, E.V. was in his office doing paperwork.

"I'm getting out of Tumwater," Frederick stated the moment he crossed the threshold. "The first chance I get to talk to the bank and make sure Pa's house is okay."

E.V. stared at him and said nothing.

That only made Frederick angrier. "Now that I don't have to worry about Pa losing the house, you bet I'm going. Just as soon as I can find someplace else to go."

The expression on E.V.'s face didn't change, so Frederick continued. "I'm not about to stay in a town where I've got accusations hanging over my head like a two-ton anvil ready to drop. You know how folks talk, especially ladies."

"Whoa, what accusations?" E.V.'s eyebrows rose.

Frederick took a few minutes to explain the situation and then waited not so patiently for E.V. to respond.

"All right." E.V. finally answered.

That stunned Frederick. "All right?"

"I know you wouldn't make a major decision like this without praying." E.V. turned his gaze back to the account book on his desk and resumed writing. "Since you know this is what God wants for you, I won't try talking you out of it."

❄

Frederick flinched. He hadn't prayed, but what was the point?

"I, uh, need to send a telegram to some friends in California about getting a logging job down there." He backed out of E.V.'s office and left before his friend changed his mind and decided to preach to him about being patient and not making rash decisions.

Frederick strode into the post office and eyed the telegram clerk. "I'd like to send a message to Eureka, California."

The clerk quickly took down Frederick's message and agreed to send it that afternoon. Frederick left the office, and when he finished his day's work, he traipsed home. He slept fitfully that night, wondering what it would be like starting fresh in California.

The next afternoon, Frederick stopped in at the post office to make sure the message had been sent. To his surprise, he found a response already awaiting him. The telegram was an offer to come work in the Redwood Forest. Men like him were needed to help clear the mammoth trees that made most pines in the Pacific Northwest look small.

Realizing the opportunity available was not just for him, Frederick flew out of the post office and made a beeline to the construction site where Willum was rebuilding a cracked roof.

"I hear you're leaving us," Will said as he sawed a board down to size.

"E.V. tell you?"

"This morning when I picked up my lumber." Will paused with the handsaw for a moment and studied Frederick. "You don't have to leave Tumwater for work. I'll hire you."

"I'm not a carpenter like you."

Willum stared at him with that same disappointed look that E.V. had yesterday. "Since I know this is what God wants for you, I won't try talking you out of it."

Frederick snapped. "Did E.V. tell you to say that?"

"No." Willum frowned. "You did pray, didn't you?"

"After I take Emma Pearson to the party at the Schmitt mansion," Frederick said to change the subject, "I'm leaving."

With a nod of acceptance, Will returned to sawing, and Frederick walked away. With his stomach rumbling for food, he headed to the tracks and boarded Inferno for the short trip back to the logging camp. As he thought of Emma, dread grew in his heart at how and when he'd tell her he was leaving.

❄

It was the end of November and a chill set in on the afternoon of the party. Emma sat in the parlor of the Wilkins' house and sewed with frantic speed on the dress she hoped to wear that evening. To her delight, the lace Frederick gave her had been long enough to encircle the collar and both sleeves, if barely. Frederick had said he would arrive at five sharp. Emma heard Abigail had been invited and was in no mood to deal with her troublemaking.

Looking forward to one last evening with Frederick, she couldn't bring herself to cancel. She thought she owed it to him to make some beautiful memories on their last night together. The last thing she wanted to do was cause him extra pain, and backing out of the party would surely do that. Why ruin the night for him by skipping the festivities?

Afterward, she and Jake were leaving for Chicago. She didn't want to think about Frederick's reaction. She kept repeating in her head that he was better off without her. Not only was she poor, with no family and no status, but she was broken inside from such a traumatic childhood. He'd probably regret it if they married. Or were these just excuses she used because she was afraid of letting him get too close?

"Oh, this cheap thread!" Emma growled as she snipped the broken ends and rethreaded her needle. How would she ever get the lace sewn when the thread kept breaking?

"Ouch!" she yelped as the needle bit into her fingertip. She stuck the sore finger into her mouth.

"Everything will be fine after tonight." Getting back to her sewing, Emma began singing "Amazing Grace," hoping to sooth her fretful mood.

An hour later, she snipped the ends of the thread and the beautiful garment was complete. Evergreen in color, it matched the name of the new state. And she would celebrate by spending the evening with the local politicians and Mr. Frederick Corrigan.

A stab of pain shot through her heart with as little mercy as was shown to her fingertip only an hour earlier. Just where the feeling had originated she didn't know, but it did nothing to change her plan.

A deafening racket of cheers arose from the street as dozens of loggers celebrated. How grateful she was that Jake had made a full recovery. She was also glad he didn't drink hard alcohol. He would join his friends at the saloon but would return home that evening as sober as a preacher on Sunday morning.

"Emma." Her brother's voice carried into the room.

She rose to greet him. "Yes, Jake?" She hoped he heard her above the whoops and hollers.

"Emma, I'm heading downtown with the men. Fred will be along shortly. You sure about things?" She could hear the concern woven into his tone. He leaned against the door jamb and studied her with seriousness written in his features.

"I'm certain, Jake. Thank you. Now if you'll excuse me, I need to dress before Frederick gets here."

"All right, but be careful now, you hear?"

Jake shook his finger at Emma and made her feel like a child. Well, she wasn't a child any longer. She huffed. Hopefully, once they arrived in Chicago, Jake would be too preoccupied with Uncle Irving to bother with her business.

With a small degree of difficulty she and Mrs. Wilkin managed to get the dress on over her head and keep it from brushing the floor and getting dirty before she ever left the house. Her friend did up the plethora of buttons that lined the back.

"Thank you so much." Emma smiled and then took the time to admire herself in the small mirror. The green yards of flowing material were beautiful. She bit back tears as she thought of the many times her mother had worn the same dress. She hoped that at least

Frederick would like it. If only she had the money to get a portrait taken. Something in her heart said it would be a night she would always remember.

❄

Frederick stood before the mirror and tied his necktie for the fourth time. After taking the time to iron it, he was worried it would get wrinkled. With a twist and a turn he managed the small feat.

Now to finish combing his hair, although sometimes he wondered why he bothered. The seemingly endless rain, from mist to downpour, ruffled his locks at every turn.

"Thanks, Willum, for letting me get ready at your place," Frederick declared when he finally finished with his tie. How he hoped Emma wouldn't get upset with him when he told her he was leaving. He said a quick prayer that she would take the news well. He didn't want to break her heart, but he couldn't bear to take her away from the only family she had left either.

Once he had readied himself to satisfaction, he strolled out the door. Sweat beaded on his forehead even though it was cold outside. His nerve endings tingled when he thought about where and when he was going to tell Emma of his departure.

With his friends in Eureka expecting him in three days, and the arrangements already made, what choice did he have but to leave?

Frederick curtailed his thoughts when he knocked on the door. When Emma pulled the door open and stood on the threshold, his heart threatened to stop beating. His breath halted in his throat. Emma stood in a green gown, hair upswept in a neatly coifed bun, her eyes blazing with passion. Frederick wondered if he'd be able to tell her he was leaving, let alone actually follow through with his objective.

"Hello, Frederick. It's wonderful to see you." Emma batted her black eyelashes and aimed a radiant smile at him that endangered his carefully laid plans.

❄

Emma smiled at Frederick and hoped it masked her sudden desire to throw herself into his arms.

"Good evening, Emma." Frederick grasped her gloved hand as she held it out to him, and he lifted it to his lips and laid a tender kiss there. How Emma wanted him to lay another kiss upon her lips, but proper ladies didn't say such things. Good heavens, how was she ever going to make it to Chicago with images of this handsome man tailing her every step of the journey?

"Are you all right?" Frederick looked at her with concern in his eyes.

"Yes, could you help me with my shawl, please?" Emma turned, allowing him to wrap the garment around her shoulders.

"Shall we?" Frederick offered his arm and motioned toward the covered buggy he had borrowed from friends. Even though it wasn't Frederick's, Emma stared at it and felt like a princess in a fairy tale being whisked away to the grand ball. The event was by invitation only, and it was by a stroke of luck that Frederick had obtained tickets from his father. All the more reason for Emma to feel like Cinderella.

Dinner was a delicious combination of roast goose and smoked salmon, along with baby red potatoes, and carrots glazed in sauce. Servants milled about, meeting the guests' every need, including Emma's. Frederick sat to her right, and every so often she noticed him staring at her with a strange expression on his face. Oh dear. She hoped he wouldn't confess to loving her.

There was much discussion regarding Mr. Elisha P. Ferry being sworn in as the new and first governor of Washington State. The orchestra played a collection of hymns, one of which was Emma's favorite. She hummed along with the comforting tune. It was also her mother's favorite. The melody caused memories of her mother to dance in her mind.

The tall woman had been the very picture of elegance, grace, and devotion to the Lord. Someone Emma had admired. Then came the day her father had died and Mama had clung to God with fiercer determination. Emma, who was angry at God for taking her father, didn't understand her mother's commitment to her faith. Things went from bad to worse when her mother hastily married someone she had courted only a short while.

Emma shook the frightening memories from her thoughts. If only she could shake them from her history as easily. Her breath came in gasps, and she couldn't draw enough air into her lungs. The tightly laced corset didn't help matters. This was her body's reaction every time she dared to entertain memories of her mother's final days. Well, she wasn't making the same mistakes, of that she was certain.

The orchestra finished the song. Emma drew courage and sat straighter in her chair as she spoke. "Frederick, I'd like to speak with you in private if I may."

The features on his face flickered with emotion before he replied. "Yes, there's something I need to discuss with you. Allow me."

Frederick rose and once again offered his arm. They strolled along the grounds of the rolling estate and discussed the stars in the heavens. Frederick pointed out the Big Dipper, holding her hand so she wouldn't fall along the path. In the cold night air, his touch lent comfort to the ache in her heart. The moon cast a glow about them.

Emma mustered courage to tell him of her plans to leave Tumwater, but he sat her down on a nearby bench before she had the chance. He sat down beside her with his hands clasped in his lap. For a brief moment she thought he might kiss her, but he acted too strangely for that.

Frederick hesitated for what seemed like an eternity. "I need to tell you something." This time an uncomfortable feeling rolled in Emma's middle. Something about his tone and tense body wasn't right.

Oh dear, please don't say "I love you"!

"Emma," he began, "I can't remain in Washington any longer. I am leaving for California day after next. Please don't be angry."

Emma's breath escaped her in one quick whoosh, and for a moment, she was unable to draw another. Frederick was leaving Washington? She had heard rumors of unrest murmured around camp, and of course, he would take them personally. She wanted to be angry with him, but couldn't, not when she was planning on leaving also.

"So you're not angry?" Frederick raised his eyebrows as if to question.

"No, I'm not angry. Perhaps disappointed." Emma blurted the statement without giving much thought as to what she was saying.

"Disappointed?" Frederick leaned back and aimed a puzzled look at her.

"I never would have expected a man of your caliber to run away from the face of difficulty." Emma bit her lip at the cruelty of her words. The blaze in his eyes told her she had hurt him and she was immediately sorry. Her soul ached with the sting of her actions. This was her last night with dear Frederick. She never expected her own heart to hurt so much.

"I don't run from anything. But I don't stand around and let folks get away with calling me a liar either. It's a matter of pride."

"Then I guess this is good-bye. I was going to tell you tonight. I'm going to Chicago with Jake." Emma lifted her chin and gave her words a minute to register.

"So you're leaving, too. Just when were you planning on sharing this news with me?" He stood, with his hands on his hips.

"I can't stand living with the camp's drudgeries another day, Frederick. It's so rough and dirty, and besides, I need to stick close to my brother. He's watched out for me for so long, I need to be there for him in return. I owe that to him." Emma paused. "I need him." All this was true, but she didn't have the heart to tell Frederick she was afraid of a man getting too close to her heart.

"Then I guess you're right, this is good-bye." Frederick stood in stony silence, and the words sank to the depths of Emma's heart like a heavy boat anchor.

Without another word, he offered his arm and escorted her back to the carriage. The entire ride back home was made without a word. Like a perfect gentleman, he helped her alight from the carriage and escorted her to her door. He then lifted her hand to his lips and placed a gentle kiss on the back of her gloved hand. She had barely enough time to get inside the door and shut it quietly behind her before the painful sobs tore loose from her heart. Outside, she heard his footsteps echo in the night as he walked away. . .forever.

❄

Two days later, Frederick boarded a train heading south to California. It had been hard saying good-bye to his best friends. Willum had taken the news with understanding, but E.V. had hardly said a word to him since he made the announcement.

Prayer and time with the Lord seemed as dry as a day-old biscuit. Much like it had before he left. This made him question whether or not he was doing the right thing. While studying his devotions at yet another stop along the way, a scripture spearheaded its way into his heart.

"Except the Lord build the house, they labour in vain that build it."

Frederick slammed his Bible shut. The last thing he needed was to second-guess his well-intentioned plans. The next time they stopped he would send a telegram to his three friends in Tumwater to see how they were doing. He missed them already.

The next afternoon, Frederick arrived at his friend's house. A telegram was waiting.

Frederick noted the return address—the logging camp. He tore open the message.

Mr. Wilkin said another accident had happened, and it couldn't be blamed on Jake or Frederick this time. Mr. Kenicky and his company were conducting an investigation and getting to the bottom of things. They begged him to come back and testify at the inquiry.

Frederick marched straight to the telegraph office and sent a message that he would be on the next train back to Tumwater. He had lost the woman he loved, so far as he was concerned, but at least he could clear his good name. Frederick wasted no time in heading back to the train station and back to Washington State.

Chapter 10

Emma stepped off the train in Chicago and searched in vain for the slightest sign of a tree, a bush, or anything that resembled nature. The racket of streetcars buzzing past nearly scared her silly. City life was going to take some getting used to. Jake wouldn't let her bring Bacon along on the train. She had to leave him with the Wilkins, and she feared he would actually become bacon!

Once at her uncle's house, Emma yearned for God's peace. The kind she had at the logging camp, in spite of the conditions. She asked her uncle about churches in town and what services he attended. The man brushed off the question like he would a pesky fly.

Her uncle then showed her where she would be living and where she would be working. Emma was highly disappointed in both. The living quarters were dirty and small. And her place of employment was a loud and smelly factory. It looked dangerous, too. She had thought the conditions at the logging camp were horrid. To make matters worse, the pay wasn't what she thought it would be.

The first night, trying to sleep in the small cot in her tiny room, Emma tossed and turned, thinking of Washington, the towering trees, the cool bubbling stream at the base of camp, of Bacon. . .and Frederick. Perhaps her heart had grown to love more than she thought it had.

Chicago wasn't anything like she expected. She wanted to go home to Washington, but she couldn't bear the thought of being away from Jake. She needed to wash his clothes and make him dinner. She needed to stand by him like he had done with her since their mother died. How could she tell him of her desires after she had begged so hard to come with him?

Working in the factory was nothing like cooking in the wide open spaces of the logging camp. The machines made a racket that hurt her ears and gave her a headache long before noon. Jake, on the other hand, was doing very well working at the newspaper behind his shiny new desk. And he was going to law school at night. He whistled on his way out the door to work and sang when he came home at night. Emma took great delight in seeing him so content.

One night, about three weeks after their arrival, her brother surprised her. "Sis, I know you're not happy here. Why don't you go back to Washington?"

"I can't leave you, Jake. Don't send me back to where I'll be all alone." Emma's mouth went dry as kindling and her eyes pooled with unshed tears.

"Emma, you won't be alone. You'll have the Wilkins and Bacon and Frederick."

"Jake, no." By now, tears streamed down Emma's cheeks like water over Tumwater Falls. "Jake, I'm afraid. I don't want to end up like Mama, hurt by a filthy man who guzzles whiskey from dawn till dusk."

"Mama remarried in haste. She had to do something to put a roof over our heads and clothes on our backs. She realized before she passed, she made a mistake in not consulting the Lord. Take a year to stay with the Wilkins and see if you can find Fred, maybe ask his friends if they know where he is. If the Lord leads you to him, take some time to really get to know the man. I've prayed about it, Emma, and I believe this is what God wants. Uncle Irving and I'll come out to visit."

"Uncle Irving. . ." Emma hiccupped and dried her tears.

"He's already agreed to escort you back. You have plenty of time to get there before Christmas and go to Christmas Eve service." Jake smiled down at her. She was pleased that he saw her as a woman who could care for herself if necessary and not some child.

The next morning, Emma and Uncle Irving were on a train headed for Washington. They arrived in Tumwater a few days later, and her uncle checked them into the hotel in town. The Christmas Eve service was that night. Emma wanted to be with people she had grown to care for, namely the Wilkins. For the first time in weeks, her heart was at peace.

When she and Uncle Irving arrived at the church, she saw the back of a tall blond man standing in front of the building. Upon closer inspection, she noted his hand on the stair railing, a hand that looked so familiar. Could Frederick be back from California? It didn't seem possible.

Emma lifted her skirts and stepped closer. She looked up just in time to see the tall blond turn.

Frederick!

The breath went out of her in a wheezy gasp as she advanced toward him with more speed than what was ladylike.

She fell against his chest and sobbed.

"I'll meet you inside." Uncle Irving planted a kiss on the top of her head then went inside the church.

Frederick held her in his arms and swore to never let her go.

"You, me, and Bacon, we're going to be a family," he teased. He leaned down and kissed her, a kiss she returned without fear and with all her heart. This evergreen night was one she would always remember.

Debby Lee was raised in the cozy little town of Toledo, Washington. She has been writing since she was a small child, and has written several novels, but never forgets home. The Northwest Christian Writers Association and Romance Writers of America are two organizations that Debby enjoys being a part of. As a self professed nature lover, and an avid listener of 1960s folk music, Debby can't help but feel like a hippie child who wasn't born soon enough to attend Woodstock. She wishes she could run barefoot all year long, but often does anyway in the grass and on the beaches in her hamlet that is the cold and rainy southwest Washington. During football season, Debby cheers on the Seattle Seahawks along with legions of other devoted fans. She's also filled with wanderlust and dreams of visiting Denmark, Italy, and Morocco someday. Debby loves connecting with her readers through her website at www.booksbydebbylee.com.

All Ye Faithful

by Gina Welborn

Dedication

To my Inky Sisters: "Be light. Be love. Believe." isn't merely my calling—it's what I see lived out in you, and for that I am blessed every day. And to Jeremy for listening patiently each time I explained why the backspace key on my laptop was broken (again) and why MS Word is having "issues" (again) and why we need to order pizza for dinner (again).

Where no wood is, there the fire goeth out:
so where there is no talebearer, the strife ceaseth.
PROVERBS 26:20 KJV

Chapter 1

I've decided to throw caution to the wind and tell E.V. how I feel," Larkin Whitworth happily announced before plopping down in the wooden chair despite the fullness of her skirts and petticoats. She handed Anna the punch cup she'd refilled for the fifth time since Emma and Frederick's wedding celebration began. Considering how quickly her adorably—and abundantly—pregnant friend downed the apricot-flavored beverage, Larkin also offered the second cup she'd brought for herself while Anna's doting husband, Jeremiah, fetched a second plate of egg salad sandwiches.

"Really?" Anna exchanged the full cup with the empty one. "I can't figure why I'm so parched all day long."

"You're expecting. I think that's expected."

"I suppose." Anna fanned her sweat-glistened forehead. "Are you hot? I'm hot. It's hot."

As the fiddling increased in volume, signaling the beginning of another dance, Larkin took the fan from Anna and attended to cooling her *tillikum*, closest friend. Mama would be proud she was at least *thinking* Chinook jargon.

"I'm fine, but the *Farmer's Almanac* did predict a warm though wet—"

At Anna's raised hand, Larkin fell silent.

"We are both too young and the wrong gender to be discussing weather." Instead of drinking her punch, Anna gave Larkin a slant-eyed look. "Are you really going to tell Mr. Heartless Renier that you love him?"

Larkin glanced at E.V. His smooth face and sun-brightened hair made him easy to find among the many bearded and mustached men in the room. "Yes, and he isn't heartless, and the almanac conveys a wealth of information even women in the bloom of their youth can appreciate."

"Again, you know my rule against almanac talk. Shh. Now what, pray tell, do you call someone who convinces a girl he loves her"—Anna sipped the punch—"and then allows almost two years to pass without proposing? Or at least asking to court her?"

Larkin smiled. "He's—he's—" Her grin faltered somewhat, and she stopped fanning Anna. "Well, he's judicious." She hoped her tone conveyed every ounce of confidence she had in E.V. despite the tinge of doubt that seemed to be growing with each passing day.

"Judicious? Someone has been spending too much time reading." With a disappointed shake of her head that caused her floral-decked straw hat to tilt a fraction, Anna muttered, "I had a different descriptive in mind."

"Like what?"

Anna shrugged. "Oh, I don't know. Maybe something that rhymes with trout." She reclaimed the fan from Larkin and resumed fanning herself.

Larkin looked to the bridal couple doing a Virginia reel in the center of the warm barn with a score of other Tumwater residents, including E.V. and Abigail Leonard. Granted, E.V. didn't seem to be enjoying the dance as much as the other dancers were. Of course, Emma and Frederick Corrigan *were* newly married and thereby unable to *not* enjoy the moment.

Besides, E.V. had never made any overt claims on any woman since arriving in Tumwater two autumns ago, so Larkin had no cause to be jealous or wary or fretful.

Still, this was his third—*third!*—dance with Abigail.

And he had been spending more time than usual with Abigail's father, who was also spending more time than usual at E.V.'s sawmill. In fact, every time Larkin had walked by Renier Lumber Company during the last week—which was only because she passed it on her way to take lunch to her father at the brewery—she'd noticed Mr. Leonard's impressive roan gelding tied to a hitching post. If he was buying lumber, wouldn't he have brought a wagon?

Gripping the empty punch glass and resting her hands on her knees, Larkin's shoulders drooped just a fraction. The corset her mother required her to wear wouldn't allow an unladylike slump under her new yellow-and-ivory-striped gown. The gown her mother had insisted they go to Olympia to buy specifically for the wedding. After all, they needed to have another fitting on her Christmas gown anyway, or so Mama had justified to Papa. Since they were at the modiste's shop, being the kill-two-birds-with-one-stone person she was, Mama also bought a new gown for Larkin to wear to Anna's twentieth birthday party in a month. That brocade dress, unlike this year's burnished-gold Christmas one, was the exact shade of the limes grown in Mama's conservatory.

Lime next to Anna's ivory-with-a-touch-of-coral complexion was beautiful.

Lime next to the copper-toned skin Larkin had inherited from her one-quarter Chinook mother was practically morbid. Not that Larkin would suggest that to Mama, whose 1891 obsession apparently was with the color green. One of these days, though, she would convince her mother that every special event did not require a new gown. Certainly not one in a greenish hue. Or yellow, the color for the year of our Lord 1890. Or purple—Mama's earlier obsession. Or 1887's dreadful Year of the Orange.

She cringed in memory.

Why did Mama have to favor vibrant, look-at-me shades? As if the fanciness of Larkin's gowns weren't attention-demanding enough, Mama had to add rich, bold color. Larkin loved beige, muted browns, and earthy golds that subtly blended in with the surroundings.

Everyone in Tumwater knew Larkin was an heiress. The white Whitworth mansion ostentatiously located on a prominent corner near the center of town was enough of a daily reminder. She didn't need to be dressed like an unapproachable china doll for people to treat her differently.

Still, remembering that others were watching, Larkin sat up like a proper lady, so as to not bring any dishonor on her parents, and refocused on her agenda. The one that had begun after E.V. escorted Abigail to the dance floor for the third—*third!*—time.

She almost felt a tad angry.

All right, she did feel a tad angry. . .in fact, more than a tad angry.

"I think I shall confront E.V. once this dance is over."

"Confront? You?"

"I *can* confront." At Anna's dubious look, she added, "Why do you think I'm incapable of confronting someone?"

"Just where did Tuck go to find those sandwiches?" Anna rested her empty punch glass atop the empty one Larkin held. She rubbed the shifting bump on her almost-nine-month tummy. "This babe is a prized whopper in the making. Larky, you can do better than E.V. Renier. I think—"

"Please don't mention—"

"Willum Tate," Anna continued without skipping a beat, "personifies faithfulness and, according to the grapevine telegraph, those green eyes have stopped many Tumwater ladies in their tracks."

Larkin said nothing because she was used to Anna's weekly Willum Tate exaltation. And, truly, letting Anna have her say was far easier than trying to explain that she had no romantic feelings toward the impeccable-though-surly carpenter. Life had been more pleasant when plucky, fun-loving Anna fished, rummaged through the woods, and swam in the creek with Larkin. Before she ever noticed that members of the opposite gender were, well, quite appealing.

Or at least Jeremiah Tucker was.

Anna leaned closer and spoke low even though they were the only two in this corner of the barn. "Kathleen said when she was in the mercantile this morning she heard Mrs. Bollen tell her daughter-in-law Martha that she heard cranky ol' Mrs. Ellis complimenting Willum Tate at the livery to Mr. and Mrs. Parker, and Mrs. Ellis doesn't compliment *anyone* but you. Ever."

"Why do you think that is?" Larkin asked to distract Anna from praising the splendidly handsome Mr. Tate, who was currently dancing with Anna's sister even while oddly focused on Natalie Bollen, who was dancing with the handsome-but-not-as-quite Mr. John Seymour, who the grapevine telegraph seemed convinced would be Natalie's first official suitor once she turned eighteen next June. Larkin quickly added, "About people saying Mrs. Ellis is cranky. She is quite a dear heart once you get to know her. I don't understand why everyone in town hates her. Poor Mrs. Ellis is truly misunderstood."

Anna didn't answer. Instead she stared at Larkin for what seemed to be a minute or two.

"My friend," she finally said, "you aren't and will never be crafty. There's nice, and then there's you—nicer than nice. You're sweet, sincere, and selfless."

"Thank you, but you're as sweet—"

"Shh. I have never heard either you or Mr. Tate say anything critical about that ornery old woman who almost shot off my left foot when I came within two feet of her back fence because I foolishly—and incorrectly—thought that the skunk chasing me was worse than Mrs. Ellis. You and Willum are clearly suited."

"And E.V. and I aren't?"

"It's been two years, Larky. If he really cared about you, he'd have asked to court you by now. E.V. doesn't deserve you. Willum Tate, though, needs a good woman."

After a sigh at hearing the name of the man Anna had championed this year as *the ideal husband. . .after mine of course,* Larkin thought back to Anna's descriptive of E.V. rhyming with trout. "There's no fitting word for E.V. that rhymes with—"

"Lout," Anna blurted.

Larkin rolled her eyes. "He isn't a lout."

"Gout."

"That's a disease."

"Indian scout, unbearably stout, German bean sprout."

Larkin fought back her smile. "Now you're being silly."

A smug grin teetered on Anna's lips. Her brown-eyed gaze shifted from Larkin to the dancers, then back to Larkin, and her voice softened with what seemed—no, felt—like sympathy. "Doubt."

Larkin dropped her gaze to the yellow shoes peeking out from the ankle-length ivory-lace hem of her gown. She poked at the straw under her toes. That tingle of doubt she'd been trying to ignore rang like the bells she'd received the last two Christmases from an anonymous admirer. She liked to dream they were from the blond man with an adorable cleft in his chin, the man who gave her such tender attention the first autumn he moved into Tumwater, the man who faithfully attended worship services and always sat in the pew one row back and to the left of her, and who bought her meal baskets at every church auction.

The quiet sawmiller who every Wednesday at a quarter past nine met her at the front steps to the Bollens' parsonage and delivered half a ham while she brought a basket of pies or fruit, and then walked her home. Even on the days it rained, which was most days, after all, because when did it not rain in the Washington Cascades?

A man that faithful, that consistent, had to care, right?

He loved her. She knew he did because he said more in the looks he gave her than in any conversation they'd ever had.

And they'd had myriad conversations in the last two years—enough for her to learn how important overcoming his father's failings was to E.V. and for him to learn she feared embarrassing her parents.

Yet that same man had not spared a glance at the two friends sitting near the entrance of the barn. No, Eric Valentin Renier III hadn't looked her way any more than Willum Tate had. Did he think she'd given up on them having a future together? Or had his feelings merely changed?

They hadn't spoken in over a week. During the last conversation, E.V. had seemed irritated, wouldn't look at her, and jerked back every time she drew close.

"Larkin, you're doing it again."

"What?" she said without looking up.

"That glazed look you get when you're deep in thought. I don't care if it's what those with Chinook blood do. It's creepy."

Oddly not humored by the good-natured ribbing, Larkin turned in her chair to face Anna, whose delicate beauty glowed with love and pregnancy. "Do you think I should tell him how I feel?" she hesitantly asked. "Say yes, and I'll do it, right here in front of everyone."

Anna's winged brows drew together in sadness. "Oh Larkin, when have you ever done anything that would intentionally draw attention to yourself?"

Larkin flinched. Never. But this was 1890, the year she'd vowed would be different, and up to this point, she hadn't done a single thing different or courageous or adventuresome because she never did anything different or courageous or adventuresome unless she was with Anna. And ever since Anna married Jeremiah Tucker, Larkin had even less opportunity to be anything but the dullard she was.

At twenty-one, she was the only female in Tumwater of courting age who had never had a suitor. Either no one had the courage to approach her father or, worse, none wanted a nicer-than-nice wife.

Why not tell E.V. that she loved him? That she wanted to marry him.

She had little to lose and all the world to gain.

A year from now she wanted to be the one sitting in a chair soothing her rounded belly while Anna brought her copious amounts of beverages.

Decision made, she reached over Anna to set the punch cups in Jeremiah's chair. She then deftly removed the pin holding her feathered hat atop her head. The last thing she wanted was to join E.V. in a dance and have her hat slide over her eyes, blocking her view, causing her to trip over his feet, and consequently crash into someone while flipping her skirts up in the air. Not that that had ever happened to her, but it could. One should always prepare for the worst while expecting the best.

She stood and placed her hat in her vacant seat. "Don't let me leave here without it."

Anna gasped. "You're really going to do this, aren't you?" She grabbed Larkin's hand and drew up to standing. Panic blanched her face. "I know I almost lost Tuck by letting him think I loved Garrick when I really loved him, but what will your parents say? Just think about what the grapevine telegraph will say. Don't do it."

As far as the grapevine telegraph went—well, people never gossiped about her, because she never did anything worth gossiping about. She could speak to E.V. here at the wedding reception without anyone listening in because, after all, why would anyone want to overhear what she had to say? She was the last person anyone would *ever* suspect of doing something noteworthy or mysterious.

Considering Papa was at home tending to Mama, they wouldn't know what happened until she told them in the morning. By then she and E.V. would be courting. And Papa would see they were in love and would agree to the marriage.

Being an heiress, being someone everyone except Abigail Leonard liked, being known as sweet and sincere and selfless—none of it mattered much if she had no one to enjoy life with. Anna had Jeremiah and soon a baby, too. Her parents had their own lives.

She didn't want to grow old alone.

She didn't want to be Mrs. Ellis, warning people away with her shotgun because she believed the pain of another broken heart was worse than being alone.

She wanted to love and be loved because she believed—no, she *knew* to the depths of her soul—she was created to love and be loved. And since her father allowed her to court— she was old enough, after all—then, logically, wouldn't it be acceptable for her to initiate the courting? Even Ruth had to nudge the honorable-yet-stubborn Boaz into action.

Time to be bold and adventuresome.

Hearing the music of the dance dwindling to the end, Larkin kissed Anna's cheek.

"I vow before you have that baby, E.V. and I will be married. No matter what it takes. No matter what I have to throw to the wind." She felt the corners of her mouth draw upward. "Within reason of course.

Chapter 2

He wasn't going to look her way. Wasn't. Not even when his position on the dance floor brought her into his direct line of sight. Because once he did, E.V. knew he would be lost in the depths of those eyes. Eyes so greenish-gold they reminded him of mossy tree bark—words not worthy of a Shakespearean sonnet and words he certainly would never share with her. He wasn't a man with much to say. And besides, he knew his girl didn't need or desire besotted praise.

Loving Larkin Whitworth made him more, made him want to share more, made him want to be more.

What he needed though was time.

And he had spent enough of that on his knees in prayer during almost two years of having his marriage proposals rejected by her father, to know he also needed a miracle in the form of a large lumber supplier. Once he'd built Renier Lumber Company into the most profitable mill in Tumwater—and one more large supplier would do it—he'd prove his work ethic, worthiness, and his ability to provide for Larkin to her wealth-focused father.

Tonight he was two steps closer to that miracle.

Literally.

All he had to do was pay enough attendance on Abigail Leonard for the other bachelors in town to realize she was an available female, even if the Caesar-like nose she'd inherited from her father was too large for her face. To be fair, she was no Larkin, but neither was she the least attractive female in the room. Considering the number of men who had already danced with Miss Leonard at the wedding, E.V. felt confident that his—and her father's—plan was succeeding.

Competition brought out the warrior instincts in every man, especially with a woman involved.

As the musicians allowed the last notes to die, E.V. graciously escorted Miss Leonard back to her father and met three other bachelors waiting, he hoped, to ask the slender blond to dance. Harvey Milton, Reverend Bollen's middle son David—the one E.V. long suspected of harboring feelings for Miss Leonard—and Frederick's new brother-in-law Jake Pearson immediately began complimenting Miss Leonard. She did look nice in her odd-shade-of-red (or maybe pink) gown. Larkin would know the exact color. Men needed wives so they didn't need to know these types of things.

As abruptly as the compliments began, the three men facing Miss Leonard fell silent, their gazes shifting from her confused expression to something E.V. would have to turn around to see. Harvey's mouth gaped a bit. Jake stood taller. David though, seemed to recover himself and looked longingly at Miss Leonard, who stepped closer to her father and, E.V. could've sworn, whispered, "Do something, Daddy."

Before E.V. could turn and look, Mr. Leonard clenched E.V.'s arm. "Renier, we need to talk."

At the harshness of Leonard's tone, E.V. felt a ripple of tension center between his eyebrows. He didn't mind helping Silas Leonard secure a husband for his oldest daughter, but his feet were aching, his mouth parched, and stomach rumbling, and if the barn grew any warmer from the body heat of all the wedding guests, he'd have to shed the black tailored coat he'd used his last bit of savings to purchase two years ago to wear to Larkin's birthday party in hopes of attracting her attention. Still, he needed the contract, and if Leonard wanted to talk, E.V. would listen.

He opened his mouth, intent on uttering his well-practiced "yes sir," when the sweetest voice he'd yearned to hear say, "Yes, I'll marry you," broke the taut silence.

"Mr. Renier, might I have a word?"

E.V. found his breath and turned to Larkin, now standing close enough for him to pull her into his arms for a lengthy kiss. Loose strands of her black hair caressed the sides of her high cheekbones. He ached to pin them back into the neat and tidy bun she always wore underneath a hat she was forever taking off and forgetting. Whenever she smiled—and he prayed she wouldn't at this moment, for his sake—the dimples on the sides of her mouth testified she'd inherited all the beauty of her part-Chinook mother and the whimsy of her Irish-English father.

Everything about her took his breath away.

"Daa—dee," Miss Leonard whispered (more aptly, whined) again.

"Yes, a word, Miss Whitworth," E.V. blurted before Silas Leonard could make another demand. "We could speak over by the punch table." He motioned that direction. "I could use a drink." Remembering the contract he needed, he met Leonard's intense gaze. "We won't be but a moment, sir."

Larkin took a step then stopped. Her sweet-natured gaze settled on Miss Leonard. "Oh Abigail, cerise is certainly your color. You look lovely today." Larkin then nodded at Jake, Harvey, and David to acknowledge their presence but spoke only to Jake. "Please express to the newlyweds my apologies for my parents' absence. Mama. . ." She looked uneasy for a split-second. Then the corners of her mouth curved softly. "The wedding was delightful."

E.V. stepped to Larkin's side, touched the small of her back in the most platonic manner he could possibly manage, and nudged her into walking before drawing his hand away from her. He focused on keeping the distance between them not too close to appear as anything but friends. When she would close the gap, he would ease to the left, keeping propriety in mind.

Since she said nothing, he remained silent also as they wove through the wedding guests joining the line for another dance. Though Larkin was several inches shorter than Miss Leonard, he couldn't—nor did he want to—shake the feeling that Larkin was perfectly made for him. To think their relationship began over a tray of cookies spilled by Miss Leonard's brother.

The words *will you marry me?* languished on the tip of his tongue. Only he couldn't ask until he'd gained her father's approval first. The Whitworth family honor was too important to them for E.V. to bring it any shame.

They stopped at the refreshment table. Larkin filled a glass of punch, handed it to him, then picked up a plate and looked over the food offerings.

Aware of how alone they were, yet at a public event, E.V. found himself admiring the curve of her neck and the finger-length strands of hair escaping from the bun, which seemed even blacker against the yellow and ivory stripes of her silky gown. He clenched the punch glass. He wasn't going to touch her. Wasn't. Not even when the distance between them was less than an arm's length.

Was there anything in life he desired more than her?

"I hope you like egg salad and smoked salmon."

E.V. blinked. "Ahhh. . ."

"They seem to be the norm at weddings here in Tumwater," Larkin continued, "which is why I intend on having something totally different when we—umm, when I marry." Her head tilted to the left as she looked up at him, and her mouth curved enough for him to see hints of her dimples. "Were you paying attention to me?"

To her words, not so much.

To her, absolutely.

And he felt as much irritation as joy in being this close to her.

Understanding exactly how a parched man viewing an oasis felt, E.V. downed his punch. Two years of waiting. Two years of once-a-week marriage requests and immediate rejections. Two years of answering even the most obscure question about his family while enduring reminders of his father's failure from Larkin's father. E.V. had been steadfast, resolute, and patient. By remembering his sinful nature was dead and Christ now lived through him, he could endure as long as needed. The reward was too great to give up now.

The prize—Larkin—was too precious to lose.

"You wished to speak to me?" he asked as the musicians began another tune. Immediately he regretted the exasperated sound of his tone. Since he couldn't explain to her the struggle between his honor and his desires, he simply mumbled, "Sorry. Please, go on."

"Yes." Looking unsure of herself, she took the punch glass and gave him a plate of finger-sized sandwiches. "E.V., I know we—you—well, at least I felt there was something special between—" She broke off, and her gaze shifted as if to see who was watching them.

E.V. glanced to his right and groaned.

Miss Leonard strode purposely toward them, her progress occasionally halted by couples exchanging partners in the brisk dance.

Larkin touched his wrist, drawing his attention. "Do you remember when Reverend Bollen preached about prayer the Sunday before Thanksgiving?" she rushed out.

He nodded.

"He said faith in action is trusting God with our future even when our prayers aren't answered." Her gaze focused on where he'd turned his hand enough to touch the inside of her wrist, yet she didn't draw away. "I am trying to trust. I also need to know that I have reason to hope my future will include—"

"Mr. Renier!" Miss Leonard called out.

Larkin pulled away, leaving E.V.'s skin chilled despite the unseasonable warmth in the barn. She turned from him and smiled at Miss Leonard. "Is there a problem?"

Miss Leonard stopped too close to E.V. for his comfort, but the table on his left blocked him from moving away. "Daddy needs to speak to you."

"About?"

She playfully tapped his arm. "About trees, silly."

E.V. took a leisurely bite of an egg salad sandwich. After a quick grimace, he chewed, swallowed, then muttered, "Miss Whitworth and I are in a conversation," before finishing off the bland sandwich.

"Daddy said *now*."

Annoyed by her demanding tone, E.V. reached behind him to pat the table in search of a punch cup. He wasn't their lackey. "Give me a moment, will you please?"

While Larkin refilled his drink, Miss Leonard's lips pursed, and if he were a gambling man, he'd swear one of her feet was tapping impatiently on the straw-covered barn floor.

"Fine. But do know if Daddy feels you aren't serious about working with him, he has an increased offer from a more established and experienced mill that he'd be a fool not to accept. Good day, Mr. Renier." Without even sparing Larkin an *I acknowledge your presence* glance, she swiveled on her heel and began walking away.

E.V. looked across the barn to spy Leonard's ashen-blond, oiled head. The man stood at least half a foot taller than any other man in the room. He was speaking to the other two sawmill owners in town. The shorter, sour-faced one was currently buying Leonard's lumber; the taller, heavily-wrinkled-despite-his-age man was the one E.V. had heard was also courting Leonard's business. His competition.

Panic welled in E.V.'s chest. Earlier this week, Leonard vowed he'd make a decision who to make a new lumber contract with at the wedding reception. So far, he had yet to say a word on the subject to E.V.

Help me, Lord. I need his lumber.

"Wait, Miss Leonard!" Once she halted, E.V. took the drink Larkin offered and lowered his voice so only she could hear. "This is important. I have to— I can't lose—"

"Mr. Renier," Miss Leonard said in that increasingly shrill voice of hers, "Daddy isn't as patient as I am."

E.V. grimaced.

Larkin waved him away. "Go on. What I wanted to say can wait."

"Are you sure?"

With a soft curve to her lips, she nodded.

E.V. downed the apricot-flavored punch as quickly as he could. "Don't leave. We haven't had our dance yet."

Larkin took his plate and empty punch cup and said nothing, which was something E.V. loved about her. Unlike most females, especially the verbose Miss Leonard, Larkin spoke only what needed to be said and not to fill silence.

"You're a gem." After snatching two of the remaining sandwiches off his plate, E.V. leaned forward to place a kiss on Larkin's cheek when he remembered Miss Leonard and no telling how many others watched them. He drew back. Until he secured her father's approval, he wouldn't do anything to slight Larkin's reputation or her family's honor. "I won't be gone long."

She merely nodded again.

E.V. caught up to Miss Leonard and walked with her to her father, who stood talking to the two sawmill owners. Unlike Jake Pearson and Harvey Milton, who seemed to have found other females to dance with, David Bollen stood against the barn wall glaring, it seemed, at E.V.

Mr. Leonard stopped talking and patted E.V.'s shoulder. "Nice to see you again, son. Burr, Odell, and I were discussing how focused you've been in building up your sawmill these last two years. Took Burr four years to achieve the same production level. Took Odell, here, seven."

"Would have taken less than seven," Odell grumbled, "but my wife kept having babies. Women are a distraction."

Burr patted the shorter man's back. "While my success came in half the time, I have a fourth of the children you do. I'd gladly trade years for more sons."

Silas Leonard nodded. "I know what you mean." His gaze settled on E.V. "When a man reaches our age, he realizes how important children and grandchildren are." His eyes narrowed a bit as his gaze shifted to his daughter then back to E.V., who immediately felt a wave of wariness. "Renier, take Abby for a spin about the room. I'll talk to you after I finish with Odell and Burr."

"Sir," E.V. started, while trying not to show his aggravation at having been called *son* by a man he wanted as nothing more than a business associate, "I don't mind discussing the lumber contract right now."

"That's all good and fine," Leonard answered, "but I need to ponder the matter more. Go dance."

"Earlier David Bollen expressed interest in dancing with your daughter. He's right over—"

"David Bollen?" Miss Leonard laughed. "I treasure my toes too much to dance with that clod." Clearly oblivious to how loud her words were, giving audience to the dozen Tumwater residents around them, including Bollen, she tugged on E.V.'s arm. "Hurry, Mr. Renier, the two-step is about to start."

Feeling deceived by the Leonards, E.V. didn't move. If tomorrow he heard folks in Tumwater were wagering on him proposing to Abigail Leonard—

The sudden taste in his mouth was more unappealing than the egg salad sandwiches.

Mr. Leonard's heavy brows rose. "Listen, Renier, I don't have to give ear to what your mill can pay me. I have other options." He nodded to the center of the barn. "Get on. I wouldn't want my daughter's day ruined."

E.V. reluctantly nodded and, with Miss Leonard clinging possessively to his arm, stepped toward the dancers already lining up. Right now he was their lackey. And within reason, he would do what they asked until he secured that five-year, nonnegotiable, fully binding contract to buy lumber from Silas Leonard. The moment he did, he would distance himself from their family.

Minus Garrick Leonard. That man had twice the character the rest of his family members had.

"Before we dance," E.V. said as socially as he could despite his grim mood, "I'd like more punch."

"Why? She's gone." The cheerfulness in her tone was undeniable. Miss Leonard stopped walking in the middle of the barn and pointed to the refreshment table. "See. Larkin left, even though you kindly asked her to stay. Imagine how dishonoring she will be to her future husband when he asks her to do something. She has such a selfish, rebellious spirit. A God-fearing man would be a fool to marry her."

E.V. gritted his teeth to keep from countering her spiteful assessment of Larkin. Confident his girl was merely somewhere else in the barn, he circled slowly, seeking her yellow-and-ivory-striped gown. Once he found Larkin, he'd ensure that she knew he loved her.

Where was she? Probably with Anna and Tuck.

He looked their direction. No, they sat contented and alone near the barn's half-open east door. Tuck laughed at whatever Anna was saying, and beyond them a light rain shower glistened in the afternoon sunshine. On the chair next to Anna was Larkin's feather-decked hat. No Larkin.

"See, I told you she left."

E.V. focused on the rain dripping down the barn door's frame. While wisdom said Larkin was too proper to walk out into the rain, he knew she wouldn't have left unless she had a good reason. "I need to make sure she gets home safely." He took a step, and with both hands, Miss Leonard grabbed his arm, stopping him.

"Oh, no need for the gallantry, Mr. Renier," she said, smiling. "While you were talking to Daddy, I watched Larkin get into the Whitworth carriage. Stop worrying." She tugged on his coat sleeve. "Let's dance. Daddy is watching, and I aim to do all I can to ensure you get that contract you want."

E.V. glanced across the barn to see her father was indeed watching them. Relieved that Larkin wasn't walking home in the rain, he escorted Miss Leonard to the other dancers, minus David Bollen, who also seemed to have disappeared. Tomorrow when Larkin was at worship services, E.V. would find a way to speak to her privately. To encourage her to be patient. To wait.

No one, not Abigail Leonard or Larkin's father, would come between them.

Chapter 3

Who had stuffed her mouth with cotton? Why was the room so hot? Without even opening her eyes, which were too tired anyway, Larkin reached for her chest to remove whatever weight was on it and found several heavy quilts. She felt—

"Awful," she croaked.

"Yes, dear," Mama said softly, "you do look terrible. I imagine you must feel it, too."

Larkin opened her heavy lids to the sunlight brightening her pristine white bedroom, only to shield them from the painful light. She tried to raise her head from the many pillows behind her, but her head, neck, and shoulders ached.

Every time she felt sick, her mother made her stay in bed for a week, not by demanding it but by "medicating" her with the honey-whiskey-herb sleep aid she'd learned from her Chinook mother, who'd learned it from her mother, who learned it from the Scottish fur trader she'd married at Fort Astoria back in 1811. One drink to cure all ills.

And it didn't taste any better with additional honey or spices.

Larkin shuddered.

Mama, sitting in one of the two Queen Anne chairs near the hearth, put down her embroidery. She lifted a crystal goblet from the circular table between the chairs and brought it to Larkin. Her crimson taffeta skirt rustled as she walked, her slanted brows rising in concern.

"Drink this, dearest." She offered the half-full goblet that Larkin didn't take. She could smell the whiskey on her mother's breath.

"I'm fine," Larkin rushed to say as she kicked off the excessive blankets. Then realizing her head, neck, and shoulders didn't ache as much as they felt stiff from nonuse, she stopped kicking as abruptly as she started. Her bladder was near close to exploding. And everything in her room seemed to spin, which made her nauseous. Remembering the frigid rain she'd walked home through after leaving the wedding, she knew—*knew*—what happened after she'd returned home last night. She closed her eyes and gripped her bed to still the spinning and to think.

Was it last night?

Larkin looked to the clock on the mantel above the fireplace. She blinked until her eyes could focus. Six minutes until eleven o'clock.

She met her mother's gaze. "What day is it?"

"Thursday."

"Thursday?" She immediately regretted yelling because it only made her head ache more. Her day had just started and was turning into one of regrets. She rolled her eyes because that seemed to be the only movement that didn't make her regretful. "You medicated me again. For four and a half days. Mama! Why?"

Tears glistened in Mama's dark eyes. "To ward off *sick tumtum*."

Sickness of the body.

Larkin never had the courage to remind her mother that the actual translation of sick tumtum was sickness of the heart.

While Maire-Dove Larkin Whitworth dressed with the elegance of any society grand dame, in moments like this, Mama looked more like the superstitious native Papa had tried for years to cure her of being. He'd even had her black hair lightened to almost a blond and required she stay out of the sun so her skin would stay more cream than copper, which caused most in Tumwater to forget she was a *Metis*, mixed-blood. Then again, a good number of Washingtonians could claim a degree of Indian blood. Even Anna boasted being Dutch-Scots so she could be included in the American crucible of races.

"I'm not—I wasn't sick," Larkin clarified.

"Your gown was soaked when you arrived. Your teeth were chattering and your nose was red." Mama paused. "I heard you cough."

"But that didn't mean you needed to medicate me."

"Darling, you're feverish."

"Not from any sickness." Although, she did feel a bit dizzy from the medication—not that she'd tell her mother—and her head felt utterly heavy. Larkin removed the last blanket and unbuttoned the neckline of the ridiculously ornate nightgown she always found herself in after waking up with sick tumtum, real or imaginary. "Mama, you're smothering me again."

"I don't wish. . ." With a broken sob, Mama sat on the edge of the bed. "I am, aren't I? My heart can't bear losing you, too."

Although she figured the pain of losing a sibling couldn't be as deep as that of losing a child, Larkin understood why Mama behaved as she did. Though it had been almost five years since her brother died, the intensity of missing him hurt more than any physical pain she'd ever suffered. Some nights she'd wake thinking Sean had once again stolen into her room and invited her to join him in another adventure that would earn them a paddling, lecture, or usually both. Unlike her, nothing about Sean had been dull. Life without him still didn't feel right.

Her heart and frustration softening with compassion, she eased forward on the bed until she could rest her head on her mother's shoulder. She wrapped her arms around Mama and prayed for patience with—and peace for—her mother. . .and for herself.

Oh Lord God, I know I shouldn't have walked home in the rain, considering Mama's fears, but I couldn't bear seeing Abigail cling to E.V. as if he were hers. Either take away my love for E.V. or show me why I should continue waiting for him.

"Loving and losing someone hurts," she whispered, "but it'll be all right, Mama. I'll be all right. You're going to be all right." Someday. She kissed Mama's shoulder. "God has us in His hands. *Naika ticky maika.*"

Mama patted Larkin's hands. "I love you, too."

Larkin closed her eyes, lids still heavy from the last dose of Mama's feeling-sick drink. While she wouldn't mind sleeping off the aftereffects of the medication, she needed to deliver pies, or something else if the pies weren't baked, to the Bollen parsonage. Bringing the family food every Wednesday was the least she could do for the service and ministry they provided Tumwater.

Considering it was Thursday, not Wednesday, she doubted E.V. would be waiting to walk with her to the Bollens'.

She glanced across the room to the mirror atop her vanity table. Her hair appeared clean yet tangled from having been washed and dried as she slept; her eyes had violet bags underneath. Overall, not the best she'd looked nor the worst. Yet if she hurried to dress and didn't run into any human obstacles on the way, she could deliver food to the Bollens and still make it to the brewery in time to share a luncheon with Papa.

Yes, a brisk walk would do wonders.

Her stomach rolled. First though, she needed to empty her stomach and bladder.

Knowing something else needed to go down the commode as well, Larkin took the cordial from her mother. "We've both had enough."

Chapter 4

Still content to pine for your ladylove? I'd have thought with Mrs. Ellis's praise, the 'impeccable Mr. Tate' would have earned the right to court any lady in Tumwater." E.V. shoved the tail ends of the freshly cut pine boards into the filled wagon then smacked his gloves together to rid them of wood shavings. With a crooked grin, he patted Willum's shoulder as Willum leaned over the side of the wagon, staring absently at the wooden planks in the bed. "Well, you know what they say."

"No, what do they say?" Willum grumbled.

"If at first you don't succeed," E.V. said, resting his elbows on the wagon's side, "try and try again. That's my motto."

The "impeccable" Mr. Tate did little more than glare in response. Any frown was hidden by his bristly winter beard, yet despite his lumberjack appearance, Willum was still the grapevine telegraph's favorite bachelor. Apparently, women liked his green eyes, shoulder-length hair, and ability to construct anything from outhouses to rabbit houses to tree houses to homes almost as large as the Whitworth mansion.

Considering how much attention Willum received from women, he should've been the first between Jeremiah, Frederick, E.V., and him to marry. Would have been if things had worked out differently.

E.V. looked to the buildings opposite the mill. At the right end of the street was the whitewashed church. At the other end of Main Street was the Whitworth Brewery, one of the many businesses in town Larkin's father owned, or partially owned. E.V. didn't want to think about the companies the man owned throughout the Pacific Northwest region.

Everything Whitworth touched turned into a financial success.

After all the thirty-minute Wednesday morning visits they'd shared since E.V. began asking for Larkin's hand in marriage one-hundred-and-two-weeks ago, E.V. knew that for every financial loss, Patrick Whitworth had a dozen successes. The man would have to face losses as catastrophic as Job had to be considered a failure. Unlike E.V.'s father, who had an uncanny ability to lose the family fortune and manage two banks and a railroad into bankruptcy over the course of ten years. For all their differences, his father and Mr. Whitworth shared one commonality: faith in money to solve all woes and none in God.

As E.V. and Willum stood in silence, their breath puffed in misty clouds into the cool December air. Not quite freezing but getting there. To think almost a week ago the afternoon temperature was twenty degrees warmer.

So much for the *Farmer's Almanac*'s prediction of a warm though wet December.

"How much of a prediction," E.V. said breaking the silence, "is it for the almanac to say it'll be wet this time of year when it's always wet this time of year?" He looked into the increasing clouds in the bright yet gray sky. "We have two hours at most before the next shower."

Willum sighed loudly. "I don't see how Whitworth can reject you when you and his daughter are the most weather-obsessed people in town." He withdrew something from his heavy yet tattered woolen coat and stared wistfully at it.

Best E.V. could tell, it was a palm-sized carving of some type of animal. If Willum ever stopped building and repairing houses, he could make a living with his intricate wood carving skill alone.

Content to let their conversation die, E.V. hummed "Joy to the World" as he watched the occasional jingle-bell-decked wagon or buggy roll past. He hoped to see the mail wagon. Any day now, the sterling Gorham bell he'd ordered for Larkin for Christmas would arrive. This year he planned on making it an engagement gift instead of a gift from an anonymous admirer.

"Eric, are you ever going to stop asking to marry Larkin?"

At that moment, E.V. realized Willum was in a more surly mood than usual, because those were the only times Willum ever called him by his given name.

From the corner of his eye, E.V. glanced at Willum. He looked wounded. Broken. Love never seemed to treat Willum well.

"No," he honestly answered. "Is there something else bothering you?"

Willum's grip tightened around the carving. "What if Whitworth never agrees?"

"He will."

"Your confidence borders on foolishness. Sometimes you need to cut your losses." Willum turned to face E.V. "You should sell the mill and start a business where you don't have to be at Silas Leonard's beck and call."

"Can't," E.V. answered. "My investment partner will lose money, and I won't go back on my word. Besides, with the mammoth amount of wood you're regularly buying from me, I need another lumber supplier to keep up with the demand."

Willum shook his head in obvious disappointment—or maybe disbelief—that E.V. would choose faithfulness over the easy solution. The latter was more likely considering Willum's past. His gaze turned from E.V. and refocused on the carving he held.

E.V. breathed in the cool air. He loved Tumwater more than any other place he'd lived. "Willum, stop worrying on my behalf. The contract I'm offering Leonard makes us equals."

"He's doing his best to ensure his daughter is part of the contract."

"I realize that." *Now.* E.V. shuddered. In all his twenty-five years, he'd never felt as much a fool as he had during the last half of Frederick and Emma's wedding reception. Silas Leonard never had any intention of discussing the contract that day. No, he'd merely wanted it to look like E.V. was courting his daughter.

Willum repocketed the carving. "I need to get back to work, and you need to stop being so optimistic about life and intervene."

"Intervene in what?"

"In *that*." He motioned to the paved sidewalk on the other side of the street.

At the intersection of Main and the street leading to the Whitworth Mansion, stood Larkin, wearing a mustard-colored cape and clutching a basket with both hands. Miss Leonard, clad in a reddish-pink cape, stood near the rear of the small buckboard she often drove around town. To say the two were having a conversation would be an overstatement because only Miss Leonard was talking, and whatever she was saying made Larkin's normally straight posture slump.

Without another word to Willum, E.V. took off running.

❄

"The perfect Larkin Whitworth is pickled. I never thought I'd see the day." Abigail covered her mouth as if to hide her laughter, but Larkin still heard it, felt it, smelled every greasy bit of it. *Smelled it?*

Larkin breathed deep and grimaced. Since the linen-covered basket she carried only contained fruit from Mama's conservatory, the rancid odor had to be emanating from the white wicker picnic basket on the back of the Leonard buckboard.

"Abigail, stop. I'm not—"

Hearing footsteps crossing the bricked street, Larkin looked to her left and her vision momentarily blurred. How was it possible she felt worse after eating a soft-boiled egg and a bowl of bouillon? Now that she'd stopped walking, she felt so sleepy. She blinked until her eyesight cleared, although the movement—odd but true—sounded as loud as hammers against wood.

E.V. ran toward them, wearing denims and a woolen vest over a flannel shirt. How could he not be cold? Just looking at him made her shiver.

"I think the almanac got this December wrong," she mused aloud. "It doesn't feel warm at all."

Abigail leaned toward Larkin until their noses almost touched. "I know what a drunkard looks like and how one talks," she whispered, and her eyes seemed sad. But the familiar spiteful glee took its place so quickly Larkin knew she had imagined any sadness. The corners of Abigail's mouth indented into a smug grin. "E.V.'s finally going to see you aren't the good Christian girl you've convinced everyone you are. I win. You lose."

Larkin blinked at the surprising and eerily cheerful admission. She'd never felt they were enemies, even though Abigail had never been receptive to her overtures of friendship.

"When did we begin a competi—?"

"Mornin', ladies," E.V. said as he stopped at the back of the buckboard, approximately equal distance between them, Larkin noted. His warm breath showed in the chilly air, the tip of his nose a little red.

Thrilled to end the confusing conversation with Abigail, Larkin tilted her head, which wasn't any less heavy since she woke up an hour ago, and studied him. Something was different. His short yellow hair was still sun-bleached to almost white at the tips because he never wore a hat. His eyes were still a lovely shade—medium brown with golden rays in the iris and possibly some orange. Rather similar in color to the vile honey-whiskey cordial she had dumped out despite Mama's protest.

He wasn't as stunningly attractive as Mr. Tate, but Larkin liked E.V.'s square-jawed, dimpled-chinned, less-than-shining handsomeness. Still, what was different about him?

"Your face is bristly," she muttered.

E.V. nodded. "I didn't shave this morning."

"Why not?" she blurted.

"I hate shaving so I only do it on Sundays, Wednesdays, and special occasions like my friends' weddings. My skin is sensitive." He looked at her oddly. "Are you all right?"

Larkin smiled and nodded and hoped that was enough of an answer—only she nodded too much. The pounding in her head increased, causing the food Cook had claimed would lessen the aftereffects of the cordial to roll in her stomach.

This was the worst Mama had ever medicated her. She needed to leave before she lost her breakfast, yet propelled by curiosity, she asked, "Then why do you shave at all?"

"Larkin Whitworth!" Abigail sniped in her irritatingly shrill voice. "I can't believe you asked Mr. Renier something so personal." She stepped closer to E.V. and touched his sleeve. "Mr. Renier, let me apologize for my dear friend. I hate to say this, but she's been imbibing."

"I haven't," and "She has?" came out in unison.

E.V. stepped around Abigail to face Larkin. "You don't look well."

"I'm fine," she muttered then realized that was a lie, because she didn't feel the least bit fine. Abigail was correct in that she was pickled—or at least suffering the after effects—but it wasn't intentional, and to clarify everything would mean sharing Mama's problem. Larkin would never bring shame to her mother. Never. Not even to protect her own reputation. "I'm sorry, I must go." She pointed to the parsonage. "The Bollens need fruit, and I don't feel. . ."

Leaving her words to hang in the air, Larkin walked away slowly. She kept her pace steady despite the unevenness of the sidewalk, the churning of her stomach, and the perspiration on her forehead.

For as cold as December was, somehow it had grown as warm as July.

❄

"Larkin's so pickled she doesn't make sense." Miss Leonard wrapped her red-gloved hand around E.V.'s arm. "It's a shame, you know, for her to behave like this, but it's best to know the truth." She gasped and covered her mouth. "Imagine marrying her and then learning about her preference for strong drink."

E.V. stayed focused on Larkin. She'd faintly smelled of whiskey. Because of his past before his salvation, he knew the scent well. Yet something was wrong. His girl wasn't a drunkard or even an occasional imbiber. During the fish fry Anna and Tuck held to celebrate their one-year anniversary, Larkin had shared with him her frustration and embarrassment over her father's ownership of the brewery and had asked E.V. to join her in praying he would sell the business.

E.V. took a breath. He felt ill trying to sort it all out.

"Mr. Renier, you are looking a bit pale. Would you like something to eat?" The concern on Miss Leonard's face wasn't the least bit believable.

"Something is wrong with Larkin."

Miss Leonard's blue eyes widened, mouth gaped open. She looked practically peeved he'd make such an obvious statement. "Good gracious, she's a drunkard. What else would explain her absence about town the past four days?" She gave a dispassionate shrug. "I hate to be the one to share this with you, but this isn't the first time Larkin's breath has smelled of whiskey. However, it is the first time I've seen her inebriated."

Still unconvinced, E.V.'s gaze slid back to Larkin. Her stride faltered. Stopping at the lamppost in front of the milliner's shop, she rested her basket on the ground and wiped her brow.

Someone stopped by on horseback, but she waved him off. Likely with a *no, thank you, I'm fine* response.

When he said nothing, Miss Leonard continued, "Hearing news of this is going to shatter her parents' hearts. For the sake of Larkin's reputation, they'll have to move, which will grieve me greatly because I value"—her voice cracked—"no, *treasure,* our friendship."

E.V. shook his head slowly in hopes of ridding it of his confusion. This wasn't his Larkin. Through his friendship with Tuck, Frederick, and Willum, E.V. had learned a true friend—a man of God—trusts what he knows of another's character. That's what they had done for E.V., even when the gossips at the university claimed the worst about him. While the evidence appeared to paint Larkin disfavorably, E.V. knew the good and right thing to do was trust the character Larkin had demonstrated prior to this moment.

"Mr. Renier, I see how disturbing this must be. I'm meeting Daddy and Garrick for lunch. Usually I drive alone"—she looked to the sky—"but with this weather, I know Daddy would prefer I have an escort."

E.V. blinked. She was always driving the buckboard around town alone.

She looked hopeful. "I've packed enough lunch for four."

"Something's wrong with Larkin," he repeated, removing Miss Leonard's grasp of him. "She needs help." He took one step before she snatched at his arm again.

"But—I—well, this morning I overheard Daddy telling Garrick he was ready to make a decision on the contract."

E.V. glanced from Miss Leonard to Larkin, still leaning against the garland-and-ribbon-decorated lamppost, now using her hat to fan her face. Miss Leonard could be speaking the truth about what she overheard, but after her—and her father's—performance at the wedding reception, he'd grown more wary of believing anything that came out of their mouths.

Willing to risk that Miss Leonard was bluffing, E.V. jerked free of her hold. "Pickled or not, Larkin needs help." *My help,* he wanted to add, but doing so would mean wasting another moment talking to a woman he had no interest in talking to.

For the second time that day, E.V. took off running.

Chapter 5

I feel poisoned." The words had barely left her mouth when Larkin felt her feet separate from the ground. She dropped her hat and reached for the lamppost. The tips of her fingers brushed the velvet ribbon encircling the metal post, but she couldn't grab hold.

"Relax, Miss Whitworth," E.V. said as two widow ladies new to town stopped next to them. He settled her in his arms. "I've got you."

"Why?"

"You're unwell so I'm taking you home." As he said it, one widow nudged the other with her elbow and grinned.

Home? She couldn't go home yet. She had to fulfill her duty, and she was not about to disappoint the Bollens. "I must deliver the fruit. I always—"

"Miss Whitworth."

At the sound of her name, she stopped squirming and turned to see who'd spoken.

"I'll see the good reverend gets the basket," the milliner, Mr. Dudley, offered as he stood in the opened doorway to his shop. He nodded at E.V. "Y'got her?"

E.V. adjusted her in his arms. "Yes sir."

One of the widows picked up Larkin's hat. "We'll take this to your father, dear, since we're headed that way to get his investment advice." And they hurried off, oblivious to Larkin's, "No, that's all right, I can carry it" response.

She sighed.

E.V. started walking. "It's only a hat."

"I know, but I seem to have a habit of losing my hats. No one returns them to me, so my theory is Papa pays a finder's fee."

"Then I ought to turn in the two in my office."

"You should, and then let me know how well he pays."

Content in the arms of the one who held her, Larkin rested her head against E.V.'s chest as he walked up the shaded alley between the milliner's shop and the barber's. She'd often dreamed of being held by him, but, somehow, she'd never imagined this scenario.

"E.V., how did Mr. Dudley know who I was taking the fruit to?"

"Sweetheart, you always deliver food to the Bollens on Wednesday."

"But this is Thursday."

"So it is."

"I also take food to Mrs. Ellis and to, umm, to other people in town," she finished. Really, her head hurt too much for her to think straight. Only—she felt like she was thinking straighter than she ever had before. And hearing better, too. To hear his calm, gentle, well-educated voice say *sweetheart* again, she asked, "What did you call me?"

Thunder rolled overhead, yet Larkin could have sworn this time he said *mine*.

And the pounding of her pulse seemed to beat all too perfectly. For a moment everything became nothing but them.

"E.V., I—"

"Shhh, rest," he said softly. His brown eyes held such kindness and love that she'd be a fool to doubt his devotion.

Larkin, again resting her head against his rough work vest, closed her eyes and listened to his steady heartbeat. Someday she'd tell him exactly how she felt. When the time was right. Magical. Lovely. When he didn't so much smell like sawdust. When she wasn't medicated. And then he would say he loved her, too, and would kiss her for the first time, and it would be spectacular. It would be the kiss to end all kisses. No! Even better.

Imagining the moment, Larkin felt her lips curve.

It would be the kiss to *begin* all kisses. Which was completely absurd of her to think as *the kiss to end all kisses,* but she was too deliriously happy to care about being logical.

E.V.'s pace increased, and Larkin opened her eyes in time to see him turn the corner to the back alley that led to the tree-lined street leading to her parents' house.

"I'll get you home as quickly as I can," he said between breaths. He glanced around as if he were looking for someone. "Not many people out right now, I'm guessing, because it's about to rain. Smell the breeze."

She breathed deep. "Sawdust."

"Interesting. I smell whiskey." His intense gaze met hers. "Larkin, what's going on?"

"I want to explain, I truly do, but I need you to trust me."

"I do," he said without hesitation.

And she believed him. Feeling warm and cozy and content despite the queasiness of her stomach, Larkin focused on his bristled jaw. It'd probably scratch when she kissed him.

"Why do you shave on Sundays and Wednesdays since it bothers your skin?" she asked as casually as she could. The pounding of her pulse was nothing like she'd ever felt before. While the beautiful overcast sky was brimming with the promise of rain, the world around them was bright. Magical.

Lovely.

His grin was small but there, and his eyes glinted as when one had a secret too amazing to keep hidden. "I have important meetings those days with two very important people in my life."

"You see me on Sundays."

"And Wednesdays."

"Who else do you meet with on Sunday?"

"The Body of Christ."

"Oh." Dreading he would say Abigail, yet ready to hear the worst, she asked, "Who else do you meet with every Wednesday?"

"I—" He paused and his grin and amusement ended. "I can't share. I want to, but I need you to trust me, too."

Larkin nipped on her bottom lip. Did she trust him? She wanted to. She had for two years, but if he loved her, why hadn't he asked to court her?

I'm impatient, Lord. That's what it comes down to.

"I do trust you." Saying the words sealed them in her heart, chasing away the doubt she'd struggled with. She *did* trust him.

He nodded. "Then be patient."

As E.V. turned the corner from the back alley to the street, Larkin noticed her house in her peripheral view. They'd be home before she could sing the first stanza of—of—well, of any song that she could remember if she could think of anything besides how sick she still felt from her toes to her eyelashes. Yet she also felt wonderful. . .and free to be honest with him.

Time to be a Ruth and motivate her Boaz into action.

She reached forward and touched—poked, really—his bristly cheek. "I. Love. You." While she meant it to sound a bit more melodically romantic, she was happy to finally say the words. She wiped the increased perspiration from her forehead with her sleeve. "Would you like to know something else?"

Smiling broadly, E.V. stepped onto the bricked path dividing the front lawn. As he walked, the sound of his boots on the pavement grew in volume. "I'm not sure how you can top that, but I'll listen."

"I think—" she started, but then he stumbled on an uneven brick.

She bobbled.

He adjusted his hold of her.

That's when she offered an apologetic grin. "I think I'm going to be sick."

And she was.

Chapter 6

Fiddling with the middle button on the black waistcoat he wore over a white shirt, E.V. sat in the chair across from Mrs. Whitworth as they waited for Larkin to join them in the formal parlor decorated in holly, ivy, myriad red candles, and bundles of fragrant cinnamon sticks. The union suit he wore kept his chest modestly covered, so he wasn't sure why Mrs. Whitworth had given him the waistcoat. The dress shirt with his denims and work boots was absurd enough. If he'd buttoned the upturned collar, the contrast would have been even worse.

He was thankful Mrs. Whitworth omitted giving him a tie.

E.V. looked around the oversized parlor that was really more of an elaborate Victorian salon, with its five distinct sitting areas and Steinway square grand piano in the far corner. Two years ago at Larkin's birthday party, he'd gazed about the empty room, from the handcrafted fireplace mantel to the crystal chandelier hanging from the middle of the fourteen-foot ceiling, and debated if talking to Larkin—whom he'd only known as *the pretty Whitworth girl* at the time—was worth enduring an evening of dancing in a home that reminded him so much in appearance to the mansion he'd spent his childhood in.

Each home after that one had grown significantly smaller. Now he lived in a one-room apartment next to his office.

Having gone from riches to rags and having learned to enjoy freedom from the trappings of wealth, he hadn't been too sure he wanted to follow the attraction he felt for a young woman used to a life of luxury. Her beauty drew him in, but her passion for Jesus and for graciously serving others had caught him hook, line, and sinker.

Two years later, he'd turned his sawmill into the most profitable one in Tumwater. Beyond marrying Larkin, E.V. had no grander ambitions.

He didn't want to own businesses and companies throughout the Pacific Northwest that consumed his every waking hour. He merely wanted to prove himself to Larkin's wealth-focused father so he could begin a life with the woman he loved. After an honest day's work, he wanted to spend his evenings and weekends with his wife and children. Not in his office mulling over stock reports.

Yet here he was, sitting in Patrick Whitworth's chair, in Patrick Whitworth's grand parlor, wearing Patrick Whitworth's shirt and waistcoat, while waiting to share tea and crumpets with the man's beloved wife and daughter, while his own scrubbed-clean shirt and vest hung next to Larkin's cape to dry beside the kitchen stove.

It wasn't that he disliked Whitworth.

He merely didn't want to become him.

The ornate grandfather clock in the front foyer bonged once.

Mrs. Whitworth glanced over the shoulder of her red taffeta gown to the two doors on the east wall—one led to the library and the other to a water closet, but which was which E.V. couldn't remember. Truth be told, since moving to Tumwater, he couldn't remember exchanging more than a dozen words with Larkin's mother.

"I suppose we can begin without Larkin." Mrs. Whitworth's hands shook as she filled E.V.'s teacup. "Why is it I find conversation easier in a crowd than with one person?"

Empathizing, E.V. admitted, "I'd say it's because with one person there is an invitation to intimacy which is often intimidating. In a crowd, there's freedom for obscurity. I'll admit I've sought the safety of anonymity." He knew Larkin did as well.

Mrs. Whitworth's head tilted in a manner much like Larkin's. Whereas her face was leaner and more rectangular than Larkin's oval face, E.V. could imagine the children he and Larkin might eventually have looking like her. Only their blond hair could be natural, unlike Mrs. Whitworth's chemically altered color.

"Are you in love with my daughter?" she finally asked.

He leaned forward in his chair to claim his teacup and saucer off the marble-topped coffee table. "You already know the answer to that, don't you?"

The edges of her wide mouth curved. "Patrick has told me of your conversations. Two years is a long time to remain faithful despite the rejections. My husband is less inclined to view your behavior as romantic." With a sad smile, she motioned to the crumpets. "Eat."

While he did, she told him stories of Larkin's childhood. She asked him if he knew who'd contracted the construction of the large house Willum Tate was building, and E.V. answered vaguely. From there, they spoke of politics, the due date of the Tuckers' baby, the approaching anniversary of his parents' deaths, the Pearson-Corrigan wedding she missed attending, church socials and the quilt auction she was organizing in the spring, the growing popularity of baseball (and how much both despised the sport), and finally the family's upcoming Christmas soiree, which E.V. did not have an invitation to. If he had, he'd have to shave and, well, that was that.

She had laughed easily.

He had laughed as much as he did when he was with Larkin.

Then she vowed to call him Eric.

He grimaced. "I prefer E.V."

"I realize sharing your father's name is something you wish to forget." All amusement left her tone. "Your heritage made you who you are but doesn't have to define who you will be. Besides, I like Eric better." She gave him a look that said it was pointless to argue.

That's when E.V. realized this was likely a test to win her approval. More importantly, he realized from their conversation how passionately Mrs. Whitworth loved her husband and daughter. . .and how much she still grieved the loss of the son whose name she never mentioned.

"I won't take Larkin from Tumwater," he promised. "I won't take her away from you."

Her eyes filled with tears.

Since Larkin still hadn't returned to the room, E.V. lowered his voice and whispered conspiratorially, "How about a pact? You call me Eric until your first grandson is born, then I go back to being E.V. That way I can honor my heritage by giving the world an Eric Valentin Renier IV, and still honor you."

She raised a hand to cover her mouth, and though she said nothing, he knew her answer.

Mountain Christmas Brides

"What's this?" barked a voice E.V. knew all too well.

As Mrs. Whitworth wiped the tears off her cheeks, E.V. looked to his right.

With the extravagant angel-and-golden-feather-decorated Christmas tree in the foyer behind him, Patrick Whitworth stood in the parlor's arched entrance beneath the mistletoe. He clenched his black Bowler hat in one hand and his greatcoat in the other, rain from both items dripping on the wood floor. His red tie was the lone bit of color on his lean frame. Contrary to their meeting yesterday morning, the few strands of brown hair that remained on the top of his head were not neatly combed to the side.

He tossed his wet items to a silent, hovering manservant who quickly scurried away.

Clearly Whitworth had gotten word about E.V. carrying Larkin home. And though his cheeks were rosy, he looked not a bit jolly over the news.

Chapter 7

Hearing Papa's voice, Larkin woke with a jolt. She'd fallen asleep against the library door as she'd waited for Mama and E.V. to stop talking. She scrambled to her feet then smoothed the navy fringe on the bodice and three-quarters-length sleeves of her pale yellow gown. Thankfully her stomach had settled, her eyes no longer burned, and the vertigo was gone. However, the mortification she felt over what had happened—

Only a man blindly in love would still wish to court a woman who'd spewed eggs and broth on his chest.

"I cannot believe I did that," she groaned.

Knowing the embarrassment she felt added needed color to her cheeks, Larkin gently opened the door leading to the parlor.

Papa, E.V., and Mama immediately looked her way from where they sat in the west end of the room.

Only E.V. stood.

With a slight grin strained by the tension she felt in every nerve, she tried to think of a logical excuse for having left Mama and E.V. alone for the last—she glanced at the clock— *oh dear*—hour and twelve minutes.

Sometimes the best explanation was no explanation.

She hoped.

As slowly as she could traverse the large rectangular room without making it look like she was stalling, Larkin moved toward the sitting area nearest the double-door entrance to the front foyer.

With one leg crossed over the other, Papa sat in the second chair opposite Mama's place on the settee. The angle at which he sat gave him a clear view of E.V.—whose chair was a good three feet from Papa's—without having to turn to look at him. While the elbow of Papa's left arm rested on the curved armrest, two of his fingers on his right hand tapped his chin. His thinking position.

His *you're about to get a lecture on decorum* position.

Because of the heavy brown mustache covering his upper lip, Larkin couldn't tell if Papa's handsome face held a frown or a grin. Not that she expected a grin.

While E.V. wasn't smiling either, he didn't seem intimidated by Papa's presence, but neither was he as at ease as he'd been talking to Mama.

"Oh, how nice, tea and crumpets." Larkin sat on the empty side of the settee, smoothing the fringe on her skirt while E.V. resumed his seat.

Mama filled a teacup and handed it to her. "How was your nap, darling?"

Not at all surprised by her mother's forthrightness, Larkin casually took a sip of her tea while raising her eyebrows as if to say—*nap?*

"Your cheek has the imprint of the carvings on the library door." Mama lifted a plate off the tea tray. "Crumpet?"

Larkin shook her head. She shuddered at the thought of putting anything into her stomach for the next twenty-four hours.

Mama put the tray down. "They're here if you change your mind. Eric enjoyed them."

At Mama's use of E.V.'s given name, Larkin looked at E.V. He hated being called by his father's name. E.V. shrugged as if the usage was of no import.

Papa cleared his throat.

Dreading the lecture but knowing Papa would wait until they were alone because he would never—*never*—air their conflicts in public, Larkin met his gaze and smiled softly. She said nothing. This was the moment where E.V. would show himself to be the true hero he was and ask Papa for her hand in marriage. Right here. In the parlor. In the very room where she and E.V. had met over a tray of spilled cookies.

Papa would then agree to the marriage because he loved her, and he wanted her to be happy. Mama would cry yet be happy. And Larkin would cry, too, because she was finally going to marry the man she loved.

All was about to be well with the world.

Papa stopped tapping his chin. "Larkin, are you in love with this man?"

Realizing her hand trembled with nervous anticipation, she rested her teacup and saucer on the tea tray. "Yes sir."

"Have you been cavorting with him?"

"No sir."

"Would you elope with him if I refused to allow you to marry?"

Confused by his line of questioning, Larkin looked to E.V., who leaned forward in his chair, his fingers steepled together, his eyes intent on her face. What did he want her to say? Yes? No? Maybe? It depends? Give me time to pray over it?

Panic welling within, she looked to Mama.

Her mother's dark eyes pleaded with her to say no.

Could she?

Help me, Lord. How do I choose between love for my parents and love for E.V.?

"Stop." E.V.'s voice was so soft, Larkin wasn't sure she'd heard him. "Stop," he repeated, rising to his feet. "I won't let you force her to choose. I'll carry the burden."

Papa's jaw shifted yet he said nothing. He didn't have to. The narrowing of his eyes conveyed his dislike of E.V., which confused Larkin all the more. How could Papa despise someone he barely knew? Someone he'd barely had half a dozen conversations with?

E.V. inclined his head to Mama. "Mrs. Whitworth, thank you for the hospitality." His gaze settled on Larkin. "Miss Whitworth, I pray all will go well with you in your future endeavors. Merry Christmas to you all."

With that, he strolled from the parlor and out the front door, allowing a chill to steal into the room.

Larkin stood. "Papa. Why?"

"Renier only cares about your inheritance."

"He loves me. Me!"

"Has he ever told you?"

She opened her mouth but didn't answer. He had never said the words, but—

"You're money to men like him," he said coolly. "He'll forget you soon enough."

She shook her head. "No. E.V. is faithful and kind and patient and. . .I will never stop believing God will work out things for us to be together."

Papa's fingers tapped his chin again. "So you choose him?"

"I—"

Mama grabbed Larkin's hand, silencing her. "Patrick, please. Don't do this to our family. I can't bear losing another child—I can't. Please make this right."

Papa stood and, without another word, followed E.V.'s path out the front door.

❄

Willum was right. He should cut his losses. Rain soaked through every layer of clothing as he walked away from the Whitworth mansion.

Hearing a door slam somewhere behind him, E.V. stopped in the middle of the street, turned around, and rolled his eyes. Wind gusts were the only thing he could think of that would make the moment worse. Or an audience. Actually *that* would be worse.

Whitworth approached with the fervor of a man on a mission. "Stop proposing!"

"What?"

"You heard me." Whitworth halted before E.V. and looked him directly in the eye—an easy task since they were nearly the same height. "I will never give my permission," he growled.

"Why not?" E.V. growled right back, having simply had enough of being patient with the man he'd thought would be his father-in-law someday.

"You don't have the character to be faithful to her in the tough times."

"I don't—" E.V. bit back his angry retort.

Knowing yelling wasn't the way to bring peace between them, he drew in a breath. *Jesus living through me, Jesus living through me.*

Focused and calm, he said, "After all the conversations we've had, how is it you *still* don't know my character? I know yours. I know that Patrick Whitworth has one of the most astute financial minds in the country. He is loyal, fair, judicious, yet will take educated risks and selflessly help his business associates prosper, too. You love your family, routinely ignore advances from other women, give generously to the community and charities throughout the Pacific Northwest, carry guilt over your son's death, work too much, and are too self-possessed and arrogant to humble yourself before God."

Whitworth's mouth clamped into a thin line. In anger? Shame? Resentment that E.V. knew all that about him?

E.V. wasn't sure and, to be frank, at that moment he couldn't have cared less. "What do I have to do to prove myself to you?"

"You are your father's son." Whitworth gave him a slit-eyed look. "You can't change that."

E.V. flinched. How many times had he accused himself? Were it not for his friends' intervention and determination to pray him to salvation, he would still be following his father's path of debauchery and greed. Yet, as the rain poured down on them, he suddenly saw his past more clearly. Mrs. Whitworth was right.

"Sir, my heritage made me who I am today, good and bad," E.V. said with a peace that could only be God-supplied, "but Jesus living in and through me, not my heritage, defines who I am and who I will be. My sawmill has grown. I'm on the verge of securing a large supplier, and I don't need Larkin's inheritance. I can provide for all her needs."

Whitworth stared in silence. Then he slowly shook his head. "This isn't about money."

E.V. gaped at the man. Whitworth lived and breathed money. "For two years, I worked day and night to build my mill and prove my work ethic to you. For two years, I've allowed you to harass me with questions about my past, and I've respected your demands and honored your rule of not telling Larkin exactly how I feel. If money is not the issue, then what's this about?"

"God may have changed you," Whitworth answered furiously, "but He can't—won't—*hasn't* changed my wife. And now, like her brother, Larkin is showing the same weakness for—" His shoulders slumped, his voice lost its intensity. "I don't hate you. I love my daughter and wife too much to risk trusting you to protect our family honor when your reputation is on the line. They're mine to protect."

"Give me a chance to prove—"

"No, Renier. This is my burden to carry alone."

Unsure of how to respond—how could he when he had no idea what weakness Whitworth was alluding to—E.V. wiped his brow, which did little good because the rain continued to run down his face.

"I don't hate you," Whitworth repeated. "Saying no to you is easier for me." With that, he turned and walked back to his house.

E.V. turned as well. Each step back to his mill took him farther away from Larkin.

Cut his losses. That's what he should do.

Chapter 8

You and a guest are cordially invited to...

In the solitude of his office, E.V. stared at the gold letters on the embossed invitation to the Whitworth's annual Christmas soiree on Saturday, December 20. Three days away. Music. Dancing. Food.

Larkin.

Not everyone in Tumwater attended, because not everyone was invited, and the list varied each year. To receive an invitation put one on the *People Significant to the Whitworth Family* list that included business associates, local clergy, politicians, law officials, close friends, family. No one under the age of sixteen allowed.

Dress: formal.

His first year in Tumwater, E.V. attended at the personal invitation of Mr. Whitworth to Tuck, Frederick, Willum, and himself as they were leaving Larkin's nineteenth birthday party. By the time the date of the soiree arrived two months later, he'd already asked Whitworth twice for Larkin's hand in marriage. At that time, Whitworth had still been cordial to him.

Last year he never received an invitation.

What was he to make of this year's invitation? Even more intriguing, who sent it? Larkin? Her mother? Why write *no reply necessary* on the back?

For the third (or eighth) time since the invitation arrived in his office last week, a few days after Whitworth confronted him in the rain, E.V. tossed it in the wooden milk crate he used to collect wastepaper for kindling. This time he wasn't taking it back out. And he wasn't attending. His heart hurt too much.

Instead, he'd help Willum cut and piece the intricate first-floor crown molding demanded by the increasingly particular owner of the house Willum was building. At the rate the owner was making changes to the design, Willum would be an old man before he'd finish building the house. See—now *that* was a situation for cutting one's losses.

E.V. grabbed his pencil off the accounting book and re-examined the month's numbers. If he sold out his shares in the mill, he could take his profits and move to anywhere he desired, do any job he wanted. He'd find a nice girl and settle down and have a bevy of children. And a dog—no, dogs. A bevy of them, too—as many as he had children, so they'd each have their own and no reason to fight over who the dog loved best.

Frustrated with his absurd thoughts, E.V. dropped his pencil. Elbows on his desk, he rested his forehead against his fingertips. *What do I do, Lord? Where should I go?*

"Wait." The word whispered again across his soul, as it had each time he'd prayed for guidance.

Could he wait? Could he stay in Tumwater?

More aptly, *how* could he stay now that the grapevine telegraph claimed Whitworth had given Harvey Milton permission to court Larkin? Harvey Milton, Esq., the very lawyer who had yet to win a case. Harvey Milton, who for the last year, had courted and stopped courting—before starting and stopping again—Miss Abigail Leonard. Every shop E.V. entered, even before and after worship services this past Sunday, someone had been talking about the news.

If that wasn't frustrating enough, the number of women who ceased talking when E.V. approached was making him wonder if someone had overheard him and Whitworth in the rain. He didn't remember seeing anyone out on the street watching them.

But in a town this size. . .with a gossip chain this strong. . .

In the two years he'd lived in Tumwater, he'd never heard anyone—except Miss Leonard—say an unkind word about Larkin. Now the descriptions ranged from princess to imposter to hypocrite to drunkard to Jezebel. The latter occurred when he overheard two of his workers repeating that Larkin had been "leading the boss man on with the goal of making Milton jealous."

With Tuck's wife, Anna, on bed rest because of sporadic contractions, only cranky ol' Mrs. Ellis remained to champion Larkin's reputation, which did little good, because Mrs. Ellis was the least-liked person in town. That left him. As Reverend Bollen had advised, telling people they shouldn't gossip silenced the talk but did nothing to restore the damage to Larkin's reputation. How could E.V. come to her defense if doing so would only cause her father to believe he was plotting a nefarious plan to kidnap Larkin and hold her for ransom? Or elope. Either amounted to the same in Whitworth's eyes. Why add fuel to the gossips' fire?

Doomed if he did, doomed if he didn't.

"Ugh," E.V. groaned. He snapped his pencil and tossed it in the trash. Then he sat listening to the saws buzz and his workers yell orders to each other. And sat. And sat.

The door to his office opened. Willum stepped inside, unbuttoning his winter coat. His bright-eyed gaze fell to the trash crate before centering on E.V. "You busy?"

"Yes—no," he corrected. "Something wrong with your order?"

"No. It's all loaded." Willum motioned to the doorway. "Thought I'd warn you, Silas Leonard just arrived with a manila envelope and his daughter." Removing his work gloves, he stepped to the enclosed stove in the corner of the room to warm his hands. "Saw a few snowflakes earlier. Think we'll get any accumulation?"

Uninterested in discussing weather, E.V. leaned back in his chair, gripped the V-edges of his tweed work vest, and stared at the remaining hat of Larkin's he hadn't had delivered to her at home with her father's shirt and waistcoat. He wasn't ready to part with the only tangible object of hers that he could hold. Larkin hadn't looked at him Sunday. Neither had she looked at Milton. Whatever day she was delivering food to the Bollens wasn't Wednesday.

No, today E.V. had delivered his customary half ham alone.

Two years without declaring himself to her.

Two years being a model of propriety.

Two years of stifling his desire to kiss her senseless.

E.V. rested his head against the back of his chair and grimaced. Two years of being a faithful yet utter fool.

Bam!

E.V. flinched and looked at his surroundings. He then glared at Willum. "Why is there a log on my desk?"

Willum shrugged. "I couldn't reach the back of your head to knock sense into you. Go sign the contract with Leonard. Then you'll at least have half of what you think you want in life."

❄

"You want *what?*" Feeling his brows draw together in stunned disbelief at what had been asked of him, E.V. stopped reading the contract and looked at Silas Leonard, who stood with his back to the door of the mill's main entrance. With the saws running and workers scrambling to load and unload the machines, this waiting area was the quietest part of the building besides his office.

"Son, it'll be one last favor," Leonard explained, grinning and putting his arm around the shoulders of his daughter's some-shade-of-red (or maybe pink) cloak that matched the bonnet she clenched with both hands.

Now that E.V. noticed what she wore, he realized in all the times he'd seen Miss Leonard since Emma and Frederick's wedding, she'd been wearing either red or pink or a shade thereof. Much like the way Larkin wore clothes in one color spectrum for an entire year—something he had never pondered the reason behind. Some of a woman's mysteries needed to stay mysterious. Though he knew this was Larkin's yellow year.

Why would Miss Leonard want to follow the behavior of someone she clearly hated? Did she want to be—

E.V. looked the young woman over and felt his frown deepen. Her blond hair was pinned in a simple bun at the back of her neck while loose strands grazed her cheekbones, similar to Larkin's preferred coiffure. The style actually made Miss Leonard's Caesar-like nose seem less—no, no it didn't. Her nose was still too large for her face.

"Renier!"

At the sound of his name, E.V. refocused on Silas Leonard. "Why?" he couldn't help asking.

"Abby can't get a husband on her own. She lost her chance with Milton now that Whitworth bought him for his daughter."

Miss Leonard's eyes widened in obvious mortification at her father's words. "Daddy, I never favored Mr. Milton. I like—"

"Hush, girl. Stop making everything about you."

E.V. glanced over his shoulder at Willum watching them unabashedly as he leaned against the doorframe. Based on Willum's smug grin, E.V. didn't want to wager on what his friend was thinking. He turned back to Leonard.

"No," he answered with complete assurance in his decision. "I will not escort your daughter to the Whitworth soiree in exchange for a lumber contract. Nor will I marry her in exchange for one."

"I'm only asking you to escort Abby to the party," Leonard countered. "If you want to marry her, that's your own decision. I won't mind though. The contract price is more than fair, especially if you want Abby, too."

"Fair? For who?" E.V. pointed at Miss Leonard. "For her? How do you think your daughter feels about being a bargaining chip in contract negotiations? She's not a commodity you can sell or trade. Show some respect."

Leonard's nostrils flared as he stepped closer to E.V. in an obvious attempt to intimidate with his Goliath size. "You insult me, boy."

While E.V. never considered himself prone to sarcasm, this was one moment he truly wanted to respond with—*you think so?*

Instead, he wisely responded with, "Sir, I would be honored to sign a contract with you, because my mill could use your lumber, but not at the expense of my self-respect or your daughter's." He returned the contract unsigned. "Have a Merry Christmas."

Leonard stormed outside. "Abigail, come!"

Miss Leonard didn't move. She looked at E.V. with such longing in her eyes that he knew, in his attempt to defend her honor, he'd unwittingly earned her devotion.

"I, uh," he stuttered, trying to think of some response.

A smile spread across her face. She wrapped her arms around him and hugged him as if she would never let go, and then she burst into tears.

Unsure of what else to do, E.V. awkwardly patted the top of her head. "There, there, it'll be all right."

"Oh Mr. Renier, no one has ever loved me like you do."

"Me?" Stiffening, E.V. felt the color drain from his face. "Miss Leonard, I, uh, you, uh. . ."

Her father yelled for her again, and she complied this time, darting out the mill's front entrance, saving E.V. from further awkwardness.

Within moments of the door closing, Willum slapped E.V.'s back. "I suppose I'll give you this instead of burning it like I'd planned." He stuffed a crumpled envelope in E.V.'s palm. "I read what she wrote, and I'm not sorry." Willum stepped to the door and gripped the handle then stopped and turned around. "E.V.?"

"Yeah?" he answered, meeting Willum's intense gaze.

"Mrs. Ellis doesn't take kindly to rejections."

Chapter 9

B *ury the booty, hide the corpse, bury the booty, hide the corpse,* Larkin repeated over and over as she carried the last two rum bottles securely against her chest with one hand while holding her black boots in the other. She wasn't too sure why the childhood chant her brother had made up resurfaced from her memory. After all, she hadn't thought of it in the last five years since Sean had died. Yet whenever he'd invited her on his nightly escapades, she'd repeat the words to calm her nervousness. He, not her, had been the bold, courageous, adventuresome one in the family.

As she twisted the knob on the kitchen door, her heart pounded. *Click.* The sound of the latch echoed throughout the dark room laden with food and serving items for the Christmas soiree. Larkin held her breath and waited for Cook or one of the maids to stagger into the kitchen and demand to know what she was up to at precisely 1:31 on a Saturday morning. *No good* would have been Sean's honest answer.

Hearing nothing, she opened the door enough to ease into the chilly night, and then she slowly pulled it closed behind her.

Seven trips and yet undiscovered. After days of searching the house, she was confident she'd found all the hidden liquor bottles and Mama's sick tumtum medication.

Larkin breathed a sigh of relief, although the action did little to settle her rapid pulse. So she breathed even deeper until her breath was no longer ragged and her chest didn't feel as if it would explode.

Then. . .she went to work.

Within minutes, she had her boots on and black riding cloak tied tight, the hood pulled securely down over her head. She wedged the bottles with the others in the wheelbarrow then covered them with a couple of horse blankets to dampen the sound of any glass clinking against glass. The cloud cover kept the moonlight from exposing her work.

Determined to accomplish her task as quickly as possible, Larkin quietly pushed the wheelbarrow down the path leading to Mrs. Ellis's property at the end of the street. The tip of her nose already felt frozen. *Please, Lord, please,* she prayed, but for what she begged, she didn't know.

Her heart ached. Her soul grieved. She felt so. . .alone.

❄

"Dig a little quicker," Mrs. Ellis ordered, raising the lamp to shine where E.V. was digging. "I'm freezing out here." She leaned on the butt of the shotgun she held in her left hand. "Make the hole deeper, too. Don't want no varmints digging where they shouldn't."

E.V. held back his grumbles and continued to shovel dirt. He wasn't about to point out that any additional varmints on her densely wooded plot were opportunities to add pelts to the multicolored fur coat she wore over a calico gown hemmed short enough to show the tops of her U.S. Army-issued boots. Likely her dead husband's. Husband one or husband two—E.V. wasn't about to ask in case it would incite her wrath.

This was the first time he'd been on her property and not been shot at.

Thankful the night was void of moisture and breeze, E.V. jammed the shovel again into the soft ground. Why dig a hole in the middle of a walking path?

"Care to tell me what the hole is for, ma'am?" he asked, adding another scoop of dirt to the shin-high mound next to him.

"Nope," came the clipped response. "I suggest you stop talking before I start disliking your worthless hide again."

He opened his mouth, intent on reminding her that other than his lone question she had done all of the talking, when the sweetest voice he hadn't heard in the last sixteen days interrupted their conversation.

"E.V.? What are you doing here?"

E.V. swiveled around and almost dropped the shovel. Larkin stood not five yards away, with a wheelbarrow of all things. Even in the shadowy darkness she took his breath away.

"I invited him," Mrs. Ellis answered crisply.

"Oh. Well, thank you, Mrs. Ellis, for having the foresight to get us aid." While her words sounded sincere, Larkin nervously looked to the left and to the right. "Is anyone else here?"

"Just us three and the good Lord." Mrs. Ellis set the lamp on the ground. "At the rate Renier is digging, we're likely to be here till kingdom come." She turned and walked away, muttering, "I knew I should have brought that second shovel. Back in a jiffy. And I mean jiffy."

The sound of her boots crunching the twigs and leaves underfoot died away.

E.V. spoke first. "I trust you."

She lowered her cloak's hood. Her skin looked pale in the lamplight. "You don't know what I'm doing."

He shrugged. "Mrs. Ellis's note said you needed help."

"I could be doing something reprehensible."

E.V. gave her a look to let her know how unlikely he believed her guilty. "Sweetheart, I have full confidence in the integrity of your character."

Her mouth moved yet no sound came forth. The dimples on the sides of her mouth appeared in one of her rare, glorious smiles.

E.V.'s heart skipped a beat. Whatever she had in the covered wheelbarrow, he didn't know, couldn't suspect, and didn't care. The fact that losing-lawyer Harvey Milton was now courting Larkin had no bearing on his thoughts either.

Two years was an awfully long time to wait to kiss the woman he loved.

Feeling no longer bound to any oaths he'd made to her father, he tossed the shovel to the ground. In hindsight, he'd say he didn't remember running over to Larkin, but he had to have because she was still standing beside the wheelbarrow in his embrace when Mrs. Ellis returned.

"Now that you two have gotten that outta the way, can we get this hole dug?"

All Ye Faithful

❄

Larkin broke free and peeked around E.V., whose hands lovingly rested on the back of her head and on her waist. Mrs. Ellis not-so-lovingly held a shovel and a second lantern in one hand and her shotgun in the other. A myriad of responses ran through Larkin's mind. The best of which—*I had a speck in my eye and I needed his help to remove it*—didn't sound remotely believable. Clearly Anna was right. She, Larkin Whitworth, wasn't and never would be crafty. Thus, this seemed to be another one of those *sometimes the best explanation was no explanation* moments. She hoped.

Besides, Mrs. Ellis's eyesight was too sharp for her not to have seen how splendidly E.V. had been kissing her. Larkin touched her lips and smiled and sighed happily and—*oh my*. Her first kiss had been a lovely and magical moment indeed.

E.V. sighed loudly (perhaps it was more of a groan). "Ma'am," he said to Mrs. Ellis, releasing Larkin and turning around, "I suspect anything I say won't endear me to you."

"Nope." Mrs. Ellis's tone likely sounded as harsh as normal to E.V., but having spent enough time with the woman, Larkin had long learned to distinguish between annoyed grumpiness and amused grumpiness.

Larkin tugged on E.V.'s woolen coat sleeve, drawing his attention. She whispered, "She has a hard time expressing love. She really likes you."

His upper lip curled. He grimaced and muttered, "Her love is toxic."

"Kiss her again, Renier," Mrs. Ellis added louder this time, "and I'll have no choice but to shoot yer worthless hide. Nothing personal, mind you, but she is courting that even more worthless Harvey Milton. You ought not be kissing another man's woman."

Stunned at the news, Larkin stared openmouthed at them. "I'm not courting Mr. Milton."

"You're not?" and "Why not?" came in unison.

Larkin glanced back and forth between the two. "Where did you hear that news?"

This time E.V. and Mrs. Ellis glanced back and forth between each other and her.

"Can't say I can recall," Mrs. Ellis answered, frowning.

With a confused frown of his own, E.V. scratched the side of his head. "Tuck told me because Anna told him. I assumed you'd told her."

"No," Larkin said barely loud enough to hear herself.

While she hadn't seen Anna in the last three days because she'd been focusing on finding all of Mama's liquor bottles, the last time they'd talked, they'd not discussed any men in Larkin's life. Or courting. Anna hadn't even given her weekly Willum Tate exaltation. Anna wasn't a gossiper, so Larkin knew her friend wouldn't have shared the information with Jeremiah unless she heard it from a reliable source. Who would make up a rumor she and Mr. Milton were courting? And why?

"With the soiree approaching, I've been distracted, helping Mama prepare." Dreading what she'd hear, she asked, "Has anything else been said about me?"

She stood in stunned silence as E.V. and Mrs. Ellis took turns sharing all they'd heard about her being a drunkard.

E.V. tucked strands of her loosened hair behind her ears. "Sweetheart, I didn't—don't—believe any of it. I've defended you when I could. Reverend Bollen says he's gone privately to those he's heard gossiping and spoken to them."

Mrs. Ellis added, "I told them all it wasn't true. People tend not to listen to what I say." Her voice had softened, reminding Larkin how wounded her heart was. Back to her normal bluster, she added, "If *you* said something publicly—"

Larkin shook her head. She wouldn't say anything that would cast negative aspersions on her mother. She'd rather people believed she was a drunkard than for them to know Mama was. Those who were her true friends would trust what they knew of her character and not believe any rumors.

Remembering her agenda, she asked, "Is the hole deep enough?"

Mrs. Ellis examined it. "A foot deeper than we need."

"You told me to—" E.V. glared at Mrs. Ellis. "Then why did you get another shovel?"

Mrs. Ellis glared right back. "What did I tell you about talking so much? Don't make me shoot you."

"I wasn't—ugh!" E.V. looked to Larkin. "I take it we're burying something?"

"Yes."

When he didn't ask what, she drew in a deep breath to still her apprehension and fear. Shame. She should have told E.V. this well before now.

"Three days after my brother's seventeenth birthday," she said, focusing on him since Mrs. Ellis already knew everything, "he told Mama he had a cough that was bothering him. Papa said he was pretending to be sick and refused to call the physician. Mama believed Sean, so she gave him the honey-whiskey cordial she always gave us when we were ill. The more Sean coughed, the more Mama medicated him."

His brows drew together. "For how long?"

"A week, maybe. He had a seizure and died. After that, we moved from Olympia to Tumwater." Larkin swallowed to ease her dry throat. "Mama believes sadness of heart also needs medicating. Birthdays, weddings, holidays, all resurface her grief."

"That's why her hands shook when she served me tea."

Larkin nodded. "She doesn't drink regularly, but when you lose someone you love, the pain is so great that you'll do anything to make it go away, to not feel anything."

Instead of giving his opinion of who was to blame or offer token platitudes such as *life is hard*, E.V. looked at her with compassion. With understanding. He brushed a kiss across her cheek, grabbed the handles of the wheelbarrow, and pushed it over to where Mrs. Ellis stood by the hole.

In the quiet of the night, with Mrs. Ellis shining a light down on them, they laid the bottles side by side in the dirt coffin. When E.V. promised he'd be at the soiree in case she needed him, Larkin paused long enough to wipe away the tear that escaped. Over the next day or two, Mama would eventually realize all her liquor was missing. She'd panic. She'd grieve. She'd break. Who knew what she'd do at the soiree if Larkin didn't confess everything first and promise to help Mama face her grief.

Dreading the conversation she would have later with her parents but loving them too much to keep living as they were, Larkin lifted the last bottle from the wheelbarrow. *Naika ticky maika, Mama. Please, Lord, draw my parents to You, and heal my mother's grief.*

After placing Mama's crystal decanter filled with the sick tumtum medicine in the hole, Larkin stood and watched as E.V. shoveled dirt over the bottles. *Bury the booty, hide the corpse.* Allowing Mama to suffer was the only way Mama was going to face Sean's death. . . and the only way Papa was going to realize Mama needed more help than he could give.

Her heart ached. Her soul grieved. Only this time she wasn't alone.

Chapter 10

As they stood next to the refreshment table, E.V. cheerfully handed Willum a punch glass filled with eggnog. That Larkin's father hadn't grabbed him by the neck and tossed him out made the evening rather. . .well, enjoyable. The candles around the room glowed brightly. The crystal chandelier glinted with every color of the rainbow. The musicians hit each note perfectly, and, thankfully, not a single person he walked past or stood next to smelled overpowering in either the bad or good range of the odor spectrum.

"Now isn't this more fun than measuring crown molding?" he said, grinning.

"No, I should be at the house working," Willum grumbled. "I'm not going to get it done in time." Yet instead of leaving, he sipped his eggnog and continued to watch the center of the Whitworth parlor where a dozen or so couples were dancing, including John Seymour and Natalie Bollen, who looked prettier than usual in her blue (or maybe green) dress.

E.V. figured Willum would know the exact shade. The man had a good eye for color. But instead of asking, since he could feel tension emanating from his friend, he drank the last of his frothy eggnog in silence. No sense asking Willum questions Willum wouldn't—or more aptly, wasn't ready—to answer.

As the music from the stringed quartet flittered through the open library door, E.V. scanned the parlor for Larkin or her parents. The silver Gorham bell E.V. had given Larkin when he and Willum arrived earlier rested on the fireplace mantel with the crystal bells from the two previous Christmases. Whatever feelings Whitworth had toward the gift, he hadn't shown them. Mrs. Whitworth, on the other hand, had kissed E.V.'s cheek and said she liked how he'd matched his burnished-gold brocade vest with a burgundy frock coat.

E.V. had never bothered much with being a dapper dresser. But the romantic in him had hightailed it to Olympia this morning to find something suitable for the soiree. After learning from Anna what Larkin would be wearing, that he'd match her burnished-gold gown had been his intention. That he had to drag Willum with him and force him to buy something new was because if anyone cared less than he about being fashionable, it was Willum, who, E.V. would acknowledge, looked quite debonair in a charcoal frock coat with a black velvet collar.

Sensing someone gazing in their direction, E.V. looked around and met Reverend Bollen's observant eyes. He and his wife rested near the piano that had been pushed to the corner of the parlor. Several other older couples lingered about the parlor's perimeter, including the mayor and his new bride and Silas Leonard and the affluent widow he was courting. Some sat, some stood, most watched the dancers.

E.V. turned his attention to the busy center of the room.

Garrick Leonard, like the man in love he was, danced with his wife Kathleen, who looked like she was trying to have a good time but, E.V. suspected, was worried about her bedridden sister who, according to Tuck, was confident their baby would be a ten-pounder, at least.

Next to Miss Bollen and Seymour, Martha Bollen danced with her husband, Isaac.

Isaac's younger brother, David, danced with Harvey Milton's younger sister, both of whom managed to step on each other's toes continually. Both, E.V. noted, were watching Abigail Leonard dance with the newest councilman, who kept glancing at Elizabeth Leonard, who'd recently begun courting Sheriff Phillips and was sitting at the piano moving her fingers above the keys as if she were playing in time with the quartet. At Elizabeth's insistence, Sheriff Phillips was dancing for the second time with the councilman's spinster sister, who was probably the most skilled dancer in the room and who, to E.V.'s amusement, occasionally cast admiring glances in Willum's direction.

The triangles of love in the Whitworth parlor could have populated a Shakespearean comedy.

All that mattered to E.V. was that he wasn't included in any love triangle, quadrangle, or hexagon. And with Miss Leonard having given him distance all evening, he held hope she'd transferred her affections from earlier in the week to a more suitable bachelor.

With a *humph*, Willum gave his empty punch cup to a server walking by.

E.V. quickly added his. "Thank you."

The server nodded and continued on.

"Are you going to ask to marry Larkin tonight?" blurted Willum.

From the corner of his eye, E.V. glanced at his friend. Willum looked. . .hopeful? "No," he honestly answered.

"Ever again?"

"No sense to. Whitworth won't ever agree."

"Maybe in time."

E.V. looked at the dancers moving—most of them—effortlessly to the music, the colorful gowns swishing back and forth like Christmas bells. People lived and loved. People died. Heartaches happened to everyone. Life was loss, and life went on. That was the order of things, and he could let reality steal his joy or focus it.

When he didn't answer, Willum said rather sadly, "You've cut your losses."

"No, I haven't. I've. . ." E.V. wasn't sure how to explain. What he couldn't tell Willum was that last night—this morning, actually—when he was burying the liquor bottles, he realized how his actions had been as misplaced as Larkin's parents' were. In order to have Larkin for his wife, he'd been desperately grasping and arranging and worrying over what he needed to do to earn Whitworth's permission to marry her. He loved her so much that he'd made her an idol in his life. Rather like Mrs. Whitworth and her need to medicate away her grief.

All he truly needed was God. All he really desired was God. God had created him to desire Him, but he'd allowed that desire to be sidetracked with something good but something not God.

The walk back to his lonely one-room apartment had brought him to the place where, once he closed the door behind him, he'd fallen on his knees in worship and repentance.

"No," he repeated. "When God is in His rightful place in my life, all my other desires fall into place. If God makes a way for Larkin to be my wife, I'm content. If He doesn't, I'm content."

This time Willum nodded and said nothing.

The dance came to an end, and several couples made their way to the refreshment table.

"I wonder where she went," E.V. heard Kathleen Leonard say.

"She's probably off having a drink," came her sister-in-law's loud reply. "Poor thing can't go a day without imbibing. Anna befriends her out of pity."

The room silenced.

Kathleen nudged her husband, who immediately glared at his sister.

"Abby," Garrick chastised, "you know that's not true. You shouldn't gossip."

Though her face flushed, Miss Leonard glanced at the dozen people around the table. Panic flittered across her features. "How come you can say you saw Larkin at the mercantile and it's not gossip, but if I say I saw her drunk then it is? The truth isn't gossip." As she spoke, more of the soiree guests crowded around. She turned to E.V., pointing in his direction. "Just ask Mr. Renier. He was there. He smelled the whiskey on her breath. He saw her stumbling about."

E.V. nipped at the inside of his cheek, debating his response. When the murmuring quieted, he noticed Larkin across the parlor standing under the mistletoe. Truth was, as he admired how the fitted bodice of her gown with its waterfall of ruffles on the skirt accentuated her lovely figure, he couldn't quite remember why everyone was looking at him for a response.

As the grandfather clock struck nine, Larkin stood in the parlor's entrance with her parents, holding the basket full of ribbon-wrapped gifts for their guests. Since Mama had abruptly stopped and grabbed the sleeve of Papa's black frock coat, halting them, Larkin assumed she wanted to say something before they handed out the gifts. Only Mama didn't talk, allowing them to hear every mortifying word Abigail uttered.

Almost directly across from them, E.V. and Willum Tate stood at the refreshment table, with their other guests forming a half circle.

Not at all fearing what E.V. would answer because she trusted he'd keep her secret, Larkin tilted her head until she could meet his gaze. His attention drifted briefly to something above her. The moment she realized what she was standing under, the corner of his mouth indented into a half smile, which made her give him a look to say—*Don't you dare*. Were it not for Mama favoring Victorian Christmas traditions, Larkin would banish the mistletoe from the house, sparing all from possible embarrassing moments.

Papa muttered under his breath, "Why is he still here?"

"Patrick, don't make a scene," Mama cautioned.

"Did you send him an invitation?" Papa asked her.

"I was wondering when you would ask."

"That's not an answer."

"No, I did not."

To Larkin: "Did you?"

"No sir," Larkin answered honestly, although she had her suspicions who had. She reached forward with the hand not holding the basket, and gripped Papa's fingers. "I love E.V., but I'd never dishonor you by marrying him or any man without your approval. I choose our family." And although she didn't want to resurrect the pain she'd brought her parents after confessing over breakfast what she'd done with Mama's liquor, she reminded him, "That's why I did what I did last night. That's why I will endure any untruths spoken of me. And that's why you will be a gracious host to *all* of our guests. Please, Papa."

His mouth clamped in a thin line.

Larkin watched his chest rise and fall underneath his cherry jacquard vest that matched in fabric and shade Mama's gown. Before the soiree began, the photographer had captured their images—Papa sitting in a chair and Mama standing elegantly behind him with her left hand gracefully resting on his shoulder. Pity the black-and-white image couldn't depict the depth of love they showed when gazing upon each other. Larkin blinked at the moisture in her eyes. Her heart ached with yearning to grow old and in love.

With another deeply drawn-in breath, Papa offered his arm to Mama. He squeezed Larkin's hand, and they walked toward the crowd together.

❄

E.V. simply didn't know what to say. It was an unsettling, unmanning, unfamiliar feeling, really. While he never considered himself a fluent conversationalist—he preferred to be known for being a good listener—when times called for him to say the right, wise, or practical thing, he'd always known what to say.

But now with all eyes on him, he was speechless.

Even Whitworth looked at him as if he expected—feared—E.V. would share everything Larkin had told him last night about her mother and brother. Only Mrs. Whitworth's hold on him seemed to keep him from intervening.

"Mr. Renier," Kathleen Leonard questioned, "do you have something to add?"

E.V. turned from Kathleen to her sister-in-law, who stood there with a smug grin on her face. And everything became clear. "You started the rumors about Larkin being pickled and about Milton courting her. Why? Because I love her instead of you?"

Everyone's attention shifted to Miss Leonard. Her mouth twisted into a scowl. "Good gracious, no!" she spat out. "I only wanted to stop her from getting another thing she wanted. Larkin is a drunkard, an imposter, and a thief."

"A thief?" Larkin pushed through the crowd. "What did I steal?"

"My friend!" The bottom of Miss Leonard's face trembled. She sniffed. "You stole the only friend I ever had. So I don't feel bad for telling everyone the truth about your drinking."

"Oh Abigail." Larkin answered, in tears. "I wanted to be your friend, too, but you pushed me away."

"Because I didn't want to be your friend! You have everything and I only had Anna. Now I have no one." She broke into sobs and ran from the room.

Garrick and Kathleen took off after her with her father and his lady-friend following.

E.V. looked about the room, seeking the right words to say to break the awful silence and knowing he would never share Larkin's secret.

"I've been everything Larkin has been accused of being," he confessed. "And worse. Thanks to Jesus, who I was isn't who I am today. Who Larkin is, is what you know her to be, and that's not anything she's been accused of. Trust what you know of her character and not any rumors you hear, because that's what you would want others to do for you."

"Renier!"

The crowd separated like the parting of the Red Sea.

E.V. swallowed what little moisture he had left in his mouth.

Patrick Whitworth motioned to one of the members of the string quartet standing outside the library entrance. "You, play something lively for my guests to dance to. Larkin, Renier, you two come with us." He swiveled around then grabbed his wife's hand and walked to the empty front foyer.

Feeling uneasy, E.V. stepped to Larkin's side, and taking care not to step on the train of her gown, he touched the small of her back and nudged her forward before dropping his arm to his side. "Does he know about—"

"Yes," Larkin interrupted. "And he knows who my accomplices are."

Somehow E.V. managed to find a little more moisture to ease the tightness in his throat. In this moment, he'd prefer fisticuffs to a lecture.

They stopped in the foyer. Standing at the end of the staircase, Whitworth rested his right foot on the bottom stair and his right elbow on the handrail, the fingers on his right hand tapping his chin.

"You've been cavorting with my daughter," he stated.

E.V. nodded.

Still holding his wife's hand, Whitworth drew her close. Gently he turned their enclosed hands, raising them so he could place a kiss on her knuckles in what seemed to E.V. to be a comforting manner. "Renier, you pegged me accurately that day in the rain. You missed one thing, though. I can admit when I've been wrong."

E.V. stared in silence.

"I've been wrong about you." Whitworth's eyes narrowed, yet the corners of his mouth pinched upward. "In some things. Others I'm still deciding. What you did last night helping Larkin—" He cleared his throat. "Your faithfulness to her then and now is why in about thirty seconds I'm going to give my wife the dance she's been asking for, leaving you two alone here in the foyer. If my daughter so happens to stand under the mistletoe and you so happen to kiss her a little longer than decorum permits and Reverend Bollen happens to see, well, considering you admitted you've been cavorting with Larkin, you'll have to marry her. You understand?"

For a moment E.V. was struck dumb. But then his mind started processing exactly what Whitworth was suggesting—was granting permission for. No wonder Larkin had such a tender spot for cantankerous ol' Mrs. Ellis. The woman was a female version of Patrick Whitworth.

Trying not to smile, E.V. nodded again. "Yes sir."

All Ye Faithful

Whitworth inclined his head. "Merry Christmas, son." Holding his wife close as she blinked away her tears, he stepped toward the parlor, pausing long enough to brush a kiss on Larkin's cheek.

Wordless, Larkin walked with E.V. to the mistletoe. A struggle of emotions graced her face as she stared at the suddenly intimidating red berries and green leaves. He knew exactly how she hated to be the center of attention.

"What are you thinking?" he whispered.

"If I *really* want to throw caution to the wind, now that the opportunity is before me." Her gaze shifted to the guests dancing and lingering about the parlor. She released a ragged breath. "I vowed to Anna that we'd be married before her baby is born. Jeremiah sent word that her labor began a few hours ago."

"Far be it for me to let you to break a vow."

"We'd have to marry tonight."

E.V. nodded in agreement even though she was more focused on her fears than on him. "If we gave proper cause, Reverand Bollen could arrange a wedding. One good kiss should do it."

"Everyone will be watching."

"I love you."

She met his gaze. "What did you say?"

"I love you?" he repeated.

"Are you not certain?"

He grinned and she grinned, and all E.V. saw was her.

"I'm *quite* certain, sweetheart."

The dimples in her cheeks deepened as her smile chased away her fears. In a movement that stunned the breath from his lungs, she drew him close, far closer than decorum allowed, and her lips found his. She kissed him. She kissed him until he forgot everyone was watching. She kissed him until he was sure *she* forgot everyone was watching, because when Reverend Bollen tapped E.V.'s shoulder and E.V. reluctantly drew his lips from Larkin's, the look on her face was exactly how he felt.

Content.

ECPA- bestselling author **Gina Welborn** worked for a news radio station until she fell in love with writing romances. She serves on the American Christian Fiction Writers Foundation Board. Sharing her husband's love for the premier American sportscar, she is a founding member of the Southwest Oklahoma Corvette Club and a lifetime member of the National Corvette Museum. Gina lives with her husband, three of their five Okie-Hokie children, two rabbits, two guinea pigs, and a dog that doesn't realize rabbits and pigs are edible. Find her online at www.ginawelborn.com.

A Carpenter Christmas

by Mary Davis

Dedication

To my son, Ben, who loves to
build and create with his hands.

Every wise woman buildeth her house:
but the foolish plucketh it down with her hands.
PROVERBS 14:1

Chapter 1

June, 1891

Natalie Bollen tried to pick out the *solid* areas of mud, if there were such a thing. But everywhere she stepped, her boots sank in at least an inch, if not three. She balanced herself with an umbrella in one hand and held her skirt up in the other. Rain tapped on the fabric of the umbrella like a soft symphony. She loved how a shower cleaned the air and made everything smell so fresh.

She stopped in front of the big house under construction. It had been in such a state for a year now. The builder not in a particular hurry to complete it. It wasn't as big and fancy as the Whitworths' mansion, but clearly it would be one of the larger houses in Tumwater. The owners must be people of importance to need such a fine home.

The hammering told her the carpenter was present, and a giddiness rippled through her. The noise came from above. He wasn't foolish enough to be up on the roof in this downpour?

As she tipped her head back to look up, her hat loosened. She dropped her skirt and slapped her hand on her hat. "Mr. Tate?" She would prefer to call him Willum, but Papa forbade it. He said it wasn't proper for a young lady to address a gentleman outside her family by his first name. Most people would think a logging town like Tumwater to be a simple backwoods place where decorum wouldn't matter. To many, it didn't. But to Papa, the town's only religious influence, it did. When decorum went, he said, so did society.

The pounding stopped, and Mr. Tate peered over the edge of the roof, hanging on to a rope tied around his waist. Sandy brown, shoulder-length waves hung in dark, wet tendrils from beneath his worn hat. He shook his head then proceeded to climb down.

Rain poured from his hat brim. He narrowed his pine green eyes, dark on the outside and lighter on the inside, like the varying shades of the forest. "Miss Bollen, you shouldn't be out in this weather."

As proper as Papa. "And *you* shouldn't be climbing around on the roof like a monkey." He shook his head again. "Come inside where it is drier."

She released her hat and collected up her skirt again. Mr. Tate guided her by her elbow up the three steps and in through the front door. He took her umbrella and set it against the inside wall.

Natalie smoothed her hands down her pink-striped dress. She looked best in pink, and today was a special day. But even after all her best efforts, mud still managed to get past the hem's mudguard around the bottom of her skirt. Papa would say that this was where vanity got a person. She had just wanted to look her best.

Mr. Tate took off his hat and shook the water from it. "Does your father know you're out in this?" He pointed to the window with his still dripping hat.

She tugged at one finger of her glove then the next and next. "Papa is out visiting members of the flock."

Mr. Tate shook his head again. His wet waves swung gently.

She pulled her hand free of her right glove. Wasn't he the least bit pleased to see her?

Across the room, Mr. Tate's orange-colored dog appeared in the kitchen doorway on her three legs and wagging her feathery tail.

Natalie smiled at the dog. "Hi, Sassy."

Mr. Tate held up a hand to the dog. "Stay, girl."

Sassy's body shook with her obedience, and she whined.

Natalie crossed the room to her and scratched the dog's head around her silky ears.

Sassy sat, and her feathery tail brushed the floor. Mr. Tate had Sassy when he arrived in town three years ago, and said he had found Sassy wandering and hungry. He had no idea how the furry orange canine had lost one of her back legs. But she got around fine on three. She'd taken a shine to him and become his faithful companion.

Sassy rolled over, and Natalie rubbed her soft tummy.

"I think she likes you better than me." Less of a criticism and more of a pleased acknowledgement.

Natalie looked back at Mr. Tate. "I doubt that. You're her master."

He scratched the whiskers on his chin. "No. She just knows where her next meal is coming from."

Natalie held her hand out to him, and he pulled her to her feet.

"I've seen the way she gazes up at you." Natalie was afraid she might have that same expression just now and looked away.

She surveyed the room. Water dripped from several places above. She could see right through the trusses of the upper floor to the underside of the roof. With all the rain they'd had lately, it was no wonder he was trying to get the rest of the shingles on. Then the interior could dry out. They were standing in the largest of the dry areas. "You certainly are taking your time with this house. Isn't your employer anxious to move in? I'm sure his wife is."

"He is not yet ready to move in."

"Not with rain pouring in."

And then he did it. His whisker-framed mouth broke into that smile that melted her heart.

"The house will be ready when *my employer* wishes to move in."

"You still are not going to tell me who it is?"

He just stared at her, grinning. "You'll have to wait until they move in, like everyone else."

"Oh bother."

She wandered into the next room. Bone dry. Not a single leak, and the floor above was finished, too. One wall was lined with bookshelves that had delicate carvings across the tops and down the sides. Mr. Tate had to be a patient man to do such fine work and a master at his craft. She ran her hand over the smooth surface.

She wished to compliment him on his workmanship so turned around. Mr. Tate stood directly behind her. Well, now in front of her. She sucked in a breath. Her heart raced like a runaway Shay engine with a full load of timber.

"Why did you come?"

Why had she come? Because today was a special day, in spite of the rain. And she had wanted him to remember it was special, too. He obviously did not. "Oh, I don't know." She sighed. "I thought it a lovely day for a stroll."

His mouth twitched up slightly at the corners. "Then let me escort you home." He moved back to the front door and retrieved her umbrella and waited.

Truly? He wasn't going to comment that a downpour did not constitute a lovely day? And one should remain indoors in such weather? Mr. Tate was as stubborn as a cantankerous mule. She shoved her hand back into her glove and marched for the door. She wanted to tell him that she could find her own way home but didn't want to be disappointed if he honored her request. If she knew he would still insist on walking her home, she would protest. A great and mighty protest. But she would rather hold her tongue and be able to enjoy his company a little longer, than have her heart crushed by his indifference.

He held the umbrella up just outside the door and extended his work-gloved hand to help her down the steps.

She took it, scooped up her skirt with the other hand, and descended the three steps into the mud. When she was a little girl and had first come to Tumwater, she had enjoyed walking barefoot in such mud, feeling it squish between her toes. "For the grandeur of the house, the porch seems a bit understated."

He laughed and tucked her hand in the crook of his elbow, and they began their promenade through the rain.

She liked his laugh. Full and jovial. Lively.

"Those steps are temporary. They are only to get me in and out of the house without killing myself. When the rain lets up and I have the roof finished, I plan to build a porch that wraps around the entire house. And a balcony off the master suite."

She could picture it. "Oh, that will be lovely."

A puddle she had skirted fairly easily earlier now stretched out before them. She looked left and right to determine the most suitable course. The land gently sloped up on the right, and the puddle ceased sooner in that direction. She stopped at the water's edge.

Before she could suggest their course, as Mr. Tate had not turned either left or right to survey the hazards, he placed the umbrella in her hand and scooped her up. He then slogged through the muddy waters. She presumed, since he was already soaked from head to toe, that a little more water made no difference to him. She stared at his whiskered face and bright eyes the multihued greens of the forest. Even if he didn't remember that today was special, being carried by Mr. Tate was well worth a soaking. She would find some way to remind him. Perhaps on Wednesday when he regularly ate supper with her family.

He set her down on the boardwalk where the stores began. Under the awnings, out of the rain and the mud, at least for the time being.

At her house just beyond the edge of town, he opened the door for her.

She stepped inside and turned. "Would you like to come in and warm up with a cup of coffee?"

He collapsed the umbrella and shook it before handing it to her. "I better not. I'm a bit of a mess." He motioned with his hands down his muddy, wet attire. "I don't want to drip all over your floor." He took off a glove and reached inside his coat pocket. He handed her a small carved animal. "Happy birthday."

He had remembered. Her heart soared. So he knew the significance of today. Now that she was eighteen, he would ask Papa to court her. But Papa was out on visitations. "Papa's not here."

He nodded. "You told me he was out visiting."

"We'll see you for Wednesday supper?"

"Wouldn't miss it." He tipped his hat. "Good day."

Natalie closed the door, leaned against it, and looked at the wooden kitten. So detailed. Mama sighed, her blond hair glowed in the firelight. "You best get that dress off. It's half ruined with the mud. I have some pink fabric goods that we can use to put a border around the bottom, add a little fabric to the collar and cuffs. No one will know."

What she meant was that Papa wouldn't know.

Natalie crossed to where Mama sat in a rocking chair by the fire, peeling last year's potatoes, and kissed her on the cheek. "I love you, Mama."

"I love you, too. Now scoot, so you can help me fix supper."

Natalie went upstairs to her room and set the carved kitten on her bureau with the dozen other animals Willum had carved for her over the past three years.

❄

Willum whistled all the way back to the construction site, kicking at clumps of dirt, causing mud to spray up. Natalie had thought he'd forgotten she turned eighteen today. He'd been surprised she had ventured out on such a dreary day. Pleasantly surprised. He'd known from the start exactly why she had come and had tempted her to admit it, but she didn't. She looked older, more mature, with her dark hair pulled up on top of her head.

He scrubbed his hand across his bristly chin. He, on the other hand, probably looked like a grizzly bear. It was time to shave off his winter beard.

Natalie had set her cap for him long ago. From the moment he'd first met her three years ago, she had intrigued him. But being seven years his junior, he'd not thought of her in a romantic way at first. Now he thought of her all the time.

His intentions were jumbled where Miss Natalie Bollen was concerned, and his heart troubled.

He knew better than to let a young lady ever manipulate him again. But wasn't Natalie too sweet for deception and games? Too sweet to play with a man's heart then casually throw it away and crush it under her pretty little shoe?

Chapter 2

Natalie sat straight as a board in the front pew at church Sunday morning. They always sat in the same order—Mama on the aisle then the children next to her from youngest to oldest. Even her oldest brother Isaac's wife sat with them. As the family of the pastor, they sat in the front pew every Sunday where everyone could see they were present and on time, and that the family wasn't distracted by the rest of the people in church. But Natalie was distracted *because* she couldn't see anyone but Papa. And today more so than other Sundays.

She could feel someone staring at the back of her head. She didn't dare turn around but was dying to know who. Willum? Nothing up front had a reflective surface that she might be able to see and scan the congregation. She tilted her head and slightly turned it in one direction then looked out of the corner of her eye at the first window. Shadowy figures, but she couldn't make anyone out. So she turned and tilted her head the other direction to see if she could see in the windows on the other side any better. Because of the shadows on the outside of the window, it was darker, and she could recognize people. She turned her head a little farther to get a better view.

Mama nudged Natalie. "Pay attention."

She turned her focus back onto Papa.

After service was over, Natalie stood next to Mama, who stood next to Papa just outside the church doors to shake hands with each member and to send them into their week with the Lord's blessing. Mr. Tate had come through the line early and now stood with his friends Mr. Tucker, Mr. Corrigan, and Mr. Renier, and their wives. She hoped he didn't leave. He'd barely stayed long enough on Wednesday to eat and spent no time alone with Papa to discuss courting her. And going through the reception line after service certainly didn't afford him any time.

John Seymour lingered close as the line drew to an end. He smiled at her. To be polite, she smiled back.

The line ended, and she could go to Mr. Tate herself, not to talk about courting but about visiting with her papa.

Mr. Seymour stepped forward and asked to speak to Papa.

Mama put a hand on Natalie's arm. "Please go invite Miss Leonard to Wednesday supper."

"But Mama?" Nobody liked Abigail. "She's the meanest girl in town."

"And she came to church. Now go."

Natalie looked toward Mr. Tate. "But. . ."

"Go."

Natalie slumped her shoulders and walked off. She heard Mama clear her throat. The meaning of that simple sound was unmistakable. *Stand up straight.* So she did and fashioned her face into a pleasant expression.

"Abigail."

The stunning blond turned with a start. "Natalie?"

She needed to make this fast so she could still talk to Mr. Tate. "Mama has invited you to supper on Wednesday night."

Abigail pulled up her lip on one side in a very unattractive manner. "I'm sure it rubs you into a rash to have to invite the most hated person in town. I can tell you don't want to be here with me, and certainly don't want me in your home."

It wasn't so much that she didn't want to be around Abigail as much as she wanted to be with someone else. "You are not the most hated person in town."

"The most hated *girl*."

Why couldn't Abigail just say yes and let Natalie be on her way? Mama would not be happy until she came back with a yes. Truthfully, Natalie didn't want Abigail at Wednesday supper, although any other night of the week would be fine. Wednesday supper was time to spend with Mr. Tate. "I believe Mrs. Ellis is more disliked than you." Mrs. Ellis had left buckshot in the backside of more than one trespasser.

Abigail's mouth turned up. "Well, at least more feared."

"Miss Bledsow?" Natalie could still feel where the schoolmarm had whacked her knuckles, even though it was years ago.

Abigail rubbed her own knuckles. "Maybe I'm number three then." And she gave a small giggle.

"You'll come to supper?"

Abigail nodded.

Natalie left Abigail with the answer Mama wanted, but Mr. Tate and his friends were gone. Maybe he was talking to Papa. She sighed. Mr. Milton stood close to Papa, deep in conversation. So she walked over and looped her arm through Mama's. "Miss Leonard said she'd come to supper."

❄

Willum woke Tuesday morning long before dawn to the school bell ringing a warning. He dressed in a hurry then rushed with Sassy leading the way to the school to see what the ruckus was about. But before he even got there, he saw the glow of the raging fire that consumed several businesses and the church. He smelled the smoke and heard the hungry crackling. Men, women, and children had formed two lines and were passing buckets of water. One line went to the fire's last victim—the building was only half burned. The other line went to the untouched building next to it, hoping to prevent it from catching fire as well.

There had been no rain since a week ago Monday. Everything had dried out then gone on drying, ripe for fire.

Willum shouted over the roaring to the nearest person, "Is there anyone inside?"

The man shook his head. "Those who live above these businesses got out."

That was a blessing.

Willum joined the volunteer firemen in setting up the water wagon and hose. What they could use was a nice downpour.

By noon the fire had been reduced to smoldering debris. People milled around in the streets, surveying the damage. Three destroyed businesses and the church.

A dripping ladle appeared before him. "Water?"

He recognized that voice. He reached for the ladle, making sure to reach high enough on the handle to partially cover his benefactor's hand. Would she move it? Or leave it there? Her hand was cool under his. He wanted to put it to his forehead to cool his face. Holding her hand this way was all he dared in public. Reverend Bollen would never allow a public display of affection.

Once his thirst was quenched and he'd held her hand on the ladle as long as he dared, Willum looked up into Natalie's rich chocolate eyes. But she was sweeter than any chocolate he'd ever tasted. Her face was sweet. Her smile was sweet. Her heart was sweet. He doubted she knew how to deceive or hurt another person. He'd seen her talking to Miss Abigail Leonard on Sunday. There were precious few who would talk to Abigail outside of a business transaction. She'd hurt too many people. Then there she was at church, and sweet Natalie had befriended her. He knew enough to steer clear of girls like Abigail. She would cast her net for a man and pull him in before he was any the wiser.

"You worked hard here today."

Her words brought him back to the vision in front of him. "A lot of people did."

She looked left then right.

Was she anxious about something?

Then she glanced down at his hand, and he did as well. It still covered hers. He released her hand slowly. He evidently hadn't completed the task when he thought about releasing her hand a few moments ago.

"I'll see you Wednesday at supper."

"See you then." He watched her walk away. Even in a drab gray dress, she looked enchanting.

A hand clasped him on the shoulder. "Looks like you will have plenty of work to keep you busy this summer."

He turned to his good friend Tuck. The last thing he needed was more work. He needed to finish the house. "I have plenty of work, thank you."

"Yes, I saw. Have you officially started courting her?"

Willum backhanded Tuck in the stomach. "Not her. Actual work."

"I saw you two. It's about time, buddy. I thought your broken heart would never mend. And Natalie is a right fine young lady."

"She's so young."

"You missed the boat on eligible young ladies your age. You let Frederick, E.V., and me woo them first. And we all thank you. Wouldn't have stood a chance if you were interested in any of 'em."

Willum gazed at Natalie offering water to her brother David.

"So, are you courting yet?"

Willum narrowed his eyes at his longtime friend. "Why do you care so much?"

Caught, Tuck rubbed the back of his neck. "Anna will have my hide if I don't come home with the information. She's been pestering me all week."

"Pestering? Just because others expect it isn't a good reason to start courting any woman."

"Ah ha. That's good. You haven't started courting Natalie yet." He turned to leave then turned back. "Anna will want to know why you haven't asked to court her yet, and when you're going to ask for permission."

Willum shook his head and walked off. But the question was valid. Why hadn't he asked to court Natalie. . .again? He'd asked just over a year ago, when she turned seventeen and he knew she was too young. Now that she was old enough, he couldn't bring himself to ask. Why?

Chapter 3

Willum sat at the Bollens' table as he had done every Wednesday since he arrived in town. He bowed his head as the reverend blessed those around his table and the food. After the "amens" of nine people echoed, Mrs. Bollen stood and dished up the first bowl of thick bean soup and passed it down the table. Willum took the full bowl and passed it on to Matthew sitting next to him, who passed it on down the table.

Willum avoided eye contact with Natalie sitting directly across from him. He knew she expected him to ask her father tonight to court her. The Reverend Bollen probably expected it, too. Willum didn't know if he could tonight or not. For the first time in three years he hadn't wanted to come to Wednesday supper because of his indecision.

But fortunately, he had other business with the reverend. "I checked the church's rock foundation. It seems solid enough to rebuild on."

The reverend nodded. "Good. We'll need to raise money before any construction can start."

"I drew up plans for a new church building." Willum passed another bowl along. "They're rough."

"I'll look at them after supper."

"The plans will let us know just how much money we'll need to purchase materials."

Then Natalie spoke up. "Mama and I are planning to organize bake sales to raise money. And we are going to ask the quilting circle to make a quilt for a drawing."

Willum glanced over at Natalie but looked away before she looked at him with that expectant expression.

Abigail set down her glass of milk. "Where will church be held until the new building is completed?"

Why had Natalie invited *her* here? She had nearly ruined two of his friends' chances with their now wives. She had meddled and tried to get between several couples in town. What was innocent Natalie learning from her? To be conniving and manipulative? No. Natalie was sweet and just being nice. Or was Abigail trying to come between him and Natalie?

The reverend took a biscuit and passed the basket on. "Service will be held in the schoolhouse. It will be a little cramped, and I'm afraid people might use that as an excuse to stay home."

David, the Bollen's second son, who was a year younger than Willum said, "Do they know what happened? How the fire started?"

Willum buttered his biscuit. "No one is quite sure."

After supper, the women cleared the table and washed the dishes. Willum sat at the table with the reverend and his three sons, Isaac, David, and Matthew. The paper plans rolled out before them. As they hashed over the details, Willum made notations on the side of the brown paper. He would draw up more accurate plans and bring them back for the reverend's approval.

❄

Natalie stayed in the kitchen while Papa and the men talked about the new church building. She heard the paper crinkle as it was rolled up, then some hearty good evenings.

Who was leaving? Wasn't Mr. Tate going to at least bid her good night? She'd hoped he'd tell her that he'd talked to Papa, and they were now courting.

Isaac called into the kitchen, "Martha, time to go."

Natalie's sister-in-law pushed her cumbersome body out of the chair. "I hope this child decides to arrive soon. I want to hold him in my arms. After losing the first one so early, and the second being stillborn, I want to know this one is healthy."

"Him?" Abigail said.

"Isaac really wants a boy." She waddled out of the kitchen.

Natalie followed her to say good evening to Mr. Tate. But he was gone.

Had he asked Papa to court her?

"David, would you walk Miss Leonard home?"

David looked from Papa to Abigail standing in the kitchen doorway, then back to Papa. He stood. "Of course." David did not look like he wanted to, but it was the family's obligation to see that Abigail arrived home safely. David opened the front door. "Miss Leonard."

Abigail thanked Natalie's mother for supper. She seemed genuine. Almost a different person.

"Papa, where's Mr. Tate?"

Papa looked at her with his sympathetic blue eyes. "He has much work to do."

"Did he say anything about me?"

Matthew, her brother who was only ten months older than her, wrapped his arm around her neck and rubbed his knuckles in her hair. "Why would he talk about you?"

Natalie wiggled. "Let me go. You're messing up my hair."

"Matthew! Let your sister go."

Matthew released her.

Natalie stood up straight and smoothed her hair. "I'm not nine anymore."

"Your sister is a young lady, and you must treat her as one."

"But Papa—"

"Even at home."

Matthew hung his head like a scolded puppy.

"Now go fill the wood bin in the kitchen for your mama."

Matthew crossed the room, and once behind Papa, he turned and made a face at Natalie. She desperately wanted to make a face back, but Papa was turned in her direction. He'd called her a lady, so she supposed she should act like one, even at home.

Then she had a horrifying thought. What if Mr. Tate was so comfortable with their family that he thought of her as his sister?

"Papa?"

Papa looked up from stirring the fire. "Yes, child."

How should she say this? She couldn't very well come right out and ask if Mr. Tate had discussed courting her. Papa would send her to her room for being so forward. "Papa, since I'm eighteen and you told Matthew that I was a young lady, I thought it would be a good time to ask if. . .if any young men have asked to court me."

Papa stood and towered over her, silent. He didn't look upset. His blue eyes had a bemused twinkle in them.

"Well?"

"Well, you haven't exactly asked a question. Yours was more of a statement."

"Papa."

Papa smiled then and laughed. "Several young men have made such a request. Don't worry, the young men in Tumwater have taken notice of you. A little more than I would like, I'm afraid."

"Who, Papa?" *Mr. Tate?*

The twinkle left Papa's eyes. "Don't you worry about that just now. Run along and finish helping your mama in the kitchen."

She turned and left. She knew when Papa had finished a conversation. No amount of begging would keep him talking. And he'd probably tell her she was being childish. If he thought that, he might suggest she needed to do a bit more growing up before courting, and make her wait until she turned nineteen. Why wouldn't he just tell her who?

Chapter 4

Over a month had gone by since the church and three businesses in town had burned. The baker, barber, and milliner had reopened their "shops" in canvas tents, but were eager to have solid buildings again. Willum had been hired by all three to work on the construction. The owners collaborated to have one structure that they all owned part of, so they could share the expenses of building. Cheaper for everyone. And easier for Willum to work with all three owners at once. With the construction nearly complete, Willum could focus on the church, which would take longer because they did not have the funds yet.

Working from sunup until sundown on construction of the new business building left Willum fatigued. He had overslept this morning and had to creep into the back of the schoolhouse while the first hymn was already in progress. There was usually a seat available in the last pew. But with the schoolhouse being smaller, he had to stand in the back corner. He yawned and leaned his head back against the wall. Before he knew it the service was over. *Lord, forgive me for falling asleep. I guess I'm more exhausted than I realized.*

He let the corner hold him up until most of the people had filed out of the building. The reverend and his wife stood at the door to send his flock on their way. Natalie and her brothers were nowhere to be seen.

Willum shook the reverend's hand then Mrs. Bollen's.

Mrs. Bollen held onto his hand with her gloved one. "Will you join us for supper this evening?"

Willum swallowed hard. Sunday supper? No one was ever invited to the Bollens' for Sunday supper. It was for family only. Willum was not family. The significance of the offer was not lost on him. He was being included with *the family*. If he said yes, they would have expectations of him. If he said no, then what would become of him and Natalie? "I would be honored."

Mrs. Bollen smiled. "Fine. We'll see you before six." She patted his hand and released it.

❄

Willum clicked open his pocket watch. Five fifty-seven. Snapping it closed, he slipped it back into his vest pocket and straightened his jacket. He'd never dressed up for supper with the Bollens before. He'd never felt as though he needed to.

He'd shaved a second time today and tied his shoulder-length hair at the nape of his neck. Should he have gotten it cut? He wasn't sure if he was ready to be that civilized again just yet. And it was too late to worry about it now. He put his palm out to Sassy to make her stay then took a deep breath and knocked.

When the door opened, Natalie's smiling face greeted him.

And he knew he'd come to the right place.

At the conclusion of supper, the reverend stood. "Willum, would you take a stroll with me?"

"Of course, sir."

Natalie smiled eagerly at him.

Sassy darted around sniffing while Willum walked beside the reverend for five minutes in silence. Raising money for the new church building was going a lot slower than the reverend wanted. He had voiced many times that he hoped to have the building complete by the end of the summer. And here they were a week into August and they barely had half the money they needed. Attendance was dropping off as people made excuses for the small, stuffy space. Or did the reverend want to talk about the actual plans for the building? Was he displeased with them? Willum could certainly get started building some of the framing with the money raised so far. Maybe when people saw it starting to take shape, they would contribute more to the building fund. But it was not his place to initiate the conversation. Reverend Bollen was the one to request his presence. He would suffer in silence.

The older man finally spoke. "About Natalie."

Willum's throat went dry, and he couldn't swallow.

"Over a year ago, you asked my permission to court my daughter, rather boldly I might add. I told you then that I would not allow her to be courted until she turned eighteen. She's been eighteen for two months and quite impatient. Have you lost interest in her?"

"No!" The word flew out of his mouth.

The reverend coughed to cover a chuckle. "May I ask what the delay is?"

Delay? "I've been quite busy with the construction in town and the church building project."

"It only takes a moment to ask. And you have had plenty of opportunities. Inviting you to Sunday supper was no oversight. Your acceptance or regrets would have told me how important my daughter still is to you. You didn't turn us down. Yet you are reluctant to ask."

Willum rubbed the back of his neck. "I was engaged three and a half years ago."

"I take it that it didn't end well."

"If you mean me standing in front of the church in my finest, waiting and humiliated, then, yes, it didn't end well."

"What happened to her?"

"She ran off with a man who had a larger wallet than I did. Three days before the wedding! Her family kept it a secret because they were too embarrassed to tell people, and so they let me stand there like a fool. Waiting. I guess they thought it was fair for me to be embarrassed, too."

"Your heart is afraid to love again."

Willum shook his head. "I love Natalie."

"But you are afraid to declare it."

"I guess I am."

"It's difficult to trust with such a wound. There are five men to every woman here. You are not the only one who has expressed interest in courting my daughter."

Willum's insides tightened.

The reverend put a hand on his shoulder. "I have thought of you as a son. I would gladly welcome you into the family. But I cannot hold off the other suitors much longer.

And Natalie's patience is wearing thin. You need to decide if you are ready to take a risk."

Willum nodded. "I'm ready." He couldn't lose Natalie. "May I court your daughter?" The moment he voiced the question, he felt as though a weight had been lifted from his shoulders.

The reverend's mouth broke out into a wide grin, and he nodded. "It's about time, son. Shall we head back so you can tell her the good news?"

❄

Natalie stood by the window, holding the curtain back. Where had Papa gone with Mr. Tate? It shouldn't take this long to ask one simple question.

Mama sighed. "Honestly, Natalie. It is unfitting for a lady to gape out the window like a miscreant. Come away from there."

Natalie swung around and into a chair. "Do you think he's asking Papa right now?"

"I wouldn't know."

Natalie hopped up and took hold of Mama's arm. "Papa must have told you. Mr. Tate *was* invited for Sunday supper."

"You'll just have to be patient and wait."

Natalie darted back to the window. "I hear voices. They're coming back."

"Get away from there and behave yourself. You'll run poor Mr. Tate off before he has a chance."

Natalie sat in the chair across from Mama by the fireplace and opened a book. Matthew made a kissing sound.

Mama pointed at him and whispered rushed words, "We'll have none of that from you. Just wait until it is your turn. I don't want to hear a sound from—" Mama turned with a smile to the opening door.

Natalie looked down to pretend to be engrossed in reading when she saw the horrifying truth. The book was upside down. She closed it quickly and set it in her lap.

Papa and Mr. Tate stepped inside. Papa gave Mama a slight nod.

Natalie's stomach danced.

Mr. Tate walked over to her with his hands clasped behind his back. "Miss Bollen, would you do me the honor of accompanying me on a stroll?"

"It would be my pleasure." She held out her hand, and Mr. Tate helped her to her feet.

Matthew made a guttural sound almost as though he were choking.

She would like to choke him.

Mama said, "Take a shawl. The night air has a chill to it."

Natalie took one from a peg beside the door and swung it on. Mr. Tate closed the door behind them then offered his arm to her. She tucked her hand in the crook of his elbow, and he covered her hand with his. Neither of them wore gloves. His hand was warm. Sassy followed along beside them.

"I spoke to your father tonight."

She wanted to jump into his arms, but he hadn't said what he'd spoken to Papa about. She knew though.

"I have gained his permission, now I'd like yours."

"Yes!" she blurted out.

He stopped their progress and smiled down at her. "I haven't even asked yet."

"Well then ask, so I can say yes."

He started walking again.

She stopped, and her hand slipped off his arm before he stopped and turned. She planted her fists on her hips. "If you don't ask me right now, I'll go back home."

He let out a jolly laugh then got serious. "Miss Bollen, may I have the honor of courting you?"

She let her hands slide off her hips. "I'll think about it."

He folded his arms, and a smile tugged at his lips.

She wanted to scream yes a thousand times that he could court her. But instead she decided for the ladylike approach. "I believe that being courted by you would be most pleasurable." She took his arm again.

He chuckled. "Now can we drop all this formality?"

She giggled and leaned into his arm. "I'd like that. Now that we're courting, you can call me Natalie. May I call you Willum?"

He seemed to think about it. "Hmm. I kind of like you calling me Mr. Tate. It makes you sound obedient."

She tried to pull her hand free again, but he held tight and kept her at his side. "You are impossible, *Willum*."

"Well, if you say it like that, I especially don't like it."

In her sweetest, most innocent voice, while batting her eyelashes, she said, "Willum."

"I like the sound of that."

She turned to face him. "Are you going to kiss me?"

He gazed down at her. "I'm not sure your father would approve."

"He gave you permission to court me. I'm sure he expects it."

He caressed her cheek and leaned closer ever so slowly, his breath fanning her mouth a moment before his lips touched hers.

Her first kiss was better than she'd imagined. Her insides turned to mashed potatoes and her knees to jelly.

Willum wrapped his arms around her, keeping her up.

Finally, Willum was hers.

❄

Willum walked home with a huge smile on his face, a smile he couldn't seem to tame, not that he really wanted to. He passed the charred ground that had been the church. He needed to do something about getting the construction started. He couldn't finish the house and the church all at once. And he knew just how to get the extra money they needed.

Chapter 5

By the beginning of September, all the funds were in place and construction on the new church could begin. Monday, the first load of lumber would be paid for and delivered to the building site.

From the kitchen, Natalie studied Mama who looked worriedly at the mantel clock again and again. Supper was always at six. Papa had never been late. Never. He always arrived home well before six. Should they eat or wait? The question on everyone's mind.

At a quarter past, David swung on his coat. "I'm going out to look for him."

Matthew grabbed his coat, but before he could shove his arms into the sleeves, the door opened. Natalie could see Mama's whole body relax at the sight of Papa.

Papa wasn't smiling. He took off his hat and coat and hung them on a peg by the door. "Mr. Whitworth and I were at the schoolhouse counting the building fund money. A man with a bandana over his face came in with a gun. He took all the money. He tied us up and shoved us in a broom closet."

Tears prickled in Natalie's eyes. Papa had been so excited at the possibility of being in the new church building well before Thanksgiving. Something to be truly thankful for. Now the dwindling congregation wouldn't have their church back even for Christmas.

Mama went to Papa and wrapped her arms around him. "I'm so glad you're safe."

Papa held Mama for a moment. "I'm going to eat quickly and walk over to Willum's and give him the bad news."

Natalie stepped through the kitchen doorway. "May I go with you, Papa?"

"If you wish."

Natalie smiled. She'd never seen Willum's place, just knew he had a cabin outside of town. She would get to see where she'd live after they married, know what kind of curtains she could start making. And if they'd need a rug in the front room by the fireplace. So many plans to make.

After supper, Natalie left with Papa. She couldn't wait to see Willum even though they brought bad news. She had seen him yesterday, but she wanted to see him every day. Off the path, Papa headed for a small plank cabin. Her feet dragged. Papa got ahead of her. Her stomach knotted. This couldn't be where Willum lived. It was too small. He worked hard and long and made a good wage. He was a carpenter. He could build a cabin as large as he wanted with many rooms. This cabin couldn't be much bigger than her bedroom.

Papa stopped and looked back. "Don't dawdle."

She quickened her step, and the knot in her stomach tightened.

Papa knocked on the door.

Someone else would answer. She was sure of it.

But Willum opened the door and smiled. "Reverend. Natalie. What brings you out here?"

Her hands began to shake. She fisted them to make them stop then gripped one in the

A Carpenter Christmas

other, but they still shook. She followed Papa through the doorway.

Papa removed his hat. "I'm afraid I have some bad news. The building fund was stolen this afternoon."

Natalie gazed around the even smaller interior. Two narrow sets of bunk beds lined each side wall with clothes and tools on three of the mattresses. A small table with two three-legged stools, a potbelly stove with Sassy curled up next to it, and a small bookshelf crammed with books made up the rest of the furnishings. One window, no curtain.

Willum said, "That's terrible. Who did it? Did they catch him?"

She faintly heard Papa and Willum's voices and tried to draw air into her lungs, but they refused to cooperate.

Papa shook his head. "Mr. Whitworth and I were tied up. We had a terrible time getting free. By the time we did, the man was long gone."

She wiped her moist palms down her skirt. Was the room shrinking? She'd been locked in here before. It hadn't been her fault.

The lights began to dim.

❄

Natalie blinked several times. Papa and Willum looked down on her, their voices muffled. They both looked quite concerned. Suddenly their voices returned.

Papa's eyebrows were knitted together. "Are you all right?"

Willum shook his head. "I think she's confused."

"I'm fine. I'm not confused." But she was. She just didn't want to admit it. What was going on?

Willum pulled on her arm. "Can you sit up?"

Papa lifted her at her shoulder.

She wasn't sitting? Mercy. She was lying down. On Willum's bunk! Double mercy.

Not only did she sit up in haste but got to her feet.

Willum grabbed her arm. "Whoa. You aren't too steady yet."

Papa had hold of her other arm, and she swayed between the two. "Maybe you should sit back down."

"No. I'm fine." The walls moved. Or did they?

Papa tightened his hold on her arm. "You fainted. You are not fine. Sit."

She waved a hand toward the door. "A little fresh air and I'll be fine."

Sucking in the cool night air in several long breaths revived her like a slap and brought her back to her senses. Mostly. She still felt weak-kneed, but she could breathe. She drew in another long breath.

Papa kept hold of her arm. "If I had known you were feeling ill, I wouldn't have brought you."

Yes, ill. That could be what it was. But she knew better. "I'm sorry, Papa."

Willum said, "Should I get a wagon to take her home?"

"I'll be fine." If she said it enough times, maybe she would believe it.

Chapter 6

Natalie pulled her shawl tighter around her against the damp air that promised rain as she walked down the opposite side of the street from the house Willum worked on occasionally. Was he there today? She heard no pounding or sawing. The house would be quite nice if he ever finished it. It sat in a semi-prominent location. It would be nothing to the grandeur of the Whitworth home that held the place of prominence. But it had a grandness in its own right.

No wonder Willum was penniless and lived in a shack. He couldn't even finish a simple house in a timely manner. He'd finished the roof, put in windows, and painted the outside her favorite color, a cheerful butter yellow. But the porch had not been put on yet—the extravagant wraparound one. And she was sure the inside still needed walls and upper floors.

He'd managed to complete a building for three businesses in no time with a crew. Why didn't he hire a crew for this house and be done with it, so the man and his wife could move in? And he could get paid for his work.

She was sounding petty. She had nothing against people of diminished means. She just didn't want to be one again. She tried not to think of those black years in her life. She was grateful for all the Lord had given her and didn't want to lose it. She was selfish and petty. And ashamed.

She hurried on to the mercantile, hoping not to run into Willum. She'd felt too sick for Sunday supper this week and had stayed in her room. But she knew her nausea was from nerves. Though her stomach was a little unsettled again on Wednesday, she forced herself to the table, grateful for the distraction of Abigail. David, of all people, had invited her. He smiled at her all through supper. Smitten beyond belief. She'd felt that way about Willum. Only just last week. She still did, didn't she?

The bell over the door jingled. She made a quick scan of the interior and breathed easier. Until she sorted out this gnawing in the pit of her stomach, she would rather not see Willum.

She quickly gathered the items Mama needed, paid, and stepped out onto the boardwalk. A light mist caressed her face. She wouldn't be arriving home dry. She had better hurry for many reasons.

A covered buggy stopped in front of the mercantile. John Seymour smiled at her and jumped down. "Let me get those for you." He took her parcel and shopping basket, placing them on the floor of his buggy. He held his hand out to her. "It looks like rain. Let me give you a ride."

It was an innocent enough invitation. And it did look and feel like rain. Almost drizzling already.

She stared at his proffered hand then took it. Immediately, a sinking feeling in the pit of her stomach told her she'd made the wrong choice. A large round raindrop splattered on the back of her glove, then her cheek and her nose. Instinct—and Mr. Seymour—propelled Natalie into the buggy.

Mr. Seymour raced around the buggy and jumped aboard, half soaked. He laughed as he shook off some of the rain. "That was close."

She laughed, too.

Her sinking feeling dissuaded for the moment.

❄

Willum stood in the shadows of the livery, watching Natalie with John Seymour. Laughing. John obviously had no compunction about escorting another man's girl without his permission.

He hadn't thought Natalie flighty. He'd seen her walk into town, stop and gaze at the house, then continue on to the mercantile. He'd watched every graceful step she took, like a hummingbird floating.

He'd seen the look on her face when she visited his pocket-sized, boxy cabin. He'd never thought she would ever have an opportunity to see it. He'd made his place small to discourage visitors, squeezing in bunk beds for his friends when they came to town from the logging camp. When he'd come to Tumwater, he wanted to be left alone and cloistered himself away to heal. It had worked. As time passed he became more and more involved in the town, looked forward to Wednesday supper with the reverend and his family. Looked forward to young Natalie's smile and laugh. Now she was laughing for another man.

He tossed the reins of the surrey he'd rented back to the livery owner. "Here, Ulysses. I won't be needing this." He'd planned to escort Natalie home so she wouldn't get wet.

Ulysses dug in his pocket.

Willum waved a hand at him. "Keep it."

"But you paid for an hour."

Willum turned up the collar on his coat and stepped out into the downpour.

❄

Natalie sat in a rocking chair by the fire, knitting.

Mama sat across from her, also knitting. "You're quiet."

She looked up. "Am I?" She'd been lost in her regrets about accepting a ride from Mr. Seymour. He'd been cordial and behaved like a perfect gentlemen, telling her how lovely she looked and how it was his pleasure to escort her home. It hadn't been a pleasure at all. It had been dishonest.

"Mama? If you do something and later realize it might have been wrong but no one got hurt or even knows about it, do you still have to tell anyone?"

"God knows about it."

God knows.

That pricked her heart. "So confession to God would be enough?"

Mama rested her knitting in her lap and looked straight at her. "If someone else were to find out, would it hurt them?"

But it was an innocent buggy ride to stay out of the rain. How could that hurt anyone?

David burst through the door. He held out a wad of cloth. "Would a girl like this?"

By "a girl" Natalie knew he meant Abigail.

Mama unwrapped the gift. A hair comb. More than modest but nowhere near extravagant. It had tiny pearls along the front edge. "This is lovely." She looked up at her son. "You haven't been courting her long. Are you sure about this?"

Mama was being nice. David had only asked to court Abigail last week. But he was besotted.

"Is it too soon?"

"I think maybe just a bit."

David smiled. "Then I'll hold onto it. But I'll have it for when the time is right."

Natalie held out her hand. "May I see it?"

David transferred the comb from Mama's hand to hers like he was entrusting her with a delicate flower that would wilt upon a single breath grazing it.

A bit of envy pricked Natalie's heart. David had bought a girl he'd only just started courting a gift. Willum had never bought her anything.

❄

The downpour had settled into a steady, gentle rain. Willum had arrived in town three years ago in the rain. It was only fitting that he left that way.

He'd stopped by the house and collected his tools. He secured a tarp around the top of his open toolbox to keep the rain out. He stuffed the rest of his belongings in his knapsack and tied on his rolled-up blankets and pillow. He glanced around the boxy room, sorry he couldn't take his books. Closing the door behind him, he set out. He turned to Sassy and slapped his thigh. "Come on, girl."

He stopped by Frederick's and knocked.

"Come in out of that rain."

Willum shook his head. "I don't want to make a mess of Emma's floor."

Frederick eyed Willum's knapsack and toolbox. "You're leaving, aren't you?"

He nodded. "It's time."

Frederick lowered his voice. "What about Natalie?"

"She's found someone else."

Frederick's mouth fell open. "Can't be."

"She was riding in his buggy. Quite close and laughing."

Frederick grabbed his coat from the peg near the door and shoved one arm in. "Who is it? Let's have a talk with him."

Willum shook his head. "I only came to tell you that I left my books at the cabin. They are yours. Please take them."

Frederick shook his head. "No. You'll come back. You have to come back."

He'd let his friend believe what he wanted. "Please don't tell anyone."

"Tuck? E.V.?"

"You can tell them but not any of your wives."

Frederick let his coat slide off his arm and onto the floor. "This isn't the way you should be leaving. Where will you go? Back to Seattle?"

"Not Seattle. I'll find someplace. Someplace with no women."

"Where would that be? The North Pole?"

"Sounds intriguing."

Frederick held out his hand. "Let me know when you get settled."

Willum shook it and left.

Willum tossed his knapsack on the bed of the boardinghouse. He'd managed to gain Sassy a warm place by the kitchen stove by agreeing to do a few repairs for the woman who ran the place. He was more than happy to help out.

Tomorrow, he would get a list from her and start. But for now, he just wanted to rest. Exhausted, he sprawled out on the bed and closed his eyes.

"Build My house."

Willum sat straight up. It was dark outside. He must have fallen asleep. He raked a hand through his hair and fumbled for the matches next to the lamp on the bedside table. He struck one and the room was cast in eerie, wavering shadows. The match began to burn his fingertips, so he blew it out. He lit another then the lamp. What time was it? He pulled out his pocket watch and opened it.

Midnight.

Mr. Seymour stepped onto the boardwalk beside Natalie. "May I offer you a ride?"

She kept walking. "No, thank you. It's not raining."

"But it has recently and the ground is all muddy. You'll ruin your shoes."

"I'll be fine, thank you." She'd been wrong once, she wouldn't be again. She would walk through a monsoon before accepting a ride she shouldn't from any man.

He gripped her arm, pulling her to a stop, and she backed up against the building. He leaned one hand on the planking next to her head. "Rumor around town is that he left. No good-byes, just left."

Natalie fought sudden tears. "He'll be back." He had to come back. She loved him. He wouldn't just leave her without saying good-bye. He had no reason to leave.

"Most folks say he won't."

She ducked under his arm and hurried off. Crossing the muddy street, she went inside the house Willum was building. He would be back. He had to finish this house for the man who'd hired him.

Natalie gazed around the living room. A thick layer of wood shavings covered the floor. The crown molding around the ceiling had a vine of delicate flowers carved into them. Even the molding at the base of the walls had the carvings. No wonder it was taking Willum so long. The details were incredible. It must have taken him hours and hours to carve each section of the moldings. This wasn't the simple house she'd thought from the outside. She'd been wrong about this house and wrong about Willum not being able to complete a "simple" house. There was nothing simple here. Willum had poured his heart into this house. She could see him in all the details.

She crossed to the middle of the room where a worktable made from two sawhorses and a wooden door stood. On the table lay a piece of the lower molding, the design penciled on, the carving barely started. His tools were gone.

Willum must have had a family emergency to not tell her or Papa or his friends where he was going.

She left the house and walked straight to Willum's cabin. She put her hand on the latch and stopped. *Please don't let the same thing happen as last time.*

What if Willum had returned and was home?

She knocked.

And waited.

And knocked again. "Willum?" She opened the door. The room was dim, cold, and damp. No one had been here in several days at least. A lamp and matches sat on the small table. She lit the lamp and a warm glow filled the room. She waited for the feeling, the dread, the shaking, the difficulty breathing, the weak knees, the nausea, the walls moving. None of that happened this time. She took a deep breath then closed the door and looked around.

On the bare bunk sat a small lump of wood. She picked it up. A partially carved doe curled up with her fawn. She hugged it to her breast. She would rather have one of Willum's carved animals that cost him nothing than a hundred hair combs in the fanciest designs.

Willum, where are you?

She slumped onto the bunk and curled up.

He had to come back.

He just had to.

❄

Natalie woke to Papa shaking her. "Natalie!"

She sat up and could see that it was dark outside.

"We were so worried about you. Are you all right?"

She shook her head. "Where is he?"

"I don't know."

She threw her arms around Papa and cried.

❄

Willum woke and looked at his watch. Midnight. He rubbed the back of his neck. That was three nights in a row. He would sleep hard until midnight, wake suddenly as though someone had shaken him, then wouldn't be able to sleep well the rest of the night. What was going on?

"Build My house."

Willum jerked around. "Who said that?"

Silence.

He lit the lamp and held it high. "Who's there?" The room was empty.

"Build My house."

The voice hadn't come from in the room, but closer. But from where? His head? But it had been so audible. Was he going mad? Or was it. . . ?

"Lord?"

"Build My house."

He sat up. The Lord was speaking to him? "Your house? The church? But the money was stolen."

"Trust Me. Build My house."

Had the Lord seen to it that the thief had been caught? "But that would mean returning to Tumwater."

"Build My house."

The thought of seeing Natalie with another man festered the hurt already inside of him. "I don't want to go back."

"Build My house."

He swung his legs over the edge of the bed. "I can't go back."

"Build My house."

He raked his hands into his hair and grabbed two fistfuls. Could he do it and not see Natalie? No. Everyone would know what he was doing once he started swinging his hammer. They would all come to gawk and laugh. He released his hair and stood. "I *won't* go back."

The voice went silent.

"Lord?"

Willum stood on E.V.'s porch in the cold. Was returning the right decision? Part of him said no. The part that was still in love with a girl who had betrayed him. But the other part, the part that knew better than to try to run from God, knew he was supposed to return. He prayed that the money was returned and he could build quickly. He knocked.

E.V. opened the door and immediately pulled him into a back-slapping hug. "Where have you been? Frederick told us you left. I'm so glad you're back. You're staying, right?"

It was nice to know he was missed. At least by his friends.

"Come in."

Willum welcomed the warmth. He sat down at the table with E.V., Larkin brought them each a cup of coffee. "Thank you."

"Did they find the man who stole the church building fund?"

E.V. shook his head. "He got clean away."

He was afraid of that. *What am I supposed to do now, Lord?*

"The church is planning a bake sale this Saturday to get the building fund going again."

"That will take too long."

E.V. furrowed his brows. "Too long for what?"

Last time, Willum had donated money from his own savings so the building could start. He'd thought it an investment in his own future. He took a deep breath. "I need you to do me a favor tomorrow."

"Anything."

"I need you to make arrangements at the sawmill to have my share of recent profits be converted into lumber and delivered to the church building site."

E.V. frowned. "You're going to supply all the lumber?"

"Apparently." Willum took a sip of his coffee.

"You can go into the mill yourself and do that."

Willum shook his head. He'd been a silent partner in the mill from the beginning to help E.V. get started. No one in town knew he was associated with the mill except as E.V.'s friend. "I don't want anyone to know I'm back yet."

"You mean Natalie."

He didn't want to talk about Natalie.

E.V. curled his hands around his cup. "I can put together a crew. Find a reliable foreman to report to you. You would never have to be at the church while it's being built."

He liked that idea. That could be the solution to his problems.

"No. You build My house."

Willum lowered his head into his hands. *Alone, Lord? That will take a long time. Even Noah had his sons to help.*

"This is not the ark."

This deal was getting worse by the minute. Willum shook his head. "No crew."

"You aren't going to build it all by yourself?"

Willum drew in a deep breath. "Apparently so." He really wanted to be gone by Christmas. Could he get it completed by then, working alone?

"Why?"

Willum raised his head. "Don't think I've lost my mind."

"I won't."

"The Lord told me. I know it sounds crazy. Every night for a week and a half I was awakened at midnight. Exactly midnight." He got up and paced. "I heard this voice. I heard it just like I hear your voice. But no one was in my room."

"What did it say?"

Willum stopped pacing and looked E.V. in the eyes. " 'Build My house.' " It sounded ridiculous. "I said no several times. But I kept hearing, 'Build My house.' When I outright refused, the voice stopped."

"So what changed your mind?" E.V. took a swig of coffee.

"I kept waking up every night at midnight. Like a silent plea. After another week of it, I said yes. That was the first night I slept all through the night. I woke up feeling more rested than I had in a very long time."

"I'll get the lumber ordered and delivered."

"You believe me?"

"Of course. Look at what happened to Jonah when he refused the Lord's calling. I don't want you to end up in the belly of a whale, my friend."

Chapter 8

Natalie stood across the street from the church ruins. Last night at supper, Isaac told Papa about the lumber being delivered to the church. Papa had claimed it was a miracle. Natalie knew Willum must be back. She had wanted to go see, but Papa wouldn't let her wander around after dark.

A horse-drawn wagon full of plank lumber pulled up to the rock foundation. Four men jumped off the wagon, two from the front seat and two from the back atop the lumber.

Where was Willum?

She waited for a buggy to pass, and a horse with a rider then crossed. She stepped around several puddles. "Excuse me."

One of the workmen turned her way. "Yes, miss."

"Where is Mr. Tate?"

"Can't say that I know." He turned to the other men. "Anyone know a Mr. Tate?"

Each man shook his head no.

"Well, didn't he order this lumber?"

The workman hefted the end of a stack of at least six planks. "E.V. gave us the order to deliver the lumber."

"Mr. Renier?" How disappointing. She was sure Willum would be building the church.

"Yes, miss." He slid out the planks and another man hoisted the other end.

"Is Mr. Renier at the sawmill?"

"Yes." Together the men carried the boards to the pile of planks stacked up beside the foundation.

Natalie hurried to the sawmill and knocked on Mr. Renier's office door.

"Come in."

Natalie opened the door.

Mr. Renier looked up from the papers he had in front of him with his easy smile, but it faded ever so slightly. He stood. "Miss Bollen, what can I do for you?"

"The men at the church said you ordered the lumber being delivered."

"Just filling an order."

"Who ordered it? The church's building fund was stolen."

He stood silent for several moments. "One of the sawmill's investors donated the lumber to rebuild the church."

Of course it had to be an investor. Willum wouldn't be able to just order a building's worth of lumber. "Who's going to build it?"

"That will be up to the investor. If that's all, I have work I really need to complete." He walked around his desk and held the door.

Natalie held her ground. "I'm sorry for taking your time. I'm just worried about Mr. Tate. He left without a word."

Mr. Renier's features softened slightly. "Willum has always been able to take care of himself. I wouldn't worry about him."

"Has he contacted you?"

Mr. Renier just stared down at her.

She wrung her hands together. "If you hear from him, would you tell him I'm anxious to speak with him? Thank you for your time, Mr. Renier." She stepped outside, and Mr. Renier closed the door behind her.

Why would Willum leave town without telling her and possibly return in the same manner? Unless he was preparing a surprise for her. She headed off in the direction of his cabin. Maybe he was there.

❅

Willum watched Natalie return from the direction of the sawmill. When she stopped briefly in front of the house, he took a step back from the upper window. He doubted she could see him, but just in case. She moved on down the street to the church building then headed in the direction of his cabin.

He'd been right not to go back to his cabin. But hiding out in the unfinished house made him feel like an outlaw. A house that would never be finished.

He waited until the supper hour when most folks would either be home eating or at one of the saloons. The fewer people who came out to see the spectacle the better. And in the evenings, he was sure Natalie would never come by. He strapped on his tool belt, took up his toolbox, and grabbed an unlit lantern. He wouldn't light it until he needed it. He didn't have much daylight left. He left the house and headed for the church. If there weren't clouds threatening to rain on him, he could work for some time in the moonlight.

He laid out several more floor beams before he needed to light the lantern. When he turned around, three shadow figures stood outside the foundation. He crossed over to them.

Tuck was the first to shake his head then the other two followed. But it was Frederick who spoke. "You would get done faster if you worked during the daylight."

E.V. said, "And if you'd hire a crew."

Tuck put on an Irish accent. "People be talkin'. Some be jokin' it be elves or leprechauns buildin' in the middle of the night."

E.V. said, "Children think it's ghosts because it's at night, and they don't see them."

"The more spiritual say it's the Holy Ghost," Frederick said.

Willum didn't want to fool anyone into thinking he was some sort of deity, and certainly not God Himself.

Tuck leaned over the foundation wall and put a hand on Willum's shoulder. "What are you afraid of? That she doesn't care for you anymore? Or that you may discover that you don't care for her? Or that you do care and don't want to be without her?"

Leave it to Tuck to get to the heart of the matter. His heart.

E.V. said, "She seemed sincerely concerned about you when she came by the sawmill today."

"You can't avoid her forever," Frederick said.

"I can try."

The following morning, Natalie ate as quickly as she could and started in on the dishes. Matthew was still at the table poking along. She stood behind him, and when he stabbed the last of his fried potatoes, she swiped his plate and turned toward the kitchen.

"Hey!"

"I waited until you were done." Natalie quickly finished the dishes, put on a cardigan sweater, and swung on a crocheted shawl. "Mama, I'm going into town. Do you need me to pick up anything for you?"

"You went to town yesterday."

Matthew made a face at her. "She wants to see if Willum is back."

Mama scowled at him. "That's enough. You better hope that one day when you fall in love, your sister doesn't tease you. Now you have work to do. You best be doing it."

Matthew slumped out.

Mama turned to her. "With the way he acts, you would think he was five years younger than you rather than a year older. He is the most worrisome of all you children." She set a basket of apples onto the table. "So Willum has returned?"

"I think so. He wasn't at his cabin when I went out there yesterday, but I think he might be staying with one of his friends."

"Natalie, you shouldn't be going to a man's cabin unaccompanied. We know Willum well, but it's still not proper."

Oops. She hadn't meant to admit that. "I'm sorry, Mama. I won't do it again." She had been so excited to see Willum that she hadn't thought about propriety. "I'm just going to go to the church and see the progress on the construction. May I go?"

Mama smiled. "If it is Willum, tell him we have all missed him at supper."

"Thank you." She kissed Mama on the cheek and hurried out.

Even before she could see the church, she heard the hammer's pounding echoing through the trees. Hoping it was Willum, she picked up her pace. As she got closer, she could see a lone figure swinging a hammer. Even though his back was to her, she recognized him.

"Willum?"

He swung the hammer three more times before turning her way. He was back.

She smiled. "I've missed you."

"I have a lot of work here."

Did he want her to leave? No, he was probably just tired. She tried to sound perky. "I can see that. Where is your crew? Did they take an early morning break and leave you with all the work?"

"No crew. Just me."

"You're going to build the church all by yourself?"

He pulled a nail from the pouch hanging from his tool belt and held it to the board. "Apparently."

"I'm sure Papa could find some men to volunteer. Men in the church."

"No thank you." He pounded the nail.

She waited until the nail had been driven all the way in. "Where did all the lumber come from?"

"Donated." He pulled out another nail and beat on it.

She waited then said, "I know that. By whom?"

"People are tired of meeting in the schoolhouse. I have work to do." He sounded cross and lifted a beam on one end.

"Are you mad at me?"

He stopped but didn't turn toward her. He just stood, holding the board.

"Do you not love me anymore?"

He dropped the board and ducked under the beams from the middle of the foundation area to her on the other side of the wall. "I saw you with John Seymour."

Natalie's stomach knotted, and she felt the blood drain from her face. Mama's words came back. *God knows. If someone found out, would they be hurt?* "I'm sorry. It didn't mean anything." She reached her hand over the nearly shoulder-high foundation to him.

Willum stepped back and into the first beam. "You gave him your hand. You were laughing. Not exactly fitting behavior for a girl who is being courted."

It had been wrong. She knew it then and knew it more so now. "It was going to rain."

"You love the rain. Probably the only person in town who does. Once upon a time, you came to see me in the pouring rain and four inches of mud."

"I'm sorry. It truly meant nothing."

He narrowed his eyes. "I can guarantee you it meant something to John. A young lady doesn't accept a buggy ride from a man unless she's interested in him."

"I never should have accepted his offer. I'm sorry. Is that not enough for you?"

He stared at her for a long moment with hard creases around his eyes. "Three and a half years ago, before I came to Tumwater, I was engaged to be married to a beautiful lady who I loved with all my heart. She was charming and funny, and I was swept away by her."

Natalie didn't want to hear about his love for another woman. Why would he hurt her like this? Had he gone back to this woman? Is that where he went when he left?

"My friends tried to warn me about her. They didn't trust her. I wouldn't listen to them. I stood in the front of a church for half an hour waiting for her to walk down the aisle to me before her parents told me she'd run off with another man."

"Oh Willum." She wanted to reach out and touch him, comfort him. "That must have been terrible."

"I won't let it happen to me again." His words were cold and bitter. "I saw the horrified look on your face when you came to my cabin with your father. I thought you just weren't feeling well. But when the next day I saw you with John, I knew better."

"Willum, you have to understand."

He folded his arms. "Understand what?"

"I was scared. I panicked. I was a little girl again, hungry, cold, and scared. All by myself."

"By yourself? You have a good family who loves you."

She had to make him understand. "I never knew my father. My mother and I begged for food. She died when I was six. I was put in a horrible orphanage. The older children would lock me in a dark closet. When I was seven, I was put on an orphan train. I was sick with a cough and no one wanted me. Until the Bollens."

His features softened. "You're adopted?"

"You couldn't tell? I don't look like anyone in my family."

"I thought you got your dark hair and eyes from a grandparent."

"When I saw your cabin, I became that hungry, scared child locked in a dark closet. I didn't want to go hungry again."

"I understand. I'm sure John can provide well for you."

"I don't love John. I love you."

He remained impassive. "You best find yourself a man that you know can provide for you in the way you want."

"I don't want someone else. I want you."

"I'm sorry. How can I trust you not to leave if things get really tough? If we do go hungry?"

"We won't. I'm sure of it." Papa and Mama would always bring them food if it came to that.

"And if we did, you'd become that frightened little girl and run off. I can't risk that. I had one woman I loved leave me. I won't go through that again. I can't. Go home." He turned and ducked back under board after board.

Tears welled up in Natalie's eyes. He couldn't mean that. He was just scared like she was. She ran home, wishing she could change the past. Wishing she hadn't reacted to his cabin. Wishing she hadn't accepted a ride from John. Wishing.

Chapter 9

Three days later, Willum had finally finished placing all the floor beams. Several good men had stopped and offered help. He thanked them but declined. The Lord had been clear that he was the only man to build the church. Then there were the onlookers who whispered about him. Some called him touched in the head and nicknamed him Noah. He'd heard rumors of others who supported his work as long as they weren't called upon to help or contribute any money for the cause. He didn't care what people called him, so long as they left him alone to do the work the Lord had unfortunately called him to do. Alone. In a town he wished not to be in.

And Natalie hadn't been around either. He'd evidently gotten through to her. He hated to hurt her, but he couldn't trust her. And that made him saddest of all. He hadn't thought her flighty, but he understood. She needed a man she could trust fully, and he evidently wasn't that man.

He reached down and lifted one end of a floorboard. He would get the floor down then raise the walls and roof. He raised his end up above the foundation to the floor level. He would have to walk along the board, keeping the first end on the foundation wall. When he felt the other end of the board lift, he looked down the length of it. Natalie smiled back at him.

He dropped his end. He hadn't meant to, but it pulled the other end out of Natalie's hands. "What are you doing here?"

"I came to help."

"I don't need your help."

"Yes you do. You don't want the church to take as long as the house has for you to build alone."

That stung. Was she goading him? "I should have the church completed in a few weeks, by Thanksgiving. Working by myself."

"I don't see how. Why won't you let me help you?"

"The Lord told me that I was the only man to work on the church."

Her smile broadened. "I'm not a man, so I can help."

"Ladies don't work in construction."

She picked up a basket by the pile of lumber. "I brought lunch. Your favorite." She pulled back a red-checkered cloth and lifted out a bowl. "Fried chicken."

"I have work to do." His stomach betrayed him with a loud growl. He didn't want Natalie doing nice things for him. "Go home." He needed her to go away and leave him alone, so he could build this church and forget about her.

❄

Natalie would not be dissuaded. She had made a terrible mistake in a moment of weakness. She would prove to Willum that she was faithful to him. She would be at his side every day while he worked on the church. He would see he could trust her.

She planted her hands on her slim hips. "I'm not going away, so you might as well give in and let me help you."

Willum glared at her.

She could be just as stubborn as he.

He finally looked away then pointed to the pile of lumber. "You can sit there. And don't move."

So he was letting her stay but wasn't going to let her help. Fine. She would sit for now but would keep a watchful eye for an opportunity to help.

❄

Willum stared at the skeleton of the church building, at the framework for the walls and half the roof trusses. Work on the church had gone slowly. Rain had made it impossible to build. Clear drying nights, and drenching days. If he could get the exterior completed, then it wouldn't matter if it was raining, he could still work on the inside. The gray sky felt heavy. The damp air sent chills clear through to his bones. He hoped the rain held off. It could rain all night every night if the days would just stay dry. It would be impossible to finish in two weeks for Thanksgiving. Even finishing before the Christmas Eve service was in jeopardy now. One drop hit his nose, another his cheek.

Lord, I could use a little help here.

"Hello, Willum."

He spun to see Natalie holding the daily lunch basket. *Not that kind of help. Less rain and a work crew.*

Natalie glanced up, blinking at the sprinkles hitting her face. "Are you going to be able to work today?"

"I'm going to have to if I'm going to have any hope of getting this finished by Christmas Eve."

"But it's starting to rain."

She wore the same worn work skirt she wore every day when she came to help, not that he'd let her. "Go home, Miss Bollen. Get out of the rain."

She made that little pinched face she made when he'd started calling her Miss Bollen again. "I brought you something."

"You don't have to bring me lunch every day. I'm capable of feeding myself."

"It's about the only thing you'll let me do around here."

And he didn't exactly *let* her bring lunch. It was more like she forced it on him. She would literally stand between his hammer and the nail until he ate.

The rain came as only a drop now and then.

She set the basket down and pulled a blue bundle from inside her coat. She shook out a sweater. "I hope I got the size right. I used David to fit it on."

She knit him a sweater?

"It's wool and should keep you warm even if it gets wet."

"I don't need a sweater."

"You've been working in the rain. You'll get sick." She held it out. "Put it on."

The set of her jaw told him she would not take no for an answer. He took the sweater and pulled it over his head. It was almost like having her arms around him. It warmed him inside as well as out. "Happy?"

She gave him a triumphant smile. "I was thinking, if you removed both sets of bunk beds, and moved the table and chairs to one wall, there would be room for a bigger bed." Her cheeks pinked. "Your bookshelf could go at the foot of the bed. A small rocking chair could go in the corner next to the potbelly stove."

She was rearranging his cabin? That was kind of cute, but she was trying too hard to *prove* his small place was fine with her, when they both knew it wasn't. He folded his arms. "Why would I want to go to all that trouble?" He didn't plan on staying around.

"Well, I just thought when. . ." She tilted her head and looked up at him with a coy smile and her big brown coltish eyes.

"When what?"

"You know after. . ."

Yeah, he knew. "After what?"

"After we get married, we'll need a larger bed, and one won't fit in that corner." Her cheeks went from their soft shade of pink to a deep red. "Maybe you could add on a bedroom."

"I never proposed." He didn't want her to think she had a legitimate hold on him.

"Well, we're courting, aren't we?" Her tone held a note of concern.

"I never asked for your hand."

"You asked Papa to court me."

"It's not the same thing."

"Well, you want to marry me, don't you?" The doubt was there in her voice and her eyes.

He did, but he knew he shouldn't.

She seemed nervous with him just staring down at her. She raised her hands and brushed them across his shoulders. "I think it fits rather well."

He grabbed her wrists. He didn't want her touching him. He didn't want to be touching her either but couldn't seem to let go. He didn't want to let go. He wanted to keep her always but didn't know how.

❄

Natalie's heart raced at Willum's touch, even if he did look a little mad. She would take whatever he would give her, so long as he didn't ignore her. She still had hope. His grip was so gentle that she could have easily pulled away. He hadn't said he *didn't* want to marry her.

His grip shifted slightly, but neither tightened nor loosened. "You don't trust me to provide for you."

"I most certainly do."

"How do I know I can trust you not to get scared and run off?"

"I'm here, aren't I?"

He didn't look convinced, but his expression softened. His gaze shifted a shade to the left, and as quick as a whip his features hardened to stone.

To her right she heard a voice. "Natalie, is everything all right here?"

She wished he wouldn't use her first name. She hadn't given him permission. "We're fine, Mr. Seymour."

Willum released her wrists and walked away.

She missed his touch. She wheeled around. "Mr. Seymour, I appreciate your gallant offer, but I'm not in need of it."

"Please, call me John."

She would not encourage his attention. *"Mr. Seymour,* thank you, but good day."

He scooped up her hand. "You deserve better than him."

"You're wrong." She pulled her hand free. "It is he who deserves better than me." She was a weak sentimental girl who thought more of her stomach than the man she loved.

Mr. Seymour tipped his hat. "When you grow tired of him, I'll be waiting. I've always held fond affection for you."

Fond affection? How unromantic. Yet if Willum had said that, she might have swooned into his arms. She guessed that was how love colored words. They sounded better coming from the one a person loved.

"What's made you smile? I hope it's me."

"Mr. Seymour, I am flattered, but I really must go." She dipped her head to him and turned in the direction Willum had gone. To the back side of the church, she thought. She caught a glimpse of movement. Had Willum been watching? She hoped so. Then he'd see there was nothing between her and Mr. Seymour.

Willum crouched near his toolbox, rattling tools. He looked up. "Where's John?"

"I sent Mr. Seymour on his way."

"You could have gotten a ride home."

She smiled. "Are you offering?"

He thinned his lips. "I have work to do. If this rain will hold off, I can make some progress."

"If you'd let me help, it would go faster."

"I'm setting trusses. Too dangerous for a girl."

She could see several A-frames for the roof lying in the grass. "I see you have some built. How do you get them up there?"

"With a rope."

"It's starting to rain again."

He picked up the end of the rope that wasn't attached to his scaffolding and tied it around the top of a truss.

Large raindrops splashed on Natalie's cheek, her glove, hat, shoulder, then everywhere at once, like a full bucket being dumped over her head.

Willum pretended not to notice the rain. He was a stubborn man. He looked so silly with rain running off his hat and him trying to tie a knot in the rope.

A giggle rose up from her tummy and burst out of her mouth.

He shook his head and let his hands drop to his side. Then he slogged through the wet grass and took her by the elbow, leading her toward the street.

She snatched the food basket as he ushered her past it. She hoped the food wasn't ruined. When Willum guided her to the livery, disappointment washed over her.

"I'd like to rent a rig."

She held up the basket. "What about lunch?"

"You're soaked through."

"So are you."

"I'm not cold."

"See, I told you that wool sweater would keep you warm even wet."

He narrowed his eyes. "You're not so lucky."

Mr. Parker hitched a buggy, and Willum helped her up into the seat. He climbed aboard and set the horse into motion, but not fast. A leisurely walk.

This was nice. She wrapped her arm through his and rested her head on his shoulder. She felt his muscles tense under the sweater, and he looked down at her with his eyebrows pinched together in question.

"I'm cold." She was.

He pulled his arm free of hers and her spirits plummeted then rose higher than the sky when he wrapped his arm around her shoulders.

"Is that better?"

She nodded and laid her head back on his shoulder. This was perfect.

Chapter 10

The week leading up to Thanksgiving broke into sunshine. Willum had finished the trusses and shingled the roof. Much to Natalie's dismay. She had been stuck below, drawing lines in the dirt with the toe of her shoe. She was cute to watch. . .when she didn't know he was looking. The church looked peculiar with open studwork for walls and a completed roof. But he wanted to get the roof on before more rain. He didn't need walls to work on the interior.

Reverend Bollen's buggy rolled up in front of the church. Natalie wasn't with him. Wasn't she coming today? He would miss her. "Hello, Reverend."

The reverend pulled on the reins then tipped his hat. "Willum."

Willum strode to the side of the buggy. "I hope everything is all right." He hoped Natalie wasn't sick.

"Everything's right as rain. I promised my daughter I'd stop by."

"Is she well?"

"Other than driving her brothers mad with all her fussing, she's fine. She wanted me to tell you that she won't be arriving until lunchtime. Her mama needs her at the house."

So he would see her. "Thank you."

"She'll be right along if she gets her work completed sooner. The way she was going at it, I'd say it will be sooner."

A smile crept across Willum's lips.

The reverend chuckled. "I see you've worked things out with my daughter."

He wouldn't say they'd worked things out, but Willum was softening to her. "We're getting there."

The reverend nodded and snapped the reins, putting the buggy into motion.

If Willum could only figure out how to trust Natalie. How long would it take to trust her again? Years? Would he need a big fat bank account to keep her? He never thought money would have mattered to Natalie—that was one of the things that drew him to her. But if money was what it was going to take for her to trust that he could take care of her, and in return get him to trust her not to get scared off, how much would be enough?

Throughout the morning, as he worked to finish the porch, these questions went through his mind. He anticipated Natalie's arrival with both longing and dread. It wasn't right to let her keep coming if in the end he wasn't going to be able to commit to a life with her. She could let John Seymour or any number of other men court her. But the idea of Natalie with any other man rankled him. Isn't that how this whole affair started?

"What's got you fretting?"

Natalie's lilting voice immediately soothed him like a cool balm. And her smile set his heart to pumping at a healthy rate. He felt a smile tugging at his lips but forced them into a frown. He shouldn't encourage her. He should let her go.

But he didn't want to.

She held up her lunch basket. "Are you hungry?"

He smelled beef stew and biscuits. His stomach gave a silent growl of approval. "You really shouldn't be coming here every day."

"Lunch is the least we can provide with you doing all this work to rebuild the church."

So would she rather not be here? Was this just serving her duty to the church? "You don't have to come."

Her smile turned to that special one that he imagined was only for him. "But I want to. If I had to choose between being here with you—rain or shine—or shopping at the biggest department store in the biggest city"—she sat down on a pile of lumber—"I'd stay right here. Do you know why?"

He couldn't imagine anyone wanting to sit in the cold with the threat of rain day after day when they could be inside a dry building in front of a warm fire. And what woman would ever turn down the chance to go shopping?

"Because I'm happy being near the man I love."

His heart flipped over and over. Was love enough for her?

"Shall we eat?"

"It smells like stew and biscuits." He sat next to her on the stack.

"It's still hot."

After his stomach was satisfied, he knew he *should* get back to work and rose to a stand. "Pie?"

"Pie?" He hadn't smelled any pie. He sat back down. "What kind?"

"Apple."

After his mouth was satisfied with the sweet taste of cinnamony fruit and flakey crust, Willum stood again, pulling on his work gloves. "I really need to get back to work."

"What are you working on today?"

"I finished the porch entrance and now I'm going to put on the siding while I wait for the hay to be delivered."

Natalie inclined her head. "I remember you putting hay in between the outer and inner walls on the house you're still building. Does it really keep a building warmer?"

He nodded. Even if he filled every crack from top to bottom, a building could still be difficult to heat from corner to corner. But with a layer of hay between the walls, the cold didn't seep in as much.

He set up a sawhorse in the middle by the side wall. He took a siding board and rested one end of it on the sawhorse and walked down the length to the other end and lifted it to where it needed to be on the wall. The other end slipped off the sawhorse. Usually, he would have had another man hold up the opposite end, but working alone didn't afford him that luxury. He'd had to get creative several times to do portions by himself he normally had help for. He replaced the board onto the sawhorse and tried again. It fell. But the third time he tried this system the board stayed and then some. It raised level with where he was trying to nail it on the side of the building.

He looked down the length of the board. Natalie stood at the other end, smiling back at him. He wanted to tell her to put it down and go back and sit, but truthfully, he could use her help, and the Lord hadn't impressed upon him that she was not allowed to help. Quite the opposite. He would be a fool to keep refusing her assistance. "Hold it right there." He reached into his tool belt and pulled out his hammer, quickly pounding in a nail then rushed to her end, raised the board even, and pounded in another nail. "You can sit now. That will hold while I hammer in the other nails."

She gave him a curtsy and sat back on the pile.

❄

When Willum turned back to the side of the church to hammer in the rest of the nails along the first board, Natalie let her feet dance up and down. He'd let her help. Maybe he was finally forgiving her. She hoped so.

She helped him with the next board and the next. When she couldn't reach high enough any longer, he set up an A-frame ladder for her.

He held out his gloved hand to her. "You be careful up there."

She put her pink-mittened hand in his. The contrast between ruffled mitten and worn leather work glove almost made her laugh. "I will." She didn't dare allow herself to be careless or get hurt, or he would banish her from ever returning.

He leaned one end of a board up against the ladder. "Don't touch that yet."

She nodded.

He positioned a couple of boards between two sawhorses and jumped up on it then lifted his end of the board. "Okay, grab that end."

She did and lifted it into place.

"I'm going to slide it your way a bit."

She held it secure.

As Willum pounded the nail, the board shook loose from her hands. She tried to hold on tighter but the board fell out of her hands and slivers jammed through her mittens into the flesh of her palms. "Ow!"

Willum jumped down and ran over to her. "What happened?" The board hung on to the wall at Willum's end.

"I'm sorry it slipped." She held her slivered hand to her stomach. The wood pieces hurt, but she couldn't let him know that.

He snagged her wrist and helped her down off the ladder. "Slivers?"

Dare she admit it?

He pulled gently on her mitten.

She sucked in air through her teeth. "Ow, ow, ow. It's catching on the slivers."

He took a slow breath. "Can you get it off?"

She put the tip of her other mitten between her teeth, but when she began to pull, she could feel a sliver in that hand, too, being embedded deeper. "Ow."

He took her other wrist as well. "Here. Let me. Which one is worse?"

She raised one a little.

He squeezed the other. "Where on this hand is the sliver?"

"I only feel one on the heel of my palm."

He slipped his index finger under the edge of her mitten to free the fibers from the sliver.

Shivers coursed up her arm at his touch.

He worked the mitten off. "That's not too bad. I see a couple of smaller ones as well. Can you get the other off?"

She worked her free fingers inside the other mitten. There were more splinter ends to catch. Once she had her fingers covering her palm and the slivers, she said, "You can pull it off now."

He pulled slowly.

"Ow. There's one in my middle finger."

He pulled the yarn away from the finger and moved it around until the fibers became free of the wood, and then he pulled the mitten off. He shook his head.

She had to have a dozen slivers in that hand.

He walked her over to the lumber pile and made her sit. Then he placed her most injured hand in his. "A few of these I can just pull out, but they might hurt."

She nodded.

He pulled out five easily with just his fingernails. Then he removed his pocketknife and opened it.

"What are you doing?"

"I'm going to use the edge of my knife to get under the end of the slivers to pull them out."

She nodded.

He pulled out three more before he ran into a difficult one. "Look away."

Her stomach flipped. "Why?"

"Trust me."

"I do, but please tell me what you're about to do."

"This one broke off inside the wound. I need to cut the skin to reach it."

"Is your knife sharp?"

He nodded. "And clean."

"Then go ahead." She didn't take her eyes off her palm.

"Don't you want to look away?" Tenderness etched in his voice.

No, she would show him she was strong. "I'm fine."

When he pressed the point of his knife on her palm, she shifted her gaze to his face and willed herself not to jerk her hand when the pain came. She would study his face. He had grown out his winter beard. Pain stabbed at her hand. She sucked in a breath through clenched teeth but did not jerk her hand away.

His worried gaze met hers. "Are you all right?"

She nodded.

"I'm sorry I hurt you."

"It has to be done or it will fester." She was glad he had the nerves to do what needed to be done. When she was younger, she had hidden a sliver once until it festered into a painful red sore that was worse than the small piece of wood that lay beneath. To distract herself, she focused on wanting to touch his wavy brown locks.

He went back to his task, finishing with the worst hand and making quick work of the other. He brushed his thumbs back and forth across both her palms, searching for unseen slivers.

The caressing sent tingles up her arm and through her body. Her heart sped up like she'd just been the victor in a three-legged race. She shivered.

He stopped. "Are you all right?"

Fine. Wonderful. There was nowhere else she wanted to be.

He stood. "Stay here. I'll be right back." He disappeared down the street.

He had let her help, and then he tended to her injury. Though it was a small gesture, he showed tenderness toward her pain. She had hope.

Willum returned with a small jar of salve and cloth bandage rolls. He dabbed salve on the palm he'd had to cut the slivers out of then wrapped it. "You shouldn't have any trouble with that."

"Thank you for taking care of me."

His gaze darted between her eyes and her mouth and back.

She licked her lips. Would he kiss her? She hoped so. Then she'd know everything was all right between them.

A dog barking down the street caused Sassy to get up from where she'd been lying and bark.

Willum turned to his dog. "Sassy, come." The dog obeyed.

The spell was broken. She wanted to get it back. "I really am sorry for ever accepting a ride from Mr. Seymour."

Willum looked to the ground. "It was never about the ride."

She realized her mistake. She'd made it worse. She shouldn't have brought up Mr. Seymour. "Then what?"

"Doubts. Trust."

"I don't have any doubts. I trust you. Can you ever trust me again?"

"You doubt I can provide. I have doubts about your steadfastness. We both have doubts. Until we settle those, neither of us can fully trust."

But she did trust him and had no doubts. If it wasn't for her doubt in the first place, he wouldn't doubt her. "What can I do to make you trust me again?"

"I don't know. But I do know I have a church to build." He pulled a pair of new leather work gloves from his back pants pocket. "These may be a little big, but they were the smallest I could get. They will protect your hands."

She took them, and they blurred. He was making it easier for her to help him instead of shooing her away because she got hurt. "Thank you."

"I don't want you getting any more splinters." He cleared his throat. "Besides it's a poor use of time. Daylight's short this time of year."

After securing one more board, Willum stopped to receive a wagonload of hay. He and the men transferred the bales from the back of the wagon through the stud wall in the front to the floor inside. She watched him work. He worked so hard. Hard enough to always provide for her.

He was right. Her thoughts always came back to whether or not he could provide. Needing the proof and not trusting. She kept picturing that tiny cabin. How did one banish doubts they didn't want to have? *Lord, take these doubts from me. Help me trust unconditionally.*

Chapter 11

For the next three sunny days, Natalie arrived at the church ahead of Willum. It pleased him to see her eager, smiling face first thing. She helped him finish the exterior siding then they moved inside to the interior walls. The work went much faster with her help, and by the first week of December, the interior walls were all up and stuffed with straw to make the building hold heat in the winter. Then he finished the surface of the interior walls and painted the church inside and out. He painted the outside, while Natalie painted the inside. The church would be done in time for the Christmas Eve service, with a week to spare.

The congregation would be nice and warm when they celebrated the Lord's birth, because he had installed a stove with pipes that ran through the floor, providing heat from front to back. The heat from the stove turned a fan that would push air through the pipes and up through vents in the floor.

The bare tree branches of the nearby oak scraped against a back window. The eerie sound prickled his flesh. He'd walked Natalie home hours ago before the storm became too strong. He had a little bit of interior work to do before moving in the pews and presenting the building to the reverend. This storm's timing was absolutely perfect. A gift from the Lord.

He lit a candle from the lamp and headed toward the closed front door. A blowing storm was just what he needed to check for drafts. He held the candle up to the frame of the door and moved it around the entire frame slowly. The flame never flickered. No leaks. He did the same with the walls and windows down one side. Sassy followed him around the room. His flame stayed steady.

As he reached the rear window, the branch became more insistent in its knocking. He hoped it didn't break the glass. Then, with a flash of light, a crack of thunder, and a huge crash, the branch careened through the window and smashed the wall around it, blowing out the candle and knocking Willum to the floor. Boards came down, and pain shot through his head and arm.

❄

Natalie sat in a rocking chair near the fire, knitting a scarf for Willum. She had decided that the only way to prove to Willum—and herself—that she was trustworthy, was to be around him as much as possible and be trustworthy. This last month of working on the church had been a challenge and made her ache in places she didn't know she had.

A dog barked at the front door. Not just any dog. She recognized that bark. Sassy! That meant Willum was here. She stood.

Papa looked her direction. "Leave it. It's probably just a stray looking for food or a warm fire."

"No, Papa. That's Sassy. I know her bark."

Papa held up a hand to her to keep her at bay and rose. "Let me check." He opened the door a crack, then wider, looking down and then out into the dark. "Where's your master, girl? Do you want to come in?"

Sassy put her front feet over the threshold and barked then hopped back out. Her coat was soaked through.

Natalie came closer. "What are you doing here without Willum?" She looked out into the darkness but didn't see him.

Sassy barked at her and ran into the storm then returned and barked again. She went back and forth several times.

Matthew came up beside her. "I think she wants us to follow her."

Mama joined them at the door. "In this weather?"

Natalie's insides knotted. "I think something must be wrong with Willum. We need to follow her."

Papa took his and Matthew's coats off the pegs by the door and tossed Matthew his. "Let's go hitch up the buggy."

Natalie grabbed her coat. "I want to go, too."

Papa sighed. "I don't suppose I can stop you. Wait here, and we'll bring the buggy around."

Papa and Matthew were fast, and soon the three were speeding in the storm toward the center of town.

Natalie twisted one mittened hand in the other. "Should we go to the church or his cabin?"

Papa wrapped his arm around her shoulders. "Sassy's heading toward the church. He was likely working to finish the inside. We'll try there first."

Matthew urged the horse faster.

As they neared the church, they saw a fire. Then a flash of lightning lit up the scene. Half of the split oak tree had fallen into the side of the church, and the other half glowed with flames.

When Matthew reined in the horse, Papa climbed down.

Natalie didn't wait for Papa to help her but jumped down behind him and ran in through the front door. A lantern glowed brightly in the middle of the room, sending eerie shadows through the spindly tree branches and fallen timber. Willum lay face-down under the wreckage.

She ran to where his arm lay exposed. "Willum!"

He didn't move or make a sound. *Please, Lord, no.*

Papa knelt beside her. "Take the buggy and get Isaac. Bring him back here then fetch your mama and David if he's come home."

"I don't want to leave Willum." She couldn't leave him.

Papa gripped her arms and turned her toward him. "Go. Matthew and I will start clearing the debris from him so your mama can look at him."

The look in Papa's eyes said what he feared but didn't speak. He didn't want her to see if Willum was dead.

Tears filled her eyes and spilled. "Papa, please save him."

Papa's expression became even more despondent. "I'll do my best. Now go, quickly."

She ran out into the rain and climbed aboard the buggy. *Lord, save him. He was building Your house. Save him. Oh please, save him.*

❄

Willum's arm throbbed and his head felt like a knife was digging around in it. He turned his head. The pain increased. He forced his eyes open. The room was strange. Ceiling beams and trusses. He did not build this room. He'd never been here before. Where was he?

He tried to focus on the rest of his body, from his searing head to his throbbing arm and aching leg. He seemed to be in a bed. Not his bunk or bedroll. A real bed.

His arm that wasn't in pain seemed to be paralyzed. He couldn't move it. He tilted his head to look at it.

Natalie lay with her head on his hand and arm, her face turned toward him.

And he knew.

Natalie didn't have to have confidence in his ability to provide. He had enough confidence for both of them. He could provide, and she would come to believe it, too. He didn't have to doubt her. He could just trust. Trust the Lord.

He wished she didn't look so distressed in her sleep, with her eyebrows pinched. He wanted to soothe away her troubles, and so he raised his other arm with that intent, but it was bound in a plaster cast. The movement shot pain through his arm, and he groaned.

Natalie jerked awake and stared at him. "Willum!"

He tried to talk but only let out a croak of sorts through his dry throat.

Sassy put her front paws up on the edge of the bed. He patted her head.

Natalie picked up a glass of water from the floor and held it to his lips.

He drank with some running out the side of his mouth. "Thank you," he whispered.

She stood. "I'll go get Mama."

He gripped her hand. "Don't leave me." He didn't want to let her go.

She smiled at him then turned her head toward the door. "Mama!"

He squeezed his eyes shut. "Ow."

"I'm sorry. Mama wanted to know when you woke up. I need to get her."

"I'm sure she heard you."

She bit her bottom lip and sat back in the chair.

Two hours later, after Mrs. Bollen had examined him and deemed he would live, Willum dressed and climbed down the stairs with much help and support of the walls, railing, and Natalie.

Natalie shook her head. "Mama, tell him he shouldn't be up."

Mrs. Bollen shook her head as well but had a look of resignation on her face. "You should be in bed resting."

Willum smiled. "I appreciate your concern, but we both know you can't stop me. I need to survey the damage. The Christmas Eve service is five days away."

Mrs. Bollen exchanged a look with Natalie. "It's three days. You were unconscious for a day and half."

How would he ever make the repairs in time for the congregation to use the church Christmas Eve?

Mrs. Bollen pointed to a chair. "You sit while Natalie and I hitch up the buggy."

Now he was the one to shake his head. "That's not for women to be doing."

Natalie put her hands on her hips. "You sit and wait, or I will be stopping you."

Mrs. Bollen smiled. "My daughter can be quite stubborn. You best do as you are told."

He obliged and was soon sitting next to Natalie on the seat of the buggy. He reached for the reins with his good arm.

She pulled them away. "I'm driving. You rest."

"I've never known you to be so bossy."

"When it comes to your well-being, I am." She snapped the reins, and the buggy lurched into motion.

He gripped his arm around her waist to catch his balance then left it there. "I'm sorry I missed going to the Whitworth party with you. Did you have fun?"

She turned to him. "I didn't go without you."

"Why not?"

"I never could have had fun with you lying in a bed half dead." She turned back to the road.

And he realized the depth of her love. "You never left my side, did you?"

"Of course not."

He saw tears rim her eyes.

"I was afraid if I left you, you would—" She blinked several times. "I was willing you to live, begging you. I didn't want you to slip away."

"Thank you." He kissed her cheek.

When Natalie reined in the horse at the church, the four Bollen men and his three best friends were pounding away, repairing the damage.

No! He was commissioned to build the church.

"You fulfilled your call."

He had built the church with Natalie's help. A peace that could only be from the Lord washed over him, letting him know that this was the way it was supposed to be. He'd been set free of the burden of working alone. The repairs belonged to others.

He turned to Natalie in the seat next to him. "Did you do this?"

"I didn't do much. I asked Papa if he could help. Papa asked your friends."

"Thank you." He leaned closer and kissed her. He'd missed her.

Chapter 12

The day of Christmas Eve, the repairs to the church were complete. Natalie stood happily with Willum's arm around her, holding him up. Willum's mother stood on the other side of him. One of Willum's friends had telegraphed his folks in Seattle about his accident, and they had arrived yesterday. Willum's father, along with Papa, her brothers, and Willum's friends unloaded another set of pews from a wagon. Apparently, in the evenings when Willum couldn't work on the church building, he'd been constructing pews and carving designs on the endcaps. Each end showed an event in Christ's life, either from the Christmas or the Easter story. The congregation could all worship together at the Christmas Eve service in the church this evening.

Willum was healing well and feeling much stronger, though he still walked with a limp. Did he really need to lean on her, or was he just using his injuries as an excuse to so boldly put his arm around her in public? She didn't mind. Part of her liked him needing to lean on her, but for that to continue he wouldn't be healing. She wanted him to heal but didn't want to lose his arm around her. He hadn't kissed her again since the day he'd woken up, but seemed content with her at his side, almost happy with her again.

Willum's arm tightened around her shoulder. "Take a walk with me."

"Are you sure you should be walking?" She worried about his bruised leg. "Maybe you should rest. You've already done too much today."

He squeezed her shoulder. "I'll be fine with you next to me." He took limping steps, Sassy following along beside them.

Why would he want to walk in his condition? But as long as he was willing to let her be with him, she wasn't going to question him. As they made their way down the street, she could feel the tension within him, like he had a huge decision to make. What if he was thinking of telling her it would never work between them? That he couldn't get past her doubt? Her stomach knotted.

Please don't let this be good-bye. Tears welled in her eyes. She blinked them away. "Willum?"

"Hmm?"

She seemed to have pulled him out of his thoughts. "Before, you said that you were only staying in town until you rebuilt the church. You aren't going to leave now, are you?"

He was silent for a moment then pointed to some steps. "Can we sit? I'm tired."

She led him over to the steps and realized it was the house he had been building for a year and a half. Did he realize it, too?

He used his good leg to lower himself to the steps. "I need to ask you a question."

She sat and folded her arms for warmth. Was this a good question or bad? "You haven't answered mine."

"Mine first. Don't answer too quickly. Think about it." He turned and looked her in the eyes. "Do you trust me?"

"Yes." The word shot out of her mouth, and she realized she did and deeply so. Her doubt completely banished.

"Do you trust that I can provide for you?"

"I believe that you will work hard and do everything in your power to provide. That's all one person can ask of another person."

He smiled. "Then to answer your question, I'm not leaving."

So there was hope for them. "Do you trust me?"

He tucked his good hand inside his coat pocket. "I have one more question."

"That's not fair. I asked you a question."

He chuckled. "If I didn't trust you, I wouldn't stay."

She leaned into him and tipped her head onto his shoulder. "Okay, you can ask another question."

"Do you mind if I give you your Christmas present tonight instead of tomorrow?"

She sat up straight. "A lot of people exchange gifts on Christmas Eve. But I don't have your present with me. So let's wait."

"I don't know if I can. You can give me mine tomorrow. I don't mind."

"I want to exchange them at the same time."

He let out a heavy sigh and frowned.

She wound both her arms around his good arm. "I love you." She wanted to bring back his good mood.

"I love you, too, and that's why I'm giving you your present right now. I'm sorry. I can't wait." He pulled his arm free of hers and his hand out of his pocket. In his hand sat a small, wooden box with a pair of connected hearts carved on the lid.

She took it and traced the carving, knowing his hands did the delicate work. "Oh, it's beautiful." Better than any fancy hair comb.

"Open it."

She shook the box, and something inside rattled. She tried to lift the lid but it wouldn't come off.

He put his thumb on the top and rotated the lid sideways.

She looked up at him. "How clever."

He raised his eyebrows. "Your gift is in the box."

She stared at the ring lying in the box.

He plucked it out and held it up. Between his thumb and index finger sparkled a diamond ring, two smaller diamonds beside a larger one. "Will you be my wife?"

She squeaked. "Oh yes. Yes, I will. Yes." She yanked off her mitten and held out her hand to him.

"I don't know. You said you didn't want this until tomorrow."

She wiggled her fingers. "No, I want it now."

He slipped it on her ring finger. A perfect fit. She tilted it in the fading afternoon light. "This is the best Christmas present. I'm afraid my gift to you isn't nearly so grand. Just a silly scarf I knitted."

"Your 'yes' is the only present I need." He tipped her chin up and kissed her.

She pulled away. "You asked Papa, didn't you?"

"Of course."

She stood. "I want to go show Mama."

He thumbed to the door behind him. "Can I show you what I've done inside?"

So he did know where they were. She nodded.

He stood and opened the door.

The interior was dark but warm. Maybe Willum kept it warm while he worked nights on it. Soon a glow showed the room. She gasped. "Oh Willum, it's beautiful."

The floor was swept and polished to a deep shine. All the carved moldings were up, the walls painted, and lights glowed on the walls. She turned to him. "Gas lights?"

"All the modern conveniences."

"Indoor plumbing?"

He nodded. "A water closet and hot water upstairs."

"You can't have hot water upstairs. Is there a stove up there or something?"

"The kitchen stove has a tank behind it, and the hot water is pumped upstairs. Let me show you." He toured her through the empty downstairs first—library, sitting room, living room, dining room, kitchen, a large pantry, and a water closet. Upstairs there were six bedrooms and a water closet with a claw-footed tub.

"This is so beautiful." She would love to take a long, hot bath in that.

After showing her the smaller bedrooms, he opened the door to the master bedroom. The only piece of furniture in the entire house, a four-poster bed, stood in the middle of the room, with delicate carvings in the headboard and footboard, and slats where the mattress would eventually go.

She went to it and traced a flower. "Are these. . . ?"

"Rhododendrons? Yes."

Her favorite. "You carved this?"

"I carved it for you."

She jerked her head around to him. "Me? But— What? How?"

He stretched out his good arm. "I built this whole house for you."

"What? How? You live— I don't understand."

"Just because a man lives modestly, doesn't mean he can't provide for the woman he loves."

"But how can you afford this?"

"I'm not a pauper."

"But your cabin."

"Was a place to hide when I first came to town. Then merely a place to lay my head. Then a place to stay while I built our house."

"But you've been building it for a year and a half, and we only just started courting this summer."

"I asked your father to court you when you turned seventeen."

"He let you?" That didn't make sense. He hadn't courted her.

"No, but I knew. I wanted to build you the most special house I could."

She looked around. She couldn't believe this was all hers. Or would be when they married. Then she realized it was just a thing. It held no real security or happiness. "All I need and want is you."

He covered her hand with his. "It's not quite finished. I still have some interior work to do and that wraparound porch, but I've put a lot of work into this house. I plan on living here. With you."

"When will we get married?"

"Whenever you want. Do you need to know everything at once?"

She just had so many questions.

His gaze shifted to her lips, and he leaned closer. His warm breath fanned her mouth, and she breathed it in.

"Mama!" She straightened. "We have so many plans to make."

He cupped his good hand around the back of her head and kissed her soundly then deepened the kiss.

All her questions floated away.

Epilogue

Willum stood at the front of the church dressed in a new suit, his father and Sassy at his side. His gut tightened a little with each passing moment. He could hear his heart thumping against his ribs. The last time he stood at the front of a church, waiting for his bride to appear, he'd waited. . .and left alone.

He wished she'd hurry. He pulled out his pocket watch. It was time. Where was she? She hadn't changed her mind, had she? All this was rather sudden. Natalie had wanted to marry that night—Christmas Eve—when they had arrived back at her home and told her family. When she was convinced to wait, she begged for Christmas Day. Finally, she was granted the day after Christmas by her parents and his.

What if she reconsidered? What if she realized this was all too fast? What if someone had talked her out of marrying him? What if. . .?

No, this was Natalie, not Wanda. Natalie would come. He was sure of it, but he still could not dislodge the rocks in his gut.

❄

Natalie stood outside the sanctuary doors on Papa's arm. She fluffed out the skirt of her pink dress with thin green plaid lines crisscrossing through it. She had begun making it when she was sixteen and had put it in her hope chest. Mama helped her finish it last night. It had small sleeves that didn't do much more than cover her shoulders. She'd always thought she'd get married in June or the summer, and the dress would be perfect. She wanted to marry Willum, and he wanted to marry her. No sense in waiting till summer because of a dress.

"Papa, Willum is at the front of the church, isn't he?"

"Yes, darling." Papa pulled her veil down over her face.

"Did you see him? Not just heard someone else say it, but *you* saw him."

"See for yourself." He opened the door.

Her breath caught.

Willum stood, dignified and straight in his suit, with his hair tied at the nape of his neck, and his arm in a sling.

My, but he was handsome.

His expression was one of pure love and adoration. . .with a little relief mixed in.

She wanted to run down the aisle to Willum but forced her feet into submission then took her first step toward her future and the man she loved.

She was getting her carpenter for Christmas.

Thank You, Lord, for making this little orphan girl's Christmas dreams come true.

Mary Davis is an award-winning author of over a dozen novels in both historical and contemporary themes, four novellas, two compilations, and three short stories, as well as being included in various collections. She is a member of American Christian Fiction Writers and is active in two critique groups.

Mary lives in the Colorado Rocky Mountains with her husband of over thirty years and two cats. She has three adult children and one grandchild. She enjoys playing board and card games, rain, and cats. She would enjoy gardening if she didn't have a black thumb. Her hobbies include quilting, porcelain doll making, sewing, crafts, crocheting, and knitting. http://marydavisbooks.com https://www.facebook.com/mary.davis.73932

Fires of Love

by Tamela Hancock Murray

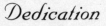

Dedication

To John, my hero who braves all the elements.

For thou, Lord, art good, and ready to forgive;
and plenteous in mercy unto all them that call upon thee.
PSALM 86:5

Chapter 1

Denver
Early December, 1913

Thalia Bloom watched white flakes drift to the hard ground in front of the Denver home she shared with her aunt. Feeling a chill seep through the drawing room window framed by heavy green draperies, she rubbed her hands together. "The snow is so pretty. I wonder if there will be enough to build a snowman."

Viewing the precipitation for herself, Dorcas Bloom shook her head, although too gently for her graying hair to fall out of place. "Not at the rate it's falling. I don't imagine we'll have more than an inch or two. Besides, snowmen are the least of your worries. Tonight's party should be your main concern."

Thalia turned to her aunt. "I'll admit I'm a bit nervous to be hosting the first Christmas party of the season."

"I wouldn't worry if I were you. Everybody on the guest list is congenial."

As long as Maximilian Newbolt stays away.

"Do you have everything set for music and parlor games?" Aunt Dorcas asked.

"Yes, I believe so. But the entertainment doesn't hold a candle to the food." Sugary smells of Cook's pastries mingled with robust aromas of spiced beef and country ham. If Thalia hadn't just eaten a light meal, the scents would have influenced her appetite. "Cook will be getting a good Christmas bonus from us this year."

"I agree. And Eliza, too."

"That's for sure." Their maid had been instrumental in the party preparations.

"But you can take all the credit for the decorations," Aunt Dorcas pointed out.

Thalia gave a contented sigh and noticed with renewed satisfaction the fresh scent and soothing look of the pine tree decorated with dried wildflowers. On the mantle and tables, cream-colored beeswax candles flickered in silver candlesticks adorned with red ribbons, adding mellow light sure to flatter everyone's complexion.

"You can credit others, but I couldn't have done any of this without you." Wistful, she drew closer and took hold of her aunt's hands. "In my whole adult life, I couldn't have done much without you. I remember all the times you wrote to me in boarding school. I wanted to quit sometimes, but you kept me going. And since I've been home, you have been so kind. If I ever lost your affections, my heart would break."

"Now, child, don't go getting sentimental on me." Dorcas released Thalia's hands. "Let's think of the party. I can't wait to see our guests."

"Assuming the snow doesn't deter them." Thalia's gaze went toward the window.

Aunt Dorcas's gaze followed. "Oh, pshaw! A little snow will only make the scene more picturesque. I daresay every guest will be talking about this event for months. Even

Maximilian Newbolt." Her pale lips curled into a wry line. "Especially Maximilian Newbolt."

Maximilian. The man who broke her heart. "I sent invitations in plenty of time, but I didn't see a response from him." Her voice sounded more hopeful than she meant.

"He wrote that he plans to be here. The letter must have gotten misplaced before you had a chance to see it."

Thalia tensed. "Maybe I shouldn't be so blunt, but I wish you hadn't invited him."

"But, my dear, he's a widower now. He hasn't been out and about in months. Not since our dear little Norma died so tragically. She was such a sweet angel." Aunt Dorcas looked heavenward. "The world is a bit colder without her." As though ice touched her shoulders, she shuddered and turned back to Thalia. "But now that she's gone, surely you wouldn't deny your cousin's widower the joy of our Christmas party, would you? After all, for Norma's sake, we need to tend to him. My regret is that we can't be more attentive since he lives in Aurora."

Thalia didn't answer. Let him stay in Aurora for all she cared. At least since he lived fifteen miles away, they didn't see him in church or feel obligated to invite him to their home except on special occasions.

Undeterred—or perhaps encouraged—by Thalia's silence, Aunt Dorcas continued. "Of course, no one could ever live up to Norma. He'll never find another love."

Thalia swallowed. Aunt Dorcas didn't present a threat to Norma, so she never had reason to be anything but sweetness and light to the older woman. Putting such an unkind thought out of her mind, she posed a question. "Do you want Maximilian to find a new love?" Why did she ask such a thing? Maximilian's romantic affairs were none of her concern.

Dorcas paused for only the slightest bit of a second. "No, I don't want him to find someone new. I don't think a remarriage for him is in anyone's best interest. He may think he'll be happy with someone else, but he never will. I feel sorry for the delusional woman who thinks she could ever take Norma's place in his heart. Now you, on the other hand—well, it's high time you married."

Searching for an excuse not to face her aunt, Thalia swiveled around. "Does the bow in the back of my dress seem straight to you?"

Aunt Dorcas paused. "Yes, I believe it does. I must say, I like the new style."

Thalia turned back around. "You mean, old style? This high waist makes me feel as though I'm a member of Napoleon's court instead of plain old Thalia Bloom."

"You are neither plain nor old. I might speculate that you'll have heads turning tonight. And as I said before, it's about time, too."

"Oh, Aunt Dorcas, please don't start up again. You know I have no intention of marrying."

"Whyever not?"

Thalia tried not to display her impatience. Her aunt had asked many times. How could she tell her that once Maximilian had broken her heart, she couldn't risk making it vulnerable again. No, better to be a spinster, to serve the Lord through church work and charitable deeds, than to be trapped in a loveless marriage.

Rather than waiting for Thalia to answer, Aunt Dorcas flitted her hand. "What a waste that would be if you didn't. Josiah Billings has been looking your way. He can hardly keep his eyes off you in church."

Josiah looked attractive enough, but they had nothing in common. "Oh, please. All he thinks about is baseball."

"I'm sure as pretty as you look tonight, you can set his mind on other things."

Thalia decided to turn the tables. "What about you? I'm sure you'll have Mr. Snead and Mr. Carmichael coming to fisticuffs over you before the night is through."

"They can come to fisticuffs, but I'm not ready to mother a brood of ten Snead children nor watch every penny Mr. Carmichael earns. In my youth I was the belle of the ball, but I never felt led by love—or the Lord—to marry any of my suitors."

"Are you sorry about that?"

She answered without missing a beat. "Not at all. I was perfectly happy tending to my brother during his last days, God rest his soul."

Thalia remembered Uncle Tyler. A strange old bird, he proved a handful for his much younger sister. Truly Aunt Dorcas was a saint.

"Enjoy this time, Thalia," her aunt advised. "This is your night."

Thalia laughed and looked at the banquet table. Their maid, Eliza, was in the process of setting out food. "Do you think this platter of sandwiches looks good here in the center, Miss Thalia?"

Thalia surveyed the table with a discerning eye. "I think I prefer to keep that spot for the soup tureen. Why don't you place the sandwiches beside it? Then everything will be perfect." She smiled. Pleasing scents drifted to her nostrils. Certainly with a table so fully stocked with beef, ham, chicken, and different types of rolls for sandwiches, along with preserved fruits and vegetables, relishes, pickles, pies, pastries, and cakes, no one would go hungry. For the hundredth time, Thalia wondered if hosting a full dinner would have been easier than setting out a buffet.

As the grandfather clock in the front hall chimed the hour, Thalia looked toward the polished curved staircase just visible from the dining room door. "Rose should be joining us any minute."

"I admit, I thought she would have appeared by now. But the poor thing was so tired from her train ride. And I didn't think you would ever let her break away from your conversation over tea long enough for both of you to prepare for the party."

Thalia's chuckle displayed more chagrin than humor. "I know. It's just so exciting to have a chance to see her after a whole year."

Just then Rose entered.

"Oh, there you are, Rose. You must have heard us talking about you." Thalia smiled. "You look refreshed after your nap."

"I feel much better, thank you. I don't usually fret over my appearance, but I hope I look all right for the party. I haven't seen so many people for so long that I want to look my best."

"You look splendid." Thalia compared their outfits. "And the color of your dress looks quite nice with your hair. A little part of me wishes my hair were the same shade of auburn."

"Oh, no. You look quite striking with those black curls framing your face, Thalia," Rose argued. "And you chose wisely in your dress, too. That shade of pink brings out the warmth in your complexion. If I weren't your best friend, I'd think your skin had never seen a drop of sunlight or winter's blast. Lucky you."

Aunt Dorcas clucked and shook her head as a guest knocked on the door.

Soon the maid announced the arrival of the new doctor in town. When they entered the drawing room, the three women wore their best smiles.

Aunt Dorcas was the first to speak. "Dr. Stanton. My, but how handsome you look tonight." She shot a look toward Thalia.

Thalia tried not to send her gaze skyward and back in response to her aunt's broad hint. Denver's new doctor was indeed handsome, but he didn't ignite sparks for her. Not the way Maximilian once did. She shook her head in small, swift motions to shoo the image from her mind.

"Is anything the matter, my dear?" Aunt Dorcas asked.

"Oh no, ma'am. I'm fine." Without further prompting, Thalia greeted the doctor and introduced him to Rose.

"Am I the first to arrive?" Dr. Stanton asked.

"Yes, but I think I hear Patricia Logan's voice in the foyer. Dr. Stanton, I must introduce you to Miss Logan. She's an old school chum of mine." Thalia ignored Aunt Dorcas's cautioning look.

A beeping horn got everyone's attention.

Aunt Dorcas put her hands to her ears. "Oh, those wretched automobiles! They will be the death of everything that's good in this world."

Thalia laughed. "You can't stop progress, especially now with mass production."

"Maybe, but who in the world would drive an automobile in this weather?" Aunt Dorcas wondered. "Whoever it is must be freezing."

"I'd venture a guess it's Natalie," Thalia said. "She loves to show off her new Cadillac Model 30."

"If I owned such a fine machine, I might put up with a little cold weather to show it off," Dr. Stanton said. "You make her out to be quite a character."

Thalia smiled. "That she is."

Soon the guests had gathered by the food and fire. Introductions were few since most were acquainted, and as more partygoers arrived, laughter and conversation filled the house. Comments about the snow sounded as brisk as the whirling wind outdoors, and occasionally a guest or two would peek out the window to see its progress, but sparse flakes concerned no one.

Everyone who promised to attend arrived. Everyone except Maximilian. Thalia felt relieved yet somehow disappointed. Fighting conflicting emotions, she told herself she didn't want to see him again. Not now. Not ever. Why, she was even glad he didn't have

Fires of Love

the nerve to show up at her party.

Thalia was surprised to hear a knock almost a quarter hour after the person she considered to be the last guest had arrived.

"Ah, a latecomer," Aunt Dorcas noted.

In her mind, Thalia ran down the guest list and came up with only one missing name.

No, it couldn't be. Maximilian couldn't have decided to appear after all.

Chapter 2

S cat, cat!" Almost dropping the package he held, Maximilian Newbolt shooed a solid black stray so it wouldn't cross the flagstone pathway, sugared with snow, in front of him. He felt relieved when the animal meowed in his direction but went on its way. The last thing he needed was even more bad luck, especially in front of Thalia's house. Prideful about his new Studebaker, he'd driven it in spite of snow-dusted roads and threatening clouds. He'd already gotten a flat tire on the way to the party and had escaped muddying his new overcoat only by inordinate care. Now snow fell with vigor. How many more pitfalls must he sidestep?

He rubbed the white rabbit's foot he carried in his pocket for luck. Tonight would determine his future. He would keep looking for signs until it became clear whether he should stay in Aurora or seek his fortune in California. His cousin Jake's offer to buy an orange grove together tempted him. Working outdoors with his hands would prove quite a contrast to managing the mining company, wasting away with paperwork in his drafty office, never seeing the light of day during winter's deep freeze, only to return after a long day to a house that was empty except for his loyal servants. But even the most dedicated staff, paid to wait on him hand and foot, couldn't—and shouldn't—replace true love or family.

His life had become cold and empty. As cold and empty as his heart. He remembered the day he discovered Thalia didn't love him. Could he change her mind? Or would God send a sign—a sign he was destined for California?

He scratched his itching nose. Surely that was a sign of impending company. Wonder who would soon be visiting him? Not that he had many visitors. The flurry of caring friends ceased a couple of months after Norma's untimely death. Not that they weren't sympathetic. His unwelcoming attitude had discouraged kind overtures. He couldn't put up a front of the truly grieving widower after such an unhappy union. The fact filled him with guilt.

Even now, with his official period of mourning over, he still felt reluctant to get back into the social scene. When he first received Thalia's invitation, he had almost responded with regrets. But his valet, Addison, had encouraged him to go. Sad how he talked to his closest servant more than anyone else these days. Indeed it was high time for him to renew his old acquaintances, whether he wanted to or not.

Which acquaintances would be at the party? The Blooms' Victorian-style house, with fussy white gables prominent against bright pink, boasted quite a few carriages and even a couple of automobiles parked in front. He recognized most of the conveyances and could gauge who appeared on Thalia's guest list based on the fact. He wondered if he could pick back up with the old crowd now that Norma was no longer at his side.

He knocked on Thalia's front door. Muffled voices coming from indoors sounded animated. As he awaited an answer, he regarded the falling snow. "I hope we don't get a blizzard," he muttered, and knocked on the first wood available, which happened to be the front entrance, in hopes of warding off such a plight.

The Blooms' maid opened the door, a look of irritation on her young face, probably because he had seemed impatient with his knocking.

He hoped a pleasant smile would put her in a better mood. "Good evening, Eliza." Shaking snow from his wool coat and stomping on the woven mat, he stepped inside and was greeted by warmth. "I see the party's in full swing. I hope I'm not too late. I had a flat tire on the way."

"I'm sorry to hear that, Mr. Newbolt. You aren't too late. Miss Dorcas has been expecting you." She took his coat and hat.

Miss Dorcas? What about Miss Thalia? He let out an "oh" without worrying if his disappointment showed. Darting his gaze to Eliza, he anticipated a comforting look but received none.

In keeping with Eliza's prediction, it was not Thalia but Dorcas, in a dress of filmy white, who greeted him first. "Oh, Maximilian, I am so glad you decided to join us." She motioned for him to enter the parlor.

"Yes, thank you for the invitation." Excitement and cheer gladdened his spirit. Maybe accepting the invitation had been the right thing to do after all.

A survey of the room, filled with men and women dressed in their best, rewarded him with a glimpse of Thalia. The instant he recognized the figure in pink, his senses tingled with anticipation. Shiny hair the color of a deep, cloudless night crowned a face fairer than any statue of Venus. He'd anticipated that seeing her again now that he was a free man would be difficult, but he hadn't realized how much of an effect she still had on him. Why did she have to be such a marvel, a marvel with an unyielding heart? His mouth dropped with awe and yearning before he gained enough awareness to compose himself.

"What's the matter?" Dorcas prodded.

He shook his head and regarded the elder Miss Bloom. "Nothing. Nothing at all." Desperate to deflect questions, he handed his hostess the package containing a small but dense fruitcake. Its sweet aroma penetrated its wrapping of cheesecloth tied with a green ribbon. "I had my cook bake this fruitcake just for you. It's her Christmas specialty. I hope you enjoy it."

"Oh, I remember Ginny's fruitcake. So dark and moist, just the way I like it. Norma always served it at Christmas." Her eyes grew misty, but she kept her voice cheerful.

"I know. That is a fond memory for me, too." One of the few, although he decided not to reveal that to Norma's aunt. "Do enjoy the cake. Ginny retired as of yesterday."

"Really? Is she ill?"

"No, thankfully. Her son's wife just gave birth to their ninth child, and he invited her to live with his family. I can't believe she took him up on it."

"My, I'm sure with all those children, they could use two extra hands."

"I'm sure." He sent Dorcas a half smile. "I even offered her a raise in salary to stay, but she respectfully declined."

"So you're eating cold sandwiches until you find another cook?"

"Oh, I have another cook." He grimaced at the memory of burned toast and under-cooked potatoes. "She's quite inexperienced. Breakfast and lunch weren't especially good today. But she's young and her family needs the money, so I don't have the heart to fire her."

"She'll improve."

"I hope so. Although I must say, I look forward to sampling some good food tonight."

Dorcas gave the cake she held a little squeeze. "Maybe you should have kept this for yourself. Really, Maximilian, you didn't have to bring a thing. It's gift enough for me knowing that you have finally gotten out of that lonely house of yours. Norma would want you to enjoy life now that your time of mourning is well over."

"That's comforting, especially coming from you." He smiled and darted his glance to Thalia long enough for his treacherous feelings to return. He felt compelled to move toward her. "If you'll excuse me, I'll take a moment to speak to Thalia."

"Oh, but you shouldn't have to chase your hostess. She'll make her way over to you soon enough." Dorcas surveyed the party guests as if desperate to find someone. Soon she smiled and tapped his forearm. "Now who do I spy but Bryant Emmet? He's some-one you need to meet. He just moved here, and he's very interested in the mining business."

Discussing business at a lively party didn't appeal to Maximilian, but he knew from experience that there was no arguing with strong-willed Dorcas Bloom.

❄

Thalia looked across the room and caught her aunt chattering with the latecomer. A guest whose silhouette she would have recognized in the darkest alley.

Maximilian.

Almost spilling her punch, she recovered her composure. Maximilian's form was unmistakable. Tall and slender but not skinny. Dark hair gleamed under the light. Despite the ins and outs of fashion, he remained clean shaven—a wise choice consider-ing his fine yet manly features. She took in a breath then swallowed. She wanted to greet him, but again, she didn't.

"Who's that you're looking at so hard, Thalia?" Josiah wanted to know. With curious eyes, he peered in Maximilian's direction. "Oh, Newbolt came, did he? It's been a long time since he's been out and about. Can't say I missed him much." He chuckled and shook his carrot-topped head. "Look at him talking to your aunt, standing there as though he's king of the world. And look at how he's dressed. He's quite the dandy, isn't he?"

"Don't make fun of him," Thalia snapped. Then, regretting her force of emotion, she softened her stance. "His official period of mourning the loss of his wife is over, and so what if he wears dashing clothes now? I do believe this is his first party since her death."

"That's right. I'm sorry. I remember now. She was your cousin Norma, right?"

Thalia nodded and tried not to stare at Maximilian too long. She could see him excusing himself from Aunt Dorcas. Since he looked in her direction, she guessed he planned to make his way toward her. But just as quickly, her aunt took him by the elbow and guided him toward Bryant Emmet. She felt grateful for the reprieve.

"Thalia?" Josiah asked. "Are you listening to a word I'm saying?"

"Something about baseball?" she guessed.

He grinned. "What else? You know, seeing Newbolt brings me a thought. I wonder if his church has a team. Maybe our church team could play a few games against them for fun."

"I doubt if he's given it any thought. Spring's a long time away," Thalia pointed out.

"You're right about that. Much too long, if you ask me."

In her head, Thalia didn't want to talk to Maximilian, but her heart insisted that she seek him. "Excuse me, Josiah, but I must greet Maximilian since he just arrived."

"Sure. I'll come along with you and ask about the teams."

If only Josiah would be lured to the table for refreshments—anything to keep him from following her. In the same instant, she realized his insistence on accompanying her would save her from speaking with Maximilian alone.

Aunt Dorcas gave Thalia a warning look when she and Josiah interrupted their conversation with Bryant. Ignoring her, Thalia smiled and hoped her face didn't reveal her excitement upon seeing him once more. Just being near him, taking in a whiff of the spicy shaving lotion he wore, being near his confident essence, sent old feelings rushing anew. "Maximilian. How nice of you to join us in our celebration. It wouldn't have been Christmas without you."

The expression in his eyes told her that he was just as conflicted about seeing her as she was him. But he locked his gaze with hers, and for her, everyone else in the room melted into oblivion.

"Thalia."

The way he caressed her name with his voice filled her with a craving to be closer to him. She felt wobbly. In spite of her desire not to look away from intense brown eyes flecked with gold, she searched for a nearby chair. Too bad Mrs. Hansen already occupied the only one in reach. Far be it from Thalia to take a seat from a frail dowager. At least now she could look back into Maximilian's eyes. Judging from his stare, he would be content to gaze at her all night.

Why did she have to react this way? She couldn't. Not after what had happened.

If Josiah noticed her reaction to Maximilian, he didn't let on. "Remember me, Newbolt?" He extended his right hand.

Maximilian returned the gesture, and the men exchanged a hearty shake. "Of course. Josiah Billings. Still a big baseball fan?"

Josiah swung an imaginary bat, almost coming into contact with a burning candle in the process. "If I keep practicing, I'll be a regular Ty Cobb."

Dorcas laughed louder than she should have. "Thalia, let us leave the men to their sports talk."

"Oh, but you have always encouraged me to take an interest in baseball." Thalia couldn't help but chide. "And look, there's Mr. Carmichael. Have you had a chance to speak with him yet?" She waved toward the balding man.

He smiled and started toward them.

Dorcas threw Thalia daggers with her stare, but Thalia smiled when he approached. "Mr. Carmichael, have you had a chance to see Mr. Newbolt?"

"Evening, Newbolt." The older man extended his hand, and Maximilian accepted.

Though they exchanged pleasantries, as Thalia expected, Mr. Carmichael didn't dwell on Maximilian too long. Instead, he focused on Aunt Dorcas.

"The food you got here tonight is mighty good, Dorcas. If you don't mind me for asking, where did you buy your beef?"

Obviously not expecting such a question, Aunt Dorcas dropped open her mouth and paused. "Uh, Swanson's."

"Swanson's?" He let out a whistle. "They're the most expensive place in town." He lifted his right index finger. "Now let me recommend a place that'll save you lots of money, especially if you tell them I sent you. . ."

Taking his victim by the arm, he led her toward the refreshment table. Thalia imagined they would go over each plate and discuss the price of every foodstuff available. She tried not to giggle—or think about the tongue-lashing she would receive later.

With her aunt at bay, Thalia had a suggestion for Josiah. "Wouldn't it be fun if we played a few records on the Victrola?"

His eyes brightened. "Sure it would."

"Maybe you could go through our collection and pick a few songs."

"Sure. That would be swell." He headed for the Victor Talking Machine, a small wooden box with a large horn. Such machines had become popular for anyone wishing to listen to recorded music.

Maximilian shook his head. "Josiah hasn't changed since the day he turned ten."

Realizing his observation wasn't far from the truth, Thalia decided not to comment.

Maximilian glanced toward the window. "If it weren't snowing outside, I'd ask you to take a walk with me in the moonlight."

"But alas, it snows. I hope this weather won't be too much of an inconvenience for my guests." She sighed at the falling flakes. "It is quite pretty, though."

"Not nearly as pretty as you," he proclaimed. "You look even lovelier than I remember." He captured her gaze with his once more.

Taken aback and yet delighted by his compliment, she forced an answer. "It—it appears the snow is falling harder."

"How do you know? You're not looking out the window."

"Oh, you are incorrigible." She broke the lock on his stare.

"I know where a window is—a window where no one else is looking. And if I were a betting man, I'd say it's right near a fire so we can stay warm as we watch the snow."

"If you mean the window in the study, you would have lost the bet. Aunt Dorcas told Eliza to keep the fire lit to accommodate the overflow. Judging from how sparse the main room has become, I would venture it's already been discovered. If it's privacy you want, I doubt you'll get it there."

"Too bad. Wonder how we can get away from Josiah?"

A giggle escaped Thalia's lips in spite of her best efforts to contain it.

"Certainly your aunt doesn't think you should yoke yourself to such a juvenile."

She felt mirth leave her expression. "She said that, did she?"

"She spoke quite approvingly of a possible match. You—you're not engaged to him, are you?"

The thought sent a shudder down her back.

His eyebrows rose just a tad. "Does that mean you can't stand the thought?"

She felt her cheeks flush. "Was I that obvious?"

He chuckled.

"I've told Aunt Dorcas time and time again that I have no desire to marry, but she won't listen. She seems to think Josiah is the perfect match for me. Probably because he has more than enough money to offer me a lifetime of security."

"So do many other men."

Discerning that he referred to himself, Thalia tried to hide her surprise and made sure not to encourage him. "There are things far more important than money."

"Watch it. People may think you're a woman who has always had more than enough."

"Do they?" Her voice snapped no less than if it had been a blow to his cheek.

He flinched. "I'm sorry. I didn't mean to sound harsh. I have no right to chastise anyone about poverty, since I've never gone to bed hungry. Forgive me. And you are right; there are other important things."

"And you are right. I shouldn't be so defensive." Ashamed, she glimpsed at the Oriental rug on the floor and back up again. "God has blessed me with enough, and because I don't have to worry about where my next meal is coming from, I can focus on ethereal things. Not everyone has that luxury."

She saw Maximilian grimace and thought he wasn't sure about what she said—until she heard Josiah.

Excited, he held a waxy red disc for their inspection. "Look, you've got 'Take Me Out to the Ball Game.' I didn't even know they'd recorded that."

"Then your night is made." Thalia's voice betrayed more sarcasm than she meant.

Josiah didn't seem to notice. "Come on in and listen. Everybody's asking for you. They want you to play the piano for a sing-along."

"That does sound fun," Thalia said with feigned enthusiasm. Sitting by the fire with Maximilian—even among other guests—seemed much more appealing. She tried not to look too vexed as she set her gaze on Maximilian. "Looks as though we'll have to delay your plan to watch falling snow."

Though she had dreaded the thought of seeing him again, her feelings for him took her by surprise. She needed to sort them out. She would definitely try to see him again in relative privacy before the party ended if it was the last thing she did.

Chapter 3

Maximilian wanted to accompany Thalia and Josiah to the music room, but he held back. Thalia proclaimed she never wanted to marry, but then again, he'd seen many women say the same and go on to wed and bear a brood of children. But with Thalia, things were even more complicated. Obviously he had stepped into Josiah's territory—at least as far as Josiah and Dorcas were concerned—and he wasn't about to interfere and offend Dorcas. Not when he still hadn't seen a clear sign about when—and if—to tell Thalia his thoughts about going to California.

Too busy catching up with friends to eat earlier, he decided to swing by the banquet table one last time before entering the music room. Besides, there was no doubt Josiah would be hanging all over Thalia. He wasn't sure he wanted to witness that.

"A penny for your thoughts, Maximilian."

Snatched from his dream world, he looked in the direction of the voice and discovered a friend of Thalia's, Edith. "You came in out of the blue. How long were you standing there?"

"Long enough to see you pondering the mysteries of the universe. I thought perhaps my penny would be well spent to learn your thoughts."

"That's where you're wrong, I'm afraid. My thoughts are hardly worth a penny."

Edith laughed. "I doubt you would find many in agreement with you." She took a small bit of an especially appealing tart. "Mmmmm. Delightful. You must try one."

"You and I are the only ones hovering around the banquet table. What does that say about us?"

"Oh, it might say that we are among the hardy souls who aren't afraid of a little snow. A lot of people left already, you know."

"Yes, I thought it seemed as though the crowd had dwindled."

"Poor Thalia." Edith brushed crumbs off her blue dress. "She worked so hard on this party. It's a shame it had to be cut short due to the weather."

"I would dispute that it's been cut short. Seems to me lots of people are still having a good time."

"I know I am with so much food. After this I won't need to eat for three days." She gestured toward him, holding the last bit of tart. "I recommend trying one before they're all gone."

"I don't know if I should indulge. I already had a piece of mince pie." The remaining two slices of pie, with rich fruit filling and flaky crust, tempted him.

Edith regarded the pie with less enthusiasm, judging from the way she wrinkled her nose. "I don't care much for mince pie myself."

"Oh, but you might put aside your distaste for it and try it around this time of year."

"Why?"

"You've never heard the old saying?" Since she obviously hadn't, he continued. "For each piece of mince pie you eat at every Christmas party you go to, you'll have a month of happiness the following year."

Edith laughed. "What a silly superstition. Are you saying I need to go to twelve parties this month and eat mince pie?"

"If you want a year of happiness, I suppose so." He smiled. "A year before I married, I managed to eat four pieces over the season, and I had the best spring of my life."

"Goodness, Maximilian, I can't believe here in the twentieth century that an educated man such as yourself—a graduate of William and Mary College in Virginia, no less—would believe in such nonsense. I would credit your happy spring to coincidence."

"Promise me you won't tell my old professors," he joked before turning serious. "I know I might sound silly, but I do have my reasons for thinking the way I do."

"Does Thalia know your reasons?"

He thought for a moment. "No, I suppose not."

"Then no wonder you and Thalia never wed. She'd never put up with such foolishness. At least not without a very good reason."

Maximilian winced. Thalia was full of vigor and fun but much too serious about religion. Sure, he went to church and had no doubt about the existence of God. He even prayed to Him when he needed something. But trusting the rabbit's foot in his pocket seemed the better bet. The rabbit's foot he could see, but not God.

"Did I say something wrong?" Edith asked. "I'm so sorry. I suppose that was insensitive of me, especially since Norma—"

"I think I'll take you up on your suggestion about that tart." Looking away from Edith, he reached for a delectable-looking puff pastry too quickly and knocked over a pepper shaker meant for a nearby platter of roast beef. Black particles of the spice scattered on the tablecloth. "Oh, no."

Edith shrugged. With a well-tended hand, she righted the shaker and swished the offending pepper onto the floor. "See? No harm done."

He shuddered at her cavalier attitude. "Don't you know a spilled pepper shaker is bad luck?"

"Not those old tales again. Honestly!" She grinned. "I have to say, coming from you, I find them quite amusing."

He wasn't sure—or perhaps he was too sure—about Edith's flirtation. Though charming, she wasn't interesting enough for him to consider complicating matters with thoughts of her other than as a food critic. He decided to taste the tart Edith recommended. He nodded his approval as sweet fruit and buttery pastry pleased his taste buds.

"Is it good?" Approaching from another direction, the female's voice was teasing.

Maximilian nodded to Mabel, an acquaintance of Thalia's since girlhood. "Edith suggested I try one. Clearly, Edith, you know your way around a buffet table."

"Thanks. I think."

A horn squawked four times. "Oh, bother," said Edith, "It's Papa. He must have come early because of the snow."

"At least you won't be stranded," Maximilian pointed out.

Edith sent him a look. "I could think of worse fates." She waved and headed for the door. "Toodles."

As soon as Edith was out of sight, Mabel shook her head. "That Edith. She's so bold. Nothing like Norma. You never could guess what she was thinking."

The observation brought back a few too many memories. "True."

"You can always tell what Edith is thinking. She wears her heart on her sleeve," Mabel noted. "I, on the other hand, believe that a woman should shroud herself in mystery."

Maximilian fought back a grin. Clearly Mabel was unaware of her own transparency.

She bit into a sandwich. "We'd better eat hearty since we'll be fighting a lot of snow and wind on the way home. In fact, I'm thinking of abandoning ship as soon as I finish my punch. Who knows? This could turn out to be a blizzard."

"Blizzard? I think this is hardly what one would call a blizzard." He took another bite of pastry and looked outside. His mouth dropped. "Oh, you're right. The snow has accumulated quite a bit. Much more than any of us imagined."

She nodded toward the entrance. "I see most of the other guests are giving us the old twenty-three skiddoo."

Though several could still be heard singing in the music room, along with the piano and a banjo, their numbers did in fact seem to be dwindling by the minute. Even then, he looked toward the front door and noticed a couple of the guests leaving. "So it seems."

"How about you? Do you plan to stay?"

He thought about the long journey back to Aurora. While not arduous in fair weather, the falling snow would increase its difficulty by automobile. With the amount on the ground, he wondered if even a horse would improve his journey's success. "I suppose I should be leaving, much to my regret. I was rather late in arriving as it was. I had a flat tire on the way."

"You don't look the worse for wear." Then, seeming to be embarrassed by her bold observation, she continued. "At least you won't be the first to leave."

"True." The word sounded strange, as though someone else had uttered it.

"Is something the matter, Maximilian?"

"I—I had some news for Thalia, but I don't know if I can tell her now." Indeed, talking proved difficult. Was this the sign he wanted?

"News?" Mabel licked her lips. "Is there something I can tell Thalia for you?"

"No." Maximilian swooshed his tongue around his mouth. Why did the inside of his mouth feel as though he'd been attacked with itching powder? His arms felt the same. He didn't want to scratch, especially not in front of Mabel, or anyone else. But he had to do something. "I'm so sorry. I have some pressing business I must tend to."

She looked doubtful, but he had no recourse except to ignore her. With as much dignity as he could muster, he walked as quickly as he could without running, down the hall to the library, certain no one else would be there. He opened the door and felt a draft in spite of the lit fire on the opposite end of the room. Undeterred, he ignored the cold

Fires of Love

and shut the door behind him, noticing the musty, leathery odor of aging books. The room was dark except for the fire and the glow from the blanket of white snow streaming through the window.

Wanting to assess his condition and stay warm at the same time, he went to the fireplace and rolled up his shirtsleeve. "Oh no! Hives!" Unable to control the urge, he scratched.

"Hives!" A female gasped.

Maximilian startled and swirled in the direction of the voice.

Her companion interrupted. "I beg your pardon, sir. Can't you see we want privacy here?"

Maximilian saw none other than Whit, a known rake and cad. Hovering behind him was a girl he had known since she was a baby—Nanette. Such a young woman had no business to be involved with a scoundrel. Though he couldn't see her expression in the dim light, he could feel her embarrassment.

Whit's eyes didn't meet his. Without a doubt, he had caught them in a stolen kiss. Maximilian squashed the urge to warn the girl about Whit. Judging from her blushing cheeks and unwillingness to look him in the eye, admonitions would only be greeted with deaf ears.

"What's that?" Whit's pointing motion brought with it a whiff of a liberal application of bay rum.

Taken aback even though he knew Whit saw the condition of his arm, Maximilian blurted, "What's what?"

Whit moved toward him and pointed to red bumps. "Look, you've got them on your face, too."

Maximilian touched his face and discovered welts.

"You don't have the measles, do you?" He cringed and stepped back. "I couldn't abide catching the measles."

"Measles? No, no. It's nothing like that, why, it's. . ." He searched for an explanation until he recalled the only cause for such symptoms. "Do I look flushed?"

They nodded.

A feeling of impending doom visited him. "Then it could only be one thing. I must have somehow eaten rhubarb. And that means trouble." His stomach tightened.

"We've got to get a doctor right away," Whit said. "That new doctor in town is here, isn't he? What's his name—Stanton?"

Maximilian tried to think, but his brain was getting too foggy to remember. "Uh, I. . . why, I think so. Yes, I was introduced to a doctor named Stanton. A charming fellow, as I recall. Forgive me. I'm not usually this muddleheaded."

"Of course not. You're sick," Nanette said.

Whit agreed. "Don't try to say anything else. Nanette, go get the doctor."

She nodded and exited the library.

"Sit on the couch," Whit advised, pointing to a short sofa upholstered in a paisley print near the fire. "I won't hear an argument." Without further ado, Whit took an unlit candle from a silver stick, lit it with the fire, and proceeded to light a lamp.

Even in his weakened and somewhat frightened state, Maximilian felt he had to argue, though on a different point. "Come here, Whit."

"I'm not sure I want to."

"Fine. Stay there by the light."

"What's so important?"

"I decided to spare you by not saying this in front of Nanette, but if you want to play games, save them for women sophisticated enough to know the score. Don't sully an innocent girl."

"I don't know what you're talking about."

Maximilian knew well that Whit knew exactly what he meant. "Nanette's children will be going to Sunday school in this town some day. Unless you mean to be the gentleman with her, find someone who doesn't expect marriage. And that goes for the other young girls around here, too."

His pleasant features darkened into a sinister scowl. "See here, sport, this is the twentieth century, not the Dark Ages. I never have and never will force my attentions on a woman. Nanette knows the score."

"It was too dim to see a lot in here, but I could feel her excitement and hear the rapture in her voice. She isn't skilled in the games you play. And you know it."

"Who do you think you are, her father?"

"No, but I know her father, and if he were here, that's what he'd say, and then some. Don't let me see you with her again unless your intentions are honorable."

"Or what?" Whit snarled.

"I know my voice is hoarse and I sound strange when I speak now, but you can take my word that you don't want to cross me when I'm at full strength." Breathing had become difficult, but Maximilian tried not to show it for fear of appearing weak.

"I won't stand here and be insulted. I'll let it slide this time since you're ill. But don't expect me to play nursemaid." He left without another word.

As soon as Whit departed, Maximilian heard footfalls of several people rushing in. No doubt they wanted to view him as though he were a sideshow exhibit. He wished he didn't have the presence of mind to be chagrined, but he did.

Thalia rushed to his side to sit beside him on the couch. "Maximilian, what's wrong?"

Though he had managed to ward off Whit from making more advances toward Nanette—or at least he hoped, at this point his tongue felt too thick for him to respond. All he could do was shake his head. He wished Thalia didn't look so alarmed.

"The doctor will be here any minute. He went to his buggy to retrieve his bag. You're in good hands," Thalia assured him.

Maximilian heard an authoritative voice. "Move aside, everyone, please. I need to see the patient."

Obeying, the partygoers vacated the room, leaving him alone with the doctor.

His consoling voice matched his concerned countenance. "How are you feeling?"

Having spent his voice protecting Nanette against Whit, at this point he could only shake his head.

"Can you breathe okay?" Even as he asked, Dr. Stanton took out his stethoscope and warmed the shiny metal tip against his palm.

Maximilian shook his head. "Throat's sore and a little tight."

"We can take care of that. Has this happened before?"

He nodded.

"How many times? Do you recall? You don't have to speak, just hold up your fingers to indicate the number."

Sensing the question's importance, he tried his best to recall every incident. The time at his aunt's had taught him a lesson but good. He hadn't gone near the fruit since. He held up one finger. Maximilian thought, trying to recall when he had felt so miserable. He couldn't remember. Except. . .except the time he encountered rhubarb at his aunt May's. But surely he hadn't eaten any rhubarb tonight.

Maximilian sighed. "Fruit. Rhubarb."

His brow wrinkled. "Have you eaten rhubarb today? I don't remember seeing any on the table."

Maximilian shook his head, feeling foolish. He always took care not to eat the cursed fruit. How he managed to encounter it now, he had no idea.

Dorcas peeked her head in the door. "Is there anything I can do?"

The doctor looked at her. "Not right now, but you could wait a minute while I question Mr. Newbolt." After Dorcas exited, he turned back to his patient. "Maximilian, when did you first notice your symptoms?"

He tried to recall. "About. . .fifteen. . .or twenty minutes ago. . .itch in my throat. . . nose started running." He reached in his pocket, pulled out a rumpled handkerchief, and blew his nose.

The doctor placed the stethoscope against Maximilian's chest. "When did you notice the rash?"

"A few minutes later." He tried not to cough but couldn't help himself. The hacking resounded throughout the library, embarrassing him with its vigor.

"Does your throat feel full?"

He tried to swallow then nodded.

"We need to figure out if you had any rhubarb." The doctor put the stethoscope into his jacket pocket. "If not, we have to find out what else you're allergic to."

He called in Dorcas, who appeared with Thalia.

"Ladies, was there any rhubarb in anything you served tonight?"

Thalia blanched. "Yes. Why?"

"From the best I can tell, Mr. Newbolt is allergic to rhubarb, and he has had a reaction."

"Oh, no!" Their hostess gasped. "Maximilian, did you eat one of the tarts with red filling?"

"Yes. . .strawberry, Edith said. Delicious. I had. . .another."

"It's all my fault." This time she wailed. "That was a new recipe that called for strawberry and rhubarb preserves. Oh, what have I done?"

The doctor stood and turned to Thalia. "We need to get him into bed. Could we move him to a guest room?"

"Of course. We have several bedrooms. Actually, one is on the first floor. It would be easier to put him there. I'll have Eliza start the fire." Dorcas moved toward the door.

"After he's in bed, we need to make a tent out of a sheet and fill it with steam. You do have a teakettle on the stove, don't you?" As he spoke, Dr. Stanton held out his hand to Maximilian. Grateful for the assistance, he accepted it and balanced himself on his feet.

"Yes, I can get whatever you want." Dorcas clasped her hands as if trying to keep them still. "Perhaps you could help take Maximilian down the hall and help him get into bed. There's an old nightshirt of my brother's in the top drawer of the bureau."

"I'll do that, and Miss Bloom, please bring a glass of water and a spoon when you return."

A glass of water sounded good to Maximilian, as did any help he could get. A few moments later, feeling woozy, he offered no resistance as the doctor helped him dress for bed and tucked him underneath the covers.

As soon as he was in bed, the doctor asked for his wrist and checked his pulse rate. Though Dr. Stanton kept his expression neutral, Maximilian didn't take comfort in his lack of consoling words. But at the moment he was too tired to ask questions.

❄

Thalia waited as long as her patience allowed before returning to the first-floor guest room.

Lord, please heal Maximilian!

She knocked on the door. "May I come in?"

"Yes," the doctor answered.

As she entered, Thalia noted with satisfaction that being sure the spare room sparkled had paid off. Even though earlier that evening, neither she nor Aunt Dorcas had any idea they'd have overnight guests, both women liked to keep every place in the house presentable whether they planned for it to be seen by visitors or not. Maximilian was sure to rest in comfort—or, at least in as much comfort as possible for someone ill—in a room as well appointed yet homey as he would find in Denver.

The doctor stood over his patient. Maximilian looked helpless lying alone in the four-poster bed with several woolen blankets and the sheets pulled up to his neck, his head nestled in fluffy down pillows. If only she hadn't served rhubarb.

For fear of disturbing them, she didn't want to make her approach too close. "Is he going to be all right?" Her worry expressed itself in her voice at the sight of the hives on his forehead.

The doctor turned a kind expression toward her. "Oh, it's you, Miss Thalia. I thought you were your aunt returning with the things I requested. Yes, I believe he'll be all right."

She hoped the doctor felt as confident as he appeared. "Is there any way I can help?"

"I've been thinking about the best way to tent him for the steam. I asked your aunt for supplies. Maybe you could get us an extra sheet. And bring a couple of towels and a bowl. Miss Bloom is bringing the teakettle and a glass of water."

"I think there's an extra sheet right here." Thalia made haste to open the bottom drawer of the cherrywood bureau. A faint yet sharp smell of mothballs greeted her as she reached for seldom-used linens. At least they were clean and would do the job.

Turning around, she saw the doctor checking Maximilian's pulse. "How is it, Doctor?"

"No change." He studied his patient. "At least he's asleep now."

"I wonder if he'll sleep through the night."

"I wouldn't count on it, although I'll make him as comfortable as I can." The doctor took a seat in the blue brocade Chippendale chair beside the fireplace and pulled it up next to the bed.

A knock indicated that Aunt Dorcas was back. Thalia opened the door and let her aunt in.

The doctor took the tray from Aunt Dorcas, set it on the bedside table, and took the sheet Thalia had draped across her arm. "Probably the best way to do this is to tuck this behind the headboard and drape it across Mr. Newbolt." He leaned toward his patient and gently shook him awake. "I really hate to disturb you, but we need to get you to sit up in the bed."

Thalia watched as Aunt Dorcas and the doctor arranged Maximilian in bed.

"Before we finish making the tent, I want to give him some bicarbonate of soda." The doctor prepared the medicine and handed the glass to Maximilian. "Drink this right up."

Maximilian took the glass without hesitation and drank a swallow, then grimaced.

The doctor seemed amused but consoling. "I know it doesn't taste good, but it should help you. If you drink it fast, you won't taste it very long."

Thalia felt sorry for Maximilian as he obeyed then let out a burp.

The doctor smiled. "See, it's already helping some."

He glanced toward the two women. "Pardon my faux pas."

Thalia smiled at him. "Think nothing of it."

She watched as the doctor and her aunt made a tent for Maximilian out of the sheets, using boiling water poured in the bowl for steam.

"Breathe in as much steam as you can," the doctor advised while taking his pulse. "Try to relax but don't fall asleep. And if you get too hot inside there, let us know. We can raise one corner of the sheet so you can have some fresh air."

Thalia hadn't expected such an elaborate remedy. Seeing the patient covered in such a way increased her anxiety. Once Maximilian was settled, she couldn't wait to ask the doctor his opinion. Seeking more reassurances, she motioned to him to step outside the door with her so the patient wouldn't overhear what was said. "Will—will he be okay?"

"I hope so."

Her stomach lurched. "You—you hope so? You mean, you don't know?"

"Most allergic reactions cause more discomfort and inconvenience than any real harm, but there is the possibility that the allergy could develop into something more serious, especially since he had such a severe reaction so quickly."

"You—you don't think he could. . ." She didn't want to say the word, but she had to. "Die?"

"I'm hoping for the best."

His noncommittal answer left her with more anxiety. No matter how much he had hurt her, Maximilian couldn't die. He just couldn't.

Thalia's gaze went to the window at the end of the hall. The night sky was almost white with falling snow.

Chapter 4

Alone in bed with only sounds of the crackling fire and his labored breathing to break the silence, Maximilian tried to take in as much air as possible. The feeling of suffocation left him fearful. He had to summon the will to keep going. Though oppressive, the steam did open his throat.

Thank you, Lord, that Dr. Stanton was here.

Contemplating his predicament, he didn't know whether to feel foolish or angry. All those years ago, Norma had told him Thalia didn't love him, but even now, she wouldn't play a mean trick on him by slipping rhubarb into strawberry preserve tarts. He could see by her unmitigated shock at his sudden illness that she didn't know he was allergic to the fruit. Then again, rhubarb wasn't a common ingredient in foods he ate, so even Norma never witnessed what effect the fruit could have on him.

There was no one to blame but himself. He should have asked before he ate any red-colored confection. He thought he had tasted something a bit different in the tart, delicious though it had been. If only he had possessed the foresight to stop eating when he had a chance. Maybe one bite wouldn't have been as devastating as two entire tarts. Then again, he had let Edith distract him with her prattle.

He could play the blame game, but it wouldn't change a thing. Without thinking, he had eaten the tarts, and now he was paying. Paying dearly. He could only pray he wouldn't pay with his life.

Three soft raps at the door got his attention.

"Maximilian?" Thalia's voice sounded sweet, concerned. He wished he hadn't ruined her party by becoming ill and disrupting the fun. "May I come in?"

He considered how he must look and what she must think of him, lying limp underneath sheets, breathing in and out laboriously like some kind of fiend. He hated for Thalia to see him in such a state. Surely every sign pointed to California—first the flat tire, the near miss with the black cat crossing his path, the spilled pepper, and now this horrid illness. But now that the signs seemed so clear, he wished he could stay in Colorado. Maybe then he could change her mind.

Unwilling to let pride stand in the way of seeing Thalia, he uttered a response. "Yes. You may come in."

The soft swishing of a skirt marked each of her steps. Recalling how she looked earlier that evening, he pictured her in a pink party dress, resembling a bouquet of delicate spring roses in defiance of the snow outside.

"How's the patient by now?" The expression in her voice sounded blithe. He wondered if she was putting on an act for him.

"Do I seem to be all right? No, don't answer that." He took in another breath and tried to swallow in spite of his tightening throat.

"Don't try to say anything. We can talk later. Just relax," she instructed.

New footfalls announced someone else's arrival.

"Thalia, let me take care of this," he heard Dorcas say. "You don't need to be in here playing nursemaid while you have other guests to attend to."

"Thank you, but it's all my fault this happened, and I'll take care of him. Anyway, everyone else is pretty tired. It's late, and I think they'd like to go to bed."

"No doubt. Thankfully we have enough guest rooms to accommodate everyone, although I do believe you should bunk with Rose tonight."

"She won't have a roommate. I'll be here. I can sleep on the chaise lounge."

In between breaths, he objected. "No. . .don't. . ."

"That seems highly improper to me." Dorcas's voice sounded sharp.

"Please Aunt Dorcas. Under the circumstances, I believe my honor will remain intact. You can check on us anytime you like."

She sighed with clear exasperation. "Oh, all right. Call me if you need anything."

Hearing Dorcas exit left Maximilian feeling relieved. He would have to thank Thalia later. Whether he could credit feeling better to the steam or just knowing Thalia remained nearby, he didn't know. Or care.

The next morning he awoke, his throat feeling less constricted. Steam poured into the tent. Obviously Thalia had kept the mist going throughout the night. How could he express his gratitude?

He lifted the sheet enough to see. Still in her party dress, Thalia had fallen asleep in the chaise lounge by the fire, which had died down overnight but still held some warmth. He tried not to awaken her, but as soon as he stirred, she moved. Her eyes opened.

"I didn't mean to wake you." Maximilian folded the sheet away from his face. He realized talking didn't take the monumental effort it had the previous night.

"That's okay." She jumped from her seat and rushed to his side. "My prayers are answered. You made it. You made it through the night. I hardly slept a wink, wanting to be sure you were okay. You seemed to be able to breathe better in the wee hours. I was so relieved!"

Her relief scared him. Had he been closer to death than he imagined?

"Do you feel better? You look better." Her body sagged, releasing emotional strain.

He nodded and caught the faintest whiff of tuberose perfume that still clung to her from the previous night. The sweet aroma made him think of his garden in spring. He could get used to the scent forever as long as Thalia wore it.

Not noticing the effect she had on him, she regarded his face. "The hives have gone down considerably, but you appear a bit flushed. Your cheeks are red—like a cherub's picture on a Christmas card." Her eyes widened and she seemed fully awake.

"That doesn't sound so flattering since I'm not a cherub." He sneezed.

Placing the back of her right hand on his cheek, she looked at him with less concern. "You're not terribly hot. I think it's probably just the steam."

Facing away from Thalia, he sneezed again.

"Or maybe you have a cold."

Groaning, he remembered changing the flat tire in the freezing weather. "Don't tell me that, even though you're probably right. I must be the worst party guest on record. Maybe I can go ahead and try to go home. I can be my valet's problem there and not yours." He tried to rise but realized he felt too weak to move.

She shook her head. "You're exhausted from the stress of trying to keep oxygen in your body. You have no business traveling anywhere. Besides, the snowstorm has dropped quite a few inches on us already, and snow is still falling. It's much too dangerous to travel. I think it's safe to say by now that we're in the midst of a blizzard. Josiah and Dr. Stanton are outside shoveling even though the snow is falling as fast as they can clear a path."

Guilt visited him faster than the storm. "I should help," he said, even though he knew he couldn't.

"Are you insane? Of course not. They understand. Do you want me to keep the steam going?"

He took in a breath. "I think I can make do without it."

Thalia's voice softened from competent nurse to dainty woman. "I feel terrible that all this happened."

"No, I should have known not to eat anything questionable after I knocked over that pepper shaker." He took a breath.

"What?"

"Spilling pepper is a bad omen. You know that."

"I know no such thing. I rely on God to keep me safe." She placed her hand on top of his. "But I don't want to argue. I'm sorry."

"I don't think I ever told you I was allergic."

"Maybe not. Now that makes me feel better. You always were considerate of others' feelings." She smiled.

Despite her attempt at cheer, he could see tiredness in Thalia's eyes. "Please go and get some rest yourself. There's no way you had a peaceful night sleeping in your party dress in a chair. Your dedication to me went far and above the call of duty of any hostess. I thank you."

She glanced demurely downward. "I—I think I will take you up on your offer to get into some fresh clothes and take a nap. I'll see you later this afternoon."

I'll see you later this afternoon.

He hadn't imagined such words when he arrived for the party. Regardless of what Norma had said so long ago, he yearned to see Thalia again. Her sweet face had not disappointed. And now he would be staying even longer. The miserable illness was almost worth it. Could it be a sign he was supposed to remain in Colorado after all? Confusion left him feeling disconcerted.

Lord, help me figure this out.

Bored yet restless, he took a few moments to appreciate his surroundings. As might be expected from the fine furnishings in the rest of the house, Thalia's guest room was well appointed. The cherrywood dresser, vanity, and wardrobe, each mellowed to a reddish brown with age, featured carved magnolias that told a bit about the Bloom family's history.

Snow still fell outside, but inside the steam kept him warm.

"Thank you, God, for Thalia," was the last thing he muttered before falling asleep.

Chapter 5

After a long nap, Maximilian awoke in a strange room. Within a flash, he remembered everything that happened—the party, the tart, the violent illness, and Thalia. Thalia. She had been there for him, nursing him throughout the night. If only he didn't still feel so wretched. Sweating despite the cold, he threw off the coverlet. Ah. Relief.

"Just what do you think you're doing?" The questioning voice didn't belong to sweet Thalia but to her aunt, Dorcas.

"Where's Thalia?"

"Where's Thalia indeed? In bed where she belongs. She stayed up all night with you. She's getting some rest now. I'm taking over." Dorcas pulled the coverlet over him. "Do you want dinner? You missed breakfast and lunch."

He shook his head.

"Well, that's too bad, because you're getting it anyway. Eliza is bringing in warm broth."

"Warm broth? That doesn't sound too appetizing, but I suppose it's best since it seems I've picked up a cold."

"True. Dr. Stanton said to force fluids. You must drink some broth. You need the nourishment in it for energy." Dressed as she was in a no-nonsense gray house frock and wearing a stern expression, Maximilian didn't doubt she knew exactly what she was talking about.

"Thalia? Where is Thalia?"

"Now don't get too attached to the idea of Thalia being your nursemaid. I'm up for the task, and she has other guests to attend to. They're in the drawing room piecing together a jigsaw puzzle now. Never liked puzzles much myself. Besides, I'm old, and no one will miss me. Tending to you is the least I can do for poor little Norma. She would have wanted me to take care of you, I know."

Maybe so. But he liked his other nurse much better.

If he had to get sick and be embarrassed, now that he was out of the makeshift tent, at least he couldn't have chosen a more comfortable place. He looked through a window framed by brocaded draperies at snow still falling outside. From all appearances, the blanket of snow had grown deep enough to cause considerable trouble walking through it.

"Looks as though there's no letup on the snow. I guess we're shut in today," he speculated.

"Yes, I suppose anyone can look outside and see there's not much traveling today. I just pray that those who left last night got where they were going."

"Me, too. I'm sure they did." He heard voices coming from the dining room. "Apparently not everybody left."

"You really are out of it, aren't you? Rose and Dr. Stanton are here. And Josiah." Dorcas sat on the nearby chair and took up some knitting.

He held back a grimace. Of all the people he wished had gotten out in time, Josiah was top on his list.

"I'm glad Josiah stayed," Dorcas said as though she had heard his thought and wanted to debate. "He's the perfect match for Thalia, don't you think?"

"The perfect match? What, has one of Thalia's hands turned into a baseball mitt?"

"Don't be silly. All men have interests that don't relate to women. She can't expect to love everything he does. For comparison, I wouldn't expect you to be interested in my knitting project." She held up a square of green yarn with two needles wrapped up in it. How those needles and thread ended up in a sweater or whatever garment the women wanted, he would never know.

"There's interest in a subject, and then there's obsession. I don't think Thalia likes to be bored."

"She won't be bored long. The Billings family has plenty of money, and she will be happy and secure. And she'll have plenty to do, especially once the babies start coming. Can you just imagine redheaded little imps?" She chuckled and kept knitting.

Maximilian could imagine them, but he didn't want to. The combination of red hair and imps conjured up little devils in his mind. The thought of Thalia having Josiah's children made his fever rise. Too distressed to pay attention to his breathing, he coughed.

Dorcas dropped her knitting and rushed to his side. She slapped him on the back. "Now, now. Let's not make your cold worse on top of everything else."

Her worried look concerned him. Still, he desperately wanted to return to Aurora, but how could he with snow falling so hard one could hardly see the sky? He tried to rise, but apparently his motions caused a stir, as Thalia entered, leaving the door open behind her. "Maximilian, what are you thinking? Don't you dare try to get up!"

"But I feel so much bet—" His spinning head forced him to realize that indeed he did not feel better. He lay back.

Thalia set a tray on the bedside table.

"Thalia, what are you doing with that tray?" Dorcas asked. "You're supposed to be in bed yourself."

"I couldn't let my guest go without a bite to eat."

"Eliza can bring his meals to him."

Maximilian wondered why Dorcas's tone was so grumpy. "She was just trying to do me a good turn. Thank you, Thalia."

"You don't look so good, but the hives seem to be gone," Thalia answered. "If you have a cold—and I think you do—Dr. Stanton will try his best to keep you comfortable."

"Thank goodness for him."

"It's fine that you want to be a good nurse, Thalia," Dorcas interrupted, "but you're not being a very good hostess, are you? You should be tending to your other guests."

"But Maximilian is a guest, too."

"You shouldn't argue. It's not becoming of a lady," Dorcas cautioned. She turned to

Maximilian. "You must excuse her, dear. She's been in a state with this party."

"No doubt."

Thalia blushed and, without a word, excused herself. Maximilian wondered what had gotten into Dorcas for her to be so willing to reprimand her niece in his presence.

Putting down her knitting, Dorcas got up from her chair and approached the patient's bed. "I'm so sorry this party had to be spoiled by a horrid fruit tart. After all, this was your first time out socially since Norma's death, wasn't it?"

He swallowed. "I—I suppose so."

"Dear, dear Norma." Dorcas clucked. "She was a jewel, one of a kind. No one can ever replace her. Her death was so tragic."

"Yes."

Dorcas placed her hand on his. "I know life alone will be hard. I've lived as a spinster all these years, and though it gets lonely at times, it's never too much to bear. But keeping Norma's memory enshrined, as if it were a pearl set in prongs of gold, will honor her and your marriage."

Maximilian wanted to point out that he never said he wanted to live life alone, but considering Dorcas's wistful demeanor, decided against it. He thought back on his brief marriage. Norma had been one of a kind, with many good qualities. If only she'd been as perfect as Dorcas thought. Maximilian had been taken by her charm and beauty, but as soon as they married, Norma's pettiness and jealousy revealed themselves. He wondered if she loved him at all. If only he had chosen Thalia when he had the chance. But Norma had said that Thalia didn't love him—that her true love was elsewhere. And Thalia never did anything to dispute Norma's claim. If only Thalia had loved him, things would have been so different. Sure, she'd been a wonderful nurse the previous night, but a display of sympathy to an ill guest wasn't the same as giving the commitment of a lifetime love.

"Even once you're better, I hope you'll avail yourself of our hospitality as long as possible. We enjoy having you around. It's been too long. Having you near reminds me of my dear Norma."

Maximilian couldn't bear Dorcas's reminiscences much longer. Cold or no cold, he would rise out of his sickbed and leave as soon as he could. Thalia had already told him that she couldn't bear to lose Dorcas's love, and the more Dorcas spoke, the clearer it was that he could never have Thalia and her aunt's approval at the same time.

The sign he had asked for had happened. He would be heading for California as soon as the snow cleared the mountain passes on the Union Pacific Railway.

Chapter 6

The next afternoon, Thalia, wearing a fresh dress with a pattern of roses, entered the drawing room.

Josiah shuffled Flinch cards for the group at the game table. "Good. Now we have a foursome."

"I'm afraid not. I'll be taking care of Maximilian today."

"Aw, come on, Thalia, you don't have to stay by that baby," Josiah chided. "You've been with him all day. Stay with us awhile."

The last thing Thalia wanted to do was play, even the most popular card game of the day. "Aunt Dorcas is much better at cards than I ever could be."

"He doesn't need you to watch him sleep." Josiah grimaced. "You should have some fun."

"I think it would do you good to play," Dr. Stanton suggested.

"Can't argue with doctor's orders, can you?" Josiah gave the physician a satisfied grin and shuffled the deck of cards once more.

Recalling how groggy Maximilian had been when she last checked on him, she reconsidered. "Oh, all right. I suppose I can join you for a few hands."

She sat at the table with the others and took a hand. Before long, she got caught up in the spirit of fun competition and for the first time since Maximilian had taken ill, enjoyed her own party. Even the snow falling outside no longer bothered her.

"Beat you again!" Josiah said after a particularly lively and close round.

"You are demonstrating talents beyond baseball," Dorcas observed, knitting in the corner.

Thalia knew the remark was aimed at her but decided not to comment as she dealt the next hand. She created the stockpile, dealt the hands, and set the stack. The players organized their cards, and Dr. Stanton started the play.

"Flinch!" Maximilian cried as he entered the room.

Thalia's heart jumped upon hearing the now familiar voice. Without rising from her seat, she swiveled to see that her patient not only stood before her, but had shaved and dressed. The hives had disappeared, and he looked like his handsome self.

"May I join in the fun?"

"Maximilian, what are you doing out of bed?" Thalia scolded.

"I felt better, so I decided it was high time for me to join in the fun." He stifled a cough.

"Are you sure you're well enough to be up?" Rose queried.

"Yeah, maybe you should go back to bed. We have enough hands to play Flinch," Josiah urged. "Isn't that right, Doc?"

"We have enough to play, but if he feels like staying up, it would be better than becoming weaker by lying in bed so long." The doctor smiled. "I'm glad to see you up.

For a while there, you were in grave danger."

"Not anymore. I'll join you, then." Maximilian pulled up a chair to sit by Thalia.

"Here," Josiah intervened. "Sit here instead." He made a dash to occupy the seat by Thalia and left Maximilian with the empty spot between him and Dr. Stanton.

Thalia waited for Maximilian to comment, but he acquiesced without a murmur. As she dealt cards, she resolved to thank him later for letting Josiah get away with his childish behavior. Josiah would never change, so there was no alternative but to give in so they could keep the peace.

She stole a furtive glance at Aunt Dorcas. The older woman, rather than pursing her lips in disapproval, smiled at what she must have perceived as a victory for Josiah. Would she ever get through to her well-meaning but stubborn aunt?

During the game, Thalia noticed that Josiah was more competitive than he needed to be, especially with Maximilian. The fact that Maximilian showed good sportsmanship and gentlemanlike conduct, in spite of holding back coughs and sniffles, did not escape her notice.

"Everyone ready for a bit of cocoa?" Thalia asked after several hands.

Maximilian peered out the window. "I think more shoveling might need to be done before dark. Then cocoa would be more than called for."

"That's a fine thing for you to say," Josiah scoffed. "You haven't had to do any work."

He stood. "That's where you're wrong. I plan to shovel right along with you and Dr. Stanton."

"We only have two shovels," Aunt Dorcas pointed out.

"In that case, I'll take a short turn since I still haven't totally shaken this cold. But I do want to contribute. After all, I owe the doctor a break after he took such good care of me."

His firm resolve worried Thalia. Maximilian always struggled with pride, and now it looked as though he wasn't going to let a cold keep him from facing hard work in freezing, snowy weather. "I don't think it's a good idea." She looked to the expert for help, making sure a pleading light showed in her eyes. "Do you, Dr. Stanton?"

"I think waiting at least until tomorrow is well advised under the circumstances."

"I know you mean well, Dr. Stanton, but I'm over the allergic reaction. As long as I don't touch more rhubarb, I'll be fit as a fiddle." Without waiting for more arguments, Maximilian rushed to the coat closet.

Thalia rose to try to stop him, but Aunt Dorcas placed a firm hand on her shoulder. "When a man is that determined to do something, there's no stopping him. If you try, you'll be viewed as a nag."

A quick glance in Rose's direction told Thalia she'd get no help from her friend. Thalia held back a grimace. "I guess you're right."

Josiah stood. "I'll go help him and make sure he doesn't keel over and fall in a snow-drift." The sardonic expression on his face took away any hint of real compassion for the other man.

Thalia let Josiah exit without protest, but then she turned to the doctor. "Can't you convince Maximilian not to go out in this?"

"I did my best, but short of tying him to the bed with a rope, there's nothing I can do to force any patient to follow my orders. If his cold symptoms get worse, common sense will prevail and he'll come in. And I'll be sure to go out soon to relieve him. I think he wants to prove to us he can do his part. Maybe letting him have that will do more than any amount of steam and hot soup."

"How can I argue with that?" Thalia smiled. "You're a good doctor."

"I think so, too." Rose's soft expression led Thalia to believe that her words were a shallow veil for deeper feelings. The thought of Rose and Dr. Stanton becoming a couple seemed sweet to Thalia.

"You know, I think I'll have a bit of tea." Aunt Dorcas placed her knitting in her basket. "Could you help me in the kitchen, Thalia?"

Thalia knew her aunt needed no help and wondered why she wanted to speak with her. "Okay. Excuse me, will you?"

She followed Dorcas into the kitchen. No matter how many times she entered the room, Thalia always noted how the yellow walls projected a summer feeling regardless of the weather. Cook was on break, so they had the room to themselves. Thalia closed the door behind them so the others wouldn't hear. "What is it?"

"You are being entirely too hard on Josiah." Aunt Dorcas reached into the cabinet for a teacup and pulled out one with a daisy pattern.

"What do you mean? He practically ran over Maximilian to get to his seat and then wasn't a very good sport over cards. Really, Aunt Dorcas, I need you to get over any thought of us ever being a couple." Thalia leaned against the counter and crossed her arms.

"But the only reason he stayed here was because of you. And I'm glad he did. I can see you are getting entirely too attached to Maximilian. He is not for you, Thalia. He's not for anybody." She set her cup down in a matching saucer with more force than needed.

Thalia knew that her aunt meant well, and she didn't want to sound snappish with the older woman. "I know your fond desire is to see me make a match with Josiah, but I just don't feel he's the one for me. Even with us being in close proximity, I don't long to be near him."

"You feel nothing for him?" Hurt, surprise, and disappointment evidenced themselves in her tone. "After all, he is attractive."

She had to stand her ground. "Yes, but still I feel nothing more than the blessings I would want for any brother in Christ. I'm sorry, Aunt Dorcas."

"Fine." She poured water into the teakettle. "What about the other men who looked your way at the party? Why, there was Andrew Stallings, Ned Jones, Thomas Callahan, even Whit Tanner."

"Whit Tanner? That scoundrel? Please, Aunt Dorcas." Exasperated, Thalia took a seat at the worn but serviceable kitchen table.

Aunt Dorcas tightened her lips while she stuffed a silver steeper full of loose black tea leaves. As soon as she was done, she covered the tea tin. "Oh, all right. I admit I have heard a thing or two about him I don't like. But the others are more than respectable. They come from fine families and would make a wonderful match for you."

"I know it seems that way, but none of them touch my heart."

Dorcas let out a harrumph of disgust as she dropped the steeper into her empty cup. "Fine then. But that doesn't mean you should go running after your deceased cousin's husband. Sullying her memory in such a way would raise a few eyebrows."

Thalia wasn't sure she agreed with her aunt, but she decided not to argue. "I have already given the situation over to the Lord. I don't want to hurt anyone, either. Please, let's see how His plan unfolds."

The steaming water Aunt Dorcas poured was no hotter than her anger. "As long as it's His plan and not yours."

❅

"At the rate you're going, we'll be here all day," Josiah chided as Maximilian shoveled.

Maximilian didn't want to admit how tired he was. Each shovelful of snow seemed heavier than the last. The coal shovel was already heavy. Almost from the moment he ventured outside, he wished he had heeded the doctor's advice to take it easy. But pride had forced him to shovel. Each day he learned more about how foolish he had been to cling to his pride. With God's help, he tried to let go. Though their efforts didn't reveal bare ground for long, at least by removing snow as more fell, a pathway remained visible.

"I'll try to move faster," he shouted to Josiah. With determination, he picked up the pace.

"You'll never beat me."

Maximilian had only been near Josiah a couple of days, and he'd been out of commission most of that time. Yet the jerk got on his last nerve. He moved toward Josiah and set his shovel in the snow, leaning ever so lightly on the handle. "Josiah, why is everything a competition with you? Life is not one big baseball game."

"Everything is not a competition with me. But Thalia's different. I may court her."

"Is that so?" he challenged. "You've had all this time to ask. And obviously Miss Dorcas has no intention of standing in your way. So what are you waiting for?"

Josiah hesitated. "I—uh, I hadn't thought about it. I—I reckon there's no good reason not to ask."

"Is that so? I think in your heart of hearts you know the reason. She's not interested in you, at least not in a romantic way."

Josiah's face blazed crimson, and not from the cold. "What makes you think you know so much? And why do you care?" He frowned. "I know. You want her for yourself, don't you? That's why you came to the party."

"Not exactly, I—"

"I'll show you who's boss."

Before Maximilian realized what was happening, Josiah punched his face, knocking him off balance and into the snow.

"Ha-ha!" Josiah pointed at him and laughed. "You deserve a comeuppance!"

Maximilian recovered as quickly as he could, staggering to his feet. He could taste blood, but a quick lick on the inside of his mouth told him his teeth were intact. Anger swelled in him. "Why, you—" He raised his fist to retaliate.

"Maximilian! Stop!"

Both men turned to see Thalia, without a coat, racing toward them.

Immediately Maximilian felt remorse. He never should have let his pride get the best of him, even to argue with Josiah, much less come at him with a fist, bloody lip notwithstanding.

"Thalia, get back in the house," Maximilian insisted. "You'll catch your death of cold."

"I saw you out here, and I could tell by the way you looked that you were arguing. What's wrong with you? Two grown men should know better."

"I'm sorry. Please go in the house." Maximilian looked skyward. "Shoveling is a waste of time for now anyway. Let's go in." He realized he had something else to say. "Josiah, I'm sorry."

"You sure are."

Ignoring Josiah and his attitude, Maximilian took Thalia by the elbow in a deliberate fashion and guided her back to the house. He noticed she seemed to hold back a grimace.

"He got you good," she said. "What were you arguing about?"

Running up beside them and keeping lockstep, Josiah glared.

Tempted though Maximilian was to tell all, he decided that to declare victory in an argument—especially over her—could do him more harm than good. "Never mind." He took her by the arm to help her up the icy porch steps. "Let's get you back inside. Dr. Stanton has all the patients he needs."

Chapter 7

After nearly a week of falling, the snow stopped. With an accumulation of forty-five inches, the area stayed shut down far beyond anyone's guess. Rapid winds pushed most of the accumulation into high drifts. For the remainder of the time they were stranded, Josiah and Maximilian lived under an unspoken truce, which relieved Thalia. Once the trains resumed running, Thalia bade good-bye to Dr. Stanton and Rose as they left her house. Judging by the way they looked at each other, she could tell romance brewed.

Though happy for Rose, Thalia felt wistful for herself the day after they departed. In the early morning, sitting alone in the library with her Bible and cup of tea, Thalia realized that the city's ability to spring back meant one thing—that Maximilian would be leaving. She never thought she'd mourn his departure, but she realized that after almost losing him, she didn't want him out of her life again. She wasn't ready for courtship as long as Maximilian's relationship with God appeared weak, but she could stay on friendly terms with him. She would have to make herself content with that.

She turned to the fifth chapter of Matthew: *And if ye salute your brethren only, what do ye more than others? do not even the publicans so? Be ye therefore perfect, even as your Father which is in heaven is perfect.*

If she didn't follow Jesus' guidance and forgive Maximilian, and even Norma, was she better than any garden-variety pagan? How could she serve the Lord as a faithful servant if she couldn't let go of past romantic disappointments?

She turned to one of her favorite verses, Psalm 86:5: *For thou, Lord, art good, and ready to forgive; and plenteous in mercy unto all them that call upon thee.*

Had Norma ever expressed a shred of remorse for ruining her chances with Maximilian? No. At least she never shared regrets with Thalia, even on her deathbed. Perhaps Norma's vanity and pride wouldn't allow her to see how much she had hurt Thalia. But she couldn't lay all the blame at Norma's feet. Maximilian had chosen her cousin, breaking Thalia's heart as easily as a toothpick.

She expected anger to surge at such distressing thoughts. But it didn't. Maybe Maximilian's appearance at her party, seeing him again, proved to be the best thing that could have happened.

Lord, is it true? Have I forgiven them both long ago, in my heart?

Thinking about her reaction to Maximilian, she realized that spinsterhood was not her desire. He was. But could he ever be hers?

A silent prayer entered her mind. She shut her eyes. "Lord, I know my thoughts about Maximilian and Norma have been unkind, but I have come to full and complete forgiveness of them. You know my sadness over Norma's death is genuine. I do miss her, in spite of everything. Please forgive me for being so hard-hearted toward her—and Maximilian."

Josiah interrupted. "Thalia, I want to speak to you."

Jumping a little, she opened her eyes and threw her hand to her chest at the same time.

"Did I scare you? Sorry."

"A little, but I'm fine." She rested her hand on the doily-covered armrest of the couch to show she had relaxed. A flash of thought that she hoped he planned to bid her good-bye occurred to her, but she squelched it. "Sure, we can talk."

Thalia could feel his anxiety as he sat by her. His twitching foot made her wonder why the usually brash Josiah seemed nervous. "I—I have something to ask you. And since I've got to get back home, I don't have much time, so I'll make it quick. I—I'd like to court you. I know your aunt approves."

Not a shred of happiness visited Thalia. Surely when a man asked to court a woman, her heart should beat strong with love. Though Josiah's appearance pleased her, she couldn't imagine being his bride. If only he had seen the signs she tried to give him. Though always civil and polite, she'd done nothing to encourage him toward romantic thoughts.

He didn't wait long to prod her. "Well? Aren't you going to say anything?"

"Uh, I'm sorry. I—I didn't mean not to answer."

"Happiness does that to a woman, right? Makes her at a loss for words?" Hope in his voice made it harder for Thalia.

"Maybe sometimes, but I'm afraid not this time." The urge to take his hand seized her, but she knew that any touch would only make matters worse. "I have no plans to marry. Ever. I'm sorry, Josiah. I know you'll make some lucky girl a very good husband someday. She just needs to be the right girl for you."

A flash of hurt crossed his face before he screwed his expression into a snarl. "It's that dandy, isn't it?"

"Dandy?"

"Yeah, Maximilian." He narrowed his eyes when he said the name.

"He's made no move toward me, if that's what you mean."

"Oh, but he will. You can count on it." He rose. "Go ahead. Stay with that sickly fool. You'll play nursemaid your whole life with that one."

Unwelcome feelings roiled within Thalia. Josiah's venom resulted from jealousy, and she knew Maximilian's illness was a unique occurrence, never to be repeated as long as he shied away from rhubarb. But the truth about Maximilian's lack of faith in the living God bothered her, enough to keep her from acting on any romantic feelings she harbored for him.

"And to think I gave him a bloody lip over you."

So the fistfight did happen because of her. She didn't respond.

"Never mind. Well, you had your chance. Don't come crying to me when you're tired of nursing that dandy back to health. Good-bye." Josiah turned and left the library. As though to emphasize the end of their friendship, he shut the door so the thud resounded throughout the house.

Thalia knew he meant what he said. She would never have another chance with him. For some reason, the thought left her sad.

She didn't have time to think about Josiah before Aunt Dorcas rushed in. "What's the matter? Josiah ran out of here as if he were a fox with hounds on his tail."

"I don't think we'll be seeing much of him around here anymore." Realizing she'd never be able to return to her Bible reading for the day, she shut the book and set it on her lap.

Aunt Dorcas gasped as she took a seat beside Thalia. "Did you discourage him?"

"I did more than that. I told him I don't want him to court me. I'm sorry, Aunt Dorcas. I know you were hoping for us to make a match."

"I just hope you won't live to regret that decision."

"If I do, I'll know the consequences are my own doing. Try not to worry about me so much. I know my life will turn out just fine, regardless of whether or not I marry."

"But once I die, you'll be alone without me."

"Is that what this is about? You're afraid for me?" Touched by her aunt's concern, Thalia softened her voice.

"I've lived my life—or most of it, anyway. Spinsterhood suited me. I had my brother and sister-in-law for company, and now you," Aunt Dorcas pointed out. "And now, I'm not afraid of death. But you, on the other hand, have no one but me. I don't think you should live your life alone. I may seem stern, but I want you to be happy."

Her aunt's unselfish sentiments made Thalia's eyes mist. She took her hands. "I'll be fine. I promise."

❄

Maximilian wished he didn't have to go back to Aurora. He enjoyed staying at Thalia's too much. Family and friends kept life at the Blooms' exciting. Never did he feel a pall about the place. Superstitions and darkness were swept aside. Maximilian contemplated the reasons for Thalia's successful home. Could her success be attributed to her faith?

Seeing Thalia again brought back so many unresolved feelings—feelings he had long forgotten. The desire to go to California had lessened since he arrived at the party. He had to tell his cousin whether he wanted to join him. The time for a final decision had come. He had to talk to Thalia.

A quick survey of the house revealed her in the library, sitting with her Bible and tea.

She greeted him when he entered. "I'm quite popular today, it seems. You're my third visitor, and I've only been here an hour."

He stopped short at the doorway. Never could a woman but Thalia make an everyday housedress appear to be a heavenly robe. Even Norma, deservedly considered a great beauty, couldn't have compared to Thalia. "I see you have your Bible. Am I interrupting your devotions?"

Her smile sweetened her face even beyond its usual angelic appearance. "They've been interrupted so many times I've given up for the day. But don't worry. God has heard my concerns." She set the Bible on the end table.

He approached her and sat on the sofa. "I wish I had such faith."

"Such faith can be yours if you trust and keep the lines of communication open with God."

"I heard you praying for me while I was ill." Maximilian wanted to reach for Thalia's hands but decided the gesture might be too bold. "Just thanking you seems so inadequate."

"I don't need your thanks. I know God's providence is the reason you recovered."

"I guess it didn't hurt."

"Your lucky rabbit's foot didn't seem to do you much good." Though her words chastised, they didn't sound harsh.

"Maybe it kept me from dying."

Thalia sighed. "Maximilian, why do you hold on to silly superstitions? You go to church—" She paused and leaned a few inches toward him, enough that he could inhale the pleasant scent of tuberose. "You do still go to church, don't you?"

He nodded. "Of course. And of course I do believe in God. I'm just not as sure as you are that He answers prayer."

"Maybe that's because you don't talk to Him enough." Her eyes glinted with sadness.

So many things he wanted to say ran through his mind, but he stopped. He couldn't say how he really felt. Not now. Clearly Thalia wanted her God more than she wanted him. Norma must have been right. Thalia never did love him. He would have to live with that.

"I—I wanted to say good-bye, and to thank you again for everything." He rose from the couch.

She followed suit. "I'll miss you. I'm sure Aunt Dorcas will want to invite you over for dinner now and again, especially since your official period of mourning is over."

"That would be nice." He paused. "I should say good-bye to Josiah."

"He's not here. He already left."

"Oh." Though he could hardly say he made friends with Josiah while they were snowed in, courtesy called for a farewell. "I'm sorry I missed him."

"He left in a hurry."

Maximilian knew his next query was nosy, but since he still considered going to California, he figured he might as well go for broke. "That's strange for a man who told me he wants to court you."

"He told you that?"

"Yes, right before he punched me in the lip." Maximilian's hand involuntarily touched his mouth at the painful remembrance. "No doubt your aunt is dancing a jig."

"I turned him down. She's not too happy with me." Thalia sighed and stared at the fireplace. "I wish I didn't have to distress her so. I don't want to lose her love, Maximilian. She's the only family I have."

Desperately he wanted to reach out to her, to take her in his arms, to tell her he could give her all the love she would ever need. But he couldn't. Dorcas had made her wishes clear. For him to marry anyone would be upsetting enough to her, but he couldn't risk pursuing Norma's cousin, the very woman who lived under her roof. He had to find the strength to remain quiet.

Chapter 8

Maximilian trudged through the snow to his motorcar. He dreaded going home. Snow still covered the ground, and driving the vehicle through it would be tough. He had never tried such a feat with the motorcar. A hay burner would have served him better. But another reason for his despair pulled at his heart. He didn't want to leave Thalia. Despite his efforts to look for signs that he should stay, he saw none.

He opened the livery barn door. His motorcar waited for him on the left, covered by a canvas tarp. He pulled off the frozen material and sat down in the cold leather seat. He grabbed the starter crank and engaged the switch, then proceeded to the engine block and inserted the crank.

The engine failed. He tried again.

It still failed. No matter how much he tried to start the Studebaker, the engine refused to turn over.

He got out of the automobile and made his way back to the house. *Lord, why are the signs so hard to read?*

Thalia greeted him at the door. "What's wrong? I thought you'd left."

He scowled even though he hated for her to see him in a bad mood. "I can't get the Studebaker to start. I need to get home. I don't know what to do."

She flitted her hand at him to dismiss his worries. "That's easy. We'll take you in our sled."

Why hadn't he thought of the obvious? Still. . . "I hate to inconvenience you in such a way."

"It's not an inconvenience. Let me get my coat and some blankets for the journey. Aunt Dorcas will want to come along. We're so tired of being confined to the house."

"Okay, but I insist you both stay the night at my house in return for the favor."

"Are you sure we should stay, considering your cook serves up raw potatoes?" Her eyes sparkled, and her mouth curved into a mischievous line.

"Maybe you'd be better off hungry." He grinned.

"Hmm. Maybe not. We'll accept your hospitality. And our driver, Jonas, is here today. He just dug out of the snow at his house himself. Now that he's here, he can drive us."

Soon Thalia and her aunt joined Maximilian just outside the carriage house. Jonas pulled the sled out with ease.

"Told you there's nothing better than horses for transportation," Dorcas declared, not bothering to conceal her glee as she settled into her seat. "You young people will rue the day you decided to rely solely on motorcars for transportation."

"I think I might already be sorry," Maximilian said only half-jokingly, remembering how he'd already had to fix a flat tire on the way to the party, and now this. Chilly, he checked to make sure all the buttons on his coat were fastened.

"Oh my!" Dorcas exclaimed during the trip as they traveled by mounds of shoveled snow in front of homes and businesses. "Look at this mess. We weren't the only ones who had trouble digging out."

"We'll have a winter mess for quite some time," Maximilian agreed. "Until spring, at least."

"Hope we don't get more snow anytime soon, but I imagine that's a dream," Dorcas ventured.

Glancing at Thalia, he noticed that though she nodded in agreement with their various observations, she remained strangely quiet.

"Maybe the blizzard, my illness, and the trouble with my motorcar are signs that I should head out to California after all," he mused aloud.

"California?" Dorcas asked. "Whatever do you mean?"

For the first time during the trip, Thalia turned her full attention to the conversation. "I want to know, too."

"I didn't tell you? My cousin has asked me to go in with him on some orange groves out there. I thought the warm weather and change of pace might do me good, what with everything bad that's happened."

"I wouldn't put so much stock in signs." Dorcas wagged her finger. "Just because your mother believed in old wives' tales, doesn't mean you need to stay in bondage to them."

"His mother?" Thalia asked.

Dorcas's eyebrows rose. "Didn't you know? Lily Newbolt was the most superstitious woman in town."

"She had reason to be," Maximilian noted.

"Why?" Thalia's voice heightened with curiosity.

"I thought everyone in the family knew that story." Dorcas jumped in. "She was supposed to go back East to some fancy school to study music. She wanted to be a concert pianist, you know."

"Really?" Thalia gasped. "Maximilian, why didn't you ever tell me that?"

He shrugged. "It never came up. She didn't enjoy talking about her past, so I never dwelled on it."

"So what made her superstitious?"

"I'll tell you as much as I know. On the day she was supposed to leave for school, she was on her way to the train station and spotted a penny, faceup," Maximilian answered. "Of course, if you see a penny, you're supposed to pick it up for good luck. Well, not putting any stock in superstition, she ignored it. She ending up missing her train, and when she went home, she found that her sister—Aunt Nettie—you remember her. . ."

"Oh, yes," Thalia said.

"Well, Aunt Nettie had suddenly taken ill, and she had to stay home—she was the only other woman in the house, you know—and nurse her back to health. Once the opportunity was missed, she never had another chance to follow her dream. To the day Mother died, she swore that if only she had stopped and picked up that penny, she would have been a famous concert pianist."

"That is the silliest thing I ever heard," Thalia blurted.

"She didn't think it was silly," Maximilian pointed out. "She taught me every superstition she knew and taught me how to look for signs."

"That hasn't helped you much, has it?" Thalia kept her voice gentle. "You've been so busy looking for superstitious signs that you may have missed true signs you could have read from real people."

Maximilian flinched. Was she telling him that if he had paid closer attention, he would have seen her true feelings for him and not listened to Norma?

"Is that true, Maximilian?" Dorcas asked. "Do you really believe in those things? Norma never mentioned it."

"I'm not surprised. Norma was very attentive to me during our courtship, but once we were married, I could have worn a powdered wig and tights, and she wouldn't have noticed." He shrugged. "It seemed as though since she'd won me, she didn't care after that."

Thalia paled.

Dorcas snapped back as though she had been walloped. "Is that so?"

He hadn't meant for his confession to upset the older lady. "I'm sorry, Dorcas. Please don't mind me. I'm not myself. I know how much you loved Norma."

"Things would have improved once children arrived," Dorcas said decidedly.

"Maybe, except she didn't want any. She told me she was too busy enjoying herself to be tied down to a brat."

Dorcas gasped. "I don't believe it!"

"I have no reason to lie. I'm sorry if I upset you with these truths, but I only have revealed them to you. . .her dear relative."

"Aunt Dorcas knows Norma wasn't perfect," Thalia said. "Don't you, Aunt Dorcas?"

"Of course," she answered with an unconvincing tone. "But we're talking about superstitions now. I don't put stock in those. I listen to God's leading."

"I try to," Maximilian answered, "but He's not always clear. I can't see God, but I can see my rabbit's foot. It's clear to me that I can avoid spilling pepper and crossing paths with black cats. I can pick up that penny rather than passing it by."

"Do you realize how ridiculous that is?" Dorcas managed to reprimand him without a tone of condemnation. She leaned over and placed a maternal hand on his knee. "If you ask God to release you from the bondage of superstition, you'll be able to hear Him."

"Wise words, Aunt Dorcas." Thalia looked thoughtful.

"I do pray to God, but I honor Mother's memory by following what she taught me."

"Your mother was no fool, but superstition was not her friend. And it's not yours. I think you want to honor her, but you can do so in other ways," Dorcas suggested.

Maximilian decided not to answer. But he resolved to give what Dorcas said some thought.

Chapter 9

Thalia couldn't digest everything Maximilian had said during the ride to Aurora. So Norma really never cared about him. She knew her cousin had been vain, but she never considered she would give up the blessings and joys of motherhood for parties. Poor Maximilian. How brokenhearted he must have been.

Soon they reached the outskirts of Aurora, and the sled pulled up to the gate of the Newbolt home. Maximilian's eyes held a longing light. She could imagine how touched he must be to return home. Surely during the darkest hours of his ill-ness, he may have pondered never seeing his childhood home again.

"The smoke really is thick today," Dorcas noted. "Everybody must have their fireplaces going trying to keep warm."

"I don't think that's it." Maximilian's happy expression soon turned to one of fear. "What's that?"

Thalia saw smoke and flames streaming from what remained of the house. "Oh, no!"

"At least the Aurora fire department is here!" Maximilian exclaimed.

As soon as the sled stopped in front of the house, the passengers jumped out and ran to the flaming structure. Maximilian's valet, maid, and a young girl Thalia assumed to be the new cook, watched as the firemen did everything they could to stop the destruction. Thalia wished there was something she could do. Maximilian stood as still as a statue. No doubt he felt helpless watching every memory of his life destroyed by vicious flames.

A woman who appeared to be in her thirties, with three young children in tow, approached. "I'm so sorry. You can stay with us as long as you need to."

"Thank you, Mrs. Daily." Maximilian introduced his neighbor to the Blooms.

"That's okay. He can come back home with us," Thalia told her. When he smiled at her answer, she knew he needed the comfort of those who really loved him and was glad she had made the offer.

After the crowd dissipated amid many other offers of kindness and shelter, the Blooms and Maximilian were left standing in front of the destruction.

Thalia looked at the rubble and noticed a singed oil portrait of Norma. "Maybe if we go through this mess, we can find a few things that were spared."

Maximilian shook his head. "I'll go through everything on my own time. But I don't care about things. I kept most of my money in the bank, so I'll be okay. And the Studebaker is at your house, for all the good it did me today. The main thing is the people. All my staff is well, and that's what matters. Maybe they can tell me how this happened."

"I think I'd rather go back to the sleigh where I can sit, if it's all the same to you," Aunt Dorcas said.

Thalia didn't want to leave. "Do you mind if I go with you to talk to the staff?

Maybe you could use the support."

Maximilian nodded. They didn't have to approach them. The valet and a pretty maid walked toward them. Thalia knew them as Addison and Minnie.

Addison spoke first. "I'm sorry, sir. This is unforgivable. I don't know what happened except it was near breakfast time, and the fire started in the kitchen. I have no choice but to think Cookie started it. That girl has got to go, Mr. Newbolt. She's nothing but trouble."

The young girl ran up to them. "I heard that. I did not start that fire. I know you want to think I did since I'm new and I'm not a very good cook yet, but I had nothing to do with it. I promise."

"How dare you," the valet snapped.

Cookie flinched and blushed but stood her ground. "The fire started in the parlor, where Minnie was dusting."

"Not true," Addison insisted.

"Yes, it is," Cookie protested. "Oh, I know no one will believe me." Tears fell from her eyes, though she covered them with her hands. Her body shook.

Thalia couldn't help but feel compassion for the girl. She wrapped a maternal arm around the bony shoulders, calming her. "I believe you." To emphasize the point, she looked up at Maximilian with a strong countenance.

"I believe you, too."

The frightened girl looked up at her employer. "You—you do?" Her voice trembled.

"Yes." Maximilian turned a sharp expression to Addison. "What is the meaning of trying to make me think Cookie started the fire?"

Minnie flushed red. "He—he was protectin' me."

Addison's eyes narrowed. "Stop it, Minnie."

"No, I'm going to tell him. I wouldn't feel right if I didn't. I dropped a lit lantern and it broke. Fuel spilled on a stack of papers on your desk, and the fire caught on. There was nothin' I could do but get out of there. I don't have the money to replace what I damaged, and I'm sorry." She looked at the ground. "I know I'm dismissed. I'll be leavin' now."

Maximilian held up his hand to stop her. "No, I am not dismissing you, Minnie, because you told me the truth. Granted, I don't have a house right now for you to dust, but as soon as I get my life back in order, you can come back."

Addison spoke. "Thank you, sir."

Maximilian's countenance didn't seem benevolent when he turned to his valet. "Addison, you're dismissed."

"What?"

"I know you're sweet on Minnie, but trying to blame the cook for something she didn't do was wrong. I can't trust you. Don't look to me for future employment or ask me for a reference. Good-bye."

Thalia wasn't surprised when Addison said nothing but glared and stomped away. Minnie didn't speak but ran after Addison.

"So—so I can stay?" Cookie's voice sounded weak with happiness.

"Yes, you can stay. I'll pay your wages while you wait to come back into my employ."

"Oh, thank you, sir. I don't deserve such generosity. I promise to practice making lots of dishes while I wait to come back."

He smiled. "That's a good idea."

"Promise not to put a trace of rhubarb in anything," Thalia cautioned. "Mr. Newbolt is deathly allergic to rhubarb, and not the first stalk of it should be in his house."

"Yes, ma'am."

Maximilian smiled. "Now run along home, Cookie. I don't want you to get sick out here in this cold."

She nodded and complied.

Thalia gave him a sardonic smile. "I hope you won't be sorry about these decisions you just made in your heightened state of emotion."

"No, I won't."

"I think you did the right thing."

He pulled the rabbit's foot out of his pocket. "And now I'm going to do something else you'll think is the right thing."

He tossed the rabbit's foot on top of Norma's half-burned portrait. "This never did me any good. I can see that now." He looked heavenward. "From now on, it's just you and me, Lord."

Chapter 10

A week later, Thalia sat at the baby grand piano in the music room and stared at the sheet music for an Irish ballad enjoying newfound popularity, "Danny Boy." Her plan had been to learn it by that evening, but her mind betrayed her, forcing her to focus on Maximilian.

The past few days, she had watched him seek the Lord with an eagerness she hadn't witnessed from any other Christian in a long time. Throwing the rabbit's foot on the burned rubble had only been a start. She could see him embracing the faith of his childhood, returning to familiar Bible passages and talking with her about their significance. And while she didn't see him pray except to bless each meal, she sensed his prayer life had increased. Truly the fire had set Maximilian free from the bondage of his past so that he could walk with the Lord in the future.

Such happy thoughts encouraged her to play.

"That sounds pretty good."

She jumped and swiveled on the piano bench. "Maximilian, what are you doing sneaking up on me? I didn't think you'd be back from Aurora already."

"I didn't mean to scare you." He grinned. "I was called by the siren song from your beautiful piano."

"You are so silly." In spite of her teasing assessment, he looked anything but silly. With his straight, tall bearing, warm brown eyes, and comely face she could stare into every day for the rest of her life, he made her wish she were a sculptor so she could preserve an image of him forever. The picture in her mind would have to suffice.

She rose from the bench. "Come into the parlor. I'll ask Eliza to bring tea. I want to catch up on how your week went."

"Very well, though I missed you. I finished my Christmas shopping. There are now a few gifts for you and Dorcas under the tree."

"You didn't have to do that, with everything you've gone through. You'll find a gift or two from us as well, though," she noted. "So were you able to save anything from the fire?"

"Yes, a few things."

"Good. I'm glad you will have some memories to hold on to."

Moments later, they sat in the parlor and waited for tea to be served. "So have you thought about rebuilding the house?" Thalia asked.

"I haven't decided yet."

"Oh." She became conscious of her heartbeat. He had mentioned going to California. Was he planning to leave Aurora after all?

"A lot of my decision depends on you."

"On me?"

"You told me to start looking at people for signs instead of trusting in superstition.

That was good advice. It's been freeing. Similar to losing almost everything in a fire." His mouth twisted into a rueful line.

Thalia thought about his words. "Perhaps losing everything did offer you a way to begin fresh."

"I'll say. I've been watching you as I recovered."

"Oh, you have, have you?" She wasn't sure what to think.

"I hope I'm not too weak at reading people now that I've thrown away my talismans. I—I'm hoping you've changed your mind about me."

"Changed my mind?" She paused. "Well, I'm glad you're looking toward the Lord now, of course. But other than that, I don't have any idea what you mean."

"Don't be coy. You know why I didn't choose you over Norma all those years ago." He seemed more hurt than angry.

Shock bolted through her. She leaned closer. "Uh, no, I don't."

His eyes widened. "Why, Norma told me the truth about you—that you didn't love me."

Taken aback, Thalia gasped. Her head spun. How could her cousin tell such a lie? Even worse, how could Maximilian believe it? "When did she tell you that?"

"Why—I—I—I don't know. Sometime before I decided to start courting her in earnest. Does it really matter when?"

"I knew she wanted you, but I didn't think she'd resort to lies." Thalia didn't know whether to laugh or cry.

"Lies? You mean you did love me?"

"Couldn't you tell?"

"I guess I should have. But Norma seemed so sure of herself. And you were so reserved and so much closer to God than I ever was. I am hoping I can follow your example and become closer to God, too."

"I know." The thought filled her with joy.

At that moment, Eliza brought in tea. The maid couldn't take her gaze from them, but Thalia didn't want to satisfy her curiosity. The couple remained silent until she exited.

Sweet tea, with its spicy aroma, would have been appealing any other time, but Maximilian and Thalia were too preoccupied to enjoy it.

He took her hands in his. Their warmth sent a tingle through her. "I don't want to talk about the past. I want to talk about the future. Do you still love me?"

Her voice came out as a whisper. "Yes."

"And I love you now more than ever. You have changed my life for the better."

"With God's help. I do nothing good alone."

"I know how important your aunt is to you. You want to stay here in Colorado, near her."

"Yes." She hoped her answer wouldn't ruin her chances with him, but she had to speak the truth.

"If that is what you want, that's what I want. I would love to build a new house for you, in any style you like, if you would live with me in Aurora."

The thought left her dizzy. "A one-room cottage would be enough, if I was with you." She paused. "But Aunt Dorcas. . ."

"I spoke with her. She knows about this, and in light of how dramatically my attitude toward God has changed, plus everything we confessed to one another on the way to Aurora that day, she has given her approval."

"I might have been surprised by that only a few weeks ago, but no longer. I know she really does want me to be happy."

Nodding, he reached into his suit pocket and took out a small box. "In the midst of all that rubble, I found a link to the past that I do want to remember. Surely the preservation of this treasure is a Christmas miracle. This is a way that I can honor my mother. Here." He handed her the box.

She opened it to discover a gold-filigreed ring with a large marquis-shaped diamond flanked by two emerald baguettes. "Oh, I've never seen a ring so beautiful!"

"I know Mother would want you to have it. Will you wear it as a token of our engagement?"

"Our—our engagement?" She wondered at how such words fell from her lips. But saying them felt fantastic beyond belief.

With a gentle motion, he took the ring out of the box and placed it on the third finger of her left hand. "There. It fits perfectly."

"It's gorgeous."

"Not as gorgeous as you. So you'll wear it?"

"I'll never take it off. Ever!"

His lips moved toward hers, and she looked into his eyes. As they kissed, everything faded into oblivion. Everything except the fires of love.

Tamela Hancock Murray is the author of over thirty novels and nonfiction works. She feels honored and humbled that her books have placed her on bestseller lists and that one of her Barbour titles, Destinations, won an RWA Inspirational Readers Choice Award. Tamela has been a literary agent since 2001 and is with The Steve Laube Agency.

Tamela lives in Virginia with her husband of over thirty years. They are the parents of two lovely daughters. Tamela enjoys church, reading, and spending time with her immediate and extended family and friends.

Tamela is passionate about edifying and encouraging other Christians through her work. She always enjoys hearing from readers. Please visit her on Facebook and Twitter.

The Best Medicine

by Lena Nelson Dooley

Dedication

This book is dedicated to my writing teammates:
Tamela Hancock Murray, Susan Page Davis, and Darlene Franklin.
Working together on this collection has been a lot of fun.

Thank you, Rebecca Germany, for giving us this chance.

Very special thanks to Dr. Richard Mabry, a friend in Dallas.
Richard was able to give me authentic practices from the
time period as well as symptoms. This is the second book he's
helped me with. Any errors are mine and not Richard's.

And as always, I dedicate this book to my wonderful husband, James.
When I married you almost fifty-two years ago, I loved you with all my heart.
You brightened my life with your love. Through all we've experienced,
the good and the bad, that love has grown stronger and deeper and provided
a beacon in this topsy-turvy world for our daughters, sons-in-law,
granddaughters, grandsons, one grandson-in-law, and now three great-
grandsons. Welcome to the family, Sebastian Alexander VanZant,
Holden Andrews, and Hudson Andrews.

A merry heart doeth good like a medicine:
but a broken spirit drieth the bones.
PROVERBS 17:22

Chapter 1

December, 1913

Metallic tapping awakened Rose Fletcher. She stretched then got out of bed, but she couldn't identify exactly what startled her. Of course not. She wasn't in her family's home in Breckenridge, or even at the house out on their ranch. Another soft clang came from the steam radiator. She hoped these knocking sounds wouldn't keep her awake after she went to bed tonight.

Rose picked up the dainty timepiece her father had ordered from France for her last birthday. She should have heard it ticking, but no sound emanated from the jewel-studded brooch. As she began to turn the stem, it felt loose. The instrument had completely run down because she had forgotten to wind it. No way to tell exactly how long she'd been asleep.

Glancing at the window to estimate how late in the day it was, Rose noticed snowflakes dancing in the dwindling winter daylight, casting a white haze over everything outside. She rushed through her ablutions and donned the new emerald green dress she'd had made just for this party. The dressmaker in Breckenridge had copied the style from *Harper's Bazaar*. The magazine kept Rose aware of what was going on in fashion even when it was *Harper's Bazar*. After Randolph Hearst bought the magazine from the Harpers and changed the spelling, the coverage improved. This lovely dress was the perfect example of how they presented up-to-date fashions. She slid her hand down the other sleeve, enjoying the soft feel of the lightweight wool.

Rose tilted the pier glass up to make sure her new coiffure was not mussed. Quite a departure from the Gibson-girl pouf she had worn all through finishing school. She felt her hair to make sure the figure-eight chignon was secure. Then she tilted the glass down so she could see all the way to the hem of the dress. Tiers on the skirt gave it definition without adding width. She turned her back and glanced over her shoulder. The gown fit like a soft kidskin glove and made her feel like a princess.

When Rose arrived downstairs, Thalia and her aunt Dorcas once again made her feel welcome. Why hadn't she made more opportunities to spend time in the city with her friends?

"Dr. Stanton has arrived," the maid announced.

He must be new. Rose couldn't remember a doctor by that name being in Denver. When Thalia had taken ill at school, she'd lamented the fact that Dr. Wetherby wasn't there to take care of her. He'd looked after her family since before she was born, and she trusted his wisdom.

Rose couldn't keep her eyes away from the stranger. He doffed his hat, took off his muffler, and handed them to the waiting servant, leaning toward the young maid and speaking softly to her before he turned toward the parlor. Surprise blossomed within Rose's chest as she beheld the handsome man. Tall with broad, muscular shoulders, he looked as if he performed hard physical labor instead of the less strenuous profession of caring for the sick.

While she stood spellbound, the man pushed at unruly dark curls, trying to make them lie down. The effort was in vain, for one drooped across his broad brow like an errant child. Dr. Stanton shrugged out of his coat and handed it to the maid before striding toward their hostess.

Rose took a deep breath and slowly let it out, more to calm herself than for the needed air. Why hadn't Thalia told her about the arrival of this young doctor in Denver? Surely she could have mentioned it in one of her letters.

Thalia glanced up, and her eyes twinkled. "Rose, I want to introduce you to the doctor who has joined old Dr. Wetherby in his practice."

The man turned intense gray eyes toward her. For a moment, they seemed familiar, but nothing else about the man did. Perhaps she had met someone who shared the same kind of serious expression. He never took his gaze from her, making her want to squirm. She pressed her hand over the bottom of the V-neckline of her dress. Hopefully, he didn't think it too daring.

Thalia slipped an arm around her waist. "Rose is one of my dearest friends."

Rose smiled at the tall man. She held out her hand for him to shake, but instead he lifted it and barely pressed his lips against the back of her fingers.

For a moment, she stared into his eyes. When his hand encountered hers, heat from his body infused the connection and began a slow journey up her arm. At the same time, a blush rushed up her neck and into her cheeks, causing them to burn. She wished she carried a fan. So much for looking poised.

After he raised his head, he continued to hold her hand captive. "I'm charmed by your presence." The tone of his words was almost familiar.

"Nice to make your acquaintance" was all she could think of to say after his greeting.

A twinkle lit his eyes, and once again she felt as if she should know this man, but no real remembrance came to mind.

❋

Thomas held Rose's hand a little longer than decorum allowed from a stranger, but he hoped she would recognize him. It had been years since he left her father's ranch to go to Harvard Medical School. Back then, Rose had turned longing eyes toward him, almost as if she didn't want him to go.

After a blush befitting her name suffused her cheeks, she tugged her hand from his. He raised one eyebrow, gave her a nod, and waited for her response. At any moment, she'd realize who he was.

"Rose!" The newest arrival rushed toward her, and the young women threw their arms around each other and started talking at the same time—in exclamations.

Thomas moved away but kept his attention on Rose, studying all the ways she had changed. A sophisticated hairstyle in dark auburn replaced her carrot-colored braids. The waves framing her face ended at the nape of her neck with a soft bun like one of the nurses at the hospital wore below her cap. He'd heard her tell one of the other nurses that it was the latest style from France. A spark of fire burned on the crests of those dark red waves. He wanted to reach out and touch one to feel its warmth. Quickly, he shoved both hands into the pockets of his slacks.

Even her freckles had faded. He'd heard her father call them her pennies from heaven that were scattered across her cheeks and forehead when she was younger. Now her skin looked translucent, like creamy porcelain. When he'd worked on her father's ranch, the girl had idolized him. She made his life miserable. The young hoyden who followed him around the ranch, riding her horse with reckless abandon, was gone. Little Rose had grown up while he had been away, and he wanted to get to know her as a woman.

The other young woman turned to take off her coat, and Rose finally noticed that he still stood close by.

"How long have you known our hostess?" He hoped his question would keep her near him until she realized who he was.

"Thalia and I were roommates in boarding school." Rose's smile lit her face like the electric lights that had come into general use in many areas of the country.

"Where did you go to boarding school?" Thomas didn't want this conversation to end too soon.

"Outside New York City." Rose glanced around the room as if looking for someone else.

What would it take to keep her attention on him? "I returned to Colorado from back East a few months ago. I attended Harvard Medical School."

That caught her attention. "You did? I know someone who is going to—"

"Thomas." Thalia's voice interrupted as she stopped beside them. "I have someone else I want you to meet. Can you come over here, please?"

At the first sound, he'd looked at their hostess. When he turned back to Rose, her brow puckered. "Thomas?" The word sounded almost strangled.

"Yes, Rose. Thomas Stanton."

A myriad of expressions that he couldn't decipher raced across her face.

"Are you coming, Thomas?" Thalia's insistence urged him along with her hand on his arm. "Rose, please excuse us."

He leaned toward Rose. "I need to go now, but we will continue this conversation later."

While Thalia took Thomas from group to group, introducing him to the other guests, a special awareness of Rose went with him. When she finally started a conversation with another young woman, he was able to concentrate more on the people he met.

❄

Rose watched Thomas walk away with Thalia. How could she not have recognized him? Evidently her heart did even though her mind hadn't. Those gray eyes and that voice, though the timbre had deepened with maturity. Her heart fluttered as butterfly wings danced in her stomach, making her breathless. What was wrong with her? This was just Thomas. She'd fancied herself in love with him when she was in pigtails, but she never really expected to see him again after he left for medical school. He hadn't even returned when his father died. She had been sure the lure of the big cities back East held him there.

They hadn't held her, either. She'd enjoyed finishing school, but the Rocky Mountains called to her heart, and she'd gladly returned to Breckenridge.

"Rose!" Natalie Daire was taking off her long coat and gloves as she hurried toward her. "I've been anxious to see you."

And she was glad to see Natalie. Now all four of the girls who had been so close at school were at the party.

"Daring Natalie, what's this I hear about you having one of those Cadillacs?" Rose's question brought a sparkle to Natalie's eyes. Her nature fit her last name so well.

"You'll have to go for a ride with me while you're in Denver." Natalie laid her coat across one arm. "I wore my driving duster and hat. There isn't any dust this evening, but it helped keep the snow off my new dress and out of my hair."

"Do you really like driving that thing?" Rose had a hard time keeping her attention on Natalie. Her gaze kept returning to the tall, handsome man across the room.

"So have you met our new Doctor Stanton?" Evidently Natalie noticed where Rose's gaze wandered.

Rose smiled at her friend. "Actually, I've known Thomas for years. His father was the foreman on my father's ranch. Thomas worked there, too, before he went to medical school."

A knowing smile crept across Natalie's face. "So that adds to his fascination, doesn't it?"

For the second time tonight, Rose felt a blush stain her cheeks. "I wouldn't say I find him fascinating. I just didn't expect to see him after all this time." In her heart, she knew she was more interested in him than what she professed to her friend.

Chapter 2

How was Thomas ever going to keep all these new people straight? His inability to remember names had plagued him all his life, and it wasn't a desirable trait in a doctor. Patients felt more comfortable with a physician who called them by name every time he met them, in the office or out in public.

No matter where he was in the house, somehow he sensed Rose's movements as she went from group to group of her friends, always staying on the opposite side of the room. A fact that wasn't lost on him. When he meandered toward the fireplace, she drifted through the archway into the dining room where the table stood laden with so many good things to eat that everyone here would probably gain a pound or two.

He, as graciously as possible, ended his conversation with those near him and headed toward the punch bowl on the sideboard near the food. By the time he arrived, Rose stood at the bottom of the staircase, talking to three other young women of similar age. After filling his cup once more with the delicious beverage, he headed toward the cluster of giggling femininity. Before he took two steps out of the dining room, the group broke apart and scattered toward other people in the parlor.

Rose began talking to a tall, thin man. If Thomas remembered correctly, his name was Newbolt. . .Maximilian Newbolt, to be exact. And if he had all the details right, the man was a young widower with no children. Could Rose be interested in him? Maybe he should mosey over and check out the situation.

The two were deep in conversation as he approached. He didn't think they noticed him until Maximilian smiled toward him.

"Rose, have you met Dr. Stanton?"

When Newbolt turned his gaze back toward her, did Thomas see a hint of proprietorship in his face? After a moment, Thomas was sure he only imagined the extra connection.

She swiveled and glanced toward Thomas. "Yes, Maximilian, I've known the doctor for a long time."

That seemed to surprise the man. "I thought he was new to Colorado."

"No." Thomas moved halfway between the other two. "I actually lived here before I went to medical school."

"Here in Denver?" Creases between Maximilian's eyebrows signaled his puzzlement. "Should I have known you?"

"No, to both questions. I lived near Breckenridge." Thomas hadn't felt this gauche since he was in his teens. He stuffed his hands in his pockets, because he couldn't think of anything else to do with them. "My father was the foreman on the Fletcher ranch."

A slow smile spread across Newbolt's face. "No wonder Rose knows you."

She peered at a young woman on the other side of the room. "Excuse me, but I need to ask Patricia something."

The object of Thomas's sensory attention turned and walked away. His gaze followed her until he heard a deep chuckle.

"So that's how it is." The twinkle in Newbolt's eyes didn't bode well for Thomas's peace of mind.

Thomas glared at the other man. "I don't know what you mean." He knew he would be considered rude, but this was the last time Rose would get away from him. "Excuse me." They needed to finish their previous conversation.

❄

Rose had worked hard to stay as far away from Thomas as possible. She didn't really want to converse with him until her mind was settled. This wasn't the boy she'd longed for as a girl in her teens. This man was even more imposing, and his effect on her was hard to understand.

She'd matured and learned how to be gracious, but all her graces fled when he came near. Disturbing, because deep in her heart of hearts, she knew there could never be any kind of romantic relationship between them—no matter how much she wished otherwise.

A scene from her childhood returned to her thoughts. She had finished a thrilling ride then cooled down her mare. Next she lovingly brushed her best friend's hide, using just the right amount of pressure to give the chestnut the most pleasure.

Thomas came through the barn door, leading his mount. "How you doing, squirt?"

How Rose hated for him to call her that. "I'm taking care of my horse." She patted the mare's flank before moving to the other side with her brush. "I think horses are some of God's greatest creations, don't you?"

A harsh laugh burst from the young man. "God? You don't believe all that stuff, do you?" Derision dripped from every word. His attitude had caused the first bit of doubt about him to enter Rose's heart.

Over the next few months, she had tried to bring up God's goodness, but only a few times. His response remained much the same. The man was not a Christian, and he didn't sound as if he would ever change his mind.

Those memories warred with the strong attraction she felt toward the mature man across the room. His reactions to her attempts to talk to him about God had made her mad when she was younger. Now his lack of interest in the Lord grieved her heart.

How could they ever really be friends, much less anything more?

Rose stood beside the heavy green draperies and gazed almost unseeing at the snow filling the scene outside. She'd always loved winter when she was home. Getting snowed in didn't have to be a problem in the house in Breckenridge, or even the log one on the ranch. Father and mother kept both stocked with games and books, plenty of things to do indoors during the extended bad weather.

No matter how much she tried to turn her thoughts to other things, they winged back toward Thomas Stanton. She didn't remember ever hearing his last name when she was growing up. Dad always called his foreman Farley and the son Thomas. No wonder she didn't recognize his name when she first heard it.

"Rose?"

Her whispered name on his lips so close to her ear made her gasp for breath. How had he come so near without her hearing him? She turned slightly. "Yes?"

Thomas moved around until she could see his face. "I'd like to continue our conversation. You didn't recognize me when I arrived, did you?"

She glanced down at her clasped hands. "Not at first."

"I immediately knew who you were." His voice carried a husky tone, entirely too intimate. "But you were no longer the boss's young daughter. I want to get to know the woman standing before me."

The heat returned to her cheeks, and she glanced back toward the window. "I'm not sure that's a good idea." Her words trailed away.

❄

This was not the reaction Thomas expected. He conjured up the memory of her beseeching eyes following his departure when he left for Cambridge, Massachusetts. Why wouldn't she want to get to know him better now?

Walking in a resolute manner, she opened the door and floated out onto the porch. He followed before she could shut the door behind her. "Have I upset you?"

She crossed her arms and whirled to face him. "Seeing you again after all this time has somewhat unbalanced my emotions. I'm trying to calm myself and cool off."

He smiled to himself. *So she felt something, too.*

The frigid wind cut through his suit. Surely her dress, as pretty as it was, wouldn't keep the air from chilling her. "You should be cool now."

"You're right. Maybe I should return to the house." She started to go around him.

He moved one step over to keep her in front of him. "Here, take my coat. We need to finish this subject." After slipping off the garment, he snuggled it around her shoulders.

Rose clutched the lapels and pulled them together. "Thank you. That feels better. But aren't you cold?"

"I'll live." Thomas leaned toward her. "Why are you shying away from me?"

"Father will want to know you're back in Colorado." The wind blew a wave of auburn hair across her forehead, and Rose brushed it away.

She hadn't answered his question. He'd have to practice patience to give her time to feel comfortable with him again.

Thomas placed his arms loosely around her and leaned his chin on the top of her head. "This should help keep you warm." He wanted to enjoy holding her in his arms for as long as he could, even if it wasn't a romantic tryst. "I'll have to go to Breckenridge to see him soon."

She pulled away, and he wondered if he'd made her feel uncomfortable. That hadn't been his intention.

Rose turned toward the snow that had grown so thick Thomas couldn't even see the iron fence at the edge of the front yard. "Thomas, I'm worried about the weather. We could end up being snowbound."

He took her hand and led her back through the door into the heated house where she relinquished his suit jacket. "Let's warm up by the fireplace. Then we'll find Thalia and share our concerns with her."

How easily Thomas had moved beyond her defenses. Rose followed him toward the blazing logs. For those few moments when Thomas sheltered her from the harsh wind, she'd felt protected. . .and even almost cherished. But that could never be.

After he stopped on one side of the fireplace, she took up a position as far from him as she could, while still taking advantage of the warmth. Her fingertips felt like icicles. She held her hands toward the flames and kept her attention on the dancing colors. She'd always been fascinated by the way fire moved and glowed.

"There you are, Rose." Thalia joined them. She looked at Thomas standing nearby. "I wondered where the two of you had gone. Catching up on old times?"

Rose glanced at her friend then back at her hands, which tingled as the warmth infused them. How could she answer without letting Thalia know how much his presence rattled her?

"Trying to." His strong baritone held a hint of laughter. "We seem to be always talking to other people."

"Didn't I see you come in from outside?" Thalia placed her hand on Rose's arm. "Weren't you cold?"

Rose nodded. "That's why we're warming up now." She peered into Thalia's eyes. "Actually, we're concerned about the weather. Thomas and I spoke about it while we were on the porch. People might have trouble getting home tonight."

"Oh pooh, Aunt Dorcas said it's just a Denver winter storm. We always have snow." Thalia's bright smile could light up a whole room. "Besides, you don't have to worry about that, since you're staying overnight."

Rose moved back from the heat, which was becoming overwhelming. "It could be snowing even more up in the mountains. What if it covers the railroad tracks?"

Thalia looked up at Thomas. "Has she always been such a worrier? I know she did a lot when we were in school."

He chuckled. "I don't remember that about her. Maybe it came later."

They were talking about Rose as if she weren't standing there. Although she didn't know what to say right now, their conversation made her feel uncomfortable. She might as well go get something hot to drink.

Thomas watched Rose glide across the floor, wishing she would come back so they could finish their conversation.

"Don't worry." Thalia's voice pulled his attention back to her. "I think the storm will be over before morning."

"Dr. Stanton!" A girl named Nanette hurried toward them. "We need your help. Maximilian is having a problem breathing!"

Thomas followed her as they hurried to the library. Maximilian's breathing was even. He didn't seem to be in imminent danger, but his skin had red splotches all over. Deciding that a better plan of action would be to have all his implements and medications with him when he examined the sick patient, Thomas wanted to get his satchel first.

"Please try to keep him quiet. I'll be with you in a moment after I retrieve my medical bag from my buggy." Thomas hurried from the library.

He shrugged into his overcoat and slapped on his hat, then slung his scarf around his neck before going out into the storm to retrieve the medical equipage from his buggy. Thankfully his vehicle was parked in the carriage house.

Why hadn't he brought his medical bag in with him? Of course, he hadn't really expected to need it, but he never left home without the black leather satchel. Much simpler to bring it in with him and leave it with his coat, hat, and scarf. A lesson learned.

❄

At Nanette's words, Rose forgot she was peeved at Thalia and Thomas. She turned back before she reached the hot chocolate and watched people scurrying around. Thomas hurried outside, and others flocked to see what was happening in the library. Why did people always want to gawk at someone who was in distress?

She knew something better to do. Not wanting to kneel in her party dress, she dropped onto an upholstered wingback chair near the fireplace. After folding her hands in her lap, she closed her eyes and began to pray silently.

Her prayers were interrupted when Thomas returned from outside. The amount of snow that had accumulated on him the brief time he was gone shocked her. She peered outside but could see nothing except white. Her father called this a whiteout. Snow so thick it was almost impenetrable. How ever did Thomas find his way back to the house? For a moment, her heart almost stopped beating when she thought about him lost in the snowstorm. No matter how much she told herself that she couldn't have feelings for the man, her heart didn't listen.

❄

When he returned to the house, he realized that even though he and Rose stood on the porch only a few moments ago, that wouldn't be possible now. Icy wind swirled the flakes, flinging them against the windows and door with a fury. He couldn't get back into the house without bringing windy swirls with him.

Thomas opened the door and entered as quickly as possible, slamming it behind him. He glanced around and found everyone looking at him while he brushed the accumulated snow from his hat and overcoat. "The storm doesn't seem to be letting up."

Varying reactions answered his pronouncement. A few of the guests talked about leaving before the conditions worsened. Thomas didn't agree that was a good plan, because the weather already looked dangerous, but he couldn't think about that right now. He needed to get to his patient. They'd have to make their own decisions without his input.

❄

A rumbling murmur that started while partygoers watched Thomas remove his outer garments grew to a dull roar. Everyone was talking at once. Many said they wanted to try to get home.

"I don't think that's a very good idea." Rose tried to make herself heard above the others, but no one paid any attention.

Soon most of those at the party were donning their coats, gloves, hats, and scarves and setting out through the dense storm. Now Rose had something else to pray about.

Evidently, everyone except Thomas, Maximilian, Josiah, and herself had started home. Josiah stood in front of the fireplace to chase away the chill caused by the door being opened so many times. Rose stayed where she sat and once again prayed for Maximilian. . .and those who ventured outside.

❄

Thomas hurried down the hallway to the library where Newbolt sat on a sofa in front of the fireplace. Other people gathered around him.

"Move aside everyone, please. I need to see the patient."

Red splotches scattered across Newbolt's face and neck—and even on his hands.

Thomas set his bag on the table at the end of the sofa and pulled his frigid stethoscope from the interior. The instrument felt much too cold to touch anyone with, so he started rubbing it with his hands. He was glad to see that everyone had left the room. "Can you breathe okay?"

Newbolt shook his head.

"Has anything like this ever happened before?"

Newbolt squinted his eyes and stared at the mantel. Thomas could tell he was thinking, maybe trying to remember.

"Has there been another time?" Thomas needed to know before he proceeded.

The other man sighed. "Fruit. . .rhubarb."

"With the rash and difficulty breathing, I thought this might be an allergic reaction to something. Is your throat closing up?" Thomas certainly hoped not. That could be really serious.

Maximilian shook his head. "Throat's sore and a little tight."

"We can take care of that." Thomas hoped he could keep the patient calm. That often helped in situations like this. "Have you eaten rhubarb today? I don't remember seeing any on the table."

Newbolt shook his head.

The culprit might be something else. Thomas needed more information. "How many times has this happened to you in the past? Do you recall? You don't have to speak, just hold up your fingers to indicate the number."

Newbolt once again stared toward the fireplace while he pondered the question. Finally, he held up one finger.

The door opened, and Miss Dorcas Bloom entered. "Can I get you anything, Dr. Stanton?"

Thomas looked at her. "Not right now, but you could wait a minute while I question Mr. Newbolt."

She glided through the door and gently closed it behind her.

"Maximilian, when did you first notice your symptoms?" Thomas studied the man's face as he prepared to answer. Sometimes he learned as much from a patient's expression as he did from the words he spoke.

Newbolt shook his head slightly as if trying to remember. "About. . .fifteen. . .or twenty minutes ago. . .itch in my throat. . .nose started running." He reached into his pocket, pulled out a rumpled handkerchief, and blew his nose.

Finally the chest piece of the stethoscope felt warm enough to use. Thomas slid it inside his patient's jacket and pressed it against his shirt. "When did you first notice the rash?"

"A few minutes later." A croupy cough punctuated the answer, followed by a gasp that ended in a wheeze.

Thomas didn't like the way the man's lungs sounded, and his throat might be closing up. "Does your throat feel full?"

This time Newbolt nodded instead of answering.

"We need to figure out if you had rhubarb." Thomas put the stethoscope into his jacket pocket. "If not, we have to find out what else you're allergic to."

He called in Dorcas, who appeared with Thalia.

"Ladies, was there any rhubarb in anything you served tonight?"

Thalia blanched. "Yes. Why?"

"From the best I can tell, Mr. Newbolt is allergic to rhubarb, and he has had a reaction."

"Oh, no!" Their hostess gasped. "Maximilian, did you eat one of the tarts with red filling?"

"Yes. . .strawberry, Edith said. Delicious. I had. . .another."

"It's all my fault." This time she wailed. "That was a new recipe that called for strawberry and rhubarb preserves. Oh, what have I done?"

Thomas turned toward their hostess. "We need to get him into bed. Could we move him to a guest room?"

"Of course, we have several bedrooms. Actually, one is on the first floor. It would be easier to put him there. I'll have Eliza start the fire." Dorcas moved toward the door.

"After he's in bed, we need to make a tent out of a sheet and fill it with steam. You do have a teakettle on the stove, don't you?" He helped Newbolt to stand.

"Yes, I can get whatever you want." Dorcas clasped her hands as if trying to keep them still. "Perhaps you could take Max down the hall and help him get into bed. There's an old nightshirt of my brother's in the top drawer of the bureau."

"I'll do that, and Miss Bloom, please bring a glass of water and a spoon when you return."

The bedroom was easy to find, and very soon Thomas helped Newbolt get undressed and slip between the sheets on the bed. When he was settled, Thomas checked his pulse rate. The rapid staccato didn't bode well. Thomas knew this night was going to be a long one. He'd heard of people dying from a severe allergic reaction, but that wouldn't happen to Newbolt. At least, Thomas would pour every effort into preventing such an outcome.

Chapter 3

When the door opened, Thomas glanced up, surprised. Miss Bloom shouldn't be back so soon.

"Is Maximilian going to be all right?" Thalia's brows knitted in concern.

Thomas quickly stood. "Oh, it's you, Thalia. I thought you were your aunt returning with the things I requested. Yes, I believe Maximilian will be all right." *At least I hope so.*

Thalia peered at Newbolt's still form. "Is there any way I can help?"

"I've been thinking about the best way to tent him for the steam." Thomas studied the headboard of the bed. "Maybe you could get us a sheet. And bring a couple of towels and a bowl. Miss Bloom is bringing the teakettle and a glass of water."

"I think there's an extra sheet in the bureau." Thalia opened one of the drawers.

Thomas once again checked his patient's blood pressure, pulse, and respirations. No change. At least the man was resting right now. He'd even slipped into slumber.

Thalia started toward the door then stopped. "I wonder if he'll sleep through the night."

"I wouldn't count on it, although I'll make him as comfortable as I can."

After pulling a chair close to the bedside, Thomas sat down and pondered the situation. He hadn't read about any recent developments that would assist him in treating an allergic reaction. Medical professionals actually didn't know a lot about what to do with them. With all the modern advances, he wished one of them had been for situations like this one.

A quick knock sounded, and the door opened again. Thomas turned to see both of the Bloom women carrying a number of items. He crossed to the door and relieved Miss Bloom of the tray she carried.

Noting that it contained what he had asked for, he set it on the bedside table. Thalia still had a folded sheet across her arm. He reached for it. "Probably the best way to do this is to tuck this behind the headboard and drape it across Mr. Newbolt."

He leaned toward his patient and gently shook him. "I really hate to disturb you, but we need you to sit up in the bed."

Miss Bloom assisted Thomas as they arranged the pillows behind the patient's back so he would be comfortable.

When Thomas turned to call Thalia forward, he found her right behind him. He took the towels, folded them, and laid them across Newbolt's lap, then placed the bowl on top of the towels.

"Before we finish making the tent, I want to give him some bicarbonate of soda." He took the glass and spooned the powder into the water. After stirring until it dissolved, he gave the elixir to the patient. "Drink this right down."

Newbolt took a tentative sip then made a wry face.

"I know it doesn't taste good, but it should help you. If you drink it fast, you won't taste it very long."

After a brief hesitation, Newbolt chugged it down. When he was finished, he couldn't contain a loud burp.

"See." Thomas had to force himself not to laugh. "It's already helping some."

Newbolt glanced toward the two women, and his face turned crimson. "Pardon my faux pas."

Thalia smiled at him. "Think nothing of it."

Thomas picked up the teakettle and carefully poured the hot water into the bowl. Miss Bloom helped him drape the sheet over Newbolt and the headboard of the bed to form the tent to keep the steam inside.

"Breathe in as much as you can." Thomas picked up the patient's wrist and checked his pulse, which was still too rapid for his liking. "Try to relax, but don't fall asleep. And if you get too hot inside there, let us know. We can raise one corner of the sheet so you can have some fresh air." *This had better work.* If it didn't, getting Newbolt to the hospital in this snowstorm could prove impossible.

After spending more than an hour with the patient, Thomas stepped out for a break, leaving Thalia sitting with Newbolt. Her aunt came out with him.

Miss Bloom looked at the parlor with only a couple of people in it. "Where are all the others?"

Rose raised her head and stood. "Miss Dorcas, most of them tried to get home. I just hope they make it."

Thomas recognized the tremble in her voice. She sounded ready to cry. He walked toward her. "I'm sure they'll be fine."

Her hazel eyes had darkened to brown, and tears wet her lashes. "I hope you're right. I tried to tell them it wasn't a good idea to leave, but I don't think anyone heard me. Everyone was talking at once."

Thomas wanted to take her in his arms and comfort her. If only he had the right.

Miss Bloom clapped her hands to get their attention. "No one else is going to leave tonight. We have plenty of bedrooms. Come with me, and I'll show you where you'll be staying."

Josiah followed her out of the room as if she were the Pied Piper, leaving Thomas with Rose.

"Aren't you going to see where you'll be staying?" Rose smiled up at him, making his own heartbeat accelerate, but not as much as Newbolt's.

And Thomas's wasn't from an allergic reaction. Just the opposite. He'd better stop this line of thinking before it got him into trouble, encouraging him to do something that would make her shy away from him even more.

"I'm not sure I'll be sleeping tonight anyway. I have a patient to take care of. The first twenty-four hours are the most critical. If he pulls through that, he should be all right." This wasn't what he wanted to be talking to Rose about, but he couldn't decide how to turn the conversation to the subject he did want to approach. Would she be offended if he asked her why she kept running from him at the party?

Rose laid her hand on his arm, and he felt the heat clear to his heart. "I'm going to retire to my room, Thomas. It's been a very long day."

Before he could answer, she was walking up the staircase. After a few steps, she stopped and turned around. "I'm so glad you were here. I don't know what we would have done about Maximilian if you hadn't been." With a brief smile, she continued out of sight.

He wanted her to be glad he was here for another reason—because she really wanted to see him again.

❄

When Rose awakened the next morning, the steam radiator had kept her room comfortable all night. Although she loved watching the flames in the fireplace, this was much better for a bedroom. Even the water she used for her ablutions wasn't too cold. Sometimes at home in the winter, the water in the pitcher would have a thin film of ice on the surface.

She arrived in the kitchen in time to help Thalia's aunt Dorcas set the table for breakfast. Even though the Blooms had several servants, the two women often worked right beside them.

Rose stood in the dining room, counting out silverware for the table settings. "Thomas, Maximilian, and Josiah stayed over. Do you think they'll all come to breakfast?" She hoped Miss Dorcas could hear her question.

"I know I'm hungry." The deep baritone voice was hard to mistake, and it didn't come from the kitchen.

Rose whirled toward the doorway. "Thomas, how is your patient?"

Although he was fully dressed, his hair was disheveled. "Maximilian made it through the night. I'm hopeful for a full recovery."

"Did you sit up all night with him?" Rose started pulling linen napkins from the top drawer of the sideboard but turned at an angle so she could watch him.

"No, Thalia helped me a lot." His smile reached across the room to her heart. "I actually was able to get a few hours of sleep. Have you checked the weather this morning?"

"I did peek outside. Nothing has changed. Will Maximilian join us for breakfast?" Rose wanted to be sure to set him a place if he did.

"I don't think so. He had a rough night. Perhaps he could have some broth. I think I'll go ask if they have some in the kitchen." He walked through the room and out the other door.

When he was gone, Rose felt as if the morning had lost some of its brightness. She would have to stop reacting to Thomas every time he came near. She took a deep breath and slowly let it out.

"Is something the matter, dear Rose?" Miss Dorcas came to her and patted her shoulder. "Didn't you sleep well? Was your room too cold?"

Rose smiled at the older woman. "Yes, I slept well, and the room was just right."

"I only hope we can keep it that way. If the snowstorm goes on too long, we might run out of coal for the boiler." A frown marred Miss Dorcas's appearance. "Of course, we have the fireplaces, but they aren't as efficient as coal for keeping the house warm."

Leaving the silverware and napkins, Rose went to look out the front window. The snowstorm hadn't let up one bit. This would be a second day of snow. How long would it last? Hopefully not long enough to cause too many problems.

❄

After breakfast, Josiah and Rose went into the parlor. She wondered what they should do today.

Josiah turned from where he stood staring into the fire. "Why don't we play charades?" Had he been reading her mind?

"Do we have enough people?" Rose knew Thalia, Thomas, and Maximilian were in the house, but they hadn't rested as well as she and Josiah evidently had.

"There aren't as many as last night, but we only need two or three on each team." He started looking through the writing desk and took out pencils and paper.

"I don't think Maximilian is well enough to participate. And Thalia and Thomas took turns staying with him. They're probably both too tired." Rose didn't want to close the damper on their fun, but the playing field had just been diminished.

"Do you want to play checkers, Rose?" Josiah wasn't going to give up. His pleading expression brought a smile to her face.

"Okay, but I'm very good." She taunted him. "I haven't been defeated in a long time."

Josiah took up the gauntlet and started setting up the game on a table he pulled near the fireplace. "We'll see about that." He was much too serious about his games.

Rose decided to make it fun. Soon the two of them were making almost as much noise as the party last night.

"What's all this racket?" Thomas stood in the doorway.

Chagrin cloaked Rose as silence descended on the room. Why hadn't she remembered there was a patient in the house? "We're sorry, Thomas. Did we disturb Maximilian?"

He strode across the Persian carpet and stopped right beside her. "He's taking his first serving of broth. With the bedroom door closed, I doubt he even heard it. I just didn't want to miss whatever is causing all the merriment."

Josiah groaned. "Rose thinks she can beat me at checkers. She's telling a lot of funny stories. Probably hoping it'll take my mind off of what I'm doing."

She giggled. "It's working, isn't it? Who has the most checkers left?"

Josiah gave a loud groan. "I may be down, but the game isn't over." He picked up a checker and jumped one of hers, which took him into the last row on her side of the board. "King me!"

"Good move, old man." Thomas pulled up a chair and sat back to watch the rest of the game.

For some reason, Rose couldn't even remember the strategy she was using to win. In less than five minutes, Josiah held all her checkers.

He jumped up with his fists pumping the air. "I won! . . . I won!"

"So you did." Rose couldn't think of anything else to say.

"How about you playing checkers with me?" Thomas gave her an enticing smile.

She rose from her chair and offered it to him. "Since Josiah was the winner, you should play him. I'm going to see if I can do anything to help Miss Dorcas."

❄

Thomas liked this relaxed, fun-loving Rose much better than the reserved Rose of last night. He watched her leave the room as if she was fleeing something. Probably him. Were they back to her staying away from him as she did last night? He'd planned to let her win the first game so she would play a second with him. They could converse while they played. Maybe she would warm up to him being here.

"Your move." Josiah leaned back and smiled.

Knowing he couldn't gracefully get out of playing, Thomas decided to win as quickly as possible. Very soon, he realized that he'd underestimated the skill of his opponent. Even though he tried to keep his mind on the board, his thoughts often strayed to the auburn waves and hazel eyes that beguiled him. Now that he was a doctor, surely he was good enough for the boss's daughter.

What a thought! Maybe that was the problem. Rose still thought of him as the foreman's son. Her father had never treated him as if he wasn't equal to them. And Rose hadn't when he had worked on the ranch. Maybe that boarding school back East had given her other ideas.

Chapter 4

Since Newbolt was no longer having trouble breathing and his rash was almost completely gone, Thomas spent the next night in his own room. He sorely needed the uninterrupted sleep. Arising before dawn, he stared out his window at the continuing snowfall, clearly visible against his window. Three days was fairly long for a storm to rage, and this one showed no signs of letting go of its fury. He should get back to the clinic in case Dr. Wetherby needed him, but traveling the streets in this mess would be next to impossible, and Thomas didn't want to subject his horse to the torture and risk losing her. He hoped the snow would let up today so he could get home.

When he descended the stairs, he realized the fire had gone out in the parlor. Already cold drafts of air were chasing the warmth from the room. He had noticed the firewood stacked on the back porch when he went out to retrieve his medical bag. After being in this house so long, he needed more exercise than climbing stairs.

The back door was frozen shut, and he had to pull hard to dislodge it. While making his way the ten feet across the porch toward the stack of split logs, he wished he'd returned upstairs for his overcoat. The wind whipped and howled, blowing drifts across the expanse of porch as well as the yard. After loading his arms with icy logs, he hurried through the door to the back hallway. When he tried to close the door, he bumped it too hard with his hip, and the door slammed behind him.

Oh, no. He hoped the noise wouldn't awaken anyone else. The other people in the house needed sleep, too.

He stacked the logs in the woodbox beside the fireplace in the parlor. He needed to get the fire started before he could put any of them in the grate. A bucket of kindling and newspaper sat on the opposite side from the firebox. Beside it rested a package of safety matches by the Diamond Match Company. All the other matches being made in the United States were poisonous because of the phosphorous. After treating various patients suffering the effects from breathing the fumes, Thomas always bought Diamond matches.

Building a fire that would start quickly was an art he learned as a young boy. Soon all the kindling caught fire, so he placed pieces of split wood on top, careful not to inhibit the fire. When the flames finally leaped and danced, Thomas added more logs. He stood and turned to warm his back, clasping his hands behind him.

"Good job, Stanton." Josiah leaned nonchalantly against the door facing. "I'll wager that's not the first fire you've built."

Thomas grinned. "You're right."

Josiah joined him beside the fireplace.

"Couldn't you sleep?"

"I slept fine." Josiah turned around so he could warm his back, too. "I hardly ever sleep longer than six hours."

"I was afraid the back door slamming woke you."

"No, I was already dressing by then."

Thomas stared into the flames. "This isn't the only fireplace I'm worried about."

"I'll help you bring in more wood to build the other fires. I'd enjoy having something productive to do."

The two men grabbed their coats and headed out to the woodpile. They soon had plenty of wood beside each fireplace in the main rooms downstairs. While they were at it, they built up the fire in the kitchen stove, which had been banked last night.

After they finished the last fire, Thomas stood. "I've been wondering about the coal supply for the boiler. I'm sure the wagons won't be making deliveries in this storm. I'm going to take a lantern down to the basement to see about it."

Josiah rubbed his hands together. "I'll go with you, but I want to put on a coat first."

As Thomas feared, the coal bin was less than half full. "Do you know how much coal a boiler this size needs in a day?"

Josiah stomped his feet, probably to keep them from getting too cold. "I'm not sure. The one at our house is smaller."

Thomas walked around to the other side of the huge furnace. "I've never seen one this big in a private home either."

He picked up the padded glove on the workbench and used it to open the metal door to the firebox. Josiah helped him load more coal into the boiler without dousing the fire. After they finished, they climbed back up the stairs.

❅

Rose was thankful that the fire in the kitchen stove was already burning. She started a pot of coffee so that soon the hot beverage could warm her insides, too.

She went to the window to check the weather. Nothing had changed since yesterday. How long would this blizzard last? Her thoughts leapt over the peaks to the valley high in the Rocky Mountains. Did Father stay in Breckenridge, or had he gone out to the ranch? If he was at the ranch, she hoped he wasn't alone in the big log house. Maybe some of the hands had gone up there for the evening. They'd be snowed in, too. Of course, they used a system of ropes and pulleys they attached to the structures at the first sign of snowfall. With them, they would be able to get around to the other buildings near the ranch house. Too bad something like that wouldn't work in town.

Behind her, the door to the cellar opened, startling her. She pressed her hand to her heart and suppressed a scream as she turned around. "Thomas, what are you. . .and Josiah doing?"

Thomas's long strides ate up the floor as he approached her. "We wanted to see how the coal is holding out."

He towered over her, the gaze from his steel gray eyes never leaving her face. The room that had felt cavernous a moment ago had shrunk with his presence. The man was just too handsome for his own good. . .or hers. She'd never known his mother. When Farley came to work for her father, he was a widower. Thomas must look more like his mother, who surely had been a beautiful woman. Farley's grizzled appearance didn't resemble his son in any way.

"And is it holding out? The coal, I mean." She felt like a stammering child around him. And yet not quite. This man standing before her made her aware that she was a woman.

Thomas blinked, releasing the hold his gaze had on her. "I'm not sure. The coal bin was not even half full."

Rose realized she still had her hand on her heart. She dropped it to her side. "The snow hasn't let up."

Thomas gazed outside for a moment. "I don't like the looks of the storm. If we run out of fuel before this stops and the coal wagons can't get through, we could be in trouble. This far from the center of town, no one will be digging us out anytime soon."

That was not what Rose wanted to hear. Once again her thoughts flew to her father. She'd worried about him ever since her mother died. Even with his housekeeper and ranch hands, he would be lonely because she hadn't returned home as planned. He probably was worried about her.

❄

Thomas noticed the sadness that invaded Rose's expression. While they were talking, Josiah had slipped from the room. Maybe Rose would open up to him now. "What's troubling you? It's more than just the weather, isn't it?"

"I'm concerned about my father. I only meant to leave him for a couple of days." Worry lines crinkled her brows.

"He's not alone, is he?" Thomas knew Mr. Fletcher had a number of employees around him, unless things had changed a lot since he left.

Her spine stiffened, and she lifted her chin. "No, but he has no family near him." With those words, she turned and left the room.

Thomas stared after her retreating figure. *What was that all about?* The pleasant aroma of coffee teased Thomas's nostrils, leading him toward the pot on the stove. Since the coffee hadn't been there before he and Josiah went to the cellar, Rose must have made it. Yet she left the room without getting a cup. Every time Thomas tried to talk to her, Rose withdrew from him. Why was she acting that way?

When Rose and Josiah played the game last night, Thomas had caught a glimpse of the Rose he had known. He wanted to see her flashing hazel eyes and the high color on her smooth cheeks. Where was the Rose Fletcher who loved spending time with him?

Chapter 5

Finally the storm was over. It had continued for six whole days, almost driving Thomas crazy. At least the coal supply hadn't run out. The men shoveled snow during the storm to keep too much from building up around the house and the carriage house. The social interaction at other times gave a pleasant break, but he'd made little headway with Rose.

Today he had to try to get to the clinic. Even though he'd washed out some of his clothes and hung them on the radiator in his bedroom overnight, he was ready for more than just what he wore to the party. And he wanted to check on Dr. Wetherby. With the storm finally over, people who were sick would find their way to the clinic.

With Josiah and Maximilian's help, Thomas dug the snow from the front sidewalk and the street along the whole block in front of the house. Other people worked on the connecting streets. By midafternoon, he hitched his horse to his buggy and set out. The trip should have taken less than half an hour, but he didn't arrive at the house until past suppertime. Exhaustion and the extreme cold weighted him down, so he could imagine how tired his horse had to be. When he unhitched the animal, he gave her a good rub-down and a bucket of oats. She deserved the extra treat.

Thomas entered the back door of the house. Silence greeted him. He wandered through each room, but no one was there, not even Dr. Wetherby. Thomas opened the front door and tested the porch to see if ice made it hazardous to cross. He found no evidence of anyone having been there during the storm. A piece of paper tacked to the front door fluttered in the gentle breeze. *If you need a doctor, come to my house.* The older physician's signature was scrawled across the bottom.

Alone, Thomas headed toward the stairs that took him up to his quarters but then turned back. He'd have to start the boiler to take the chill out of the house, and he needed to bring in wood for the fireplace and stove. Since no one had been here for the duration of the storm, his supply of coal wasn't depleted.

Two hours later, Thomas sat in his favorite chair with his Bible open on his lap. A bath, clean clothes, and a shave made him feel like a new man on the outside. Now to take care of the inside. Too many days lately, he'd let busyness crowd out his private times with the Lord. In his silent apartment above the empty clinic, this was the perfect time to reconnect.

Thomas read then reread two chapters in the New Testament, letting the words burrow themselves deep inside him. One of the doctors he'd interned under had introduced him to Jesus, and he still felt like such a baby in Christ. He closed his eyes and prayed for a long time until his spirit finally felt refreshed. Why did he so often neglect his time alone with the Lord?

He foraged in the pantry for something easy to fix. All he could come up with was a can of Campbell's Pork and Beans and a can of peaches. He opened the beans and dumped them in a pot on the stove. While they warmed, he opened the peaches and set the can on the table. Why get a bowl dirty since he was alone? He stirred the beans to keep them from sticking and set the pan on a folded towel on the table to prevent a scorch mark.

He bowed his head and thanked the Lord for the food, such as it was. Eating alone had never been his favorite activity, even though he often had to while he was in Cambridge. This meal looked meager after the abundance at the Bloom house.

His thoughts turned to Rose. He couldn't understand why she was unapproachable most of the time they were snowbound at the Blooms' home. He stuffed a spoonful of hot food into his mouth and chewed away. *Could you give me some discernment here, Lord?*

Another bite of beans was followed by a thick slice of peach. They tasted better together.

"Give her time." The words resounded inside his head.

"Okay, Lord, what does that mean?"

After they repeated again, he heard nothing more, even though he tried to listen while he finished consuming his meal.

He washed the pot and spoon and pondered the phrase. What could it mean? Give her time for what?

By the time he finished cleaning up his mess, he'd come up with a plan.

❄

After Thomas left the Bloom house, Rose missed him. Every room she entered held memories of his presence. His smile, the laughter they shared over games, even his caring ministrations to Maximilian. Everything pointed to what a wonderful person the man was. If only he were a Christian, she could stop fighting her attraction to him.

Not even wanting to spend time with anyone else, Rose went to her room. She pulled out her well-worn black leather Bible. The book had been such a comfort to her while she was in boarding school—almost like a real live friend.

She sat in the wingback chair by a small round table. Letting the book fall open in her lap, she started reading in Proverbs. The verses found in this particular book of the Bible had affected most of her life. Her parents started reading them to her when she was very young. Probably one of the reasons she'd wanted to learn wisdom and discernment. But her powers of discernment seemed to have deserted her. Or the desires of her heart overruled them.

If she didn't gain control of her wayward emotions, she might be tempted to forget the admonition not to be yoked to an unbeliever. *Father God, please help me.* Rose spent a long time communing with her heavenly Father, asking Him to help her close the door on her attraction to Thomas.

Maybe it was a good thing he left today. She wouldn't see him again unless he waited to go to Breckenridge to see her father until after she returned home.

She felt the need to read one of the wonderful stories about a woman who listened to God instead of her own desires. The much-loved story of Queen Esther thrilled her with every word she read. When she finished, Rose knew that like the woman who saved her people, she could control her emotions and follow the path God set before her.

Before she finished with the Bible, she turned to Ephesians 4. The last verse caught her eye. *And be ye kind one to another, tenderhearted, forgiving one another, even as God for Christ's sake hath forgiven you.*

Kind. . .tenderhearted. Rose knew she had used the excuse that Thomas had scoffed at her belief in God all those years ago to turn a cold heart toward him. She knew she did it to protect herself, but she hadn't been showing God's love to him. How could he come to know the Lord if every Christian treated him the way she had the last few days? With her new resolve to keep a tight rein on her emotions, she wanted to express God's love to Thomas, to draw him into the fold.

After lunch the next day, Rose decided to get out of the house for a while. She bundled up in her coat and scarf and pulled on her gloves. When she reached the front edge of the porch, she held on to the column and took in all the surroundings. The men had dug a deep path to the street. As she contemplated strolling down the walkway, someone entered from the street end.

If she hadn't glimpsed his face before he trained his eyes on the ground, Rose would have known who he was anyway. His every movement was familiar. "Thomas, what are you doing here?"

He looked up as he took another step. His foot slid before it found traction, and one arm windmilled to compensate. Finally, both feet were stationary. A smile lit his face. "Rose, I came to see how you're doing."

She clutched the column even tighter. "I just wanted a breath of fresh air. I was trying to decide whether to venture down the walk. Maybe I should just stay here since it's so slick."

"There are icy patches you have to avoid." He continued toward the house, this time missing all the other slick places. "Why don't you have a hat on? It's too cold to be out here without one."

Rose laughed. "Is that the doctor talking or just the friend?"

He stood beside the bottom step and stared deep into her eyes. "Which one do you want me to be, Rose?"

The way his voice caressed her name sent chills up her spine that didn't have anything to do with the temperature. She couldn't stop the shiver they brought.

Thomas climbed the few steps to the porch. "Are you too cold?"

If only he knew, his presence caused warmth to invade her whole body. "Not. . . really." Why did she stammer so much around him?

"We can go in." The concern in his tone tugged at her heartstrings.

"I've been in the house so long." She pulled one end of the long scarf up around her head and tucked the end into her coat. "I'd rather stay here."

Thomas blew out a deep breath that instantly became a white cloud before it dissipated. "Fine. Are you doing okay, Rose? Do you need anything?"

Rose laughed. "This storm has really changed all my plans."

He leaned closer to her, and she could feel the warmth emanating from him. "What plans?"

"I would already be home by now. I had planned to go shopping here in Denver before returning home, but that wouldn't have taken long." Rose wanted to stand this close to him for hours. *Lord, I asked you to help me with my emotions.*

"I could take you shopping tomorrow." His murmured words surprised her.

"You like to go shopping?"

He chuckled. "I didn't say that. I just offered to accompany you. We could go to Daniels & Fischer department store."

"I'd like that. I need to get some more clothes. I've been washing things out at night." Rose wondered if she should have mentioned that, sure he'd know the type of clothes she was talking about. A blush brought even more heat to her face. "But I also want to get some candy and other things to take back home."

"Let's make a day of it." Delight twinkled in his gray eyes, lightening them. "Then when the railroad is cleared, you'll be ready to head to Breckenridge."

❄

As Thomas walked back home, he whistled "Sweethearts." His heart was light, and the future looked promising. The time he spent with Rose today gave him hope. Not once did he sense her retreating from him. Tomorrow would be a wonderful opportunity to do what he'd been wanting to for a week. Get to know her as the woman she'd become.

Even though he slept well that night, he awoke far too early. So after he ate a quick breakfast of a bowl of cornflakes, he sat down with his Bible again. Usually he didn't have any trouble concentrating on the words before him, but a beautiful face crowned with glorious auburn waves kept intruding. Finally he closed the book.

Lord, forgive me for not finishing the chapter. Once again, he poured out his heart to God then listened in his spirit. He didn't feel God cautioning him about his interest in Rose.

Thomas dressed with care, wanting to look dapper for her. He carried a hot brick wrapped in a blanket out to the carriage house. Before he hitched up his horse, he placed the bundle in the floor of the sleigh. He even placed a second heavy blanket on the seat.

Rose was ready when he arrived to pick her up. Thomas helped her into the sleigh before unwrapping the brick and placing it under her feet. He gave her one blanket to wrap up in and placed the other around her skirt.

"Thomas, how thoughtful of you, but we won't be traveling that long." Rose smiled down at him.

He hurried around the front of the sleigh, only giving his horse a cursory pat before he climbed up beside Rose. "Can't have you getting too cold."

First they stopped under the clock tower of the Daniels & Fischer department store. Immediately, the clock chimed ten times.

Thomas helped Rose alight from the sleigh then held out his elbow. She slipped her gloved hand into the opening and rested it on his forearm. He could get used to the feel of her hand on his arm.

Knowing that she might need to buy some personal items, he turned toward her after they entered the imposing front door. "I have a few things I need to pick up, so why don't we meet here in half an hour?"

❄

How thoughtful of Thomas to suggest this. Rose had decided not to buy more unmentionables, since he accompanied her to the store. Now she could make her purchases freely. If she wasn't careful, she'd find herself caring far too much for him. He was not at all like the boy she had known before he went to medical school. Over the last few days, she'd seen his kindness exhibited in many ways. Thomas had been funny and serious, and he put the good of others in front of seeking his own needs. So many wonderful qualities, but the one missing was the most important. She would continue to pray for him to find the Lord.

Thomas waited near the front door with several bulging paper bags. "Are you finished shopping here?"

"I have all I need." Rose held up her purchases.

"Let me take them to the sleigh." He put his bags under one arm and hers under the other. "I'll put our sacks on separate sides so we won't be confused and get the wrong purchases."

Rose watched him through the glass in the door, knowing she'd be terribly embarrassed if he opened hers. As promised, he kept the bags separate. She heaved a sigh of relief.

Thomas returned. "Would you like to walk around and see what else they have in the store?"

She agreed, and they sauntered through several different departments. The store even had a rather large book section. "I want to look at some of the titles. I love to read."

"I do, too."

They walked along the shelves, commenting on books they'd read. Thomas picked up a book before Rose could read the title. "I've heard about this one. I think I'll buy it."

"What is it?" Rose craned her neck, trying to see.

Thomas turned the spine toward her. "*The Secret Agent* by Joseph Conrad. I read *Lord Jim* when I was younger and have been wanting to read this one."

Rose didn't think she'd try either of them. She lifted a volume from the shelf. "This one looks more interesting to me." She turned it over in her hands. "*A Room with a View* by E. M. Forster."

Thomas held out a hand. "Let me see." After she gave it to him, he studied the first few pages. "How about if we buy both of the books? Then when we are finished with reading one, we exchange them."

"That sounds good to me." Not the only thing that sounded good to Rose. Evidently, Thomas expected them to see each other again later.

After strolling through the store, they went to the counter to pay for the books. Thomas hadn't given hers back, and she expected him to when they got there. But he didn't. He paid for both of the books.

They arrived back at the sleigh, and Thomas settled her into the seat. After he climbed in beside her, she asked, "Why didn't you let me pay for my own book?"

"I wanted to give you a little memento of the day." He picked up the reins and clicked at his horse. "Where else did you want to go, Rose?"

"I really wanted to buy a few special things. Some tea bags for Mrs. Barclay. You remember our housekeeper. She has really taken a liking to them. Some Hershey bars. I like the plain ones, and Daddy likes the newer ones with almonds in them."

"Let's go to the emporium." Thomas turned the corner and headed another direction. "They'll have those things and much more."

Rose loved going to the emporium when she came to Denver, so she laughed and agreed. They walked up and down the aisles looking for the tea and candy. Rose bought several Hershey bars while Thomas looked at other confections. He had another clerk measuring out some bulk candy for him while she paid for her purchases.

When she turned away from the counter, Thomas stood beside her. "I have something else I want you to try."

"Okay." Rose waited expectantly.

He took out a small piece and slowly unwrapped it, never taking his gaze from hers. "Open your mouth."

She complied, and he dropped in a lump of chocolate that immediately started melting. Her lips tingled where his fingers had brushed them. She savored the sweetness until the confection had completely dissolved. "What was that?"

"A kiss, Rose." Thomas paused a moment. "A Hershey's Kiss."

Rose loved the chocolate, but his words caused a riot in her emotions, and her lips still felt his touch. *A kiss indeed!*

Chapter 6

Rose sat beside the dressing table and brushed her hair, arranging it into her favorite chignon at the nape of her neck. The past week since the storm ended had been full of activity. Besides the times she spent with Thalia and her aunt, she enjoyed Thomas coming in the evenings. The knowledge that he was a thoroughly nice man grew with every visit.

When she allowed her thoughts to dwell on the man, she had to admit he was more than nice. Such an insipid word, falling far short of describing Thomas. Thoughtful...handsome...intelligent. She could compile a long list of adjectives if she had time.

She heard a knock on the front door, and soon a timid tap on the door to Rose's room. "Miss Fletcher, that nice Dr. Stanton is here to see you."

Thomas was here? *But it's morning.* "Thank you, Eliza. I'll be right down."

Rose slipped the last hairpin into her coiffure and studied her reflection in the pier glass. She pinched her cheeks and rubbed her lips together several times to bring more color into her face. Then she went downstairs.

Thomas waited at the foot of the steps with his hat in one hand. "Good morning, Rose. How lovely you look."

She held out her hand for him to shake, but as he had done at the party, he lifted it and pressed his warm lips to the back of her fingers. She held her breath for a moment and felt a blush stain her cheeks. Why had she pinched them? Now they were probably too red.

"Thank you, Thomas. What brings you here this morning?" Her gaze traveled up his broad chest to the twinkle in his gray eyes.

"Isn't it enough that I wanted to see you?" His deep chuckle rumbled around her.

She extracted her fingers from his clasp and nervously brushed both hands across the front of her skirt. "Yes... Did you just want to see me?" She liked this teasing exchange.

"Actually, I came to get you and take you to the train station."

"The tracks are clear?" Rose almost shrieked. However, her training came to the fore, and she was able to maintain decorum. "After all the trouble with the railroad this year, I was afraid they'd use this storm as an excuse to shut down service to Breckenridge. Of course, I could at least get to Frisco and take a horse from there."

He brushed the brim of his hat with his other hand. "One of the workers brought his sick wife to the clinic late last night. He told me service is restored all the way to Breckenridge."

"I wonder if I can make the morning train." Excitement at the possibility of seeing her father today warred with disappointment that she wouldn't continue to see Thomas every day.

"That's why I'm here, Rose. Hurry and pack your things. I'll accompany you home."

Relief flooded through her along with a sense of panic. How would they ever get to the station in time? "Won't Dr. Wetherby need you?"

Thomas shook his head. "I've run the clinic the last week. He said he could take over now, and I could go with you."

Rose turned and almost ran up the stairs. She'd quickly pack then tell her hostesses good-bye.

❄

Thomas drove the horse-drawn sleigh as fast as he felt was safe, but they barely made it before the train was scheduled to pull out from the station. The livery would send someone to retrieve the conveyance. The conductor agreed to hold the train while Thomas ran in and purchased two tickets. Thomas boarded and found Rose seated halfway down the car. By the time he dropped into the seat beside her, the wheels were already turning and the engine building up steam.

The conductor, who had continued down the car, returned and took the tickets from Thomas.

"Why is the train so short?" Rose smiled up at the man.

"With all the bad weather, miss, not too many people even know that the tracks are cleared. They decided to just pull two passenger cars besides the caboose. I think they only brought the second one in case more people wanted to take the return trip to Denver." He tipped the bill of his cap and continued on.

❄

Even though the passenger car was heated, the extreme cold seeped in. Thomas took a blanket from his bag and offered it to Rose. "I brought this for you to use. I know how cold it can get on the trip over the mountains."

"How thoughtful of you, Thomas." She spread the cover around herself and clutched it tight.

When she gazed at him, his heartbeat accelerated, and he felt as if he could lose himself in the depths of her eyes. Today they took on a dark blue hue to match her traveling coat and hat, and golden flecks sparkled in their depths. Since their shopping trip in Denver, Thomas had enjoyed the change in Rose. He'd begun to hope that soon she would have the strong feelings for him that he experienced every time he looked at her. Actually, he didn't even have to be in her presence to feel the depth of his emotions and longing for her. Could this be love?

If love was more intense than what he felt now, he wasn't sure he could handle the emotion. *Love!* This was the first time he'd actually allowed himself to dwell on that word. In his mind, love led to marriage, and that was what he wanted. To marry Rose. Even though he had dismissed the crazy idea he had earlier about him not being worthy of her because of his father working for hers, he wanted to proceed with caution. He had to be sure she felt the same way.

"Miss Dorcas gave me a package of food." Rose tipped her face toward Thomas. "She said we'd need to eat before we arrived in Breckenridge."

Thomas didn't want to think about food. He wanted to lean his head toward hers until their lips met. The day he'd fed her the chocolate kiss often lingered in his mind. The velvet touch of her lips on his fingers made him want to experience their touch on his own lips. He jerked his attention away from the temptation.

"The mountains look beautiful, don't they?" That should be a safe topic of conversation.

❄

Rose glanced at the glass window veiled with moisture that clung to the inside. How could Thomas see a thing through them? "I've always loved the textures of the trees against the thick blanket of snow. Each trunk and limb outlined by the stark white. Of course, the evergreens add a welcome touch of dark green." Why was she babbling?

When she looked up at Thomas a moment ago, she felt a strong connection. Although she wanted to feel only tender-hearted toward him until he came to know the Lord, controlling her emotions was hard in the close confines of the railroad car. And as the train went around curves, their shoulders often touched. Each time, tingles went all the way through her. Maybe his ploy of conversation would keep her mind off her emotions.

The farther they went, the more questions Thomas asked, and Rose told him more about herself than she had ever told anyone else. How she worried about her father now that her mother was gone. How much she enjoyed living at the boarding school back East. How much she missed seeing friends on a more regular basis. Even how she wondered about her future, how out of place she sometimes felt. He kept her talking about herself, but she had a hard time turning the conversation toward him and his desires. He was closemouthed on that subject.

Rose leaned toward the window and rubbed the glass, clearing away the mist. "Look at that, Thomas."

She could hardly believe what she saw. Where the Keystone water tank should have been, she saw a wondrous frozen waterfall cascading to the ground and down the incline away from the tracks. She noticed the conductor making his way through the car.

She leaned around Thomas and waved toward the other man. "Sir, what happened here?"

"The blizzard was a real doozy, miss. The workers were able to keep most of the water tanks from bursting, but they didn't make it to this one soon enough."

"Many of them leak." Thomas stood beside the man. "We've seen the large icicles hanging from all the others."

Rose once again glanced out the window. "I know that's a problem, but the icy sculpture is beautiful."

The man ducked his head and squinted against the vast whiteness. "I guess you could say that. Most people would only see the damage though."

He continued on down the car, and Thomas returned to his seat. "Since this is Keystone, we're not too far from Breckenridge."

She grasped his hand. "Oh, Thomas, I will be so glad to see my father. I hope he hasn't been too worried about me. And I'm sure he'll be glad to see you."

❄

When they arrived at the station in Breckenridge, Thomas shoved one of Rose's traveling bags under his arm then picked up the other one as well as his suitcase.

"Thomas, I can carry my own bags."

"There's no need. I already have them."

He led the way down the car to the landing where they could exit the train. After his feet touched the platform, he set down the baggage and offered her a hand for the last long step. He'd like to do things like this for her for the rest of their lives. He cleared his throat and turned back to pick up the luggage.

"I'll get you settled in the station, Rose. Then I'll go to the livery and get a sleigh to take you home."

Thomas watched Rose stare around at Breckenridge as if she hadn't seen it for years before heading toward the station door. "Okay, the sooner I get home the better."

He left her and hurried down the street. He didn't want to be out in the bitter cold longer than he had to. Right before he reached the livery, he encountered one of the ranch hands who'd worked for Mr. Fletcher when Thomas's father had been foreman.

"Petey, do you remember me? I'm Thomas Stanton." He held out his hand for the man to shake.

The old-timer looked him up and down before he gave him a crooked smile. "Wal, I wouldn'ta known you if you hadn'ta said somethin'. Yur all growed up."

Thomas laughed. "That I am."

"What ur you doin' here in Breckenridge since yur Pa's gone?" Petey pulled his hat off and placed it over his heart. "God rest his soul."

"I've accompanied Rose Fletcher home from Denver. I'm heading to the livery for a sleigh. She's real anxious to see her dad." Thomas hoped the other man understood his need to hurry away.

"Wait a minit there, son. The boss's out t' the ranch." Petey scratched his bearded cheek.

"Thanks. I'll get horses instead, so we can ride out there."

When Thomas arrived back at the station with two horses in tow, Rose stared at him. "How are we going to carry these bags on horses? I'm not dressed to ride."

Thomas explained about meeting Petey.

"This suit has a full skirt. I could ride in it." Rose glanced down toward the bags. "What will we do with these?"

"I have enough rope to tie them on the horse." Thomas squatted and started tying her two bags together. "These will balance my bag, so I'll tie them on behind me. We only have a few miles to ride."

❄

Even though the ride wasn't long, Rose felt like that frozen waterfall back in Keystone by the time they reached the ranch house. Thomas dismounted and helped her down, bringing the blanket he'd insisted she wrap around her as protection from the icy breeze. Her stiff legs almost gave out, and she slumped. He pulled her against him and slipped his arms around her back.

"Can you walk, or should I carry you into the house?" His breath against her hair infused her with warmth.

She leaned back so she could see his face. "I can walk now. I was just a little stiff."

He released her, and she hurried up the walkway to the front porch, clasping the blanket around her like armor. Her heart needed protection.

Before she reached the door, it flew open, and Mrs. Barclay gave a shout. "Land's sakes, come in here, child. It's freezing out there."

Rose fell into her waiting arms and returned her bear hug. "I'm so glad to be home." When the older woman pushed the door closed, Rose shook her head. "You'll need to see if Thomas could use any help with the bags."

Mrs. Barclay pulled the door wider. "Is that Farley's Thomas?" The smile she turned on the man should have blinded him it was so bright.

Thomas came in and set down the bags he carried. "Is that your famous stew I smell, Mrs. B.? I hope so, because I'm starving."

The housekeeper led the way to the kitchen and poured them each a cup of steaming coffee before she reached for the bowls to serve the stew.

Rose had always loved this homey kitchen, but one thing was missing. "Where's Daddy, Mrs. Barclay? I expected him to meet us at the door, or at least join us in here."

"Oh, Miss Rose, it's so sad. Your dear father has been sick in bed for several days. It's all I can do to get him to drink a little broth." She tsked and shook her head.

Rose's heart dropped to her stomach. She had a hard time remembering the last time her father was sick, and she knew he didn't stay in bed more than one day. *Please, Lord, don't let anything happen to him.*

Chapter 7

R ose slammed her steaming cup down, sloshing coffee on the table and rushed out the door of the kitchen. "He has to be all right."

Thomas went to his suitcase and extracted his medical bag, then followed her. "I'm sure he will be. I'll check him out."

She stopped and whirled around. "I'm so glad you came with me." She grabbed him and gave him a big hug before continuing up the stairs and down the hall.

When she reached the closed door of her father's bedroom, she gave a gentle knock.

"Come in, Mrs. Barclay." The thready voice didn't even sound like her father's. "I'm not asleep."

Rose pushed the door open and gasped. Her father looked old and frail. She'd never seen him like this.

"Is that you, Rose?" This time his voice carried a little more strength.

Before Rose could step into the room, Thomas stopped her. "I don't want you in there if this is what I think it is."

"Thomas?" Her father tried to raise his head but quickly dropped back on his rumpled pillow. "Is that. . .really. . .you?" He had a hard time getting the words out.

She wanted to go to him, but she knew Thomas wouldn't have prevented her from doing it if it hadn't been important. She put her hand on Thomas's arm. "Please take care of him."

Thomas put his arm around her and gave her a comforting squeeze. "Wait out here. I'll let you know what I find."

❄

Thomas closed the door behind him, thankful he'd left Rose in the hall when a paroxysm of coughing came from the older man. After hurrying to the bedside, Thomas pulled up a chair and sat beside his patient.

When the coughing spell ceased, Thomas placed his hand on Mr. Fletcher's forehead. The man definitely had a fever. "Mr. Fletcher, how long have you been feeling bad?"

The older man swallowed then croaked, "About. . .a week. . . . Is Rose. . .okay?"

"She's fine. I just want to take care of you before she comes in here. When you got sick, you didn't stop working right away, did you?" Thomas studied the sick man's flushed face and watery eyes.

Mr. Fletcher shook his head a little but quickly stopped and closed his eyes as a tear trickled down one pale cheek.

"Does it hurt to move your head?"

His eyes slowly opened. "Yes."

"I heard your cough. Does your chest hurt?"

The Best Medicine

The older man placed a trembling hand on his chest. "Yes." The word came out on a whisper.

Thomas took out his thermometer and shook the mercury down before placing it under the patient's tongue. He didn't like what he saw. The Spanish flu. Every year many people contracted the disease. He had treated a number of them, and some of them didn't survive. Without a doubt, Mr. Fletcher was suffering from influenza. No matter how much Thomas learned about different ailments, he often felt helpless against them. But he would use everything he knew to save this man who'd had such a profound influence on him.

He took the instrument from the man's mouth and frowned at the high number that registered. First he'd have to get the temperature down, if he could, but he also needed to use steam to break up the congestion in his chest. The dilemma all physicians faced. What was the best way to treat this patient? And such an important one, at that.

After sterilizing the thermometer with alcohol, he returned it to his bag. Thomas would need to get help, but he didn't want Rose in the room with her father. He wanted to protect her from the disease. Although he and Rose had slowly drawn closer, he hoped they would develop a deep and abiding love. He knew he already had.

❉

Trying to picture what could be going on in her father's bedroom, Rose paced the hallway and prayed. *Lord, please don't let Daddy die. I need him. He's all the family I have left.* As if God didn't know that.

Memories of the way Thomas cared for Maximilian flitted through her mind. Thomas was the best thing that could happen for her father. *Give him wisdom, Lord, even if he doesn't know You.*

Mrs. Barclay came up the stairs then approached down the hallway. "Rose, I brought your coffee. You're probably still chilled."

Rose took the proffered heavy mug and wrapped her fingers around its warmth. "Thank you. I really did need this." She took a sip of the steaming liquid, finally realizing just how cold she was, even though the log house kept them snug from winter's cold winds.

"So how's your father?" Worry brought deep grooves to the older woman's brow.

"I don't know. Thomas wouldn't let me go all the way into the sickroom." Tears breached her lower eyelids and slid down her cheeks.

Mrs. Barclay wound her arms around Rose and held her close against her cushiony bosom without spilling the coffee Rose clutched between them. "The good Lord's watching over him."

Rose nodded. "And Thomas is a very good doctor."

"And how do you know that for sure?"

Maybe telling her about what happened at the party would make the time pass more quickly. "He was at Thalia's party when one of the guests became sick. He knows what he's doing." Her words brought herself comfort, too.

"I hope you're right. I have been real worried about your father."

The door opened, and both women turned toward it. Thomas stepped through and closed it behind him. "I believe that Mr. Fletcher has the Spanish flu."

The women gasped in unison.

"I know, it's serious, but I'll do everything I can to help him." He raked his fingers through his dark hair, making it stand out in all directions.

Rose had never seen him like this. His coat and tie had been discarded, and his sleeves were rolled up, revealing muscled forearms. A stethoscope hung around his neck. He'd never looked better to her, because this was who he was—a doctor through and through. A glimmer of hope for her father entered her heart.

"How can we help?" Mrs. Barclay stood with her fists pressed against her ample hips.

"Have you given him any aspirin?"

She shook her head. "I don't think we have any out here on the ranch. I have some at the house in town. I could make sure one of the hands brings some back the next time anyone goes to town."

"That's okay, I have some in my bag." He took a deep breath and huffed it out. "I need a washbasin of cold water and some cloths to help me bring down his fever. After we get that lowered, we'll use steam for the congestion in his chest."

"I'll get them right away." Mrs. Barclay hurried toward the stairs.

Rose marched over and stopped so close she could almost feel his heartbeat. "I want to see my father now." She started to go around him, but he gently held her arm.

"I can't take a chance on you getting influenza. I'll take care of him." His gaze bored into her, making her feel as if he could see everything in her heart.

"You don't understand." She heaved a deep sigh. "I will stay with him and help you. I don't want to be anywhere else." Her emphasis on the last words echoed in the silence of the hallway.

Thomas stared at her; then his frown softened. "All right, Rose, you can come in, but you must do everything I tell you."

She nodded. If that was the only way, so be it.

❄

For hours, Thomas watched Rose sit beside her father's bed and bathe his face and chest with cool water and then place the folded cloth on his forehead until the fabric warmed. Over and over she repeated the process until the cloth finally remained cool to the touch.

Thomas wondered exactly what time it was. Midnight had passed long ago. "Rose, you need to get some rest."

"And what about you? You've been here longer than I have." Her eyes looked strained and weary, and her pale face had a pinched look about it.

"I'm used to taking care of patients." His reminder didn't seem to shake her resolve.

Another bout of deep coughing wracked the patient. Thomas didn't know how long Mr. Fletcher could keep this up. He looked so frail, not the strong man Thomas remembered so well.

"We have to ease that congestion in his chest." Thomas brushed thick black hair peppered with gray from Mr. Fletcher's forehead.

Rose stood, but didn't let go of her father's hand. "How do we do that?"

"With steam."

After sending Rose for the teakettle, a bowl, and some towels, Thomas studied the bed. Built differently from the one where he took care of Newbolt, this bed would be harder to tent.

The older man's hand snaked out and latched onto Thomas's. "Should. . .my Rose. . . be in here?"

Compassion touched Thomas's heart. "I know what you're thinking, but Rose wouldn't stay away. I'll just have to pray that the good Lord protects her."

"Good. . .Lord? When did. . . ?" The man's eyes begged for an answer.

Thomas dropped into the chair Rose had vacated. "Yes, I know Jesus now."

A faint smile veiled his old mentor's face.

"Because of all the things you told me, I was finally ready to listen when one of the doctors I interned under shared the Lord with me." Thomas clasped the other man's hand. "But I wouldn't have listened to him if it hadn't have been for you and your influence. And I don't mean the money to go to medical school. The most valuable thing you did for me was prepare me to hear Dr. Denison's words."

"I'm. . .glad." Tears squeezed out of the older man's eyes after he closed them.

Thomas loved this man, but he loved his daughter even more. If he had thought about it before, he would have admitted he had loved Rose as a girl, but that early love was more as he'd love a younger sister. The love he felt for the woman she had become had nothing brotherly about it. He loved her as he would love the woman he married. A forever kind of love.

❄

When Rose arrived at the top of the stairs, she wondered how she would open the door. Her hands were full. She walked carefully so none of the boiling-hot water would spill from the teapot.

The bedroom door opened, and Thomas glanced out. "There you are, Rose." He hurried to take some of her burdens.

They placed the items on a table near the bed.

"We also need a sheet." Thomas couldn't keep his eyes off Rose. Even after staying awake most of the night, she looked beautiful to him. He wanted to brush back a loose auburn curl that probably tickled her cheek.

As if she felt his glance, she whisked the offending lock of hair back and stuffed the end behind her bun. "Has he been awake since I left?"

"Yes, we had a short discussion."

"That's a good sign, isn't it?" Her pleading expression almost broke his heart.

"I certainly hope so." He watched her leave the room to fetch the sheet.

While she was gone, he folded the towels into thick pads. When she returned they worked together to help her father sit up, then draped the tent over him with a steaming bowl of water resting on the padded towels in his lap.

For the next couple of hours, they continued to change the water in the bowl so her father breathed in the steam. Finally, most of his coughing settled down, but the heat had brought back the fever.

Rose only left the sickroom for short periods of time. Thomas spent all the time she was gone in fervent prayer for his patient and the man's daughter. By midafternoon the next day after a long bout with chills and fluctuating high temperatures, the fever finally broke.

Thomas sent Rose away and cleaned up his patient, dressing him in a fresh nightshirt. He helped the man sit in a comfortable chair while Mrs. Barclay changed the sheets on the bed. After Thomas returned Mr. Fletcher to his bed, Rose walked into the room.

Remembering the verse in Proverbs about a merry heart being good medicine, Thomas started regaling them with funny stories from his days in medical school. Soon the room rang with laughter. The laughing Rose he remembered had returned. Her laughter blessed his heart. Even her father roused much of the time and joined in. Could things be looking up for Thomas?

Chapter 8

Rose hadn't wanted to leave her father's room, but now she agreed that Thomas was right. After a hot bath and a long nap, she felt refreshed. She wouldn't have left if her father hadn't been better. Even though she'd been afraid she'd sleep a long time and miss something, she awoke early in the evening. She dressed and fixed her hair quickly so she could get back up there and be sure Daddy hadn't had a relapse.

When she started up the stairs, she heard Thomas talking to someone. She knew she shouldn't eavesdrop on a private conversation, but she didn't want to miss any detail about her father he might not want to share with her. So she crept quietly up the stairs, skipping the third one from the top that always squeaked. Thomas's voice receded then moved toward her. He must be pacing the hallway.

"Father God, I praise You for the miracle You worked in this house. Thank You for healing Mr. Fletcher. I wasn't ready to let him go, and I'm glad it wasn't Your will to take him right now. And thank You for protecting Rose from this dreaded disease. Lord, my medical degree can't do a single thing to heal anyone, but with You, I can help people. Thank You for being with me this time."

Once again his voice faded away until she couldn't understand the words. How could she have been so wrong about him? Those memories from childhood when he jeered at her for her faith in God had colored her perception of him far too long. She had changed. Grown and matured. Why hadn't she considered the possibility Thomas could have learned to love the Lord during those years he was away?

The spark of love she kept trying to extinguish in her heart became a flame, fed by the knowledge that Thomas was a true man of God, someone she could spend her life loving. Knowing she didn't have to hold a tight rein on her emotions made her heart light and brought a smile to her face.

She stepped into the hallway and found it empty. Where was the object of her affections?

He'd been up longer than she had. Maybe he was in one of the other bedrooms. She hurried to the door of her father's room and knocked before opening it. Her father sat in a chair near the window, and Thomas stood beside him.

"Well, look who's here." This time her father's voice sounded strong, and no cough punctuated his words.

Rose rushed across the room and threw her arms around him, careful not to be too rough. "Daddy, I'm so glad you're better." She planted a kiss on his leathery cheek.

"I'm right as rain now, thanks to Thomas." Her father shook his forefinger at him. "He's a really good doctor."

"Because of you and Harvard Medical School." Thomas's laugh rolled around the room.

"You don't have to tell anybody else about that." Her father sounded stern. "It's just between you and me."

Rose looked from one man to the other. "What's going on here? What did I miss?" Both men started talking at once.

She threw up her hands. "Wait. . .wait! One at a time, please."

"I said, 'Nothing,'" her father growled.

"And I was trying to tell you that your father paid for me to go to medical school." Rose crossed her arms and gave her father her full attention. "Is that so?"

He clasped his hands in his lap. "I could see the potential in him, and we needed a doctor in Breckenridge."

"But Dr. Whitten came about a year after Thomas left." Rose was trying to figure this all out.

"That's why I went to Denver when I came back, instead of Breckenridge." Thomas stuffed his hands into his pockets and gave her a tight grin.

She leaned down and kissed her father's other cheek. "You're really an old softie under all that gruffness. I'm proud of you, and I agree that no one else needs to know."

Rose hadn't noticed how tense Thomas had become until he relaxed at that last statement. She turned toward him. "It's time you got some rest, too." She shooed him out. "I want to spend time with Daddy."

After Thomas left, Rose pulled a chair beside her father and sat down. "How do you really feel?" Her hands itched to touch his forehead to make sure his fever hadn't returned.

"I'm fine. Just a little weak. Won't be long until I get my strength back." He tried to look stern, but she could see right through his ruse. "Now tell me about your trip to Denver."

For the next few minutes, she regaled him with tales of the party, the storm, Maximilian's illness, and even about Thomas taking her shopping. Of course, she left out a few details of that trip. Especially about the Hershey's Kiss. Too much emotion was attached to that moment.

When she was talked out, her father's eyes roved over every feature of her face. "Something's different about you. You've changed somehow. . .even since you came home. You have a glow that you didn't have yesterday." Shrewd eyes peered from under his thick brows. "Want to tell me about it?"

What was there to tell besides how she felt about Thomas? Did she really want to talk to her father about that?

He waited patiently at first. Finally, he said, "You won't be able to keep it from me very long. We've always talked about everything."

Rose knew he was right. She started with the party. How Thomas had affected her. Then she recounted how he scoffed at her faith years ago before he went away to medical school, so she tried to hold her emotions in check.

He laughed when she said that. "So what changed your mind?"

"When I came up the stairs just now, I heard Thomas praying, thanking God for healing you and protecting me from the Spanish flu. The way he was talking to the Lord,

I could tell He was an old friend to Thomas." She stopped and looked down at her hands folded in her lap.

"So do you love him?" Her father had always been direct with her.

"I think so." She looked up at him. "How can I know that I'm truly in love?"

He started to laugh but stopped after the first hoot. "You'll know. No mistaking how I felt for your mother, and she returned the feelings."

Rose remembered how the love they felt for each other gave them a glow anyone could see. She wondered if she had a radiance like that.

"Just trust your instincts and let the Lord work it out for you. You know you can trust Him."

That's what she really wanted. To experience the love God ordained between a man and a woman. She was more than halfway there. If only she knew what Thomas felt for her.

❄

Thomas awakened to the enticing aromas of frying bacon and baking biscuits. He'd slept all night. Evidently Mr. Fletcher hadn't needed him. A good sign the crusty rancher was on the mend. After dressing, Thomas stopped by his old boss's bedroom and knocked on the door.

"Come in." This time the voice sounded strong.

When Thomas opened the door, Mr. Fletcher sat on the side of the bed, fully clothed. "It's good to see you, sir. Especially since you dressed yourself."

"I don't see any sense in lying in bed all day today." His patient huffed out a breath. "Took me longer than usual, but I managed."

"Maybe you could take breakfast up here before you tried to venture out. I'll bring it to you." Thomas knew he would help Rose's father down the stairs if he insisted.

"Sounds good to me. I'll be waiting for you." The older man stood and slowly made his way over to the chair near the window.

When Thomas arrived in the kitchen, Rose was setting four places at the table. "How did you sleep, Thomas?"

"Very soundly."

She looked rested, too. Instead of her usual waves and bun, Rose had pulled her hair back and braided it. Wisps framed her face like a halo of morning sunlight.

"Is Daddy coming down to eat, or do I need to take him a tray?" She placed the last utensil beside a plate.

"If it's all right with you, I'd like to take the tray up to him. I know he's improved today, but I'll eat with him. It'll help me evaluate how much better he really is."

Rose agreed and started fixing a tray with two breakfasts on it. When she finished, Thomas took it upstairs. This time when he knocked on the door, Mr. Fletcher opened it.

Thomas carried the tray to the table. The two chairs had been placed on opposite sides. While they ate, he observed the vast difference in the rancher. Although the man hadn't regained all his strength, Thomas was amazed at how far he'd come. After they finished with the food, they lingered over heavy mugs of coffee. Thomas lifted his to take a drink of the fragrant brew.

"So, Thomas, what are your feelings for my daughter?"

Thomas sputtered and almost spit out the liquid. How did the man know?

"Did you really think I couldn't see the way your eyes follow her every move?"

Thomas tried to detect any censure in the question but found none. "I like her very much."

Mr. Fletcher's eyes narrowed. "Is that all?"

Thomas shifted in his seat and placed one ankle across the other knee, resting his forearm on the raised knee. He tried to relax. "Actually, sir, I think I'm falling in love with her."

"You think?" The older man snorted. "You really need to know, son."

Thomas dropped his foot to the floor and stood, then rubbed the back of his neck. He turned to face Mr. Fletcher straight on. "I love Rose, sir, and would like your permission to court her."

"All right!" The old man slapped his knee. "It took you long enough to tell me." He cackled. "I'd be right proud to have you for a son-in-law."

Thomas laughed right along with him. Relief felt good.

❄

Now that her father was well, Rose remembered the presents she had bought. She went to her bedroom and returned to the kitchen with the tea bags for Mrs. Barclay. "I picked these up while I was in Denver."

"You always were such a sweet girl." The housekeeper gave Rose one of her famous bear hugs. "Should we try some of these now?"

"No, you go ahead. I bought Daddy some Hershey bars with almonds. I'll take them upstairs."

Before Rose could knock on her father's door, she heard a loud hoot of laughter. She wondered if she should bother the two men, but then she decided she wanted to know what that laughter was about. She waited until the noise quieted down, because she knew they would never hear her knock through all the racket.

"Come in." Her father's voice still contained a remnant of mirth. That was a good sign. She opened the door. Thomas stood beside the table with both hands shoved in his pockets. She'd noticed he did that when he was agitated or nervous. For a moment, she wondered which one he was this time.

"Hey, girl, come on over here." High color marked her father's cheeks, and his eyes twinkled. He peeked at Thomas. "You want to tell her, or do you want me to?"

"Tell me what?" Rose would have put her hands on her hips if she hadn't been holding the chocolate bars. She studied each man in turn. Something was up. That was for sure.

Thomas cleared his throat. She'd never heard him do that before. Maybe something was wrong with him. "Your father and I were discussing..." He left the sentence hanging while he expelled a deep breath. He crossed his arms and stood tall. "I want to court you, and he's given me his blessing."

Everything around her faded away while Rose stared at the man she loved. "Court? . . . As in?"

Thomas dropped his hands to his sides and took a step toward her. "As in learning whether we could love each other."

Her father harrumphed in the background, but she didn't take her eyes from Thomas. "Love. . .each. . .other?"

Thomas reached for her and gently clasped her shoulders. "Rose, may I court you?"

All she could do was nod.

❋

The next day Thomas rode into Breckenridge. He wanted to buy some small gifts for Rose. Something to give her every day. The mercantile contained a large selection. He perused the displays and bought a book of poetry and a copy of *The House of Mirth* by Edith Wharton. He hoped she'd like them. In another section, he found a display of the new teddy bears named for Teddy Roosevelt, so he purchased one. He knew Rose liked to sing, so he bought sheet music to "Sweethearts" by Robert B. Smith. The words should tell her how he felt. He picked up some of the new Crayola crayons, because he hoped their relationship would always be filled with fun.

"Is that you, Thomas Stanton?" A booming voice behind him alerted everyone in the store of his presence.

He turned around. "Brandon Stone, I'd know you anywhere, but where are the overalls?"

Brandon laughed. "I could beat you in any footrace, even if I was barefooted."

"That you could." Thomas studied the man before him.

Now his school chum wore a suit and bowler hat. "I work at the bank. Just made vice president."

What a change.

"Congratulations."

"Didn't I hear you finished medical school and came back to Colorado?"

Thomas nodded.

"Why are you working in Denver?"

Thomas wasn't thrilled that everyone in the store had stopped what they were doing and eavesdropped on their conversation. However, it might not be considered eaves-dropping, since Brandon talked so loud.

"You already had a doctor, so I'm sharing a practice—"

"Don't have one now." Brandon's assertion raised Thomas's eyebrows.

"What do you mean?"

Brandon removed his hat and circled it in his hands. "Doc Whitten left town on yesterday's train, and he isn't coming back. His father is very sick, and he asked Doc to come home and take over his business until he gets well. I told him if he left, we'd have to replace him. Didn't bother him a bit."

Thomas thought he knew where this was leading. What would he do if Brandon asked him to move here?

Rose accepted the mail Thomas brought home. She shuffled through the few pieces and found an envelope addressed to her. She tore it open; then a smile crossed her face.

"What is it, Rose?" Thomas leaned toward her and enjoyed the floral fragrance of her hair.

"An invitation from Natalie Daire. Her birthday is Christmas Eve, and she's having a party." She sighed.

"What's the matter with that?" Thomas wanted to slay dragons for her, or at least work out her problems.

"I'd like to go, but I can't be in Denver on Christmas Eve and at home on Christmas Day. That won't work."

Thomas took her hand and peered into her eyes. "Do you want to go to the party?"

"Yes, but—"

"No buts." He dropped a swift kiss on her forehead.

"Thomas, will you be back in Denver by then?"

He squeezed her hand. "Would you like for me to stay in Breckenridge?"

Rose took a deep breath. "How could you do that?"

His smile gave her hope. "I saw Brandon Stone at the mercantile. He told me that Breckenridge needs a doctor right away."

Rose heard her father get up from the squeaky leather chair across the room.

"What're you talking about?" He came to stand beside her. They both waited expectantly.

"The other doctor left, and Brandon asked me if I would take his place."

She wanted to shout, "Hallelujah!" but didn't. "Do you want to take the position, Thomas?" She held her breath.

"That's the main reason I went to medical school." He looked at her father. "So I could return to Breckenridge to practice medicine."

Her father let out a whoop then clapped Thomas on the back.

"So, Rose," Thomas asked. "What about the party?"

Her father smiled at both of them. "Why don't we just celebrate early, and then you two can go to your party?"

After they had read the Christmas story and exchanged gifts the night before Christmas Eve, Thomas watched Rose's father excuse himself and head upstairs to his room. She turned toward her own bedroom.

"Rose." Thomas stood beside the Christmas tree where he'd been blowing out the candles. "I have another gift for you. Can you stay a few minutes?"

She hurried to his side. "You've been giving me a gift almost every day. What more could you have left?" She stared up at Thomas. Her nearness almost made him speechless.

"This, Rose." He handed her a tiny package overpowered by a big red bow.

He leaned down so close that their foreheads almost touched. She fumbled with the wrapping, finally uncovering the small box. Inside she found a gold ring with a pearl nestled on soft cotton.

She turned her gaze to his. "It's beautiful, Thomas."

He gently took the box from her and set it on the table. He lifted the ring and slid it on her ring finger while gazing deep into her fathomless eyes. "Rose, would you marry me?"

"Yes." The word came out on a breath.

He slid his arms around her and pulled her close. "I love you."

Just before his lips touched hers, she whispered, "I love you, too."

Her eager acceptance of his kiss sealed that love for all their lives.

Laughter isn't the best medicine—love is.

Multi-published, award-winning author **Lena Nelson Dooley** has had her books appear on the CBA and ECPA bestseller lists, as well as some Amazon bestseller lists. She is a member of American Christian Fiction Writers http://www.acfw.com/ and the local chapter, ACFW - DFW. She's a member of Christian Authors' Network, and Gateway Church in Southlake, Texas.

Her 2010 release Love Finds You in Golden, New Mexico, won the 2011 Will Rogers Medallion Award for excellence in publishing Western Fiction. Her next series, McKenna's Daughters: Maggie's Journey appeared on a reviewers Top Ten Books of 2011 list. It also won the 2012 Selah award for Historical Novel. The second, Mary's Blessing, was a Selah Award finalist for Romance novel. Catherine's Pursuit released in 2013. It was the winner of the NTRWA Carolyn Reader's Choice Award, took second place in the CAN Golden Scroll Novel of the Year award, and won the Will Rogers Medallion bronze medallion. Her blog, A Christian Writer's World, received the Readers Choice Blog of the Year Award from the Book Club Network.

She has experience in screenwriting, acting, directing, and voice-overs. She has been featured in articles in Christian Fiction Online Magazine, ACFW Journal, Charisma Magazine, and Christian Retailing.

In addition to her writing, Lena is a frequent speaker at women's groups, writers groups, and at both regional and national conferences. She has spoken in six states and internationally. She is also one of the co-hosts of the Along Came a Writer Blogtalk radio show.

Lena has an active web presence on Facebook, Twitter, Goodreads, Linkedin and with her internationally connected blog where she interviews other authors and promotes their books.

Website: www.lenanelsondooley.com
Blog: Http://lenanelsondooley.blogspot.com
Pinterest: http://pinterest.com/lenandooley/
Facebook: www.facebook.com/lena.nelson.dooley
Twitter: www.twitter.com/lenandooley
Official Fan Page: www.facebook.com/pages/Lena-NelsonDooley/42960748768?ref=ts
Goodreads: http://www.goodreads.com/author/show/333031.Lena_Nelson_Dooley
http://www.christianbook.com/Christian/Books/cms_content?page=1728796&sp=67
484&event=67484|1728796|67484
Blogtalk Radio: http://www.blogtalkradio.com/search/along-came-a-writer/
www.linkedin.com
www.instagram.com/lenanelsondooley
Amazon Author Page: http://www.amazon.com/-/e/B001JPAIDE

Almost Home

by Susan Page Davis

Dedication

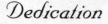

To Axel Clark Ballard, a true westerner.
Thought you'd like a cowboy story.
Once you learn to read, tell me what you think!

Love you,
Marmee

Ponder the path of thy feet, and let all thy ways be established.
PROVERBS 4:26

Chapter 1

December, 1913

Patricia stared out the window of the train as it pulled into the depot at Colorado Springs. Snow fell fast, and she could barely make out the boardinghouse across the street. Her hopes of making it home to the Logan ranch tonight plummeted.

When she stepped down onto the platform, she didn't see John Ryder. She looked about anxiously until he suddenly appeared out of the driving snow.

"Mr. Ryder! Thank you for meeting me!" The wind snatched Patricia's words as she hauled her leather bag out of the passenger car.

"Glad you made it through, Miss Logan." Ryder reached to take her luggage, and Patricia pulled her wool scarf across her face. "This wind is mighty fierce. Just stick close to me, and we'll get over to the house." He set off with his head lowered.

Patricia followed, stepping in his deep boot prints in the snow. Even in the street, it was nearly a foot deep, and she felt the cold crystals falling down inside the tops of her boots.

They gained the porch of the Ryders' boardinghouse, and he slammed the door behind them, shutting out the storm. The quiet warmth of the entry enveloped her. Mrs. Ryder, plump and maternal, came to the front door to meet her. Patricia longed to remove her wraps, shake off the snow, and sit before the cozy fire she could see through the parlor doorway.

But an even deeper longing prompted her to ask instead, "Will we be able to leave right away?"

Mr. Ryder eyed her as he unwound his red wool muffler. Patricia almost laughed because she could see the snowflakes that had clung to his arched eyebrows melting as she spoke.

"Can't go anywhere tonight, Miss Logan."

"Are you certain?" She'd anticipated his answer, but that didn't ease her disappointment.

"Oh no, child," his wife said. "The storm is too wild. I misdoubt the car could get down Main Street in this weather, let alone all the way to your uncle's ranch."

"Not a chance tonight," John Ryder said. "Probably not tomorrow, either. You were lucky the train got this far."

"But I need to get home." She stopped, realizing the futility of her pleas. The conductor on the train had come through the car before they pulled up at the depot, advising all passengers to disembark as the locomotive would not likely go on tonight.

"We've got a room all prepared for you," Mrs. Ryder said.

Patricia nodded in defeat. "I appreciate that. And I expect you'll have extra guests tonight from the train."

At that moment, a robust knock on the door sounded, and Mr. Ryder went to open it.

"Hello," called the new arrival. "Any chance of getting a room tonight? The train is stopping here until morning."

"Come on," Mrs. Ryder said to Patricia in a conspiratorial whisper. "I knew you'd be disappointed that you had to stay over, but I've kept the best room for you."

Patricia sighed and picked up her bag. Mrs. Ryder puffed up the stairs ahead of her and led her down the hall.

"Maybe a sleigh could get through tomorrow," Patricia suggested. "Does Mr. Ryder have a sleigh?"

Her hostess shook her head. "We don't keep horses anymore, Miss Logan, since we got the car. It's too bad your uncle doesn't have a telephone at the ranch so you could call him and tell him you're safe. Here now. Your room is all snug and waiting for you."

"Thank you." Patricia entered the bedroom and realized how tired she was. When she'd left the Christmas party at her friend Thalia Bloom's home, she rode to the train station in Denver with another friend, Natalie Daire, arriving on the platform at the last possible moment. She'd anticipated traveling late into the night, but now the four-poster bed with its handmade patchwork coverlet did look inviting.

When she was alone, she undressed and blew out the lamp. Pushing aside the ruffled curtains at the window over the street, she looked out. No automobiles or wagons traveled through the storm. The only movement was the blowing, drifting snow—falling fast, in a thick, swirling mass. No one would leave Colorado Springs until the storm was over.

❄

A gray light streamed in through the window when Patricia woke. She hopped out of bed and hurried across the cold, bare floor. The clouds lowered and light snow was still falling, but the wind seemed to have abated. The deep snow that drifted unbroken across Main Street looked daunting, but Aunt Edna needed her, and Patricia was determined she would get home today.

She dressed and packed her things then went downstairs to the parlor, where she waited impatiently for Mrs. Ryder to serve breakfast. The stranded travelers who had filled the boardinghouse to capacity the night before began to fill the dining room. Patricia joined them, and all made introductions and exclaimed about the inclement weather. When Mr. Ryder appeared in the doorway and greeted them with a cheery "Good morning, all," Patricia pounced on him.

"Mr. Ryder, is there any chance. . . ?"

"I'm sorry, Miss Logan." He gave a mournful shake of his head. "I don't expect to take that car out of the carriage house until spring."

"But. . ." Patricia stared at him. Her brained whirred, trying to come up with a solution.

Almost Home

Mrs. Ryder brought a platter of pancakes and a pitcher of warm syrup from the kitchen.

"You'd best hunker down here with us until your uncle Bill can fetch you in his sleigh." She set the platter down before a hosiery salesman and a mine supervisor who had come in after Patricia the evening before.

Patricia sat down and ate her breakfast, thinking as she chewed. She refused coffee afterward and pushed back her chair. "I believe I'll walk down to the livery stable and see if they can help me."

Mr. Ryder blew on his steaming cup and sipped the hot liquid, then set it down. "Mrs. Ryder's right. You won't get out of this town today. It's still snowing."

"But it's not so bad as it was." Patricia eyed him, her hope shrinking like a snowdrift in bright sunlight.

He shook his head. "There's more coming, if you ask my opinion. Not that you did."

"Well, I'm going to give the livery a try." Patricia turned to her hostess. "Thank you, Mrs. Ryder. Breakfast was delicious. If I find transportation, I'll be back in a jiffy for my things."

"Surely you're not going out this morning," Mrs. Ryder protested.

"I'm sure I can make it a few yards down the street to the stable."

Mr. Ryder set his fork down and grimaced. "Won't nobody be leaving town today. I suppose they might break the roads tomorrow if it doesn't snow more."

She swallowed hard. "I really can't wait. My aunt needs me, and I promised her I'd only be gone two nights. I'm already a day overdue."

He winced and shook his head doubtfully. "You might hire a sleigh from Ned Peakes at the livery. Perhaps. If the snow's not too deep."

"And a driver?"

Ryder shrugged. "Doubtful. Very doubtful."

She stood thinking for a moment. She didn't feel confident enough to set out on her own, driving a horse in winter, and she wasn't at all sure she could find her way home alone in the snow-covered landscape. If Mr. Peakes couldn't supply a driver, she would have to find someone willing to take her. She decided to face that hurdle when she reached it.

She went to the entry and wriggled into her coat, hat, and gloves, then opened the front door and ventured out into the glaring white world.

She would not allow herself to think that she would be stuck for another day in the town ten miles from Uncle Bill's ranch. Somehow she would get home.

Well, Lord, I guess this is when I should ask You to show me how to get home. She refused to consider that it might be God's will to delay her trip home. How could it be? Of course He wanted her at Aunt Edna's side. Uncle Bill had married late in life, and he and Edna expected the arrival of their first child any day. Aunt Edna was a sweet and wise woman and had become dear to Patricia in the three years she had been Mrs. Bill Logan. Now, at age thirty-eight, she faced her first delivery. Uncle Bill was ecstatic about the coming child but worried that Edna would have a difficult birth. Patricia knew she had to get home, as much for Uncle Bill as for Aunt Edna.

The livery stable down the street seemed her only hope, and she headed toward it, wading through the deep snow. It came in over her boot tops almost at once and sent shudders up her spine, but she forced her way onward through the unbroken whiteness. A few flakes still fell, but surely they would stop soon.

Inside the stable was dim, and the warmer air smelled of hay, manure, and horses. Two men conversed at the far end of the building while one of them saddled a horse, and Patricia walked toward them.

"Help you, miss?" The older man turned toward her and left the other to finish his job.

The one who spoke must be Peakes, the stable's owner. Patricia walked toward him and put on the most confident smile she could muster. "Yes, I wondered if you had a sleigh and a driver available today. I need to get to my—"

"Nope."

She caught her breath. "It's very important, sir."

"Still nope."

"Mr. Peakes, I must get home today. It's only ten miles, and—" She shot a glance toward the other man and stared in disbelief. It was dim inside the stable, but still. . . Could it be?

"Jared? Jared Booker?"

The younger man turned toward her, and her heart pounded. Her mouth was suddenly dry, and her stomach turned handsprings. She couldn't be mistaken, even in the poor light. His straight nose, his gentle brown eyes, the quirk at the corner of his mouth.

He studied her, a puzzled frown wrinkling his brow. "Patricia Logan?"

She laughed and hurried forward to grasp his hand. "Jared! Yes, it's me. And you used to call me Trisha."

She looked him over and shook her head. He had changed, gaining maturity, of course, and his form had a new solidity. His shoulders had broadened, and he was taller, too. Of course, he'd been only fifteen years old the last time she saw him. He looked wonderful, better even than her girlish memories of him.

She scowled at him. "Why didn't you write to me?"

Jared stared down at her and slowly began to smile. "I can't believe it! What are you doing so far from home in this weather?"

"I've been to a party in Denver. My old school friend Thalia Bloom threw an early Christmas celebration, and when I left last night, the storm was at its peak. The train barely made it this far. All the passengers had to stop here last night at the Ryders' boardinghouse."

"Imagine our meeting like this. I take it you didn't intend to stay in town last night?"

"No, Mr. Ryder had said he would drive me home, but the storm prevented that. Now he can't get his car out in the deep snow. He may not run it again until spring. So I came here to see if I could find some other mode of transportation to the ranch. I didn't see you at Ryders', though. Where did you stay last night?"

"I bunked here at the stable with Mr. Peakes. As a matter of fact, I was heading out for your uncle's place this morning."

She grabbed his arm and squelched a scream of joy. "That's perfect! Take me with you!"

"Oh, I don't know. It'll be hard riding. Do you have a horse?"

"No, and Mr. Ryder seemed to think the snow is too deep even for sleighs."

"That's true," Peakes said. "Can't send a team out in these drifts. They wouldn't get to the edge of town."

"Please, Jared?"

He opened his mouth then closed it.

"What is it?" she asked.

Jared looked uneasily toward the stable owner. "No offense, Trisha, but I'm not sure I'd want to be responsible for you. They say there may be more snow before the day's out."

She gulped down the lump forming in her throat. No matter what, she would not let Jared ride out of her life again so easily. "Perhaps we could go down the street to Ryders' and get a cup of tea, and you could tell me—"

"No time. The traveling's not good, and I want to get to the ranch before it gets worse."

"Oh, please don't leave me here! I need to get home."

Jared looked toward Peakes, as if hoping to be rescued from a snare, but the livery-man just spit toward a pile of manure and looked away.

"Mr. Peakes, do you have a horse she can rent?" Jared asked.

"Afraid not, in this deep snow. I gave you my opinion. You ought to wait here until the weather breaks. Likely your nags will get in a deep drift and flounder around 'til they exhaust themselves."

Jared sighed. "So you won't rent Miss Logan a mount?"

Peakes shook his head. "If you did get through all right, I wouldn't get him back till who knows when. Now, if you want to *buy* a horse—"

Patricia said hastily, "No. I'm sorry, I don't have the funds for that."

Jared pushed his hat back and scratched his head. "I need to hit the trail, Trisha. I'm sorry about your predicament, but maybe your uncle can send someone down for you tomorrow."

"Please, Jared!" She clutched his sleeve, unwilling to let him ride off alone. "There must be a way."

Again he looked down at her, and Patricia felt the strange, unsettled feeling she'd had when she recognized him. For hundreds of lonely evenings at the boarding school she had told herself that eventually she would hear from him and see him again. Uncle Bill and Aunt Edna would welcome him home. Thoughts of Jared had grown into dreams of a future together. She had allowed herself for a long time to dream of winning Jared's heart. In those reveries, he rode back into her life a beloved hero. They bought a ranch of their own and raised superior horses, and they were supremely happy. Obviously, those fantasies were far from the truth. He was heading toward the Logan ranch but not to see her.

Jared cleared his throat and looked at Peakes. "This one was my shadow when my father and her uncle ran the ranch together."

"I take it that was some time ago."

"Oh yes, she was just a half-grown tomboy. Wanted to be a cowpoke."

The livery owner smiled, and Patricia knew her face was beet red now.

"Well, I've grown up, Jared. I promise I won't be any trouble to you if you'll take me along."

"I don't see a way to do that, Trisha. I need to get moving."

"But. . .we haven't even had a chance to get reacquainted." She looked to Peakes for support. "Jared's father and my uncle were old army buddies, back in the eighties. They were stationed together at Fort Garland, and when they mustered out, they bought a ranch as partners."

Peakes nodded. "I heared your uncle tell about the old days."

She felt some encouragement and raced on. "Yes, well, Uncle Bill and Rupert Booker had a bit of a falling out ten years ago. Rupert moved his family to Texas, and Jared and I haven't seen each other since."

"I'm really sorry," Jared murmured. He moved toward the back of the barn, but instead of untying the horse he had saddled, he opened another stall door.

Peakes's eyes glittered, and for the first time he showed some enthusiasm for the conversation. "He's got some fine horses, Miss Logan. Now, Booker, if you ever want to sell one—"

"I'll let you know." Jared entered the stall and emerged leading a magnificent, coal black stallion. The young horse snorted and lifted his feet extra high as he pranced beside Jared.

Patricia stared at the black's fine head, the sculpted ears and bright eyes. His deep chest rippled as Jared led him toward the paint gelding and untied the saddled horse from the ring in the wall.

"He's beautiful!"

"Easy, now." Jared stroked the colt's neck, and the black nickered and snuffled his coat collar.

Patricia's heart leaped. "How old is he?"

Jared frowned. "I know what you're thinking, and the answer is no."

"But—"

"No."

She clamped her lips together to keep from arguing, but she couldn't help clenching her gloved hands into fists and giving a tiny stamp on the straw-strewn dirt floor.

Jared and Mr. Peakes laughed, and once more she felt a blush creeping up her cheeks, this time from shame at her childish frustration. If she wanted Jared to believe she had grown up, this was no way to show it.

Jared led his two horses toward the door, and when he was close to her, he stopped and smiled at her.

"Listen, any other time, I wouldn't mind taking you. In fact, I'd enjoy the company. It's really good to see you again."

Patricia felt her insides thawing in the warmth of his wistful smile.

"But with this snow, I can't risk it. This stallion is only three years old. He's barely saddle broke, and besides, he doesn't belong to me. I couldn't let you ride him."

"But you could ride him." Immediately she knew she should have kept quiet.

Jared's smile faded.

"No, Trisha. I'm sorry."

Chapter 2

Jared led his paint horse, Patches, toward the big stable door. The colt followed a few steps behind, as much following the gelding as he was responding to Jared's gentle tug on the lead line.

Trisha scrambled around to walk beside him.

"Aunt Edna is expecting a baby anytime now, Jared. I'd hate not to be there when she needs me."

"Aunt Edna?" Jared had no idea what she was talking about. Peakes eased past Patches and slid the big door open.

"That's right, you don't know. Uncle Bill got married at last!"

"Not really!" Jared couldn't help smiling. He remembered Bill Logan as a gruff old bachelor. Getting married was about the last thing he'd expect of Bill.

"Yes. Three years ago, almost. And Edna is as sweet as they come. But she's thirty-eight, and this is her first baby. The midwife woman said sometimes older women have a...a difficult time." Patricia's cheeks went scarlet, and she avoided looking toward Mr. Peakes, concentrating instead on Jared. "If I don't get out of here now, I may be stuck in this place for a week or more! Jared, please. I'm begging. It's very important that I get home."

Jared felt himself wavering. He looked out into the stable yard. It wasn't snowing at the moment, but the gray clouds still threatened more. Ten miles to the Logan ranch. They could do it in an hour in summer. But this time of year?

"This stud colt is really green, Trisha."

"But you're such a good rider."

He sucked in a breath, trying not to laugh. She'd always had a way of wrapping him—and Uncle Bill and all the ranch hands, for that matter—around her little finger. "Have you kept up your riding since I last saw you?"

Patricia lowered her lashes and eyed him cautiously. "Of course! I ride all over the ranch with Uncle Bill and Joe Simmons. You remember Joe?"

"Sure I do. He was always good to me when we lived at the ranch."

"Well, he's still an old softie. Takes me on rambles. And I'm a good rider. You know I am!"

Jared sighed. She was always persistent. Stubborn, her uncle Bill called it. "I suppose if I showed up alone and they found out I'd seen you here and left you stranded, it wouldn't set well with your folks."

Patricia's heart leapt. "Thank you! Oh, thank you, Jared!"

"But I can't let you ride the colt," he said quickly.

"That's fine. The paint looks steady."

Jared looked down into her vivid blue eyes—still as bright and lively as he remembered. He gave himself a mental kick. He had to be crazy to tell her he'd take her with him. But her face was so eager. How many nights had he dreamed of those china-blue eyes?

"All right, little girl, I guess I have no choice."

"You won't regret it!"

He sensed a new layer of reserve behind her enthusiasm. In the old days, he reflected, she would have launched herself at him and hugged him ferociously. The years of separation had changed things, but they both remembered how close they had been. Those memories tipped his hand.

Jared looked over at Peakes. "I don't suppose you can let us borrow a saddle?"

Peakes closed the barn door. "Guess I can let you take one. I've got an old cavalry-issue rig."

Jared winced. "All right, if that's the best you can do."

"Can't let you take one of my good saddles. You got a bridle for him?"

"Yeah." Jared handed Patches's reins to Trisha and tied the young stallion to an iron ring in the barn wall. "Easy, Chief." He took the extra bridle from Patches's saddlebags and slipped it over the colt's face. Chief took the jointed bit easily—something Jared was proud of. He had trained all of his father's colts to let their trainers handle them easily and safely.

"You got your stuff?" he asked Trisha.

"I left it at the Ryders'."

"Well, get on over there and get it. You've got ten minutes. If you aren't back, I'm leaving." He tried to scowl at her, but she laughed at him, handed over Patches's reins, and opened the big door just enough so she could squeeze through. As soon as she'd left, he regretted sending her for her luggage. He should have told her to leave it and let her pick it up later. He dropped Patches's reins. The gelding wouldn't go one step until Jared told him to.

Peakes brought the saddle and a worn blanket. Jared eyed it for a moment and took the military gear with distaste. Next to no padding in those old things. He knew he would be uncomfortable all day.

"You want me to pay you for this miserable thing?"

Peakes waved his hand. "I'll trust you or Bill Logan to get it back to me sometime."

Jared folded the blanket and smoothed it over Chief's withers. He slung the saddle onto the young stallion's back.

"You're asking for trouble, you know," Peakes said.

Jared grunted and tightened the cinch.

"Shoulda told that gal to wait here."

"Tell me something I don't know." Jared tried not to remember how close he and Trisha had been ten or twelve years ago. She was always a bit bossy, and he wasn't above giving in to her to keep peace when they played together. He suspected her uncle did the same thing. So she was a little spoiled. She had also become a beautiful woman. He tugged on the leather strap. The saddle would stay on Chief. Too bad he'd gotten so fond of Trisha when he was a boy. By the time he and his father moved away, when Jared was fifteen, he was even dreaming of marrying her one day.

"I never knew why Logan ended up raising that girl," Peakes said, sticking the end of a straw in his mouth.

"Her parents died when she was five. Her pa was Bill's brother. Someone shipped her out here to the ranch after her folks died. My pa and Bill were working the ranch together then. I was seven." Jared shook his head. "I recall when she came, I couldn't decide if I was glad to have a playmate or mad that someone else started getting all the attention."

"So you two grew up like brother and sister?"

"More or less."

Peakes shook his head. "Making a mistake, that's what I say."

Jared was surprised how quickly Trisha returned with her bag. He rolled the door open and led the horses outside. Her face glowed with the effort of hauling her bag, and Jared caught his breath. In all his dreams, she'd never grown to be this beautiful. Good thing he hadn't been around her lately. She probably had dozens of young men swarming about. The funny feeling in his stomach told him he would have been jealous if he'd seen it. He took her bag and tied it securely to the back of Patches's saddle.

"You ready?"

"Sure am."

She smiled up at him, and his heart beat a strange, quick rhythm. What would Bill Logan do to him if anything happened to her? Too late to think about that now.

She swung into the saddle without waiting for assistance. Her skirt billowed for a moment in the wind. Patches stood rock still for her, but Chief pulled at his reins and snorted. Jared turned to speak to him, calming him down. He hadn't thought about Patricia riding in a skirt. She used to tear around the ranch in dungarees, but he supposed she didn't wear them anymore, now that she was a lady. He mounted Chief, and the colt pranced a little.

"Easy, now." Jared patted the horse's neck. He lifted a hand to Peakes. The stable owner waved back and shut the big door. "Will you be warm enough?" he asked Trisha.

"I'm fine." She smoothed her skirt and tucked it in here and there. "I'll follow you."

Jared nodded and turned Chief toward the ranch.

The snow began to fall again lightly as they trotted out of the stable yard. Someone had gotten out and rolled a short section of the street, but as soon as they hit the end of it and got into the loose snow, the horses slowed to a walk. The young stallion whickered and tossed his head. He had almost no experience in snow. If he didn't settle down, he'd quickly wear himself out.

Jared looked back at Trisha. He ought to insist they give up and go back to the stable. She smiled and waved, her eyes bright.

"I can't tell you how much this means to me," she called.

Jared turned forward and concentrated on finding the best path for Chief.

Almost Home

❄

They followed the contour of the road, although Patricia couldn't tell where the road ended and the prairie began. Jared seemed to observe every tree and house closely and to have an innate sense of where to guide the horse.

After they got out onto a flat stretch, the going was easier, though snow was falling again. The wind had blown all night, and in places the snow was only a few inches deep. Patricia realized that the snow must have drifted into hollows and piled up much deeper in other spots.

She urged Patches up alongside the black colt, and he responded to her eagerly. The young stallion gave a whicker from deep in his throat and eyed Patches, his ears twitching.

Patricia laughed. "He's absolutely gorgeous, Jared. And he's behaving very well."

"I hate to push him hard." Jared shifted in the saddle and stroked the colt's neck. "His mother was a thoroughbred."

"He's got the long lines. I'll bet he's fast."

He didn't answer but frowned up at the gray ceiling of clouds above them. "I think the snow's getting heavier."

"We'll just take it slow. We've got all day." She smiled at him, but Jared's worried expression didn't lighten. "I'm so glad we met up this morning."

Jared rode in silence for several paces, as though thinking it over. At last he nodded. "Me, too."

Her spirits lifted on hearing that declaration, and she nudged Patches a little closer. The black stretched his neck around and nipped at the gelding. Patches squealed and hopped to the side.

"You all right?" Jared stopped the stallion and watched her bring her mount under control.

"I'm fine. I just expected Chief to have more manners, I guess."

"He's still young. I've been working with him, but you know stallions are unpredictable."

She nodded. "You're right. I know better. We'll keep our distance. It's just so good to have you close at hand again. I've missed you terribly. Uncle Rupert, too, but especially you, Jared."

He looked off at the hills in the distance. "I thought about you some, too."

"If only Uncle Bill hadn't gotten so mad at your father."

"Well, he did." Jared sighed. "Pa was angry, too. And too stubborn to give in. So he up and moved us to Texas."

"Yeah." Patricia brushed a light coating of snow from Patches's mane. "Uncle Bill missed Rupert, but he won't admit it. For years he's complained about how he took the best horses with him when he left."

"Well, your uncle got the ranch. It was only fair for Pa to get a string of mares to go with the stallion he captured."

"I guess so." She sighed. "I always felt as though that fight tore our family apart. You and your dad were part of the family, as far as I was concerned."

"Yeah. Dad and Bill were like brothers." Jared turned and looked into her eyes. "I'll tell you something."

"What?"

"I believe this horse is a peace offering."

Patricia caught her breath. "You mean. . .Uncle Rupert sent that stallion to Uncle Bill?"

"Yeah."

"That's wonderful."

Jared pressed his lips tight together and stared straight ahead. He didn't speak for a long time. The snow grew deeper, and Patches stumbled. Patricia let him fall back behind the black and walk in Chief's footsteps. The snow pelted down in small, dry flakes now. She hoped the squall didn't last long. She couldn't see nearly as far ahead as she could when they headed out of town.

She could see Jared's ramrod-straight back, however. He'd always been a pensive boy, but now he seemed even more serious. Had he changed so very much? Surely he still had the same tender heart he'd had when he helped her rescue a motherless ground squirrel. Of course he'd grown up. But still. . . She didn't like the thought that her old, childish love for Jared still colored her reactions to him. Better keep a checkrein on those meandering thoughts.

Chapter 3

Patricia hadn't paid attention. The snow was deeper, and the path of the roadway was obscured now. Jared must be navigating by dead reckoning and what few landmarks he could see. The young stallion floundered into a drift and whinnied shrilly. Jared pulled Chief's head around, forcing him to move his front feet to the side.

"Easy, now. Get up, you."

Patricia's throat constricted as she watched. There was nothing she could do to help him. The black horse pawed at the ground for a moment, and she realized they had strayed off the roadbed and into a low spot.

In an instant, the black found his footing and leaped onto solid ground again. Patricia exhaled and rode up on the other side of the stallion.

"Are you all right?" she called.

"Yes, but Chief's getting tired."

She looked about, but the driving snow made it difficult for her to orient herself.

"Stay close to me," Jared said, "but not so close that you follow me into a hole like that."

"I will." If Jared were traveling alone, would he have reached the ranch by now? She felt like apologizing for begging him to bring her, but that wouldn't do any good now. She pulled Patches in behind Chief and tugged her scarf up over the lower part of her face.

❄

The young stallion moved slowly, head down, putting one foot in front of the other. Jared looked back. Tricia and Patches had fallen behind, and he could barely make out the horse's bulk as he plodded along.

"Whoa." Chief stopped and gave a big sigh. Jared turned him so his tail was to the wind and waited.

Patches trudged slowly up to him and stopped. Patricia's muffled form was covered in snow. She raised a gloved hand and brushed the loose, white coating from the scarf that covered her mouth.

"I'm sorry, Jared. I promised I wouldn't slow you down."

"It's not your fault. But this storm isn't going to let up. I think it's time we admitted that and looked for a house where we can stop."

Her shoulders straightened. "I can keep on if you can."

Stubborn, as always. His attempted smile cracked his bottom lip, and he winced. "Trisha, I was wrong to set out when I did, with or without you. I'm sorry I led you into this."

She eyed him for a moment then ducked her head. "I put you on the spot. That was really low of me. If you think it's best to find shelter..."

He thought she sounded relieved. "I do. We've been riding for more than two hours, but I don't think we're more than halfway to the ranch."

Her blue eyes flared for a moment. "I guess we could be in serious trouble if one of these horses plays out on us."

Jared nodded. "Let's stick close together. I think there's a fencerow off that way." He pointed to the left, where he'd been watching an erratic ripple in the snow a few yards away, but it was becoming less distinct every minute. "We can't be far from a house."

He turned Chief into the wind again and set out. The snow was up to the young stallion's knees, making progress difficult.

At this rate, night could overtake them. He scoured the landscape for a building, but he couldn't see more than a few yards in any direction. His ears ached with cold, and his toes were starting to go numb. *Lord, we need some help here. Please guide us to shelter.*

After what seemed like a long time, he heard Patricia call out behind him, and again he stopped and turned his horse to face hers. Patricia urged Patches up close to Chief and pushed her scarf away from her mouth.

"Are you sure we're still on the road? Whenever we drive to town, we pass several ranches between Uncle Bill's and Colorado Springs."

He gritted his teeth. No use glossing over it. "I'm pretty sure we've lost the trail, Trisha."

She nodded. They sat in silence for a long moment. The wind howled around them, blowing clouds of snow about the horses' still forms.

"What should we do?" Patricia had to yell to be heard above the wind.

"We'll have to keep going in as straight a line as we can and pray for a place to take shelter."

"All right."

He hesitated, knowing she and Patches were both exhausted. Chief had stumbled several times, and if they got into a deep drift, he would be too tired to fight his way out this time. But what else could they do? He sent up another silent prayer and turned his horse toward what he figured was northwest.

Patricia's fingers and toes were numb. They'd been plodding along for what seemed like hours, but she couldn't tell if they were making any progress. They might be heading away from the ranch, for all she knew. At least the ground was fairly flat, but the horses had reached a dangerous level of fatigue. The gelding stumbled again, and she spoke to him, stroking his neck and giving him a minute to rest. When she looked up, she could barely make out the hindquarters of Jared's horse. She hated to push Patches any farther, but she knew she'd be left behind, alone in the blizzard, if she didn't.

"Up, boy. Come on. Just a little farther."

Patches lifted his right foreleg and pushed forward two steps then stopped again. Patricia's chest tightened.

"Jared!"

Almost Home

At first she thought he hadn't heard her, but slowly his horse turned and came back toward her.

"Patches is about done in," she yelled.

Jared looked around and waved at something off to her right. Patricia squinted and made out a small stand of pine trees. The stunted pines might offer slight shelter from the wind.

Patches floundered into deeper snow, and she sat still, speaking gently to calm him. Once he stopped thrashing, she stroked his neck and squeezed him with her legs.

"Come on, fella. See those trees? That's where we're going. You can do it." She urged him on in the messy path Chief had broken. Patches bunched his muscles and leaped forward. In just a few strides, they were among the trees.

Jared dismounted and let Chief's reins trail. The colt immediately lowered his head and turned his hindquarters to the wind. Patricia started to swing her leg over the saddle and realized how stiff and cold she was. Jared shuffled to her side and held up his arms. She slid down Patches's side, glad to have Jared steady her when she landed.

"I've got a tinderbox in my saddlebag," he said, close to her ear. "Help me break some small twigs off the low branches. We might be able to get a fire going."

Twenty minutes later, Patricia sat in relative comfort with her hands and feet extended toward the small blaze he had kindled. They had stomped the snow down in a circle around the fire, giving them a recess where they could huddle mostly out of the wind.

Jared waded back to the hollow with an armful of small pine branches. "These won't burn for long, but they'll get us warmed up," he said.

Patricia noticed that he didn't have to shout. The wind had eased, and the snowfall seemed lighter. She pulled her scarf away from her face.

"Any idea what time it is?" she asked.

He shrugged and glanced toward the sky. "Hard to say, but I'm hungry."

She smiled. "I hadn't honestly thought about it, but I am, too."

"I've got some coffee. Maybe we can keep this fire going long enough to melt snow and make a pot. We'd both feel better, I'm sure."

"Let me help." She started to rise, but he placed a hand on her shoulder.

"No, you stay there. Take your boots off and get your feet good and warm."

"Well, I . . ." She gazed up at him, certain she'd be blushing if she wasn't so chilled.

"Do it." He turned away to where the horses stood nose-to-tail, offering each other some body heat.

❄

As he filled his small coffeepot with snow and worked to position it over the coals without putting the small fire out, Jared considered their options. They could hole up right here with the possibility of freezing to death—the limited supply of small branches dry enough to break off and burn wouldn't last through the night—or go on. He didn't really like that alternative any better. The horses were near exhaustion. It might be better to stop here than to ask more of them. If one of them went down out in the open, they would have small chance of survival.

Patricia seemed embarrassed at his suggestion that she remove her boots, but that was of little consequence. Jared was beginning to fear he had brought her into mortal danger. He returned to Chief's side and took his small sack of coffee from the saddlebag. He didn't dare unsaddle the horses. There was no place to stow the saddles, and he didn't want to put them down in the snow. Besides, resaddling them would involve working the stiff leather straps. The weather would not be generous.

He removed his gloves and warmed his hands over the flames for a minute before removing the lid to the coffeepot. The snow was melted, but now the pot was only a third full. He pulled on his gloves and scooped up more snow to add to it. They'd been stopped at least half an hour before he had a passable brew.

"Drink this." He handed Trisha his tin cup, half full of murky liquid.

"You go ahead," she said, arranging her skirt hem carefully.

He almost laughed. Was she still worried about showing off her ankles? "Drink it." The words came out gruffly, and he immediately regretted it.

She reached out and took the cup meekly. Jared smiled grimly to himself. Maybe he'd hit the right tone, after all. Her stubbornness and defiance seemed to have vanished.

"Listen, Trisha, I'm wondering if we should stay right here for the night and heap up the snow for shelter."

Her eyes narrowed. "Stay here all night?"

He nodded.

"Do you think. . ." She looked around. "Jared, we wouldn't be able to get enough wood to burn all night, would we? If we had a hatchet. . ."

A small stick of burning wood fell and rolled to the edge of the fire, and he edged it back in with the toe of his boot.

"You're right, but if we made a snow cave, it would protect us some. We could survive the night."

He could see the fear now. She stared at him for a long time. At last she squeaked out, "But what about the horses?"

He sighed. They might live through a night in this storm, but he doubted it.

Trisha rose to her knees and passed him the empty cup. "Jared, I'm ready to go on whenever you are. I don't think we should dig in here. It might mean our deaths, and Patches's and Chief's, too."

He took his time pouring his coffee then returned her gaze. "I can't guarantee getting us through, and once we leave these trees, we're in the open. We might not find another place to stay—or make camp—before dark."

She swallowed hard and looked up at him with those huge blue eyes. "I'll do whatever you think is best, but. . ."

"But what?"

"I think we should try. The storm seems to have slacked a little, and we might be just yards from a house."

He sipped the coffee. Grounds floated in it, but he swallowed them down. "All right. But if you've got extra clothing in your bag, I want you to put it on. Extra stockings, another dress, anything you've got that you can layer."

He trudged through the loose snow again to the horses. He had to remove his gloves, and even then he couldn't work free the leather thongs that tied her bag behind the saddle. After a few fruitless minutes, his fingers were numb again. He pulled out his knife and sliced the thongs.

"Here." He dropped the bag beside her and went to the other side of the fire to warm his hands. "I mean it, Trish. Put on every stitch you can. If I had an extra pair of trousers along, I'd give them to you."

Her lips twitched, and she cleared her throat. "Can you, uh. . ."

He realized she wanted him to turn his back. "Yeah, I was going to try to get some more wood, anyway." He pulled on his stiff gloves and waded toward the few trees he hadn't already stripped of dry branches.

When he returned a few minutes later, she had pulled a fancy blue dress on over her wool traveling skirt. She looked funny with the shiny material showing below her coat. The skirts stood out around her, giving her a pouffy, round form. *Must have added a petticoat or two.*

"Do you have any extra clothing?" Trisha asked as he dumped his scant load of branches on the fire.

"Just a shirt, but I have a blanket I can wrap around me. He squinted up at the sky. "It's let up some." He could see a lighter streak in the clouds where the sun was lowering in the west.

He shook out his blanket and draped it over Chief's saddle, then turned to give Trisha a boost. When he mounted the young stallion, he took his bearings and made his best guess as to the direction of the ranch.

"All set?"

"Sure am." Trisha smiled, and his heart lurched. He had to have been crazy to bring her out here. How could he face Bill Logan if anything happened to her? He clucked to Chief and squeezed the horse's ribs with his legs. The black snorted and set out with his head low.

An hour later the light was nearly gone. The storm lashed out with new fury, throwing grainy snow in their faces. Jared no longer expected to find shelter. Only a tiny part of him cared. Chief's steps had slowed to a crawl. Jared reminded himself of Patricia and slowly swiveled to look behind him. He couldn't see her. Any part of him that wasn't numb ached. He couldn't feel his fingers or feet.

"Trisha?"

Out of the swirling snow in the blackness, something moved toward him. He realized it was Patches, with an inch of snow piled on his head and neck. Jared made out Trisha's bulky form on the gelding's back.

Her dull eyes peered at him from between the snow-caked folds of her scarf.

There was nothing to say. He turned forward and squeezed Chief's sides. The colt took a step then stopped. Jared squeezed harder but got no response. He kicked his mount, but Chief only drooped his head lower. Vapor rose from the horse's breath.

Jared stared ahead of him. Something about the snow had caught his eye. Just beyond Chief's nose, stretched out but covered in a thick layer of ice and snow, was a strand of what could only be barbed wire.

He stared at it stupidly for a long moment then slowly wormed around in his saddle. Patches was right on Chief's haunches.

"Trisha!"

She raised her chin and met his gaze.

"We've hit a fence."

Chapter 4

Patricia leaned forward in the saddle and raised her right leg behind her. Her thigh muscles screamed, and her leg seemed outrageously heavy. With a jerk, she got it above the saddle and pulled it over to the near side. She kicked loose from the stirrup and slid to the ground.

The soft snow engulfed her, and she sank to her knees, with her skirts spreading out around her.

"Are you all right?" Jared sounded more alert now, which was probably good. He stirred in his saddle.

"Yes," she said. "Don't get down. This is awful."

She grabbed Patches's mane and pulled herself forward, propelling one leg at a time in agonizing slowness. She reached the fence line and knocked the snow off with her hand. Her gloves were caked and stiff with it, but she was able to uncover a couple of the barbs that were spaced along the wire. In the twilight, she bowed to peer at them.

"Jared!"

"What is it?"

"I know where we are."

"You do?"

"Well, not exactly where we are, but within a couple of miles. This is Uncle Bill's fence."

"Are you sure?" He pushed Chief around and bent down out of the saddle.

"Yes. He bought new fencing last spring to enclose his south range. The barbed wire is different from the old stuff and different from any of the neighbors'. Everyone remarked on it at the time. See how it's got these flat metal slices twined in at every barb?"

Jared squinted. He was so stiff, he couldn't lean lower without falling out of the saddle. "If you say so."

"I do." Hope surged up inside her. "We're at the boundary of the ranch. I'm not certain where along that boundary, but if we follow the fence, we'll eventually get home."

Jared was silent for a minute. Neither of them spoke the thought that hung in the frigid air. The horses wouldn't last long enough to trace miles of fence around the Logan Ranch's outer boundary. They could freeze to death on Bill Logan's land.

"Can you get back on Patches?"

"I'll try."

Getting her foot up to the stirrup was a feat, but she managed. When she tried to swing up into the saddle, her heavy skirts weighed her down in the deep snow.

"Jared, I don't know if I can do it."

He nudged Chief up close on the other side of Patches and reached across the empty saddle. "Take my hand."

She reached up and tried to grasp his gloved hand, but her cold fingers didn't want to bend around it. How would she ever hold the reins? He seized her wrist with icy, leather-covered fingers and hauled her upward. She gave a jump and sprang free of the drifted snow and almost overshot the saddle, but Jared steadied her.

"Here you go." He leaned down and snagged Patches's trailing right rein. "Can you keep on for a while?"

"We've got to." She eyed the black colt with concern. He stood with his head and neck lowered and his eyes closed. "Is Chief all right?"

"He's exhausted."

"Maybe Patches could go first for a while and break trail."

Jared hesitated then gave a nod. "He's a tough old cow pony. Let's give it a try."

Patricia lifted the reins, and without her guidance, Patches began to walk slowly along the fence. They traveled obliquely to the wind now, and it blew across her cheek, more gently it seemed.

They had gone only a matter of yards when she spotted a bulge on a fence post and leaned to examine it.

"Jared! It's a gate."

He brought Chief up next to Patches and bent low to work at the wire. It was only a spot where the wires were looped over the top of a fence post, so that they could be taken down if the ranch hands wanted to ride a horse through. He couldn't pull it free, so he dismounted. After a minute, he had worked it loose and laid the wire back toward the next fence post.

"Wait," he called. "There may be another strand lower down, under the snow."

She nodded and waited while he waded into the gap.

"I feel it." Jared shuffled to the fence post and dug down through the snow with his hands.

"Can I help?"

He shook his head and kept working. At last he straightened, holding another loop of wire. He carefully pulled it back, yanking it up through the deep snow.

Patricia urged Patches forward. A moment later they were inside the fence, on Logan land. *Well, Lord,* she prayed silently, *I wanted to be home for Christmas, and here I am. Thank You for getting us this far.*

Jared led Chief through and mounted. Patricia peered around but couldn't make out any landmarks in the darkness.

"What now?" she called.

"Follow the fence."

She turned Patches in the direction they had been traveling and sent up more soundless prayers. With each step, the horse dragged his feet up out of the snow. Once he floundered, belly-deep, in a low spot. Jared came alongside, grabbed Patches's reins and spoke to him. The horse calmed and found his way out. They went on for what seemed like hours, and Patricia became aware of something ahead—something large and dark in her path. Patches took two more steps and stopped. They stood outside a small structure.

❄

Jared squeezed Chief's sides, but the colt refused to take another step.

"I think it's a line shack," Patricia yelled over her shoulder.

"Oh, thank You, Lord!" Jared slapped Chief's withers, none too gently. "Come on, boy. We're here." The colt pushed forward a few more steps.

Patricia swiveled in her saddle and screamed, "Smell that?"

Jared inhaled deeply. The cold air filled his lungs, and he caught a whiff. "Wood smoke!"

She laughed and turned forward, drumming Patches's sides with her heels.

A few steps closer, and Jared could make out a faint glow. The golden light seemed to come from a small window in the cabin wall.

"This looks like the shack in the south forty," Patricia said. "See the lean-to?"

Jared nodded and swung down off Chief's back. He remembered riding out here as a youngster with his father to check on the herd grazing the south range. Those were great times. This line shack was probably as far as it could be from Bill Logan's house and still be on his ranch. At least two miles, as the crow flew.

He tugged the reins gently, and Chief followed him into the dark lean-to. Only a few inches of drifted snow had made it inside. Using his teeth, he pulled off one glove and felt along the wall. *Thank You, Lord!*

He let Chief's reins fall and went back to the opening.

"Trisha! Bring Patches in here. There's hay and a barrel that might have some feed in it."

She plummeted to earth just outside the lean-to. Jared reached out to grab her by the shoulders.

"You all right?"

"Yes, but my legs are numb."

He pulled her farther inside, out of the wind, and she collapsed against him for a moment. He held her close just for a second. "We're safe now."

She pulled away. "What do you need me to do?"

"Nothing. Let's get you inside. These horses won't go anywhere." Already he could hear them munching the hay they'd found. "I'll come out and unsaddle them after I thaw my hands."

They plunged out into the blowing snow once more and around the few steps to the door of the shack. It bothered him that no other horses were in the lean-to. But someone had lit the fire inside.

"Hey!" Jared raised his fist and pounded on the door. A moment later, it was pulled open a few inches, and a weather-beaten, wrinkled old woman squinted out at him.

❄

"Annie?" Patricia stared at the old woman who served the area as a midwife. A new fear grew in her chest with the realization that Aunt Edna must do without Annie's services, at least for tonight.

"Land sakes, child! Where did you come from? Get in, get in! Out of the storm. Quick, now."

Patricia and Jared tumbled into the cabin, and the old woman slammed the door on the wind. The quiet and warmth enveloped them. Patricia looked around. Two bunks, a small table with benches, a box stove, a few wooden crates stacked for storage. She gravitated toward the woodstove and struggled to unwind her scarf.

"Let me help you, Miss Patricia." Annie tugged the uncooperative scarf around until it came free.

Patricia pulled off her hat. "Oh, we're getting snow all over the floor."

"Don't worry about that now. You must be half froze."

"More than half, I'm afraid," Jared said.

The old woman turned and looked him up and down. "Who might you be, mister?"

"Annie, this is Jared Booker," Patricia said. "You remember his father, Rupert Booker, was my uncle Bill's partner when he bought the ranch?"

Annie squinted at the tall, snow-covered man. "Don't look like that scrawny Booker boy to me."

Jared laughed a deep, rich chuckle that warmed Patricia more than the sputtering little stove did.

"Well, it's really him, Annie. He was on his way to visit Uncle Bill, and I tagged along, coming home from a trip to Denver. But what are *you* doing here?"

The old woman began to work Patricia's coat buttons. "Get your things off. We'll thaw you out. Why, don't you know, I smelled the storm coming yesterday, and I set out for the ranch house. Thought I'd go over and stay with Edna in case she needed me. I know she's not due for a couple of weeks yet, but I didn't want to be stuck at my house three miles away when her time came. Might turn out that no one could fetch me when that babe took a notion to come."

"And so you're stuck here now instead," Jared said.

She nodded grimly. "That's right. The snow comes on sudden in these parts. Got so I could hardly see where I was going. Almost missed the fence and kept on out into nowhere."

"Oh, Annie! I'm glad you found this shack," Patricia said.

"Me, too. I decided to hole up here until the snow let up, and I've been here one night and the better part of two days." She pulled Patricia's coat sleeve. Patricia let the heavy garment slide off. "Sit down on that bench now, and let me get those boots off you." Annie pushed her gently toward the table.

Jared used his teeth to help peel off his gloves.

"Get your coat off, Booker, or whoever you are," Annie said.

"I'll just warm my hands up for a minute. Then I need to go out and tend to the horses."

"How many you got?" Annie asked.

"Two, in the lean-to outside."

"They'll want water. We'll have to melt lots of snow." Annie scooped up a clump that had fallen from Patricia's clothing and threw it into a steaming pan on the stove. "I've got two buckets. When you go out, you can fill them and set them inside. I'll work on melting it down while you tend your critters. Then, if you're not frozen stiff, you can get more."

"Sounds good." Jared flexed his fingers and then spread both hands again, closer to the stovetop. "I need to get their saddles off and bed them down."

Patricia winced as Annie eased her left boot off. "At least I can feel that one."

"You can't feel the other foot?" Annie asked. "I hope you ain't frostbit."

"Ouch!" Patricia gasped as the blood tingled her fingers. She rubbed her hands together. "Pins and needles."

"That's a good sign." Annie's face wrinkled into more canyons and valleys as she bent over Patricia's other foot. "I may not be able to untie this until the ice melts a bit."

"I could cut the lace," Jared said.

"No, but let's move this bench closer to the stove."

Jared worked diligently at the lacing until at last it loosened. He grasped the heel and pulled the boot off. "There! Now let Annie give you some of that tea she's fixing. I'll go see to Chief and Patches."

"I'll have tea and hot oatmeal ready for you when you're done," Annie said.

Patricia grimaced. "Oatmeal?"

"Can't be choosy." Annie's beady eyes sparked. "We've got some canned beans and peaches, too. If you don't like the vittles, tell your uncle Bill he needs to stock his line shacks better."

Chapter 5

Jared could see that Patricia was worried about her aunt, knowing the midwife hadn't made it to the ranch. Of course, for all they knew, Edna didn't need Annie's services yet. But babies were known to arrive at odd times. As he scooped snow into the two pails, he assessed the swirling, drifting flakes. A rip-roaring blizzard. He wouldn't want to go more than a few steps from the cabin. He sent up a swift prayer for the Logans. *You know what's best, Father. We'll wait on You for direction. Can't do much else. But I thank You from the bottom of my heart for letting us find this cabin.*

He set the buckets inside the cabin door and took the lantern from Annie. Wading through the thigh-deep snow to the lean-to took all his energy. Already the cold sapped his body heat. Both horses had their heads down and their hindquarters to the entrance. He called out to them and slapped Patches's white rump. The gelding snuffled and sidled over enough toward Chief to let Jared in beside him. The colt let out a soft whinny but returned immediately to munching hay.

If we'd been out any longer, these horses wouldn't have made it. Jared shook off the thought and felt about for the barrel he had spotted earlier. The top was secured with a clamp to keep animals from getting into it. He set the lantern down and quickly removed the clamp. The barrel was more than half full of crimped oats. He wished they had some sweet feed for the horses. He would have to ask Annie if their limited supplies included a jug of molasses. That would perk these animals up and give them a little more nourishment to fight the cold. He scooped out a coffee can full of oats for each horse and dumped the rations on the ground, on top of the hay they were nibbling.

The knots in the leather straps that held the saddles on were stiff. He held the lantern up close but despaired of warming the leather enough to make it pliable. His own hands weren't warm enough for that either. He considered slicing through the cinches, but when he got out his knife, he found he could dig at the knot on Patches's saddle with the tip, and though he gouged it somewhat, after several minutes he got it loose.

At last the horses were free of their burdens. He stored the tack on an overhead rack and plunged out into the storm again. The irregular mound to one side of the door must be a woodpile. With great effort, he dug the snow away. His hands were already numbing, but he managed to pull out several sticks of firewood. All he could think of was getting warm. He stumbled toward the stoop, wondering if he could make those few steps.

He couldn't open the door to the cabin with his arms full, so he kicked the lower boards. Patricia opened it.

"Oh, Jared, you're covered with snow. Come in, quick!"

A lovely smell of cooking food met him, and the interior of the little shack seemed overly warm. The snow on the roof and banked all around the cabin no doubt insulated it, and heating the twelve-by-twelve room was not a problem. He lowered his armful of wood into the rough box near the stove and stepped back nearer the door to remove his snowy outerwear.

"Don't want to get the floor all wet," he explained as he handed Patricia his hat and gloves.

"I'll sweep it down the cracks in the floor before it can melt," Annie said. She advanced with a sorry-looking broom and attacked the little clumps of snow that had fallen from his boots and coat.

The plain food filled his hollow belly, and afterward Jared sat on a bench with his back against the edge of the table and stretched out his long legs toward the stove. Patricia helped Annie gather up the dishes. All day, he'd thought of her mostly in terms of her danger and the desperate situation they'd put themselves in. Now he noticed anew how lovely she was, even in this shabby cabin. Her dark hair swirled about her shoulders as she worked. Her mouth, set in a determined line, had a shape that made his stomach flutter. She'd been at a fancy party in Denver before they met up. They lived in different worlds now.

She looked over at him and smiled. "How are you doing? Did you get enough to eat?"

"Yes, thanks." Jared turned to look at the older woman. "Annie, that may not have been the most elegant meal I've ever eaten, but it was the most welcome."

"Thankee." Annie stacked the dirty dishes. "We'll save these for later. I can wash dishes anytime, but those horses haven't had a drink of water all day. We'll melt snow until they've had what they need, then we'll think about wash water."

"I hate to send you out again to take it to them," Patricia said to Jared. "Maybe I could go this time."

"No." He climbed to his feet. It was too dangerous to send either of the women outside in the howling storm. "I know it's not far to the lean-to, but I can't touch the cabin wall all the way because of the woodpile. I brought my rope in off my saddle, and I'm going to tie one end of it to the door handle outside. Didn't see anything else it would hold on. And I'll fix the other end to something in the lean-to. Then I won't take a chance on missing my way."

"It's that bad?" Annie asked. "You could get turned around just from here to the shed?"

"Easy." Jared pulled on his damp boots. Good thing he'd greased them well before he set out on this adventure.

"Take these two kettles and fill them with snow," Annie said. "I hate to keep opening that door, but we'll have to melt snow all night if we want enough water for those animals and our own needs."

"It's all right, Annie," Jared said. "Just make me a place to sleep on the floor when I come in. I'm tired to the bone." He pointed to a space between the table and the stove. "There. I'll be able to keep the fire up in the night without disturbing you two any more than necessary."

"Now there's a gentleman." Annie nodded at Patricia. "You're young. You take the top bunk."

Patricia started to protest then shrugged. "Yes, ma'am. I guess that makes sense."

"You're exhausted." Annie propelled her toward the bunks against the far wall. "While Mr. Booker tends to the horses, you pile into bed. And I don't want any arguing from you."

An hour later, Jared settled down on the floor with a wool blanket under him and a tattered quilt as a covering. The two women seemed to be asleep already. There was no question about Annie; her gentle snores, with occasional louder snorts, reminded him of the night noises in the bunkhouse at home. He assumed Patricia lay beneath the mound of blankets on the top bunk, having seen no sign of her since his last foray outside for more snow to melt.

He blew out the lantern and pushed it carefully to one side on the floor. He could still see a glow of orange through the draft holes on the box stove, but the night was so dark that he couldn't tell where the two windows were. The wail of the wind keening about the little shack soon obliterated even Annie's snores.

Was this whole trip a mistake? His father had bequeathed the three-year-old stallion to Bill Logan. The copy of the will Jared carried in his inner coat pocket was indisputable. But what if Bill was still angry with his old friend and wouldn't accept his final gift? Patricia seemed friendly enough, although their perilous situation today hadn't left much opportunity for them to renew their acquaintance. He'd like to. All these years, he'd thought of her as a cheerful little pest. He'd missed her plenty and had wished he could see her again. But he'd never dreamed she'd grown into such a beautiful woman. How would she and Bill react when he revealed the purpose of his journey? Had she absorbed her uncle's resentment of Rupert's behavior?

Jared rolled over and tried to find a comfortable position on the cold board floor. Patricia's attitude was very important to him. More than anything, he wanted her to forgive his father. Unless she did that, she probably wouldn't welcome Jared back into her life. And he wanted to be in it. He'd come back to Colorado to stay. If the Logans wouldn't welcome him, life could be miserable. His last waking thought was the beginning of a garbled prayer. *Lord, let her forgive us. . .and let Bill accept Chief.*

❋

Patricia awoke in a dim gray room. Someone was moving about. She opened her eyes and pushed the blankets aside and saw an old woman dipping hot water from a kettle on the stove into a dented blue coffeepot.

Of course. Annie, the midwife. The cabin. The storm.

It came back in a rush. She sat up and looked around the small room. Jared must be outside. She pushed back the covers and noted that the cabin had stayed toasty warm all night.

Annie glanced up at her. "Come on down and make your ablutions before that feller comes back. Did you say he's Rupert Booker's boy?"

"That's right. Jared." Patricia grasped the edge of the bunk and slid down, landing with a thump on the floor.

Annie went about preparations for breakfast while Patricia quickly took her skirt from the bedpost and pulled it on over her petticoat.

"Still snowing, I take it." She looked toward the nearest window, but frost coated it.

"Yup. Doesn't look like stopping now."

The wind moaned about the eaves, and the stovepipe shivered where it met the wall. The door opened, and Jared kicked his boots against the top step before entering. Even so, he brought a great deal of snow in with him. He stood a long-handled shovel against the wall by the door and pulled off his gloves.

"Good thing they left that shovel in the lean-to. I didn't see it last night."

"How deep is the snow?" Patricia asked.

"Past my waist. About up to the window ledges, I guess. Of course, it's drifted in around the buildings. Took me awhile to make my way out to the horses, but we've got a path now, provided the wind doesn't throw all the snow I've shoveled back into it. How much water have we got, Annie?"

"Enough for one bucket full." Annie lifted one pail off the stove. "Bring me back some more, and I'll melt it for the other critter."

"How many buckets of snow does it take to make a bucket of water?" Patricia asked. The process seemed painfully slow with their few containers.

"Four or five, I reckon." Jared took the pail from Annie.

"Coffee and hot porridge will be ready in about half an hour," Annie told him.

Jared went out once more into the swirling storm.

"What can I do to help you?" Patricia asked. The old woman nodded toward the shelf on the wall above the table. "Pick out something to go with this porridge. I reckon there's a little brown sugar in that small crock, and the canned fruit doesn't seem to have frozen."

"Aunt Edna's applesauce!" Patricia reached eagerly for a pint jar on the shelf. "I helped her put this up last fall, and we sent a few jars out to each of the line shacks."

"Bless her for thinking of it." Annie plunked three tin plates on the table. "I reckon we've got food for another three or four days. A week if we go half rations."

Patricia stood still and stared at her. "Do you think we should do that?"

"No guarantee we'll be able to get out of here sooner. This storm ain't over yet, and no one knows we're out here."

"But. . .Aunt Edna and the baby. . ."

Annie patted her shoulder. "There, now. Don't think about that. It's not like she's alone. She's got your uncle Bill and a dozen cowboys."

"But Uncle Bill's never delivered a baby. Not a human baby, anyway."

"Just pray, child. It's all we can do."

Patricia recognized her wisdom and prayed silently as she finished setting the table. After Jared had filled all their empty pails and kettles with snow and brought in several more armfuls of wood, they sat down together to eat.

"So what brings you back to Colorado after all these years?" Annie asked Jared. "I thought your pa moved you down to Mexico."

"Southern Texas," Jared said. "Well, you see, ma'am, my father died about three weeks ago."

Patricia caught her breath. "Jared, you didn't tell me."

"I wanted to." His brown eyes filled with contrition. "It didn't seem like the right time when we were at the livery stable, and then we had all we could do to deal with the storm."

"I'm so sorry to hear about Uncle Rupert."

"Well, thanks." Jared picked up his tin cup and looked down into his steaming coffee. "It's because of his passing that I'm here."

"What do you mean?" Annie asked.

Jared looked at her and smiled grimly. "Before my father died, he wrote a will, and in it he left the stallion I've got out there in the lean-to—Chief, we call him—to Bill Logan. I'm here to deliver the bequest."

Patricia gaped at him. "But why would Rupert send a horse to Uncle Bill?"

"Weren't they friends in the old days?" Annie asked.

"Well, yes. But they had a big fight, were so angry that they split up their friendship. Uncle Rupert took Jared and left us." Patricia felt the heat rise above her collar, into her cheeks. Uncle Bill had fumed about the situation for years. He still got riled up whenever anyone mentioned Rupert. She rounded on Jared. "He and Uncle Bill had worked together twenty years. But that didn't count with your father. He tore our family apart."

"Trisha, you know we're not really related."

"You can say that if you want to. When I came to this ranch, I was all alone. Uncle Bill and you and your parents were the only family I knew. Then your father started chasing that pesky stallion. Uncle Bill told him to stop, but he wouldn't. And after he finally caught it, he packed up and took you away." Tears filled her eyes, and she turned her face away. He didn't understand at all. Apparently the rift hadn't affected Jared nearly as deeply as it had her. It was almost as if a married couple had two children and one left, taking one child, while the other kept the second child. Patricia had lost her own parents early. Losing Uncle Rupert and Jared had been a second bereavement for her. Even though she knew Uncle Bill loved her to distraction, his awkward attempts at fatherhood couldn't make up for her sorrow and the wounds of abandonment that Rupert's defection had left.

She glared at him. "If your father hadn't insisted on chasing that wild stallion and spending all his time and money on horse racing, we'd still be a family."

❄

Jared stared at Trisha. He wanted to deny the things she said, but he couldn't. He'd felt the sting of his father's actions himself. But he'd learned to live with the situation and become accustomed to their new life. He saw the good things about it and enjoyed helping his father raise and train horses. But he could not refute her argument that his father's pursuits had put the Logan ranch in danger and made life more difficult for Trisha and Bill Logan. How many times had he asked himself what would have happened if his father had stayed out of horse racing?

"Trisha," he said gently.

She looked up at the sound of her name. Would she listen if he told her how he had suffered as well and gave her his perspective on the changes he had undergone? He cleared his throat.

"You're right about a lot of things. I know that you were hurt when we left the ranch. And I know your uncle was more than just angry. He was hurt."

"How do you know that?" Her blue eyes glinted like cold steel. "How do you know what we felt?"

Jared set down the coffee and inhaled deeply. "Because I was hurt, too. I didn't want to leave. I had no desire to go into horse racing then, but we did it. We left here with a fast stallion and a half dozen decent mares. My father built his racing stable from the ground up. I've worked for Pa these ten years. But I never liked the racing life. And I told my father that. I told him I didn't want to stay in it."

"What'd your pa say to that?" Annie stood and reached for the coffeepot and refilled her cup.

"He didn't like it. But he knew that was what began the trouble between him and Bill. Pa wanted to go into horse racing, but Bill preferred sticking with cattle ranching. Pa didn't see much future in the ranch. After twenty years, they still hadn't made good, at least not in my pa's eyes." Jared took a sip of his cooling coffee and went on. "My mother's family, the Contreras, are established in Mexican horse racing, and his brother-in-law—my uncle Manuel—tried for a long time to get Pa to go down there and get into racing."

"I never knew that." Trisha wiped her eyes with her hand and sniffed. "You mean, after your mother died in '02?"

"Yes, but before that, too. I don't think Mama wanted to do it. She liked the ranch, and she liked being with you and Uncle Bill. She felt Bill was a stable influence in my father's life. Despite her family's leanings, she had a calm nature. She saw her brothers get mixed up in a lot of devilment, and she didn't want to see Pa get into it."

Patricia seemed to mull that over while she sipped her coffee. "I recall when your father caught that wild stallion. He wanted to race him."

Jared nodded. "He took him to the fair in Denver, and he won."

Trisha nodded, her eyes wide and thoughtful. Annie ate her breakfast quietly, but Jared could tell she hadn't missed a word.

"My pa wanted to breed the stallion to some of the ranch mares, but Bill refused to let him. The horse was ugly and ornery, it was true. Your uncle said the only thing he was good for was running, and his colts wouldn't make good cow ponies."

"I didn't know all that," Trisha admitted. "I knew they fought at the last and that Rupert wanted to race, but Uncle Bill never told me the details."

"Well, I guess they realized at last that they had different dreams, so they split up. Pa took the wild stallion and moved us to Texas. Uncle Manuel lived about fifty miles away, just over the border. He encouraged Pa to race, and pretty soon we started racing the stallion and other horses at the tracks in Texas and Mexico."

"Did you win?" Annie asked.

"Sometimes. That wild stallion had speed and heart. His earnings set my father up pretty well. And Pa bred him to a lot of mares." Jared chuckled and shook his head. "The colts were all ugly, but they were fast."

"Well, that colt you're bringing Uncle Bill isn't ugly," Trisha said. "He must not be the wild one's offspring."

"But he is." Jared leaned forward and looked into her sober eyes. "He's a grandson of the wild one, Trisha. Pa bred the stallion to a beautiful Arabian mare and got a fast mare that didn't look too bad. He went another generation, breeding her to a thoroughbred stallion, and Chief was the result. Finally he got a colt without the Roman nose and stubby ears."

"Can he run?" Annie asked.

They both laughed, but Trisha's eyes still held that wary, defiant glint.

"Yeah," Jared said. "I think he can. But we haven't raced this one. Not yet."

"But why did your pa leave Chief to Uncle Bill?" Trisha asked.

"I'm not sure, exactly." Jared sat back. This was a question he had wrestled with on his trip north.

"Probably just to prove his point to Uncle Bill that he was right all along and racing paid off."

Jared's jaw clenched. "That's a pretty mean thing to say."

"Well, leaving us alone was a pretty mean thing to *do*."

"Yeah? Well, just 'cause you're still mad at Pa, doesn't mean you should yell at me."

They both shoved their chairs back and stood on opposite sides of the table.

Trisha's eyes snapped blue fire. "Who's yelling at whom?"

"You are!"

Annie whacked the table with her spoon. "Here, now! You two pups settle down and quit your barking at each other. I thought I was stuck here with two adults, but it seems I was wrong."

A wave of shame washed over Jared, immediately followed by a splattering remnant of anger. How could he have imagined that Trisha had become a refined, sweet, and gentle woman? She was as stubborn and ornery as she'd been at twelve.

Chapter 6

The next morning dawned gray and quiet. At first Patricia thought the snow had stopped, but when Jared opened the door to go to the lean-to, she realized it was still falling hard. The little cabin was nearly buried in it, and for that reason, the wind no longer buffeted the walls.

"Looks like my path has a foot or more of new snow in it," Jared observed. "It's drifted on the far end, near the lean-to. I'd best clear it before I take the water out." He reached for the shovel and went outside.

Trapped. Patricia threw a bleak glance at Annie, but the old woman calmly went about preparing their breakfast. Remorse tugged at Patricia's conscience, and she hurried to help.

When the three of them sat down together to eat it later, Annie asked a blessing.

"Lord above, You've stuck us here, and we don't know why. But You do, so that's good enough. Thank You for these vittles. Amen."

Jared and Annie picked up their spoons and plunged them into their portions of oatmeal. Trisha noted that Annie had prepared less of the porridge than she had yesterday. Instead of opening a jar of fruit, they'd added a few raisins to the oatmeal. That and coffee was all they would eat until noon. If they could tell when it was noon. None of them had a watch, and the dim light that reached them through the windows was barely enough to get by with, but they'd agreed the night before to save the lamp oil as much as possible, and so they sat in the twilight.

Patricia cleared her throat. Annie kept eating, but Jared glanced up at her, an uneasy frown touching his mouth and eyes.

"I want to apologize for the mean things I said about your father yesterday, Jared. I mean. . .about the horse racing and. . .and his character in general. I loved you and your father. I admit I was repeating things I heard Uncle Bill say in his worst moments. I shouldn't have done that. Will you forgive me?"

Jared's dark eyes softened. He laid down his spoon. "Trisha, I believe Pa missed Bill—and you, too—after we left Colorado, and I think he hoped someday he could reconcile with Bill."

"You do?"

Jared nodded. "Pa enjoyed his life in Texas, but that fight with Bill bothered him all these years. When he became ill and suspected he would die, he talked to me about the business. I'd told him before that I didn't want to stay in horse racing, but Pa had hoped I'd change my mind. But at the end, he could see that I hadn't. After he got sick, he sold the racing stable."

"Well now," said Annie.

Patricia just stared at Jared, feeling more miserable than before.

Jared picked up his tin cup, looked at it, and set it down. "I inherited a large sum of money, because Pa had done well the last few years. I came here for two reasons. To bring Chief to your uncle and to look around for a place of my own."

"You want to stay in Colorado?" Patricia asked, a surge of hope rising in her.

He nodded. "That's my dream. A ranch of my own, near where I grew up. I've always remembered the Logan ranch, and that's where my heart is. I want to live in this area and raise cattle."

Patricia sighed. "I wish you success, Jared. And. . .welcome back."

"Thank you."

Annie leaned over and snaked her arm out to reach the coffeepot off the stove. "Seems to me you're tenacious enough to make your dream come true, boy."

Jared smiled, and Patricia's heart lifted just looking at him. There was the boyish Jared, the optimistic, confident Jared.

"I hope so, Annie. But there was one thing that's always been more important to me than where I lived or what I did for a living. That was my dream of seeing my father receive Christ."

Annie clucked in sympathy and refilled his coffee cup. "Did it happen?"

Jared glanced over at Patricia, his face somber once more. "You know your uncle Bill led me to Christ when I was a little boy."

Patricia ducked her head. "Yes. I'd almost forgotten that."

"Your uncle is a good man, Trisha. I've always been grateful. And I witnessed to my pa many times, right up to his death, but so far as I know, he never believed."

Patricia felt her heart soften and melt. How could she have been angry with Jared because of things his father did so many years ago? She had been unjust and immature in her judgment of him. Tears sprang into her eyes. She reached over and grasped his wrist gently. "I'm so very sorry, Jared. I acted despicably yesterday."

He closed his hand over hers and gave her fingers a squeeze. "Forgiven. All forgiven."

Even Annie's eyes glistened.

Patricia reluctantly pulled her hand away and fumbled in her pocket for a handkerchief. "Perhaps we could pray together this morning. For our safety, and for Aunt Edna and the baby."

"A good idea." Annie nodded. "You start, boy." She sniffed and wiped her eyes with her sleeve.

❄

That afternoon, Jared allowed Patricia to brave his path with him to the lean-to and help him feed and water the horses. The snow was now shoulder-high to him on each side of the path, and as high as Patricia's head, so they were able to reach the horses while staying out of the fierce wind.

The blowing continued, but by evening, Jared was sure the snow had stopped falling, though the gale still flung the loose stuff on the surface all about.

On a top shelf, Annie discovered a board marked off in squares and a tin containing dark and light rounds of wood. Half were charred, half were not, and she immediately recognized the primitive checkers game. This welcome diversion helped them pass the hours in the cramped cabin, and they used some of their precious lamp oil to continue the play into the evening hours.

The next morning they awoke eager to do something—anything—to free themselves from their prison. The storm had ended, and the sun sparkled on the snow. Jared climbed on what was left of the woodpile and surveyed the range. The dips and slopes of Bill Logan's south forty kept him from seeing more than half a mile, but he knew exactly in which direction the house lay. Two miles. So close.

He wondered if they would be able to dig out. The snow had drifted deep around the shack, but perhaps out on the open rangeland, it was not so deep. The wind had surely scoured some of the accumulation away. Was it best to wait for the sun to do its work and compact the snow? He glanced toward the lean-to, where Chief and Patches were snuffling their morning ration. They had already ingested most of the hay, and the oat barrel wouldn't hold out longer than two or three more days.

He climbed down and went to the door, kicked the snow off his boots, and went inside. Annie and Patricia looked toward him expectantly.

"I think I could make it to the ranch house by riding across the range."

Patricia's jaw dropped. "Isn't the snow over my head?"

"Not in the open. It's probably still belly-deep to a horse in most places, but I think Patches could do it. Chief might panic if he got mired in a drift, but Patches is steady. I think I should try. If I can even get within sight of the house, maybe I can get their attention."

Annie's eyes glittered as he spoke. "You don't have a gun, do you?"

"No."

"Well, too bad. But you can take some tinder and a few matches and start a fire. They might see that. Then they could take that workhorse team of Bill Logan's and break trail out here to get us."

"I don't know if they'd be able to do that yet," Jared said. "But they could bring me some snowshoes, at least. We can walk out if we have snowshoes."

"Well, come on, then," Annie said. "Let's pack up your gear."

"Travel light, for Patches's sake," Patricia said. "Dress warmly, but don't carry anything you won't need."

They argued good-naturedly over what he might need and what his chances were of making it through or getting stuck somewhere between the cabin and the ranch house.

Annie insisted he take a small amount of food in his pockets, and Patricia carefully packed his fire-making supplies in a saddle-bag while he layered on his extra shirt and socks.

"Hey." Patricia's head jerked up, and she looked toward the door. "Did you hear that?"

Jared and Annie stopped what they were doing and listened. Sure enough, Jared heard what sounded like a muffled shout.

He threw the door open and dashed outside. Climbing on the woodpile, he looked out over the range and whooped.

Three cowboys from the Logan ranch wallowed through the snow a hundred yards out, riding the big draft horses Bill used to haul hay wagons in summer and logs for firewood in winter.

"Hey!" Jared waved his hat in the air. A yodeling call from one of the men answered, and another of the cowboys fired a rifle into the air.

"How many people you got?" came the faint cry.

"Three," Jared shouted. "We've got the midwife."

The three men seemed to consult and changed course, heading the big horses toward the cabin. The largest took the lead, but the snow was up to his breast, and he tired quickly. After a few yards, the next horse moved ahead and broke trail for a few yards.

Jared hopped down from the woodpile and ran inside.

"It's men from the Logan ranch. Put your woolies on, ladies! We are leaving here before you know it." He seized the shovel and ran out to carve a way out of the drifts around the buildings. By cutting into the side of his path, he hoped he could move enough powder so Chief and Patches could work their way up to the level of the draft horses and follow their messy trail home.

❄

In no time, Patricia had her boots, coat, scarf, hood, and gloves on. She hurried outside. Jared was throwing shovelfuls of snow as fast as he could out of the recess he'd dug earlier.

"Where are they?"

He raised his head and stood on tiptoe to look. "Just up the knoll. Fifty yards now."

"What can I do to help?"

"Go throw the blankets and saddles on the horses. The bridles and saddlebags are inside. We can be ready by the time they reach us."

"Those men will want to warm up and have a cup of coffee," Patricia said. "I'll tell Annie." She ran inside and returned carrying the two bridles and Patches's saddlebags. "Annie's putting on some flapjacks. She says their horses will be exhausted and need to rest a bit."

Jared straightened and looked again. "She's right about that. It's heavy work for them. But we can give them some melted snow and a small ration of oats." He stomped the snow underfoot and realized he could walk up his enlarged pathway now. Soon he stood, from the waist up, above the higher level of the snow, looking out across the surface. The low point of the path, at the cabin's doorstep, was five feet below him. He waved to the cowboys, who were now within easy talking distance.

"Did you say you've got old Annie there?"

"Yup. She was trying to get to Miz Logan and got snowed in here."

"Hallelujah," the man shouted back. "We was headed down to her place in the holler. Miz Logan thinks today's the day!"

Jared turned and called to Patricia, who was inside the lean-to, "Did you hear that, Trish?"

"No, what?"

"These men were on their way to fetch Annie. Miz Logan says it's time for the baby."

Patricia came to the opening of the lean-to. "Oh, Jared! We've got to hurry. Annie needs to be there."

"We're working as fast as we can," he replied.

Behind him, the door opened. "I heard that," Annie said. "I've got our clothes and such all packed up."

Patricia took a few steps toward her along the snow-walled path. "Annie, what if we don't get there in time?"

"Don't worry, child. First babies take their time gettin' here. Still, we won't lollygag none."

The man on the lead horse called to Jared, "The snow's getting deeper. I don't think we should bring the horses any closer."

"No, don't," Jared told him. "It's a good five feet deep here near the cabin. Just let them rest, and I'll shovel the last few yards out to you. We've got oats and a little melted snow they can have. And Annie's got hot coffee and flapjacks inside."

"Sounds good," the man said.

Jared squinted at him. "Aren't you Joe Simmons?"

"Yup. Do I know you?"

"I'm Jared Booker."

Joe's face broke into a toothy grin. "Well now! Welcome back, sonny."

Patricia scrambled up beside Jared, floundering through the snow, and he reached out a hand to boost her.

"I knew he'd remember you," she said.

Joe's mouth opened and his eyes flared. "Is that you, Miss Trish? What on earth are you doing here? Your uncle was sure you'd used your head and stayed in Denver with that school chum of yours."

"Well, it's a good thing he didn't know otherwise, or he'd have worried about me."

"Can't believe you've got Annie here. That'll save us a good two hours or more. We're not even halfway to Annie's place. I wasn't sure these nags could make it that far, but the boss said to try."

Another cowboy added, "We saw your smoke from the stovepipe here and figured some poor soul got caught out in the blizzard."

Patricia laughed. "Three poor souls. And we're mighty glad to see you."

Joe hopped down from his horse and staggered to his feet, waist deep in snow. "Let me come help you shovel, Jared. You must be tuckered out."

❄

Half an hour later, they set out with the strongest draft horse in the lead. Annie went next on Patches, at Jared's insistence.

"And if we get to where the path is easygoing, Miss Annie, you just go right on ahead and ride up to the ranch house," he told her. "We'll follow as quick as we can."

The other two workhorses fell in behind Patches, with Trisha riding double behind Joe Simmons. Jared brought Chief along last, hoping the trail would not be too hard for the colt after the bigger horses had trampled it twice. The going was slow, and the horses soon dragged their feet, but they kept on with lowered muzzles.

Before long, they could see the ranch house, and shortly afterward they entered a pasture where the cattle had trampled down the snow. A herd of about a hundred head huddled together where the hired men had thrown hay for them that morning. Annie broke away from the line of horses and loped Patches across the field toward the house.

Soon they were all on better footing. Jared sighed with relief when they reached the barnyard. He jumped out of the saddle and ran his hands down each of Chief's legs in turn.

"Is he all right?"

He straightened to find Patricia standing near him.

"I think he is, praise God."

She smiled. "Let's put him in a nice, comfy loose stall and rub him and Patches down."

Jared shook his head. "You go on into the house. I know you want to see how your aunt's doing. I'll take care of these critters."

Half a dozen cowboys had come from the bunkhouse to greet them, and one of them seized Patches's trailing reins where Annie had left him ground tied and led him into the barn.

Patricia hesitated. "You gave me my wish, Jared. You got me here on time."

"Go on," Jared said with a grin. "After all we went through, you don't want to miss the big event."

She leaned toward him and placed her gloved hands on his shoulders. Before he realized what she was doing, she'd stood on tiptoe and kissed his cold, scratchy cheek. Then she backed away from him, her blue eyes gleaming, turned, and streaked for the ranch house.

Jared led Chief into the big, airy barn. On both sides of the aisle, horses were champing hay. Because of the weather, all of the cow ponies were inside, and all the tie-up stalls were full. Chief snorted and pranced as Jared walked him farther down the row.

"Bring him on down here," a man called. "Got a spot here for your stallion."

Jared recognized the large foaling stall. He nodded at the cowboy who held the door open. "I appreciate it."

"The boss hasn't got a stud right now," the man said. "Will that one behave himself in here?"

"I think so," Jared said. "He's young, but he's fairly docile. Needs a good rubdown and a blanket. We had a rough trip up here from Texas."

He set about grooming Chief. A cowboy brought him a soft brush and a hoof pick, and another brought a bucket of water for the colt.

Jared worked methodically around from the horse's near shoulder to his rump and up the off side. He took a loaned blanket off the half door of the stall and spread it over Chief's back, pinning it at his chest, then stroked his face and glossy neck.

"There, now. Feeling better, fella?"

"Jared Booker."

Jared froze at the words and straightened slowly, turning his head toward the doorway. Bill Logan stood just outside the stall, peering in at him and Chief.

Chapter 7

J ared hesitated only an instant. He hadn't planned what he would say to Bill Logan when he met him, and it might have been easier if Patricia or one of the cowpokes had stuck around. But no, this had to be man-to-man.

"Mr. Logan."

He stepped over to the door, shifting the brush to his left hand and extended his right. Bill reached out to shake it over the top of the closed bottom stall door.

"Well now. You've grown some."

"Yes, sir."

"Patricia told me you'd brought her from town, and I figured to come out here and skin you alive. Foolhardy business, setting out in the storm like that."

Jared swallowed hard and forced himself to meet Bill's gaze. "I can't disagree, sir. At the time, it seemed like an easy ride in the lull of the storm, but looking back, I'd be the first to admit it wasn't the wisest thing I ever did. We were sure happy to run across your line shack and find it had wood and foodstuffs and rations for the horses."

Bill nodded soberly. "You'll have to give me the details later. I know Trisha's head-strong, and she claims she forced you to bring her. It's probably true."

Jared shrugged, but he couldn't help a grim smile. "I understand you're to be con-gratulated, sir. I'm pleased to hear you found a fine woman."

Bill nodded, but a worried frown took up residence between his eyebrows. "Edna's one of the best things that ever happened to me. I'm just praying now that things go well today. You. . .know about the baby?"

Jared nodded. "That was Trisha's trump card, if I can be so blunt. She was sure her aunt needed her, and she couldn't stay put in Colorado Springs."

"Well, I'm glad she's here, and Annie, too. When I think that she might have frozen to death out on the range. . ." He shook himself and leaned on the door. "God has been merciful to us all."

"Amen," Jared said softly.

Bill straightened and focused beyond him on the coal black colt. "That's quite a horse you've got there, Jared."

A smile started deep inside Jared and worked its way up to his lips. "Yes, sir. This is the crowning jewel in my father's string. We call him Chief. Mr. Logan, I brought him to you as a gift from my father."

Bill's face clouded. He turned away from the doorway. "I don't need any racehorses. I told Rupert that ten years ago."

Jared quickly unlatched the stall door and hurried after him. Bill's long strides had already taken him to the other end of the barn, and he was about to open the door.

"Mr. Logan! Please, sir. I have a letter here from my father." Jared hurried toward him, reaching inside his coat for the sealed letter he had carried from Texas.

Bill stopped and turned to face him. "I don't care what your father has to say in that letter, Jared. He was always a hardheaded man, and he would never listen to me. Why should I listen to him now?"

Jared stood five feet from him with the envelope in his hand, unsure of what to say.

At that moment, the door swung open. Patricia stood silhouetted against the bright, snowy yard outside, her eyes bright and her cheeks rosy.

"Uncle Bill! Come on! Edna's asking for you."

Bill whirled toward her. "Is she all right?"

Patricia grinned. "She and your daughter are just fine."

"Praise be!" Bill sprinted for the ranch house.

❄

Patricia laughed and shot a glance at Jared. "Uncle Bill's going to be so happy now."

"Yeah."

Jared's tone was doubtful, and she looked closer at him. "What's wrong?" She noticed then that he held an envelope.

He tapped the letter against his other hand. "He says he doesn't want Chief, and he won't read the letter Pa wrote him."

Jared looked so forlorn that Patricia stepped closer and laid her hand on his sleeve. "I'm sorry, Jared. You didn't tell me that your pa wrote him a letter before he died."

Jared stood still for a moment, his lips compressed. "You know, I don't think I told him that Pa passed on. You didn't tell him, did you?"

She shook her head. "No, I forgot to mention it in all the excitement over the baby." She threw her shoulders back and forced a smile. "Listen, everyone's distracted now, but Uncle Bill is bound to be in a more jovial mood. Let's give him time to get to know his daughter, and I'll help the cook prepare a nice dinner. After he's eaten and calmed down a little, you can talk to him again. Tell him everything."

"I don't know, Trish. He sounded like he knew his mind."

"But he doesn't know the circumstances. Look, I know Uncle Bill can be stubborn. But I also know that he loves the Lord, and once he sees things laid out plain and simple, I think he'll back down. We both know he loved your father. It was Rupert's deserting him that's kept him so bitter all these years. But now he's found Edna, and you're here with a wonderful peace offering. Surely he won't keep holding a grudge against an old friend who's died."

"Well. . ."

She could see that he wavered, so she slid her hand through the crook of his arm. "Come on in the house. You're tired. We all are. Grab your saddlebags, and I'll show you to a room where you can clean up and rest for a while."

"Oh, no, Trish. Don't do that. I'll go over to the bunkhouse."

"Nonsense. After what you did for me this week? You are an honored guest in this house."

With a little more coaxing, she persuaded Jared to collect his gear and go with her into the low ranch house. Sarah, the wife of one of the cowboys, served as the Logans' cook now, and when Patricia took Jared in through the back kitchen door, she gladly told Patricia to show Jared to the spare room where Edna and Patricia did their sewing.

"Isn't it wonderful?" Sarah asked, her eyes swimming with tears. "A new little baby in this house!"

"It's delightful," Patricia agreed. "Have you seen her yet?"

"No, but I heard the boss shouting, 'Praise God,' until Mrs. Logan hushed him. He's so happy! We'll celebrate today."

Patricia and Jared laughed.

"I intend to help you prepare for that celebration, Sarah. Excuse us while I show Mr. Booker his room, and then I'll be back to put on my apron."

As they walked through the big main room that Edna referred to as the parlor and Bill called the settin' room, all was quiet. Jared walked silently beside her into the hall.

"Jared," she said softly, "I'm sure Uncle Bill will come around. But just in case we're not clear, I want to tell you straight out, I forgive you and your pa for all the past hurts, whether real or imagined."

He gave her a little smile. "Thank you. That means a lot."

"Deep in my heart, I never was angry with you. I think I just absorbed Uncle Bill's attitude about your father, though, and that wasn't right."

He shrugged. "You were loyal to your uncle, and that's not all bad."

They heard Annie's practical voice coming from the master bedroom. As they walked past the open doorway, the old woman said, "There the kids are now."

Suddenly Uncle Bill filled the doorway, holding a soft white bundle in his arms. Patricia and Jared stopped, and Patricia reached out to lift the edge of the blanket, exposing the new infant's little red face.

"Oh! She's sleeping!"

Uncle Bill nodded with a smile. "Jared, Patricia," he said formally, "I would like to introduce you to my daughter."

Patricia had already seen the baby, but she could play along.

"We're charmed, sir. And what is this adorable creature's name?"

Bill's smile extended to nearly split his face in two. "We've decided, finally. May I present Hazel Dorothy Logan?"

Tears sprang into Patricia's eyes. "My mother's name," she whispered.

Bill nodded. "Jared, my lad, are you still walking with the Lord?"

Jared cleared his throat. "Yes, sir. I'm doing my best, with His help."

Bill nodded. "Would you give a prayer of thanks for this little one's safe arrival?"

Jared lowered his saddlebags gently to the floor. "I'd be happy to, sir."

❄

After Jared's prayer of thanks, little Hazel began to fuss, and Bill hastily handed her over to Patricia. "If you wouldn't mind, Trish, could you please take her back to Edna? I think she wants her momma, and I need to speak to Jared for a minute."

"I'd love to." Patricia cuddled the baby, wrapped in a soft white blanket, against her shoulder and carried her into the bedroom.

Jared and Bill walked back to the living area together.

"Have a seat, Jared," Bill said.

Jared sat down on a leather-covered chair. His skin prickled all over, and he made himself sit still and not scratch, but he couldn't deny he was nervous.

"Boy, I want to apologize."

Relief washed over Jared, and he closed his eyes for an instant. "No need for that, Mr. Logan."

"Yes, there is. I had no call to be upset with you. Well, if the truth were known, I've no right to stay mad at your father, either, after all this time. I'll give it to you straight. I deliberately nourished bitterness in my heart for the last ten years. I was angry with Rupert. I admit it. He was wrong. Well. . .so was I." Bill looked Jared in the eye. "Can you forgive me?"

"Oh yes, sir. That's not hard at all. I've missed you and Trisha something awful, and I hoped you'd let me stop a day or two with you while I look around for some land."

"Land? You want to move back up here? What about your father?"

Jared bit his upper lip. He reached in his pocket for the envelope and leaned forward with it in his hand.

"Seems I went about this all backward, sir. The first thing I should've told you is that my pa died three or four weeks ago, down in Texas. And shortly before he passed away, he wrote this letter to you. One of the last things he did was to ask me to bring the letter and the black colt that's out in your barn. That's why I came, sir. That's how I met up with Patricia. I was on my way to deliver this letter to you, along with Chief."

Bill's hand came forward, an inch at a time, until his fingers touched the envelope. Tears shone in his eyes. "I've been a big old fool."

Jared swallowed hard and said nothing.

Bill ripped open the envelope and withdrew the paper that was inside. Jared winced as he saw the lines written in his father's shaky hand. He looked toward the window. The sun still shone outside, and it appeared the storm was truly over.

Bill let out a big sigh. "You should hear this, too, Jared. Do you mind if I read it to you?"

"No, sir."

"It says, 'Bill, if you're reading this, it means that I'm gone. Well, there are some things you need to know. When your turn comes, we'll meet again. My son has told me many, many times that I needed Jesus. I admit I was pretty mean to him about that. Told him he could believe that if he wanted, but I was doing fine on my own. Rupert Booker didn't need "saving," as you called it.'"

Jared bowed his head as he heard the words. So often he'd tried to tell his father about Christ. Hearing again how annoying he found that made his eyes burn and his nose stuff up.

Bill went on reading, his voice choking now and then. " 'Yes, Bill, the truth is, I

Mountain Christmas Brides

resented your part in getting my son to be religious. That was your doing. You told Jared when he was a boy that he needed to be saved, and Jared went along. I didn't. I guess that was the beginning of my bad feelings toward you.'"

Tears poured from Jared's eyes, and he swiped at them with the back of his hand.

"'And then the whole thing with the wild horse herd. I wanted that stud. He was faster than anything I'd ever seen. Well, it's time to put all that behind us. You were right, Bill. About God and about a lot of things. I believe in Him now. He's forgiven me all the things I did to you and Jared and my wife and anybody else who crossed my path over the years. And I'm asking you to forgive me, too. I want you to have the black colt, Chief. He's the best colt I ever bred, and I hope you'll take him as a reminder of the friendship we did have in the past. He's black like my heart used to be. But I'll see you again one day, up in heaven. Very truly yours, Rupert Booker.'"

A huge lump in his throat prevented Jared from speaking. He stared at Bill Logan, knowing his face was streaked with tears and not caring. A slow smile spread over Bill's face as he folded the letter.

"My father believed," Jared croaked out.

"Sounds like it. I'm really glad, son."

Jared nodded and pulled in a deep breath. "I do hope you'll accept his gift, sir."

"Well now." Bill sat back, looking very pleased. "You know, Jared, this isn't a good time to buy land. Everything's under a heap of snow. Why don't you stay here with us until spring? I could use you. We do a lot of repairs and such in the winter. Get our wood for next year down out of the hills—you remember."

Jared nodded.

"Well, if you want to stay on here, I'll give you a job. And next spring, when the snow is off, I'll help you find a good place for ranching. There's a fellow over on the North Branch who was talking about selling out last summer. I don't know if he did or not, but we could find out. It's a decent spread."

Jared cleared his throat, wondering if he could trust his voice. "Thank you, sir. I'd like that a lot, but there's something else I need to tell you."

"What's that?" Bill fixed his gaze on him, and Jared sat a little straighter.

"I love Patricia, sir. I think I always have. I'd like your permission to court her."

❄

Patricia couldn't keep a smile off her face as she watched her aunt hold the sweet baby. Dinner was over and the kitchen put to rights. Uncle Bill and Jared had drifted out to the barn, and she'd settled in for a cozy chat with Aunt Edna.

"I like your young man." Edna shifted on her snowy white pillows. "I expect I'll be up and about tomorrow, and I look forward to getting to know him better."

"You'd best take it easy for a few days." Patricia leaned forward and touched the baby's hand with her fingertip. "She's so soft!"

Edna smiled. "I think she's sleeping now. I'm feeling a little tuckered myself."

"Let me take her. I'll put her in the cradle. Or maybe I'll just hold her and watch

396

her sleep for a while, if that's all right." Patricia looked eagerly at her aunt. Edna did look weary.

"Go ahead. But if Bill comes in, tell him not to stay away. I want to see him even if I've dozed off."

Patricia stood and bent over her to ease the slumbering infant into her own arms. Edna sighed, adjusted the covers, and closed her eyes. "Thank you, dear."

Tiptoeing out of the bedroom, Patricia nuzzled the baby's silky hair. "You darling."

Uncle Bill and Jared were coming in from the barn. They stomped the snow from their boots and wiped their feet on the rag mat inside the door to the sitting room.

"Aunt Edna's resting, but she wants you to go in anyway, Uncle Bill," she said.

"All right, but that's my daughter you're holding, missy. You take good care of her." Bill hung up his coat.

Patricia grinned and sank gently onto the sofa. "You needn't worry about that. I'm going to cuddle her for a few minutes, and then I'll put her in the cradle for a nap."

Her uncle left the room, and Jared came hesitantly to stand beside her. He looked down at little Hazel.

"Isn't she an angel?" Patricia asked.

He smiled.

She looked up at him and tucked her skirt against her thigh. "Sit down, Jared. She's just the sweetest thing I ever saw."

"I recall you mothering a rabbit kit when you were about eight years old." He folded down onto the seat beside her, looking at the baby.

The memory brought a flash of joy. "Lulu! I loved her so much."

"She kept getting in the garden."

"Yes, we did have a time with her."

"Well, I expect you all will have a handful with this one, too." The smile still played at his lips. "Think a human kit is better than a bunny?"

She wrinkled up her face at him. "You're horrid! Of course it is. I want one of my own someday—that's for certain sure."

Suddenly she realized that he had inched closer and extended his arm along the back of the sofa.

"Trisha, if you can give me just a teeny, weeny bit of attention here, I'd like to say something."

"What is it?" She turned her head and found Jared's brown eyes, warm and tender, assessing her. She swallowed hard but didn't draw back.

"Your uncle and I had a chat earlier."

Her heart skipped a beat. "What about?"

"About us."

"You and Uncle Bill?" she asked.

"Well, that, too, but I meant you and me."

It was a moment before she could respond to that. "Was he upset with you? I told him you were a perfect gentleman, and that you saved my life. It wasn't your fault that we almost—"

He reached out and brushed back a strand of her hair, and she sat very still, looking deep into his eyes.

"That wasn't what we talked about."

"Oh." It was a mere squeak.

"Trisha, this may seem kind of sudden, but. . .well, I don't know how else to put it. I love you. I asked Bill if I could court you."

"What did he say?" she whispered.

"He said it was up to you. Said he couldn't force you to let me, but if you decided you cared for me, he wouldn't be able to stop you, either."

She smiled. "Smart man."

Hazel whimpered and stirred, and Patricia looked down at her. "There now, baby. Shh." She glanced up at Jared again. "Do you want to hold her?"

"Who? Me?" His eyes widened. "I don't think so. She'd probably cry if I did."

Patricia chuckled and nestled the baby closer, brushing her cheek against Hazel's head. "You do want children, don't you, Jared?"

"Who? Me?"

She widened her eyes at his repetition, and he had the grace to blush. "Yes, you. I'm speaking to the man who just said he wanted to court me. It's important."

"Well, sure. Someday. I mean. . ." He hesitated and then held out his arms.

Patricia leaned over and kissed his cheek, then carefully transferred Hazel to him. Jared gulped and sat back, staring down at the baby.

"Don't be so stiff," Patricia whispered. He shifted slightly, easing Hazel's tiny head into the crook of his arm.

"She hardly weighs anything." He glanced up and shot her a tentative smile. "Pretty amazing."

"Yeah." Their gazes locked.

"Hey, you two." Uncle Bill emerged from the hallway and came to the back of the sofa. "Let me see that little dumpling."

Jared stood and passed the baby to him over the back of the sofa.

"You don't mind, do you?" Bill asked.

"No, sir. But she sure is a pretty little thing."

"Oh yes, she is."

Patricia laughed as Uncle Bill walked back toward the bedrooms, uttering baby talk all the way.

Jared sat down again, suddenly shy it seemed. His smile flickered then disappeared as he sucked in a deep breath.

"Jared, I'd be honored if you'd court me."

They both sat stock-still for an instant. His expression cleared, and everything about him seemed to soften: his eyes, his lips, the set of his shoulders. He lifted his arm behind her and slid closer. She met his kiss with exultant anticipation.

Epilogue

Patricia and Jared leaned together on the bottom half of the foaling stall's door.

"He's absolutely magnificent," she breathed.

Jared smiled. "Not yet, but he's got the lines to be in a couple of years." He slid his arm around Trisha and squeezed her.

"I suppose I'd better get into the house and get ready. But I had to see the new arrival first."

"I knew you'd want to see him."

"It was very considerate of Lady to drop her foal on our wedding day."

"Wasn't it?" Jared drew her into his arms and kissed her.

Patricia lingered for a moment and then pulled back. "Here now, you're not even supposed to see me before the ceremony."

"Aw, your Aunt Edna's the superstitious one. Just sneak in the kitchen door, and don't let her know we came out here to see the foal."

"What if she's in the kitchen now?" Patricia stifled a giggle and met his next kiss with enthusiasm.

A moment later, Jared released her and turned her away from the stall, his arm about her shoulders. "All right, I suppose we have to go in."

"Yes, we do. Our guests will be arriving in less than an hour." They walked to the barn door. Jared's wagon was already loaded and sitting on the barn floor, loaded with her hope chest, assorted household goods, and the bags that held her clothing. "I'm glad we'll only be a few miles from Uncle Bill and Aunt Edna."

"Me, too. God must have had that ranch waiting for me to buy and your uncle primed to help me find it."

"We'll raise the best beef in Colorado," she said with a sigh.

"And a whole tribe of little Booker cowpokes." Hand in hand, they crossed the yard to the kitchen door of the ranch house.

Susan Page Davis is the author of more than sixty Christian novels and novellas, which have sold more than 1.5 million copies. Her historical novels have won numerous awards, including the Carol Award, the Will Rogers Medallion for Western Fiction, and the Inspirational Readers' Choice Contest. She has also been a finalist in the More than Magic Contest and Willa Literary Awards. She lives in western Kentucky with her husband. She's the mother of six and grandmother of ten. Visit her website at: www. susanpagedavis.com.

Dressed in Scarlet

by Darlene Franklin

Dedication

To Anita Gardner, who joins me on my writing adventures.
We shared an unforgettable weekend at the Brown Palace Hotel.
Thanks for all your support, Mom!
A special thanks to the staff at the Brown Palace for their
marvelous service and patience with my questions.

*Who can find a virtuous woman? for her price is far above rubies. . . . She is not
afraid of the snow for her household: for all her household are clothed with scarlet.*
PROVERBS 31:10, 21

Chapter 1

Fabrizio Ricci glanced around the garage at the Brown Palace, making sure everything was in order. Peerless Roadsters jostled next to Cadillac Phaetons and a single Ford Model T, a bit of an oddity for the Brown's well-heeled clientele. Big or small, fancy or plain, he loved all his charges, even the smell of motor oil that permeated the air. His job was to keep the cars running and available to hotel guests. He loved driving cars he could never otherwise afford. Whatever money he didn't give to help his family, he saved toward having his own shop.

No one would drive anywhere tonight in the storm that hit Denver yesterday. More than twenty-four hours later, the snow had not even slowed down. Anyone would be a fool to drive in weather like this. Even the trolleys that he sometimes took had stopped running. It was a good thing he kept a pair of Nordic skis in the garage. If he didn't leave soon, he would have to spend the night at the hotel, or longer, if the snow kept up. As the only son remaining at home, he knew his parents depended on his help.

Fabrizio changed his work shoes for boots and strapped on the skis. He hadn't planned for the cold, but he didn't think that would be a problem, not with the long woolen scarf knitted in green and yellow by Mama. He would dress like that character in the Christmas story. What was his name? Bob Cratchit, that was it. *A Christmas Carol* had to be one of the best stories in the English language. Not as beautiful as Italian, of course, or that's what Papa would say.

Fabrizio looked out the window at the swirling snow, wishing he had taken the time to go to the kitchen for a last cup of hot coffee before he left. Too late now. The snow danced in the air before landing gracefully on the ground. *Bella neve.* Beautiful snow.

Wrapping his scarf around his nose and throat before winding its length around his body, Fabrizio pulled his cap as far down on his head as it would reach and turned the collar of his coat up over the scarf. He hadn't brought any mittens, but his work gloves should do the job. He pulled them on and hoped the oil stains wouldn't get on his clothes. Mama complained about his soiled work clothes; four sisters created enough laundry without him adding any more.

Fabrizio opened the door and headed out into the snow. He shivered, tugging his coat closer. It wasn't usually this cold when it snowed. He looked down the street. Where he should see the Daniels & Fisher tower lit against the night sky about a mile away at the other end of downtown, he saw nothing but a curtain of snow, obscuring all but a few feet ahead. Still, following the street should not present a problem.

The ground outside the garage was packed down, trampled by horses and guests who came and went at the hotel. The snow fell rapidly, filling in even the most recent footsteps. Wind flung handfuls back into the air, redistributing them across the ground.

He dug his poles into the snow and pushed forward to the front of the hotel.

"*Buona notte*," the doorman called. "Be careful tonight. See you tomorrow."

"Buona notte," Fabrizio called back. He headed west from the hotel, down Sixteenth Street toward the D&F tower, and then across the bridge to his home.

He picked up speed, getting into rhythm, feeling rather like a four-legged creature as he used the skis and poles. The push-and-pull gave way to the grace of gliding over the snow as if weightless. The exertion warmed him. He kept his eyes to the ground to avoid the sting of the snow, looking up only when warned by the jingle of a horse's harness or the crunch of car tires. He breathed deeply, his nose aching from the rush of cold air. He closed his mind against the cold and thought instead of the bowl of warm, fragrant minestrone that Mama would have waiting for him. Three miles, that was all. He had walked the distance many times. He would be home soon.

❄

Natalie Daire looked at the bright lights inside the train station where she had dropped off her friend Patricia Logan. She debated about stopping for a cup of hot chocolate. She was very cold, in spite of the red woolies and warm scarf and the driving bonnet that cut some of the wind. Father would have forbidden her attendance at Thalia's party if he had known the snow would last so long. She knew he must be worried about her; that's why she left the party early instead of spending the night as she had planned.

Her car, the Cadillac Model 30, had proved its worth as "The Standard of the World" on the drive from Thalia's house. The train station stood halfway to her home in Westminster. She decided to drive to the Brown Palace, only a few blocks away. They must have a phone. She would call home and purchase a hot drink while she was there.

She leaned forward, breathing warm air against the front windshield, rubbing a small patch clear. She managed to move her feet in the correct clutch-release pattern to start the Cadillac moving forward again. The car slipped as she turned right toward the Brown Palace.

The tall buildings of downtown Denver provided some protection against the wind. The windshield wipers did their best, but she could only see a few feet ahead of her. Heaven and earth met and melted into a dotted wall of white in front of her. She slowed the car even further. One car passed, a silver ghost under the veil of snow. The Brown Palace couldn't be much farther.

A figure loomed in front of her, bent against the wind, gliding over the snow, and straight in her path. Natalie slammed on the brakes. Tires skidded on the slippery street.

She didn't know what happened next. One foot on the brake pedal tried to stop the car. The other on the accelerator veered away from the approaching figure. Her car spun in a circle and crashed into a wooden stall on the sidewalk. Natalie flung her head forward between her arms.

"*Signorina*, are you all right?" A deep voice penetrated the blackness behind her closed eyes.

The world stopped spinning. Natalie opened her eyes. A tall, black-haired man stood beside the car, dark eyes burning with concern. *This must be the man who caused the accident.*

"What were you doing in the middle of the street?" she demanded. "I was trying to avoid running into you."

"I am sorry. You are unhurt?" He repeated his concern.

Natalie took another look at the man. He presented an improbable sight, a pole in each hand, feet ending in long skis, his coat tugged as tightly as possible against his body, a bright scarf wound around face and neck and torso like a barber pole, only burning black eyes visible beneath the visor of his cap.

No, she wanted to say. *I'm cold and hungry, and I want to be at home with my family.* Instead, she checked herself for injuries. Her hands had not loosened their grip on the steering wheel. Her feet had slid off the pedals. She shook herself. Her head complained, but the rest of her seemed fine. Fine particles covered her coat. Snow?

That was when she noticed the shattered windshield, the wiper blade paused in midair as if trying to rid the air itself of snow.

"Oh no. My car."

"I can help." He extended a hand to assist her from the carriage, removed his skis, and took her place in the driver's seat. He turned the key, and the engine restarted. "The car, it is in good condition. Only the windshield is broken."

"But I can't drive home if I can't see," Natalie wailed.

"Come with me. I will fix it." He brushed glass and snow off the passenger seat with a dark-stained glove and invited her to sit. "Let us go to the Brown Palace. You can spend the night, and tomorrow the car will be ready to go."

"That's where I was headed," Natalie said. "I can use the hotel telephone to call my father and tell him what happened."

After the man packed his skis in the backseat, he drove the car without regard to the snow that flowed through the broken window pane.

"Thank you for helping me." She wondered where he was going when she had her accident. Away from the hotel.

"It is right to help others," he said. "I can fix your windshield tonight."

"No, no," Natalie said. "Tomorrow is soon enough." She hoped to see him again, to look at him in better light. Did his appearance match his deep, lightly accented voice?

"As you wish." He did not speak again during the short drive.

They arrived at the hotel. The man carried her luggage inside the lobby. Natalie reached for her purse to tip him.

"*Non,* it was my pleasure, signorina."

"It's Natalie. Natalie Daire."

"Signorina Daire." The man did not offer his own name. He disappeared through a back door.

Half an hour later, Natalie sipped hot tea and looked out through the window from her top floor accommodations. Snow painted the windowpanes with a puzzle of crystals. "Thank You, God, for bringing me here safely."

Tomorrow she would see her mysterious rescuer again.

Chapter 2

Fabrizio stirred, ready to start the day. He had lain awake for some time in the double bed he shared with Patrick O'Riley, the front desk clerk. More staff than usual stayed in the servants' quarters; many spent the night at the hotel rather than risk the weather. He liked the Irishman well enough, but he had grown since the last time he had shared a bed before his brother married and left home. The bed felt cramped with two of them in it. He bundled up his coat for a pillow, and the blanket didn't quite cover both of them. Cold wind pounded on the window, building up ice and creating drafts.

He welcomed the arrival of dawn. Would the hotel expect him to stay through the storm? Common sense suggested that no one would want their horseless carriages in this weather. Then again, Signorina Daire had tried driving through the snow, and look what had happened. Anyone should learn from her mistake.

No. He shook his head. It was unfair to blame the young woman for an accident that he caused by appearing out of the darkness. The good Lord had protected both of them. He would replace the windshield in Signorina Daire's car and then ask if he could go home. Mama and Papa would need his help more than ever with this snow.

He hurried through breakfast in the hotel kitchen, gobbling eggs and biscuits and drinking a cup of coffee as hot as he could stand it. *"Grazie."* He set his plate beside the sink and headed for the garage.

No new cars had arrived since the Cadillac on the previous evening. Snow covered the windows set high in the garage doors. He hoisted himself on a box and looked out. The driveway he had shoveled yesterday afternoon had already filled again. No one should drive in this weather. If the streets were cleared, snow would fill them again within minutes. He hoped the manager would allow him to leave.

First, he would repair the young signorina's windshield as promised. He had a piece of glass that was the right size. He did not worry whether she could pay for the work. She came from money; anyone who owned a fine piece of machinery like the Cadillac Model 30 did. He ran his hands over the Dewar Trophy–winning auto. Well built. Sleek. *Expensive.* In the same class as its owner. So why could he not get her soft blond curls, frozen in place by the snow, or those expressive gray eyes out of his mind? *Fabrizio, Fabrizio,* he scolded himself. *You must not let a pretty face fool you.* Someone like Signorina Daire had no place in the dreams of a poor immigrant.

If only his heart would listen. He finished replacing the windshield.

John Livingston, the hotel manager, lifted an eyebrow when Fabrizio asked if he could go home and stay until the snow stopped. "Do you think that's wise?"

"I do not know," Fabrizio admitted. "But I must try. They will worry."

"You have my blessing. It's my guess that no one will require your services for a few days." Livingston shook his head at Fabrizio's foolishness. "But if you can't make it home, you're welcome to stay here. There'll be plenty for you to do."

Fabrizio thought of his worried parents and the cramped quarters he had shared last night. He must try to reach his family's home located in the Highlands district of Denver. Once again he wrapped his bright green and yellow scarf around his neck, strapped on the skis, and slipped his hands into his gloves. He looked over the world gone white, took a deep breath, and braced himself for the cold air.

Once outside, he could get no rhythm going. Instead of gliding over the surface, his skis sank into deep snowdrifts. Memories of the lovely Signorina Daire interfered with his concentration. Her face swam in front of his eyes, adding color to the landscape. He made it as far as the place where the accident had occurred the previous evening. Snow covered the wooden stall, obliterating any hint of what had happened only twelve hours before. The sight reminded Fabrizio of one of his favorite Bible verses. "Come now, and let us reason together, saith the Lord: though your sins be as scarlet, they shall be as white as snow; though they be red like crimson, they shall be as wool." Isaiah could have been looking down Sixteenth Street in Denver when he wrote those words.

Was Signorina Daire looking at the same scene? Did she like snow? How foolish to drive in such weather. What father would allow his daughter to drive in a blizzard? His own papa would not allow his daughters to drive at all, even if they could afford a horseless carriage. But he suspected that the spirited young woman would not accept any curtailment of her activities without a protest. She might even be one of those—what was the word?—suffragettes.

Fabrizio realized he had been staring at the stall for several minutes. Thank the good Lord that neither of them was hurt. Now he must get moving before he turned into a statue made of ice. He pushed ahead with his ski pole. It broke through the crust into a deep pocket, plunging several feet. He toppled forward and flailed his arms, catching himself on the edges of the stand before he could fall.

The street stretched before him. Tall buildings protected it; snow would drift even higher away from the center of the city. He faced the truth. He could not make it home. Mama and Papa would trust the Lord for his safety; and he must do the same for their needs.

He made a wide circle and started back for the Brown Palace. Already snow had filled in his tracks. He prayed the Lord would keep his family safe and warm. Somehow he didn't mind returning to work. He might see the enigmatic Signorina Daire again.

❄

The clock was striking ten when Natalie stirred on Wednesday morning. It took a moment to orient herself. She snuggled under a dark green comforter. The mattress on the immense four-poster was soft but unfamiliar. She stretched and banged into the headboard. The nudge set up a complaint in her head. Natalie ran her hands over her forehead and discovered a bump.

The events of the previous night came back to her in a rush. The drive from Thalia's house. The decision to spend the night at the Brown Palace. The mysterious stranger who appeared out of the darkness and caused an accident—who then in turn rescued her and brought her safely to the Brown. Her entire body ached, her head most of all.

She rubbed her eyes and stared at the clock, not believing the hour. Surely it couldn't be that late. The light coming through the window suggested early morning. Natalie tugged her negligee about her and walked over to the window. Where she expected sunshine—after more than twenty-four hours, surely the storm had stopped—instead she saw the same wall of white, snow flying in ten directions at once. She doubted that she could leave today. Still, it wouldn't hurt to find out if that nice young man had repaired the Model 30 as promised.

Natalie rang the bell for one of the hotel maids. A brief glance in her dressing room mirror confirmed that her forehead sported a bump the size of a mothball that was coloring. She touched it gingerly. She remembered the shattered windshield and thanked God that she wasn't hurt more severely. Not a single scratch. Perhaps it was just as well that she could not return home today. Father would worry if he could see her face or the car.

She wanted hot tea and a warm breakfast; then she would search out the young man who had been both the cause and savior of last night's accident. Perhaps he was visiting the Brown from Europe. He spoke with some kind of accent. French perhaps? She didn't think it was Spanish; several of their household help came from Mexico, and she knew a little of the language. He called her "Signorina." Italian, definitely.

Sunny Italy. Given the blizzard, he might wish he had decided to stay home for the holidays. What was he doing on Sixteenth Street in the middle of a blizzard, wearing skis? Perhaps he was an angel, sent from heaven because of the accident. Natalie smiled to herself. She doubted that angels wore bright scarves or had such handsome dark looks.

She debated on whether to don the dress she had worn to Thalia's party for a second day or to wear a different gown. She thought of the handsome stranger and opted for a new outfit. Fur trim accented the tiered skirt, and the robin's egg blue of the material flattered her coloring. After the maid helped her dress, she studied her reflection in the mirror. What could be done about the bruise on her forehead? She fingered her hair and teased a few curls over it. Perhaps it would deflect attention from the multicolored hues. Satisfied at last with her toilette, she left her room and headed down the stairs in search of brunch.

Walking into the foyer of the Brown Palace always gave Natalie a thrill. She loved the sight of liveried doormen, the low hush of voices from tables, the magnificence of the stained glass overhead, even when obscured by snow as it was now. In addition to the cosmopolitan mix of guests, she could usually count on meeting acquaintances, more often than not one of Daddy's fuddy-duddy business associates. Unlike that handsome stranger. She intended to find the mysterious Italian; she could ask him about the car as an excuse for seeking him out.

She rang the bell at the front desk, and a young man whose lilting voice and bright red hair proclaimed his Irish heritage appeared. "May I help you, miss?"

"I am looking for one of the guests." Natalie felt heat rise in her cheeks. Maybe the clerk would attribute her color to the blast of warm air from the vents. "He assisted me last evening, and I wanted to thank him properly."

"What is his name?" The clerk, whose name tag read "PATRICK," smiled.

"You see, that's the problem." Natalie twisted a handkerchief in her hands. "He disappeared without introducing himself.

He appeared to be Italian. Tall, dark, in his twenties." *Do I dare say* handsome? "Oh yes, and he was wearing a very distinctive scarf. Yellow and green stripes, as bright as a summer day."

The front door crashed open, and cold air blasted in. Patrick's eyes widened in recognition. "You're in luck. I believe this is the man you are looking for."

He's here? Natalie rotated on her heels. First she noticed a snow-crusted cap covering dark hair, then the bright yellow and green scarf. She suddenly was very glad that she had decided to wear her most becoming frock.

"Fabrizio! I see that you decided to return." Patrick greeted him warmly.

Fabrizio. So that was his name. The syllables rolled around in her mind. It tasted exotic, like basil and garlic and maybe a hint of sweet tomatoes. But why was he traveling in this weather? On foot?

"Miss Daire, is this the gentleman?" Patrick spoke in a low tone. She appreciated his discretion.

"Yes." God must be behind this encounter; she didn't expect to run into him so soon. "You should know. . ."

Fabrizio approached the counter before Patrick finished his sentence.

"Fab—" Natalie stopped. They had never been properly introduced, after all. She coughed and spoke again. "I wanted to thank you for your assistance last night."

"Signorina Daire." The snow on Fabrizio's head melted in the warm lobby, and his dark hair sprang into curls. "Your car, it is ready." He paused. "But you will do well not to leave today. The snow, it is too deep."

Natalie shook off his admonition. "I intend to wait out the storm at the Brown. But thank you for seeing to my car." She took in features of Fabrizio's appearance that she had missed in the dark the previous evening. His coat was frayed around the edges. A faint oily odor clung to him. And his shoes—her father would never wear such shoddy workmanship. She looked into his beautiful brown eyes with growing suspicions.

"Miss Daire." Patrick interrupted her thoughts. "I see you have already made the acquaintance of our coachman, Fabrizio Ricci."

"You may tell Patrick when you will leave. I will bring the car for you." Fabrizio nodded respectfully and walked away.

Her mysterious rescuer was not a guest from the Continent. He was one of the hired help. Natalie stared thoughtfully at his departing back.

Chapter 3

N atalie!" A familiar voice called her name. It belonged to Eleanor Royal, one of the circle of friends she palled around with in Denver. She could be outspoken but fun, the kind of person her father expected her to associate with. Unlike her mysterious rescuer from the previous evening. Natalie cast a longing look at the door through which the coachman had disappeared and greeted her friend. They entered the dining room together and observed as a waiter floated a fresh tablecloth over a window table and laid out two place settings.

"I expect we shall be here several days." Eleanor tucked her napkin in her lap. "I love the Brown, but I fear it will become boring."

"Not at all. We shall just have to organize parlor games and other activities, as we did at school." Natalie paused. "Speaking of school, I expected to see you at Thalia's party. We had a wonderful time."

"Father refused to let me go when the snow started falling. It's just as well. Have you ever seen a storm like this?"

Natalie stared out the window. Down here on the ground level the prospect was truly frightening. Snow climbed the lower half of the window.

A querulous voice interrupted her thoughts. "Waiter!" An older woman, hair falling in precise silver waves, bellowed and jutted out her chin. A small, round man rushed to her side. "Yes, Mrs. Rushton?"

"I have two butter knives and no dinner knife. The standards at the Brown have deteriorated."

The poor man dashed away and returned with a fresh set of silverware. The cantankerous older woman didn't bother to thank him.

I hope I can avoid her at mealtimes. Natalie chastised herself for the unkind thought. No, God said to love everyone, not only pleasant people. Perhaps she could do something to cheer the older woman.

Natalie realized that she was staring. She turned her attention back to Eleanor. What would her friend think if she told her she wished she could go outside and build a snowman as they had when they were children? Eleanor had always preferred to stay inside where it was dry and warm. So instead, Natalie described her arrival at the Brown the night before.

"You mean to say that you drove in this weather? I don't want to drive those scary things. But you go bravely about in that splendid car of yours." Eleanor peered at Natalie's forehead. "Were you hurt in the accident?"

Natalie tugged at the curl covering the bruise. "Only a small bump. Really, it was nothing."

"And tell me more about the handsome stranger who rescued you. How romantic."

"How *providential*," Natalie corrected. "God sent me help when I needed it." She paused. She wasn't ready to tell her friend about her rescuer's true identity as the hotel's coachman. Nor would she admit her interest in him. She wanted to discover more about him, and she thought she knew how to make that happen. "I expect you shall see him soon enough. Now, let's see if the desk clerk will show us to a room that we can use for parlor games."

Natalie waited until Eleanor returned to her room to freshen up before she approached Patrick. "I believe the guests will become restless because of the snow." She smiled in the way that usually won her way. "I am planning some parlor games, and I would appreciate the help of someone on the hotel staff."

The redheaded clerk smiled back, a coconspirator. "And did you have someone particular in mind, Miss Daire?"

"I thought perhaps some of the staff cannot perform their normal duties because of the snow. Someone like—Mr. Ricci?" She blushed as she said his name.

"Certainly. No one will require his services in the garage today. Did you have a room in mind for the party?"

"I was thinking of the Ladies' Ordinary." Natalie mentioned the facility used for ladies' club activities. "Only for this occasion we will welcome male guests and children." Patrick confirmed the availability of the room and completed arrangements for a high tea service.

Later in the day, Natalie made her way to the room by herself. She was envisioning the arrangement of chairs when she heard the door open. Eleanor swept in, followed by Fabrizio. He looked as handsome as ever, if a bit uncertain. "Mr. Ricci. I'm so glad you could join us." She walked toward him, hands outstretched.

He bowed low over her hands, a lovely Continental gesture. "I am glad to be of service."

"And have you met my friend, Eleanor Royal?"

"Signorina Royal." Fabrizio acknowledged the introduction.

Natalie loved the way "signorina" rolled off his tongue. She would have to study Italian.

"Oh, do let's dispense with formalities." Eleanor insisted in her usual blunt style. "We are planning a party, after all. We must be on a first-name basis. As you know, I'm Eleanor, and Miss Daire's given name is Natalie."

"As in *Buon Natale*."

For a brief moment, Natalie thought that Fabrizio was calling her pretty, and she felt heat creep into her cheeks.

"In Italian, *Natale* means *Christmas*." Fabrizio's explanation deflected some of the heat.

"Why, that's the same thing Natalie means in English. Her birthday is the day before Christmas, you know," Eleanor gushed.

"Which is still a few weeks away." Natalie wanted to get the attention off herself. She did not want to mention her coming-of-age party, and the inheritance that came with it, in front of Fabrizio. She suspected that the quiet coachman would retreat even further into himself if Eleanor revealed that. "While today we are holding a party for people stranded here at the hotel. What do you think? Shall we arrange the chairs in small circles or in a large grouping?"

"I understand that Molly Brown seats everyone in a large U-shape." Eleanor giggled. "So her guests can meet new people."

Molly Brown did not set Denver's society standards, but Natalie liked the plain-spoken, kindhearted matron. "Then that's what we shall do. We may be spending several days together, and it would be good to become better acquainted at the outset. Let's get started."

Natalie's hopes to learn more about Fabrizio seemed doomed to failure. Never speaking unless spoken to, he moved with quick, precise movements, never a step out of place. She remembered how easily he moved over the snow on the skis. Every now and then a smile passed across his face. Perhaps he was thinking about his sweetheart. He could even be married. Why did the possibility leave her with a pang in her heart?

They finished arranging the room with time to spare. Eleanor wrote the names of people, places, and things from the Christmas story for a get-acquainted game. Fabrizio clasped his hands together and trained his eyes on the floor when he spoke to her. "May I do anything else to help you, signorina?"

She wished he would say "Natalie" again. It warmed her heart like the glow of Christmas candles and a cup of hot, spiced cider. But he wouldn't; Eleanor's suggestion to use first names probably made him uncomfortable. Guilt hit her. The poor man had arisen hours before she had, repaired her windshield, braved the weather, and then spent the afternoon helping them set up for the party.

"I hope you will join us for the tea—as our guest." She made it an invitation, not an order.

"That would not be wise." Fabrizio seemed determined to respect the social boundaries that separated them.

Natalie racked her brain for an excuse to see him again. The perfect answer came, one that would address two problems. "There is one thing you could do for me."

"Anything, signorina."

"Please invite Mrs. Rushton to join us for tea. And escort her if she needs help." Natalie suppressed a giggle at the surprise that flitted through his eyes.

"*Fino ad allora.* Until then, Signorina Daire." He sketched a bow and left the room.

❄

Fabrizio's feet whispered along the plush carpet to Mrs. Rushton's room. He could have left word of Natalie's invitation at the front desk. He should have left it there. Everyone in the hotel avoided the old lady if possible. Her temper was legendary, and she expected perfect service, regardless of the circumstances. She would not welcome his intrusion.

But Fabrizio could not bring himself to disappoint Natalie. In his private thoughts, he savored the sound of her name. It suited her, with her golden hair shining like an angel's halo around her head, her richness of spirit, as well as purse, that spoke in everything she did. Her dress probably cost more than his entire family spent on clothing in a year's time. But away from her, he allowed his thoughts to linger on how the blue fabric brought out the color in her eyes. He scolded himself. The likes of Natalie Daire were not for the likes of Fabrizio Ricci.

He hesitated at the door to Mrs. Rushton's room then knocked. He expected a maid to answer, but instead Mrs. Rushton herself cracked the door open. "Yes?" Dressed in a robe and shoulder wrap, she looked elderly and frail, not at all like the terror of the entire hotel staff.

Fabrizio cleared his throat. "Signorina Natalie Daire invites you to tea in the Ladies' Ordinary this afternoon." He handed her an ivory envelope.

"Nonsense. I always have tea in my room."

"The signorina asks for you especially." Fabrizio didn't know why he made the extra effort. The guests would enjoy the party more without the presence of the grumbling older woman. Still, Natalie asked for Mrs. Rushton in particular. "She thinks the guests, they will be bored in all this snow." He paused and added a final word. "She asks me to escort you to the tea."

Mrs. Rushton's face lined in a frown, but she did not speak.

"I will come for you in an hour." Fabrizio left before Mrs. Rushton could refuse. He had done as Natalie wanted. Maybe now he could get the lovely heiress out of his mind. Hotel gossip buzzed about the fortune she would inherit from her grandfather on her next birthday. Fabrizio smiled. He also received a legacy from his grandfather—his name. If he could be the man his grandfather was, as brave in coming to a new country and as dedicated to his family, he would consider himself rich.

Fabrizio went to the kitchen for a bite of lunch. Conversation centered on the news from St. Clara's Orphanage.

"Those poor *Kinder*, freezing in this terrible snow. They say the place has run out of coal." Braum, the heavyset German cook, stirred soup at the stove.

Fabrizio winced. St. Clara's housed a multitude of orphans, many of them from Denver's Italian community. They would indeed suffer without coal to heat the home.

"The *Denver Post* has offered to send wagonloads of coal," a maid mentioned. "But I don't see how they'll get through the snowdrifts."

Fabrizio's thoughts flew to his own family. Did they have enough coal? He looked at the able-bodied men sitting around the staff table. How he wished he could have made it home. His parents counted on him to help with the heavy work. His only brother, the eldest child, had married and lived with his new wife and their little ones. His four younger sisters could only do so much. If only he could find a way home. Maybe he could hitch a ride with one of the *Post*'s wagons. The road to the orphanage passed near his house. Perhaps, if his manager would release him from work. . .

An hour sped by, and he returned to the fourth floor to escort Mrs. Rushton to the tea. He determined not to let Natalie cajole him into staying. Staff did not dine with guests. A smile tugged at his mouth. Not only that, but he did not want to be the only gentleman present. Since the Ladies' Ordinary was the hotel's clubroom for women, men might hesitate to brave the gathering.

A transformed Mrs. Rushton answered his knock. Her beaded dress shimmered with Christmas splendor. A hint of a smile suggested her pleasure at Natalie's invitation.

"*Signora* Rushton, you are lovely."

The smile vanished. Had he spoken aloud? Fabrizio could not believe his folly. Mrs. Rushton might accuse him of familiarity to the manager. But aside from a little color in her powdered cheeks, she did not respond. "Shall we take the elevator, Signora Rushton?" He feared the steps to the eighth floor, where the tea was located, would prove too much for the older woman.

"I am not an invalid, young man." That was classic Mrs. Rushton.

"Signorina Daire asked me to escort you."

"Daire's daughter? She's a sweet young thing." The compliment surprised Fabrizio, and he almost missed the fact that she handed him a small mesh bag. "Since Natalie insists, you may carry my reticule."

Mrs. Rushton paused on the eighth-floor landing to catch her breath. Natalie must have spotted their approach, because she dashed forward to greet them. "Mrs. Rushton! I am so glad that you decided to join us." Natalie took her arm and led her to the open door. She looked over her shoulder and mouthed "thank you" to Fabrizio. At that moment, he felt as though he would do anything she asked. He followed close behind.

Loud voices laced with laughter leapt through the door. Eleanor greeted Mrs. Rushton and pinned a piece of paper to the back of her dress. INNKEEPER'S WIFE. Fabrizio wondered if the appellation was intentional; he could imagine Mrs. Rushton turning away a young couple, even if the wife was pregnant. Through the open doorway, he could see a few men and several children mingling with female guests. Natalie led Mrs. Rushton to the seat of honor.

Fabrizio hovered near the door, watching the gaiety, remembering happy gatherings at home. He was preparing to leave when Natalie returned. "You will join us for tea, won't you?" Steady gray eyes pleaded with him.

A few minutes ago, Fabrizio had felt ready to do anything this beautiful woman asked of him.

He would do anything, that is, except to cross the social barriers that stood between them, as thick as the Great Wall of China.

Chapter 4

Natalie watched Fabrizio's departing back. He looked good in his uniform, so broad shouldered, so quietly strong. If only he would have agreed to stay. Not a single man at the tea captured her interest as he did. How had he managed to convince Mrs. Rushton to attend the party? Natalie had sent the invitation but had not expected the woman to accept. She surprised her by showing up, dressed to the nines, and a kind word for "that nice young man who carried my reticule." A brave young girl hovered near her, giving her clues about the name pinned to her back.

Natalie lingered a moment, until Fabrizio disappeared around a corner, and then wandered to the window. Snow swirled in the air. She doubted that anyone would leave the hotel tomorrow either, whether staff or guest. Patrick had assured her that the hotel generated its own electricity and drew water from an artesian well. They did not have to fear the loss of power.

The afternoon tea achieved a moderate success. Too late, Natalie realized that she had not invited the staff, and none attended. They must be as bored and stressed as the guests. Social distinctions paled in the face of their shared experience, snowbound by the weather. People already referred to the storm as "Denver's big snow." It was certainly the worst that she had ever seen. She decided that she would plan a mixed activity for staff and guests together, perhaps a carol sing. Everyone sang the same songs of the season. Even better, she knew the right man to help her set up the music room. She invited her guests to return that evening for another event.

After the tea ended, Natalie sought out Patrick. She reserved the Ladies' Ordinary for the following day. "Tonight I'd like to hold a carol sing and invite the staff to join in. What time is most convenient for them to attend?"

The clerk murmured a protest, but Natalie insisted. He agreed that most of the kitchen staff as well as the maids would be finished by half-past nine. She beamed. "Please be sure to let everyone know that they are invited."

"And would you be needing Mr. Ricci to help you set up for the party?" Patrick suggested.

"Please." Natalie knew her cheeks must look nearly as red as the Irishman's hair.

❄

The carol service dominated conversation during the staff supper. Fabrizio had not decided whether to join the celebration.

Braum stirred a bubbling pan. "I am making hot cocoa to bring." He hummed a few phrases in German.

What was that tune? "Oh, Christmas Tree," that was it.

Most of the hotel staff intended to go. Fabrizio was torn. He loved music. His family probably whiled away hours of snowbound tedium singing around the fireplace.

The thought tugged at his heart. Did he dare spend more time in Signorina Daire's presence? She already occupied more of his thoughts than she should; she crept in at all hours of the day. That afternoon, he had helped her move the piano and chairs. When she sat down to play, the chords flew like an arrow from the keys to his heart and lodged there.

After the music started, he could not stay away. He found a chair next to Patrick in the back row. Natalie had changed into an emerald green dress, and lights from the chandeliers danced on her golden hair. She announced each selection in her clear soprano voice. Fabrizio lost himself in the songs, humming through unfamiliar verses, adding a bass line to others. Patrick sang tenor. When Fabrizio closed his eyes, he could almost imagine he was at home with his family, singing in four-part harmony.

When they started "Silent Night," Natalie changed her routine. "I've heard a story about this carol. I'm not sure if it's true or not. The organ at St. Nicholas Church in Oberndorf, Austria, broke down on Christmas Eve. So the assistant pastor, Joseph Mohr, wrote a song that he could accompany with his guitar. It would be lovely to hear the song in the original language. Surely someone here speaks German?"

"Ja, I do." The chef, Braum, raised his hand.

"Splendid." Natalie smiled. "Would you be willing to sing it for us in German? We would all enjoy it so much."

The rotund man stood. Still dressed in uniform, he hesitated. Someone—Natalie's friend Eleanor, perhaps?—clapped, encouraging him forward. Red flooded his face more than when he stood over a hot stove. He sucked in a deep breath and nodded at Natalie. In a pleasant baritone, he began singing. *"Stille Nacht! Heil'ge Nacht!"*

A hush descended. Fabrizio closed his eyes and repeated the words in Italian, envisioning the holy family in the stable that first Christmas night. *Thank You, God, for sending* Cristo il Salvatore *to us.*

When Braum finished, the group sang the same carol in English. Natalie made another suggestion. "Next, let's sing 'Angels We Have Heard on High.' I've heard some lovely harmony from the group. Mrs. Rushton—"

Fabrizio had not anticipated the older woman's presence at the caroling. He looked around the gathering and saw her seated near the heater vent. She looked startled.

"I heard your lovely alto voice. Please come sing with me."

Pink colored Mrs. Rushton's high cheekbones as she made her way to the piano. Natalie twisted on the bench and sought Fabrizio in the crowd. "Mr. Ricci? Mr. O'Riley? We would welcome four-part harmony."

Patrick jumped to his feet. The Irishman loved to put on a show. Fabrizio took more time. When he stood, Natalie's eyes sparkled as if the very stars of heaven shone in them. She arranged the quartet so that Fabrizio stood next to her. He felt her nearness, the warmth of her shoulder. It confused him so that he missed the introduction and joined on the second note. Once he started, he lost his self-consciousness in the music, imagining the wonder of the angel choir on that first Christmas night. "Gloria in excelsis Deo." Glory to God in the highest. His voice deepened and slid down to low bass notes, while Natalie's soared into the highest.

A worshipful silence greeted the end of the song. Then Natalie thanked the quartet and invited them to sit down. Eyes shining as bright as a silver coin, she swiveled on the bench. "The singing has been wonderful. Let's end our party by sharing Christmas memories."

Fabrizio tensed. Would she talk of the elaborate gifts she must have received? Of fancy holiday parties her family had hosted?

"My birthday is on Christmas Eve." Natalie glanced at the floor, as if embarrassed to share a personal detail. "My grandfather tells me that I am blessed to share my birthday with the Savior of the world. Somehow I've always known that my cake and candles were also for that other Christmas baby, Jesus. On my twelfth birthday, I realized that God had given me the best present I could ever hope for: His Son. So Christmas is my birthday twice over: I was born the first time; then I was born again as God's child." Joy that only came from the Holy Spirit shone in her eyes. "Would anyone else like to share?"

Fabrizio's heart danced. Natalie believed in his Lord. They both belonged to the family that truly mattered, with God as their Father and Jesus as their brother. A few others mentioned special memories. Braum described the German Christmas tree tradition.

Food filled Fabrizio's memories of Christmas. Rather than the turkey and ham that Americans enjoyed, they ate *baccala*, salted codfish. His mother competed with his grandmother over homemade pasta and melt-in-your mouth molasses cookies. But those memories, though pleasant, would not lift up the Savior whose birthday they celebrated.

"That's so interesting, Mr. Braum. Thank you for sharing. I love learning about Christmas traditions in other countries." Natalie scanned the rows of carolers. Her gaze drew Fabrizio to his feet like a puppet on a string.

"My family, we came to Denver from a small village outside of Potenza, in Italia. Three weeks before Christmas, we bring a *presepio* into our home. The presepio is a manger such as the one the baby Jesus slept in. Every time we help someone, we add hay to the presepio. We want it to be as soft as possible for the Christ child." He ran out of words and sat down.

"What a wonderful tradition! Let's practice the same thoughtfulness ourselves. Instead of complaining about the snow, we can think of what we can do for others." Natalie beamed as if Fabrizio had given her the perfect conclusion to the evening. "I hope all of you will join us upstairs in the Ladies' Ordinary for more games tomorrow afternoon. We have something planned for your children in the morning. Feel free to come and go as your duties allow."

From the look Natalie sent in his direction, Fabrizio suspected she would require his assistance again. Somehow, after the memories they had shared, it no longer seemed like such an impossible idea. What would the alluring signorina decide to do next?

Chapter 5

Fabrizio had predicted Natalie's intentions correctly. Patrick contacted him early in the morning. "Miss Daire would like to see you in the music room. After breakfast, to be sure. She was mentioning that baby Jesus crib you described last night."

Fabrizio forced himself to sit down for a cup of coffee and a cinnamon roll first. Music bubbled inside him, echoes of last night's carols, Natalie's lovely soprano soaring above them all. What plans had she made for the day? A scant fifteen minutes later, he joined her.

"Fabrizio! I'm so glad to see you. The boys will be here any second."

Wood sat in a neat pile in the center of the room, as well as a bale of hay in one corner. A variety of tools were spread across a table.

She explained. "I had planned for the children to draw some Christmas decorations. But the crib you described would be so much more fun for the boys." She hesitated. "You do know how to *make* the crib, don't you? I figured with your talent for fixing cars. . ."

Fabrizio nodded his head. He had learned how to build a crib at his grandfather's side.

"That's good. Do we have everything we need?"

"There is plenty, signorina."

"Oh, good. Patrick gathered wood for us. After the boys finish the—what did you call it? presepio?—we can get everyone involved in filling it with hay. I love the idea of preparing for the baby Jesus." She paused. "I hope you will join the adult party later this afternoon. Patrick said he was certain several of the morning staff would join us. Please say you will."

"I do not know, signorina." The *Denver Post* might attempt to deliver coal to St. Clara's today. If they did, he intended to go with the wagons. He looked into her eyes, bright in their eagerness, and lost all reservations. If he was still in the hotel, he would come.

※

Natalie hung the homemade Christmas cards around the Ladies' Ordinary. They added a homey, festive atmosphere. She almost wished the room used candlelight, instead of the electric fixtures, bell-like lamps hanging from a chandelier. Who would come today? Her maid had promised to attend with some friends. Perhaps games could break down the awkwardness between staff and guests. Denver's big snow could become a magical memory for those staying at the Brown.

Why did that thought bring the tall, dark Italian to her mind? But would the one person she most wanted to see join them? Her mind darted to his deep voice booming in celebration of the coming of the Christ child. To the memories he shared. To his patience with the boys while they built the crib. He was good with children. He would make a good father someday. The thought shocked her. She had no business thinking about such things.

At the appointed hour, the room quickly filled. Most of yesterday's guests returned, even Mrs. Rushton. The gentlemen must have convinced more of their friends to join them. Her maid came with a handful of friends. They sat at one end of the circle, as far as possible from the guests. Nearly every seat was filled when at last Fabrizio made his entrance. He nodded at her, and her heart soared.

Natalie looked at the seating arrangement—guests to the right, staff to the left—and knew she had to do something to encourage the people to mingle. She already had decided on the game.

"I will be 'it.' I will ask one of you, 'Do you love your neighbor?' If you say 'no,' you must change places with one of the people on either side of you. I will try to take your seat." Natalie smiled as she said this. "And I warn you that I am fast. Or. . ." She shook her finger around the circle. "You can say, 'I love all my neighbors except for everyone wearing blue, or with brown hair,' or whatever you like. Then everybody who is wearing blue has to change seats. If you say, 'I love everyone,' all of you have to change seats."

The people nodded in recognition of this variation on a familiar game.

The men removed the few extra chairs while Natalie debated who to approach first. Eleanor, who else? Her friend would jump into the spirit of the game. She stood in front of her friend and asked, "Do you love your neighbor?"

Eleanor glanced around the circle. Mischief danced in her blue eyes. "I love everyone except people who are younger than ten years old." Giggles erupted from the children. They jumped to their feet, shrieked, and ran in every direction. Natalie slipped into the chair Eleanor vacated. The game picked up pace. The children delighted in saying, "I love everyone," and making the whole group run around. Natalie passed Fabrizio a few times. He kept quiet, reserving his brilliant smiles for the youngest children, who loved to tease him.

Natalie called a halt to the game before the older guests could tire. "Let's enjoy some of the marvelous refreshments before we start our next game."

Servers had arranged platters of the Brown's famous macaroons and carafes of beverages. Natalie stood guard to discourage children from grabbing more than a couple of the meringue-light coconut cookies at a time. She poured a cup of tea for herself and turned face-to-face with Fabrizio. His hand hovered over the sweets as if he didn't dare to take one.

She handed two of them to him on a napkin. "Please eat these. I don't want the children eating too much sugar."

"The *bambini*, yes." He smiled at a pair of young girls giggling in the corner. "The girls, they remind me of my sisters." He looked sad.

"Do you come from a large family?" Some families among the Italian community burgeoned with as many as ten children. She could not imagine it herself.

"One older brother and four younger sisters. I worry about them in the storm." He bit into a macaroon then looked guilty, as if regretting his pleasure when his family suffered elsewhere.

"God will watch out for them. As He looked over the Christ child in the presepio." She smiled. "I checked the crib after lunch. People have already added a thin layer of hay. Thank you for sharing your tradition with us."

"I am glad to learn we both believe in the Christ child." Fabrizio's dark eyes lifted long enough to gaze into hers. Then he took another bite of macaroon.

Natalie sensed that he wanted to convey more than their common faith. "We all kneel before the same manger, whether we are shepherds or wise men from far away. He is the King of us all."

"*Sì*. Yes, He is the Lord of lords, and He even made the snow." He gestured to the window where they could see white swirls in the air.

"Maybe He sent the snow so that we could become friends?" *Or more than friends? Why did that thought even cross her mind?*

Thanks to the storm, they shared a magical experience outside the normal social boundaries. But as soon as Denver dug out from the big snow, they would return to their normal roles. The thought sent a shadow across her heart, dimming her joy.

"Sì. Maybe He did," Fabrizio whispered.

The shadow fled in the light of his smile. For a brief moment they stood in a silent circle of delight, oblivious to everything around them. Then Eleanor's voice interrupted them.

"The macaroons are almost gone. Perhaps we should start again?"

Fabrizio nodded at the two women and walked back to his seat. Natalie clapped her hands to gain everyone's attention. The guests rejoined the circle, and Natalie explained the next game, You're Never Fully Dressed without a Smile.

Natalie took the first turn as "it." She made comical faces while everyone else tried to keep their faces solemn. As she expected, Eleanor was the first to smile in return. "Now you're 'it.'"

Eleanor coaxed grins and outright laughter from a number of guests. One "it" after another told jokes and made faces. Laughter echoed throughout the room. Fabrizio won by keeping a straight face the longest. This time his silence did not bother Natalie. He had joined in the fun of the marvelous afternoon.

"I saved a couple of macaroons for the winner—Fabrizio Ricci!" He bowed over her extended hand and for a moment she wondered if he would kiss it. She hoped he would. Instead he straightened and said a simple "grazie." He left when the party ended a few minutes later.

She couldn't wait until tomorrow. Surely Fabrizio would return.

❄

Fabrizio rose before dawn. This morning, the *Denver Post* would deliver coal to St. Clara's orphanage. He had determined to accompany the coal wagon in an effort to reach his family. He slipped a couple of rolls from the previous evening's dinner into his coat pocket, wrapped his scarf around his neck, and strapped on his skis. He arrived at the *Post* building as the wagons pulled out. Stalwart horses lowered their heads and began their slow progress through downtown and across the river.

Fabrizio ate one roll in slow mouthfuls. In addition to the rolls, he carried the macaroons he had won during yesterday's festivities. The smiles that he had suppressed during the game escaped. Natalie made playing games as much fun for the adults as for the children, for the staff as for the guests.

In fact, Fabrizio almost had not gone with the coal wagons today. For the first time in his life, he longed to remain in the company of a young woman rather than take care of his sisters. He wished that he could remain at the Brown until the snow melted and the magical interlude ended. But in the end he did his duty. Snow still blanketed the sky, whether from fresh powder or the wind whipping the accumulation into a frozen batter. Even with the wagons traveling in front of him, he could barely ski over the ground. In a few more blocks, he would need to leave the safety of the horses' trail for home.

The wagons' slow progress stalled as they approached West Twenty-Sixth Street. Away from the center of town, the snow drifted deeper, and the horses could no longer move.

Fabrizio ate his second roll while the wagon drivers talked together. What could they do? He sent up a prayer that God would make a way. Noise pierced the air, a sound foreign on the snowy day—the trumpet of elephants. Could it be? Barnum and Bailey's circus spent the winters in Denver.

The mammoth animals rounded the corner, towering over the snow, complaining with loud voices about their forced departure from their warm barns. Wrapping their trunks around the rear axles, they lifted the wagons off the ground and began to push. Terrified that they would be run over by their own wagons, the horses reared and plunged into the snow. Once again they moved forward. Fabrizio wondered if anyone would believe the story.

With the snow now packed by horses' hooves, wagon wheels, and elephant feet, Fabrizio skied effortlessly over the ground. Two blocks later, he came to the intersection where he had to turn to his parents' home. The wagons continued in the direction of the orphanage, the elephants' trumpets announcing their progress.

How could he reach his home? Snow drifted as high as his shoulders in some places. He searched the walls for a break, where he could clamber to the top, but found none. If he could remove the skis, perhaps he could climb a tree and search the horizon. But if he removed the skis, he could not traverse the ground. He found a spot low enough to look across the blanketed city. Although his family's home lay only half a mile away, he could not see it. Even the smoke from the hearth fires blended into the white sky. He could not possibly make his way through the snow.

Behind him snow lined the trampled-down path. He shivered, tightened the scarf around his neck and under his arms, and headed back to the light and warmth of the Brown Palace.

To the place where Natalie waited.

Chapter 6

Disappointment nettled Natalie when she failed to catch a glimpse of Fabrizio during the morning. *He's probably working somewhere else,* she told herself. *The hotel needs his services.* When he didn't appear at the afternoon gathering, disappointment deepened into a disturbing sense of loss. After tea, Natalie approached Patrick. "Is Mr. Ricci working elsewhere today?" She hoped she did not sound overly eager.

The Irishman shook his head. "No, miss. He followed the coal wagons headed to the orphanage, trying to reach his family. He's been mightily worried about them."

"He went out? In the storm?" Natalie remembered Fabrizio's mention of younger sisters, and for the first time she considered his family, snowbound without his strong back. "Then I shall say a prayer for his safety." The evening hours dragged by. When had Fabrizio's presence come to mean so much to her? She examined the shelves of books thoughtfully provided in her room, only to discover that most of the titles were in other languages. She recognized several of the romance languages—French, Spanish, Italian—and others that appeared to be in Swedish. At last she found a book in English, American short stories and essays, and whiled away an hour reading an excerpt from *The Autocrat of the Breakfast-Table.*

When Sunday morning dawned, Natalie checked outside. The storm had slowed; only a few flakes drifted lazily through the air. She said another prayer for Fabrizio and slipped into her green gown, freshly laundered by the hotel staff.

One of the guests, a visiting minister, had offered to lead a worship service in the Grand Salon. It should be a lovely spot, if any sunlight could come through the stained-glass windows. She ate breakfast in her room before descending to the second floor.

To her surprise, she saw a dark head and broad shoulders seated toward the back of the room. *Fabrizio.* She felt her cheeks flush, and she held her Bible close to her chest like a shield. He caught sight of her and moved over a seat. She took that as an invitation and joined him on the hard-backed chairs.

The congregants sang a few hymns. Fabrizio's bass voice vibrated through the book that they shared and up her arm. She thanked God for his safe return. What had happened to his trip home? Surely the Brown had not required him to return to work the following day. She forced herself to concentrate on the sermon.

After the final amen, Natalie turned to her companion. Aside from windburn on his cheeks, he looked as handsome as ever.

"I prayed for you yesterday. Patrick told me you tried to go home?"

Regret flickered in Fabrizio's dark eyes. "I followed the wagons as far as I could. From there, I could not break through the snow. So I returned."

The breath caught in Natalie's throat. Was it so terribly wrong of her to take pleasure in his forced return? She pointed to the window. "Sunshine is starting to break through the clouds. Soon the snow will stop falling and begin to melt." *And you will be able to leave, and so will I.* The thought saddened her.

Fabrizio nodded. "We will shovel tomorrow."

Natalie stilled. Their time together would end as surely as the snow would melt.

"*Fino a domani*, Natalie. Until tomorrow. I must return to work." For a moment, he bowed his dark head as if in prayer and then strode out of the temporary chapel.

Natalie. He called her *Natalie*. So why did she feel so downcast?

❄

On Monday morning, Fabrizio joined the male staff at the front door of the Brown. As Natalie had predicted, the snow had stopped falling. Today they must begin the process of clearing the areas around the hotel. They all dressed as warmly as they could, but few had adequate protection. Still, he expected exercise would keep them warm. He wrapped his scarf around his angular body and considered his gloves. If he didn't wear them, cold would bite and then numb his fingers. If he did wear them, he might ruin the soft leather that he prized for working on cars. He sighed. If only he had a pair of Mama's knitted mittens, as darned and patched as they were.

An outburst of giggles drew his attention to Natalie and the children gathered around her. She waved at him, and warmth spread through Fabrizio's body even as someone opened the door and cold air struck him breathless. He plunged into the narrow space under the awning, which had not collapsed under the weight of the snow. The slight protection kept the drifts to under a foot deep. A glance down the intersecting streets in front of the Brown told the real story. Snow tapered to knee height in a few places and surged past shoulder height at others, a nature-made miniature of the Rocky Mountains that dominated Denver's western horizon. Not that they could see the mountains today. The men divided into teams and worked east, north, and south from the front entrance.

Fabrizio's group worked past the music room, where Natalie entertained the children. He waved at a boy who pasted his face against the glass, the longing to frolic outside instead of spending yet another day indoors written on his face. The child waved back, and Natalie joined him at the window. Sunlight glinted on a length of scarlet fabric dangled over her arm. She smiled widely when she saw Fabrizio. He returned the gesture, wishing he could stay basking in the warmth of her presence. The men around him moved ahead. He tipped his cap and bent back into the job of snow removal.

The men worked in shifts, wanting to persevere as long as the sun remained high in the sky. In the distance, other voices rang out, suggesting that people were digging out from the snow across Denver. When the sky paled behind the mounds of snow, the manager called a halt for the day. They had made good progress; another hour in the morning would see a path cleared all the way around the hotel. The weary men stumbled into the lobby, grateful for the reprieve.

Once inside, an aroma of hot chocolate greeted them, bowls of the warm liquid sparkling on white-linen-covered tables. Eleanor ladled the steaming drink into cups. But where was Natalie? Fabrizio found her at the opposite end of the table, tying together paper-wrapped bundles. She waved him over.

"Fabrizio! I have something to give you."

How he loved the sound of his name on her tongue, the American pronunciation softening the r sound. He shook off the snow that caked his hair and unwound his long scarf in the heat of the lobby.

"Natalie?" He could get lost in the depth of her eyes, blue streaks darting through calm gray.

She gestured at the table. "I saw you outside with the others today. You all looked so cold and miserable. Oh, I didn't give you a chance to get a cup of hot chocolate. I'm sorry." She dashed over to Eleanor and returned with a cup and saucer.

"Grazie." Fabrizio sipped the rich drink. Its warmth fought against the cold and sent shivers to his extremities. "It is good. It will give warmth."

Behind the table, Natalie bounced on her feet. "But you need more when you're outside. I wondered if there was something I could do, and I came up with an idea." She pointed to the packages on the table. "When the ladies learned what I was doing, they all supplied some material and helped me cut and sew a few things. It's not much, but I hope it helps. Will you help me distribute them?" She handed the last one she had wrapped to him. "Open it and see."

The paper crackled and flexed in his hands, suggesting something soft within. Fabrizio wiggled his still-cold fingers and untied the ribbon. A hat, mittens, and scarf set, sewn in bright scarlet wool, nestled against the plain wrapping. It reminded him of. . . He blushed. The ladies had offered their unmentionables, what they wore to bed at night. He fingered the material and imagined its warmth in the biting cold. They were perfect.

"They're clean. My maid, Annette, helped me launder the material before we used it." Natalie sounded apologetic.

"They are wonderful." The admiration Fabrizio felt for Natalie colored his voice.

She is not afraid of the snow for her household: for all her household are clothed with scarlet. Fabrizio remembered King Lemuel's words, repeated in the book of Proverbs in the Bible.

He had found the virtuous woman he wanted to treasure above precious jewels: Natalie Daire. He turned away before she could see the tears in his eyes. He had fallen in love with a woman who could never be his.

"The mittens, I will tell the others." He trained his eyes on the floor and made his escape. Back to the garage where he belonged.

Chapter 7

What did I do to offend Fabrizio? Natalie wondered when he disappeared so quickly. She fingered the red wool. Did the source of the material embarrass him? She hadn't worried about that when she hatched her plan. She only knew how cold the men looked and how light-headed she felt when she thought of a way to provide them with warm clothing. No one should catch cold and get sick because of digging out from this storm. Least of all the handsome Italian man who occupied so much of her thoughts.

She followed Fabrizio's progress through the crowded lobby. The workers made their way to her. She thanked each of them for his hard work and for making the guests' snowbound experience almost magical.

But the person she most wanted to thank did not return. Fabrizio had done so much more than shovel snow that morning. From the night he had returned to the Brown with her car instead of going home, he had helped her in every way. She thought about the way he pitched in with the daily activities, even joining in the games, although they made him uncomfortable. The night of the carol sing, his bass voice added so much to the music. He had shown the boys how to make a presipio such as the one his family had at home.

Her eyes drifted in the direction of the music room, where she knew hay filled more than half of the manger. Wistfulness washed over her. Would anyone bother to fill the manger once the snowbound guests left and no one else knew the story? She hoped so. The staff at least could continue the tradition. She had observed so many small deeds of kindness, perhaps inspired by Fabrizio's story. He epitomized the spirit of cooperation. And more. Her self-made grandfather would approve of the coachman.

Natalie's heart cried after him. She did not want their friendship to end. She wanted it to grow into something more. For the first time in her life, she felt the weight of her father's money dragging her down. It stood like the snow that flanked the hotel, cold and impenetrable. She would simply have to find a way to melt it.

On Tuesday morning, the workmen finished clearing a path around the hotel. The sky shone brilliant blue, and the sun had begun melting the ice crystals on her window. However, aside from lanes carved through the drifts here and there, snow still stretched as far as Natalie could see. The street level had risen several feet, transforming windows into doors. She could not drive her Cadillac on the street today. Even horses would have trouble wading through the drifts. At least one more day remained to enjoy their snowbound family.

For today, she could still join the excitement downstairs. Perhaps she could organize a few outdoor games for the children, who began misbehaving out of boredom. After braiding her hair, she donned her warmest dress—a jacketed outfit with fur trim that added layers. She arranged with Patrick to invite children to a snowman-making contest in the early afternoon. Fabrizio did not appear in the lobby.

"Mr. Ricci is by way of going back to the garage." Patrick must have noticed her searching gaze. "The guests will be needin' their cars soon."

The news drained some of the warmth out of the sunlight that streamed through the stained glass overhead. Then she heard excited chattering behind her. A couple of boys had seen the notice about the snowman contest and cheered the idea. Natalie pushed Fabrizio to the back of her mind. She looked forward to experiencing the wonder of four feet of snow with the children.

Shortly after dinner, the children assembled with Natalie in the lobby. She assigned five captains and let them choose teams. Their astonished gasps when they walked into the wintry playground made her decision worthwhile. Even though the melting snow was starting to compact, it was still piled higher than anything she had ever seen. Soon the children packed handfuls of snow and rolled them along the edge of the shoveled path. The balls fell apart easily.

Wind stirred snow from the top of the drift and scattered it on the children's heads. A little girl looked up, confused.

"Is it snowing again?"

Natalie rushed over and brushed away the powder. "No. It's only the wind. See? The sun is shining." She wondered if she should have asked more adults to supervise the contest.

At that moment, she spotted a bright green and yellow scarf over the top of a snowdrift. *Fabrizio.* God had heard her unspoken prayers and sent the help she most wanted.

"The day, it is beautiful." The scarf wrapped around his throat and mouth muffled the deep voice. Delight filled Natalie when she saw bright red mittens on his hands and a red hat on his head. Fabrizio continued speaking. "No one has called for their cars. I thought, maybe Natalie needs my help. And so here I am."

A snowball one of the older boys had tossed hit Fabrizio in the chest. "You want a snowball fight, eh?" He scooped snow, bright white against the red mitten, and patted it together. "This snow, it is not good for snowball fights." He whispered. "It is like—soap powder." His dark eyes asked permission to initiate a game. She nodded. He smiled, teeth almost as white as the snow that surrounded them, and tossed a handful at her. She laughed and joined in the fun.

Soon white powder covered everyone, melting and seeping through their clothes, and a few children shivered. Natalie's nose started dripping. She called a halt even though none of the teams had finished their snowmen. The snowball fight substituted for the snowmen, and she did not think the children minded the change of plans. A healthy color spread over their cheeks, and they gave one last yell before returning to the quiet of the lobby.

She paused for a moment at the main entrance while the children dashed inside. Fabrizio waited beside her. *I don't want this to end.* Had she spoken aloud?

Fabrizio removed his mittens and reached for her face. *Is he going to kiss me? I want him to kiss me.* She closed her eyes and felt his fingers tuck a curl behind her ear. A whisper of a touch, which disappeared almost as if she had only imagined it.

"They are waiting for us." Did his voice reflect the same regret that she felt?

Dressed in Scarlet

When she opened her eyes, Fabrizio had opened the door for her. He would not meet her eyes.

Natalie did not see Fabrizio again that day or the next. She thought about him, though, longing for another opportunity to spend time with him. A bad case of the sniffles kept her confined to her room. From her window she observed people out clearing the streets. She wasn't surprised when Patrick called her room on Thursday to announce that her father had sent the Daire family driver, Bob Cochran, to take her home by sleigh.

At the news, she arose from bed and called Annette to help her dress. How tired she was of the three dresses she had taken to Thalia's party. She laughed at how extravagant she had felt, packing two additional outfits for a one-day trip. Now she would gladly give them all away. Didn't Fabrizio have four sisters? Would he take offense if she offered them? Men liked to provide for women and not the other way around. She probably shouldn't make the suggestion. How silly to worry about something she could do so easily.

Fabrizio. She couldn't go without saying good-bye. She wouldn't leave him still stranded at the hotel. He was desperate to return to his family. As soon as she descended to the lobby, she asked Patrick to ring for him.

During the time she had spent sequestered in her room, she wondered if she had exaggerated the dark splendor of his eyes, the curls that sprang on his head, the broad cut of his shoulders. When he entered the lobby, dressed as usual in his uniform, she knew that, if anything, she had forgotten how marvelously handsome he was.

"Signorina, you asked for me?"

Signorina. The return to formality disappointed Natalie. She rushed into her explanation. "My father has sent a driver to bring me home." She gestured toward Cochran, dressed in a uniform almost identical to the one Fabrizio wore. "I know how anxious you are to reach your family. We can take you there on the way to Westminster. Are you free to leave?"

Chapter 8

Fabrizio had managed to push Natalie to the back of his mind during the time she had spent in her room. Her reappearance made his heart sing, informing him his longing for her had only been hiding. He could not, must not, allow it to continue fermenting. He backed away, shaking his head. "Signorina, I cannot ride with you."

"Of course you can." Natalie said the words with such fervor that she coughed. "Do you have permission to leave?"

Fabrizio looked to Patrick for help, but he shrugged. "I suggest you accept Miss Daire's offer. I'll tell the manager you've gone." A hint of a smirk played with the clerk's lips.

"So it's settled then." Natalie looked relieved.

Fabrizio couldn't say no to those pleading eyes. "I will come with you."

"We'll wait for you while you collect your things."

Fabrizio dashed down to the basement and gathered his skis and scarf, as well as the red hat and mittens that Natalie had made. He had filled the empty hours of her absence polishing every inch of every car. No duties kept him at the Brown. Heart racing with excitement and exertion, he ran back up the stairs, eager to leave. Any excuse to spend another few minutes with Natalie.

She had donned a lovely navy coat with matching hat, mittens, and scarf made out of some kind of soft wool. Gray eyes peeked over the scarf and sought him out. He hurried to her side.

"Cochran—that's the driver—is waiting with the sleigh out front." Her eyes sent a different message. *Do I have to leave?*

Fabrizio opened the front door and held on to Natalie's elbow to steady her. For one breathless second, he allowed himself to imagine entering the Brown as a paying guest, with the lovely young woman on his arm. The illusion played itself out as he lifted her onto the sleigh and joined her on the seat, tucking a blanket around their legs and another around their shoulders. She appeared to be cold, her cheeks as bright red and cheerful as Christmas morning.

Sunshine threw white-encrusted roofs into sharp contrast against the blue sky. The horses trotted down the quiet street, rising and falling as the snow had melted more in some places, less in others. They turned onto Sixteenth Street, where Fabrizio could make out the black hands on the D&F clock tower in the distance. Snow still coated most of the tower. Here a plow had cleared the street, and the sleigh made better progress.

"It's so beautiful." Natalie sighed. "It's like a Currier and Ives lithograph come to life." Her voice sounded lower than her usual lilting soprano, roughened by a cold.

The sleigh followed the same route the coal wagon had taken a few days earlier. After they made their way across Cherry Creek, Natalie asked, "How do we get to your home from here?"

She sounded wistful. Did she feel the same sadness that he did to see their time together end? *Let her go.* It was time to say good-bye, *arrivederci,* and not until tomorrow, *fino a domani,* as it had been during the days the storm kept them housebound together. The boundary between her world and his was as clear as the horizon that marked the white snow and the blue sky. He straightened his back, increasing the space between them.

"Leave me when we get to Tejon Street. I will tell you when." He gestured to his cross-country skis. "Now that the snow has stopped, I can ski home."

Natalie shook her head. "We will take you to your door. I insist." Her blue hat fell off, and a few strands of blond hair lay loose around her shoulders. Overly bright eyes looked at him. "Are you so eager to say good-bye?"

No! Fabrizio's heart shouted. "There is no need to trouble yourself, signorina." *Natalie.*

After that, silence reigned between them, broken only by distant cries of children at play and the jingle of the horse's harness. Beside him Natalie started humming. "Dashing through the snow. . ."

He joined in. "Oh, what fun it is to the ride in a one-horse open sleigh!"

Natalie broke into a paroxysm of coughing after the last note and fell over in a heap. *Natalie!* Without thinking, Fabrizio picked her up and carried her toward his house.

❄

Natalie struggled to wakefulness. Where was she? Not at the Brown. Not at home. Half dream, half memories flitted through her mind. She recalled strong arms bearing her across the snow as though she were as light as a snowflake, lips brushing her forehead. Had that actually happened? The mere possibility made her blush. *I'm at Fabrizio's house.*

"The signorina is awake." An older woman, hair flecked here and there with gray, bent over the bed. She poured water from a pitcher.

"You must be Mrs. Ricci." *Fabrizio's mother.* She could see the resemblance in their lively brown eyes, their well-formed ears.

"Call me Rosa."

"What happened?"

"You passed out from the fever. The doctor told us to keep you here until you were better. Now you are awake again." Rosa fiddled with a packet and took out two pills. "The doctor said for you to take these."

Natalie swallowed them with the glass of water.

"Now I will fix you a bowl of soup. Sofia, come here! I promised Fabrizio that we would not leave you alone," Rosa explained. "He is outside helping his papa with firewood."

Not one, but four young women ranging in age from maybe ten to eighteen, crowded around the doorway. *Fabrizio's sisters.*

"We heard voices." The smallest girl scooted forward under her older sisters' arms. "And we're all anxious to meet the signorina." She took a step toward the bed and curtsied. "Pleased to meet you, Miss Daire. I'm Isabella. The youngest."

Mrs. Ricci disappeared while the others came forward. Natalie made mental notes. Sofia, the eldest, lived at home while waiting for her upcoming wedding in the spring. Angela, the next oldest, wore an apron and refilled Natalie's water glass. Studious Maria wore glasses perched on top of her nose, a book of poetry in her hand. After brief introductions, Sofia shooed the rest of the family away. Soon Natalie fell back asleep.

When she woke again, Natalie sat up in the bed and looked around the room. The presence of a framed wedding picture and a man's pipe on the nightstand suggested it was the Riccis' room. Her maid at home had larger quarters. She felt embarrassed. *I kicked them out of their own room.*

"Can I get you something, signorina?" The studious girl appeared in front of Natalie. *What was her name?* Maria, that was it. The girl straightened the glasses on her nose.

Before Natalie could answer, she heard a brisk knock at the door, and a stranger entered, followed by Fabrizio.

"I see our patient is awake. This is good." The doctor put a thermometer into Natalie's mouth and placed his stethoscope against her chest. "Much better. The Riccis have taken good care of you."

"I am well enough to leave?" The warmth of the loving family invited her to stay, but she couldn't. She shouldn't inconvenience them any longer than necessary.

"Not yet. You need to rest and regain your strength. You may get up for a short time today if you feel up to it. I will return tomorrow, and we will see."

Mrs. Ricci chased the girls out of the room after the doctor, leaving Natalie alone with Fabrizio.

With a start, Natalie realized that she had never before seen Fabrizio dressed in everyday clothes. He looked every bit as handsome as he did in his uniform. But the same dark curls sprang from his head, and the same impressive muscles rippled underneath a plain white cotton shirt. He settled into the rocking chair beside the bed and dangled his hands between his legs. Before Natalie could speak, he began. "Natalie. I was so worried. You should not have left the Brown so soon."

Speaking of the Brown, why wasn't Fabrizio at work? Did he stay at home for her sake? Natalie waved aside his apologies. "I can't thank you and your family enough for everything they've done. This is your parents' room, isn't it?"

Fabrizio nodded. "Papa joined me in the attic room, and Mama is sleeping with Sofia." He smiled. "It is a good thing that *Nonno* Fabrizio is staying with my older brother."

"Nonno Fabrizio? Who is that? Are you named for him?"

"*Certamente.* My brother, Giacomo, is named for Papa's father, and I am named for Mama's father. It is the custom among Italians. I would like for you to meet my nonno. You would like him."

I will, if he's half as wonderful as you are. "I hope I will, someday." *Will his family become my family?* At that moment, Natalie realized how much she wished it could happen. *Did he kiss me?* Heat rushed to her cheeks.

Concerned, Fabrizio jumped out of the chair. "We have tired you out."

"No, I'm fine." Natalie protested. But she slipped down on the pillow and allowed him to tuck the corners of the quilt around her shoulders. She relished the strength of his hands, his nearness, and wished he would kiss her again. If he had indeed kissed her and it wasn't just a dream.

"*Fino ad allora, cara* Natalie. Rest well." He closed the curtains against the sunshine and left as Mrs. Ricci returned.

When Fabrizio had passed beyond earshot, Natalie asked Rosa, "What does 'cara' mean?"

The woman smiled secretively. "It means *beloved*."

Natalie tingled from head to toe. "Cara Fabrizio," she whispered under her breath.

Chapter 9

Fabrizio paced the tiny attic loft that he shared with his father. Today was the last day Natalie would spend in his house. The doctor had called the Daire home when she had improved enough to travel. And it was time, past time, for him to return to his job at the Brown Palace. He had used the phone at a nearby cheese factory and called the manager, pleading a family emergency.

"Take as long as you need," came the reply.

Fabrizio examined his memories of the past few days. Who ever would have imagined that the rich young heiress who ran her Cadillac into a vegetable stand would bring so much joy into his life? He had glimpsed her warm nature at the Brown, in the way she included Mrs. Rushton in the parties, in the activities she planned for the children, in the hats and mittens she fashioned out of scarlet wool.

These last few days had shown him a new side of his beloved. She listened to Maria read poetry; she ate every dish his mother served without question—with relish, even. She discussed wedding plans with Sofia as if she were a member of the bridal party. She acted as though she *belonged* in their household, unselfconscious and unpretentious. When he came across Sofia and Angela exclaiming over two lovely dresses, he knew that the ever-generous Natalie had even given away her clothing. He loved her more than ever.

And today he could lose her. Cochran, the driver, would return and escort her back to the world that awaited her. Could she care for him? Mama told him that Natalie had repeated his words, calling him "Cara Fabrizio." But first he must speak with her father, and that prospect frightened him almost more than the big snow.

"Are you coming down?" Little Isabella peeked around the door. "You must say good-bye."

"I am coming." Fabrizio turned away from the window and followed his sister, who skipped down the stairs. He made the final sharp turn in the narrow stairs that climbed from the basement pantry to the attic and came upon Natalie in the front room. She was wearing his favorite blue dress, one that floated about her like angels' wings. She must have sensed his presence, for she turned and smiled at him. For one unguarded moment, he let his feelings camp on his features, all the longing and impossible love he felt for her. Then he reined in his emotions. "Natalie." The effort spent on restraining himself made her lovely name come out curt, sharp.

"Fabrizio." In contrast, her voice softened, almost capturing the exact accent on the *r*. She gestured to his mother. "I was just telling your mother that you and Sofia must come to my birthday party on the twenty-fourth. I would be most pleased."

Natalie's birthday. Hotel gossip said that on the day she turned twenty-one, she would inherit a fortune. *She will forget about me.* He paused on the last step.

Her gray eyes locked with his, sending a silent plea. *I want you there. You are special to me.*

432

The soft sound of a horse's nicker interrupted their silent communication. Out the window, Fabrizio could see the fancy Daire sleigh. The driver, Cochran, had returned, bringing a stranger with him. A well-dressed, imposing man who could only be Natalie's father approached the house. Cochran remained in the driver's seat. A lump the size of a snowball formed in Fabrizio's throat.

Sweet Isabella dashed forward and flung open the door. *"Benvenuto, Signore!* You must be Natalie's father. Welcome to our home."

Daire did not reply right away. His bulk filled the doorway while his gaze surveyed the small quarters, crowded today with the entire Ricci family eager to welcome him. With his hair expertly barbered and his coat tailored to an exact fit, he looked as out of place as a flower blooming on Christmas Eve. His gaze settled on Natalie, and the solemn expression on his face eased.

Hesitant, almost shy, Natalie approached and kissed her father on the cheek. Although the quiet greetings didn't match the exuberant welcome his father received every evening, Fabrizio could not deny the affection in their reunion. Daire held his daughter at arm's length. "We were so worried."

"There was no need. The Riccis have taken good care of me. Let me introduce you."

Natalie introduced each member of the family with a brief biography. Again, she amazed Fabrizio with how much she had learned about them in such a short time, in spite of her illness. Last of all, she introduced the two men.

"Father, this is Fabrizio Ricci. The man who rescued me during the storm and who brought me into his house when I fell ill. We—we spent a lot of time together at the Brown."

Although Natalie didn't mention the fact, her father must know that he worked at the hotel.

"So you're the one who let my daughter travel when she was already sick."

Fabrizio gulped. "I did not realize..."

A twinkle appeared in Daire's eyes, and the snowball in Fabrizio's throat began melting. "If I know my daughter, she did not leave you much choice." He greeted each family member by name. At last he asked Mama, "Is there a place where I may speak privately with your son?"

The melting snowball re-formed in Fabrizio's throat. Mama led them to the kitchen. Neither man spoke while she made a fresh pot of coffee. While it brewed, she sliced some cream cake and laid it on her best china. After she poured the coffee, she left the room and shut the door on the waiting family.

Fabrizio sipped the coffee, hoping its warmth would ease the tension freezing his muscles. It did not.

"I understand that you work as a coachman at the Brown Palace." Daire broke the silence.

"Yes, sir." Something compelled Fabrizio to share a dream he had told few people. "Although some day I hope to open my own garage. I am good with the engines."

"Hmm." Daire's fingers drummed the polished surface of the table that had seen so many family dinners. He looked out the kitchen windows without appearing to see. "Did your family pay for the doctor? Medicine?" He reached into his pocket.

"Non, I mean, yes, we paid, but it was our privilege. We do not need your money." *Now I sound like an ungrateful child. How can I ask this stranger for permission to court his daughter?* Fabrizio sent a prayer heavenward and opened his mouth to speak.

But what Daire said next stopped Fabrizio from speaking. "Ricci, I have the impression that you care for my daughter."

Is it so obvious? "*Molto*, very much." Fabrizio set the cup on the saucer and looked straight at Daire. Natalie's eyes looked at him out of her father's face. "I would like permission to court your daughter."

Daire met his gaze. "I, too, was once young and in love and ambitious. In fact, I was brash enough to ask the richest man in Denver for permission to court his beloved child."

Fabrizio held his breath.

"That was so long ago. I've forgotten what it was like." Daire spoke more to himself than to Fabrizio. "But seeing your family here reminds me of my own beginnings." Daire took a bite of the cream cake. "This is delicious. I'll have to applaud your mother." He didn't speak again while he finished the food.

Fabrizio couldn't eat, even though he loved Mama's cream cake. He watched Daire's mouth opening and closing around his fork and imagined all the terrible things he would say.

Daire drank the last of his coffee. His lips curved in the same way Natalie's did when she felt mischievous. "Yes, you have my permission to court my Natalie."

❄

What is going on in the kitchen? Natalie wished she could have remained in the front room with her ear pressed to the kitchen door. Instead, she had retired to the second floor bedroom that Angela shared with Maria. All the girls waited with her.

"Perhaps Fabrizio is asking for your hand in marriage." Isabella spoke the words that Natalie dreamed. "Would you like to be our *sorella*, sister, Natalie?"

"Hush, bambina." Mama Rosa quieted her youngest. But her eyes asked the same question.

"I. . ." Natalie was saved from answering by the sound of Father's shout from below. "Natalie?"

"Coming, Father." Natalie hugged each of the Ricci women in turn. They followed her down the steps, forming a human staircase. Fabrizio waited at the bottom. The uneasiness she had sensed in him earlier had disappeared, his shoulders straightened as if relieved of a heavy weight.

Father's face betrayed no emotion. "Go ahead, my dear. I will join you in a moment." Perhaps he intended to pay Mrs. Ricci for her care.

"I will walk you to the sleigh." Fabrizio had slipped the familiar green and yellow scarf around his neck. He held her coat for her to put on. Once outside, he slipped her hand into his. "Your father, he has given me permission to court you. I think that you will not mind."

Natalie felt light-headed, as if her illness threatened a relapse. "Oh, Fabrizio, I was so afraid. . ."

"You were afraid of me?" Fabrizio's teasing voice somehow stilled the tempest in her heart.

"Of course not. I was afraid that you would let. . .things. . .come between us." The light-headedness persisted, and she grabbed his hands to steady her. "I have loved being with your family, in your home. I am not afraid of what the future holds. As long as it is with you."

"That is good." Fabrizio brushed his lips over the small portion of her cheek exposed to the elements. "I will see you again. Soon."

❄

Two weeks later, Natalie held on to the memory of Fabrizio's kiss while she dressed for her birthday party. Choosing the right outfit with the seamstress had proven harder than she expected. She wanted to look her best, but she did not want to look, well, *expensive*. She did not want Fabrizio to think she expected fine clothes and the latest fashions.

When she first left the Ricci home, she felt certain that she was living out her own fairy story, a God-ordained match made in heaven. The days since then had blurred her initial joy. She and Fabrizio had spoken twice by phone. The conversations left her unsettled, neither of them able to express their true feelings, knowing that others could listen in. She could not see those beautiful dark eyes that gave away his feelings when his words did not, or the hands that moved so surely over anything he touched. Even the hoped-for visit when he had returned her Cadillac did not occur. He left before she finished with the dressmaker.

She had told a few friends about her own private big snow miracle. "How romantic," they all chimed; but she knew they made fun of her behind her back. Tonight she would show them differently. She would walk through the door to her party on the arm of Fabrizio, and they would see his sterling quality for themselves. The only ones who seemed to understand were the same group of friends who attended Thalia Bloom's party. In fact, she had learned that the early Christmas snow had brought romance to all four of them.

She looked forward to seeing her friends again this evening. They understood how ambivalent she felt about receiving control of her inheritance today. She had plans for the money, plans she had not even told her father. Plans that would make sure the money would do good and not come between her and Fabrizio.

Natalie fidgeted while her maid adjusted the stiff collar of her dress around her neck. She hoped Fabrizio liked her outfit, a pretty claret-colored linen with an ecru bib. Next, Annette dressed her hair in her favorite Grecian style. Natalie tugged a few tendrils to curl around her face. Fabrizio seemed to like it that way.

Deep voices drifted up the stairs, and Natalie sprang to her feet. "Is that. . ."

"I'll look." Annette tiptoed to the top of the stairs and ran back. "Mr. Ricci is here."

She sounded as excited as Natalie felt, her stomach happy and bubbling like hot cider. She checked the mirror one last time and descended the stairs slowly, the way a lady should.

Fabrizio—her Fabrizio—waited at the foot of the stairs. Dressed in a new suit that showed off his broad shoulders; hair cut to a perfect curl above the collar; tall, dark, and handsome as ever—he took her breath away. He had braved her world to come to her party. He bowed low, as courtly as an Italian count, and presented her with a single red rose. "Many happy returns of your birthday, Natalie. A rose to dress you in scarlet." Did she imagine it, or did a faint blush tinge his dark cheeks?

Natalie fingered the rose, lifted it to her nose, and inhaled the scent. The color red would forever symbolize their love.

"I will put the rose in a vase, miss." Annette took the flower from her hands. "In your room."

"Perfect. I can fall asleep looking at it." And Fabrizio would not feel embarrassed comparing his single perfect rose with the abundant bouquets lining the ballroom.

Natalie accepted Fabrizio's arm and walked toward the waiting guests.

Chapter 10

Dressed in his first-ever new suit, Fabrizio felt almost worthy of Natalie. He drank in the warmth shining in her eyes, her exclamations over the rose he had found for her. But the splendor of the Daire mansion dazzled him. The initial feelings of goodwill evaporated when they entered the ballroom.

What am I doing here? Fabrizio wondered. This one room alone was almost as big as the first floor of his house. A dozen vases filled with hothouse flowers decorated various tables. His new clothes suffered in comparison to the well-tailored men and women who thronged Natalie.

Natalie introduced him without apology and even with pride to one and all. Her special school friends welcomed him eagerly. Those names he remembered: Thalia Bloom, Maximilian Newbolt, Rose Fletcher, Dr. Thomas Stanton, Patricia Logan, and Jared Booker.

"Natalie tells us that you were the one who rescued her during the big snow."

"I would never drive a car like that. She was blessed that you were there."

"She says you have a wonderful voice. Promise you'll sing for us tonight?"

No wonder Natalie had formed a lasting friendship with these women. They were as kind as she was. Fabrizio relaxed a tiny bit.

Everyone else treated him with distant civility. Behind gloved hands and polite glances, Fabrizio heard the whispers start. "Who is that man? Look at his clothes. Where did Natalie find him?"

At last Fabrizio saw a familiar face, Eleanor Royal, the young woman who had helped Natalie with the activities at the Brown. He allowed a smile on his face and bowed in her direction. "Signorina Royal. It is good to see you again."

Eleanor raised an eyebrow and took Natalie aside. "What is *he* doing here?" She whispered in her friend's ear.

Humiliated, Fabrizio stumbled back. Eleanor had treated him well at the Brown. He thought—well, no matter *what* he thought. Her reaction to his arrival proved that he did not belong in Natalie's world. He never would. He grabbed a cup of hot cider from the table and looked for a corner to hide in.

A hand clapped down on his shoulder and a deep voice drawled, "Some women don't know when to keep their traps shut." It was Jared Booker, Patricia's escort. "Let's get some air." The two men walked out of the ballroom into the courtyard.

Jared looked as uncomfortable in his suit as Fabrizio felt. "I hope Patricia doesn't expect me to attend many of these affairs. Give me the open range any day."

"Signorina Logan seems to be a lovely young woman. You are blessed."

"And so are you, if I'm reading the signals right. Don't let the whispers bother you."

Fabrizio looked through the doors, where he could see Natalie arguing with her father. He shook his head. Daire must regret his decision to give Fabrizio permission to court his daughter. His spirits sank even lower. Everyone at the party could see what a mistake it was.

Patricia Logan appeared at the door. "There you are, Jared! I wondered where you had gone."

"Duty calls. I'll take it like a man." Jared moved toward her with an easy grace. "Remember what I said."

Jared's departure left Fabrizio alone in the nippy air of the courtyard. He would rather endure the cold than face the party. The starlit sky taunted him, teasing him with his dreams of a life with Natalie. The sky under which he hoped to profess his love for her now suffocated him.

"Fabrizio?"

The gentle sound of Natalie's voice froze him in place more effectively than the chill air. He calmed his features and turned to face her.

"Signorina."

"You call me Natalie." Tears glittered in her eyes.

"It is best that I call you signorina." Why did he still want to dry the tears from her eyes?

"You heard what Eleanor said." She made it a statement, not a question.

"She is right. I do not belong...here." He made a sweeping gesture meant to indicate the house, the gaiety—her.

"Father said you might feel like that. He told me I should come after you." Natalie tugged his arm. "Let's go for a walk. The paths are cleared."

Fabrizio agreed. After he made his apologies, he could return to his own place.

They walked among the trees, blue spruce intermingled with denuded oaks and aspens. Natalie shivered, and Fabrizio reprimanded himself. She should not be out in the cold after she had been so ill. He gave her his jacket and slipped his arm around her shoulders.

Natalie stopped underneath a spreading elm tree, moonlight gilding its bare branches. "Father told me you felt uncomfortable with the guests tonight. What Eleanor said was inexcusable."

So that is what they were arguing about. "She only said what others were thinking. Me, I should not have come."

Natalie shook her head. "You're wrong. Oh, I won't pretend people weren't thinking mean things. But they're not important. They only came to my party because my father is rich, and now that I'm of age, I have money of my own. But you—I think you see the real me." She took a deep breath. "You know that today I received my inheritance. What you don't know—what I haven't even told my father yet—is how I plan to use the money. I want to help support that orphanage that needed coal during the storm, St. Clara's. And I want to invest it in new businesses—businesses opened by young men with the same drive that made my grandfather's and father's fortunes—maybe even a garage run by an excellent mechanic?"

She was offering his dream to him on a plate. Words froze in Fabrizio's throat.

When at last he could speak, he said, "Do you know why I brought you a *red* rose?"

Natalie shook her head. "It's a beautiful flower, but you meant something more?"

"You dressed the staff at the Brown in scarlet. You gave of your own bounty to keep us warm. King Lemuel, in Proverbs, he said that describes a virtuous woman. 'She is not afraid of the snow for her household: for all her household are clothed with scarlet.' You are that virtuous woman. The king said a man should treasure her like a precious jewel. I love you, Signorina Natalie. I want to treasure you above all others. But I am a poor man. I am unworthy of your love."

Natalie swiveled in his arms, facing him, starlight streaming across her face. Fabrizio allowed all the love and longing that he felt for her to show. She ran a gloved finger across his chin. "It is I who am unworthy of *you*, Fabrizio. You have been my champion, protector, my hero, since we first met." She lifted her face to gaze at him.

Fabrizio met her lips in a kiss. In this place, on this night, he knew that one day they would become man and wife before the good Lord who had made them both.

Epilogue

A year had come and gone since Denver's big snow. Such momentous news filled the intervening months that the six-day blizzard began to fade into memory. A great war had engulfed Europe after the assassination of Archduke Ferdinand in Sarajevo. So far, Fabrizio's beloved Italy maintained a neutral stance.

But the big snow of 1913 would always remain the fulcrum of Natalie's life. That's when she met the man who today had become her husband.

Natalie changed out of her wedding dress into a red woolen afternoon suit and white linen blouse that coordinated well with the roses woven into her hair. She passed through the kitchen of their second floor apartment, decorated with much affection by Mama Rosa.

"Signora Ricci!" Her husband called to her from the street, where he waited by the Cadillac Model 30 that had brought them together during the storm. Friends who had attended their small wedding ceremony had tied a banner reading HAPPILY MARRIED to their bumper.

"I'll be right down!" she called. They planned to spend their wedding night in nearby Colorado Springs. They wanted to return to Denver in time for Thalia and Maximilian's wedding on New Year's Eve. Rose had married her doctor early in the year, and Patricia and Jared had wed at Thanksgiving. Love had fallen on all four of the school chums during Denver's "big snow."

Natalie heard feet on the stairs, and a door flung open. "I can't wait any longer." Fabrizio twirled her in a circle and kissed her soundly. "We must go soon, or I will not want to leave."

Natalie allowed Fabrizio to lead her down the stairs. She paused on the steps, looking out over the showroom. New cars gleamed, and a faint smell of oil suggested motor repair in progress. Ricci Motors, a dream come true.

Fabrizio followed the direction of her gaze. "Cara Natalie," he murmured as he covered her lips with kisses. "Today God has given me a good wife worth more than all the silver in the mountains."

"And I will strive to deserve your trust, to always clothe you in scarlet."

Hand in hand, Mr. and Mrs. Fabrizio Ricci stepped forward into the future together.

Bestselling author **Darlene Franklin's** greatest claim to fame is that she writes full-time from a nursing home. She lives in Oklahoma, near her son and his family, and continues her interests in playing the piano and singing, books, good fellowship, and reality TV in addition to writing. She is an active member of Oklahoma City Christian Fiction Writers, American Christian Fiction Writers, and the Christian Authors Network. She has written over fifty books and more than 250 devotionals. Her historical fiction ranges from the Revolutionary War to World War II, from Texas to Vermont. You can find Darlene online at www.darlenefranklinwrites.com

Looking for More Christmas Romance?—Check Out...

A Patchwork Christmas
by Judith Miller, Nancy Moser, and Stephanie Grace
Whitson
Join three of today's bestselling inspirational fiction
authors in a collection of Christmas stories from
Victorian-era America that are full of second-chance
romances. Jilted by her fiancé, Karla packs away her
wedding quilts and her plans for marriage. Widow
Jane travels to marry a prosperous man she barely
knows in order to give her daughter a better life—then is stranded in a
winter storm. Victoria, a wealthy ingénue, inadvertently causes grave injury to a poor man she once considered quite a catch. Each must search
her heart, change her plans. . .and patch together a tender, unexpected
life filled with love.

Includes:
A Patchwork Love by Stephanie Grace Whitson
Seams Like Love by Judith Miller
The Bridal Quilt by Nancy Moser

Paperback / 978-1-63409-022-3 / 400 pages / $9.99